Raves for the novels of *Alliance Space*:

Merchanter's Luck:

"MERCHANTER'S LUCK is a story of transformation, not magical or mysterious but accomplished slowly through hard work. It is also about the power of misunderstanding and the courage of trust. . . . Filled with background details, customs, and a past, MERCHANTER'S LUCK is another exceptional C.J. Cherryh novel." —*Science Fiction Review*

"Cherryh's talent for inventing fully realized and detailed societies improves an already good adventure."
—*Library Journal*

"Well worked out, fun and well worth your money. Enjoy."
—*Analog*

40,000 in Gehenna:

"Cherryh tantalizes our minds with these enigmatic aliens, captures our hearts with her characters, and involves us completely with her mix of broad and narrow views of a culture's rise. Once again, Cherryh proves herself a consistently thoughtful and entertaining writer."
—*Publishers Weekly*

"When Cherryh is writing at her best, there are few in the field who can touch her, and this is very close to being her very best. . . . One of the most thoughtful novels of the past few years." —*S. F. Chronicle*

"In the guise of crisp, science-oriented speculation and adventure, (*40,000 in Gehenna*) proves to be a wider exploration of alienness, sexual roles, and humanity." —*Locus*

ALLIANCE SPACE

MERCHANTER'S LUCK
40,000 IN GEHENNA

C. J. CHERRYH

DAW BOOKS, INC.
DONALD A. WOLLHEIM, FOUNDER
375 Hudson Street, New York, NY 10014

ELIZABETH R. WOLLHEIM
SHEILA E. GILBERT
PUBLISHERS
http://www.dawbooks.com

First Printing, March 2008
2   3   4   5   6   7   8   9

DAW TRADEMARK REGISTERED
U.S. PAT. AND TM. OFF. AND FOREIGN COUNTRIES
—MARCA REGISTRADA
HECHO EN U.S.A.

PRINTED IN THE U.S.A.

ALLIANCE
SPACE

Merchanter's Luck

Their names were Sandor and Allison . . . Kreja and Reilly respectively. Reilly meant something in the offices and bars of Viking Station: it meant the merchanters of the great ship *Dublin Again*, based at Fargone, respectable haulers on a loop that included all the circle of Union stars, Mariner and Russell's, Esperance and Paradise, Wyatt's and Cyteen, Fargone and Voyager and back to Viking. It was a Name among merchanters, and a power to be considered, wherever it went.

Kreja meant nothing at Viking, having flourished only at distant Pan-paris and Esperance in its day: at Mariner, under an alias, it meant a bad debt, and the same at Russell's. The Kreja ship was currently named *Lucy*, and she was supposedly based at Wyatt's, which was as far away as possible and almost farther away than reasonable for such a small and aged freighter, claiming to run margin cargo for a Wyatt's combine. Customs always searched her, though she called here regularly. Small, star-capable ships on which the crew was not related by blood, on which in fact there were only two haggard men, and one not the same as at last docking . . . such ships were not comfortably received at station docks, and received careful scrutiny.

Lucy was a freighter by statement, a long-hauler which ran smallish consignments independent of its combine's close direction, since the combine had no offices on Viking. She was a passenger carrier when anyone would trust her—

no one did, though the display boards carried her offer. She took merchanter transfers if she could get them.

That was how Sandor Kreja lost his crew at Viking, because the crew, one old and limping sot who was paying work for his passage, found his own ship in port and headed for it without a by-your-leave. The old man had only signed as far as Viking; he had been left behind at Voyager for a stay in hospital, and he was simply interested in catching his own ship again and rejoining his family: that was the deal.

It made Sandor nervous, that departure, as all such departures did. The old man had been more curious than most, had nosed about contrary to orders, had been into everything—lied, with epic distortion, about where his *Daisy* had been, lied about deals they had made and what they had done in the wars and what he had done in dockside sleepovers, entertaining as it was. His departure left Sandor solo on *Lucy,* which he had been before and had no wish to try more often than he had to, running a freighter blind tired. But more, the old man left him with a nagging worry that he might have turned up something, and that his considerable talent for storytelling might spread tales in stationside bars that *Lucy* had peculiarities. Viking had tightened up since *Lucy*'s last docking: warships had pulled in and rumors surmised pirate trouble. They were nervous times; and a little talk in the wrong places could get back to station offices. It might, Sandor thought, be time to move on.

But he had conned his way onto the loading schedule, which meant they were going to fill his tanks and he was going to get cargo if he could only subdue his nervousness and keep from rousing suspicions this trip round. Forged papers labeled him and *Lucy* as Wyatt's Star Combine, which had a minor interest-bearing account at Voyager and Viking, outside its territories, a fund meant for emergency use if ever one of its ships should have to divert over from regular WSC ports. It was his seventh call here on the same faked papers—in fact he foresaw the time when the stamp sheets in the book would be filled and station would have to renew his papers with the real thing, a threshold he had crossed before, and which made life for a time much more secure . . . until some needed repair ran him over his margin and the questions got sharp and closer.

He was not a pirate: *Lucy* was too small for piracy and her smallish armament was a joke. He was, in his own reckoning, not even completely a thief, because he skimmed enough to keep him going, but nothing on a large scale. He delivered his cargoes where they belonged and let the money right back into WSC accounts. He made a very little profit, to be sure, and that little profit could be tipped right into the loss column if *Lucy* got stalled at dock without cargo, if *Lucy* needed some major repair. It was the reason why no combine would accept her honest application. She was small and carried small cargoes, across the too-large distances the bigger ships could cross much more quickly. She had gone into the red now and again at Viking, losses that would have broken an independent, without the forged papers to draw credit on. But all a big company like WSC would notice when the accounts cycled round at year's end was that the main fund had neither increased nor decreased. As long as *Lucy* paid back what she took out by year's end, the excess could stay in her illicit working account, to cushion her future ups and downs of profit. WSC spread over light-years and timelag. Alarms only rang down the system at audit time . . . and Sandor had no desire at all to go beyond small pilferage, no ambition to reach for profits that might get him caught. He was twenty-seven and impossibly rich, in terms of being sole remaining heir to a star-freighter, however small, which had been a legitimate trader once, before the Company War created pirates, and pirates stopped and looted her, and left her a stripped shell mostly filled with dead. Now *Lucy* survived as best she could, on her owner's ingenuity, under a multitude of names and numbers and a succession of faked papers. Now selling out was impossible: his scams would catch up with him and eat away even the thirty of silver he would get for his ship. Worse, he would have to sit on station and watch her come and go in the hands of some local combine—or see her junked, because she was a hundred and fifty years old, and her parts might be more valuable than her service.

He kept her going. She was his, in a way no stationer-run combine could understand. He had been born on her, had grown up on her, had no idea what the universe would be like without the ship around him and he never meant to find out. The day he lost *Lucy* (and it could happen any day, with one of the station officers running up with attachment warrants from somewhere, or with some sharp-eyed dockmaster or customs agent taking a notion to run a test on his forged papers), on that day he figured they would have to kill him; but they would take him in whole if they could, because station law was relentlessly humane and Union took as dim a view of shootings on dockside as they did of pilferage. They would put him in the tank and alter his mind so that he could be happy scrubbing floors and drawing a stationside living, a model Union citizen.

Stations scared him spitless.

And that talkative old man who had gone back to his ship scared him.

But he had it figured out a long time ago that the worst thing he could do for himself was to look scared, and the quickest way to rouse suspicions was to act defensive or to stay holed up in *Lucy*'s safety during dockings, when any normal merchanter would use the chance to go out bar-hopping dockside, up the long curve of taverns and sleepovers on the docks.

He was smooth-faced and good-looking in a gaunt, blond way that could be a stationer accountant or banker bar-hopping—except that the gauntness was hunger and the eyes showed it, so that he laughed a great deal when he was scouting the bars, to look as if he were well-credited, and sometimes to get drinks on someone else. And this time—this time, because his life depended on it . . . he aimed for more than a free drink or a meal on some other combine's credit. He needed a crewman, someone, *anyone* with the right touch of minor larceny who could be conned and cozened aboard and trusted not to talk in the wrong quarters. This was flatly dangerous. Merchanter ships were family, all of the same Name, born on a ship to die on that ship. Beached merchanters were beached only for a single run, like the old man he had gotten from hospital; or if they were beached permanently, it was because their own ships' families had thrown them out, or because they had voluntarily quit their families, unable to live with them. Some of the latter were quarrelsome and some were crimi-nal; he was one man and he had to sleep sometimes . . . which was why he had to have help on the ship at all. He scanned the corners of the bars he traveled on the long green-zone dock of Viking, trying not to see the soldiers and the police who were more frequent everywhere than usual, and looking constantly for someone else as hungry as he was, knowing that they would be disguising their plight as he disguised it, and knowing that if he picked the wrong one, with a shade too much larceny in mind, that partner would simply cut his throat some watch in some lonely part of the between, and take *Lucy* over for whatever purposes he had in mind.

It was the first day of this hunt on the docks, playing the part of honest merchanter captain and nursing a handful of chits he had gotten on that faked combine account, that he first saw Allison Reilly.

The story was there to be read: the shamrock and stars on her silver coveralls sleeve, the patches of worlds visited, that encompassed all known space, the lithe tall body with its back to him at the bar and a flood of hair like a puff of space-itself in the dim neon light.

In his alcohol-fumed eyes that sweep of hip and long, leaning limbs put him poignantly in mind of sleepovers and that other scanted need of his existence—a scam much harder than visa forging and far more dangerous. In fact, his life had been womanless, except for one very drunk insystem merchanter one night on Mariner when he was living high and secure, which was how Mariner knew his name and laid in wait for him. And another insystemer before that, who he had hoped would partner him for good: she had lost him Esperance when it went bad. He was solitary, because the only women for merchanters were other merchanters, who inevitably had relatives; and merchanters in general were a danger to his existence far more serious than stations posed. Stations sat fixed about their stars and rarely shared records on petty crime for the same reasons the big combines rarely bothered with distant and minor accounts. But get on the bad side of some merchanter family for any cause, and they would spread the word and hunt him from star to star, spread warnings about him to every station and every world humans touched, so that he would die; or so that some station would catch him finally and bend his mind, which was the same to him. There were no more women; he had sworn off such approaches.

But he dreamed, being twenty-seven and alone for almost all his days, in the long, long night. And at that silver-coveralled vision in front of him, he forgot the tatter-elbowed old man he had been trying to stalk, him with the vacant spot in the patches on his sleeve, and forgot the short-hauler kid who was another and safer prospect. He stared at that sleek back, and saw that fall of hair like a night in which stars could burn—and saw at the same time that arm resting on the bar, patched with the Reilly shamrock, which burned green in the green neon glare from the over-the-bar lighting, advising him that among merchanters this was one of the foremost rank, a princess, a Name and a patch which was credit wherever it liked, that walked wide and did as it pleased. Nothing like *Lucy* had a prayer against *Dublin Again,* that great and modern wonder which meant clean corridors and clean coveralls and credit piled in station accounts from Cyteen to Pell. They were Dubliners with her, cousins or brothers, big, dark-haired men of varying ages. He saw them in a fog beyond her, talking to her; and her arm lifted the glass and her hair swung with the spark of the changing neon like red stars . . . she was turning on her elbow to set the glass down, a second swirl of starry night.

Ah, he pleaded to God fuzzily, not wanting to see her face, because perhaps she was not beautiful at all, and he could look away in time and make that beautiful back and cloud of hair into his own drink-fogged dream to keep him company on the long watches—as long as she had no face. But he was too paralyzed to move, and in that same long motion she turned all the way around, shook back the living night from her face that was all blue now in the changing neon lights.

He was caught then, because he forgot to laugh and forgot everything else he was doing in that bar, stared with his mouth open and his eyes showing what they showed when he was not laughing—he knew so, because she suddenly looked nettled. She stood straight from the bar, which movement drew his eyes to the A. REILLY stitched over the blue-lit silver of a breast, while she was looking him over and sizing him up for the threadbare brown coveralls he wore and the undistinguished (and lying) E. STEVENS his pocket bore, and the gaudy nymph with *Lucy* ribbonned on his sleeve . . . the nymph was a standard item in shops which sold such things. It decorated any number of ships and sleeves, naked and girdled with stars and badly embroidered with the ribbon blank, to be stitched in with any ship's name. Insystem haulers used such things. Miners did. He did, because it was what he could afford.

She stared a good long moment, and turned then and searched her pocket . . . her crewmates had gone elsewhere, and she paused to glance at one who was himself making slow stalk of a woman of another crew off in the dim corner. She tossed a chit down on the water-circled counter and walked for the door alone, while Sandor stood there watching that retreating back and that cloud of space-itself enter the forever day of the open dock outside.

He called the bartender urgently and paid . . . no tip, at which the man scowled, but he was used to that. He hurried, trying not to seem in haste, thinking of the woman's cousins and not wanting to have *them* on his tail. His heart was pounding and his skin had that hot-cold flush that was part raw lust and part stark panic, because what he was doing was dangerous, with the docks as tense as they were, with police watching where they were never invited by merchanters.

He had dreamed something in the lonely years, which was—he could no longer remember whether the dream *was* different from what he had seen standing alive in front of him, because all those solitary fancies were murdered, done in cold pale death in that collision, because he had seen the one bright vision of his life. He was going to hurt forever—the more so if he could not find out in brighter light that her face had some redeeming flaws, if he could not have her herself murder the image and his hopes at once and give him back his common sense. You'll not have tried, kept hammering in his brain. You'll never know. Another, dimmer self kept telling him he was drunk, and yet another self cursed him that he was going to lose everything he had. But the self that was in control only advised him that he was lost out here in the glare of dock lights, that she had gotten away into another bar or a shop somewhere close.

He looked about him, at the long upcurve of the dock which was curtained by section arches and peopled with hundreds of passersby, battered with music and bright lights and sounds of machinery. Tall metal skeletons of gantries ran skeins of umbilicals to the various lighted caverns that were ship-accesses across the dock, but she surely had not had time to reach one. He went right, instead, to the next bar up the row, looked about him in the doorway of the dim, alcohol-musked interior, which drew attention he never liked to have on him. He ducked out again and tried the next; and the third, which was fancier—the kind of place where resident stationers might come, or military officers, when they wanted a taste of the docks.

She was there . . . alone, half-perched on a barstool in the silver extravagance of the place, a waft of the merchanter life stationers would come to this dockside bar to see, a touch of something exotic and dangerous. And maybe a stationer was what she was looking for, some manicured banker, some corporation man or someone she could run a high scam on, for the kind of inside information the big ships got regularly and the likes of *Lucy* never would. Or maybe she wanted the kind of fine liquor and world-grown luxury a local might treat her to and some liked. He was daunted. He stood just inside the doorway, finding himself in the kind of place he avoided, where drinks were three times what they ought to be and he was as far as he could possibly be from doing what he had come to do—which was to find some crewman in as desperate straits as he was.

She saw him. He stared back at her in that polished, overpriced place and felt like running.

And then, because he had never liked running and because he was a degree soberer than he had been a moment ago and insisted on suffering for his stupidity, he walked a little closer with his hand in his pocket, feeling over the few chits he had left and wishing they posted prices in this place.

She rested with her elbow on the bar, looking as if she belonged; and he had no cover left, not with her recognizing him, a man with a no-Name patch on his sleeve and no way to claim coincidence in being in this place. He had never felt so naked in his life, not even in front of station police with faked papers.

"Buy you a drink?" he asked, the depth of his originality.

She was—maybe—the middle range of twenty. She bar-hopped alone with that shamrock on her sleeve, and she was safe to do that: no one rolled a Dubliner in a sleepover and planned to live. It might be her plan to get very drunk and to take up with whomever she fancied, if she fancied anyone; she might be hunting information, and she might be eager to get rid of him, not to hamper her search with inconsequence. She was dangerous, not alone to his pride and his dreams.

She motioned to the stool beside hers and he came and eased onto it with a vast numbness in the middle of him and a cold sweat on his palms. He looked up nervously at the barkeeper who arrived and looked narrowly at him. "Your choice," Sandor said to A. Reilly, and she lifted the glass she had mostly finished. "Two," he managed to say then, and the bartender went off.

Two of that, he was thinking, might be expensive. They might be the most expensive drinks he had ever bought, if a bad bar bill brought questions down on the rest of his currently shaky finances. He looked into A. Reilly's mid-night eyes with a genuine desperation, and the thought oc-curred to him that being arrested would be only slightly worse than admitting to poverty in the Dubliner's presence.

"*Lucy.*" She read his patch aloud, tilting her head to see the side of his arm. "Insystemer?"

"No," he said, a hot flush rising to his face. His indigna-tion won him at least a momentary lift of her hand and deprecation of the question she had asked, because a jumpship was far and away a different class of operation from the insystem haulers and miners. In that sense at least, *Lucy* and *Dublin* were on the same scale.

"Where are you based, then?" she asked, either mercy-killing the silence or being sensibly cautious in her barside contacts. "Here?"

"Wyatt's," he said. The bartender returned with two drinks and hesitated, giving him the kind of look which said he would like to see a credit chit if it were him alone, but the barman slid a thoughtful eye over the shamrock patch and moved off in silence. Sandor took both glasses and pushed the one toward A. Reilly, who was on the last of her first.

"Thanks," she said. He limited his swallow to less than

he wanted, hoping to make it last, and to slow her down, because they laid down more in tips in this place than he spent on meals.

And desperately he tried to think of some casual question to ask of her in return. He could not, because everyone knew where *Dublin* was based and asking more sounded like snoopery from someone like himself.

"You in for long?" she asked.

"Three days." He pounced on the question with relief. "Going to fill the tanks and take on cargo. Going on to Fargone from here. I don't have a big ship, but she's *mine*, free and clear. I'm getting a little ahead these days. Trying to take on crew here."

"Oh." A small, flat oh. It was apprehension what class he was.

"I'm legitimate. I just had some bad luck up till now. You don't know of any honest longjumpers beached here, do you?"

She shook her head, still with that look in her eyes, wary of her uninvited drinking partner. Sometimes such uncrewed ships and such approaches by strangers in bars meant pirate spies; and even huge *Dublin* had *them* to fear. He saw it building, foresaw an appeal to authorities who would jump fast when a Dubliner yelled hazard. There were fleet officers drinking at a nearby table. Security was heavy out on the docks, with rumors of an operation against the pirates; but others said it had to do with Pell, or inter-zone disputes, or they were checking smuggling. He smiled desperately.

"Pirates," he said. "Long time back. . . . My family's all dead; and my hired crew ran on me and near robbed me blind, one time and the other. You know what you can hire off the docks. It's not safe. But I haven't got a choice."

"Oh," she said, but it was a better oh than the last, indeterminate. A frown edged with sympathy, and hazardous curiosity. "No, I don't know. Sometimes we get people wanting to sign on as temporaries, but we don't take them, and we haven't had any at Viking that I've heard of. Sorry. If station registry doesn't list them—"

"I wouldn't take locals," he said, and then tried the truth. "No, I would, if it got me out on schedule. Anyway, *Lucy's* mine, and I was out hunting prospects, not—"

"You rate *me* a prospect?"

She was laughing at him. That was at least better than suspicion. He grinned, swallowing his pride. "I couldn't persuade you, could I?"

She laughed outright and his heart beat the harder, because he knew what game she was playing at the moment. It was merchanters' oldest game of all but trade itself, and the fact that she joined the maneuvering in good humor brought him a sweating flush of hope. He took a second sip of the forgotten glass and she took a healthy drain on her second. "Lost your crew here?" she asked. "You can't have gotten in alone."

"Yes. Lost him here. He'd been in hospital; he hired on for passage, and caught his ship here, so that was it." He drank and watched in dismay as she waved at someone she knew, an inconspicuous wave at a dark-bearded man who drifted in from the doorway and lingered a moment beside them.

"All right?" that one asked.

"All right," she said. He was another Dubliner, older, grim. The shamrock and stars were plain on his sleeve, and he carried a collar stripe. Sandor sat still under that dark-eyed, unloving scrutiny, his face tautened in what was not quite a smile. The older man lingered, just long enough to warn; and walked on out the door.

Sandor stared after him, turned slightly in his seat to do so, still ruffled—turned back again with the feeling that A. Reilly would be amused at his discomfiture. She was.

She took the second drink down a third. Her cheeks were looking flushed. "What kind of hauling is your *Lucy*? General?"

"Very."

"You don't ask many questions."

"What does the A. stand for?"

"Allison. What's the *E.?*"

"Edward."

"Not Ed."

"Ed, if you like."

"Captain."

"And crew."

She seemed amused, finished the drink and tapped a long, peach-lacquered fingernail against the glass, making a gentle ringing. The barkeeper showed up. "I'll stay with the same," she said, and when he left, looked up with a tilt of her head at Sandor. "I mixed that and wine on Cyteen once and nearly missed my ship."

"They don't taste strong," he said, and with a sinking heart cast a glance at the bartender who was mixing up another small glass of expensive froth . . . and a second one for him, which was a foul trick and one they could pull in a place like this.

"Love them," she said when the bartender came back and set both down. She picked up hers and sipped. "A local delicacy, just on Viking and Pell. You come all the way from Wyatt's, do you? That's quite a distance for a smallish ship. What combine is that? I didn't hear you say."

"WSC." He was close to panic, what with the bill and the questions which were hitting into areas he wanted left alone. Misery churned in his stomach which the frothy drink did nothing to comfort. "I run margin, wherever there's room for a carrier. I'm close to independent. But *Dublin* fairly well runs her own combine, doesn't she? You go the whole circle. That's independent." He talked nonsense, to drag the question back to *Dublin*, back to her, staring into her eyes and suspecting that all this was at his expense, that some kind of high sign had just been passed between her and her bearded kinsman who had strayed through the door and out again. Possibly someone was waiting outside to start trouble. Or she was going to have her amusement as far as frustrated him and walk off, leaving him the bill. He was soberer after this one more drink than he had been when he came in here, excepting a certain numbness in his fingers, and while she looked no less beautiful, his desire was cooled by that sobriety, and by a certain wry amusement which persisted in her expression. He put on a good face, as he would do with a curious customs agent or a dockside dealer who meant to bluff his price down. He grinned and she smiled. "None of the chatter means anything to you," he said. "What questions am I supposed to ask?"

"You buy me a drink," she said, and set hers down, half-finished. "You don't buy anything else, of course, being wiser than some stationers I know, who don't know how far their money goes. Thank you, Stevens. I did enjoy it. Good luck to you, finding crew."

The bartender, operating on his own keen reflexes, was headed his way in a hurry, seeing who was leaving and who was being left to pay. Sandor saw that with his own tail-of-the-eye watch for trouble, felt in his pocket desperately and threw down what he had as Allison Reilly headed for the door and the lighted dock. He was off the stool and almost with her when the voice rang out: "*You!* You there, that's *short.*"

Sandor stopped, frozen by that voice, when in another place he might have dodged out, when in ordinary sanity he would not be *in* that situation. The military officers had looked up from their drinking. Others had. He felt theatrically in his pocket. "I gave you a twenty, sir."

The bartender scowled and held out the palm with the chits. "Not a twenty. Demis and a ten."

Sandor assumed outrage, stalked back and looked, put on chagrin. "I do beg pardon, sir. I was shorted myself, then, next door, because I should have had a twenty. I think I'm a little drunk, sir; but I have credit. Can we arrange this?"

The bartender glowered; but there came a presence at Sandor's shoulder and: "Charge it to *Dublin,*" Allison Reilly said. Sandor looked about into Allison Reilly's small smile and very plain stare: they were about of a size and it was a level glance indeed. "Want to step outside?" she asked.

He nodded, fright and temper and alcohol muddling into one adrenalin haze. He followed that slim coveralled figure with the midnight hair those few steps outside into the light, and the noise of the docks was sufficient to cool his head again. He had, he reckoned, been paid off well enough, scammed by an expert. He smiled ruefully at her when they stopped and she turned to face him. It was not what he was feeling at the moment, which was more a desire to break something, but good humor was obligatory on a man with empty pockets and a Dubliner's drinks in his belly. There were always her cousins, at least several hundred of them.

"Does that line work often?" she asked.

"I'll pay you the tab," he said, which he could not believe he was saying, but he reckoned that he could draw another twenty out of his margin account. He hated having been trapped and having been rescued. "I have it. I just don't walk the docks with much."

She stared at him as if weighing that. Or him. Or thinking of calling her cousins. "I take it that all of this was leading somewhere."

She did it to him again, set him completely off balance. "It might have," he said with the same wry humor. "But I'm headed back to my ship. You got all my change and I'm afraid *Lucy*'s accommodations aren't what you're used to."

"Huh." She looked in her pocket and brought out a single fifty. "Bradford's. I know it. It's a class accommodation."

He blinked, overthrown again, trying to figure if she had believed him anywhere down the line, or what she saw in the likes of him. She might be setting him up for another and worse joke than the last; but he wanted her. *That* was there again worse than before, obscuring all caution and choking off all clever argument. Years of dreaming solitary dreams and looking to stay alive, barely alive, which was all it came to . . . and one night in a silver bar and a high-class sleep-over. He had gotten hazardously drunk, he told himself, floating in an overload of senses; and so had she gotten drunk. She was deliberately picking someone like him who was a risk, because she was curious, or because she was bored, or because Bradford's was a *Dublin* hangout and one shout was going to bring more trouble down on him than he could deal with. His hand was still cold-sweating when they linked arms and walked in the direction she chose, and he wiped his palm on his pocket lining before he took her cool, dry hand in his.

They walked the dock, along which gantries pointed at the distant unseen core, towers aimed straight up beside them as they walked, and farther along aimed askew, so that they looked like the veined segments of some gigantic fruit, and the dock they walked unrolled like some gray spool of ribbon with a tinsel left-hand edge of neon-lit bars and restaurants and shop display windows. Viking dock had a set of smells all its own, part food and part liquor and part machinery and chemicals and the forbidding musky chill of open cargo locks; it had a set of sounds that was human noise and machinery working and music that wafted out of bars in combinations sometimes discordant and sometimes oddly fit. It was a giddy, sense-battering flow he had never given way to, not like this, not with a silver Dubliner woman arm in arm with him, step for step with him, weaving in and out among the crowds.

They reached Bradford's discreet front, with the smoked oval pressure windows and the gold lettering . . . walked in, checked in at the desk with a comp register presided over by a clerk who might have been a corporate receptionist. They stood on thick carpets, under fancy lighting, everything white and gold, where the foyer door shut out the gaudy noise of the docks. She paid, and got the room card, and grinned at him, took his arm and led the way down the thick-carpeted hall to a numbered doorway. She thrust the card into the slot and opened it.

It was a sleeper of the class of the bar they had just come from, a place he could never afford—all cream satin, with a conspicuous blue and cream bed and a cream tiled bath with a shower. For a moment he was put off by such luxury, which he had never so much as seen in his life. Then pride took hold of him, and he slipped his arm about Allison Reilly and pulled her close against him with a jerk which drew an instinctive resistance; he grinned when he did it, and she pushed back with a look that at once warned and chose to be amused.

He took account of that on the instant, that in fact his humor was a facade, which she had seen through constantly. It might not work so well—here, with a Dubliner's pride, on a Dubliner's money. He reckoned suddenly that he could make one bad enemy or—perhaps—save something to remember in the far long darks between stations. She scared him, that was the plain fact, because she had all the cards that mattered; and he could too easily believe that she was going to laugh, or talk about this to her cousins, and laugh in telling them how she had bought herself a night's amusement and had a joke at his expense. Worst of all, he was afraid he was going to freeze with her, because every time he was half persuaded it was real he had the nagging suspicion she knew what he was, and that meant police.

He steadied her face in his hand and tried kissing her, a
tentative move, a courtesy between dock-met strangers. She
leaned against him and answered in kind until the blood
was hammering in his veins.

"Shouldn't we close the door?" she suggested then, a
practicality which slammed him back to level again. He
let her go and pushed the door switch, looked back again
desperately, beginning to suspect that the whole situation
was humorous, and that he deserved laughing at, even by
himself. He was older than she was; but he was, he reckoned, far younger in such encounters. Naïve. Scared.

"I'm for a shower," Allison Reilly said cheerfully, and
started shedding the silver coveralls. "You too?"

He started shedding his own, at once embarrassed because he was off balance in the casualness of her approach
and because he still suspected humor in what with him was
beginning to be shatteringly serious.

She laughed; she splashed him with soap and managed
to laugh in the shower and tumbling in the bed with the
blue sheets, but not at all moments. For a long, long while
she was very serious indeed, and he was. They made love
with total concentration, until they ended curled in each
other's arms and utterly exhausted.

He woke. The lights were still on as they had been; and
Allison stirred and murmured about her watch and *Dublin,*
while he held onto her with a great and desperate melancholy and a question boiling in him that had been there
half the night.

"Meet you again?" he asked.

"Sometime," she said, tracing a finger down his jaw. "I'm
headed out this afternoon."

His heart plummeted. "Where next?"

A little frown creased her brow. "Pell," she said finally.
"That's not on the boards, but you could find it in the
offices. Going across the Line. Got a deal working there.
Be back—maybe next year, local."

His heart sank farther. He lay there a moment, thinking
about his papers, his cargo, his hopes. About an old man
who might talk, and fortunes that had shaved the profit in
his account to the bone. Year's end was coming. If he had
to, he could lay over and skim nothing more until the new

year, but it would rouse suspicion and it would run up a dock charge he might not work off. "What deal at Pell?" he asked. "Is that what's got the military stirred up?"

"You hear a lot of things on the docks," she said, cautious and frowning. "But what's that to you?"

"I'll see you at Pell."

"That's crazy. You said you were due at Fargone."

"I'll see you at Pell."

The frown deepened. She shifted in his arms, leaned on him, looking down into his face. "We're pulling out today. Just how fast is your *Lucy?* You think a marginer's going to run races with *Dublin?*"

"So you'll be shifting mass. I'm empty. I'll make it."

"Divert your ship? What's your combine going to say? Tell me that."

"I'll be there."

She was quiet for a moment, then ducked her head, and laughed softly, not believing him. "Got a few hours yet," she reminded him.

They used them.

And when she left, toward noon, he walked her out to the dockside near her own ship, and watched her walk away, a trim, silver-coveralled figure, the way he had seen her first.

He was sober now, and ought to have recovered, ought to shrug and call it enough. He ought to take himself and his ideas back to realspace and find that insystemer kid who might have ambitions of learning jumpships. He had knowledge to sell, at least, to someone desperate enough to sign with him, although the last and only promising novice he had signed had gotten strung out on the during-jump trank and not come down again or known clearly what he was doing when he had dosed himself too deeply and died of it.

Try another kid, maybe, take another chance. He talked well; that was always his best skill, that he could talk his way into and out of anything. He ought to take up where he had left off last night, scouting the bars and promoting himself the help he needed. He had cargo coming, the tag ends of station commerce, if he only waited and if some larger ship failed to snatch it; and if a certain old man kept his gossip to his own ship.

But he watched her walk away to a place he could not reach, and he had found nothing in all his life but *Lucy* herself that had wound herself that deeply into his gut.

Lucy against *Dublin Again.* There was that talk of new runs opening at Pell, the Hinder Stars being visited again, of trade with Sol, and while that rumor was almost annual, there was something like substance to it this time. The military was stirred up. Ships had gone that way. *Dublin* was going. Had a deal, she had said, and then shut up about it. The idea seized him, shook at him. He loved two things in his life that were not dead, and one of them was *Lucy* and the other was the dream of Allison Reilly.

Lucy was real, he told himself, and he could lose her; while Allison Reilly was too new to know, and far too many-sided. The situation with his accounts was not yet hopeless; he had been tighter than this and still made the balance. He ought to stick to what he had and not gamble at all.

And go where, then, and do what? He could not leave *Dublin*'s track without thinking how lonely it was out there; and never dock at a station without hoping that somehow, somewhen, *Dublin* would cross his path. A year from now, local . . . and he might not be here. Might be—no knowing where. Or caught, before he was much older, caught and mindwashed, so that he would see *Dublin* come in and not remember or not feel, when they had stripped his *Lucy* down to parts and done much the same with him.

He stood there more obvious in his stillness than he ever liked to be, out in the middle of the dock, and then started for dockside offices with far more haste than he ever liked to use in his movements, and browbeat the dockmaster's agent with more eloquence than he had mustered in an eloquent career, urging a private message which had just been couriered in and the need to get moving at once to Voyager. "So just fill the tanks," he begged of them, with that desperation calculated to give the meanest docksider a momentary sense of power; and to let that docksider recall that supposedly he was Wyatt's Star Combine, which might, if balked, receive reports up the line, and take offense at delay. "Just that much. Give me dry goods, no freezer stuff if it takes too long. I'll boil water from the tanks. Just get those lines on and get me moving."

There was what he had half expected, a palm open on the counter, right in the open office. He sweated, recalling police, recalling that ominous line of military ships docked just outside these offices on blue dock, two carriers in port, no less, with troops, troops like Viking stationers, unnervingly alike in size and build and manner, the stamp of birth labs. But tape-trained or not, Union citizens or not, there was the occasional open hand. If it was not a police trap. And that was possible too.

He looked up into eyes quite disconnected from that open palm. "You arrange me bank clearance, will you?" Sandor asked. "I really need to speed things up a bit. You think you can do that?"

Clerical lips pursed. The man consulted comp, did some figuring. "Voyager, is it? You know your margin's down to five thousand? I'd figure two for contingencies, at least."

He shuddered. Two was exorbitant. Dipping to the bottom of his already low margin account, the next move went right through into WSC's main fund: it would surely do that with the current dock charges added on. There had been a chance of coming back here—had been—but this would bring the auditors running. He nodded blandly. "You help me with that, then, will you? I really need that draft."

The man turned and keyed a printout from a desk console. Comp spat out a form. He laid it on the counter. "Make it out to yourself. I can disburse here for convenience."

"I really appreciate this." He leaned against the counter and made out the form for seven, smiled painfully as he handed it back to the official, who counted him out the money from the office safe. . . . Union scrip, not station chits; bills, in five hundreds.

"Maybe," said the clerk, "I should walk with you down there and pass the word to the dock supervisor about your emergency. I think we can get you out of here shortly."

He kept smiling and waited for the clerk to get his coat, walked with him outside, into the busy office district of the docks. "When those lines are hooked up and when the food's headed in," he said, his hand on the bills in his pocket, "then I'll be full of gratitude. But I expect frozen goods for this, and without holding me up. You sting me like I was a big operation, you see that I get all the supplies I'm due for it."

"Don't push your luck, Captain."

"I'm sure you can do it. I have faith in you. If I get questioned on this, so do you. Think of that."

A silence while they walked. There were the warship accesses at their right, bright and cheerful as merchanter accesses, but uniformed troops came and went there, and security guards with guns stood at various of the offices on dockside. Birth-lab soldiers, alike to the point of eeriness. Perhaps stationers, many of them from like origins, found it all less strange. This man beside him now, this man was from the war years, might have been on Viking during the fall, maybe had memories, the same as a merchanter recalled the taking of his ship. Bloody years. They shared that much, he and the stationer. Dislike of the troops. A certain nervousness. A sense that a little cash in pocket was a good thing to have, when tensions ran high. There was a time they had evacuated stations, shifted populations about, when merchanters had run for the far Deep and stayed there for self-protection, while warships had decided politics. No one looked for such years again, but the reflexes were still there.

"Hard times," Sandor said finally, when they were on blue dock's margin and walking through the section arch to green. "Big ships take care of themselves, but small ships have worries. I really need those goods."

Continued silence. Finally: "You hear anything down the line?" the man asked.

"Nothing solid. Mazianni hitting ships—Hang, what can I do? I don't have the kind of margin I can take out and not haul for months like some others might do. I don't have it. Little ships like me, combine forgets about us when trouble hits on that scale. WSC is stationer-run, and they're going to say haul, come what may. And some of their big haulers are going to hide out while the likes of me gets caught in the middle. But who'll keep the stations going? Marginers and independents and the like. I'd really like those frozen goods."

"Cost you extra."

"No way. You stung me for the two. I do it again and I get closer and closer to a company audit, man. You think two thousand's nothing? In an account my size it's something."

"You think your combine's pulling you out of here?"

"Don't know what they're going to do."

"Running under-the-table courier, it sounds like they want you out of here."

"I don't know."

Silence again. "Bet they're not going to check that account too closely. Bet they'll be more than glad to get their ships herded in to safer zones if there's action around here. They're realists. They know their ships have got to protect themselves. In all senses. You know the gold market?"

His pulse sped. "I know I'm not licensed to transport."

"Times like these, value goes up. The less on a station, value goes up. A lot of merchanters like to carry a little in pocket."

"I can't do that kind of thing. WSC'd have my head."

"Get you, say, some oddments. Little stuff. You put fourteen more with that extra thousand, and I know a dealer can get you a station standard price plus fifteen percent, good rate for a merchanter, same as the big ships get."

The station air hit his face with a sickly chill, touching perspiration. "You know you're talking about felony. That's not skimming. That's theft."

"How worried are you? If your combine pulls you out, if it gets hot, maybe it's going to cost you heavy. As long as you put it in again where you're going, you're covered, and you can pocket the increase it's made."

"Won't increase that much, going away from the trouble."

"Oh, it will. It always does. It's the smart thing. Always good on stations. Can't be traced. Buys you all kinds of things. And if there's any kind of trouble—it goes up."

He swallowed the knot in his throat. "Right. Well, you get me that check and I'll do it, but I don't handle it at any stage."

"It'll cost you another thousand on all that deal: my risk."

"If I'm first on the docking schedule and those goods get aboard while I'm filling."

"No problem."

*   *   *

He was loaded in two hours, signed, cleared, and belted in, undocking from Viking with a gentle puff of *Lucy*'s bow vents, which eased him back and back and tended to a little pitch. He let the accustomed pitch increase, which was a misaimed jet, but he knew *Lucy* and had never fixed it. The pitch always set her for an axis roll and a little aft venting sent her over and out still within her given lane, because she was small and could pull maneuvers like that, which were usually for the military ships. He never showed more flash than that in a station's vicinity. He had more potential attention than he wanted. He had committed felony theft, faked papers, faked IDs, had unlicensed cargo aboard, and it was time to change *Lucy*'s name again—if he had had the time.

He put on aft vid and saw *Dublin Again,* had gone right past her, that silver, beautiful ship all aglow with her own running lights and the station's floods, in station shadow, so that she shone like a jewel among the others. Not so far away, a Union dartship stood off from dock, dull-surfaced and ominous, with vanes conspicuously larger than any merchanter afforded. It watched, its frame bristling with armaments and receptors. Viking's sullen star swung behind it as he moved, silhouetting it in bleeding fire, and he lost sight of *Dublin* in the glare—shut vid down, listening to station central's ordinary voice giving him his clear heading for the outgoing jump range, for a supposed jump for Voyager Station.

It was no small job, to clear *Dublin Again* for undock.
Gathering and accounting for the crew was an undertaking
in itself: 1,882 lives were registered to *Dublin,* of which the
vast majority were scattered out over the docks on liberty,
and most of those had been gone for four days, in one and
the other sleepovers around the vast torus of Viking, not
alone on green dock, but spread through every docking
section but blue and the industrial core. They knew their
time and they came in, to log their time at whatever job
wanted doing, if there was a job handy—to shove their ID
tags into the slot when they were ready for absolute and
irrevocable boarding, passing that green line on the airlock
floor and walls that let them know they were logged on
and would be left without search or sympathy if they re-
crossed that line without leave of the watch officer.

One hundred forty-six Dubliners were entitled to wear
the green stars of executive crew; of that number, 76 wore
the collar stripe of senior, seated crew, main-day and alterday. Four wore the captain's circle, one for each of four
duty shifts; 24, at one level and the other, were entitled to
sit in the chair in theory, or to take other bridge posts. And
16 were retired from that slot, who had experience, if not
the physical ability; they advised, and sat in executive council. It took seven working posts at com to run *Dublin* in
some operations, at any one moment; eight posts at scan,
with four more at the op board that monitored cargo status.
Twenty-five techs and as many cargo specialists on a watch

kept things in order; and with all told, posted crew and backup personnel, that was 446 who wore the insignia of working crew; and 279 unposted, who trained and waited and worked as they could. There were the retired: over 200 of them, whose rejuv had given out and whose health faded, some of whom still went out on dockside and some of whom took to their quarters or to sickbay and expected to die when jump stress put too great a burden on them. There were the children, nearly 200 under the age of twenty, 120 of whom had duties and took liberty when *Dublin* docked, and 40 of those on the same privilege as the crew, to sleepover where they chose.

And at mainday 1550 hours, *Dublin*'s strayed sons and daughters headed aboard like a silver-clad flood, past the hiss and clank of loading canisters. Some of them had had a call for 1400, and some for 1200, those in charge of cargo. All the Reillys—they *were* all Reillys, all 1,082 of them, excepting Henny Magen and Liz Tyler, who were married aboard from other ships (everyone forgot their alien names and called them Reillys by habit, making no distinction)— all the Reillys were headed in, out of the gaudy lighted bars and glittering shops and sleepovers, carrying purchases and packages and in many cases lingering for a demonstrative farewell to some liberty's-love on the verge of *Dublin*'s clear-zone. No customs checked them off the station: they came as they liked, and Allison Reilly walked up the ramp and through the yellow, chill gullet of the access tube to the lock, carrying two bottles of Cyteen's best, a collection of microfiches, two pair of socks, a deepstudy tape, and six tubes of hand lotion—not a good place to shop, Viking, which was mostly mining and shipbuilding: there was freight and duty on all of it but the microfiches and the tape, but they were headed Over the Line into Alliance territory, and most everyone was buying *something,* in the thought that goods in that foreign territory might be different, or harder to come by, and there was a general rush to pick up this and that item. She needed the socks and she liked the particular brand of hand lotion.

Crossing the green line, she fished out her dog tags and pulled them off one-handed as she reached the watch desk just the other side of the lock, smiled wearily at her several cousins of varying degree who sat that cheerless duty, and stuck the key-tag into the portable comp unit while Danny Reilly checked her off. It was Jamie and little Meg behind her; she turned and nodded them a courtesy, they seventeen and nineteen and herself a lofty twenty-five, that made her ma'am to them, and them a merest nod from her. She took her packages on to the check-in desk, stripped the packing materials off and put the merchandise in the lidded bin a cousin offered her, with a grease-penciled ALLISON II on the end amid the smears of previous notes. Nearly a thousand Dubliners returning with purchases, with most of their quarters inaccessible during dock and only an hour remaining before departure: it was impossible, otherwise, to handle that much personal cargo; and it had to be weighed and reckoned against individual mass allotment. There would be a scramble after first jump, while they were lazing their way across the first nullpoint on their way to Pell, everyone going to the cargomaster to collect their purchases. There was something psychological about it, like birthday packages, that everyone liked to have something waiting for that sort-out, be it only a bag of candy. And when a body went over-mass, well, one could weigh it out again, too, and trade off, or consume the consumables, or pay the mass charge with overtime and sell off one's overmass at the next port liberty, along dockside, or (at some stations with liberal customs) in merchanters' bazaars, themselves a heady excitement of barter and docksiding stationers looking for exotica. A bin waited for packing materials; she stripped it all down, closed the lid and watched her purchases go down the chute to cargo, walked on, burdenless. When *Dublin* had collected all the packing and the debris, down to the last moment before the cargo hatch was sealed, out would pop a waste canister, everything from paper to reusable nylon, and station recycling would seize it and carry it off to be sorted, sifted, and used again. *Dublin* shifted nothing through jump but what was useful; station threw nothing away that had to be freighted in, not even worn-out clothing.

"Are we still on schedule?" she asked the cousin nearest.

"Last I heard," the woman said. "The bell goes in about forty-five minutes."

"Huh." She threw an involuntary glance at the desk clock and walked on through, burdenless, putting her dog tags to rights again, dodging past cousins with last-minute business in cargo, mostly maintenance who were taking wastage to the chute, and now and again someone with a personal bit of debris to jettison, a nuisance that should have been run through comp before now, but there was always someone trying to break through the line of in-comers with something outgoing.

There was at least a reasonable quiet about the traffic toward the lift . . . a few others her seniors, a few her junior, with some of the other unposteds . . . people in a hurry in uncommonly narrow spaces, because the great cyl-inder that was *Dublin*'s body still sat in docking lock, and no one in dockside boots could take any corridors but the number ones. The rest remained dark, up the upcurve of the intersecting halls, waiting the undock and start of rota-tion which would restore access to the whole circumference of the ship.

The pale green of outer corridors became Op Zone white, the dock smells which wafted in from the lock gave way to bitingly crisp air, tiles and corridors and lighting panels in pristine pallor that would show any smudge or streak—notoriously clean, because Dubliners in their youth spent hour on aching hour keeping the corridors that way. The lift, in the white zone, had a handful of cousins waiting for it; Allison nodded to the others and waited too—a glance and a hello to Deirdre, of her own year, another of her unit; got of a *Cato* man on Esperance liberty, so it ran. Deirdre had that knit-browed absentia of a four-day binge, a tendency to wince at noise. Allison folded her own arms and disdained to lean against the wall, being unposted exec, and not general crew, but her knees ached and her feet ached from walking, while she thought with longing of her own soft bunk, in her quarters topside.

"Good night?" someone asked. She blinked placidly at another unposted who had been with her in Tiger's last night.

"Yes," she said, thinking about it for a moment, drew in a breath and favored Curran with a thoughtful glance. "What happened to yourself?"

Curran grinned. That was all. The lift arrived, and seniors went on first; there was room for the three of them, herself and Deirdre and Curran, and a jam of others after that.

The lift whisked them up to the second level, and they lost the juniors, who were bound for their own territory; it stopped again on main, and they let the seniors off first, then followed through the corridor into the main lounge, into the din of laughter and conversation in a room as big as most station bars, curve-floored and with the float-based furniture now tilted out of trim with the ship's geometries. Posted crew and seniors gathered in the lounge beyond, and Allison wove her way through the center standing area to the archway, looked inside to find her mother, Megan, who was posted scan 24.

"I'm back," she hand-signed past the noise, the gathering in the two lounges. Megan saw her and walked over, across the white line into the unposted lounge to talk to her. "I worried," Megan said.

"Huh. I'm not about to miss the bell. Have a good stay?"

"Got some new tapes."

"Nothing else?"

Her mother grinned and went sober again, irrepressibly reached out and straightened her collar. "The number ones are still in conference. We think we're going to get undocked on schedule. The military's talking to the Old Man now."

"No question about clearance, is there?" She straightened her collar herself, minor irritance. "I thought that was settled."

"Something about some papers on the cargo. Trans-Line protocols. Viking stationmaster is insisting we re-enter Union space via Viking; we make no promises, and the military's backing us on it. The bell's going on schedule, I'm betting."

"I don't see it's Viking's prerogative."

"Balance of trade, they say. They'll raise a fuss all the way to Council."

She frowned—glanced about as a heavy hand came down on her shoulder; it was her mother's half-brother Geoff, dark-bearded, brows knit. "Allie," her uncle said, "you mind how you go on the docks."

"He was safe," Allison said.

"Huh," Geoff said, and looked past her at Megan. "Mind this one, Meg. Did that fellow ask questions, Allie? Did you answer any?"

"He wasn't curious and no, nothing he couldn't get by asking anywhere. I asked the questions, Geoff, sir, and I was soberer than he was."

"Stay to Names you know," Megan said. "Nowadays particularly."

"Ma'am," Allison said under her breath. "Sir." Drew breath and ducked past with a pat on the shoulder as her half-sister Connie showed up to report in, relieving her of more discussion. There was no great closeness between herself and Connie, who was pregnant and occupied in that, whose study was archives and statistics. " 'Lo, Connie," and "Hello, Allie," was all that passed between them. Curran was closer, Geoff was, or Dierdre, but Megan loved freckled Connie, so that was well enough with Allison, who moderately liked her, at the distance of their separate lives. "Hello," she said to Eilis, who made a touch at her as she passed through the crowd; and "Ma'am" to her grandmother Allison, who on rejuv was silver-haired, sterile, and looked no more than forty (she was sixty-two). And there was greatgrand Mina, scan 2, who also looked forty, and was twice that—seated crew, Mina, who was back in unposted territory talking to Ma'am herself, who was sitting down on one of the benches—Ma'am with a capital M, that was Colleen, whose rejuv was fading and who had gone dry and thin and wrinkled, but who still got about in the lounges during maneuvers despite brittle bones and stiffening joints. Ma'am was the point at which she was related to Curran and Deirdre both. Ma'am was retired com 1, and kept the perks she had had in that post, but evidently chose not to be in council at the moment. Ma'am and Mina deserved courtesy on boarding, and Allison worked her way across the room and the noise and paid it, which Mina answered with a preoccupied nod, but Ma'am grabbed her hands, kissed her on the cheek as if she had been one of the toddlers, and let her go again, talking past her to Mina nonstop in a low tone that involved the military and the rights of merchanters. Allison lingered half a breath, learned nothing, strayed away again, past other hellos and the delicate tottering of a two-year-old loose in the press.

She found a bench and sat down, lost in the forest of standing bodies, glanced across the tops of red contoured furniture which wrapped itself up the curve of the room: some of the unposteds had stretched out sideways on the benches with their eyes shielded. Too much celebration, too late. The inevitable bands of knee-high youngsters yelled and darted as high on the floor curve as they could, occasionally taking a spill and risking being collared by one of their elders if their antics knocked into someone. Someone's baby was squalling, probably Dia's; it always did, hating the noise. The older children squealed: it was their time to burn off all the energy, and it was part of their courage, the racing and the play and the I-dare-you approach to undock that made a game of the maneuvers *Dublin* went through. It gave them nerve for the jump that was coming, which merchanter babies went through even unborn. These were the under fives, the youngsters loose among them. The sixes through sixteens were up in the topside of the cylinder, where they spent most of their dockside time (and all of it for the six-through-nines) in a topsy-turvy ceiling-downside nursery, where a padded crawlthrough made *G* reorientation only another rowdy, rumbling game. Every Dubliner remembered, with somewhat of nostalgia, how much better that was than this adult jam-up in the downside lounge.

They gained no numbers in a generation: the matrilineal descent of merchanters generated new Dubliners of sleepover encounters with more concern for too few children than too many: another was always welcome, and if one wanted half a dozen, and another wanted none, that was well enough: it all balanced out from one generation to the next: Ma'am and Mina and Allison Senior came down, among others, to Megan and Geoff. Geoff had no line on *Dublin*, being male; but Megan had her and Connie, which balanced out; and Connie was already taking the line down another generation. Only rejuv kept five and sometimes six generations living at once: like Ma'am, who was pushing a hundred fifty and had faded only in the last decade, Ma'am, who had been Com 1 so long her voice was *Dublin*'s in the minds of everyone. It still made shockwaves, thin as it had gotten, when Ma'am made it snap and handed out an order; and there was still the retired Old Man, who had been the Old Man for most of Allison's life, and seldom got about now, snugged in his cabin that was downmost during dock, attended by someone always during jump, listening to tapes for his entertainment and sleeping more and more.

Allison herself . . . was Helm 21, which was status among the unposteds, Third Helm's number one of the alterday shift. What do you want to be? Megan had asked her as early as she could remember the question. When a Dubliner was taking his first study tapes he got the Question, and started learning principles before awkward fingers could hold a pen or scrawl his letters, tapestudy from *Dublin*'s ample library. So what do you want to be? Megan had asked, and she had wanted to be bridge crew, where lights flashed and people sat in chairs and did important things, and where the screens showed the stars and the stations. What do you want to be? The question came quarterly after that, and it went through a range of choices, until at ten: I want to be the Old Man, she had said, before she had hardly gone out on a station dock or seen anything in the universe but the inside of *Dublin*'s compartments and corridors. The king of the universe was the Old Man who sat in the chair and captained *Dublin,* the Number One mainday captain, who ruled it all.

Be reasonable, Megan had told her then, taking her in the circle of her arm, setting her on the edge of the bed in her quarters and trying to talk sense into her. Only one gets to be the Old Man; and you know how many try the course and fail? Maybe one in four survives the grade to get into the line; and one in fifty gets to Helm 24, up where you're even going to sit a chair on watch; and after that, age is against you, because the sitting captains are too young. You go ask in library, Allie, how long the sitting captains are going to live, and then you do the math and figure out how long the number two chairs are going to live after taking their posts behind them, and how long it takes for Helm 24 to work up to posted crew.

Can't I try? she had asked. And: yes, you can try, Megan had said. I'm only telling you how it is.

Maybe there'll be an accident, she had thought to herself, with a ten-year-old's ruthless ambition: an accident to wipe out everyone in Second Helm.

You study everything, Megan had said, when she had complained about learning galley maintenance; the Helm course fits you for everything. So if you fail, you drop into whatever other track you're passing. You think Helm's just sitting in that chair: it's trade and routings; law; navigation and scan and com and armaments; its jack and jill of all trades, Allie, ma'am, and doing all the scut before you hand it out, and you can always *quit*, Allie, ma'am.

No, ma'am, she had said, and swallowed all they gave her, reckoning to be stubbornest the longest, and to make it all the way, because there was a craziness in her, that once launched, she had a kind of inertia that refused to be hauled down. She was Helm 21, and when Val retired as she was likely to, Helm 6 and on the fading edge of rejuv, she would be Helm 20, and one more Dubliner got a post as Helm 24. He walked wide among the unposteds, being Helm. It had its perks. But Lallie, over there, Maintenance 196, was Second Maintenance second shift alterday at barely twenty-one, posted main crew before her hair grayed, while Helm 21 had little chance indeed, with a possible forty years until another seated Helm decided to give it up and retire. She would be on rejuv before the list got her past Helm 20, would still be lording it over the unposteds, silver-haired and still not able to cross the line into the posteds lounge, still waiting, still working the number two bridge to stay current.

She shut her eyes, leaned back, seeing blue dock again, and soldiers in their black uniforms. They talked about opening up Sol trade, shut down since the war; about opening the mothballed stations of the Hinder Stars. They talked new routes and profits to be made—putting their hand into Alliance territory, creating a loop that would link the Union stars to the Pell-based alliance. Trade and politics.

So much she knew, sitting in on *Dublin* executive councils, which was all of Helm and only sitting crew of other tracks. She knew all the debate, whether *Dublin* should take the chance, whether they should just sit out the building and wait for the accomplished fact; but *Dublin* had always stood with one foot on either side of a crisis, always poised herself ready to move to best advantage, and the Merchanter's Alliance, once an association of merchanter captains who disputed Union, now held the station at Pell's Star for a capital, declared itself a sovereign government, passed laws, in short . . . looked like a power worth having a foot inside. A clean record with Union; a clean record with the Alliance thus far, since *Dublin* had operated far out of the troubled zones during the war—she could get herself a Pell account opened and if that new trade really was opening up there, then *Dublin* could get herself dual papers. Union Council was in favor of it, wanted moderates like themselves in the Alliance, good safe Unionside haulers who would vote against Pell-side interests as the thing got bigger. Union talked about building merchant ships and turning them over to good safe Unionsiders like *Dublin* to increase their numbers—which talk quickened Allison's pulse. A new ship to outfit would strip away all the Second Helm of *Dublin,* and get her posted on the spot. She had lived that thought for a year.

But more and more it looked like a lot of talk and a maintenance of the status quo. Rapprochement was still the operative word in Union: Alliance and Union snuggling closer together after their past differences. Recontacting Sol, after the long silence, in an organized way. Clearing the pirates out. All merchanters having equal chance at the new ships that might be built.

Hopes rose and fell. At the moment they were fallen, and she took wild chances on dockside. Geoff was right. Stupidity. But it had helped, with the soldiers crawling all over station that close to crossing the Line into foreign space. So she scattered a bit of her saved credit on a fellow who could use a good drink and a good sleepover. In a wild impulse of charity it might have been good to have scattered a bit more on him: he looked as if he could have used it . . . but touchy-proud. He would not have taken it. Or would have, being hungry, and hated her for it. There had been no delicate way. He fell behind her in her mind, as Viking did, as all stations did after they sealed the hatch. If she thought persistently of anyone, it was Charlie Bodart of *Silverbell,* green-eyed, easygoing Charlie, Com 12 of his ship, who crossed her path maybe several times a loop, *Silverbell* and *Dublin* running one behind the other.

But not now. Not to Pell, across the Line. Good-bye to *Silverbell* and all that was familiar—at least for the subjective year. And it might be a long time before they got back on Charlie's schedule—if ever.

A body hit the cushion beside her, heavy and male. She opened her eyes and turned her head in the din of voices. Curran.

"What," Curran said, "hung over? You've got a face on you."

"Not much sleep."

"I'll tell you about not much sleep."

"I'll bet you will." She looked from him to the clock, and the bell was late. "I got along. I got those fiches too. And a couple of bottles."

"We'll have those killed before we get to Pell."

"We'll have to kill them at dock if they don't get the soldierlads organized and get us out of here."

"I think they've got it straightened away," Curran said. Helm 22, Curran, right behind her in the sequence. Dark-haired, like enough for a brother; and close to that. "I heard that from Ma'am."

"I hope." She folded her arms, gathered up her cheerfulness. "I had an offer, I want you to know. My friend last night was looking for crew. Number one and only on his own ship, he said. Offered me a Helm 2 chair, he did. At least that's what I think he was offering."

Curran chuckled. It was worth a laugh, a marginer making offers to *Dublin*. And not so deep a laugh, because it touched hopes too sensitive, that they both shared.

"Cousin Allie." That shrill piping was aged four, and barrelled into her unbraced lap, to be picked up and bounced. Allison caught her breath, hauled Tish up on her leg, bounced her once dutifully and passed her with a toss over to Curran, who hugged the imp and rolled her off his lap onto the empty cushion beside him. "Going to *go*," Tish said, having, at four, gotten the routine down pat. "Going to walk all round *Dublin*."

"Pretty soon," Curran said.

"Live up *there*," Tish said, jabbing a fat finger ceilingward. "My baby up *there*."

"Next time you remember to bring your baby down," Allison said. "You bring her with you the next time we dock."

There had been no end of the wail over the forgotten doll at the start of their liberty. Middle zones of the ship went inaccessible during dock; and young Will III had offered to eel through the emergency accesses after it, but no, it was a lark for Will, but a good way to take a fall, and Tish learned to keep track of things. Everyone learned. Early.

"Go," Tish crowed, anxious. Prolonged dock was no fun for the littlest, in cramped spaces and adult noise.

"Bye," Allison said, and Tish slid down and worked her way through adult legs to bedevil some of her other several hundred cousins, while Allison shut her eyes and wished the noise would stop. Her wishes were narrow at the moment, centered on her own comfortable, clean-smelling bed.

Then the bell rang, the Cinderella stroke that ended liberty and liberties, and the children were shushed and taken in arms. Conversations died. People remembered hangovers and feet and knees that ached from walking unaccustomed distances on the docks, recalled debts run up that would have to be worked off odd jobbing. "I lied," someone said louder than other voices, the old joke, admitting that after-the-bell accounts were always less colorful. There was laughter, not at the old joke, but because it was old and comfortable and everyone knew it. They drifted for the cushions, and there was a general snapping and clicking of belts, a gentle murmur, a last fretting of children. Allison bestirred herself to pull her belt out of the housings and to clip it as Eilis settled into the seat next to hers and did the same.

Bacchanale was done. The Old Man was back in the chair again, and the posted crew, having put down their authority for the stay on station, took it up again.

Dublin prepared to get underway.

3

Lucy was never silent in her operation. She had her fan noises and her pings and her pops and crashes as some compressor cycled in or a pump went on or off. Her seating creaked and her rotation rumbled and grumbled around the core . . . a rotating ring with a long null *G* center and belly that was her hold, a stubby set of generation vanes stretched out on top and ventral sides: that was the shape of her. She moved along under insystem propulsion, doing her no-cargo best, toward the Viking jump range, outbound, on the assigned lane a small ship had to use.

Sandor reached and put the interior lights on, and *Lucy*'s surroundings acquired some cheer and new dimensions. Rightward, the corridor to the cabins glared with what had once been white tiles—bare conduits painted white like the walls; and to the left another corridor horizoned up the curve, lined with cabinets and parts storage. Aft of the bridge and beyond the shallowest of arches, another space showed, reflected in the idle screens of vacant stations, bunks in brown, worn plastic, twelve of them, that could be set manually for the pitch at dock. Their commonroom, that had been. Their indock sleeping area, living quarters, wardroom—whatever the need of the moment. He set *Lucy*'s autopilot, unbelted and eased himself out of the cushion: that was enough to get himself a stiff fine if station caught him at it, moving through the vicinity of a station with no one at controls.

He found the pulser unit in under the counter storage,

taped it to his wrist and handed himself across the bridge, fighting the spiral drift along to the right-hand corridor, a controlled stagger with right foot on the tiled footing curve and left on the deck. He got the pharmaceuticals he wanted and brought them back to his place on the bridge, another stagger down the footings and swing along the hand grips. Then he knelt down in the pit and used tape and braces to rig her as she had been rigged before, taped the drugs he would need for jump to the side of the armrest where he could get at them; taped down some of the safety controls—also illegal; he set up the rig for the sanitation kit, because he would need that too, much as he dreaded it.

A second trip, rightward, this time, past sealed cabins, into the narrow confines of the galley and galley storage. He filled water bottles, and took an armful of them back to the bridge, jammed them into the brace he had long ago rigged near the command console . . . scared, if he let himself think about it. He swallowed such feelings, bobbed his head up now and again to check scan, down again to open up the underdeck storage where he had shoved some of the dried goods, not to have to suit up for the chill of the holds to hunt for them. He knelt there counting the packets out, taped them where he could get at them from the chair. His braced limbs shook from the strain of *G*. He dropped a packet and lunged after it, taped it where it belonged.

The lane still showed clear. He crawled up and held onto the back of the cushion, staring at the instruments, finally edged his way back to one of the brown plastic bunks at the aft bulkhead, to give his back a little relief from the strain. His eyes stung with fatigue. He rested his hands beside him, arms pulled askew by the spiral stress of acceleration, leaned his head against the bulkhead, not really comfortable, but it was a change from the long-held position in the cushion, and he could get the com or the controls from here if he had to.

There were compartments all about the ring, private quarters. Diametrically opposite the bridge was the loft, where the children had been . . . he never went around the ring that far. This was home, this small space, these bunks aft of the bridge, plastic mattresses patched with tape and deteriorating with age. One had been his when he was ten, that over there, nearest the partition spinward; and there had been Papa Lou's, which he never sat on; and one his mother's; he had had brothers and sisters and cousins once, and there had been three children under six, cousins too. But Papa Lou had vented them and old Ma'am too, when their boarders turned ugly and it was clear what they were going to do. They had had *Lucy*'s armament, but that had been helpless against a carrier and its riderships; they had had only two handguns on the ship . . . and the boarders who had ambushed them in the nullpoint had said they were not touching crew, only cargo. It had been *Lucy*'s clear choice then, open the hatch or be blown entirely. But they lied, the Mazianni, pirates even then, in the years when they had called themselves the Company Fleet and fought for Pell and Earth. They respected nothing and counted life nothing, and into such hands Papa Lou had surrendered them . . . not understanding.

He himself had not understood. He had not imagined. He had looked at the armored, faceless invaders with a kind of awe, a child's respect of such power. He had—for that first few moments they had been aboard—wanted to be one of them, wanted to carry weapons and to wear such sleek, frightening armor—one brief, ugly temptation, until he had seen Papa Lou afraid, and begun to suspect that something evil had come, something far less beautiful inside the armor, that had gotten into the ship's heart. He always felt guilt when he recalled that . . . that he had admired, that he had wanted to frighten others and not be frightened—he reasoned with himself that it was only the glitter that had drawn him, and that any child would have reacted the same, in the confusion, in the shaking of reliable references, in ignorance, if not in innocence. But he always felt unclean.

Most of it had happened here, on the bridge, in the commonroom and the corridor, in this widest part of the ship where they had gathered everyone but the children, and where the boarders started showing what they meant to do. But Papa Lou had gotten to the command chair and voided the part of the ship where the children and the oldest had taken refuge, before they shot him; and most of them had died, shot down in the commonroom and on the bridge; and some of them had been taken away for slower treatment.

But three of them, himself and old Mitri and cousin Ross, had lain there in the blood and the confusion because they were half dead—himself aged ten and standing with crew because he had slipped around the curve and gotten to his mother's side. They had not died, they three, which was Ross's doing, because Ross was mad-stubborn to live, and because after they had been left adrift, Ross had dragged himself from beside the bunk where he had fallen on him and Mitri, and gotten the med kit that was spilled all over where the pirates had rifled it for drugs. That was where his mother had been lying shot through the head: he recalled that all too vividly. She had gotten one of the boarders at the last, because they had given the women the two guns—they needed them most, Papa Lou had said—and when Papa Lou vented the children his mother had shot one of the boarders before they shot her, got an armored man right in the faceplate and killed him, and they dragged him off with them when they left the ship, probably because they wanted the armor back. But Aunt Jame had died before she could get a clear shot at any of them.

Here they had fallen, here, here, here, twelve bodies, and more in the corridor rightward, and himself and Mitri and Ross.

Those were his memories at times like this, fatigued and mind-numbed, or cooking a solitary meal in the galley, or walking past vacant cabins, sights that washed out all the happier past, everything that had been good, behind one red-running image. Everywhere he walked and sat and slept, someone had died. They had scrubbed away all the blood and made the plastic benches and the tiles and the plating clean again; and they had vented their dead at that lonely nullpoint, undisturbed once the pirate had gone its way—sent them out in space where they probably still drifted, frozen solid and lost in infinity, about the cinder of an almost-star. It was a clean, decent disposal, after the ugliness that had gone before. In his mind they still existed in that limbo, never decayed, never changed . . . they went on traveling, no suit between them and space, all the starry sights they had loved passing continually in front of their open, frozen eyes—a company of travelers that would stay more or less together, wherever they were going. All of them. Only Ma'am and the babies had gone ahead, and the others would never overtake them.

Mitri had died out on the hull one of the times they had had to change *Lucy*'s name, when they had run the scam on Pan-paris, and it had gone sour—a stupid accident that had happened because the Mazianni had stripped them of equipment they needed: Ross had spent four hours and risked his life getting Mitri back because they had thought there was hope; but Mitri had been dead from the first few moments, the pressure in the suit having gone and blood having gotten into the filters, so Ross just called to say so and stripped the suit and let Mitri go, another of *Lucy*'s drifters, but all alone this time. And he, twelve, had sat alone in the ship shivering, sick with fear that something would happen to Ross, that he would not get back, that he would die, getting Mitri in.

Leave him, he had yelled at Ross, his own cowardice, before he had even known that Mitri was dead; he remembered that; and remembered the lonely sound of Ross crying into the mike when he knew. He had thrown up from fright after Ross had come in safe. Another lonely null-point, those points of mass between the burning stars that jumpships used to steer by; and he could not have gotten *Lucy* out of there, could not have handled the jump on his own, if he had lost Ross then. He had cried, after that, and Mitri had haunted him, a shape that tumbled through his dreams, the only one of *Lucy*'s ghosts that reproached him.

Ross had died on Wyatt's, dealing with people who tried to cheat him. The stationers, beyond doubt, had cremated him, so one of them was forever missing from the tally of drifters in the deep. In a way, that troubled him most of all, that he had had to leave Ross in the hands of strangers, to be destroyed down to his elements . . . but he had had only the quick chance to break *Lucy* away, to get her out before they attached her, and he kept her. He had been seventeen then, and knew the contacts and the ports and how to talk to customs agents.

He slept in Ross's old bunk, in this one, because it was as close as he could come to what he had left of family, and this one bed seemed warmer than the rest, not so unhappily haunted as the rest. Ross had always been closer than his own mind to him, and because he had not cast out Ross's body with his own hands, it was less sometimes like Ross was dead than that he had gone invisible after the mishap at Wyatt's, and still existed aboard, in the programs comp held—so, so meticulously Ross had recorded all that he knew, programmed every operation, left instructions for every eventuality . . . in case, Ross had said, simply in case. The recorded alarms spoke in Ross's tones; the time signals did; and the instruction. It was company, of sorts. It filled the silences.

He tried not to talk to the voice more than need be, seldom spoke at all while he was on the ship, because he reckoned that the day he started talking back and forth with comp, he was in deep trouble.

Only this time he sat with his eyes fixed on the screens on the bridge, with his shoulder braced against the acceleration, and a vast lethargy settled over him in the company of his ghosts. Ross, he thought, Ross . . . I might love her; because Ross was the closest thing he had ever had to a father, a personal father, and he had to try out the thought on someone, just to see if it sounded reasonable.

It did not. There were story-tapes, a few aged tapes Ross had conned on Pan-paris when they were young and full of chances. He listened to them over and over and conjured women in his mind, but he knew truth from fancy and refused to let fancy take a grip on him. It had to do with living . . . and solitude; and there were slippages he could not afford. He had been drunk, that was all; was sober now, and simply tired.

He had been crazy into the bargain, to have paid what he had paid to get clear of station. And he was outbound, accelerating, committed. . . . He was headed for a real place out there, was about to violate lane instructions, headed out to new territory with forged papers. It was a real place, and a real meeting, where a dream could get badly bent.

Where it could end. Forever.

(Ross . . . I'm scared.)

No noise but the fans and the turning of the core, that everpresent white sound in which the rest of the silence was overwhelming. Little human sounds like breathing, like the dropping of a stylus, the pushing of a button, were whited out, swallowed, made null.

(Ross . . . this may be the last trip. I'm sorry. I'm tired. . . .)

That was the crux of it. The certainty settled into his bones. The last trip, the last time—because he had run out of civilized stations Unionside. Even Pell, across the Line—they had called at once, when it was himself and Ross and Mitri together; and *Lucy* had been *Rose*. They owed money there too, as everywhere. *Lucy* was out of havens; and he was out of answers, tired of fear, tired of starving and sleeping the way he had slept on the way into Viking, marginally afraid that the old man he had hired might rob him or get past the comp lock or—it was always possible—kill him in his sleep. And once, just once to see what others had, what life was like outside that terror, with the fancy bars and the fancy sleepovers and a woman with something other than larceny in mind—

He had never had a place to go before, never had a destination. He had lived in this narrow compartment most of his life and only planned what he would do to avoid the traps behind him. Pell, Allison Reilly said; and deals; and it agreed with the rumors, that there were routes opening, hope—hope for marginers like him.

It was a joke of course, the best joke of a humorous career. A surprise for Allison Reilly—she would turn and stare open-mouthed when he tapped her on the shoulder in some crowded Pell Station bar. He knew what *Lucy* could do, and what he could do that great, modern ship of hers would never try—

Stupid, she would say. That was so. But she would always think about it, that a little ship had run jump for jump against *Dublin*. And that was something of a mark to make in his life, if nothing else. There was, in a sense, more of *Lucy* left than there was of him . . . because there was no end to the traveling and no end to the demands she made on him. He had given all he had to keep her going; and now he wanted something out of her, for his pride. He had no Name left; *Lucy* had none. So he did this crazy thing—in its place.

He shut his eyes, yielded to that *G* that pressed him uncomfortably against the bulkhead, drowsing while he could. The pulser was taped to his wrist so that the first beep from the out-range buoy would bring him out of it.

Station would have his head on a plate if they knew; but it was all the chance he had to go into jump with a little rest.

The pulser stung his wrist, brought him out of it when it only felt as if he had fallen asleep for a second. He lurched in blind fright for the controls and sat down and realized it was only the initial contact of the jump range buoy, and engine shutdown, on schedule.

Number one for jump, it told him; and advised him that there was another ship behind. A chill went up his back when he reckoned its bulk and its speed and the time. That was *Dublin*, outbound, overtaking him much more slowly, he suspected, than it could, because of their order of departure—because *Lucy*, ordinarily low priority, was close enough to the mark now that *Dublin* was compelled to hang back off her tail. The automated buoy was going to give them clearance one on the tail of the other because the buoy's information, transmitted from station central, indicated they were not going out in the same direction.

And that was wrong.

He checked his calculations, rechecked and triple-checked, lining everything up for an operation far more ticklish than calculating around the aberrations of *Lucy*'s docking jets. Nullpoints moved, being more than planet-sized mass, in the complicated motions of stars. Comp had to allow for that. No one sane would head into jump alone, with a comp that had no backup, with trank and food and water taped to the board: he told himself so, making his prep, darting glances back to comp and scan, listening to the buoy beeping steadily, watching them track right down the line. He put the trank into his arm. It was time for that . . . to dull the senses which were about to be abused. Not one jump to face . . . but three; and if he missed on one of them, he reckoned, he would never know it.

There was speculation as to what it was to be strung out in the between, and speculation about what the human mind might start doing once the drugs wore off and there was no way back. There were tales of ships which wafted in and out of jump like ghosts with eerie wails on the receiving com, damned souls that never came down and never made port and never died, in time that never ended . . . but those were drunken fancies, the kind of legends which wandered station docksides when crews were topping one another with pints and horror tales, deliberately frightening stationers and insystem spacers, who believed every word of such things.

He did not, above all, want to think of them now. He had little enough time to do anything hereafter but keep *Lucy* tracking and keep his wits about him if things went wrong. If he made the smallest error in calculation he could spend a great deal of time at the first nullpoint getting himself sorted out, and he could lose *Dublin*. The transit, empty as he was, would use up a month or more subjective time; and *Dublin* would shave that . . . would laze her way across the space of each nullpoint, maybe several days, maybe a week resting up, and head out again. *Lucy* did not have such leisure. He had no plans to dump all velocity where he was going, could not do that and hope to outpace *Dublin*'s deeper stitches into the between.

The trank was taking hold. He thought of *Dublin* behind him, and the hazard of it. He reached for the com, punched it in, narrow-focused the transmission, a matter between himself and that sleek huge merchanter that came on his tail. "*Dublin*, this is US 48-335 Y *Lucy*, number one for jump. Advise you the buoy is in error. I'm bound for Pell. Repeat, buoy information is in error; I'm bound for Pell: don't crowd my departure."

Lucy's cold eye located the appropriate reference star, bracketed it, and he saw that. The terror he ought to feel eased into a bland, tranked consciousness in which death itself might be a sensation mildly entertaining. He started the jump sequence, pushed the button which activated the generation vanes while the buoy squalled protest about his track—felt it start, the sudden, irreversible surety that bizarre things were happening to matter and to him, that things were racing faster and faster. . . .

. . . conscious again and still tranked, hyper and sedated at once, a peculiar coincidence of mental states, in which he was aware of alarms ringing and *Lucy* doing her mechanical best to tell him she was carrying dangerous residual velocity. The power it took to dump had to be measured against the power it took to acquire—

No dice throws. Calculate. Move the arm, punch the buttons. Dump the speed down to margin or lose the ship on the next—

Wesson's Point: present location, Wesson's Point, in the appropriate jump range. Entry, proceeding toward dark mass: plot bypass curve down to margin; remember the acquire/dump balance—

"*Sandy.*" That was Ross's comp's voice. "*Sandy, wake up. Get the comp.*"

There were other voices, that sang to him through the hum of dissolution.

Dead, Sandor. All dead.

Sandy, wake up. Time to wake up.

Vent!

. . . acceptable stress. Set to auto and trank out for time of passage; set cushion and pulser; two hours two minutes crossing the nullpoint, set, *mark.*

Dead, Sandor. All dead.

He came out of sleep with the pulser stinging his wrist and with an ache all the way to his heels, unbelted and leaned over the left side of the cushion to dry-heave for a moment, collapsed over that armrest weighing far more than he thought he should and caring far less about survival than he should, because he had gone into this too tired, with his defenses too depressed, and the trank was not wearing off. He ought to be attending to controls. He had to get something to eat and drink, because he was going again in half an hour, and that was too little time.

He reached down and got one of the foil packets, managed with palsied fingers to get it open, and got the ripped corner to his lips—chewed food which had no taste but salt and copper—felt after the water and sucked mouthfuls of that, dropped the empty foil and the empty bottle, felt the food lying inert in his stomach, unwanted. He got the other shot home, beginning to trank out again . . . forced his eyes to focus on the boards, while *Lucy* shot her way along at a hairbreadth margin from disaster. Sometimes there was other junk ringing a nullpoint, a dark platelet of rocks and ice and maybe, maybe lost spacers who used the deep dark of this place for a tomb. . . .

He held his eyes open, alternately trying to throw up and trying to cope with the flow of data which comp itself had to sort and dump in a special mode because it came so fast . . . still blind, ripping along at a velocity that would fling even a smallish planet into his path before the computer could deal with it. *Lucy* headed for the other side of the nullpoint's gravity well with manic haste, but in that close pass they had gotten bent as light was bent, and the calculations had to take that into account. He sat there ignoring the scan-blindness into which they were rushing, trying to tell by the fluttering passage of data whether the numbers converged, reality with his calculations, trying to learn if there was error in position, and how that was going to translate in jump.

And screaming in the back of his mind was the fact that he was playing tag with a very large ship which could play games with distances which *Lucy* barely made, in a time differential he could not calculate, and that on some quirk of malign fate he could still run into them, if they just happened to coincide out here. *Dublin* was either here now or out ahead of him, because his lead was going to erode and change to lag somewhere in the transit. Ships missed each other because space was wide and coincidences were statistically more than rare; but not when two ships were playing leapfrog in the same nullpoints. . . .

Second jump . . . statistically better this time . . . a vast point, three large masses in juxtaposition, a kink in the between that hauled ships in and slung them along in a complicated warping. . . . Dump it now, dump the speed down. . . .

"Wake up, Sandy."

And his own voice, prerecorded: "The referent now is Pell's Star. Push the track reset, Sandy. The track reset. . . ."

He located the appropriate button, stared entranced at the screen . . . no rest possible here. The velocity was still extreme. His tongue was swollen in his mouth. He took another of the water bottles and drank, hurting. Food occurred to him; the thought revolted him; he reached nonetheless and located the packet, ate, because it was necessary to do.

He was crazy, that was what—he swallowed in mechanical, untasting gulps, unable to remember what buttons he had pushed, trusting his own recorded voice giving him the sequences as comp needed them, trusting to that star he saw bracketed ahead of him, if that was not itself a trick of a mind which had come loose in time. He recalled *Dublin;* if Allison Reilly knew remotely what he was doing this moment she would curse him for the risk to her ship. He ought to dump more of the velocity he had, right now, because he was scared. Tripoint was deadly dangerous, with no margin for high-speed errors. . . .

But *Lucy* was moving with the sureness of a woman with her mind made up, and he was caught in that horrible impetus and the solid power of her, because a long time ago she had hollowed him out and taken all there was of him. He moved in a continual blue of slow motion, while the universe passed at much faster rates. There was debris in this place. He was passing to zenith of the complicated accretion disc . . . so he hoped. If he had miscalculated, he died, in an impact that would make a minor, unnoticed light.

He dumped down: the recorded voice told him to. He obeyed. The data coming in sorted itself into more manic strings of numbers. He punched in when the voice told him, froze a segment, matched up—found a correspondence with his plotted course. He grinned to himself, still scared witless, human component in a near C projectile, and stared at the screens with trank-dulled eyes.

He kicked into Pell jump range with velocity that had the incoming-range buoy screaming its automated indignation at him, advising whatever lunatic had just come within its scan that he was traveling too fast and headed dead-on for trafficked zones.

Dump! it warned him, dopplered and restructured by his com. Its systems were hurling machine-to-machine warnings at *Lucy*'s autoalert, which *Lucy* was primed to obey. She was kicking in the vanes in hard spurts, which shifted him in and out of realspace in bursts of flaring nausea. There were red lights everywhere until he hit the appropriate button and confirmed the dump order *Lucy* was obeying.

4

The velocity fell away: some time yet before the scan image had time to be relayed by the buoy to Pell central, advising them that a ship was incoming, and double that time before central's message could come back to *Lucy*. Sandor extricated himself from his nest with small, numb movements, offended by the reek of his own body. His mouth tasted of copper and bile. His hands were stiff and refused coordinated movement. He rolled out of the cushion in the pit and hit the deck on his knees in a skittering of empty water bottles and foil papers sliding under his hand. "Wake up, Sandy," comp was telling him. He reached the keyboard still kneeling, hooked an arm over it and managed to code in the one zero one that stopped it, about the most that his numbed brain was capable of doing in straight sequence.

Wake up. Not that much time left before they would want answers out of him, before his absence from controls would be noticed. He had the pulser still on his wrist. He levered himself up by his arms on the counter, looked at the blurring lights and the keys, trying to recall the sequence that would put it on watch. Autopilot was still engaged: *Lucy* was following lane instructions from the buoy. That was all right.

He located the other control, which his stomach spasmed and his vision grayed, got the code in—no acceleration now. He could not have stood with any stress hauling at him. He groped for the edge of the counter at his right and worked his way up out of the pit, walked blind along the counter until he blinked clear on the lighted white of the corridor that led to maintenance storage, and the cubbyhole of a shower in the maintenance section. He peeled everything off that he was wearing, shoved it in the chute and hoped never to see it again, felt his way into the cabinet and leaned there while the jets blasted off filth and dead skin and shed hair. Soap. He lathered; found his razor in its accustomed place and shaved by feel, with his eyes shut and the water coursing over him. He felt alive again, at least marginally. He never wanted to leave the warmth and the cleanliness . . . could have collapsed to the floor of the cabinet and curled up and slept in the warm water.

No. Out again. There was not that much time. He shut the water off, staggered out into the chill air and gathered clothes from the locker there. He half-dried, pulled the coveralls on and wiped his wet hair back from his eyes. The pulser, waterproof, had not alerted him: *Lucy* was still all right. He went out into the corridor with an armload of towels and disinfectant and went back to clean up the pit, smothering the queasiness in his stomach.

He disposed of all the untidiness, another trip back to storage and disposal, then came back and fell into the cushion that stank now of disinfectant . . . shut his eyes, wilted into the contours, fighting sleep with a careful periodic fluttering of his eyelids.

They already had his ID, lying though that was. It was automatic in *Lucy*'s computer squeal, never ceasing. He had the station scan image from the buoy, estimates of the positions of all the ships in Pell System, large and small—and when he brought his mind to focus on that, on the uncommon number of them, a disturbance wended its way through his consciousness, a tiny ticking alarm at the scope of what he was seeing. Ships in numbers more than expectation. Traffic patterns, lanes in great complexity, shuttle routes for approach to the world of Downbelow, to moons and mining interests. A collection of merchanters, who got together to set rates and to threaten Union with strikes; who served Union ports and disdained the combines. . . . That was all it had been. But it had grown, expanded beyond his recollections. Sol trade—sounded half fanciful, until now.

Harder to run a scam here, if they were short and overcrowded. Or it might even be easier, if station offices were too busy to run checks, if they were getting such an influx on the strength of these rumors that a ship with questionable papers could lose itself in the dataflow . . . no, it was just a matter of rethinking the approach and the tactics. . . .

"This is Pell central," a sudden voice reached him, and the pulser stung him mercilessly, confusing him for the instant which to reach for first. He shut the pulser down, keyed in the mike, leaning forward. "You have come in at velocity above limit. Consult regulations regarding Pell operational restrictions, section 2, number 22. This is live transmission. Further instruction assumes you have brought your speed within tolerance and keep to lane. If otherwise, patrol will be moving on intercept and your time is limited to make appropriate response. Query why this approach? Identify immediately . . . We are now picking up your initial dump, *Lucy*. Please confirm ID and make all appropriate response."

It was all ancient chatter, from the moment of station's reception of his entry, the running monologue of lightbound com that assumed he would have begun talkback much, much earlier.

"We don't pick up voice, *Lucy*. Query why silence."

He reached lethargically for the com and punched in, frightened in this pricklishness on station's part. "This is Stevens' *Lucy* inbound on 4579 your zenith on buoy assigned lane. I confirm your contact, Pell central. Had a little com trouble." This was a transparent lie, standard for any ship illicitly out of contact. "Please acknowledge reception." In his ear, Pell was still talking, constant flow now, telling him what it perceived so that he would know where he was on the timeline. "Appreciate your distress, Pell central. This is Stevens talking, of Stevens' *Lucy*, merchanter of Wyatt's Star Combine, US 48-335 Y. Had a scare on entry, minor malfunction, put me out of contact a moment. I'm all right now. Had a backup engaged, no further difficulty. Please give approach and docking instructions. I'm solo on this run and wanting a sleep-over, Pell central. I appreciate your assistance. Over."

Communication from Pell ran on, an overlapping jabber now, as the com board gave up trying to compress it and created two flows that would drive a sane man mad. He slumped in the seat, which embraced him and held his aching bones, unforgiving even in its softest places. He blinked from time to time, kept his eyes open, to make sure the lines on the approach graph matched. He listened for key words out of the com flow, but Pell seemed convinced now that he was honest—still possible, another, dimmer voice insisted in his head, that some patrol ship could pop up out of nowhere, meaning business.

Station op, in the long hours, began to send him questions and instructions. He was on the verge of hallucinating. Once station queried him sharply, and he woke in a sweat, eyes scanning the instruments wildly, trying to find out where he was, how close—and too close, entering the zone of traffic.

"You all right, *Lucy?*" the voice was asking him. "*Lucy*, what's going on out there?"

"All right," he murmured. "I'm here. Receiving you clear. Say again, Pell central?"

Getting in was nightmare. It was like trying to line up a jump blind drunk. He stared slackjawed at the screens and did the hairbreadth lineup maneuvers on visual alone, which no larger ship could have dared try, but he was far too fuzzed to use comp and read it out, only to take its automated warnings, which never came. He was proud of himself with a manic satisfaction as he made the final touch, like the same drunk successfully walking a straight line: only one beep out of comp in the whole process, and *Lucy* nestled into the lockto dead center.

He was so satisfied he just sat there. Dockside com came on and told him to open his docking ports, and his hands were shaking so violently he had trouble getting the caps off the switches.

"This is Pell customs and dock security," another voice came through. "Have your papers ready for inspection."

He reached for com. "Pell customs, this is Stevens of *Lucy*. We've come in without cargo due to a scheduling foulup at Viking. You're welcome to check my holds. I'm Wyatt's Star Combine. I'm carrying just ship-consumption goods. Papers are ready." He tried to gather his nerves to face official questions, suddenly recalled the gold stored in a drop panel in the aftmost hold, and his stomach turned over. He reached and opened the docking access in answer to a blinking light and a repeated request from dock crews on the shielded-line channel, and his ears popped from the slight pressure change as the hatch opened. "Sorry, Pell dock control. Didn't mean to miss that adjustment. I'm a little tired."

A pause. "*Lucy*, this is Pell Dock Authority. Are you all right aboard? Do you need medical assistance?"

"Negative, Pell Dock Authority."

"Query why solo?"

He was too muddled to think. "Just limped in, Pell Dock." The fear was back, a knot clenched in the vicinity of his stomach. "This is a hired-crew ship. My last crew met relatives on Viking and ran out on me. I had no choice but to take her out myself; and I couldn't get cargo. I limped in all right, but I'm pretty tired."

There was a long silence. It frightened him as all thoughtful reactions did, and sent a charge of adrenalin through him. "Congratulations, then, *Lucy*. Lucky you got here at all. Any special assistance needed?"

"No, ma'am. Just want a sleepover. Except—is Reilly's *Dublin* at dock? Got a friend I want to find."

"That's affirmative on *Dublin*, *Lucy*. Been in dock two days. Any message?"

"No, I'll find her."

A silence. "Right, *Lucy*. We'll want to talk to you about dock charges, but we can do the paperwork tomorrow if you're willing to leave your ship under Pell Security seal."

"Yes, ma'am. But I need to come by your exchange and arrange credit."

A pause. "That was WSC, *Lucy*?"

"Wyatt's Star, yes, ma'am. A twenty, that's all. Just a drink, a sandwich, and a place to sleep. Want to open an account for WSC at Pell. Transfer of three thousand Union scrip. I can cover it."

Another pause. "No difficulty, *Lucy*. You just leave her open all the way and we'll put our own security on it while customs checks her. What's your Alliance ID?"

Apprehension flooded through him, rapid sort in a tired brain. "Don't have that, Pell Dock. I'm fresh from Unionside."

"Unionside number, then."

"686-543-560-S."

"686-543-560-S. Got you clear, then, *Lucy*, on temporary. Personal name?"

"Stevens. Edward Stevens, owner and captain."

"Luck to you, Stevens, and a pleasant stay."

"Thank you, ma'am." He reached a trembling hand for the board, broke contact and shut down everything, put a lock on comp and on the log; and already in the back of his mind he was calculating, about the gold, about turning that with a little dockside trade, a little deal off the manifest, very quiet, putting the profit into account, making it look right. There were ways. Dealers who would fake a bill. It might be good here. Might be the place he had hoped to find. And *Dublin*. . . .

She was here.

He hauled himself out of the cushion and walked back to the access lift at the side of the lounge, opened the hatch below and got a waft of mortally cold air. He got a jacket from the locker, shrugged it on and patted his coveralls pocket to be sure he had the papers, then committed himself and took the lift down into the accessway, got out facing the short dingy corridor to the lock, and the yellow lighted gullet of the station access tube at the end. He shivered convulsively, zipped his jacket, and walked down and through the tube into the noise of the dock and the thumping of the machinery that was busy blowing out *Lucy*'s small systems.

Customs was there. Police were. A noisy horde of stationers beyond the customs barrier, a crowd, a riot. He stopped in the middle of the access ramp with the customs agents walking toward him—neat men in brown suits with foreign insignia. His expression betrayed shock an instant before he realized it and tried to ignore it all as he fumbled his papers out of his pocket. "I talked with the dockmaster's office," he said, offering them. His heart beat double time as it did at such moments, while the crowd kept up the noise and commotion beyond the barricade. The senior officer looked over the forged papers and stamped them with a seal. "Your office is supposed to put my ship under seal," Sandor went on, trying not to look at the police who waited beyond, trying not to harass the agents at their duty. "Got no cargo this trip. They fouled me up at Viking. I'm bone tired and needing sleep. No crew, no passengers, no arms, no drugs except ship's use pharmaceuticals. I'm headed for the exchange office right now to get some cash."

"Carrying money?"

"Three thousand Union scrip aboard. Not on me. They promised me I could do the exchange papers later. After sleep."

"Items of value on your person?"

"None. Going to a sleepover. Going to get a station card."

"We'll locate you on the card when we want you." The man looked up at him. It was the same face customs folk gave him everywhere, hardly welcoming. Sandor gave it back his best, earnest stare. The man handed the false papers back and Sandor stuffed them into his inside breast pocket, started down the ramp.

The police moved in. "Captain Stevens," one said.

He stopped, his heart jumping against his ribs.

"You'll want to pick up a regulations sheet at the office," the officer said. "Our procedures are a little different here than Unionside. Did they give you trouble clearing Viking, then?"

He stared, simply blank.

"Lt. Perez," the officer identified himself. "Alliance Security operations. Was it an understandable scheduling error? Or otherwise?"

He shook his head, confused in the crowd noise that echoed in the distant overhead. The question made no sense from a dockside policeman. From Customs. From whatever they were. "I don't know," he said. "I don't know. I'm a marginer. It happens sometimes. Somebody didn't have their papers straight. Or some bigger ship snatched it. I don't know."

The policeman nodded, once and slowly. It looked like dismissal. Sandor turned, hastened on through the barrier and toward the milling crowd, afraid, trying not to walk like a liberty-long drunk and trying to figure out why they chose his section of the dock to gather and what it all was.

"Hey, Captain," someone yelled as he met the crowd, "why did you do it?"

He looked that way, saw no one in particular, cast about again as he pushed his way through. Panic surged in him, wanting out, away from this place. Hands touched him; a camera bobbed over the shoulders of the crowd and he stared into the lens in one dim-witted moment of fright before ducking away from it.

"What route?" someone asked him. "You find some new nullpoint, Captain?"

He shook his head. "Nothing like that. I just came through Wesson's and Tripoint." He kept walking, terrified at the stationers who had come to stare at him. Someone thrust a mike in his face.

"You know the whole station's been following your com for five hours, Captain? Did you know that?"

"No." He stared helplessly, realizing—his face . . . his face recorded, made public, with *Lucy's* name and number. "I'm tired," he said, but the microphone persisted, thrust toward him.

"You're Captain Edward Stevens, right? From Wyatt's Star? What's the tie with *Dublin? She,* you said. Personal?"

"Right." A small voice, a tremulous voice. His knees were shaking. "Excuse me."

"How long have you been out?" The mike followed him, persistent. "You have any special trouble running solo, Captain?"

"A month or so. I don't know. I haven't comped it yet. No. I don't know."

"You're meeting someone of Reilly's *Dublin,* you said."

"I didn't say. It's personal." He hesitated, searched desperately for a way of escape that would get him to the offices. Blue dock. That was where he had to go. Stations were universal in that arrangement, if not in their interiors. He was on green. It could not be far. He tried to recall the docks from years ago—he had been eleven—with Ross and Mitri by him—

"What's her name, Captain? Is there more to it?"

"Excuse me, please. I'm tired. I just want to get to the bank. I didn't do anything."

"You cleared Viking to Pell in a month in a ship that size, solo? What kind of rig is she?"

"Excuse me. Please."

"You don't call what you did remarkable?"

"I call it stupid. Please."

He shoved his way through, with people surging all about him, his heart hammering in panic. People—people as far as he could see. And of a sudden. . . .

She was there. Allison Reilly was straight in front of him, wide-eyed as the rest of the crowd.

He shoved his way past the startled curious and at the last moment kept his hands off her—stood swaying on his feet and seeing the anger on her face.

"You're *crazy*," she said. "You're outright crazy."

"I told you I'd see you here. I'm tired. Can we talk . . . when I get back from the bank?"

She took his elbow and guided him through the crowd. The microphone caught up with him again; the newswoman shouted questions he half heard and Allison Reilly ignored them, pulled him across the dock to the line of bars—toward a mass of quieter folk, a line of spacers. Fewer and fewer of the stationer crowd pursued them; and then none: the spacer line closed about them with sullen and forbidding stares turned toward the intruding stationers. He paid no attention then where she aimed him—headed through the dark doorway of a bar and fell into a chair at the nearest available table. He slumped down over his folded arms on the surface in blessed quiet and tried to come out of it when someone shook him by the shoulder.

Allison Reilly put a drink into his hand. He sipped at it and gagged, because he had expected a stiff drink and got fruit juice and sugar froth. But it was food. It helped, and he looked up fuzzily into Allison's face while he drank. A ring of other faces had gathered, male and female, spacers ringing the table, silver-clad, white, green and gold and motley insystemers, just staring—all manner of patches, all the same silent observation.

"Sandwich," someone said, and he looked left as a male hand set a plate in front of him. He disposed of as much of it as he could in several graceless bites, then stuffed the rest, napkin-wrapped, into his jacket pocket, a survival habit and one which suddenly embarrassed him in the face of all these people who knew what the odds were and what kind of poverty would drive a man to push a ship like that. *Dublin* knew what he had done. Someone on *Dublin* had talked, and they knew he had done it straight through, stringing the jumps, the only way the likes of *Lucy* could possibly have tailed *Dublin*. They would arrest him soon; someone would talk it over with some official in station central, and they would start running checks and talking to merchanters all over this station, some one of whom might have a memory jogged: his now-notorious ship, his face, his voice carried all over station on open vid. He could not deal quietly, take that fourteen thousand gold off the ship, deal as he was accustomed to deal, quietly, on the docks. Not now. He was dead scared. Allison Reilly was there, and the look on her face was what he had wanted, but he was up against the real cost of it now, and he found it too much.

"Allison," he said, when she sat down in the other chair and leaned on her arms looking at him, "I want to talk to you. Somewhere else."

"Come on," she said. "You come with me."

He pushed the chair back and tried to get up . . . needed her arm when he tried to walk, to keep his balance in station's too-heavy gravity. Some spacer muttered a ribald and ancient joke, about a man just off a solo run, and it was true, at least as far as the mind went, but the rest of him was dead.

He walked, a miserable blue of lights and moving bodies—the dock's wide echoing chill and light and then a doorway, a confusion of bizarre wallpaper and a desk and a clerk—a sleepover, a carpeted hall in either direction from here. . . . He leaned on the counter with his head propped on his hand while Allison straightened out the details and the finances. Then she took his arm again and led him down a corridor.

"Keep them out of here," she yelled back at someone, who said all right and left; she carded a door open and put him through, into a sleepover room with a wide white bed.

He turned around then and tried to put his arms around her. She shoved him in the middle of his chest and he nearly fell down. "Idiot," she said to him, which was not the welcome he had hoped for, but what he reckoned now he deserved. He stood there paralyzed in his misery and his mental state until she pulled him over to the bed and pushed him down onto it. She started working at his clothes with rough, abrupt movements as if she were still furious. "Roll over," she hissed at him, and pulled at his shoulder and threw the covers over him.

And he fell asleep.

5

He woke, aware of bare smooth skin next to his own, of a warm arm about him, and turned, blinked in confusion. She was still here, in the room's artificial twilight. "Allison," he said hoarsely, hoarse because his voice like the rest of him was not in the best of form. He stroked her hair and woke her without really meaning to ruin her sleep.

"Huh," she said, looking up at him. "About time." But when he tried with her, there was nothing he could do. He lay there in wretched embarrassment and thinking that at this point she would probably get up and get dressed and walk out of his life forever, about the time he had just spent.

"What could you expect?" she said, and patted his face and took his hand and carried it against her mouth, all of which so bewildered him that he simply lay there staring into her eyes and expecting her to follow that statement with something direly cutting.

She did not. "I'm sorry," he said finally. "I'm really sorry."

"There's tomorrow. A few more days. What are you going to do, Stevens? Is it worth the handful of days you bought with this stunt?"

He thought about it. For a moment he found it even hard to breathe. It really deserved laughing about, the whole situation, because there was something funny in it. He managed at least to shrug. "So, well, maybe. But I think I'm done after this, Reilly. I don't think I can do it again."

"You're absolutely out of your mind."

He found a grin possible, which at least kept up his image. "I don't make a habit of it."

"Why'd you do it?"

"Why not?"

She frowned. Scowled. She shook her head after a moment, got up on her elbow, looking down at him, traced the old scar on his side, a gentle touch. "What are you going to tell your company?"

He lay there, stared at the ceiling with his head on his arms, considered the question and truth and lies, grinned finally and shrugged with what he hoped was monumental unconcern. "I don't know. I'll think of something good."

A fist landed on his ribs. "I'll bet you will. No cargo. No clearance. You jumped out of Viking on the wrong heading. What are they going to *do* to you, Stevens?"

"Actually," he said, "it's a minor problem." He shut his eyes, still with a smile painted on his face and a weariness sitting on his chest that seemed the accumulation of years. "I'll talk my way out of it, never fear." And after a moment: "Why don't we try it again, Reilly? I think it might work."

It did, oddly enough—and that, he thought, lying there with Allison Reilly tangled with him and content, was because he had started thinking again how to con his way through, and about saving his skin and *Lucy*'s, which got his blood moving again, however tired and sore he was. He was remarkably placid in contemplating his ruin, which he figured he could at least postpone until Allison Reilly had put out of Pell Station aboard *Dublin* some few days hence. And there was the gold: he had that. If by some miracle no one had known his face, he might get himself papers, get himself cargo—go back to Voyager without routing through Viking, a chancy set of jumps, then come in with appropriate stamps on his papers to satisfy Viking—if *Dublin* had not reported that message about his change of destination. . . .

He could find out. Allison might know. Would tell him. And maybe, the irrepressible thought occurred to him, he could claim some tie to *Dublin* for the benefit of Pell authorities, use that supposed connection for a reference, at least enough for dock charges. She might do it for him. He thought of that, lying there with her arms about him, in a bed she had paid for, that he might work one remarkable scam and get himself a stake charged to *Dublin*'s account, which would solve all his problems but Viking and, with the gold, get him a real set of papers.

He turned his head and looked at her, into eyes which suddenly opened, dark and deep and warm at the moment; and his gut knotted up at what he was thinking to do, which was to beg; or to cheat her; and neither was palatable. She hugged him close and he fell to kissing her, which was another pleasure he had discovered was different with Allison Reilly.

It was hardly fair, he thought, that he himself had fallen into such hands as Allison's, who could con him in ways he had never visited on his most deserving victims. She was having herself a good time, not even maliciously, while he was paying all he had for it.

And it was finished if she knew, in all senses. She might not, even then, turn him in; but she would know . . . and hate him; and that was, at the moment, as bad as station police.

"Actually," he said during a lull, "actually I'll tell you the truth. I'm not in trouble. It's all covered, my shifting to Pell."

"Oh?" She stiffened, leaned back and looked at him. "How?"

"Because I've got an account to shift here. I'm a small enough operator the combine gives me quite a bit of leeway. All they ask is that I make a profit for them. They let me come and go where I can do that. Wyatt's can't be figuring down to the last degree where to have me break off an operation: that's my decision to make. You made Pell sound good. I heard the rumors. And you just tipped the balance."

"Huh." There was a sober look on her face. "Not me at all, was it?"

"I could have taken my time getting here. I wanted to see you. That part's so."

The sober look became a thinking look, a different, colder one. "Well, then, I guess you *will* get out of it all, won't you?"

"I will. No question."

"Huh," she said again. She rolled for the edge of the bed and he caught her wrist, stopping her.

"Where are you going?"

"Can't stay any longer. I have duty."

"What did I say?"

"You didn't say anything. I just have my watch coming up."

"It was something. What was it?"

Her face grew distressed. She jerked at his hand without success. "Let go."

"Not until you tell me what I said."

"If you put a mark on me, Stevens, you'll regret it. You want to think that through?"

"I'm trying to talk to you. I told you the truth."

"I don't think you know the truth from your backside. You didn't tell me the truth and I'll bet you didn't tell it to customs out there."

His heart slammed against his ribs, harder and harder. "So does *Dublin* tell the whole truth to customs? Don't ask me to believe that.".

"Sure. I figure there are all kinds of reasons someone would give me one story and customs another; but maybe only one reason a ship would dog us the way you have, and I don't like the smell of it. You never have answered me straight, not once, and I gave you your chance. Now maybe you can break my arm and maybe you even figure you can kill me to shut me up, but, mister, I've got several hundred cousins who know who I'm with and where and you'll find yourself taking a slow voyage on *Dublin* if you don't let me out of here right quick."

"Is *that* why you stayed? To ask questions?"

"What do you expect?"

He stared at her with more pain than he had felt since Ross died, let go her arm so suddenly she almost rolled off her edge of the bed; and she sat there rubbing her wrist and glaring at him. He had no wish to be looked at. "Go on," he said. "I'm not stopping you."

"Don't tell me I've hurt your feelings."

"Impossible. Go on, get out of here and let me sleep."

"It's my room. *I* paid the bill."

That hurt. "I'll take care of it. I'll put the fifty in *Dublin*'s account. And the fifty before that. Just take yourself off. No worry about the cash."

"It really looks like it. What are you doing, following us to get me to pay your bar bills? You going to hit me up for finance?"

"I don't charge," he said bitterly. His face burned. "Go on. Out."

She stood up, stalked over, collected her clothes from the chair and started pulling them on—paused, sealing up the silver coveralls, and looked back at him.

"Probably I'd better pay your rent for the week," she said. "I think you've got troubles, Stevens. I think your combine's going to have your head on a platter. You're not going to turn a profit on this."

"Don't bother yourself. I don't want your money and I don't want your help. I'll handle my combine."

"Oh, sure, you're going to explain how it all seemed a good idea at the time. This story's going to be told over and over again, bigger every time it hits another station. How you did it to see me again, how you did it for a bet, how you took out of Viking the wrong direction and triplejumped solo through Tripoint, that you're a Mazianni spotter or a Union spy with a hyped-up ship or an outright thief, and you know how much *Dublin* wants herself mixed into the story? The tale'll get back to Viking without our help. They'll hear it on Wyatt's real early; they'll hear it everywhere ships go . . . because they're all here, every ship, every family, every Name in the Merchanter's Alliance and then some. And Union military's coming in to call. It's going to spread. You understand that?"

He thought about that, with a chill feeling in his stomach. "So, well, then, it looks like I've got a bigger problem than you do, don't I? I'm sure *Dublin*'s going to survive it."

"Bastard."

"You came out on the dock, Reilly. That was your doing. I didn't arrange it."

"I've no doubt you'd have come to *Dublin* asking for me. You used our name over com. What more did it lack?"

"Out."

"You're flat broke, Stevens. Unless you're carrying something under the plates. And they'll look. You're going to get your ship attached. At the least."

"I've got funds."

"*What* have you got?"

"Maybe it's none of your business."

"You don't. Not worth this trip."

"None of your business."

"Huh."

He stared at her, unwilling to fight it out. Watched her walk to the door—and stop. She stood there. Looked back finally, dropping her hand from the door switch. "You tell me," she said, "really, why you pulled this."

"Like you said."

"Which?"

"Take your pick. I'm not going to argue the point."

"No. You tell me, Stevens, how you're going to rig this. I really want to know."

He shrugged, sitting up, hooked his arm in the pillows and propped himself against the headboard. "I told you already what I'm going to do. It's no problem."

"I think you're in bad trouble."

"Nothing I can't solve."

"So I'm flattered I made such an impression on you. But I'm not why you came. What made you?"

He tried a wry smile, reckoning he could hold it. "Well, it seemed reasonable at the time."

"I keep wanting to believe you. And I'm not getting any encouragement."

"I'm used to running solo," he said in a lingering silence. "It's no big deal. I've jumped her alone and I've two-jumped. She's good, *Lucy* is. She kept up with your fancy *Dublin*, for sure. I'll tidy it up with WSC when I get back to Viking. I wouldn't mind seeing you, then."

She came back and sat down on the edge of the bed, leaned with her hand on his and looked into his face at too close an interval for comfortable pretenses. "Possibly," she said, "you can claim fatigue and they'll let you out of this. Maybe it was just being out there too long."

"Thanks. I hadn't thought of that one. I'll try it."

"I'd guess you'd better try something. You are in trouble. Aren't you?"

He said nothing.

"Stevens. If it is Stevens . . . How much truth have you told me? At any time?"

"Some."

"About what you are—how about that, for a start?"

He tried to shrug, which was not easy at close quarters. "I'm what I told you."

"You're broke, aren't you? And in a lot of trouble. I think maybe you thought I could finance you. I think maybe that's what this is all about, that you really did come chasing after me—because you've overrun your margin at Viking, haven't you; and maybe your company's going to be asking questions—and now you've got a combine ship where she doesn't belong."

"No."

"No?"

"I said no."

"You know, Stevens, I shouldn't ask this, but it does occur to me that you just may not be combine."

He stared at her, at a frown which was not anger, his hold on his silence loosened for no good reason, but that she knew—he knew that she knew. She was headed back to her ship, to talk there, for certain.

"Not, are you?"

"No. I'm not. I'm—" His arm went out to stop her from bolting, but that shift had not been to get up, and he was left embarrassed. "Look, WSC never noticed me. I *made* them money. I never cost them a credit. . . ."

"Before now."

"I'll put it back."

"You *are* a pirate."

"*No.*"

"All right. So I wouldn't sit here if I thought that. So you skim. I'm not sure I want to know the details." She heaved a sigh and turned to sit sideways on the bed, slammed her fist into her knee. "Blast."

"What's that?"

"That's wishing I minded my own business. So I know. So I can't do anything about it. I'm not going to. You understand that? It's worth no money to you, whatever you planned to get."

Heat rose to his face. "No. I'll tell you the truth: it was getting tight there. Really tight. So you made me think of Pell, that's all. I figure maybe I've got a chance here."

"Just like that."

"Just like that. That's when I know to move. I feel the currents move and I go. It keeps me alive."

She stood up, thinking about the law: there was that kind of look on her face. Thinking about conscience, one way and the other. About police.

"I'll tell you," he said, and rolled over on his side, searching for his clothes. He located them on the floor and sat up, swung his feet out of bed to dress. "Reilly—I don't like it to go sour like this. I swear to you—any way you like—I know you're worried about it. I don't blame you. But that ship's *mine*. And that's the truth."

"I don't want to listen to this. I'm Helm, you hear me, and I keep my hands clean. We've got our Name, and I swear to you, mister, you crowd me and I'll protect it. I'm sorry for you. And I'll believe what you've told me in the hope that once a day you do tell the truth, and that I don't need to pass the word about you on the docks, but I don't think I want to hear any more about it than I have. And I don't think I'll be meeting you elsewhere. I don't think you'd better plan on that."

"You wait a minute. Just wait a minute." He pulled his clothes on, caught at disadvantage, zipped the plain coveralls and caught his breath and his dignity. "Listen—I'm sorry about that mess on the docks. It was crazy. I never—never intended that. I didn't expect them to be crazy here."

"Pell Operations is always on vid.—You didn't know that. You know how you sounded, coming in? Like a crazy man. Like someone crazy aiming a ship at the station; and then like somebody in trouble . . . it was on the news channel, and thousands of people were punching in on it. Misery, Stevens, it's Pell. Alliance captains are coming in here, big Names, flash ships . . . *Finity's End* and *Little Bear*, one after the other. *Winifred*. Pell folk *know* the Names. And some of these free souls don't take to regulations and some of them have privilege with a capital P. When something comes in like you came—they appreciate style, these Pell stationers. And being stationers they're just a little ignorant about what a stupid move you pulled and what dice you really shot out there at Tripoint. You've got a death wish, Stevens. Deep down somewhere, you're self-destructive; and you scare me. You're trouble. To me. To yourself. To a system full of ships and a station full of innocent people who had the goodheartedness to worry about you after they realized you weren't going to hit *them*. They think you did it on skill. On dockside they think something else. They think you're an ass, Stevens, and I'm embarrassed for you, but I got you in here because I was stuck with you after that scene on the docks; because you at least had the conscience to warn *Dublin* when you risked *our* lives at Viking, and my Old Man called me in on the carpet and looked me right in the eye and asked me what you were. When this liberty's over or before, I'm going to have to go on the carpet again and answer why I got *Dublin* involved with you. And I still don't know."

He stood and took it. It was the truth. It was all the things that had shivered down his backbone when he came in. "I've done the like before," he said in a quiet voice. "I told you that. Sometimes I've had to do it. I've had no choice. I came in high in the range. But I miscalculated myself, not the ship; too long on the dock at Viking, too little sleep, too little food—I wasn't fit for it; that, I admit to. But the solo runs—*Lucy's* not *Dublin*. I bend the regulations. That's how someone like me has to operate. You've got to sleep; you do it on auto, wherever you are. You're redlighting and you've got to see to it; and you run on auto. And you have to know that, even on *Dublin*, you have to know that all those marginers like me, we're running like that. It's not neat and failsafed. I thought I could do it. And I did it on luck at the end, and I should have let you pass me at Viking. I wanted out of there. If I'd delayed my run when I had a clearance—there were questions possible. And I went, that's all."

"And the interest in *Dublin*?"

He shrugged, arms folded.

"You make me nervous," she said.

"You. I wanted to see you."

She shook her head uneasily. "Most can wait for that privilege."

"Some don't have that much time."

"What's that supposed to mean?"

A second shrug, less and less comfortable. "I don't stay in one place very long. And I'll be gone again. I'll stay low till you go. I think that's about the best thing I can do under the circumstances. When you pull out, I'll set about getting myself out of this. But no mention of *Dublin*. I promise that."

She stared at him sidelong, a good moment. "I'm not posted. You understand—my getting involved here—can keep me from being posted. Ever. It's not a lark, Stevens. It was." She walked to the door, looked back. "I've got maybe ten thousand I can lay my hands on. I can maybe keep you clean here, if you take that and pay your dock charge and clear out of Pell. Understand me, it's all I can get. I'll be another year working off the last thousand of it. But I want you off *Dublin*'s record. I don't want you in trouble again until somewhere a long, long way off our trail."

He shook his head, his mouth gone dry. He hurt inside.

"Blast you, there's nothing more you can get."

"I don't want your money. I don't want your help. I'll take out of here. I can pay the dock charges, and I'll take out."

"With *what?*"

"That three thousand. Maybe I can get a little cargo on the side. I've got, well, maybe a little more than that."

"How much worth of cargo?"

"That's my business. You answer questions to strangers about *Dublin*'s holds? I'd think not."

She set her jaw. "I want you out of here."

"Tell your Old Man I'm going."

"I'll tell you you're taking the ten thousand. You're going out of Pell with some kind of a load, mine and yours together, that at least looks honest. And you forget the debt. Don't try to pay it. Don't talk about it. Or me. Or I go to station authorities."

"I understand you," he said very quietly. "I'd take your ten. And I'd promise to get it back to you, but I don't think you'd believe it. And it wouldn't be the truth. You're throwing it away, Reilly. I very much doubt I'm going to clear this dock at all."

"Someone here you know?"

"More than likely someone here that knows me. It's the publicity, Reilly. I'm usually a lot quieter."

"What," she asked in a lowered voice, "can they get you for? What's the worst?"

"Bad debts."

"Less than likely any merchanter would go to the police on that score. But something else—"

"I'm not one of the Names. They don't know what I might be. A pirate. They could think that. But I'll tell you the whole truth this time. I've got two thousand cash I'm not declaring. For dockside deals. —And fourteen thousand worth of WSC money in gold under the plates. That's why I ran out of Viking like my tail was afire. —Look, this stationer there, this clerk—I *had* to deal; he could have blown it all. It wasn't my idea. So I have the money. I can pay dock charges and I can deal for cargo."

"With sixteen lousy contraband thousand?"

"You think ten more is going to help? No. And if they catch me, you can believe they're going to inventory everything I've got; and they'd find me with more scrip than I'm supposed to have; and ten thousand in Pell currency, right? One question to comp and they'd have those serial numbers and a ten thousand transaction in your name. Take it from me. I know the routines."

"I'll bet you do."

"So you keep it. Against my problems, it's nothing, that ten. I'll get out of it my way." He picked up his jacket and put it on, checked his papers in his pocket. "I'll go take care of the finance, go to station offices. You just call it quits and go hang out with your cousins and say it's all nothing. Find somebody else to sleepover with and publicize it. Fast. That'll kill it. I know how to cover a trail. That, too."

"I wish you luck," she said, sounding earnest. "You'll need it."

He opened the door for her. Grinned, recovering himself. "Thanks," he said, and walked out, ahead of her in the hall, hands in pockets, a deliberate spring in his step.

Time to visit *Lucy*. Time to go under the eyes of the powers that be on Pell and try to pull it out of the fire. Or at least get some of the heat off. Station officers would unseal her for him if he could eel his way past a customs agent who might want to do a thorough check in his presence.

Then to get out of Pell with as much cash as he could save. Maybe check the black market—there was always that. Change the name and number out at Tripoint, trade black, market at the nullpoints and hope no one cut his throat. Buy another set of forged papers. If he could get out with money; and if . . . a thousand things. His mind began to work again more clearly, with Allison Reilly set behind him. With bleak realities plain on the table.

He looked back. She was there, at the door of the sleepover, just watching. A craziness had come on him for a time. Self-destructive: she was right. On the one hand he wanted to survive; and on the other he was tired of trying, and it was harder and harder to think his way through the maze . . . even to recall what lies he had told and how they meshed.

There were troops here too. He saw them . . . a jolt. Not the green or the black of Union forces, but blue. Alliance militia. He recalled the buildup at Viking and the rumors of pirate-hunting and had a presentiment of times changing, of loopholes within which it had been possible for marginers to survive—being tightened, suddenly, and with finality.

He had a record at every station in Union now; and soon a record with the Alliance; and he was almost out of places.

"What happened?" Curran asked, joining her in the shadow of the sleepover doorway, and Allison frowned at the intrusion. "Been there," Curran said with a nod toward the bar next door. "Some of us had a little concern for it . . . hung around. In case. What's he up to? You know the Old Man's going to ask."

"He's going back to his ship. I'm afraid it's a case of misplaced assumptions. We're quits."

"Allie, they've got a guard out there."

She straightened, dropped her arms from their fold. "What guard?"

"On his ship. That's what's had us upset. We weren't about to break in on you, but we've sure been thinking. That's military, that."

She hissed between her teeth, "More than customs seal?"

"More than customs. They say one of *Mallory*'s officers is on station."

"I heard that."

"Allie, if they haul him in, is there anything he can say he shouldn't?"

"No." She turned a scowl on her cousin, sharp and quick.

"Are you making assumptions, Currie me lad? Don't Allie me."

"When our watch senior sleeps over with a man the militia's got their name on . . . we come asking questions. Third Helm has a stake here."

"You don't oversee me."

"That's thanks. —We've backed you. Get back to the ship. We're asking. Now."

She said nothing. Followed the distant figure with her eyes. There was not so much traffic now as main-day. A new set of residents had come out to work and trade in the second half of Pell's nevernight—more industrial traffic than in mainday; passersby wore coveralls more than suits, and traffic on the docks was heavy moving, big mobile sleds hauling canisters, whining their way along through a straggle of partying merchanters.

And troops.

And others. Pell orbited a living world. Natives worked on the station, small and furtive, wearing breather-masks that hissed when they breathed. They were brown-furred and primate . . . moved softly on callused bare feet. And watched, two of them perched on the canisters stacked nearest *Lucy*'s dock. She made out another of them near the security rail. They moved suddenly, took themselves elsewhere, a vanishing of shadows.

She shook her head slowly, took Curran by the arm and saw the rest of her watch standing by, Deirdre and Neill. "Back," she said.

"He got a gun?"

"No," she said. "That, I know for sure. But we've no need to be bystanders, do we?"

6

The customs seal was still in effect, *Lucy*'s access presenting deep shadow, a closed hatch where other ships had a cheerful yellow lighted access tube open. No lights here, only the customs barrier still in place, and grim dark metal of an idle gantry beyond—no cargo for *Lucy*, to be sure, but the abundant canisters of the ship in the next berth, which had been offloading, a busy whine of conveyers, a belt empty now, while they sorted out some snarl inside, perhaps. Native workers hovered about, idle . . . alien life, persistent reminder of possibilities. Man had found nothing else but the quiet, avowedly gentle Downers of Pell.

It was perhaps out there, a star or two away. It might happen in his lifetime, some merchanter, disgruntled with things as they were, diverting his ship off to probe the deep . . . but the finding of nullpoints took probes, and probes took finance, and *Lucy* could never do it. Every route, everything that was settled in the Beyond rode that kind of maybe, that maybe this year . . . maybe someone . . . Sandor took some perverse comfort in that, that no one's prerogatives were that secure.

This running gnawed at him. And it was rout, this time. He was a contamination, a hazard. He thought about Allison Reilly and knew it for the truth, the things she had said.

Maybe he should have taken the money. Or anything else he could get.

He walked along the line of canisters, saw nothing out

of the way—Downers peered down at him from a perch atop the cans, suddenly scampered out of sight. He looked about him, walked the shadows closer and closer to the access. *Lucy* was not a large problem for customs, nothing that deserved as much fuss as his anxiety painted. Likely— he earnestly hoped—they had gotten some junior agent to suit up and walk through the holds to check out his claim that they were empty. The plates under which the gold was hidden were inconspicuous in hundreds of other like places, in the empty cavern of the badly lighted hold. They had looked, that was all, gone offshift—it was alterday.

He walked around the bending of the huge can-stacks, came face to face with blue uniformed militia, two grim-faced men. Blinked, caught off balance for the moment, then shrugged and strolled the other way, suddenly out of the notion to prowl about the customs barrier.

So. Too many troops, everywhere. Viking, and here. He shifted his shoulders, persuaded his frayed nerves to calm. Better to go to the offices, get it settled up there and not go try security out here. He walked lightly still, the more so when he had gotten the shock out of his system, tucked his hands into his pockets and looked about him as he walked, anonymous again, among the passing mobile sleds, the passersby that were mostly spacers or dockworkers— flinched once when a knot of stationers pointed at him and talked among themselves. But the mainday crowds were gone: the stationers who had seen his face on vid and gathered on the dock were decently in their beds, with the alterday shift awake. No one troubled him. He sealed off the experience back there, sealed off the nightmare of the docking, sealed off too the sleepover with Allison Reilly, getting himself focused again, sorting his wits into order. He might be on any station, at any year of his adult life. He had done the like over and over. His knees still felt like rubber, but that was hunger: he fished up the crushed sandwich out of his pocket—a prudent idea, that, after all; and that was his breakfast, dry, pocket-squelched mouthfuls while he walked the edge of the loading zones and headed for blue dock and the offices.

The Combine had me carry the gold in case, sir— personal funds, no, sir, not transporting for general trade.

He started composing his arguments in advance, against every eventuality they might haul up. The unsettled state of affairs, sir, the military—

No. Maybe not such a good idea to invoke that particular reason unless he had to. Unsettled state of affairs was close enough.

And with luck, they had not found the cache in the hold at all; with luck, he could pay his dock charges and get out of here with some show of trying to arrange cargo. Best not to contact the black market here: they were likely to check him closer going out than coming in. But he could change *Lucy*'s name again, out at Tripoint—could risk a blown ship or a cut throat to do some nullpoint trading, sans customs, sans police, lying off at some place like Wesson's and waiting for some ship that might be willing to trade with a freelancer, and better yet, some other marginer who might deal in forged paper. Risky business. Riskier still . . . with the military stirring about. An operation to tighten loopholes in which piracy was possible—also tightened loopholes in which marginers survived.

Union and Alliance in cooperation. He had never foreseen that.

He swallowed the last of the dry sandwich, wadded the wrapper and thrust it back into his pocket, spacer's reflex. The section seal was ahead, the office section, the military dock where militia were even more in evidence. He watched the overhead signs to find his way, finally located the customs office adjunct to the Dock Authority, halfway down the dock, and walked through the door. It was getting close to mainday. A line of applicants stood inside, spacers and ships' officers with their own difficulties. A sign advised a separate window, a different procedure for ship clearance.

He fished his papers out of his pocket and presented them at the appropriate window, and the young woman looked him in the eyes and glanced down again at the ID and *Lucy*'s faked papers. "Captain Stevens. There's a call in for you."

It started his heart to pounding; any anomaly would, in places such as this. "What ship?"

"Just a moment, sir." She left the counter, took the papers with her. Terror verged on panic. He would have bolted, perhaps, with the papers—

No. He would not. With the security seal on *Lucy* there was no way. A long counter, a bored clutch of clerks and business as usual, separated him from his title to *Lucy*, and making a row about it would draw attention. He leaned there, locked his hands on the counter to brace himself in his studied weariness and exasperation, hoping, still dimly hoping, that it was Allison Reilly with a parting message—but she would not, never would, wanting no connection with him—and they would give him his papers back and unlock his hatch for him. He cursed himself for ever agreeing to that seal; but he had been tired, his mind had been on Allison Reilly and his wits were not what they had been.

The official came back. His heart leapt up again. He leaned there trying to look put upon. "I'm really pretty tired," he said. "I'd like to get that message later if I could." That was what he should have said in the first place. That he finally thought of it encouraged him. But she looked beyond his shoulder at someone who had come up behind him, and that little shift of the eyes warned him. He turned about, facing station police.

It was not the scenario he had planned—his back to a customs counter, an office full of people who had no involvement in the situation; no gun in his pocket, *Lucy's* papers in someone else's possession, his ship locked against him. "Captain Stevens," the policeman said. "Dockmaster wants to see you."

Perhaps his face was white. He felt himself sweating. "It's alterday."

"Yes, sir. Will you come?"

"Is something out of order?"

"I don't know, sir. I'm just asked to bring you to the offices."

"Well, look, I'll get up there in a minute. I need to settle something here with customs."

"My orders are to bring you now. If you would, sir."

"Look, they've got my papers tangled up here.— Ma'am, if I could have my papers back—" He turned belly to the counter again, expecting a heavy hand and cuffs on the instant. He tried, all the same, and the woman handed him the papers, which he started to put into his inside breast pocket. The officer stopped that reach with a grip on his wrist, patted his coat with a small, deft movement even those standing closest might have missed, patted the other two pockets as well. "That's all right, sir," the officer said. "If you'll come along now."

He put the papers in his pocket, left the counter and went. The policeman laid no hand on him, simply walked beside him. But there was no escaping on Pell.

"This way." The officer showed him not to the main elevator in the niner corridor, but to a service elevator on the dock. Other police waited there, holding the door open.

"I think I have a right to know what this is about," Sandor protested, not sure that Union rights applied here at all, this side of the Line.

"We don't know," the officer in charge said, and put him into the lift with the other police, closed the door behind. "Sir."

The lift whisked them up with a knee-buckling force, two, four, six, eight levels. Sandor put his hands toward his pockets, nervous habit, remembered and did it anyway, carefully. The door opened and let them out into a carpeted corridor, and one of the police took a scanner from his belt and took him by the arm, holding him still while he ran the detector over him. Another finished the job, waist to feet.

"That's fine," the officer said then, letting him go. "Pardon, sir."

Maybe he had rights this violated. He was not sure. He let them take his arm and guide him down the corridor, a corporation kind of hall, carpeted in natural fiber, with bizarre carvings on the walls. The place daunted him, being full of wealth, and somewhere so far from *Lucy* he had no idea how to get back. Perhaps it was the shock of the strung-together jumps he had made getting here; maybe it was something else. His mind was not working as it ought; or it lacked possibilities to work on. His hands and feet chilled as if he were operating in a kind of shock. He was threadbare and shabby and as out of place here as he would be in *Dublin*'s fine corridors. Lost. There was money here that normally ignored nuisances his size, and somehow the thought of arguing a three thousand credit account in a place like this that dealt in millions—

One of the police strode ahead and opened a door with a key card, let them into an office where a militia guard stood with a large, ugly gun at his side; and two more station security officers, and a man at a desk who might be a secretary or a clerk.

"Go on in," that one said, and pushed a button at the desk console. The militiaman opened the farther door and Sandor hesitated when the police did not bid to move. "Go on," the officer said, and he went, far from confident, down an entry corridor into a large room with a U-shaped table.

All its places were filled, mostly by stationers silver-haired with rejuv; but there were exceptions. The woman centermost was one, a handsome woman in an expensive green suit; and next to her was another, a militia officer in blue, a pale blond man with bleak, pale eyes.

"Papers," the woman in the center said. He reached into his pocket and handed them to a security agent on duty in the room, who walked to the head of the U and handed them to her. She unfolded them in front of her and gave them a cursory scrutiny.

"Why am I here?" Sandor ventured, not loud, not aggressive. But it had never seemed good to back up much either. "They just asked me to come up here. They didn't say why."

She passed the papers to the militia officer beside her. She looked up again, hands folded in front of her. "Elene Quen-Konstantin," she identified herself, "dockmaster of Pell." And he recalled then what was told about this woman, who had defied a Union fleet. He swallowed his bluffs unspoken, taking her measure. "There's been some question about your operation, Captain Stevens. We're understandably a little anxious here. We have statements by some merchanters that you're under ban at Mariner, under a different name. On unspecified charges. This is hearsay. You don't have to answer the questions. But we're going to have to run a check. We're quite careful here. We have to be, under circumstances I'm sure I don't have to lay out for you. Your combine will be reimbursed for any unwarranted delays and likewise your housing and your dock charges will be at Pell's expense during the inquiry. Unless, of course, something should turn up to substantiate the charges."

It took a great deal to keep his knees steady. "There

ought to be something a little more than hearsay for an impoundment. And the damage to my reputation—what repairs that?"

"This is Alliance space, Captain. You're not in Union territory any longer. Alliance sovereignty. You came here of your own decision, without a visa, which we allow. But you have to have one to operate here. I'm personally sorry for the inconvenience, and I assure you Pell's inquiry will be brief, three days at maximum. There are several merchanters in from Mariner. We'll be talking to them. You have a right to know that the investigation is proceeding and to confront complainants and witnesses whose testimony is filed to your detriment. You have a right to counsel; this will be billed to your combine, but should the charges prove false, as I said, Pell will stand good for the—"

"I don't have that kind of operation." Panic crept into his voice. It was in no wise acting. "I'm an independent under Wyatt's umbrella. I pay all my own costs and I'm barely making it as it is. This is going to ruin me. I can't afford the time, not even a few days. That comes out of the little profit I do make, and you're going to push me right over into the loss column. They'll attach my ship—"

"Captain Stevens, if you'd allow me to finish."

"This is something trumped up by some other marginer who doesn't want my competition."

"Captain, this is not the hearing. You have a right to counsel before making statements and countercharges and I would advise you to be careful. There are penalties for libel and malicious accusation, and the ship making charges against you will likewise be detained, likewise be liable for damages if the accusation is proved malicious."

"And where do I get counsel? I haven't got the funds. Just company funds. What am I supposed to do?"

Quen looked down the table to her left. Someone nodded. "Legal Affairs will help you select a lawyer."

"And prosecute me too?"

"Captain, Pell is the only world in Alliance territory . . . unless you want a change of venue to Earth itself. Or extradition to Mariner. At your hearing you can make either request. But your appointed defender should make it only after you've had a chance to consider all the points of the matter. I repeat, this is not the hearing. This is only your formal advisement that allegations have been made, of general character and as yet undefined, but of sufficient concern to this station to warrant further investigation. Particularly since you are Union registry, since you're not familiar with Alliance law, I do suggest you refrain from comment until you have a lawyer."

"I'm not one of your citizens."

"Presumably you're seeking Alliance registry, which is the only way you can trade here. Now on the one hand, you'll be seeking to prove the charges false; and on the other, if they are proved false, if your record is established, then your registry would be a matter of forms. So if there's really no problem, it should after all save you time you might spend waiting for forms and technicalities, and I might add, at station expense. If you hoped to clear all your papers and get cargo in a three-day stopover under normal circumstances, Captain, I'm afraid you were misled."

"If it's processed *in* that time and not after it—" He played for conciliation, took an easier stance, felt a line of sweat running down his face all the same.

"Quite so. I assure you it will be simultaneous."

"I appreciate it." He folded his hands behind him and tried to look comforted. He felt sick. "Where am I supposed to stay, then? I'd like to have access to my ship."

"Not yet."

"Accommodations dockside, then?"

"At any B class lodging."

"Captain." That from the militia officer. The voice drew his eyes in that direction. The blue uniform—was wrong somehow. Foreign. He was not used to foreignness. He had never imagined any current military force outside Union, which was all of civilization. The emblem was a sunburst on the sleeve, and several black bands about the cuff. "Commander Josh Talley, Alliance Forces. Officially—why *are* you here?"

"Trade."

"For what?"

"Is that," Sandor asked, looking back at Quen, "one of the things I should wait for a lawyer to answer? I don't see I have to make my business public."

"You're not obliged to answer. Use your own discretion."

He thought about it—looked back at Talley: a precise, military bearing, cold and clean, with a hardness unlike any merchanter he had ever seen. The eyes rested on him, unvarying, virtually unblinking, making him uneasy. "For the record," he said, "I get some latitude from my combine. I was on the Viking-Fargone run. It never paid; and I thought maybe I could widen my operation a little, set up an account here and do better on a cross-Line run . . . my discretion. I have a margin to operate in. I moved it. Am moving it."

"How much margin, Captain? Three thousand, as you claimed? And you look to compete with larger, faster ships? We're interested in the economics of your operation. What do you haul, when you can get cargo? Small items— of high value and low mass?"

Suddenly the room was all too close and the air unbearably warm. "I couldn't do much worse than where I was, that was all. Yes, I haul things like that. Station surplus. Package mail. Licensed pharmaceuticals. All clean stuff. Dried foods. Sometimes I carry passengers who aren't in a hurry and can't afford better. I'm slow, yes."

"And WSC has interest in a Pell base of operations?"

He weighed his answer, trying to remember what he might have said over the com when he was accounting for himself coming in. "Sir, I told you—my own risk. I figured I could get some station cargo. I heard it was good here."

"Captain, I know something about Union law. The legal liabilities and the risks of your operation don't leave much room for profit; and it seems to me very doubtful that your combine would leave a step like yours to an independent."

"It's not a company move. It's a simple shift of a margin account." He grew desperate, tried to make it sound like indignation. "I never violated the law and I came here in good faith. There's no regulation against it on Unionside."

"Financial arrangements on both sides of the line have been—loose, true. And you fall into a peculiar category. I perceive you're an excellent dockside lawyer. Most marginers are. And I'd reckon if your log and ledgers are put under subpoena . . . we'll find they don't exist, in spite of regulations to the contrary. In fact you'll keep no more records than the Mazianni do. In fact it's very difficult to tell a marginer from that category of ship—by the quality of the records they keep. What do you say, Captain? Could that account for your economics in a cross-Line run?"

If ever in his life he would have collapsed in fright it would have been then, under that quiet, precise voice, that very steady stare. His heart slammed against his ribs so hard it affected his breathing. "I'd say, sir, that I'm no pirate, and having lost my family to the Mazianni, I don't take the comparison kindly."

The eyes never flinched, never showed apology. "Still, there is no apparent difference."

"*Lucy* doesn't carry arms enough to defend herself." His voice rose. He choked it down to a conversational tone as quickly, refusing to lose control. "You admit she can't make speed. How is she supposed to be a pirate?"

"A Mazianni carrier could hardly pull up to a station for trade and conversation. But there *is* a means by which the Mazianni are trading with stations, in which they do scout out an area and the ships trading in it, mark the fat ones, and pick them off in the Between. Marginers undoubtedly figure in that picture, trading in the nullpoints, picking up cargo, faking customs stamps. Would you know any ships like that?"

"No, sir."

"She moves fast when she's empty, your *Lucy*."

"You can inspect her rig—"

"We have an unusual degree of concern here. The allegations made against you include a possible charge of piracy."

"That's not true."

"We advise you that the Alliance Fleet is making its own investigation, apart from Pell Dock Authority. That investigation will take longer than three days. In fact, it will be ongoing, and it involves a general warrant, along with a profile of your ship and its internal identification numbers, a retinal print and voice print, which we'll take before you return to dockside, and all this will be passed to Wyatt's Star Combine and Mariner through diplomatic and military channels. Should it later prove necessary, that description will be passed to all ports, both Union and Alliance, present and future. But you won't be detained on our account, once that printing has been done."

"And what if I'm innocent? What kind of trouble am I left with? That kind of thing could get me killed somewhere, for nothing, some stupid clerk punching the wrong key and bringing that up, some ship meeting me at a null-point and pulling that out of library—you're setting me up for a target." He cast a desperate look at Quen. "Can I appeal it? Have I got a choice?"

"Military operations," Talley said, "are not under civil court. You can protest, through application to Alliance Council, or through a military court. Both are available here at Pell, although the Council has finished its quarterly business and it's in the process of dispersing as ships leave. You'd have to appeal for a hearing at the next sitting, about three months from now. Military court could be available inside a month. You'd be detained pending either procedure, but counsel will be provided, along with lodging and dock charges, if you want to exercise that right. And you can apply for extensions of time if you need to call witnesses. Counsel would do that for you."

"I'll see what counsel says."

"That would be wise," Quen said. An aide had come in, padded round the outside of the U and slipped a paper under her hands. She read it and spoke quietly to the messenger, folded her hands over the paper on the table as the messenger slipped out again. "There is an intervenor in the case, Captain Stevens, if you're willing to accept."

"I don't understand."

"Reilly of *Dublin Again* has offered his onboard legal counsel. This would be acceptable to Pell."

The blood drained toward his feet. "Am I free to make up my own mind in the matter?"

"Absolutely."

"I'd like to talk to them."

"I think our business with you is done, pending your appointment with the military identification process."

"But maybe I don't want to go through that. Maybe—" He stared into a row of adamant faces. Stopped.

"Captain," Talley said, "you have your rights to resist it. The military has its rights to detain you. Your counsel can interview you in detention and advise you. If you wish."

He thought of jails, of a Dubliner arriving to fetch him

out, one of Allison's hard-eyed cousins. "No," he said. "I'll go along with the ID."

"That ought to do it, then," Quen said, and looked aside at Talley. Talley nodded, once and economically. "Sufficient, then," Quen said. "We hope, Captain Stevens, that there's nothing but a mistake involved here. You're free to address the board in general. We'll listen. But I'd advise selecting your attorney before you do that. And prepare your statements with counsel's advice."

"I'll reserve that, then."

"Captain," Talley said, "if you'd go with the officer."

"Sir," he said, quietly, precisely. "Ma'am." He turned and walked out with the security officer, through the outer office and into the hall, trying in his confusion to remember where he was and which way the lift was and to reckon where he was being taken now. He was lost; he was panicked, inside corridors which were not *Lucy*'s, a geometry which was not the simple circle of dockside.

There was a small office down the corridor, two desks, a counter full of equipment. He stood, waited: a technician in militia blue showed up. "General ID," the officer said, and the tech took him in charge, walked him through it, one procedure and the next, even to a cell sample.

It was done then, irrevocable. The information was launched, and they would send it on. The tech gave him a cup of cold water, urged him to sit down. "No," he said. Maybe it was the look of him that won the sympathy. He failed at unconcern—looked back at the officer who had acquired a companion.

"Your party's waiting for you," the second officer said, "out by the lift."

Allison, he thought, at a new ebb of his affairs. He should have accepted jail; should have refused the typing. He had fouled things up. But confinement—being shut up in a cell for Dubliners to stare at—being shut up inside narrow station walls, in places he knew nothing about—

The officer indicated the door, opened it for him, pointed down the hall to the left. "Around the corner and down."

He went, turned the corner—stopped at the sight of the silver-coveralled figure standing by the lift, a man he had never met.

But Dubliner. He walked on, and the dark-haired young man gave him no welcome but a cold stare. C. REILLY, the pocket said, on a broad and powerful chest. "Curran Reilly," the Dubliner said.

"Where's Allison?"

"None of your business. You're through getting into trouble, man. Hear me?"

"I'm headed down to the exchange. I'm not looking for any."

"You hold it." An arm shot out, blocking his arm from the lift call button. "You got any enemies in port, Stevens?"

"No," he said, resisting the impulse to swing. "None that I know about. What's your percentage in it?"

Curran Reilly reached in his coveralls pocket and pulled out several credit chits, thrust them on him and he took them on reflex. "You take this, go get breakfast, book into the same sleepover as last night. You don't go to the exchange. You don't go near station offices. You don't sign anything you haven't signed already."

"I've been printed."

"A great help. Really great."

He thrust the credits back. "Keep your handout. I've got my own funds."

"The blazes you have. Shut your mouth. You go to that sleepover and stay there and that bar next door. We want to know right where to find you. We don't want any complications and we don't want anything else stupid on your part. Keep that money and don't try to touch what you arrived with. You've got enough troubles."

He stared into black and angry eyes, smothered his own temper, afraid to walk away. "So how do I find the place? I'm lost."

The Dubliner reached and pushed buttons on the lift call. "I'll get you there."

"Where's Allison?"

"Don't press your luck, mister."

"That's Captain, and I'm asking where Allison is. Is she in trouble?"

"Captain." The Dubliner hissed, half a laugh, and the scowl darkened. "Her business is her business and none of yours, I'm telling you. She's working to save your hide, and I'm not here because I like the company."

"She's not spending any money—"

"You've got one track in your mind, haven't you, man? Money. You're a precious dockside whore."

"Go—"

"Shut your mouth. You take our charity and you'll do as you're told." The car arrived and the door whipped open. The Dubliner held it for him and he got in, with rage half blinding him to anything but the glare of lights and the realization that they were not alone in the car. Curran Reilly stepped in: the door shut and the car shot away with them. A pair of young girls stood against the rail on the far side of the car, an old man in the front corner. Sandor put his hands in his pockets and felt the Reilly money in his left with the sandwich wrapper, with the adrenalin pulsing in him and Curran Reilly standing there like a statue at his right. The girls whispered behind their hands. Laughed in adolescent insecurity. "It's *him*," he heard, and he kept staring straight ahead, an edge of raw terror getting through the anger, because his face was known—everywhere. And he had to swallow whatever the Dubliner said and did because there was no other hope but that.

If the Reillys were not themselves plotting revenge, for the stain on their Name.

A long, slow trip on *Dublin*, Allison had warned him, if he crossed her cousins. Revenge might recover *Dublin's* sullied Name, when the word passed on docksides after that.

But he went where he was told. He knew well enough what station justice offered.

7

It was executive council on *Dublin,* and to be the center-piece of such a meeting was no comfortable position. Seventy-six of the posted and the retired crew . . . and the Old Man himself sitting in the center seat of the table of captains which faced the rest of the room: Michael Reilly, gray-haired with rejuv and frozen somewhere the biological near side of forty. Ma'am was in the first row after the Helm seats, in that first huge lounge behind the bridge that was the posteds lounge when it was not being the council room. And with Ma'am was the rest of Com; and Scan on the other side of the aisle, behind the rest of Helm, and that was Megan and Geoff and others. Allison sat with impassive calm, hands folded, trying to look easy in the face of all the power of *Dublin,* all the array of her mother and aunts and grandmother and cousins once and several times removed. She was all too conscious of Curran's empty seat beside hers, Helm 22; and Deirdre missing from 23; and Neill sitting in 24 and trying to look as innocent as she. The Old Man and the other captains had a nest of papers on the long table in front of them. She knew most of the content of them well enough. Some of it she did not, and that worried her.

The Old Man beckoned, and Will, who was the senior lawyer in the family, came up to the table and bent over there and talked a while to the captains in general. Heads nodded, lips pursed, a long slow conversation, and not a paper shuffled elsewhere in the room. The rest of the council listened; eavesdropping; and words fell out like *papers* and *liability;* and *piracy,* and *Union forces.*

Will went back to his seat then, and the board of captains straightened its papers while Allison tried not to clench her hands. Her gut was knotted up; and somewhere at her back was her mother, who had to be feeling something mortal at her daughter's insanity. People never quit their ships. Kin stayed together, lifelong; and daughters and sons were there, forever. There was Connie left, to be sure—Connie, waiting elsewhere, not posted, and not entitled here. There were friends and cousins, Megan's support at a time like this. Allison was numb, convinced that she was committing a betrayal of more than one kind—and still there was no more stopping it than she could stop breathing. Win or lose, she was marked by the attempt.

"Your entire watch," the Old Man said, "21, isn't represented here."

"Sir," she said quietly, "they're settling a situation involving *Lucy.* Before it gets out of hand."

"I'll refrain from comment," the Old Man said. "Mercifully."

"Yes, sir."

"I'm going to approve the request for financing. Contingent on the rest of your watch applying for this transfer as you represent."

"Yes, sir." A wave of cold and relief went through her. "Thank you, sir."

"You've phrased this as a temporary tour."

"Yes, sir."

"You'll retain your status then. Your watch in Helm will not be vacated."

"Yes, sir," she said. That was the risk they had run. Council supported them, then. "Thank you for the others, sir."

"I'll be talking to you," the Old Man said. "Privately. Now. Council's dismissed. Come to the bridge."

"Sir," she said very softly, and caught Neill's eye, two vacant seats removed, as others began to rise—Neill, whose brow was broken out in sweat. He gave her a nod. She got up, looked back across the rows of chairs for Megan and Geoff, and met her mother's stare as if there were no one else in the room for the moment. Her mother nodded slowly, and it sent a wave of anguish through her, that small gesture: it was all right; it was—if not understood—accepted. *Thank you,* she said: her mother lipread. Then she turned away toward the forward door the Old Man had taken, which led down the corridor to the bridge.

Little was working . . . in this heart of hearts of *Dublin,* most of the boards dark and shut down. Most of the work they did now besides monitor was connected to the cargo facility and to the com links with station. The Old Man had taken his seat in his chair among the rows and rows of dormant instruments and controls, with the few on-duty crew working in the far distance forward on the huge bridge. She went up to that post like a petitioner going to the throne, that great gimballed black chair in the pit which oversaw anything the captain wanted to look at. Anywhere. Instantly.

"Sir," she said.

The Old Man stared at her—white-haired and powerful and young/old with rejuv that took away more hope than it gave . . . for the ambitious young.

"Allison." Not Allie; Allison. She was always that with him. He rested his elbows on the arms of the chair and locked his hands on his middle. "You'll be interested to know that it's all stalled off. *Dancer*'s the ship that made the complaint. I've talked to their Old Lady. Says she doesn't have anything personal involved, and there hasn't been word from other witnesses. I take it you're still set on this."

"Yes, sir." Soft and careful. "By your leave, sir."

He stared at her with that humorless and unflappable calm that came from being what he was. "Sit down. Let's talk about this."

She had never sat in the Old Man's presence, not called in like this. She looked nervously to her left, where a small black cushion edged the main vid console, there for that purpose. She settled, hands on her knees, eye to eye with Michael Reilly.

"Applying to take a tour off *Dublin,*" the Old Man said. "Applying for finance into the bargain. Let me see if I can quote your application: 'a foot in Pell's doorway, a legitimate Alliance operation . . . outweighing other disadvantages.' You know where the sequence of command falls, 21, if we buy into another ship. Could that possibly have occurred to you?"

"I know that council could have voted it down, and Second Helm approved."

"If I thought you were the mooncalf dockside paints you, I'd give you the standard lecture, how a transfer is a major step, how strange it can be, on another ship, away from everything you know, taking orders from another command and coping with being different in a crew that—however friendly—isn't yours. But no. I know what you're in love with. I know what you're doing. And I'm not sure you do."

"There's worse can happen to him than *Dublin's* backing."

"Is there? You look at your own soul, Allison Reilly, and you tell me what you'd do and what you're buying into. You come making requests we should throw our Name behind a ne'er-do-well marginer, we should stop a complaint an honest ship has filed—all of that. And I'll remind you of something you've heard all your life. That every Dubliner is born with one free judgment call. Always . . . just one. Once, you've got the right to yell trouble on the docks and have the Old Man blow the siren and bring down every mother's son and daughter of us. And every time you do it right, that buys you only one more guaranteed judgment call. No Dubliner I can think of has taken much more on himself than you. You know that?"

"I know that, sir."

"And you apply to keep your status."

"To guarantee the loan, sir, begging your pardon."

"Not so pure, 21."

"Not altogether, no, sir."

"You're jumping over the line of succession; you're ignoring the claims your seniors might make ahead of you, if we bought that ship outright. Alterday command right off, isn't it, and not waiting the rest of your life without posting. It's a maneuver and every one of us knows it. It's a bald-faced conniving maneuver that oversets those with more right, and you're doing it on a technicality. And how do I answer that?"

Her heart was beating more than fast, and heat flooded

her face. "I'd say they voted and passed it, sir. I'd say they
have the same chance I'm taking, and there's dozens more
marginers like *Lucy*. Maybe they don't want to take that
kind of chance; and maybe they don't want it that bad. I
do. Those with me do. Third Helm's alterday watch—has
stayed unitary blamed long, sir; and begging your pardon,
sir, it functions."

"It functions," Michael Reilly said, looking into her eyes
with eyes that missed nothing, "because they've got one
bastard of a number one who's been number one in her
watch too long, who's infected with god-hood and who finds
the stage too small."

"Sir—"

"Let me tell you about smallness, 21. That ship you're
going to is small. There's no privacy, no amenities. No luxuries. No safeties and no relief and no backup."

"Better to reign in hell—"

"Yes. I thought so. And what about this Stevens?"

"He's better off with us."

"Is he?"

"Than being beached here with Pell owning his ship,
yes, sir."

The Old Man nodded slowly. "He'll thank you—about
that far. And what will you assign him—when you've got
his ship?"

"That becomes a council problem, sir, as I believe."

"Let me tell you something, young ma'am." Michael
Reilly leaned forward and jabbed a forefinger at her. "That
lies in your watch. Don't you hand it to council to settle.
Clear?"

"Clear, sir."

"So." He turned to the console beside him, searched
among the papers there, powered the chair around again
and offered her a handful of them. "There's a communication from *Dancer*. They'll withdraw the charge without protest. Understandable nervousness on their part . . . finding
a ship in port they know isn't clean. But that's no hide off
them, if we guarantee it's been taken thoroughly in hand.
The word's gone out by runner: no one else will file a
complaint on that ship without going through *Dublin* first,
and they've had an hour now to think it over. Something
would have come in if it was going to, so I tend to agree

with your judgment, that it's a financial problem the man has, no merchanter grudge. So he's clear in that respect. About the military, *that* inquiry can't be stopped; and that's going to be another problem that lies in your watch."

"Yes, sir."

"There's a voucher that will pay the dock charge; and a document of show-cause from Will that's going to clear up the matter with Pell Dock Authority. They'll have to come up with an official complaint with witnesses or drop the charge on the spot and free the ship, and since *Dancer*'s not going to stand behind the charge, it's going to die. So *Lucy*'s cleared, at least on civil charges. There's the loan agreement, for dock charges and cargo; and whatever else is reasonable in the way of outfitting. Do it proper, if you're going to rig out; no need economizing. And you remember what I told you. You come between somebody and his ship, you take that from him, and you know, in your heart of hearts, you know what you're doing. And we know. And he will. You remember that. You remember your Name, and you remember who you are."

"Yes, sir," she said softly.

"Dismissed."

She took the precious papers, stood up, nodded in respect and walked for the door—stopped for a moment, a look back at the bridge, the spacious, modern bridge of *Dublin,* the real thing that she had desired all her life. A knot welled up in her throat, a final anger, that there was no hope of this—that it had to be the sordid, aged likes of *Lucy,* because that was the only way left for *Dublin*'s excess children.

She went to say good-bye, to begin the good-byes, at least, a courtesy to Megan and Connie and Geoff and Ma'am, which was not as hard as that to *Dublin* herself.

8

There looked to be no change out across the docks. Sandor kept his eye on *Lucy*'s berth, covertly, from the doorway of the sleepover. Workers moved, pedestrian traffic went its unconcerned way up and down—mainday now, and he kept his face in the shadows. Downers shrilled and piped their gossip, busy at tasks like human dockworkers, moving canisters onto ramps or off, making distant echoes over the drone and crash of machinery.

He entertained wild thoughts . . . like waiting until station lights dimmed again in the half hour of twilight which passed mainday to alterday: like slipping over to that security barrier and decking some unfortunate workman—seeing if he could not liberate a cutter to get past that lock they had on *Lucy*'s hatch. Improbable. He thought even of going to some other marginer and pleading his way aboard as crew, because he was that panicked. The thought whisked through his mind and out again, banished, because he was not going to give *Lucy* up. He would try the cutter first; and they would take him in for sure then, with a theft and maybe an assault charge to add to the complaints already lodged against him.

Antisocial conduct. Behavior in willful disregard of others' rights. That was good for a lockup. Behavior in willful disregard of others' lives: that was good for a mindwipe for sure. Rehabilitation. Total restruct.

A cutter was as good as a gun, when it came to someone trying to get it away from him. It might bring about shooting. He thought that he preferred that, though he balked at the idea of using a cutter on any living thing. He was not made for this, he thought, not able to kill people; the thought turned him cold.

There was *Dublin,* and whatever hope that gave. He held onto that.

Militia passed in a group, male and female, blue-uniformed: he retreated inside the foyer and waited until they had gone their way with some other business in mind. Militia. Alliance Forces, Talley had said. Alliance Forces. There was talk that the militia of Pell had at its core a renegade Mazianni carrier; one of Conrad Mazian's captains— Signy Mallory of *Norway,* who had fought for the old Earth Company . . . the name the Mazianni used while they were legitimate; but a Mazianni captain all the same. Talley . . . upstairs: that was an officer of what Pell called its defense, maybe a man who had worked with Mallory. *That* was what was doggedly investigating him, a pirate hunting other pirates, who played by civilized rules in port.

But outside port—even if some miracle got him clear of Pell—

A flash across his vision, of armored troops on *Lucy's* bridge, of fire coming back at them, and the Old Man dying; and his mother; and the others—of being hit, and Ross falling on him—

And Jal screaming for help, when the troopers dragged him back through that boarding access and onto their ship; Jal and the others they had taken aboard, for whatever purposes they had in mind. . . .

The Alliance played politics with Union; and maybe they wanted, at the moment, to manufacture a pirate threat to Pell interests, to justify the existence of armed Alliance ships. And if they hauled him in—the mind-wipe could make sure he told the story they wanted. A paranoid fancy. Not likely. But he was among strangers, and too many things were possible . . . where pirates hunted pirates and might want to throw out a little deceiving chaff.

A step approached him on his left. He looked about and a hand closed on his arm and he looked straight into the face of Allison Reilly. "Told you to stay inside," she said.

"So I'm here." The shock still had his pulse thumping. "Find out anything?"

She pulled papers from her pocket, waved them in front of him. "Everything. It's covered. I've got you off clear."

He shook his head. The words went through without touching. "Clear."

"*Dublin* got *Dancer* to withdraw the allegations. We've got a show-cause order for station and they're not going to be able to come up with anything to substantiate it. We just filed the papers. And this—" She thrust one of the papers at him. "That's an application for your Alliance registry and trade license. And *Dublin*'s standing witness. That'll get you clear paper for this side of the Line. That's to be signed and filed, but it's all in order: our lawyer set it up." A second paper. "That's a show-cause for customs, to get that seal off. They can't maintain that without the charge from *Dancer*. This—" A third paper. "A loan, enough for dock charges, refitting, and cargo. I've got you crew. I've got you all but cleared to pull out of here. A way to outfit you with what you need. Are you following me?"

He blinked and tried. Stopped believing it and looked for the strings: it was the only thing to do when things looked too good. "What's it cost?" he asked. "Where's the rest of it? There is a rest of it."

She nodded toward the bar next door. "Come on. Sit down and look through it."

He went, dragged by the hand, into the noise and closeness of the smallish bar, sat down with her at a table by the door where there was enough light to read, and spread out the papers. "Beer," she ordered when the waiter showed, and in the meantime he picked up the loan papers and tried to make sense of them. Clause after clause of fine print. Five hundred thousand cargo allowance. A hundred thousand margin account. He looked at numbers stacked up like stellar distances and shook his head.

"You're not going to get a better offer," she said. "I'll tell you how you got it. I'm going with you. The whole Third Helm alterday watch of *Dublin* is signing with you for this tour. Crew that knows what they're doing. I'll vouch for that. My watch. And it's a fair agreement. You say that your *Lucy* can make profit on marginer cargoes. What do you think she could do given real backing?"

That touched his pride, deeply. He lifted his head, not stupid in it, either. "I don't know. My kind of operation I know—how to get what's going rate on small deals. *Lucy*'s near two hundred years old. She's not fast. I strung those jumps getting here. Hauling, she's slow, and you come out of those jumps feeling it."

"I've seen her exterior on vid. What's the inside rig?"

He shrugged. "Not what you're used to. Number one hold's temperature constant to 12 degrees, the rest deep cold; fifteen K net—It's not going to work. I can't handle that kind of operation you're talking about."

"It'll work."

"I don't know why you're doing this."

"Business. *Dublin*'s starting up operations here, wants a foot on either side of the line; putting you on margin account is convenient. And if it helps you out at the same time—"

The beers came. Sandor picked his up and drank to ease his dry mouth, gave the papers another desperate going over, trying to find the clause that talked about confiscations, about liability that might set him up for actions, about his standing good for previous debts.

"A few profitable runs," she said, "and you build up an account here and you clear the debt. You want to know what *Dublin* clears on a good run?"

"I'm not sure I do."

"It's a minor loan. Put it that way. That's the scale we're talking about. It's nothing. And there's a ten-year time limit on that loan. Ten years. Station banks—would they give you that? Or any combine? You work that debt down and there's a good chance you could deal with *Dublin* for a stake to a refitting. I mean a real refitting. No piggyback job. Kick that ancient unit off her tail and put a whole new generation rig on. She's a good design, stable moving in jump; some of the newest intermediate ships on the boards borrow a bit from her type."

"No," he said in a small voice. "No, you don't get me into that. You don't get your hands on her."

"You think you can't do it. You think you'll fail."

He thought about it a moment.

"What better offer," she asked him, "have you ever hoped to have? And if charges come in, who's going to stand with you? Hmn? You sign the appropriate papers, you take the offer.—I've gone out on a line for you; and for me, I admit that. I get a post I can't get on my ship. So we both take a risk. I don't know but what there's worse to you than you've told. I don't know who your enemies might be; and I wouldn't be surprised if you had some."

He shook his head slowly. "No. I don't. Hard as it may be to believe, I've never made any I know of."

"Smart, at least."

"Survival. —Reilly: if I sign those papers, I'm telling you—there's one captain on *Lucy,* and I'm it."

"There's nothing in those papers that says anything to the contrary."

He drank a long mouthful of the beer. "We get a witness on this?"

"That's the deal. Station offices."

He nodded slowly. "Let's go do it, then."

It made him less than comfortable, to go again into station offices, to confront the dockmaster's agents and turn in the applications that challenged the station to do its worst. The documents went from counter to desk behind the counter, and finally to one of the officials in the offices beyond—a call finally into that office, where they stood while a man looked at the papers.

"How long—" Sandor made himself ask, against all instincts to the contrary. "How long to process those and get the seal clear? I'd like to start hunting cargo."

An official frown. "No way of knowing."

"Well," Allison said, "there's already a routing application in."

A lift of the brows, and a frown after. None too happy, this official. "Customs office," he said, punching in on the com console. "I have *Lucy*'s Stevens in with forms."

And after the answer, another shunting to an interior office, more questions and more forms.

Nature of cargo, they asked. Information pending acquisition, Sandor answered, in his own element. He filled the rest out, looped some blanks, letting station departments chase each other through the maze. *Clear* was a condition of mind, a zone in which he had not yet learned to function.

Legitimate, he kept telling himself. These were real papers he was applying for. In the wrong name, and under a false ID, and that was the stain on matters: but real papers all the same.

They walked out of the customs office toward the exchange, and when he got to that somewhat busier desk, to stand in line with others including spacers with onstation cards to apply for . . . Allison snagged his arm and drew him over to the reception desk for more inner offices.

"Sir?" the secretary asked, blinking a little at his out at the elbows look and the silvery company he kept.

Embarrassed, Sandor searched for the appropriate papers. "Got a fund transfer and an account to open."

"That's Wyatt's?" *Everyone* knew his business. It threw him off his stride. He put the loan papers on the desk.

"No," he said, "that's an independent deal."

"*Dublin* has an account with Wyatt's." Allison leapt into the fray. "This is a loan between *Lucy* and *Dublin*. The ship is collateral. Captain Stevens hopes to straighten it up with his own combine, but as it is, *Dublin* will cover any transfer of funds that may be necessary: escrow will rest on Pell."

"What sum are we talking about?"

"Five hundred thousand for starters."

"I'll advise Mr. Dee."

"Thank you," Allison said with a touch of smugness, and settled into a waiting area chair. Sandor sat down beside her, wiped a touch of sweat from his temples, crossed his ankles, leaned back, willed one muscle after another to relax. "You let me do the talking, will you?" he asked her.

"You take it slow. I know what I'm doing."

His fingers felt numb. A lot of him did. *Clear,* he thought again. There was something wrong with such a run of luck. Ships that tossed off half a million as if it were pocket change—rattled his nerves. He felt a moment of panic, as if some dark cloud were swallowing him up, conning him into debts and ambition more than he could handle. He had no place in this office. It was like stringing jumps and accumulating velocity without dump—there was a point past which no ship could handle what it could acquire.

"Captain." The secretary had come back. "Mr. Dee will see you."

He stood up. Allison put her hand on his back, urging

him, intended for comfort, perhaps, but it felt like a fatal shove.

He walked, and Allison went behind him. He met the smallish man in his office . . . a wise, wrinkled face, dark almond eyes that went to the heart of him and peeled away the layers. So, well, one sat down like a man and filled out the forms and above all else tried not to display the nervousness he felt.

"You'll have claims from WSC," Dee advised him.

"Minor," Allison said.

Again a stab of those dark, fathomless eyes. An elderly finger indicated the appropriate line and he signed.

"There we go," Allison said, approving it. He shook hands with the banker and realized himself a respectable if mortgaged citizen. Allison shook hands with Dee and Dee showed them to the outer office in person. They were someone. He was. He felt himself hollow centered and scared with a different kind of fear than the belly-gripping kind he lived in on stations: with a knowledgeable, too-late kind of dread, of having done something he never should have done, a long time back, when he had walked into a bar on Viking and tried to buy a Dubliner a drink.

"You come," Allison said as they walked out empty of their bundle of applications, with a set of brand new credit cards and clear ship's papers in exchange. "Let's get some of the outfitting done. I don't know what you're carrying in ship's stores. Blast, I'll be glad to get that customs lock off and have a look at her."

"Got some frozen stuff. I outfitted pretty fair for a solo operation at Viking."

"We've got five. What's our dunnage allotment?"

"I really don't think that's a problem."

"Accommodations?"

"Cabins 2.5 meters by 4. That's locker and shower and bunk."

"Sleep vertical, do you?"

"Lockers are under and over the bunk."

"Private?"

"Private as you like."

"Nice. Good as *Dublin,* if you like to know."

He considered that and expanded a bit. "If you have

extra—there's always space to put it. Storage is never that tight."

"Beautiful.—Hey." She flagged one of the ped-carriers that ran the docks, a flatbed with poles, hopped on: Sandor followed, put his own card in the slot as it whisked them along the station ring with delirious ease. He had never ridden a carrier; never felt he could afford the luxury, when his legs could save the expense. All his life he had walked on the docks of stations, and he watched the lights and the shops blur past, still numb in the profusion of experience. "Off!" someone would sing out, and the driver would stop the thing just long enough for someone to step down. "Off!" Allison called, and they stepped off on white dock, in the face of a large pressure-window and a fancy logo saying WILSON, and in finer print, SUPPLIER. It was all white and silver and black inside. He swore softly, and let Allison lead him into the place by the hand.

Displays everywhere. Clothing down one side, thermals and working clothes and liners and some of them in fancy colors, flash the like of which was finding its way onto dock-sides on the bodies of those who could afford it. New stuff. All of it. He looked at the price on a pair of boots and it was 150. He grabbed Allison by the arm.

"They're thieves in here. Look at that. Look, this isn't my class. *Lucy* outfits from warehouses. Or dockside."

She wrinkled her nose. "I don't know what you're used to, but we're not going to eat seconds all the way and we're not using cut-rate stuff. You don't get class treatment on dockside if you don't have a little flash. And we'll not be dressing down, thank you; so deaden your nerves, Stevens, and buy yourself some camouflage so you don't stand out among your crew."

He looked up the aisle at clothes he could not by any stretch of the imagination see himself wearing, stuffed his hands in his pockets. The lining of the right one was twice resewn. "You wear that silver stuff into *Lucy*'s crawlspaces, will you? You fit yourselves out for work, Reilly."

"There's dockside and there's work. Find something you like, hear me?"

He studied the aisle, nothing on racks, no searching this stuff for burn-holes and bad seams. One asked, and they hunted it out of computerized inventory. "So I get myself the likes of yours," he muttered, thinking he would never carry it well. "That satisfy you?"

"Good enough. What kind of entertainment system does she carry?"

"Deck of cards," he muttered. "We can buy a fresh one."

She swore. "You have to have a tape rig."

"Mariner-built Delta system."

"Lord, a converter, then. We'll bring our own tapes and buy some new."

"I can't afford—"

"Basic amenities. I'm telling you, you want class crew, you have to rig out. What about bedding?"

"Got plenty of that. Going to have to stock up on life support goods and some filters and detergents and swabs—before we get to extravagances. I'd like to put a backup on some switches and systems that aren't carrying any right now."

A roll of Allison's dark eyes in his direction, stark dismay.

"Two of them on the main board," he added, the plain truth.

"Make a list. This place can get them."

"Will. Going to be nice, isn't it, knowing there's a failsafe?"

He walked down the aisle alone, looking at the clothes. And all about him, over the tops of the counters, were other displays . . . personal goods, bedding, dishes, tapes and games, utility goods, cabinets, ship's furnishings, interior hardware, recycling goods, tools, bins, medical supplies, computer software. Music whispered through his senses. He turned about him and stared, lost in the glitter of the displays he had never given more than a passing glance to—had never come *in* a place like this, where his kind of finances could get a man accused of theft.

A kind of madness afflicted him suddenly, like nerving himself for a bad jump. "Help you?" a clerk asked down his nose.

"Got to get some clothes," he said. And yielding to the recklessness of the moment: "Like to have it match, jacket and the rest. Some dockside boots. Maybe a few work clothes." Allison was out of sight: that panicked him in more than one sense. She was probably off buying something. And the clerk was giving him that look that bartenders gave him. He pulled his new card from his pocket. "Stevens," he said, and clerkly eyes brightened.

"You're the one that came in yesterday."

"Yes, sir." Lord, was it only yesterday? His shoulders ached with the thought. "Got in with nothing but my account money and I need a lot of things."

The eyes brightened further. "Be happy to help you, Captain Stevens."

Flash coveralls. A 75 credit pair of boots; a jacket; a stack of underwear. He looked at himself in the fitting room, haggard and wanting a shave, and took off the fine clothes and ordered it all done in packages.

And he found Allison Reilly at the commodities counter, perched on a stool and going through the catalogue. "Ordered anything?" he asked with a sinking feeling.

"Making a list." She tapped the screen in front of her, a display of first line meals with real meat and frozen fruits and boxed pastries.

"Chocolates," he added in a sense of fantasy. He had had chocolate once.

"Chocolate," she said. "There we go."

"Cancel that. It's too expensive."

"Chocolate and coffee. Real stuff. Leave it to me."

"Allison—do you—get this stuff usually?"

He would have cut his throat rather than ask her an hour ago. He looked into her face and suspected something as childish as his chocolates.

"For special days," she admitted. "I got some staple stuff too."

"I have 75 standard frozens. You can wipe that off."

"Good enough." She wiped the stylus over part of the order. "What about those hardware items we need?"

We, it was. He took up the seat next to her and keyed up the catalogue. "I can get better prices," he muttered.

"There's a discount system. Do your whole rig here and you get some off."

"Better." After the moment's euphoria, his stomach was upset. He ticked through the things they really needed. He felt conspicuous sitting here, at the counter in this place, dressed as he was. The list went on growing, more and

more expensive, because systems were, more than crew
luxuries.

"That do it?" Allison asked finally.

He punched for the total. 5576.2 came up on the screen.
He shook his head in shock. "Can't go that."

"Five of us, remember? And the hardware. That's not
out of line. Put the card in, there."

He shoved it into the slot. It registered. THANK YOU,
the screen said. He stared at it like some oncoming mass.

Took his card back.

She patted his shoulder. "Haircut for us both," she said.
"And clean up. We're meeting someone for dinner."

"Who?"

"The rest of us, who else? And why don't you get yourself a proper patch, while we're at it? I looked in the direc-
tory. There's this place does them to order, all computer
set up. Anything you like, on the spot. It's really amazing
how it works."

"Lord, Reilly—does it matter?"

"I'd think it would." She touched the misembroidered
nymph on his sleeve. "You could do yourself a class job.
Or they've got the over-the-counter stuff. If you really
want it."

That was low. He scowled and she never flinched. "Mind
your business," he said. "If I like the tatty thing it's my
business."

"You're really going to go blank like that. They'll think
you're a pirate for sure."

"I'll just get me a handful of tatty ones. Thanks."

Lips pursed. So she knew how far she had pushed.

"The name's not Stevens," she said.

"That's what you're asking, is it?"

"Maybe."

"That's my business." And after a moment: "I'll get
some blamed patch. I don't care what. But no shamrock.
I'll promise you that."

"Didn't think so."

He nodded, gathered up his packages, all of them but
the stuff they had ordered on catalogue, that would see
ship delivery when they made the loading schedule.

When.

9

He had his doubts—had them following Allison to the patcher; and getting trimmed and shaved and lotioned at the barber—his first time, for a haircut that gave him a sleek, blond look of affluence. Doubts again in sleepover, spoiling the hour he snatched for sleep: his privacy, he kept thinking; the life that he had—It was a miserable life, but he controlled it; there was comp, with its peculiarities; and the sealed rooms that these Dubliners would demand to open. There were things they would hear and see that were worse than public nakedness to him; that undercut his pride, and rifled through his memories.

But it had to be, he reasoned with himself. He had never had such a chance. Never could dream of such a chance. He looked at Allison looking at him in the mirror—and the warmth of that drove the chill away. "You look good," she said, to the silver-suited image of him, and he faced about toward her with a surge of confidence that sent some feeling back into his hands and feet. "Reckon so?" he asked.

"No question."

So it fed him his courage back. He drew a deeper breath, reassessed himself and the pathetic ridiculousness, the childishness of the things stored in comp, the nature of the sealed compartments and the relics he lived among. So if she thought that, so if she *felt* that, then she would not laugh—and the others, these strangers they went to meet— she could handle. As long as she was with him; as long as she found nothing humorous in a man trying to be what he was not—who listened to voices instead of family, who had never had the strength to clear out all the debris of the past; who kept a secret voice that talked to a child who should have long ago grown up; excruciating things. A lifetime of illusions.

There was always the alternative, he reminded himself. He could wait for the military; in his mind he heard the laughter of the dockside searchers who might get into such privacies. Or the techs who might strip his mind down, when his scams caught up to him, discovering the twisted child he was. They would put it all together, taking it all apart; and the thought of that—of the questions; the exposure of himself—

He wore a patch, had sewn it on: LUCY, it said, white letters on a black, blue-centered circle; and that was as close as he dared come to the old one. It looked naked, too, without the swan in flight that belonged there. But someone might know *Le Cygne*, and Krejas; and he and Ross and Mitri had always agreed, in all the scams, to keep the Name out of it. So it was not possible now to go to station offices and say—I lied; change the name; put it the way it ought to be. That would finish everything.

And maybe, he thought, a lifetime would get him used to looking at the patch that way.

"Coming?" Allison asked him.

He walked into the restaurant arm in arm with Allison—one of those places he expected of Allison, ornate and expensive, where flash and fine cloth belonged, and stationer types occupied tables alongside spacers of the big ships, men and women with officers' stripes: a lot of silver hair in the place. A lot of money. A waiter intercepted them—"Reilly," Allison said; and the waiter nodded deferentially and showed them the way among serpentine pillars to the recesses of the place, deep shadows along the walls.

A silver company occupied the table he located for them, a company that rose when they arrived—Sandor did a quick scan of lamp-lit faces, heart thumping, hand already extending in response to offered hands and a murmur of courtesies—and found himself face to face with Curran Reilly.

No hand offered there. Nothing offered. "Curran," Allison said. "Helm 22 of *Dublin,* my number two. Captain Stevens of *Lucy.* But you'll have met."

"Yes," Sandor said, the adrenalin hazing everything else; and in belated time, Curran Reilly took the hand he offered, a dry palm clenched about his sweating one. A grip that he expected, hard and unfriendly like the stare. And other hands, then, earlier offered, "Deirdre," Allison said, "number three"—a freckled, solid woman, dark-haired like all the Reillys, but with a grin that went straight to the heart, punctured his anger and half made up for Curran. Happiness. He was not accustomed to cause that in people.

"Neill," Allison said of the third, another offered hand; a lank and bearded man with an earnestness that persuaded him Curran was at least unique in the lot. "Neill," he murmured in turn, looked at the others. The waiter hovered, offering chairs. They settled again, himself between Allison and Deirdre, facing Curran and Neill.

"Would you like cocktails?" the waiter asked.

"Drinks with dinner," Allison said. "That's all right with everyone?"

Nods all about. The waiter whisked forth a set of menus, and for a merciful time there was that amenity among them.

He was buying; he reckoned that. The prices were enough to chill the blood, but he nerved himself and ordered the best, maintained a smile when his guests did. It was, after all, one night, one time—an occasion. He could afford it, he persuaded himself. To please these people. To give them what they were accustomed to having. On their own money.

The waiter departed. A silence hung there. "Got everything in order?" Curran asked Allison finally.

"All settled."

"Megan sends her regards."

A silence. A glance downward. Sandor had no idea who Megan might be; no one offered to enlighten him. "I'll talk to her," Allison said. "It's not good-bye, after all. We'll be meeting on loops."

"I think she understands," Deirdre said. "My people—they know. They know why."

"Everyone knows *why,*" Allison said. "It's forgiving it."

She laid her hand briefly on Sandor's arm. "Ship politics."
To the others: "—We got the outfitting done. First class.".

"What kind of accommodations have we got?" Neill
asked.

The adjoining table filled, with all attendant disorganiza-
tion. Sandor sat and listened to Reillys talk among themselves, plans for packing, for farewells, discussion of what
supplies they had laid in. "Private cabins and no dunnage
limit?" Deirdre exclaimed, eyes alight. "I'd thought we
might be tight."

"No limit within reason," Sandor said, breaking out into
the Reilly dialogues—expanded at the reaction that got
from the lot of them. "That's one advantage of a small-
crew ship, few as there are. Bring anything you like. Any
cabin you like."

"You and Allison plan to double up?" Curran asked.

It was not the question; it was the silence that went after
it. The look in Curran's eyes.

"Curran," Allison said.

"Just wondering."

The meal started arriving, wine first; the appetizers when
they had scarcely settled from that. Sandor sat and smol-
dered, out of appetite with the temper that was boiling in
him. "I'll tell you," he said, jabbing a serving knife in Curran's direction as the waiter passed finally out of earshot,
"Mr. Reilly, I think you and I have a problem. I'm not
sure why. Or what. But it started up there in blue section
this morning and I'm not going to have it go on."

"Stevens," Allison said.

"I think we'd better settle it."

"All right," Curran said softly. "The number one says
you're all right, that goes with me. Let's start from zero."

"My rules, mister."

"Absolutely," Curran said. "Chain of command. As soon
as we get that lock off."

"Ought to be soon," Allison said. "How about that routing application?"

"Got it," Curran said. His sullen face lighted instantly.
"Clear. We're routed to Venture and Bryan's, Konstantin
Company commodities, on *Dublin*'s guarantee."

Sandor had ducked his head to eat and stay out of it. He

looked up again. "You're talking about our route and cargo."

"Right."

"You take it on yourself—"

"Part of the package."

"No. Not part of the package. You don't set up routes or make agreements."

"Come down, man. We've got you a deal better than you could get. A deal that's guaranteed profit. With a station commerce load that doesn't cost you, and guaranteed rate for the delivery. How do you do better than that?"

"I don't care what you've got. No. I decide where *Lucy* goes and if she goes."

"Slow," Allison said, patted his arm, once, twice. "Hold it. Listen: it *is* part of the package. I was going to tell you. It's a good deal. The best. The Hinder Stars opening up again, the stations being set up to operate—you know what a chance it is, to get in on the setup of a station? *Dublin* herself is taking on cargo and looping back to Mariner. But we go out to the Hinder Stars. Toward Sol. You see how it works? That's Sol trade: luxuries, exotics. We take a station load out and do small runs; and as the Sol trade starts coming in, we start picking up Sol cargo. We run small cargo at first, then see about doing that conversion that'll boost her up to speed. . . ."

"You've got that planned too."

"Because I know this kind of economics, if you don't. We're not talking about dockside trading. We're talking about running full and being where trade can build."

"We get backing that way," Deirdre said. "Eventually we schedule to catch *Dublin*'s Pell loop and funnel Sol goods into Union territory; and that's big profit. *Dublin*'s not doing a total act of charity."

"They'll cut our throats. Alliance traders. Locals won't stand for that."

"Stop thinking like a marginer," Allison said. "You're linked to the *Dublin* operation. They won't touch us the way they won't touch *Dublin* herself. And after one run, we'll be local. We'll have Alliance paper."

"And I take what deals *Dublin* offers."

"Fair deals."

He thought about it a moment, avoiding the sight of Curran Reilly, took a drink of wine. "Hinder Stars," he said, thinking that if there was a place least likely for his record to catch up to him it had to be that, the forgotten Earthward stations. Sol goods, expensive for their mass. Rarities and luxuries. "So *Dublin* wants a trade link."

"Believe it," Allison said. "Both sides of the Line are interested . . . Pell, absolutely; Union, in keeping the flow of trade across the Line. You think Union wants Pell and Sol in bed together alone? No. Union's supporting Unionside merchanters that want to trade across the Line; and there's nothing that says we can't set up an operation on this side."

"We."

"Any way you like it. You needed the bailout. And we saw the advantage. You. We. You and the lot of us on *Lucy* can develop a new loop that's going to pay."

He thought about it again, excited in spite of himself. "You plan to stay on—how long?"

"We don't necessarily plan to go back. It's like I said . . . too far to the posted ranks. We're coming to stay."

He nodded slowly. "All right," he said, even including Curran in that. "All right, I'll take your deal. And the lot of you.— What about charts?"

"Got that arranged," Curran said. "No problem with that."

"From what I know," Allison said, "we're going to have a double jump to Venture and a double to Bryant's."

"Lonely out that direction."

"Pell's got some sort of security out that way."

"Patrol?"

"They don't say. They just put out they've got it watched."

"Comforting." He doubted it all. It was likely bluff. Or Pell was that determined to keep the Sol link open.

He looked up again, at the strangers who looked to share with him, to come onto *Lucy*'s deck—permanent company. So they were not all what he would have chosen. But with a Curran came a Deirdre, whose broad, cheerful self he liked on sight; and Neill Reilly, who had said little of anything and who seemed set in the background by all the others—They were Family, like any other, the rough and the smooth together. He had not known that kind of closeness . . . not since Ross. He wanted it, and Allison, with a yearning that welled up in his throat and behind his eyes and throughout. And it was his. It came with the wealth, the luck he still could not imagine. But it was real. It was all about him. He made himself relax, limb by limb, up to the shoulders, looked across the table at his acquired crew and felt something knotted up inside unsnarl itself.

And when dinner was done, down to a fancy fruit dessert, when they had drunk as much as merchanters were apt to drink on liberty—they found things to laugh at, Dubliner anecdotes, tales on each other. He laughed and wiped his eyes, as he had not done in longer than he had forgotten.

The bill was his: he took it without flinching, gave a tip to the waiter—left a happy man in their wake and strolled out into the chill air of the dockside with his flock of Dubliners.

"Go to the offices," he suggested, "see if we can't get the lock off my ship."

"Let's," Allison agreed. "Is it past alterdawn? We can get something done."

"Get a ped carrier," Deirdre said.

"Walk," said Neill. "We might be sober when we get there."

They walked, along the busy docks, past *Lucy*'s barriered berth, weaving a good deal less when they had covered all of green dock, sweating a bit when they had come into blue, and near the customs offices.

But he came differently this time, in company, with the knowledge of *Dublin*'s lawyer behind them, and papers on file that put him in the right. He walked up to the desk and faced the official with a plain request, brought out the papers. "I need the lock off," he said. "We seem to have everything else straightened away but that."

"Ah," the official said. "Captain Stevens."

"Can we get it taken care of?"

The official produced a sealed envelope, passed it over.

"What's this?"

"I've no idea, sir. I'm told it relates to the hold order."

He was conscious of the others at his back—refused to look at them, tore open the seal on the message slip and read it once before it sank in. "Report blue dock number three," he read it, looking back at Allison then. "*AS Norway,* Signy Mallory commanding."

Curran swore. "Mallory," Allison said, and it might as well have been an oath. "On Pell?"

"Arrived two hours ago," the official said, a roll of the eyes toward the clock. "The message is half an hour old."

"What's the military doing in this?" Curran asked. "Those papers are clear."

"I don't know, sir," the official said. "Answering ought to clear it up."

The fear was back, familiar as an old suit of clothes. "I'd better get out there and take care of this," Sandor said. "I don't see there's any reason for you to go."

They walked out with him, that much at least, back out onto the dock facing the military ships . . . the schedule boards showed it plainly: NORWAY, the third berth down occupied now, conspicuously alight. He looked at the Dubliners, at worried faces and Curran's scowl.

"Don't know how long this may take," he said. "Allison, maybe I'd better call you after I get back to the sleepover. Maybe you'd better go on back to *Dublin.*"

"No," Allison said. "If you don't get out of there fairly soon, we'll be calling some legal help. They don't bluff us."

That was some comfort. He looked at the rest of them, who showed no inclination to take any different course. Nodded then, thrust his hands into his pockets, crumpling the message in the right.

He prepared arguments, countercharges, mustered the same indignation he had used on authorities before. It was all he knew how to do.

But it was hard to keep the bluff intact walking up to the lighted access of *Norway,* where uniformed troops—these *were* troops, far different from any stationside militia—took him in charge and searched him. They were rejuved, a great number of these men and women—old enough to have fought in the war, silver-haired and some of them marked with scars no stationsider would have had to wear. They were not rough with him in their searching, but they were more thorough than the police had been. They frightened him, the way that ship out there frightened him, behind that cheerful lighted access, a huge carrier bristling with armaments, a Company ship, from another age. They brought him toward the ramp that led up into the access. And standing in the accessway . . . Talley, grim and waiting for him.

He kept walking. So the man was part of this action. He was somehow not surprised. The Dubliners, he was thinking, ought to get back to their ship. The military would think twice about demanding that a merchanter family of the Reillys' size give up some of its own to questioning. But alone, far from *Dublin,* they were vulnerable, unused to authorities who ran things as they pleased.

He encountered Talley, a bleak, pale-eyed stare from the Alliance officer, a nod in the direction he should go. So he had acquired a certain importance: a man with commander's rank took him in personal charge and escorted him into the heart of this narrow-accessed monster. Dim corridors: a long walk to a wider area and a lift to the upper levels. He stared through Talley on the way up in the car. Conversation could do him no good. One never gave anything away. One always regretted it later.

A walk afterward down a narrower corridor—bare, dull metal everywhere, nothing so cheerful as *Lucy*'s white, age-scarred compartments. Coded identifications on the exposed lines, on the compartments. Everything was efficiency and no comfort. They reached the door of an office and got a come-ahead light: the door opened, and Talley brought him through.

"Captain," Talley said, "Stevens of the merchanter *Lucy.*"

The silver-haired woman was already looking at him across her desk, already sizing him up. "Mallory," she identified herself. "Sit down, Captain."

He pulled the chair over and sat facing her across the desk, while Talley settled himself against the cabinet, arms folded. Mallory pushed her chair back from the desk and leaned back in it—rejuved, young/old, staring at him with dark eyes that said nothing back.

"You're getting clearance to go out," she said. "On the Venture run. I understand there's some question about your ID, Captain."

His wits deserted him. It was not the question. It was the source. One of the nine captains, one of the Mazianni from the war years, who had gotten supply by boarding merchanters, by taking supplies and personnel. Who had killed. It might have been this one, those years ago, this ship that had locked onto *Lucy* and boarded. He might be that close to the captain who had ordered it, among troops who had been inside the armor, who had killed all his family. He had thought if he met one of them he would kill barehanded, and he found himself sitting still and staring back, paralyzed by the quiet, the tenor of the moment.

"You don't have any comment," Mallory said.

"I thought it was settled."

"*Is* there an irregularity, Captain?" Softly. Staring straight at him.

"Look, I just want the lock off my ship. I've got a cargo lined up, I've got everything else in order. Because some muddled-up merchanter mistakes my ship. . . ."

"Let me see your papers, Captain."

It took the breath out of his argument. He hesitated, off his mental balance, pulled them out of his pocket and leaned forward as she did, passing them into her extended hand across the desk, close, that close to touching. She leaned back easily, looked through them, lingered over them.

"But these are new," she said. "Except for the title papers, of course." She felt of the older paper, the title, itself false. "You know this kind of paper gets traded on the market. Has to get from one station to the other, after all; and across docks, and I know places where you can get it. Don't you, Captain?"

"I'm legitimate."

"So." She passed the papers back to him, and he thrust them quickly back into his pocket, his fingers gone cold. "So. Linked up with *Dublin Again*, are you? A very respectable operation. That does say something for you. Unionsider."

"I plan to operate here. On the Alliance side."

"Oh, relations are very good with Union at the moment. They're supplying ships and troops all along the Line. We have no quarrel with Union origins. You plan to stay here, do you? Operate as *Dublin's* pipeline out of the Sol trade?"

"I don't know how things will work out." He stepped slowly through the argument, aware of maneuvering on the other side, not understanding it. Mallory was not taken in. Was prodding at him, to find some provocation.

"Your certification comes through us," she said. "We've got a problem, Captain. We've got Mazianni activity between us and Sol, into the Hinder Stars. Does that bother you?"

"It bothers me."

"They'd like to cut us off, you understand. It's a lot of territory to patrol. And they win, simply by scaring merchanters out of that run. We've got two stations coming back into operation, and we're doing what we can to keep the zones clear. We'll be out at the nullpoints, making sure you're not ambushed there. We've got a rare agreement on the other side of the Line. Union's sealing up Tripoint and Brady's and any other point you can name." The eyes shot up to lock on his, abrupt and invasive. "You play the shy side of legal, do you? Marginer. I'll reckon you're no stranger to the fringes. Lying off in space. Operating out of the nullpoints. Doing trading on the side, without customs looking on. I'll bet you have a fine sense of what's trouble and what's not. A fine sense."

He said nothing. Tried to think of an excuse to look away and failed in that too.

"Might stand you in good stead," she said. "It's a place out there—that makes raw nerves survival-positive. We'll be there, Captain. I really want you to know that."

It was delivered very softly, with the same stare. It promised—he had no idea what.

"You can go," she said. "You'll find the obstacles clear. But I have news for you. Your Konstantin Company cargo is cancelled. You'll be carrying military cargo. You'll be paid hazard rate. An advantage. You'll be taking it aboard in short order and undocking at 0900 mainday."

"Like that."

"Like that."

"I thought—I was under military investigation."

"You are," she said. "Good evening, Captain."

"Maybe I don't want this. Maybe I want to change my mind."

"Do you, Captain? I'd prefer not."

The silence hung there. "All right," he said. "You protect us, do you?"

"As best we can, Captain."

Never Stevens. She never used the name. He stood up, nodded a reflexive courtesy. Not a response: dead eyes stared into him. He turned then and walked out, and Talley followed him into the corridor, hand-signaled a trooper who came down the corridor to walk him out.

Down the lift and out to the ramp again, the cold of the dockside coming as a shock after the metal closeness of the warship. He walked down the slant past the guard that stood there, past uniformed troops and idle, hard-eyed stares. . . . He reached the dockside and walked away, taking larger breaths the farther he got from the perimeter. He felt as if he had been picked up and shaken. Dropped hard.

He saw the Dubliners waiting for him, out by the lighted fronts of the offices. Allison and the others. He went toward them with the consciousness that the military might be watching his back, taking notes on his associations.

"What was it?" Allison asked. "Trouble?"

He shook his head and swept them up with a motion of his arms. "Come on. We've got our clearance. They're going to load."

"Like that?"

"Like that." He looked at Curran as the five of them headed down the dock at a good pace. "The Konstantin cargo just got cancelled. We've been handed military stuff. Hazard rate. Immediate loading, undocking at 0900 mainday."

"Military." For once Curran was taken aback. "What, specifically?"

"No word on that. I talked with Mallory. The lock was hers. The cargo's hers. I think she wants rumors spread, or she wouldn't spill what she spilled."

"Like what?"

"That Union's occupying the nullpoints along the Line, hunting Mazianni, and Alliance is doing the same."

"Lord, you've got to tell that to the Old Man."

He walked along in a moment's silence—that it took that much for them to suggest him and Reilly talking face to face. They were scared. He saw that. Deirdre's face had lost all its cheer, pale under its freckles. Allison's had a hard-eyed wariness like Curran's. Neill just looked worried. "I'll make a call from *Lucy*," Sandor said. "When I get clear and boarded."

"They're on a hunt?" Neill asked.

"I think I was told what she wants told in every bar on dockside. And I don't know what the percentage is."

"She say anything else?" Curran asked.

"She knows about the deal. She talked about the profit there might be for a route from Sol into Union. Direct to the point. Said they're going to be at the nullpoints of the Hinder Stars, keeping an eye on things."

"For sure?" Allison said.

"I don't trust anything I was told.—I know I want to be down there if they're taking the security seal of the hatch. I want to see what they've had their fingers into on my ship."

"We're going to take a look and go straight back to *Dublin*," Allison said, "as soon as we're sure we've got that lock open. Got some good-byes to say, all of us. If they're going to load for a 0900 undock, then you can use some crew over there."

"Could," he agreed. "Could."

He had help, he was thinking, an unaccustomed comfort. He had his Dubliners, who were not leaving him at the first breath of trouble. He felt a curious warmth in that thought.

Legitimate, he kept reminding himself. With connections, Mallory could not touch him. Might not want to, wanting to keep on the good side of a powerful Unionside merchanter, with all its connections.

He tried to believe that.

But he had looked Mallory in the eyes, and doubted everything.

Downers surrounded the lock, the barriers having been removed . . . Downers in the company of one idle dockworker, who rose from the side of the ramp and gave them all a looking at. "Business here," the man asked.

"Stevens," Sandor said. "Ship's owner."

The dockworker held out his hand. "Be happy to turn her over to you, sir, with ID. Otherwise I have to report."

It was insane, such bizarre security interwoven with the real threat of Alliance military. It was Pell, and they did things in strange ways. He took out his papers and showed them.

"He good?" a Downer asked, breather-masked and popping and hissing in the process. Round brown eyes looked at them, one Downer, a whole half-circle of Downers.

"Good paper," the dockworker confirmed. "Thank you, sir. Good day to you, sir; or good night, whichever."

And the dockworker collected his assortment of Downers, who bowed and bobbed courtesies in the departure, trooped off with shrill calls and motion very like dancing.

"Lord," Allison said.

"Pell," Sandor said. He turned, led the way up the ramp in deliberation, into the lighted access, with thoughts now only for his ship. He walked the tube passage, into the familiar lock. Home again. He kept going to the lift—five of them to fill the space, to make an unaccustomed crowd in the narrow corridors. The lift let them out on the main level, into the narrow bowed floor of the indock living quarters and the bridge; and he stood by the lift door and watched them walk about the little zone of curved deck that was accessible . . . silver-clad visitors come home to scarred *Lucy,* to pass their fingers over her aged surfaces, to touch the control banks and the cushions, to look this way and that up the inaccessible curve of her cabin space and storage corridors, wondering aloud about this and that point of her design. He was anxious in that scrutiny, watched their faces, their smallest reactions, more sensitive than if they had been looking him over.

"Not so comfortable in dock," Allison said, "but plenty of room moving." She fingered the consoles. He had cleaned the tapemarks off because of customs, disposed of all the evidence, but she found a sticky smudge and rubbed at it. She looked back at him. "She's all right," she pronounced. "She's all right."

He nodded, feeling the knot in his chest dissolve.

"Handle easy?" Curran asked.

"A crooked docking jet. That's her only wobble. I use it."

"That's all right," Curran said, surprisingly easy.

"You going to call the Old Man?" Allison asked.

". . . it's likely," he said into the com, "that all of it's planted rumors. But if you're headed for Union space, sir— it seemed you might want to know what was said."

"Are you in trouble with them?" the voice came back to him.

"It's still possible, yes, sir." And aware of the possibility the transmission was tapped, shielded-line as it was: "I hope they get it straightened up."

A silence from the other end. "Right," Michael Reilly said. "You'll be taking care, Captain."

"Yes, sir."

"Thanks for the advisement."

"Thank you, sir."

"Yes," the Reilly said, "you might do that."

"Sir."

"Information appreciated, *Lucy*."

"Signing off, *Dublin*."

He shut it down, alone in the quiet again. The Dubliners were on their way back to their ship. For good-byes. For gathering their baggage. He sat in the familiar cushion, staring at his reflection in the dark screens and for a moment not recognizing himself, barbered and immaculate and in debt over his head.

Mallory's face kept coming back at him, the scene in her on-ship office. Talley's ace, and the meeting on Pell. The old fear kept trying to reassert itself. He kept trying to put it down again.

He clasped his hands in front of him on a vacant area of the console, lowered his head onto his arms, tried for a moment to rest and to recall what time it was—a long, long string of hours. He thought that he had slid mostly into the alterday cycle; or somehow he had forgotten sleep.

He did that, slept, where he sat.

It was com that woke him, the notice from dockside that he had cargo coming in, and would he prepare to receive.

10

Leaving *Dublin* was a tumult of good-byes, of cousin-friends hugging and looking like tears; Ma'am with a look of patience; and Megan and Connie—Connie snuffling, and Megan not—Megan with that data-gatherer's focus to her stare that most acquired in infancy, who got posted bridge crew, wide-scanning the moment, too busy inputting to output, even losing a daughter. And in that, they had always understood each other—no need for fuss, when it stopped nothing. Allison hugged her pregnant sister, listened to the snuffles: hugged her mother longer, patted her shoulder. "See you," she said. "In not so many months, maybe."

"Right," her mother said. And when she had begun picking up the duffel and other baggage in a heap about her feet: "Don't take chances."

"Right," she told Megan, and shouldered strings and straps and picked up the sacks with handles. She looked back once more, at both of them, nodded when they waved, and then headed out of the lock and down the access tube to the ramp, leaving her three companions to muddle their own way off through their own farewells.

Her leaving had an element of the ridiculous: instead of the single duffel bag she might have taken, she moved all her belongings. It was not the way she had started. But she found excuses to take this oddment and that, found sacks and bags people were willing to part with, and ended up going down the ramp and across the docks loaded with everything she owned, a thumping, swinging load she would have done better to have called a docksider to carry. But it was not that far to walk; and the load was not that heavy, distributed as it was. She had her papers, her IDs and her cards and a letter-tape from Michael Reilly himself that advised anyone they cared to have know it that *Lucy* was an associate of *Dublin Again*—in case, the Old Man put it, you have credit troubles somewhere.

God forbid they met someone with some grudge Stevens had deserved for himself in his precious career.

Or trouble with the military out there. She was far less sanguine about the voyage than she had been when she conceived it. The neat control she had envisioned over the situation had considerably unraveled.

But she went, and the others would, for the same reasons, and if it should get tight out there, then they would handle it, she and her cousins. To sit a chair before she died of old age—it was that close; and no threat, no sting of parting was going to take it from her.

She kept walking—the first, she knew, of her unit to leave *Dublin,* headed for *Lucy*'s dock. She had had to go up the emergency accesses to get her belongings, and pack while clambering back and forth down the angle of deck and bulkhead, no easy proposition; she was tired and had visions of bed and sleep. There was no question of spending her last night on *Dublin.* There was no room, the onboard sleeping accommodations filled with others with more seniority. Her leaving had the same exigencies as her life aboard, no room, never room; and she made her over-loaded way down the dockside with a knot in her throat and a smothered anger at the way of things, worked the anger off in the effort of walking, burdened as she was. So good-bye, once and for all. It hurt; she expected that. So did giving birth, and other necessary things.

There was *Lucy*'s berth at last, aswarm with loading vehicles, with lights and Downers and dockers. Chaos. The sight unfolding past the gantries drained the strength out of her. She stopped a moment to take her breath, then started doggedly toward the mess, closer and closer. There was Stevens, out there on the dockside, in a disreputable pair of coveralls, shouting orders for the dockers who were rolling canisters onto the loading ramp in rapid sequence.

She walked into it, into a sudden confluence of Downers

who tugged at the straps and sacks. "Take, take for you,"
they piped, and she tried to keep them. "It's all right,"
Stevens called to her: she surrendered the weight. "Air
lock," she instructed the Downers, shouting over the clank
of loading ramps and canisters; and they whistled and
bobbed and scampered off with the load, blithe and light.
Her knees ached.

"When did this start?" she asked Stevens, who looked
wrung out.

"Too long ago. Listen, I've got a call the supplies are
coming in any minute. You want to do me a favor, get on
that. Ship's stores are core, bridge-accessed for null *G* stuff;
or stack it in the lift corridor if it's personal and heated-
area stuff; and in the core if it's freezer stuff too, because
we can't get at the galley yet. You'll have to suit up."

"Got it." She gathered her reserves and headed up the
ramp to look it over. It was going to be that way, she
reckoned, for the next few hours; and with luck the rest of
the unit would come trailing in shortly.

She hoped.

And the supplies started coming.

Curran and Neill came in together, with notions of sleep
abandoned; Deirdre came trailing in last, with most of the
real work done, and Stevens a shell of himself, his voice
mostly gone, checking the last of the loading with the
docker boss, signing papers. Most of it was his job—had to
be, since he was the only one who knew the ship, the shape
of the holds and where the tracks ran and how to arrange
the load for access at Venture.

They all trailed into the sleeping area finally, sweating
and undone, Stevens bringing up the rear. Allison sat down
on one of the benches, collapsing in the clutter of personal
belongings she had struggled to get to main level—sat among
her cousins likewise encumbered and saw Stevens cast himself down at the number four bridge post to call the dockmaster's office and report status; to feed the manifest into
comp finally, a matter of shoving the slip into the recorder
and waiting till the machine admitted it had read it out.

So they boarded. They sat there, in their places, too tired
to move, Neill stretched out on a convenient couch with a
soft bit of baggage under his head.

"Still 0900 for departure?" Allison asked. "Got those charts yet?"

Stevens nodded. "Going to get some sleep and input them."

"We've got to get our hours arranged. Put you and Neill and Deirdre on mainday and me and Curran on alterday."

He nodded again, accepting that.

"It's 0400," he said. "Not much time for rest."

She thought of the bottle in her baggage, bent over and delved into one of the sacks, came up with that and uncapped it—offered it first to Stevens, an impulse of self-sacrifice, a reach between the sleeping couches and the number four post.

"Thanks," he said. He drank a sip and passed it back; she drank, and it went from her to Curran and to Deirdre: Neill was already gone, asprawl on the couch.

No one said much: they killed the bottle, round and round, and long before she and Curran and Deirdre had reached the bottom of it, Stevens had slumped where he sat, collapsed with his head fallen against the tape-patched plastic, one arm hanging limp off the arm of the cushion. "Maybe we should move him," Allison said to Curran and Deirdre.

"Can't move myself," Curran said.

Neither could she, when she thought about it. No searching after blankets, nothing to make the bare couches more comfortable. Curran made himself a nest of his baggage on the couch, and Deirdre got a jacket out of her bags and flung that over herself, lying down.

Allison inspected the bottom of the bottle and set it down, picked out her softest luggage and used it for a pillow, with a numbed aching spot in her, for *Dublin*, for the change in her affairs.

The patches in the upholstery, the dinginess of the paneling . . . everything: these were the scars a ship got from neglect. From a patch-together operation.

Lord, the backup systems Stevens had talked about: they were going out at maindawn and there was no way those systems could have been installed yet. He meant to get them in while they were running: probably thought nothing of it.

Military cargo. The cans they had taken on were sealed.

Chemicals, most likely. Life-support goods. Electronics. Things stations in the process of putting themselves back in operation might desperately need.

But Mallory being involved—this military interest in *Lucy*—she felt far less secure in this setting-out than she had expected to be.

And what if Mallory was the enemy he had acquired, she wondered, her mind beginning to blank out on her, with the liquor and the exhaustion. What if he had had some previous run-in with Mallory? There was no way to know. And she had brought her people into it.

She slept with fists clenched. It was that kind of night.

11

Moving out.

Sandor sat at the familiar post, doing the familiar things—held himself back moment by moment from taking a call on com, from doing one of the myriad things he was accustomed to doing simultaneously. No tape on the controls this run: competent Dubliner voices, with that common accent any ship developed, isolate families generations aboard their ships—talked in his left ear, while station com came into his right. Relax, he told himself again and again: it was like running the ship by remote, with a whole different bank of machinery . . . Allison sat the number two seat, and the voices of Curran and Deirdre and Neill softly gave him all that he needed, anticipating him. Different from other help he had had aboard—anticipating him, knowing what he would need as if they were reading his mind, because they were *good*.

"There she goes," Allison said, putting *Dublin* on vid. "That's good-bye for a while."

Another voice was talking into his right ear, relayed through station: it was the voice of *Dublin* wishing them well.

"Reply," Allison said to Neill at com; and a message went out in return. But there was no interruption: no move faltered; the data kept coming, and now they did slow turnover, a drifting maneuver.

"Cargo secure," the word came to him from Deirdre. "No difficulties."

"Got that. Stand by rotation."

"Got it."

He pushed the button: the rotation lock synched in, and there began a slow complication of the cabin stresses, a settling of backsides and bodies into cushions and arms to sides and minds into a sense of up and down. They were getting acceleration stress and enough rotational force to make the whole ship theirs again. "All right," he said, when their status was relayed to station, when station sent them back a run-clear for system exit. "We get those systems installed. Transfer all scan to number two and we'll get it done."

"Lord help us," Curran muttered—did as he was asked and carefully climbed out of his seat while Sandor got out of his. "You always make your repairs like this?"

"Better than paying dock charge," Sandor said. "Hope they gave us a unit that works."

A shake of Curran's head.

They had time, plenty of time, leisurely moving outbound from Pell. The noise of station com surrounded them, chatter from the incoming merchanter *Pixy II*, a Name known all over the Beyond; and the music of other Names, like *Mary Gold* and the canhauler *Kelly Lee*. And all of a sudden a new name: "*Norway*'s outbound," Neill said.

For a moment Sandor's heart sped; he sat still, braced as he was against the scan station cushion—but that was only habit, that panic. "On her own business, I'll reckon," he said, and set himself quietly back to the matter of the replacement module.

The warship passed them: as if they were a stationary object, the carrier went by. Deirdre put it on vid and there was nothing to see but an approaching disturbance that whipped by faster than vid could track it.

"See if you can find out their heading," Allison asked Deirdre.

Station refused the answer. "Got it blanked," Deirdre said. "She's not tracked on any schematic and longscan isn't handling her."

"Bet they're not," Sandor muttered. "Reckon she's on a hunt where we're going."

No one said anything to that. He looked from time to time in Allison's direction—suspecting that the hands on

Lucy's controls at the moment had never guided a ship through any procedure: competent, knowing all things to do, making no mistakes, few as there were to make in this kind of operation that auto could carry as well. He did not ask the question: Allison and the others had their pride, that was certain—but he had that notion, from the look in Allison Reilly's eyes when control passed to her, a flicker of panic and desire at once, a tenseness that was not like the competency she had shown before that.

So she had worked sims, at least; or handled the controls of an auxiliary bridge on a ship the size of *Dublin,* matching move for move with *Dublin* helm. She was all right.

But he got up when he saw her reach to comp and try to key through to navigation, held to the back of her cushion. "You don't have the comp keys posted," she said. "I don't get the nav function under general op."

"Better let me do the jump setup," he said. "This time. I know her."

She looked at him, a shift of her eyes mirrored in the screen in front of her. "Right," she said. "You want to walk me through it?"

He held where he was, thinking about that, about the deeper things in comp.

(Ross. . . . Ross, now what?)

"You mind?" she asked, on the train of what she had already asked.

So it came. "Let me work it out this time," he said. "You're supposed to be on alterday. Suppose you take your time off and go get some sleep. You're going to have to take her after jump."

"Look, I'd like to go through the setup."

"Did I tell you who's setting up the schedules on this ship? Go on. Get some rest."

She said nothing for the moment, sitting with her back to him. He stayed where he was, adamant. And finally she turned on the auto and levered herself out of the cushion. Offended pride. It was in every movement.

"Cabins are up the curve there," he said, trying to pretend he had noticed none of the signals, trying to smooth it over with courtesy. It hurt enough, to offer that, to open up the cabins more than the one he had given to his sometime one-man crews. ("I sleep on the bridge," he had always said; and done that, bunked in the indock sleeping area, catnapped through the nights, because going into a cabin, sealing himself off from what happened on *Lucy*'s bridge—there was too much mischief could be done. —("Crazy," they had muttered back at him. And that thought always frightened him.) "Take any one you like. I'm not particular. —Curran," he said, turning from Allison's cold face—and found all the others looking at him the same way.

("Crazy," others had said of him, when he occupied the bridge that way.)

"Look," he said, "I'm running her through the jumps this go at it. I know my ship. You talk to me when it gets to the return trip."

"I had no notion to take her through," Allison said. "But I won't argue the point."

She walked off, feeling her way along the counter, toward the corridor. He turned, keyed in and took off the security locks all over the ship, turned again to look at Curran, at the others, clustered about the console where they were installing the new systems. He had offended their number one's dignity: he understood that. But given time he could straighten comp out, pull the jump function out of Ross's settings. And the other things . . . it was a trade, the silence Ross had filled, for live voices.

Putting those programs into silence—sorting Ross's voice out of the myriad functions that reminded him, talked to him—(Good morning, Sandy. Time to get up. . . .)

Or the sealed cabins, where Krejas had lived, cabins with still some remnant of personal items . . . things the Mazianni had not wanted. . . . things they had not put under the plates. And the loft, where Ma'am and the babies had been. . . .

"Curran," he said, daring the worst, but trying to cover what he had already done, "you're on Allison's shift too. Any cabin you like."

Curran fixed him with his eyes and got up from the repair. "That's in," Curran said. Being civil. But there was no softness under that voice. "What about the other one?"

"We'll see to it. Get some rest."

We. Neill and Deirdre. Their looks were like Curran's; and suddenly Allison was back in the entry to the corridor.

"There's stuff in there," she said, not complaining, reporting. "Is that yours, Stevens?"

"Use it if you like." It was an immolation, an offering. "Or pack it when you can get to it. There's stuff left from my family."

"Lord, Stevens. How many years?"

"Just move it. Use it or pack it away, whichever suits you. Maybe you can get together and decide if there's anything in the cabins that might be of use to you. There's not that much left."

A silence. Allison stood there. "I'll see to it," she said. She walked away with less stiffness in her back than had been in the first leaving. And the rest of them—when he looked back—they had a quieter manner. As if, he thought, they had never really believed that there had been others.

Or they were thinking the way other passengers had thought, that it was a strange ship. A stranger captain.

"Going offshift," Curran said, and followed Allison.

Neill and Deirdre were left, alone with him, looking less than comfortable. "Install the next?" Neill said.

"Do that," Sandor said. "I've got a jump to set up."

He turned, settled into the cushion still warm from Allison's body, *Lucy* continued on automatic, traversing Pell System at a lazy rate.

Of *Norway* there was now no sign. Station was giving nothing away on that score.

A long way, yet, for the likes of a loaded merchanter, to the jump range. Easy to have set up the coordinates. He went over the charts, turned off the sound on comp, ran the necessities through—started through the manual then, trying to figure how to silence comp for good.

(I'll get it on tape, Ross. For myself. Lose no words. No program. Nothing. Figure how to access it from my quarters only.)

But Ross knew comp and he never had, not at that level; Ross had done things he did not understand, had put them in and wound voice and all of it together in ways that defied his abilities.

(But, Ross, there's too much of it. Everywhere, everything. All the care—to handle everything for me—and I can't unwind it. There's no erase at that level: not without going into the system and pulling units. . . .

(And Lucy can't lose those functions. . . .)

"We got it." Neill was leaning on the back of the cushion, startled him with the sudden voice. "Got it done.—Is there some kind of problem, there?"

"Checking."

"Help you?"

"Why don't you get some sleep too?"

"You're in worse shape."

"That's all right." A smooth voice, a casual voice. His hands tended to shake, and he tried to stop that. "I'm just finishing up here."

"Look, we know our business. We're good at it."

"I don't dispute that."

Deirdre leaned on the other side of the cushion. "Take some help," she said. "You can use it."

"I can handle it."

"How long do you plan to go on handling it?" Neill asked. "This isn't a solo operation."

"You want to be of help, check to see about those trank doses for jump."

"Is something wrong there?"

"No."

"The trank doses are right over there in storage," Neill said. "No problem with that."

"Then let be."

"Stevens, you're so tired your hands are shaking."

He stared at the screens. Reached and wiped everything he had asked to see. The no-sound command went out with it. It always would. It was set up that way.

"Why don't you get some rest back there?"

"I've got the jump set up," he said. He reached and put the lock back on the system; that much he could do. "You two take over, all right?" He got up from the chair, stumbled, and Neill caught his arm. He shook the help off, numb, and walked back to the area of the couches to lie down again.

They would laugh, he thought; he imagined them hearing that voice addressing a boy who was himself, and they would go through all of that privacy the way they went through the things in the cabin.

He should never have reacted at all, should have taken the lock off and let her and the others hear it as a matter of course. But they planned changes in *Lucy;* planned things they wanted to do, destroying her from the inside. He sensed that. And he could not bear them to start with Ross.

He was, perhaps, what the others had said, crazy. Solitude could do that, and perhaps it had happened to him a long time ago.

And he missed Ross's voice, even in lying down to sleep. What he discovered scared him, that it was not their hearing the voices in *Lucy* that troubled him, half so much as their discovering the importance the voices had for him. He was not whole; and that had never been exposed until now—even to himself.

He did not sleep. He lay there, chilled from the air and too tired to get up and get a blanket; tense and trying in vain to relax; and listening to two Dubliners at *Lucy*'s controls, two people sharing quiet jokes and the pleasure of the moment. Whole and healthy. No one on *Dublin* had scars. But the war had never touched them. There were things he could have more easily said to Mallory than to them, in their easy triviality.

Mallory did not know how to laugh.

They reached their velocity, and insystem propulsion shut down; Allison felt it, snugged down more comfortably in the bed and drifted off again.

And waked later with that feeling one got waking on sleepovers, that the place was wrong and the sounds and the smells strange.

Lucy. Not *Dublin* but *Lucy.* Irrevocable things had happened. She felt out after the light switch on the bed console, brightened the lights as much as she could bear, rolled her eyes to take in the place, this two meter by four space that she had picked for hers . . . but there was a clutter in the locker and storage, a comb and brush with blond hair snarled in it, a few sweaters, underwear, an old pair of boots, other things—just left. And *cold* . . . the heat had been on maybe since last night, had not penetrated the lockers. A woman's cabin. Newer, cleaner than the rest of the ship, as if the ship had gotten wear the cabin had not.

Pirates, Stevens had said; pirates had killed them all. If it was one of those odd hours when he told the truth.

There was nothing left with a name on it, to know what the woman had been, what name, what age—not rejuved: the hair had been blond. Like Stevens' own.

Or whatever the name might have been.

And how did one man escape what happened to the others? That question worried her: why, if pirates had gotten the others—he had stayed alive; or how long ago it had been, that a ship could wear everywhere but these sealed cabins. Questions and questions. The man was a puzzle. She stirred in the bed, thought of sleep-over nights, wondered whether Stevens had a notion to go on with that on the ship as well, in cabins never made for it.

Not now, she thought; not in this place. Not in a dead woman's bed and in a ship full of deceptions. Not until it was straight what she had brought her people into. She was obliged to think straight, to keep all the options open. And keeping Stevens off his balance seemed a good idea.

Besides, it was business aboard—and no time for straightening out personal reckonings, no time for quarrels or any other thing but the ship under their hands.

The ship, dear God, the ship: she ached in every bone and had blisters on her hands, but she had sat a chair and had the controls in her hands—and whatever had gone on aboard, whoever the woman who had had this room and died aboard—whatever had happened here, there was that; and she had her cousins about her, who would have mortgaged their souls for an hour at *Dublin*'s boards and sold out all they had for this long chance. She could not go back, now, to waiting, on *Dublin,* for the rest of a useless life.

Hers. Her post. She had gotten that for the others as well, done more for them than they could have hoped for in their lives. And they were *hers,* in a sense more than kinship and ship-family. If she said walk outside the lock, they walked; if she said hands off, it was hands off and quiet; and that was a load on her shoulders—this Stevens, who figured to have a special spot with her. They might misread cues, her cousins, take chances with this man. No, no onboard sleepovers, no muddling up their heads with that, making allowances when maybe they should not make them. It was not dockside, when a Dubliner's yell could bring down a thousand cousins bent on mayhem. Different rules. Different hazards. She had not reckoned that way, until she had looked in the lockers. But somewhere not so far away, she reckoned, Curran slept in someone's abandoned bed and spent some worry on it. And the others—

She turned onto her stomach, fumbled after an unfamiliar console, punched in on comp.

Nothing. The room screen stayed dead.

She pushed com one, that should be the bridge. "Allison in number two cabin: I'm not getting comp."

A prolonged silence.

Everything unraveled, the presumed safety of being in Pell System, still in civilized places . . . the reckonings that there were probably sane explanations for things when all was said and done . . . she flung herself out of bed with her heart beating in panic, started snatching for her clothes.

A maniac, it might be; a lunatic who might have done harm to the lot of them. . . . She had no real knowledge what this Stevens might be, or have done. A liar, a thief— She looked about for any sort of weapon.

"Allison." Neill's voice came over com. "Got lunch ready."

"Neill?" Her heart settled to level. In the first reaction she was ashamed of herself.

In the second she was thinking it was stupid not to have brought her luggage into the cabin; she had a knife in that, a utilitarian one, but something. She had never thought of bringing weapons with her, but she did now, having seen what she had seen . . . sleeping in a cabin that could become a trap if someone at controls pushed the appropriate buttons.

"You coming?" Neill asked.

"Coming," she said.

It was better, finally, Sandor reckoned, with all of them at once in the bridge sleeping area, with trays balanced on their laps, a bottle of good wine passing about. It was the kind of insane moment he had never imagined seeing aboard *Lucy*, a thing like family, unaffordable food—Neill had pulled some of the special stuff, and the wine had been chilling since loading; and it all hit his empty stomach and unstrung nerves with soothing effect. He listened to Dubliner jokes and laughed, saw laughter on Allison's face, and that was best of all.

"Listen," he said to her afterward, catching up to her when she was taking her baggage to her quarters—he met her at the entry to the corridor, loaded with bundles. "Allison—I want you to know, back then with the controls—I wasn't thinking how it sounded. I'm sorry about that."

"You don't have to walk around my feelings."

"Can I help you with that?"

She fixed him with a quick, dark eye. "With ulterior motives? I don't sleepover during voyages."

He blinked, set hard aback, unsure how to take it—a moment's temper, or something else. "So, well," he said. "Not over what I said . . . Allison, you're not mad about that."

"Matter of policy. I just don't think it's a good idea."

"It's hard, you know that."

"I don't think I'd feel comfortable sharing command and bed. Not on ship. Sleepover's different."

"What, command? It's home. It's—"

"Maybe *Dublin* does things differently. Maybe it's another way on this ship. But it's not another way that quickly. You know, Stevens, I'll share a sleepover with an honest spacer and not care so much what name he goes by, but on ship, somehow the idea of sharing a cabin with a man whose name I don't know—"

"You handed me half a million credits not knowing—"

"I rate myself priceless, man. One of a kind. I don't go in any deal."

"I didn't say that."

"I'll bet you didn't."

"Allison, for God's sake, you twist everything up. You're good at that."

"Right. So you know you can't talk your way around me." She thrust past with the baggage. He caught a strap on her shoulder, peeled half the bundles away, and she glared back at him through a toss of hair. "Don't take so much on yourself, mister."

"Just the baggage."

"I don't need your help." She snatched at the straps he held and failed to get them back. "Just drop them in the corridor. I'll come back and get them."

"You can't take any help, can you?"

She walked off. "From the man who took a half million credits with never a thanks—" She stopped and looked back when he started after her with the bag, almost collided. "You choke on the words, do you, Stevens?"

"Thanks," he said. "That do it?"

"Just bring the bags." She turned about again, stalked one door farther and opened the compartment, tossed her belongings through the door and stood aside outside it, a wave of her hand indicating the way inside.

He tossed them after the first. "What about thanks?" he said.

"Thanks." She shut the door, still outside it.

"Look, you think you have to go through this to tell me no? I can take no. I understand you."

"What's the real name?" Quietly asked. Decently asked.

"Think it'd change your mind?"

"No. Not necessarily. But I think it says something about no trust."

"First name's Sandor."

A lift of both dark brows. "Not Ed, then."

"No."

"Just—no. Nothing further, eh?"

He shrugged. "You're right. It's not dockside, is it?" He looked into dark eyes the same that he had seen one night in a Viking bar, and he was as lost, as dammed up inside. "Can't break things up when they get tangled."

"Can't," she said. "So you understand it: I might sleepover with you when we get to Venture. I might sleepover with someone else instead. You follow that? I came. But if you reckon I came with the loan, figure again."

"I never," he said, "never figured that."

She nodded. "So we take this a little slower, a lot slower."

"So suppose I say I'd like to take it up again at Venture."

She stared at him a moment, and some of the tenseness went out of her shoulders. "All right," she said. "All right. I like that idea."

"Like?"

"I'm just not comfortable with it the other way."

"Might change your mind someday?"

"Ah. Don't push."

"I'm not pushing. I'm asking whether you might see it differently."

"The way you look at me, Stevens—"

"Sandor."

"—makes me wonder."

"I understand how you feel. About being on the ship. Maybe my talking like that, in front of the others back there—is a good example of what you're worried about. I didn't think how it went out. I know you know what you're doing. I just had my mind full . . . I've just got some things with the ship I haven't got straight yet. Things—never mind. I just have to get over the way I'm used to doing things. And dealing with the kind of crew I'm used to getting."

She tightened her mouth in a grimace that looked preparatory to saying something, exhaled then. It seemed to have slipped her. "All right. I understand that too. You mind fixing comp in my quarters while we're at it?"

His heart did a thump, attack from an unexpected direction. "I'll get it straightened out. Promise you. After jump."

"Security locks?"

"They seemed like a good thing when I had unlicensed crew aboard."

"Well, it's a matter of the comp keys, isn't it?"

It was not a conversation he wanted. Not at all. "Look, we haven't got time for me to get them all down or for you to memorize them. We're heading up on our exit."

"Is there something I ought to know?"

"Maybe I worry a bit when I've got strangers aboard. Maybe that's a thing I've got like you've got attitudes—"

Her back went stiff. "Maybe you'd better make that clear."

"I don't mean like that. I'm dead serious. That's all I've got, those keys, between me and people I really don't know that well. And maybe that makes me nervous."

The offense at least faded. The wariness stayed. "Meaning you think we'd cut your throat."

"Meaning maybe I want to think about it."

"Oh, that's a little late. A little late. We're on this ship. And we're talking about safety. Our safety. If something goes wrong on my watch, I want those keys. None of this nonsense."

"Look, let's get through jump first. I'll get you a list then."

"Through jump, where we're committed. I don't consider the comp a negotiable item." She jabbed a thumb toward her cabin door. "I want my comp in there operative. I want any safety locks in this ship off. I want the whole system written down for all of us to memorize."

"We haven't got time for that. Listen to me. I'm taking *Lucy* through this jump; I don't want any question about that. I'll see how you handle her; and then maybe I'll feel safe about it. You look good. But I'm reckoning you never handled anything but sims in your life. And I'm sleeping on the bridge if I have to, to see no one makes a mistake. I'm sorry if that ruffles your pride. But even I haven't a good notion of what *Lucy* feels like loaded."

"*Don't* you?" Suspicion. A sudden, flat seizure of attention.

"I'll take the locks off when I know who I'm working with." He thrust his hands into his pockets, started away, to break it off. Instinct turned him about again, a peace offering. "So I'm a bastard. But *Lucy's* not what you're used to, in a lot of senses. I haven't nursed her this far or got you out here to die with, no thanks. I'm asking you— I want you all on the bridge when we go into jump."

"All right," she said. A quiet all right. But there was still that reserve in her eyes. "You watch us. You see how it is. Sims, yes. And backup bridge. But you catch me in a mistake, you do that."

"I don't think I will," he said softly. "I don't expect it."

"Only you're careful, are you?"

"I'm careful."

They approached jump, a sleep later, a slow ticking of figures on the screen—a calm approach, an easy approach. Sandor checked everything twice, asked for data from supporting stations, because jumping loaded was a different kind of proposition. Full holds, an unfamiliar jump point— there were abundant reasons to be glad of additional hands on this one. "Got it set," he said to Allison, who sat number two. "Check those figures, will you?"

"Already doing that," Allison said. "Just a minute."

The figures flashed back to him.

"You're good," he said.

"Of course." That was the Dubliner. No sense of humility. "We all are. We going for it?"

"Going for it.—Count coming up. Any problems?—Five minutes, *mark*. Got our referent." He reached for the trank and inserted the needle. There was no provision on this one but a water bottle in the brace, for comfort's sake. No need. They would exit at a point named James's, and laze across it in honest merchanter fashion; and then on to Simon's Point, and to Venture.

The numbers ticked on.

"Message from Pell buoy," Neill said, "acknowledging our departure."

No reply necessary. It was automated. *Lucy* went on singing her unceasing identification, communicating with Pell's machinery.

"Mark," Sandor said, and hit the button. . . .

12

. . . Down again, into a welter of input from the screens, frank-blurred. Sandor reached in slow motion and started to deal with it. Beside him, the others—and for a moment his mind refused to sort that fact in. There was the mass which had dragged *Lucy* in out of the Dark . . . they were at James's Point, Voyager-bound; and Ross's voice was silent.

"Got it," Allison was saying beside him, icy-cold and competent. "Just the way the charts gave it. . . . "

He was still not used to that, a stranger-voice that for a moment was desolation . . . but it was *her* voice, and there was backup on his right, all about him. "Going for dump," he said.

And then Curran's voice: "We're not alone here."

It threw him, set his heart pounding: his hand faltered on the way to vital controls. Velocity needed shedding, loaded as they were, tracking toward the mass that had snatched them. Things happened fast in pre-dump, too fast—

"Standing by dump," Allison said.

"That's *Norway*," Neill said then.

He hit the dump, kicked in the vanes, shedding what they carried in a flutter of sickening pulses. "She still with us?" he asked, meaning *Norway*. Sensor ghosts could linger, lightbound information on a ship which had left hours ago. No way to discern, maybe—but he wanted his crew's minds on it. Wanted them searching. Hard.

"Better set up the next jump in case," Allison said. "I don't trust this."

"Outrun that?" Sandor focused on the question through the trank haze. "You're dreaming, Reilly." They kicked off velocity again, a numbing pulse that scrambled wits a moment. He blinked and reached an unsteady hand toward comp, started lining the tracking up again.

"We're in," Allison said. "That's got us on velocity."

"Getting nothing more than ID transmission," Neill said.

"Got a solid image," Curran said. "They're *close*. That's confirmed, out there, range two minutes."

The image hit his screen, transferred unasked. "Should I contact them?" Neill asked. "I'm getting no com output."

"No." He blinked, the sweat running on his face, concentrated on the business in front of him—and that ship out there, right on them as a warship reckoned speed, silent, sullen—was Mazianni in all but name. He got a lock on the reference star, saw the figures come up congruent, fed them in and sent the information over to Allison's console.

"Got it clear," Allison said. "Still want me to take it, or do you want to hold it?"

He caught his breath, sent a desperate look over all the board in front of him. Vid showed them nothing but stars; other sensors showed the *G* well itself, the mass, the heat of an almost-star that was the nullpoint. And the pockmark that was *Norway*. A situation. A raw Dubliner recruit asking for the board, maybe not particularly anxious to have control at the moment. He shunted things over to the number two board. "She's yours." His voice was hoarse. He pretended nonchalance, let go the restraints, reached for the water bottle and drank. "Here."

Allison looked aside, a distracted flick of her eyes, took the bottle and drank a gulp, passed it back. He slipped it back into the brace and hauled his way out of the cushion.

Looked back again, toward the screens, with a tightness about his throat.

Norway. And Mallory was saying nothing. The presence did not surprise him. Somehow the foreboding silence did not either.

"Mainday shift," he said, "let alterday have it."

"Sir," Neill muttered, the first courtesy of that kind he had gotten out of them. Natural as breathing from a

Dubliner on a bridge. Spit and polish, and he finally got it out of them. Neill stirred out of his place.

"Got another one," Deirdre said suddenly. "Got another ship out there."

Sandor crossed the deck to his chair in a stride and a half, flung himself into it.

"ID as Alliance ridership *Thor*," Deirdre said. "Coming out of occupation with the mass."

"One of Mallory's riders," Allison muttered.

"If they've got the riders deployed—" Neill said, back at his own post.

No one made any further surmises.

"Second signal," Deirdre said. "The ID is ridership *Odin*."

"Deployed before we dropped in here," Sandor said.

"What do you know about it?" Curran asked.

"*Sir*" Sandor said.

Curran turned his head. "From back at Pell, *sir*—did you expect this? What was it Mallory said?"

"That she's watching the nullpoint. I'm not at all surprised she's here. Or that she's not talking. What would you expect? A good morning?"

"Lord help us," Allison muttered. "And what kind of cargo have they handed us, that we get Mallory for a nursemaid?"

"I don't ask questions."

"Maybe we should have," Curran said. "Maybe we should get ourselves a couple of those canisters open."

"I'm reckoning you'd find chemicals and station goods," Sandor said. "I'd even bet it's Konstantin Company cargo, the same as we would have gotten. I don't think that's what Mallory's interested in at all. I think we're being prodded at."

"Because they're still breathing down your neck: that's what we've inherited—your own record with them. It's some kind of trap, something we've walked into—"

"You applied for Venture routing, Mr. Reilly. *Dublin* handed a marginer a half a million, stifled an inquiry, and headed us for Pell's most sensitive underside. A Unionsider. Put it together. Union and Alliance may be at peace, but Mallory's got old habits. Maybe you'd better think like a marginer, after all. Maybe you'd better start figuring angles,

because they have them in offices, the same as dockside.
And the powers that be on Unionside had them, when they
got cooperative and wanted *Dublin* this side of the Line.
But maybe you'd know that. Or maybe you should have
sat down and figured it."

"If you've got it figured, then say it. Let the rest of us
in on it."

"Not me. I *don't* know. But we're not making any noise
we don't have to. We tiptoe through this point and get that
cargo to—"

"Moving," Deirdre said. "*Thor*'s moving on intercept."

Sandor dived for the board, a sweat broken out on his
sides, sickly cold on his face. He stopped his hand short of
the controls, clenched it there in the reckoning that there
was nothing they could do. . . . No arms the equal of that;
no ability to run, loaded as they were.

(Ross? . . . Ross. . . . What's to do?)

"Contact them?" Allison asked.

"No."

"Stevens . . . Sandor . . . what precious else can we do?"

"We keep going on our own business. We let them escort
us through the point if that's what they have in mind. But
we don't open up to them. Let the contact be theirs."

She said nothing. Helm was still under her control. The
ship kept her course as she was, no variances.

"Message incoming," Neill said: "They say: Escort to
outgoing range. They say: request exact time and range our
departure from Pell."

"They're tracking us," Curran muttered.

"They repeat. They want acknowledgment."

"Acknowledge it," Sandor said. "Tell them we're figuring." He sat down at comp, keyed through and downed the
sound, started calling up the information.

"Sir," Neill said. "Sir, I think you'd better talk to them.
They're insisting."

He snatched up the audio plug and thrust that into his
ear, adjusted the mike wand from the plug one-handed.
"Feed it through."

". . . accurate," he caught. "Lives ride . . . on absolute
accuracy, *Lucy*. Do you copy that?"

"Say again.—Neill, what's he talking about, lives?"

"To whom am I speaking?" the voice from the rider-ship asked. "To Stevens?"

"This is Stevens, trying to do your calculations if you'll blasted well give me time."

"Your ship will proceed to Voyager as scheduled. You'll dock and discharge Voyager cargo. You have three days for station call, to the hour. And you'll return to this jump point on that precise schedule."

"Request information."

"No information. We're waiting for that departure data."

"Precise time local: 2/02:0600 mainday; locator 8868:0057:0076.35, tracking on recommended referents, Pell chart 05700."

"2/02:0600 precise?"

"You want our mass reckoning?" He was scared. It was a track they were running, no question about it. He flung out the question to let them know he knew.

"You carrying anything except our cargo, *Lucy*?"

"Nothing." The air from the vent touched sweat on his face. "Look, I'll run that reckoning on my own comp and give you our RET."

"Is 0600 accurate?"

"0600:34."

"We copy 0600:34. Your reckoning is not needed, *Lucy*."

"Look, if you want data—"

"No further questions, *Lucy*. We find that agreeing with our estimate. Congratulations. End it."

"We're in trouble," Allison said.

"They're accounting for our moves," he said. "Just figuring. I'd reckon Pell buoy scheduled us pretty well the way they set it up." He shut down comp, back under lock. "So they know now what our ETA is with the mass we're hauling: every move we make from now on—"

"I don't like this."

"Every point shut down. Everything monitored. We make a false move—and we're in trouble, all right." He thrust back from controls. "Nothing's going to move on us here while *that's* out there. Shut down to alterday. Mainday, go on rest."

"Look," Curran said, twisting in his cushion. "We're not going through Pell System lanes anymore. We're not sitting here to do autopilot, not with them breathing down our necks and wanting answers."

"I'm here," he said, looking back. "I'm not leaving the bridge: going to wash, that's all; and eat and get some sleep right back there in the downside lounge. You call me if you need anything."

"Instructions," Allison said sharply, stopping him a second time. "Contingencies."

"There isn't any contingency. There isn't any blasted thing to do, hear me? We've got three days minimum crossing this point, and you let—" He saw her face, which had gone from appeal to opaque, unclenched a sweating hand and made a cancelling gesture. "They're one jump from Mazianni themselves, you know that? Let's just don't give them excuses. We're a little ship, Reilly, and we don't mass much in any sense. Accidents happen in the nullpoints. Now true a line crosspoint and don't get fancy with it."

She gave him a long, thinking stare. "Right," she said, and turned back to business.

He walked, light-headed, back to the maintenance area shower, not to the cabins; *had* no cabin. The others had. He was conscious of that. And he had to sleep, and they chafed at the situation. He stripped, showered, alone there with the hiss of the water and the warmth and a cold knot in his gut that did not go away. Mazianni ships out there . . . and they had died out there, in the corridor, on the bridge, bodies fallen everywhere. Reillys sat and joked and moved about, but the silence was worse than before, deep as that in which *Lucy* moved now, with Mallory.

(Armored intruders, a name—a name on them, on the armor; but he could never focus on it, never get it clear in his mind; he had never talked about that with Ross; never wanted to know—until it was too late, and Ross never came back to the ship. . . .)

He had thought for a day on Pell that he was free, clear. But it was with them. It ran beside them, the nightmare that had been following *Lucy* for seventeen years.

They took it three and three, she and Curran, on a twelve-hour watch: three hours on and three off by turns, their own choice. Allison sat the number two chair on her offtime or padded quietly about the bridge examining this and that, while their military escort kept its position and maintained its silence.

From Sandor/Stevens, who had made his bed aft of the bridge in the indock lounge—not a sound, although she suspected that he wakened from time to time, a silent, furtive waking, as if he only grazed sleep and came out of it again. And from Neill and Deirdre, asleep in cabins four and five respectively, no stirring forth. Exhausted: none of them was used to this, and what kept Stevens going—

What kept Stevens going bothered her, at depth and at every glance back in his direction. Something wrenched at her gut—the memory of an attraction; the indefinable something that had made her crazy on Viking, that had gotten her linked with a no-Name nothing in the first place. Owner of his ship, he had said, in that bar; and maybe that had been enough, with enough to drink and a mood to take chances.

Not quite dead, that gut-feeling. And she had watched the man drawn thinner and thinner, from haggard to haunted—not sleeping now, she was sure of it. Not able to sleep. That ship out there, that was one good cause. Or the cumulative effect of things.

And he was not about to trank out, no, not with the comp locked up and a warship on their necks; with two Reillys at the controls.

She and Curran talked, when they sat side by side at the main board, spoke in low tones the fans and the rotation could bury. They talked operations and equipment and how a man could have run a ship solo, what failsafes would have to be bypassed and how a man could talk his way past station law.

She reckoned all the while that they might be overheard. Quiet, she signed when Curran got too easy with the remarks. Curran rolled his eyes to the reflective screens and back again, reckoning what she reckoned. *No sleep, he signed back, the kind of language that had grown up over the years on *Dublin*, practiced by crew at work in noise, embellished by the inventive young and only half readable by outsiders. *Watching us.

*Yes.

*Crazy.

She shrugged, That was a maybe.

*Care? A touch at the heart, a swift touch at the head, sarcastically.

She made a tightening of her jaw, an implied gesture of her chin to the ship that paced them. *That. That concerns me.

*He keeps the comp keys.

*He's afraid.

*He's crazy.

She frowned. *Probable, she agreed.

*Do something.

There was no silence in sign. It translated as I won't. She turned a degree and looked Curran in the eyes.

This was her rival, this cousin of hers, the one that pushed, all the way, all the years. It was yang and yin, the both of them, that made alterday Third what it was, and carried Deirdre and Neill. Curran never stopped, never let up. She valued him for that, knew how to reckon him, how he wanted the number one seat, forever wanted it. It was one thing when there were twenty ahead of them—and another when they sat sharing a command. Watch it, she made her look say; and he understood. She read it in his eyes as easy as from a page.

Number two, she thought of him. And she caught herself thinking it with a stab of cold, that that was how it was. There was a man who had this ship, and there was a working unit of Reillys who knew each other's signals and had no need of explaining how it worked, who looked down familiar perspectives and knew what they were to each other and where all the lines were. Number two to her: it fell that way in seniority by two days between her and Curran, between her and a man who would have been as good, at least in his own reckoning. Who could not have gotten them what she had gotten—

—not the same way, she could reckon him saying, raw with sarcasm.

But Curran never saw any way but straight ahead. Would never have blasted them out of their inertia. Would never have taken any chance but the one he was born with: dead stubborn, that was Curran. And it was his flaw. Possibly he knew it. It was why he was loyal: the same inability to swerve. It was different loyalty from Deirdre's, which was a deep-seated dislike of a number one's kind of decisions;

or than Neill's, which was a tongue-tied silence: Neill's mind went wider than some, so it took him longer to put his ideas together—a good bridge officer, Neill, but nothing higher. She knew them. Knew what they were good for and how the whole worked, stronger than its parts. She looked down from where she sat and their reflexes all went toward each other and toward her in a sequencing so smooth no one thought about it.

She was number one to them. To Curran she had to be. To justify his taking orders and not giving them, she had to be. And the others—it all broke apart without herself and Curran at their perpetual one-two give and take. Curran was jealous of Stevens, she realized that all in a stroke, a jealousy that had nothing to do with sex; with a pairing, yes; with a function like right hand and left. For her to form another kind of linkup, taking another man in a different way, in which an almost-brother could not intervene, in which he had no place—

What was Curran then? she thought—too proud to settle to Deirdre and Neill's partnership, and cast out of hers in favor of a stranger met in a sleepover. He had to go on respecting her judgment: that was part of his rationale. But that left him. That flatly left him.

She cast a second and sidelong look at her cousin, settling deeper into the cushion, folding her arms. "I'll think of something," she said.

"Going to eat?" he asked after a moment.

She looked at the elapsed time. 1101. She nodded, got out of the seat and walked off toward the galley.

A cold sandwich, a cold drink from storage . . . mealtime, as they reckoned time aboard, from the time of their arrival at the nullpoint. There was no need to force a realtime schedule on tired bodies, no need to reckon realtime at all except in communications, and they were getting no more of that. They had become introverted in their passage, disconnected from other timescales. And there was, when all the movement and human noise was absent—a silence that made her eat her sandwich pacing the small floor space of the galley; that sent her eye to the vacant white plastic tables and benches of the galley mess, and her mind to spacing out the number that could have sat at the tables—

Thirty. About thirty. Double that for mainday and alterday shifts, a ship's crew of about sixty above infancy. And the vacant cabins and the silences. . . .

She had expected a lot of 1 *G* storage on the ship, a lot of the ring given over to cargo. Customs would expect that. It was a question how far customs would break with courtesies and search the cabins: more likely, they contented themselves with the holds and did a tight check of the flow of goods on and off. A perfect setup for a smuggler, nested in a ship like this, with a good story about pirates and lost family.

But a woman had lived in her cabin before her. Another of Stevens' women, might be . . . but there were the other cabins, all lived in like the first several—they assumed. She had clambered in and out of the barren, dark-metal core storage, entered all the holds they used in dock . . . but the ring beyond the downside area and the cabins and the galley she had not seen. None of them had. They were still visitors on the ship they crewed.

She finished the sandwich, tossed the drink container into the waste storage, and the sound of the chute closing was loud.

1136. There was time enough, in her free hour, to walk round the rim. To come up on Curran from the other corridor that let out onto the bridge.

She left the galley area, rejoined the central corridor that passed through that, walked past other doors, all cabins, by the numbers of them. She tried a door, found it unlocked. The interior was dark and bitter cold. Power-save. A cabin, with the corner of an unmade bed showing in the light from the door. Rumpled sheets. She logged that oddity in her mind, closed the door and walked on, to an intersecting corridor. She entered it, found another bank of cabins behind the first, a dark corridor of doors and intervals. The desolation afflicted her nerves. She walked back to the main corridor, kept going, the deck ahead of her horizoning down as she traveled.

A section seal was in function: she came on it as a blank wall coming down off the ceiling and finally making an obstacle of itself. Maybe four seals—around the ring. Four places at which the remaining sections could be kept pressurized, if something went wrong. It sealed off the docking-topside zone, the loft.

She stopped, facing that barrier, her heart beating faster

and faster—looked at the pressure gauge beside the seal manual control, and it was up.

The loft . . . was the safety-hole of the young on every ship she knew of. Farthest from the airlock lifts; farthest from the bridge, farthest from accesses and exits. And sealed off. It might open. It might; but a section seal was for respecting: gauges could be fatally wrong, for everyone on the ship.

And no one was ass enough to keep hard vacuum in the ring, behind a closed door.

She hesitated one way and the other. Caution won. She reckoned the time must be getting toward 1200—no time and no place to be late. She turned about again—faced Stevens.

"*Hang* you, coming up on a body—"

"It's cold in there," he said. He was barefoot, in his robe, his hair in disarray.

"What's there?" she asked. Her heart had sped, refused to settle. "Cargo space?"

"Used to be the loft. Sealed now. I'll turn the heating on in my watch. I didn't think of it. Never needed to go there."

"You give me the comp and I'll fix it."

He blinked. She wished suddenly she had not said that, here, her back to the section seal, halfway round the ring from Curran. "I'll fix it," he said. "I'll do it now if you like."

"You're supposed to be off. You have to follow me around?"

Another slow blink. "Got up to get a snack. Thought you were in the galley."

"I'm supposed to be on watch." She walked toward him, past him, and he fell in with her, walked beside her down the corridor into the galley. She stopped there and he stopped and stood. "Thought you were going to get something."

He nodded, went over to dry storage and rummaged out a packet, tore it with his teeth and got a glass. His hands shook in pouring it in, in filling it from the instant heat tap.

"Lord," Allison muttered, "your stomach. You shouldn't drink that stuff when you've got a choice."

"I like it." He grimaced and drank at it, swallowed as if he were fighting nausea.

"You're wiped out, Stevens."

"I'm all right." His eyes had a bruised look, his color sallow. He took another drink and forced that down. "Just need to get something in my stomach."

"You watching us, Stevens? You don't want us loose unwatched? I don't think you've been sleeping at all. How long are you going to keep that up?"

He drank another swallow. "I told you how it's going to be." He turned, threw the rest of the brown stuff in the glass into the disposal and put the glass in the washer. " 'Night, Reilly. Your noon, my midnight."

"Why don't you go get in a real bed, Stevens, a nice cabin, turn out the lights, settle down and get some sleep?"

He shrugged. Walked off.

1158. She was due. She walked behind him, watched his barefoot, unsteady progress down the corridor, walked into the bridge behind him and stood there watching him find his couch in the lounge again. He lay down there on his side, pulled the blankets about him, up to his chin, stiff and miserable looking.

The gut-feeling was back, seeing the disintegration, a man coming apart, biological months compressed into days—hell on a solo voyage while Reillys sipped Cyteen brandy.

She looked at Curran, whose eyes sent something across the bridge—impatience, she thought. She was late. Curran would have seen Stevens leave; she imagined his fretting.

"Your turn," she said, coming to dislodge him from the number one seat. "Any action?"

"Nothing. Everything as was."

She settled into the cushion. Curran lingered, tapped her arm and, shielded by the cushion back, made the handsign for question.

*Negative problem, she signed back. And then a quick touch at Curran's hand before he could draw away. *We two talk, she signed further. *Our night.

*Understood. A moment more he lingered, knowing then that something was on her mind. She gave a jerk of her head toward the galleyward corridor. *Out, she meant; and he went.

Watch to watch: it was the tail of her second, 1442, when Neill came wandering out of the cabins' corridor, shaved and combed and fresh-looking. Deirdre followed, pale and sober, looked silently at Stevens sleeping there. *All right? The uplifted thumb. It was a question.

Allison nodded, and they padded back again, to the little personal time they had in their schedules. She had the ship on auto, their escort running placidly beside them. She watched Curran at his meddling with the comp console, quiet figuring and notetaking. There was not a chance he could crack it. Not a chance.

A bell went off, loud and sudden, down the corridors the way Neill and Deirdre had gone. She looked up, a sudden clenching of her heart, at the blink of a red light on the life support board. The bell and the light stopped. The section seal had opened, closed again. "Deirdre," Curran was saying into com. "Neill. Report."

A weight hit Allison's cushion, Stevens leaning there. "Section seal's opened," she said. "Are they all right, Stevens?"

"No danger, none."

She believed it when Neill's voice came through. "Sorry. We seem to have tripped something."

Exploring the ship. Trying to do the logical thing, going around the rim. "You all right?" Curran asked.

"Just frosted. Nothing more. Section three's frozen down, you copy that."

"You got it shut?"

"Shut tight."

"Here," Stevens said hoarsely, tapped her arm. "Vacate. I'll get the section up to normal. Sorry about that."

"Sure," she said. She slid clear of the cushion and he slid in.

"Just go one," he said. "I'll take care of it, do a little housekeeping. Take a break, you and Curran. We don't need to keep rigid schedules. God knows she's run without it."

Curran might have gone on sitting, obstinate; she gathered him up with a quiet, meaningful glance, a slide of the eyes in the direction Neill and Deirdre had gone. "All right," he said, and came with her, walked out of the bridge and down the corridor.

And stopped when she did, taking his arm, around the curve by the galley.

*He might hear, Curran signed to her. Pointed to the com system.

She knew that. She cast a look about, looking for pick-ups, found none closer than ten feet. "Listen," she said, "I want you to keep it quiet with him. Friendly. I don't know what the score is here."

"What's he running around there, with a sector frozen down? Contraband, you reckon?"

"I don't know.—Curran, have you tried the doors on the cabins—the other cabins? Something terrible happened on this ship. I don't know when and I don't know what. Hit by the Mazianni, he says; but this— The loft is frozen; the cabins left—you know how they were left . . . there's a slept-in bed around there, frozen down."

"I tell you this," Curran said in the faintest of whispers, "I don't sleep well—in that cabin. Maybe he's worried for himself—about us doing to him what occurs to him to do to us. I don't like it, Allie. Most of all I don't like that comp being locked up. That's dangerous. And you know why he got us out of there . . . not to look over his shoulder while he works, that's what. I wouldn't put it past him, spying on us. Or murder, if it came to it."

"No," she said, a shake of her head. "I don't think that. I never have."

"You ever been wrong, Allie?"

"Not in this."

He frowned, a look up from under his brows. "Maybe the record's still good. And maybe we go on like this and we have a run-in with the military—what's he going to do, Allie? Which way is he going to jump? I don't like it."

"He's strung out. I know it. I know it's not right."

"Allie—" He reached out, touched her shoulder, cousin for the moment and not number two. "Man and woman—he thinks one way with you and maybe he thinks he can get around you; but you let me talk it out with him and I'll straighten it out. And I'll get those comp keys. No question of it."

"I don't want that."

"You don't want it, I don't want it. But we're in trouble, if you haven't noticed. That man's off the brink and he's going farther. I propose we have it out with him . . . we. Me. No chaff with me. He knows that. You just stay low, stay out of it, go to your cabin and we'll put the fear in him."

"No."

"You think of something that makes as good sense? You going to ask him and he'll come over? I'll figure you tried that."

She bit at her lip, looked up the corridor, where Neill and Deirdre came down the horizon. "Sorry," Neill said again; and Deirdre: "Who's minding the ship?"

"He is.—What was it, around there?"

"Loft," Deirdre said. She clenched her arms about her. "A mess—things ripped loose—panels askew—didn't see all of it, just from the section door. Dark in there.— Allie. . . ."

"I know," she said. "I figured what was in there." She thrust her hands into her pockets, started back.

"Where are you going?" Curran asked.

"To my cabin." She looked back, straight at Curran, straight in the eyes. "I'm off. It's your shift. Maybe you'd better get back to the bridge. I'll be there—a while."

13

Lucy had gotten along, running stable under auto: Sandor shut down comp and stared a moment at scan, numb, the dread of the warship diminished now. It was not going to jump with them: had no capacity to do that. Mallory herself was sitting still, watching—he could not imagine that much patience among the things they told of Mallory. He did not believe it: she was waiting for something, but it had nothing to do with him. He began to hope that she just wanted them out of her way.

And if it was other Mazianni she was hunting—if she expected other traffic—

He got up, looked once and bleakly at the couch he had quit. There was a little time left in main-night. But the effort to sleep was a struggle hardly worth it, lying there awake for most of the time, to sleep a few minutes and wake again. He had done that all the night. Nervousness. And no chance of tranking out. Not as things were.

He headed for the shower, trusting the autopilot—a scandal to the Dubliners: he imagined that. They wore themselves out sitting watch and he walked off and left it. There were things that wanted doing—scrubbing and swabbing all over the ship, work less interesting to them, he was sure: but he began to think in the long term, a fleeting mode of thought that flickered through his reasonings and went out again. There was the loft—

They had never done anything about the loft, he and Ross and Mitri: no need of the space—*Lucy* was full of empty space; and walking there—they just avoided it. Put it on extreme powersave. The cold kept curious crew out. When he was alone on the ship he had never gone past the galley. It was dead up there . . . until the Reillys started opening doors and violating seals. Opening up areas of himself in the process, like a surgery. He gathered his courage about it, the hour being morning: a man was in trouble who went to bed with panic and got up with it untransformed. He tried to look at it from other sides, think around the situation if not through it.

A little time, that was what he needed, to break the Reillys in and get himself used to them.

But the comp—

(Ross . . . they wouldn't have given out that money for no reason. No one's that rich, that they can spill half a million because a few of their people take a fancy to sign off—half a million for a parting present. . . .

(People don't throw money away like that. People aren't like that.

(Ross . . . I know what they want. I loved her, Ross, and I didn't see; I was afraid—Pell would have taken the ship—and what could I do? But they think I've sold her; and maybe I have. What do I do, Ross?)

The warm water of the shower hit his body, relaxed the muscles: he turned up the cold on purpose, shocked himself awake. But when he had gotten out he had a case of the shivers, uncommonly violent . . . too little food, he reasoned; schedule upset. He reckoned on getting some of the concentrates: that was a way of eating without tasting it, getting some carbohydrates into his body and getting the shakes out.

They had to make jump tomorrow maindawn. He had to get himself strung back together. Mallory was not going to take excuses out there. Mallory wanted schedules and schedules she got.

He dressed, shaved, dried his hair and went out into the corridor, back to the bridge.

Curran was sitting against a counter—Neill and Deirdre with him. "I'm for breakfast," Sandor said. "I think we could leave her all right, just—"

"Want to talk to you," Curran said. "Captain."

He drew a deep breath, standing next to the scan

console—leaned against it, too tired for this, but he nodded. "What?"

"We want to ask you for the keys. There's a question of safety. We've all talked about it. We really have quite a bit of concern about it."

"I've discussed that problem. With Allison. I think we agree on it."

"No. You don't agree. And we're asking you."

"I'll take up the matter with her."

"Are you sure there's no chance of our reasoning with you?"

"I told you."

"I think you'd better think again."

"There are laws, Mr. Reilly. And they're on my side in this." He started away from the counter, to break it off. The others moved, cutting off his retreat—his eye picked Deirdre, the one he could go over—but there was no running. He turned about and looked at Curran. "You want to settle this the hard way? Let's clear the fragile area and talk about it."

"Why don't we?" Curran got off his counter edge and waved them all back, a retreat into the lounge area among the couches, but Sandor went for the corridor, toward the cabins, a slow retreat that drew all of them in that direction.

Allison was in her cabin. He was sure of that, the way he measured his own frame and Curran's and knew who was going to win this one, especially if Curran got help. He reached for the door switch, and Curran caught him up and knocked his hand aside.

He landed one, a knee to the groin and a solid smash to the neck that knocked Curran double—a knee to the face, and Curran hit the wall as he spun about to see to Neill.

A blow at his legs staggered him and Neill and Deirdre moved all at once as Curran tackled him from behind and weighed him down.

He twisted, struck where he had a moment's leverage, over and over again—almost flung himself up, but a wrench at his hair jerked him hard onto his back and they had him pinned. "Out of it," Neill ordered someone. "Out." He kept up the struggle, blind and wild, hunting any leverage, anything. "Look out."

A blow smashed across his jaw, for a moment absorbing all

his wit, a deep black moment without organization: he knew they had his arms pinned, and his coordination was gone.

"Look at me," a male voice was saying. A shake at his hair, a hand slapping his face and steadying it. "You want to use sense, Stevens? What about the keys?"

There was blood in his mouth. He figured they would hit him again. He heaved to get a hand loose.

A second blow.

"Stop it." Neill's voice. "Curran, stop it."

Again the hand shook at his face. He was blind for the moment, everything lost in dark. "You want to think it over, Stevens?"

He tried to move. The blood was shut off from his right hand; the left had life in it. He heaved on that side, but the lighter weight on that arm was still enough. "Curran." That was Deirdre. ":Curran, he's out—stop it."

A silence. His eyes began to clear. He stared into Curran's bloody face, Neill and Deirdre's bodies in the corner of his eyes, holding onto his arms. "You shouldn't have hit him like that," Neill said. "Curran, stop, you hear me, or I'll let him loose."

Curran let go of his face. Stared down at him.

"He's not going to give us anything," Deirdre said. "We've got trouble, Curran. Neill's right."

"He'll give it to us."

"Curran, no."

"What do you want, let him up, let him back at controls where he can do what we can't undo? No. No way. You're right, we've got trouble."

Sandor gave a heave, sensing a loosening of Deirdre's arms. It failed; the hold enveloped his arm, yielding, but holding. "Get Allison," he said, having difficulty talking. And then he recalled it was her door they were outside. She might have heard it; and stayed out of it. The realization muddled through him in the same tangled way as other impressions, painful and distant. "What do we do?" Neill asked. "For God's sake what do we do?"

"I think maybe we'd better get Allison," Deirdre said.

"No," Curran said. "*No.*" He took hold again of Sandor's bruised jaw. "You hear me. You hear me. You're thinking how to get rid of us, maybe; not the law—that's not your way, is it? Thinking of having an accident—like

maybe others have had on this ship. We'll find you a comfortable spot; and we've got all the time we like. But we're
coming to an agreement one way or the other. We're having
a look at the records. At comp. At every nook and cranny
of this ship. And maybe if we don't like what we find, we
just call Mallory out there and turn you over to the military.
You can yell foul all you like: you think that'll make a difference if we swear to the contrary? Your word against ours—
and what's yours worth without ours to back it? They'd chew
you up and swallow you down—you think not?

He started shivering, not from fear, from shock: he was
numb, otherwise, except for a small quick area of shame.
They picked him up off the floor and had to hold him up
for the moment; he got his feet under him, did nothing
when Curran grabbed his arm and pushed him into the
wall. Then he hit, once and proper.

Curran hit the wall and came back off it. "No," Neill
yelled, and got in the way of it. And suddenly Allison was
there, the door open, and everything stopped where it was.

No shock. Nothing of the kind. Sandor stared at her,
a reproach.

"Sorry," Curran said in a low voice. "Things seem to
have gotten out of hand."

"I see that," she said.

"I don't think he's willing to talk about it."

"Are you?" she asked.

"No," Sandor said. His throat hurt. He said nothing else,
watched Allison shake her head and glance elsewhere, at
nothing in particular.

"How do we settle this?"

She was talking to him. "Forget it," he said past the
obstruction in his throat. "It was an idea that won't work.
We go on and forget it. I've got no percentage in carrying
a grudge."

"I don't think it works that way," Curran said.

"No," she said, "I don't either."

"There's cabins," Curran said.

"Lord—"

"It's done. I figure a little time to think about it— Allie,
we don't sleep with him loose."

"You can't lock them," she said, "without the keys."

"I'd laugh," Sandor said, "but what comes next? Cutting

my throat? Think that one through: you kill me and you've got no keys at all. We'll go right on out of system."

"No one's talking about that."

"I'll lay bets you've thought about it.—No, I'll go upsection. Close a seal. An alarm will ring if I leave it. You have to have everything laid out for you? You're inept, you Dubliners. Ought to take you several days to work yourselves up to the next step."

He walked off from them, toward the section two cabins, reckoning all the while that they would stop him and devise something less comfortable. There was silence behind him.

He passed the section seal, pressed the button.

The seal shot home.

Allison sat down on the armrest of the number two cushion and looked at her cousins—at Curran, who sat on the arm of number one, blotting at a cut lip. Neill and Deirdre rested against the central console, slumped down and very quiet. "How?" she asked.

Curran shrugged—looked her in the eyes. "It just got out of hand."

"When?"

Curran ducked his head. He was bloodstained, sweating, his right eye moused at the cheekbone. "He swung," he said, looking up again. "Caught me. He won't bluff." It was possibly the worst moment of Curran's life, being wrong in something he had argued. Her own gut was tied in a knot.

And after that, silence, all of the faces turned toward her, where the decisions should have come from in the first place. She leaned her arms on her knees, adding it up, all the wrong moves, and the first was abdicating. It made her sick thinking of it. All the good reasons, all the rationale collapsed. It was not only an ugly way to have gone, for good reasons—the game had not worked, and now it was real: Stevens understood it for real—or knew that they knew it had to be. "It's stupid," she objected, slammed her fist into her hand. She looked up at faces that had no better answer. "No ideas?"

Silence.

"We could get him off this ship," Curran said in a subdued voice. "We could ask the military to intervene. Say there was an argument."

"You reckon to do that?"

"We're talking about our lives. Allie, don't mistake him like I did: he backed up on the docks, but he's been running hired crew and he's survived; there's those cabins. And the loft."

"It was depressurized," Deirdre said. "Maybe he got holed in some tangle; but little ships don't survive that kind of thing. The other answer is some access panel going out; and you can blow it from main board, can't you?"

"So what do we do? We've got twenty-four hours to get those comp keys out of him or to get him back at controls, or we go sliding right past our jump point and out of the system. And he knows it."

Silence.

"Allie," Curran said, "he's a marginer. At best he's a liar and a thief. He's lied his way from one end of civilization to the other. He's conned customs and police who know better. At the worst—at the worst—"

"You think he's conned me?"

"I think he was desperate and we gave him a line. But he's keeping the keys in his hands and maybe he's had other crew aboard who never made it off. We don't know that. We can't let him loose."

"You got another idea? Calling the military—that still doesn't give us the keys. They'd have to haul us down; or we lose the ship. Might as well apply to leave the ship ourselves. Hand it back to him. Go back to Pell, beached. In a year, maybe we can explain it all to the Old Man. And go back to *Dublin* and go on explaining it. You think of that?"

"What do we do, then?"

"He's got no food in that section," Deirdre said. "There's that. There're things he needs."

Allison drew a long breath, short of air. So they were around to that, the logical direction of things. "So maybe we come up with something more to the point than that. That's what he was saying, you know that? He knows what kind of a mess we're in. We can't rely on him at controls—how much do you think you can rely on comp keys he might give us if we put the pressure on? He's out-thought us. He's not going to bluff."

Silence.

She rested her hands on her knees and stood up. "All right. It's in my watch. So I'll talk to him. I'm going up there."

"Allie—"

"Al-li-son." She frowned at Curran. "You stay by com and monitor the situation. Only one way he's going to trust us halfway—a way to patch up things, at least; make a gesture, make him think we think we've straightened it out. God help us." She headed for the corridor, looked back at a trio of solemn faces. "If you have to come after me, come quick."

"If he lays a hand on you," Curran said, "I'll break it a finger at a time."

"Don't take chances. If it gets to that, settle it, and call the military." She walked on, raw terror gathered in her stomach. Her knees had a distressing tendency to shake.

There was no more chance of trusting him. Only a chance to make him think they did. He was, she reckoned, too smart to kill her even if it crossed his mind: he would take any chance they gave him, come back to them, bide his time.

She hoped to get them to Venture Station alive: that was what it came to now. And if they were lucky, there might be a strong military authority there.

He sat in the corridor—no other place in section two that was heated: he had the heat started up in number 15, and if the sensors worked, the valve that shut the water down in 15 would open and restore the plumbing. He never depended on *Lucy*'s plumbing. At the moment he was beyond caring; he was pragmatic enough to reckon priorities would change when thirst set in.

And in an attempt at pragmatism he made himself as comfortable as he could on the floor, nursed bruised ribs and wrenched joints and a stiff neck, trying to find a position on the hard tiles that hurt as little as possible. The teeth ached; the inside of his mouth was cut and swollen: there was a great deal to take his mind off more general troubles, but generally he was numb, the way the area of a heavy blow went numb. And he reckoned that would start hurting too, when the shock of betrayal had passed. In the meantime he could sleep: if he could find a spot that did not ache, he could sleep.

The alarm went off—the door down the curve opened from their side, jolting his heart. He scrambled up— staggered into the wall and straightened.

Allison by herself. The door closed again; the alarm stopped. He stared at her and the numb spot gained feeling and focus, an ache that settled everywhere. "So, well," he said, "got around to figuring how it is?"

"Look, I'm here. You want to talk or do you want me to let be?"

"I won't give it to you."

She walked closer, the length of the corridor between them. Stopped near arm's length. "I won't pass it to Curran. I'm sorry.—Listen to me. I reckoned maybe we were too close for reason. I just figured maybe Curran could get the sleepover out of it; maybe— Hang it, Stevens, you're strung out on no sleep and you're risking our lives on it. Not just mine. Theirs; and I got them into it. You don't trust them. Maybe not me. But I figured if you and Curran could sort it out—maybe it would all work. That maybe if you got it straight with them, if all the heat blew out of it—"

"Misfigured, did you?"

"Don't be light with me. Say what you think."

"All I want—" His throat spasmed. He thrust his hands into his pockets and disguised a second breath with that. "I don't give you the time of day, Reilly. Let alone the comp keys. Now we can go on like this. And maybe you'll think of other clever ways to get at it. But you loaned me money; you didn't buy me out. You figure—what? To trump up something to get me between you and the police at Venture? And then to offer me another deal? Sorry. I've got that figured out. Because if they get me, Reilly, you're stuck on a ship you can't even get out of dock. Embarrassing. Might raise questions about your title to her. Might cost you a long time to get that straightened out, long-distance to Pell and wherever *Dublin* might be. Not to mention—if they send me in for restruct—I'll spill what happened here, all in the little pieces of my mind. And there goes the Reilly Name. So refigure, Reilly. Nothing you do that way's going to work."

"You're crazy, you know that?"

"You know, I really took precautions. I signed on drunks and docksiders and insystemers, and I got through with all of them. I figured a big ship like *Dublin* might try to doubledeal me, but you're pirates, Reilly—I never figured that. Mallory's out there hunting Mazianni and here's a ship full of them."

Her face flushed. He had that satisfaction. "You don't take that seriously, do you?"

"I don't see a difference."

"Stevens—"

"Sandor. The name's Sandor."

"I'm sorry for what happened. I told you why; I told you—Look, Curran thought you'd bluff. That was his thinking. Now he knows better. So do all of us. You want to come back to the bridge and sort this out?"

He ran that through his mind several ways, and none of it eased the ache. Stood there, obstinate, only to make it harder.

"Stevens—what's it take?"

"Worried, are you? We're not even near the jump point. And what when we're across it? A replay? I only go for this once, Reilly. The next time you lay a hand on me it's war. You'll get me. Sure you will. I've got to sleep, after all. But let's just lay it on the table. You may not be able to haul it out of me. And then what? Then what, Reilly?"

"It's crazy to talk like that."

"How much do you want this ship?"

"A lot. But not that way. I want us working with each other. I want our hands clean and all of us in one piece, not killed because you're still running a loaded ship like a margin cargo—you're blind crazy, Stevens. Sandor. You've got too many enemies in your own head."

"It doesn't work. You take it on my terms. That's all you've got. Up the ante, and that's still all you've got."

"All right," she said after a moment, stood there with a look in her eyes that seemed halfway earnest. She nodded toward the section seal. "Let's go."

He nodded, walked along with her. "They're listening," he said in a low voice. "Aren't they?"

She looked at him, a sudden, disturbed glance. They reached the section seal and she stopped and reached for the button. He was quicker, his hand covering it. He looked her in the eyes, that close, and the closeness murdered reason for the instant. The scent of her and the warmth and the remembrance of Viking and Pell—

"You could have had it all," he said. "You know that."

"You never trusted us. Not from the start."

"I was right, wasn't I?"

She was silent a moment. "Maybe not."

The quiet denial shot around the flank of his defenses. He turned his head, pressed the button.

The siren went. The door shot open. He was facing Curran and Neill. He was somehow not surprised.

"He's coming back," Allison said. She closed the door again. The siren stopped. "We've got it settled."

The faces in front of him did not believe it. He reacquired his own doubts, nerved himself with the insolence of a thousand encounters with docksiders. Offered his hand.

Curran took it, a small shudder of hesitation in the move, a grip that spared bruised knuckles—but Curran's hand was in no better condition; Neill's next—Neill's earnest expression had a peculiar distress.

"Sorry," Neill said.

He meant it, Sandor reckoned. One of them meant it. And knew it was all a sham. He felt a pang of sympathy for Neill, which was insane: Neill would be with the rest of them, and he never doubted it.

"Deirdre's on watch, is she?"

"Yes."

"I'm going to have my breakfast and wash up. And I'll rest after that . . . find myself a cabin and rest a few hours. You'll wake me if something comes up."

He walked on—away from them. Stopped in the galley and opened the freezer, pulled out a decent breakfast, pointedly keeping his back to the rest of them as they passed.

It was a quiet supper, hers with Curran. Curran was eating carefully, around a sore mouth, and not in a mood for idle conversation. Neither was she. "You think he'll go along with it all the way to Venture?" Curran asked once. "Maybe," she said. "I think he's had the angles figured for years. We just walked into it."

And a time later: "You know," Curran said, "the whole agreement's a lie. Look at me, Allie. Don't take on a face like that. He's a liar, an actor—he knows right where to take hold and twist. I knew that from the start. If you hadn't stepped in when you did—"

"*What* would you have done? I'd like to have known what you would have done."

"I'd have beaten a straight answer out of him. He says not. But that's part of the act. He's harder than I thought, but I'd have peeled the nonsense away and gotten right where he lives, Allie, don't think not. Wouldn't have killed him; not near. And it might have settled this. You had to come out the door—"

"It didn't go your way the first time. How much would it take? How many hours?" Her stomach turned. She pushed the food around on her plate, made herself spear a bite and swallow. "You heard what he said. We've got him working now. Another set-to—"

"You go on *believing* what he says—"

"What if it is the truth? What if it's the truth all along?"

"And what if it's not? What then, Allie?"

"Don't call me that. I don't like it."

"Don't redirect. You know what the stakes are. We're talking about trouble here. You sit the number one; you've got to have the say in it. But you're thinking below the belt."

"That's your assumption."

"Don't tell me a male number one wouldn't have gotten us in this tangle."

"Ah. There we are. What if it were a woman and it were you calling the shots? Dare I guess? You'd take it all, wouldn't you? You think you would. But would you sleep sound in that company? No. You think it through. I'm not sleeping with him. And he even asked."

"Maybe you should have."

She was reaching for the cup. She slammed it down, spilling it. "You need your attitudes reworked, Mr. Reilly. You really do. Maybe we really need to figure the logic that carries all that. Let's discuss your sleepovers, Mr. Reilly— or don't they have any bearing on your fitness to command?"

His face went red. For a moment he said nothing at all. Then his eyes hooded and he leaned back. "Hoosh, what a tongue on ye, Allie. Do you really want the details? I'll give you all you like."

She smiled, a move of the lips, not the rest of her face. "Doubtless you would. No doubt at all. You had your try;

and he knocked you flat, didn't he? So while we're discussing my personal involvement here, suppose we add that to the count: is it just possible you have something personal at stake?"

"All of that's aside. The question's not what we see; it's what Stevens is . . . and where we are. And what we do about it."

"And I'm telling you it didn't work."

"You stopped it. It's ugly; it's an ugly thing; I don't like it; but it would have settled it and your way hasn't got us anywhere but back behind start. Way behind."

She thought that over, and it was true. "Where did we ever get off doing something like this? Where did we ever learn to think about things like this?"

"It's not us. It's the company you came up with."

"Suppose he told the truth. Suppose that for a minute."

"I don't suppose it. You're back where you were, falling for a good act. And you think every customs agent and banker who ever believed him didn't think he looked sincere? Sincere's his stock in trade, him with that fair, blue-eyed innocence."

She took a napkin, blotted the spilled coffee, wiped the bottom of the cup and took a drink, and a second.

"So we go on," Curran said. "Next jump—and him running it."

"What would you do?"

"No more than I had to."

She shook her head. Got up and cleaned the plate and tossed the cup, put things in the washer.

"Alli-son. I'm not willing to risk my life on your maybe."

She looked back at him. "You're my number two. Isn't that your job?"

"If there's reason—"

"My reason is a judgment call. And I'm making it."

"On what percentage? It gets us into another spot like this one. On that understanding—just so we agree where we're going—it's my job. Right."

She walked over and squeezed his shoulder, walked past and out of the galley.

14

"That's five minutes to range limit," Allison said. "Transmitting advisement to our escort."

"Got it," Sandor murmured back, busy at final adjustments. The reports from the other stations came in, routine and indicating all stable. It had an especially valuable feel, the familiar cushion, the rhythm of operations, his hands on the controls again, as if nothing had happened. Wild thoughts came to him, like stringing the next two jumps, seeing whether his Dubliner companions had the stomach for that—he imagined screams of terror and shouts of rage; and maybe they could not haul the velocity down—would become a missile traveling out into the Deep beyond any control, too much mass for her own systems and exponentially doomed. . . . Or even minutely fouling up the schedule they had given to the military that still ran beside them. Being hauled down by Alliance military—that would give the Dubliners something to worry about . . . if it was worth falling into the hands of the military himself. He still preferred his Dubliners to either fate. Allison and Curran and Deirdre and Neill—Allison. Allison. It hurt, knowing what she had wanted; what, subconsciously, he had seen—that for her it was *Lucy* herself. She wanted what he wanted, the way he wanted—and the loneliness in her was filled without him. She had *family*. He had known. It was his solitude that gave him strange ideas. It was listening to stationer tapes and forgetting what family was, and what right and wrong was.

Forgetting Ross and Mitri and all the voyagers in the dark. Forgetting what *Lucy* contained . . . as if Dubliners could forget their own ways.

He had had time in the hours shut in his cabin—in the cabin that had been Papa Lou's, amid the remnant of things that he and Ross and Mitri had not sealed away under the plates, taking everything that might have identified the Kreja name to customs—he had had time to reckon what had happened. He might have hated them. He reckoned that. But it was too tangled for hate. It was survival, and maybe it had started out as something better than that.

He understood Allison, he reckoned: generous sometimes, and where it touched her Name, hard enough to cut glass. She would not have come to him in worthlessness, the way he would not have left *Lucy* and gone to her penniless; she came with her crewmates about her, her wealth, her substance in the account of things. And he could not blame her for that.

Even—he had reckoned, with more painful slowness—there was worth in Curran Reilly, if he could only discover what it was. He believed that because Allison believed it, and what Allison valued must be worth something. He took that on faith. There was worth in all of them.

But he meant to break Curran Reilly's arm at next opportunity.

And meanwhile he had come out of his cabin, nodded a pleasant good day, sat down at controls and proceeded with jump prep as matter of factly as if he were only coming on watch.

"Set it and retire?" he had asked of Allison, as blandly innocent a face as he knew how to wear, his customs-agent manner. "Or shall I take her through?"

"You'll take her," Allison had to say. There was no safe alternative, things being as they were with comp. And Curran's face, a twist of his head and a look in his direction, had had the look of a man with a difficult mouthful going down.

No word to him yet of warnings. Maybe they felt threats superfluous. They were. Data came to him on schedule, to screens, to his ear, quiet voices and businesslike.

"Two minutes to mark."

"All stable."

"M/D to screen three. All on mark."

"Scan to four. *Norway*'s moving."

His heart did a turn. The image came up on screen four. Mallory was underway—had been, for some lightbound time.

"Message incoming," Neill said. "Acknowledge?"

"Put it through," he said . . . *he* said, and not Allison. The realization that the moment was thrown in his lap and not routed to Allison shocked him. But they had to: the military would expect him. "That's a tight transmission," Neill said. "Same mode reply . . . We're receiving you, *Odin*."

"This is *Odin* command," the answer came. "Captain Mallory sends her compliments and advises you there are hazards in the Hinder Star zones. Wish you luck, *Lucy*."

That was polite. The tone surprised him. He punched in his own mike. "This is Stevens of *Lucy*: do we expect escort at our next point?"

A silence. "Location of Alliance ships is restricted information. Exercise due caution in contacts."

"Understood, *Odin* command." On the number four screen, *Norway* was in decided motion, gathering speed with the distinctive dopplered flickers of a military ship on scan.

"*Odin*'s just braked," Curran said. "Losing them on vid."

"Up on scan," Deirdre said, and that was so: the image was there, the gap between them widening.

"Twenty-four seconds to mark," Allison said. "Jump point minus fifteen minutes twenty seconds."

He checked the belts, the presence of the trank on the counter. His eyes kept going back to that ominous and now closer presence coming up on them. *Norway* could lie off and make nothing of their days of passage when she woke up and decided to move. He tried to ignore that monumental fact, bristling with weapons, bearing down by increments scan was only guessing. He went about his private preparations as his crew had begun to do: settling in, being sure of comfort and safety for the jump to come.

"Minus ten minutes," Allison murmured. "Hang, what's Mallory up to?"

"She won't crowd us," Sandor said. "She's not crazy, whatever else."

He put the trank in. Began to glaze over. . . . His concern for everything diminished. He stared at the scan image for an instant, hyper and fascinated, recalled the necessity to track on other things and focused his mind down the tunnel it required. "Take her through," he said to Allison—caught the roll of a dark eye in his direction . . . suspicion; question—"Take her," he said again, as if nothing else had happened, as if it were only the next step in checking out his novice crew. Allison's face acquired that panic the situation deserved, one's first time handling jump. He shunted control to her board and she diverted her attention back where it had to be. "Eight minutes," he said, reminding her. He was crazy: he knew so. The trank had blurred all the past, created a kind of warmth in which he was safe with them simply because they had no alternatives. Relinquishing things this way, he was in command of all of them . . . and Allison Reilly had failed another prediction. He sensed her anger at him; and Curran's hate; and the perplexity of the rest—smiled a trank-dulled smile as they flashed toward their departure—

"Five minutes," he said, on mark. Allison gave him another look, as if to judge his sanity, diverted her attention back to the board.

The seconds ticked off. His Dubliners, he thought. Possibly they would begin it all again where they were going. Maybe they would do more than they had already done. In one part of his soul he was cold afraid. But he was always afraid. He was used to that. He knew how to adjust to things he was afraid of, which was to grin and bluff— and he had that faculty back again.

"Minus forty-five seconds."

"All stable," Curran said.

"We're going," Allison said, and that was that: she had uncapped the switches.

(Ross . . . it's not me this time. But she knows what she's doing. In most things. Let's go, then. The first time— without my help. She's good, Ross . . . they all are. And I don't know where we go from here. They don't know either. I'm sure of that. And I think they're scared of what I'll make them be. . . .)

The vanes cycled in, *Lucy* tracking on the star that gave them bearings, and they went—

*   *   *

—in again, a pulse *down* that made itself felt all along the nerves . . .

And no need to move, no need: Allison was there, giving orders, doing everything that ought to be done. "Dump," she ordered: comp, on silent, was bunking alarm. Sandor performed the operation, neat pulses which slipped them in and out of here and now, loaded as they were, shedding velocity into the interface,· while the dark mass lent them its gravitation, pockmark in spacetime sufficient to hold them . . . friendly, dangerous point of mass. . . .

They made it in, making more speed than they had used at the last point . . . Allison's choice. "Will she handle it?" she asked on that account.

"Ought to," Sandor said. "In a hurry, Reilly?"

No answer.

"It's lonely here," Curran said. "Not a stir anywhere."

"Lonelier than the average," Allison said. "Didn't they say they were monitoring all the points?"

No answer from any quarter. Sandor took the water bottle from beside the console, took a drink and set it back again. He unbelted.

"Going back to my quarters," he said. "Good luck with her, Reilly."

"Alterday watch to controls," Allison said. "Change off at one hour."

Maybe there was something she wanted to say. Maybe— he thought, in a moment of hope—she had come to her senses. But there was nothing but fatigue in her face when she had gotten up from controls. Fatigue and a flushed exhilaration he understood. So she had gotten the ship through: that was something to her. He had forgotten the peculiar terror of a novice; had taken *Lucy* into jump for the first time when he was fourteen. Then he had been scared. And many a time since then.

He walked to his quarters without looking back at her and Curran and the others, solitary . . . back to the museum that was his cabin, and to the silence. He closed the door, keyed in on comp with the volume very low.

"Hello, Sandy," it said. That was all he wanted to hear. "How are you?"

"Fine," he said back to the voice. "Still alive, Ross."

"What do you need, Sandy?"

He cut the comp off, on again. "Hello, Sandy. How are you?"

He cut it off a second time, because while they could not access the room channels from the bridge without the keys, someone would see the activity. He stood there treasuring the sound, empty as it was. He could get one of the instruction sequences going, and have the voice for hours—he missed that. But they would grow alarmed. His quarantine gave him this much of Ross back; in that much he treasured his solitude.

He showered, wrapped himself in his robe, went out to the galley—found Allison and Curran, still dressed, standing waiting for the oven he wanted to use. He stopped, set himself against the wall, a casual leaning, hands in pockets of the robe, a studious attention to the deck tiles.

A clatter of doors and trays then. He looked toward them, reckoning that they were through. Watched them pour coffee and arrange trays for the rest of them. "Here," Allison said to him, "want one?"

He passed an eye over them: four trays. "I'll do my own, thanks. It's all right."

"Galley's yours."

He nodded, went to the freezer, pulled an ordinary breakfast. His hands were shaking: they always did that if he was late getting food after a jump. "Did the jump real well," he said to Allison, peace offering while she was gathering up the trays.

Small courtesies had to be examined. She looked up, two of the trays in her hand while Curran went out with the other two. Nodded then, deciding to be pleased. "Better," she said, "when I can do all of it."

She had to throw that in. He nodded after the same fashion, not without the flash of a thought through his mind, that it was several days through the nullpoint and that they might have something in mind. "You'll be all right," he said, offering that too.

She went her way. He cooked his breakfast, shivering and spilling things until he had gotten a spoonful of sugar into his stomach and followed the nauseating spoonful with a chaser of hot coffee. That helped. The tremors were at least less frequent. The coffee began to warm his stomach—

real coffee. He had gotten used to the taste of it, after the substitutes.

The oven went off. He retrieved his breakfast, sat down, sole possessor of the galley and the table. It was a curious kind of truce. They retreated from *him,* as if they found his presence accusatory. And he went on owning his ship, in a solitude the greater for having a ship full of company.

When? he kept wondering. And: what next? They could go on forever in this war. He kept things courteous, which was safest for himself; and they knew that, and played the game, suspecting everything he did.

He wandered back to the bridge when he was done. He had that much concern for the ship's whereabouts. The Dubliners sat on the benches at the rear, having the last of their coffee—a little looser than they had been, a little more like Krejas had run the ship, because it was safe enough to sit back there with *Lucy* on auto. Not spit and polish enough for some captains; not regulation enough: there was a marginal hazard, enough to say that one chance out of a million could kill them all before they could react—like ambush. Unacceptable risk for *Dublin Again,* carrying a thousand lives; with ample personnel for trading shifts—but here it was only reasonable. Four Dubliner faces looked up at him, perhaps disconcerted to be caught at such a dereliction. He nodded to them, went to the scan board—heard a stir behind him, knew someone was afoot.

Nothing. Nothing out there. Only the point of mass, a lonely gas giant radiating away its last remnant of heat, a star that failed . . . a collection of planetoid/moons that were on the charts and dead ahead as they bore, headed toward the nadir pole of the system. Nothing for vid to pick up without careful searching: the emissions of the gas giant came through the dish. But no sign of anything living. No ship. That was nothing unusual at any nullpoint. But Mallory had made a point of saying that the points were watched.

He straightened and looked at the Dubliners—Curran and Allison on their feet, the others still seated, no less watching him. "Got our course plotted outside the ring," he said quietly, "missing everything on the charts. Old charts. You might keep that in mind. In case."

"You might come across with the keys," Curran said.

He shrugged. Walked the way he had come, ignoring all that passed among them.

"*Stevens,*" Curran's voice pursued him.

He looked back with his best innocence. No one moved. "Thirty-six hours twenty-two minutes to mark," he said quietly. "What do you think you'll find where we're going? A station Pell's size? Civilization? I'd be surprised. Do you want to start this over—try it my way this time?"

"No," Allison said after a moment. "Partners. That's the way it works."

"Might. Might, Reilly."

"If we go at it your way."

"This isn't *Dublin*. You don't get your way. You signed onto my ship and my way is the way she runs. Majority vote wasn't in the papers. Cooperative wasn't. My way's *it*. That's the way it works. You sit down and figure out who's on the wrong side of the law."

He walked off and left them then, went back to his own quarters—entertained for a little while the forlorn hope that they might in fact think about that, and come to terms. But he had not hoped much, and when no one came, he curled up and courted sleep.

A suited figure tumbled through his vision, and that was himself and that was Mitri. He opened his eyes again, to drive that one away; but it rode his mind, that image that came back to him every time he thought of solitude. He shivered, recalling a boy's gut-deep fear, and cowardice.

("Ross," he had called, sick and shaking. "Ross, he's dead, he's dead; get back in here. I can't handle the ship, Ross—I can't take her alone. Please come back— Ross. . . .")

The feeling was back in his gut, as vivid as it had been; the sweating cowardice; the terror—He swore miserably to himself, knowing this particular dream, that when it latched onto his mind for the night he would go on dreaming it until *Lucy*'s skin seemed too thin to insulate him from the ghosts.

He propped himself on his elbows in the dark, supported his head on his hands. . . . finally got up in the dark and turned up the light, hunting pen and paper.

He wrote it down, the central key to comp, and put it in

the drawer under the mirror, afraid of having it there—but after that he could turn out the lights and go back to bed.

Mitri gave him peace then.

He slept the night through; and waked, and fended his way past Deirdre and Neill at breakfast. In all, there was a quiet over all the ship, less of threat than of anger. And a great deal of the day he came and sat on the bridge, simply took a post and sat it—because it was safer that way, for the ship, for them. He took his blanket and his pillow that night and slept there, so that there was that much less distance between himself and controls if something went wrong.

"Give it up," Allison asked of him, on her watch.

He shook his head. Did not even argue the point.

And Neill came to him, when they were minus eight hours from mark: "It was a mistake, what we did. We know that. Look, Curran never meant to get into that; he made a mistake and he won't admit it, but he knows it, and he wishes it hadn't gone the way it did. He just didn't expect you'd go for him; and we—we just tried to stop someone from getting hurt."

"To stop Curran from getting hurt." He had not lost his sense of humor entirely; the approach touched it. He went serious again and flicked a gesture at the Dubliner's sleeve. "You still wear the *Dublin* patch."

That set Neill off balance. "I don't see any reason to take it off."

And that was a decent answer too.

"I'm here," Sandor said, "within call. Same way I've run this ship all along. You're safe. I'm taking care of your hides."

They left him alone after that, excepting now and again a remark. And he lay down and went to sleep a time, until they reached minus two from mark and he had jump to set.

His crew had showed up, quiet, businesslike. "So we go for civilization," he said. And with a glance at Allison, at Curran: "A little liberty ought to do good for all of us. Sort it out on the docks."

He imagined relief in their faces, on what account he was not sure. Only they all needed the time.

And he was glad enough to quit this place, dark and

isolated as the well-traveled nullpoints of Unionside had never been isolated.

He took his place at the number one board, began working through comp on silent . . . They might have stood over him, put it to a contest; they declined that.

Perhaps after the station liberty, he told himself, perhaps then he could get his bearings, mend what was broken, find a way to make his peace with them. A ship run amiss could become a small place indeed. They wanted different air and the noise of other living humans but themselves.

They were that close to safety; and if they could get into it, head home with a success to their account—then they were proved, and the record was clear; and everything might be clean again.

Then there was hope for them.

15

... Venture system: a star with a gas giant companion and a clutter of debris belting it and the star. And a small, currently invisible station that had been the last waystop for Sol going outward. FTL had shut it down; Pell's World, Downbelow . . . had undercut Sol prices for biostuffs, closer, faster. A rush for new worlds had run past it, the Company Wars had cut it off for half a century—But there was a pulse now, a thin, thready pulse of activity.

No buoy to assign them routing: they had been warned of that. Sandor dumped down to a sedate velocity closer to system plane than a loaded ship should—but there was no traffic.

"Lonely as a nullpoint," Allison muttered, beside him. "If we didn't have station signal—"

"Never expected much here," Sandor said. "It's old, after all. Real old."

"Com's silent," Neill said. "Just noise."

"Makes me nervous," Curran muttered. "No traffic, no buoy, no lanes—can't run a station without lanes. They're going to get somebody colliding out here, running in the dark."

"I'm going after a sandwich," Sandor said. "I'm coming back to controls with it."

"You stay put," Allison said. "Neill, see to it for all of us. Anything. Make it fast."

Neill slid out. Functions shunted: com and cargo to Deirdre, scan one and two to Curran; Allison kept to her sorting of images that got to number one screens, his filter on data that could come too fast and from confusing directions. Nothing was coming now . . . only the distant voice of station.

"We're coming up on their reply window," Curran said.

"Ready on that," Deirdre said.

Neill came back, bearing an armful of sandwiches and sealed drink containers. Sandor opened his, wolfed down half of it, swallowed down the fruit juice and capped it. The silence from station went on. No one said anything about it. No one said anything.

"Picking up something," Curran said suddenly. "Lord, it's military. It's moving like it."

The image was at Sander's screen instantly. "Mallory," he surmised.

"Negative on that," Neill said. "I don't get any *Norway* ID. I don't get any ID at all."

"Wonderful," Allison muttered.

"Size. Get size on it." Sandor started lining up jump, reckoned their nearness to system center. "Stand by: we're turning over."

"You'll get us killed. Whatever it is, we can't outrace it."

"Get me a calculation on that." He sent them into an axis roll, cut in the engines as drink containers went sailing, with a collection of plastic wrap, half a sandwich and an unidentified tape cassette. "Cargo stable," Deirdre reported, and he reached up through the drag that tended to pull his arm aside, kept on with the calculations.

"We can't do it," Allison said. "We won't clear it, reckoning they'll fire. I've got the calculations for you—"

No word of contact: nothing. He flicked glances at the scan image and Curran's current position estimate . . . saw number three screen pick up Allison's figures on plot. The intersection point flashed, before the jump range.

"You hear me?" Allison asked sharply. "Stevens, we can't make it. They're going to overtake."

"They still don't have an ID pulse," Neill said. "I don't get anything."

"They're going to overtake."

"What do you expect us to do?" Sandor stopped the jump calculation while they hurtled on their way. His body was pressed back into the cushion, his pulse hammering in his ears, drowning other sounds.

"Haul down," Allison shouted at him. "Lord, haul down before they blow us. What do you think you're doing?"

His mind was blank, raw panic. Instinct said away; common sense and calculations said it was not going to work. And excluding that—

"*Stevens!*"

"*Cut it,*" Curran shouted at him. "Stevens, you'll kill us all; we can't win it."

He looked at the Dubliners, a difficult turning of his neck. "Suit up. Hear? I'll cut back. Allison, Deirdre, Neill, get below, suit up and hurry about it. Curran, I want you. The two of us—get that Dublin patch off. *Move,* hang you all."

He cut the power back—buying them time and losing some. The Dubliners moved, all of them, nothing questioning, not with a warship accelerating in pursuit. They scattered and ran, crazily against the remaining acceleration. The lift worked, behind him: only Curran stayed, zealously ripping at the patch.

"What's the score?" Curran asked. "Set up an ambush for them aboard?"

"No. We're the only crew, you and I. You signed on at Pell, got thrown off *Dublin.*" He reached to the board, put cabins two, four, and five on powersave. "Get up there and strip down their cabins; shove everything into yours. Move it, man."

Curran's face was blanched. He nodded then, scrambled for the corridor, staggering among the consoles.

The gap was narrowing. No hail, no even yet; no need of any. The ship chasing them knew; and they knew; and that was all that was needed. It all went in silence. The other posts were shut down, all functions to the main board now.

"We're suiting," Allison's voice came to him over com out of breath. "I'm suited. Now what?"

"Got all kinds of service shafts down there. Pick one. Snug in and stay there—whatever happens. If they loot us and leave us, fine. If they take us off the ship—you stay put."

"No way. No way, that."

"You hear me. You get into a hole and wait it out. I know what I'm talking about and I know what I'm doing."

"I'm not hiding in any—"

"*Shut up, Reilly.* Two of us is the maximum risk on this and I picked my risk . . . two of us of Curran's type and mine—look like smugglers. You want to get Deirdre and Neill killed, you just come ahead up here. You got the hard part down there, I know, but for God's sake do it and don't louse it up. Please, Reilly. Think it through. That ship's a Mazianni carrier. They have maybe three thousand troops on that thing. Do what I tell you and make the others do it. We got a chance. They don't hang around after a hit. Maybe you can do something; maybe there're people left at Venture. Maybe other ships coming in here—If nothing else, they may leave.—And Reilly—you listening to me?"

"I'm hearing you."

"Comp access code's in my cabin. Top drawer."

"Hang you, Stevens."

"Sandor. It's Sandor Kreja."

Silence from the other side. He could hear her breathing, soft panting as with some kind of exertion.

"You'll be taking water with you," he said. "You don't use that suit oxygen unless you have to. You might have to last a day or so in there. Now shut that com down and keep that flock of yours quiet, hear?"

"Got you."

He cut the acceleration entirely. The stress cut out; and with equal suddenness his contact with Allison went out. He felt cold, worked his hands to bring the circulation back to them.

He had it planned now, all of it, calm and reasoned. He looked up as Curran came back, out of breath and disheveled. "Just talked to Allison," Sandor said. "They're going into the service shafts and staying put. I gave her the comp code. You keep your mouth shut and swallow that temper; we're going to get boarded and we've got no choices. You're my number two, you don't know anything, we've got a military cargo and we've run together since Viking. We're running contraband gold and we'd run anything else that paid."

Curran nodded, no arrogance at all, but a plain sober

look that well enough reckoned what they were doing. . . . So here's the good in the man, Sandor said to himself, in the strange quiet of the moment. He's got sense.

He turned a look to the screens. The com light was flashing.

"Belt in," he said to Curran. "They're coming on."

There was the muted noise and shock of lockto. Allison lay still in the light *G* of their concealment, in absolute dark, felt Deirdre move slightly, a touch against her suit, and Neill was back there behind Deirdre. Her fingers rested on the butt of one of the ship's three guns—they had gotten that from the locker . . . taken two and left one, in the reckoning that any boarders might suspect a completely empty weapons locker. Likewise the suits: two were left hanging. They must have done something about the cabins topside, she reckoned; they *must* have.

A second crash that resounded close at hand: and that was the lock working. Allison shivered, an adrenalin flutter that made her leg jerk; Deirdre could feel it, likely, which sent a rush of shame after it. It would not stop. She wanted to do something; and on the other hand she was cowardly, glad to be where she was.

And Curran and Stevens up there—Sandor. *Kreja.* She chased the name through her mind, and it meant nothing to her, nothing she had known. Curran and Sandor. They thought they were going to die. Both of them. And she had followed orders because she was blank of ideas, out of her depth. Like hiding in her cabin while her unit tried to settle things with the man who had title to the ship. Like not knowing answers, and taking too much advice. She had a new perspective on herself, hiding, shivering in the dark while she threw a cousin and a man she had slept over with to the Mazianni, men who would keep their mouths shut and protect them down here—

Not for the ship, not for the several million lousy credit ship, but for what a ship was, and the lives it still contained, down here in the dark.

Another sound, eventually, the passage of someone through the corridors, not far away, sound carried clear enough into the pressurized service shafts, into her amplified pickup. They could come out behind the invaders, maybe cut them down with their pathetic two handguns if surprise was on their side—

But a thousand troops to follow—what could they do but get themselves hauled down by the survivors?.

She added it up, the logic of it, a third and fourth time, and every time Stevens/Sandor came out right. He knew exactly what he was doing. And had always known that she did not. She lay there, breathing the biting cold air that passed through her suit's filters, with a discomfort she did not dare stir about to relieve, and added up the sum of Allison Reilly, which was mostly minuses—No substance at all, no guts; and it was no moment to try to prove something. Too late for proofs. She had to lie here and take orders and do something right. Grow up, she told herself. Think. And save everything you can.

They were topside now, the invaders. Suddenly she began thinking with peculiar clarity—what they would have done, leaving some behind to secure the passage between the ship, some to guard the lift. Going out there would mean a firefight and three dead Dubliners.

That did no good. She started thinking down other tracks. Like saving *Lucy,* which was for starters on a debt, and hoping that the most epic liar she had ever met could con the Mazianni themselves.

He had a fine survival sense, did Stevens/Kreja. Supposing the Mazianni left him and Curran in one piece—

Supposing that, they might need help. Fast.

Her foot started going to sleep. The numbness spread up her leg, afflicted the arm she was lying on. Holding her head up was impossible, and she let it down against the surface of the shaft, found a way to accommodate her neck by resting her temple just so against the helmet padding. Small discomforts added up, absorbed her attention with insignificant torments. The air that came through the filters was cold enough to sting her nose, her face, her eyes when she had them open. The numbness elsewhere might be the cold. She could lose a foot that way, if the heating failed somewhere and that was the deep cold that had sent that leg numb.

She kept her eyes shut and waited, let the numbness spread as long as she dared, felt Deirdre move, perhaps because Neill had moved, and took the chance to shift to the other side.

No communication from the other two. Wait, she had told them. And they still waited, not using the lights, saving all the power they could.

Then came the sound of the lift working, and her heart pounded afresh. Whatever was done up there was done: they were leaving. Or someone was. She heard the tread of heavy boots in the corridor, the working of the lock.

If they were alone up there, if they were able—there were the suit phones. Sandor and Curran would try to contact them—

Then they started to move, a hard kick that dislodged all of them, converted the shaft in which they were lying into a downward chute.

Neill stopped them: a sudden pileup of suited bodies against the bulkhead seal a short drop down, Neill on the bottom and herself and Deirdre in a compressing tangle of limbs, weighed down harder and harder until there was no chance to straighten out a bent back or a twisted limb. The gun was still in her hand: she had that. But her head was bent back in the helmet that was jammed against something, and it was hard to breathe against the weight.

They'll break the cargo loose, she thought, ridiculous concern: they were in tow, boosted along in grapple by a monster warship, and it could get worse. Maybe four *G*; a thing like that might pull an easy ten. Maybe more, with its internal compensations. Her mind filled with inanities, and all the while she felt for hands—Deirdre's caught hers and squeezed; she knew Deirdre's light grip; and Neill— she could not tell which limbs were his or whether he was unconscious on the bottom of the heap—O God, get a suit ripped in this cold and he was in trouble. She had picked their spot in the shaft with an eye to reorientation, but she had not reckoned on any such startup; had never in her life felt the like. Her pulse pounded in cramped extremities. A weight sat on her chest. It went on, and she grew patient in it, trying to reconcile herself to long misery—

Then it stopped as abruptly as it had begun and *Lucy*'s own rotation returned orientation to the shaft wall. She crawled over onto a side, chanced the suit light. Deirdre's went on, underlighting a disheveled face; and then Neill's, a face to match Deirdre's. She gave them the Steady sign.

*Station, Deirdre said.

*Affirmative, she answered. There was no other sane answer. They have the station.

*Question, Neill said. *Question. Get out of here.

*Stay. She made the sign abrupt and final, doused her light. The other lights went out.

Two hours, the MET suit clock informed her, a red digital glow when she punched it. Two hours ten minutes forty-five seconds point six.

They might make the station in a few hours more. Might be boarded and searched and stripped of cargo. They might hijack the ship itself. She imagined hiding until they were weak with hunger, with never a chance to get at food, and then to have the ship start out from station again, with a Mazianni crew aboard, and themselves trapped.

Or short of that, a search turning up cabins full of recent clothing, unlike the rest of *Lucy*'s oddments. Clothing with shamrock patches. And the Mazianni would know what they had—a key to a prize richer than Mazianni had ever ambushed.

They knew too much.

The armored troops moved about the bridge, looking over this and that, and the one unarmored officer sat the number one post, doing nothing, meddling with a great deal. Sandor was aware of him, past the ceramics and plastics bulk of the trooper who held a rifle in his direction and Curran's; he sat where they had set him, on a couch aftmost in the downside lounge, and waited, while troopers got up into the core, and visited the holds. And all the while he kept thinking about the acceleration that had for a time pressed them all against the bulkhead, and how service shafts running fore and aft could become pits that could break bone. Allison had thought of that; surely she had taken some kind of precaution. The sweat beaded on his temples and ran, one trail and another, betraying the calm he tried to keep. *Australia*, the stenciled letters said on the armor of the man/woman who stood nearest: and a number, meaningless to him. The trooper had no face, only reflective plastic that cast back his own diminished image, a blond man with his back against the wall; Curran's reflection behind him, with another trooper's back—both of them under the gun. *Australia* meant Tom Edger; meant Mazian's second in command, of no gentle reputation. And he kept seeing the bridge as it had been in that first boarding—felt the ghost of the pain in the scar in his side; and the dead about him—He had let them board, *he* had, when all that he knew was against it. He understood that day finally, in a way he had never understood. He sat paralyzed, and trying to think, and his mind kept cycling back and back . . . staring down the rifle barrel that was aimed at his face.

No shots fired yet. No damage taken. They were limpeted to the belly of a monster, frame to frame; and he had never appreciated the power in the giant carriers until he felt it slam a loaded freighter's mass along with its own into a multiple *G* acceleration. They could not have outrun it . . . had gained most of the time they had had simply in the delicate maneuvers that brought airlocks into synch. And maybe the Mazianni had been as patient as they had been because he had cooperated.

Thinking like that led to false security. He had a rifle muzzle in front of his face to deny it. He had time to notice intimate detail in the equipment, and still did not know if it had been this ship or *Norway* or still another that had caught *Lucy/Le Cygne* before. He had a sense of betrayal . . . outrage. Venture Station was doing nothing to stop what had happened: the station belonged to the Mazianni, was in their hands. A vast horror sat under the cracks in that logic, the suspicion that there were things even Alliance might not know, when they made an ex-Mazianni like Mallory the chief of their defense.

A military cargo, Mallory had said. A delivery to Venture, where *Australia* waited. Supplies—for allies? The thought occurred to him that a power like Alliance, which consisted of one world and one station—besides the Hinder Stars and the merchanters themselves—could be threatened by a power the size of the Mazianni . . . a handful of carriers that now came and went like ghosts through the nullpoints, struck and vanished. The Mazianni could *take* Pell.

Especially if Mallory had rethought her options and decided to go the other way.

A handful of independent merchanters, he reckoned, were not going to be allowed to go their way. There was no hope of that at all. And possibly the Mazianni had a use for a merchanter ship that was scheduled to return to Pell.

The focus of his gaze flicked between the gun and the Mazianni who worked over the controls. And when the man turned the seat and got up, he had a panicked notice what the question was.

The man moved up beside the trooper . . . for a moment the gun moved aside and came on target again. "I need the comp opened up," the officer said. "You want to give it to me easy?"

"No," Sandor said quietly. And something settled into place like an old habit. He took a deeper breath, found his mind working again. "I trade. Maybe run a little contraband here and there. I've dealt the far side of the law before this. And before I trade my best deal off, I'll talk to Edger himself."

"You know, I wouldn't recommend that."

"I'm not stupid. I don't plan to die over a cargo. I figure we're going to offload it at Venture. Figure maybe you've got that sewed up tight. Fine. You want the cargo—fine. I'm not anybody's hero. Neither is my partner. I'll talk to Edger and I'm minded to deal, you can figure that. Might work out something."

The Mazianni studied him a long moment—a seam-faced, pale man, the intruder onto *Lucy*, of indefinite age. He nodded slowly, with eyes just as dead. Sandor let it sink in, numb in his expectation that it was all prelude to a pounce . . . realized then to his own astonishment that the deal was taken. "We'll go with that," the Mazianni said, and walked back to controls.

Sandor looked up at the trooper's faceplate—not for sight of that, but for a look at Curran without turning about; the Dubliner sat still, not a muscle moved. His own heart was beating double-time, a temptation to self-congratulation tempered by a calculation that the other side had an angle. Not stupid either, the Mazianni. Suddenly he reckoned that Mazianni and marginers must have similar reflexes, similar senses—living on the fringes of civilization, off the fat of others. It was like the unrolling of a chart laid out plain and clear; no enigmatic monsters out of his childhood—they were quite, quite like himself, out for profit and trade and unparticular how it came. Always the best advantage, the smart move—and the smart move at the moment was not taking apart the man with the comp key, the man with a ship that had Alliance papers and clearance to dock at Pell.

He knew how to play it then. What he had to trade. But it was not a question now of a scam, minor wounds on a vast corporation. He was not unimportant any more. And he earnestly wanted his obscurity back.

(Ross . . . got a problem, Ross. You got a tape that covers this one? I might save my crew. Curran . . . and Allison . . . Where's right? Do we play it for the ship or for some station and people we don't know; and how does anybody else figure in it when it's our precious delicate selves in Mazianni hands? . . .) His mind drew pictures and he shoved them out again, preferring the gun in front of him to the images his mind could conjure.

He settled his mind, trusted himself to ingenuity. He was thinking again, and his blood was moving—like sex, this necessity to figure. No preconceptions, but a fair idea what the opposition would be after . . . a knowledge of all the angles.

He was still figuring when the ship dumped velocity—an interface dump that shocked his mind numb with the unexpectedness of it. Military maneuver, a brush with jumpspace with such suddenness he found a tremor in his muscles—Curran swore softly, almost the first word Curran had spoken. Sandor looked that way—met the Dubliner's eyes that for once showed fright. No gesture between them: nothing—Curran was too smart for it. He had picked well, he thought, another matter of instinct. There was no soft center to Curran Reilly. What made them enemies made the Dubliner a good wall at his back. Not a flicker, beyond that startlement.

A shock then that rang through the hull—and Sandor glanced instinctively in its direction, his heart lurching: but they had ungrappled, nothing worse. They were loose, and *Lucy* was under her own helm, with a stranger at the controls.

They were headed in to dock. He felt the small shifts of

stress and focused his eyes beyond his guard, where he could see the glimmer of screens without making out the detail.

They were headed for a reckoning of one kind and the other. He felt his own nerves twitch in response to this and that move the ship made under foreign hands—felt a ridiculous anxiety that they might come in rough, as if a scrape was the worst they had to worry over.

It was rough, a jolting into dock that sent a shudder through his soul. He swore, for the guard to hear, but not for the man who had done it, whose good will he wanted, if it could be had.

16

The silence had gone on for a long time . . . since dock. Rotation was stopped. The ship had all the attendant sounds of coming and going for a while—

And then nothing. Nothing for a very long while. Allison fretted, ate and drank in the long dark hours because she had reached the point of fatigue, and she had to, not because her stomach had any appetite for it.

Neither Deirdre nor Neill offered suggestions—not since the first, when they felt the breakaway from the grapple and knew that they were going in on their own.

Now there were machinery sounds missing, like the noise of unloading. That took comp, to open the holds and run the internal machinery . . . and that meant that the Mazianni had not gotten the keys—in some sense or another. Bravo, she tried to think; but the other chance occurred to her too, that they were dead up there. And the silence continued, from the part of the ship they could hear.

She could make a fatal mistake, she reckoned, foul it all up—either by sitting too long or by rushing ahead when she ought to sit still and wait—and take their losses and hope—

For what? she thought. Sandor had never reckoned on being hauled into station, docked and occupied at leisure. There was no percentage in waiting for Mazianni to get what they wanted and move a crew in. She conceived a black picture, herself and her crew surviving in the crawlways, waiting a chance when some Mazianni crew should try to take *Lucy* out—and launching an attack. But they would be debilitated by hunger and inactivity, at disadvantage, underarmed—the Mazianni could crew *Lucy* with a dozen, and tilt the odds impossibly against them.

She turned on her suit light. *Going up, she signed to the others, making out only blank faceplates casting back her light in the darkness. But the blank heads nodded after a moment, and Neill patted her ankle with a clumsy glove. They were willing.

She moved ahead in the shaft, reckoning that somewhere toward the bow had to be a crawlspace leading to main level: they were under the bridge/lounge area, and she recollected the geography of main level, went on the best estimate she had reasoned out over the hours, where the access shaft might be. It was slow-motion movement, carrying the weight of the suits and slithering forward, trying not to hit metal against metal—She kept the light on, and turned and signed *quiet to the others—needless caution. They knew. A slip, the banging of a plastic clip or metal coupling against the metal of the shaft might set any occupation wondering.

She had to stop from time to time—stopped when she had found what she had hunted for, staring up into the access shaft—disgusted with herself because she was out of breath and doubting she could make the climb in one *G*.

She had to, that was all. Could not send Neill up there to get killed because he was strongest. She had to be ready to use the gun and use it right; and none of them had ever fired a gun except in light-sensor games.

She sucked in a breath and started, a slow upward climb, taking the same cautions. The weight of the pack dragged at her arms, threatened to tear her hands from the rungs, bruising bones in her fingers even through the gloves. She took it on her legs as much as possible, a dozen rungs, a few more; and reached a hatch beside the ladder in the shaft. She hooked an elbow around the rungs, almost disjointed by the weight, got the gun from its holster and hooked the edge of that hand into the unlock lever of the access panel. It hung, took another shove that tore muscles all the way to the groin, gave with a crash her pickup magnified.

The door swung out: a coveralled man had stood up from the number one seat, whirling in an adrenalin-stretched instant. She fired, a panic shot—watched in cold disbelief as the man folded and fell. She thrust her leg over and through the access threshold, at the corner of the maintenance corridor, stumbled out and fell skidding to one knee as terror, the deck slope, and the weight of the suit combined to take her feet out from under her. She came up with the gun trained wide on the bridge—but there was no one, only the one man, who was not moving.

No sign of Curran or Sandor. Nothing. They were gone.

Taken somewhere, she thought, struggling to her feet as Deirdre and Neill followed her. She staggered across the deck and stopped, hanging on the arm of the number one cushion, the gun trained downward at a corpse in blue coveralls. She swallowed her nausea and fired again for good measure, greatly relieved that the body prone on the floor failed to react. Then she shoved off from the command pit and circled the area through the other consoles, staggering from the weight and sucking too-warm air through a sore throat. She fumbled the oxygen on, felt for the corridor wall, her vision limited by the helmet, got the door open to Sander's cabin and used the still-burning suit light to find her way in the dark of it. She cast about for the drawer he had named, pulled open the toiletries drawer under the mirror and rummaged among the dried-up remnants of some previous tenant—a man, that one—shoved jars and tubes aside, found it, a slip of paper that her gloved hands could not unfold. She ripped a glove off, found a number.

Good luck, he had written along with it. *If you've got this, one of two things has happened. In either case, take care of her.*

She blinked, caught by an impulse of guilt . . . remembered what she was about, then, and what was at stake, and headed out of the cabin—past Neill in the doorway. She went for the bridge, staggering and leaning back in the downward pitch of the deck Neill followed her, as reckless and reeling.

Deirdre had gotten her helmet off, and set it on the console and dragged the body out of the way. Allison jerked the other glove off, fought with the helmet catches and

lifted it off. The backpack weighed on her—she started to
shed that, and abandoned the thought in her anxiety to get
at comp.

She bent over the keyboard and keyed the number in.

"Hello, Sandy," a voice said, nearly stopping her heart.
A menu of functions and code numbers leapt to the screen
in front of her. *"How are you?"*

She picked the security function, keyed it through. A list
of accesses came to the screen with x's and o's.

*"Sandy, is there some problem? I can instruct insecurity
procedures if you ask me. In any case, secure the bridge;
this is always your last retreat. Stay calm. Always keep food
and water on the bridge in case. Keep a gun by you and
power down the rest of the sectors if it comes to that."*

"Lord," Neill muttered. "What's it *doing?*"

"It's right," she decided suddenly, looking about her.
"We put the locks on. He's gone; and Curran is; and
they've got them out there somewhere. We've got to be
sure there's no one left in the holds." The computer went
on in its monologue, unstoppable. She keyed the doors
closed, one and the other, and took comp back to its listing.

"What can I do for you?" it asked.

And waited. She stared at the boards, panting under the
weight she carried. A wild idea occurred to her, that they
might all go out onto the docks and try whether some resistance might be left on Venture Station: if they could join
up with stationers trying to fight off this intrusion—

No, she thought, it was too remote a chance. Too likely
to end in a shooting: there were probably Mazianni guards
right outside.

And the Mazianni would expect to change guards on the
ship at some reasonable interval.

She kept running through the listings, finance, and
plumbing and navigation. Customs, one said; and Law; and
Banks; and Exchange; and In Case, one said. She pushed
that one.

"Sandy," the voice said gently, *"if you're into this one,
the worst has happened, I guess; and of course I don't know
where or who—but I love you, Sandy—I'll say that first.
And there are several things you can do. I'll lay them out
for you—"*

She stopped it with a push of the key, collapsed into the

cushion under the weight of the pack, under the weight of shock. Sandy. Sandor. It was indisputable title—to *Lucy* and what it held.

"That was some*body*," Deirdre said. "Lord, Allie—what kind of rig is this?"

She started shedding her pack, struggling out of her suit. "I don't know. But it's *his*. Sandor's. And whoever it was thought things through."

"They've got him and Curran," Neill said. "If we knew where—"

"Wrong odds," she said. She freed her upper body, stood up and shed the rest of it. Panting, she settled back again and looked up at them. At both of them. "I'll tell you how it is. We hold onto the ship; and if they try to take it we get ourselves some of them. That's it."

They nodded, helmetless both. She loved them, she thought suddenly. Everything had come apart. She had just killed someone . . . had gotten herself and her crewmates into a situation without exit, a dead end in all senses. Sandor and Curran gone—taken off the ship—lost. . . . Everything had gone foul, everything from the moment she had planned to have her way in the world, and her two cousins stood there, able to have added it all up, and gave her a simple consent. The way Curran had done. And Sandor, for whatever tangled reasons.

Her throat swelled, making it painful to swallow. Her mind started working. "I'm betting they're still alive," she said, "Curran and Sandor—or the Mazianni would have gone at the ship with a cutter. They still reckon to get the ship intact."

She reached and punched in on com, scanning through it, trying to pick up Mazianni transmissions, but there was nothing readable. Only the station pulse continued. . . . false indication of life. She turned on vid as it bore—and it produced a desolate image of a primitive torus, vacant except for the vast bulk of a carrier that breathed near them, and another object that might be yet another freighter docked farther on, indistinct in the dark and the curve of the station.

"Got ourselves a target if we wanted to take it," Neill said. "Even a creature that size—has a sensitive spot about the docking probe."

"Might," she agreed. "Wonder what the guns are worth." She went for the comp listing, called it up. The voice began, talking in simple terms, advising against starting anything.

"Shut up," she told it softly.

It kept on, relentless, and got then to what the guns were worth, which was not much.

But there was that chance, she reckoned; and then she got to reckoning what the bristles were on the frame of the monster next to them . . . and what that broadside would leave of them and a good section of Venture Station.

"Don't try to fight," the young-man's-voice of the computer pleaded with them. *"Use your head. Don't get into situations without choices."*

It was late advice.

17

"I told you," Sandor said, "I've got no inclination to heroics. You want to deal, I'll deal."

It was a tight gathering, that in the cold dockside office—a dozen Mazianni, mostly officers, in a dingy, aged facility, heated by a portable unit, with some of the lights burned out—a desk cluttered with printouts. And burn-scars on the walls, that spoke of violence here at some point. There was no sign of the former occupants, nothing. He stood across the desk from Edger himself, and Curran was somewhere behind him, back among the guns that kept the odds in this meeting to Edger's liking.

"What have you got to deal with?" Edger asked him.

"Look, I don't want any trouble. You keep your hands off my ship and off my crewman."

"Might have need of personnel," Edger said.

"No. No deal at all on that. Look, you want cargoes—I'm not particular. You feed me goods and I'll shift them where you like. You want some of your own people to go along, fine." There was a chair a trooper had his foot in. Sandor gestured at it, looking at Edger. "You mind? Captain to captain, as it were—" Edger made a careless, not quite amused gesture and he captured the chair from the trooper, dragged it over and sat down, leaned on the desk and jabbed a finger onto it amid the papers. "Do I figure right, you've got your sights on Pell? Maybe Mallory's playing your game out there; maybe you're going to pull it off."

"Mallory."

He sat back a fraction, playing it with a scant flicker; but the hate in Edger's eyes was mortal—So, he thought, having tried that perimeter. Play it without principles. All the way. "Her cargo aboard," he said. "She hauled me in before undock, said she was watching. And she's out there. Overjumped us. Just watching. That's what I know. I'm not particular. You want Mallory's cargo, welcome to it. And if you want trade done somewhere across the Line I'm willing—but not Pell. Not and answer questions back there."

Edger was a mass murderer. So was Mallory. But there was a febrile fixation to Edger's stare that tightened the hairs on his nape. No dockside justice ever promised Edger's kind of dealing.

"Suppose we discuss it with your man back there," Edger said.

"Discuss what?"

"Mallory."

"*I'll* discuss Mallory. I've got no percentage in it."

"Where is *Norway?*"

"Last time I saw her she was off by James's Point."

"Doing what?"

"Waiting for something. She's working with Union. That's the rumor. They've got all the nullpoints sewed up and Union's working with her. So they say."

Edger was silent a moment. Shifted his eyes to his lieutenant and back again. "What cargo?"

"I don't know what cargo. I didn't want Mallory on my neck. I didn't break any seals."

"Junk, Captain Stevens. *Junk*. We looked. Recycling goods." Edger's voice rose and fell again; and Sander's mind went to one momentary blank.

"She set me up," he exclaimed. "That bastard bitch set me up. She *knew* what was here and sent me into it."

No reaction from Edger; nothing. The eyes stayed fixed on him, feverish and still, and the noise of his protest fell into that silence and died.

"Look, I don't know anything. I swear to you. I'm a marginer with legal troubles; and Mallory offered me hazard rate for a haul—offered me a way out, and a profit, and she set me up. She bloody well set me up."

"I'm touched, Stevens."

"It's the *truth*."

"It's a setup, Stevens, you're right in that much.—Hagler, take a detail and persuade Stevens he's hired; get that ship working."

"Hired for what?"

"Don't press your luck, Stevens. You may survive this voyage . . . if you learn."

A hand descended on his shoulder. He got up, without protest, calculating wildly—to get back aboard again, get sealed in there with a crew and take care of them. . . . Allison and her cousins would be there; and there was suddenly a way out—

Everyone was moving, the gathering adjourning elsewhere with some dispatch. They were pulling out, he reckoned suddenly. They could not afford to sit at rest if they suspected Mallory was on the loose. A warship out of jump, not dumping its velocity—he did the calculations mentally, fogged in the terror of them, let himself be taken by the arm and steered for the door, a gun prodding him in the back. A ship like *Norway* could be down their throats scant minutes behind its lightspeed bow wave of ID and interference . . . could blow them out of this fragile antique shell of a station.

There never had been a major settlement here, he surmised. It was a setup, all of it, all the leaks of routes and trade—and he had not betrayed Mallory: Mallory had primed him with everything she wanted spread to her enemies. Canisters of *junk* for a cargo—

He looked about him as they went out onto the open dock, so chill that breath hung frosted in the air and cold lanced to the bone. They herded him right, the jab of a rifle barrel, all of them headed out . . . and he looked back, saw them taking Curran off in the other direction.

"Curran!" he yelled. "Hold it! Blast you, my crewman goes with me—"

Curran stopped, looked toward him. Sandor staggered in the sudden jerk at his arm, the jab of a rifle barrel into his ribs—

Kept turning, and hit an armored trooper a blow in the throat that threw the trooper down and sent a pain through his hand. He dived for the gun, hit the floor and rolled in a patter of shots that popped off the decking. The fire hit,

an explosion that paralyzed his arm. He kept rolling, for
the cover of the irregular wall, the gun abandoned in panic.

"Move it," someone yelled. "Get him."

A second shot exploded into his side, and after that was
the cold pressure of the deck plates against his face and a
stunned realization that he had just been hit. He heard
voices shouting, heard someone order a boarding—

"Give up the freighter," he heard called. "You just shot
the bastard and it's no good. Come on."

He was bleeding. He had trouble breathing. He lay still
until the sounds were done, and that was the best that he
knew how to do.

Then he lifted his head and saw Curran lying face down
on the plates a distance away.

He got that far, an inching progress across the ice cold
plates, terrified of being spotted moving. The wounds were
throbbing, the left arm refused to move, but he thought
that he could have gotten up. And Curran—

Curran was breathing. He put his hand on Curran's back,
snagged his collar and tried to pull him, but it tore his
side. Curran stirred then, a feeble movement. "Come on,"
Sandor said. "Out of the open: come on—let's try for the
ship."

Curran struggled for his feet, collapsed back to one knee;
and blood erupted from the burn in his shoulder. Sandor
made the same try, discovered he could get his legs under
him, offered a hand to Curran and steadied him getting up.
"Get to cover," he breathed, looking out at all that vacant
dock, foreign machinery more than a century outdated, a
dark pit of an access. That was *Australia* back there, two
berths down, dark and blank to the outside; and *Lucy* was
in the other direction . . . *Lucy—*

They made it twenty meters along the wall; and then the
cold and the tremors got to them both. Sandor hung onto
the wall, eased down it finally, supporting Curran and both
of them leaning together. "Rest a minute," he said.

"They'll blow the station," Curran predicted. "Hard
vacuum.—Come on, man. Come on." It was Curran hauling
him up this time; and they walked as far as they could, but
it was a long, long distance to *Lucy*'s berth.

Curran went down finally, out of strength; and he was.
He held onto the blood-soaked Dubliner, both of them

tucked up in the cover of a machinery niche, and stared at what neither one of them could reach.

Seals crashed. *Australia* was loose, preparing for encounter. Sandor went stiff, and Curran did, anticipating the rush of decompression that might take them; but the station stayed whole.

Then a second crash of seals.

"Allison," Sandor said, and Curran took in his breath.

Lucy had prepared herself to break loose.

Someone with the comp keys was at controls.

"They're wanting an answer," Neill said from com—turned a sweating face in Allison's direction.

"No," Allison said.

"Allie—those are *guns* out there."

"They know comp's locked and their man might not answer. *No,* don't do it."

"They're moving," Deirdre said.

Vid came to her screen, a view of a monster warship, the twin of *Norway,* a baleful glow of running lights illuminating the angular dark surfaces of the frame. Cylinder blinkers began their slow movement as the carrier established rotation.

"They've broken communication," Neill said, and Allison said nothing, waiting, watching, hoping that the behemoth that passed near them would reckon their man's silence a communications lockup. And that they would not, in passing, blow them and the station at once.

"Movement our starboard," Deirdre said, and that image came too: another ship had been around the rim, and it was putting out. "Freighter type," Deirdre said.

"One of theirs," Allison surmised.

There was a silence for a moment. "Get down there," she said then, "and get those port seals complete. We'd better be ready to move."

"Both of us?" Deirdre asked.

"Go."

All the functions came to her board; her cousins scrambled for the lift back in the lounge that would take them down to the frame. They had to get the seals complete or blow the dock and damage themselves, with no dockside assistance in their undocking.

And meanwhile the warship glided past them, while they played dead and helpless.

That was a panic move, that. The Mazianni had picked up something on scan: she dared not activate her own, sat taking in only what passive sensors could gather . . . no output, no visible movement on the exterior, except the minuscule angling of the cameras that she reckoned they would miss.

A force left on the docks might have spotted that closure of seals; it might have been better to have done nothing. Might have—

She could be paralyzed in might haves. She had two of her own out there—on that ship; on the station—no way of finding that out. It hurt. And there was no remedy to that either. She cleared it out of her mind for the moment, focused finally, functioning as she had not been functioning since somewhere back on Viking. So things were lost; lives were lost. She had several more to think of, and the captain of that ship out there was her senior in more than years and firepower. No match at all: the only chance was to go unnoticed, to prepare the ship to ride out the destruction of the station as a bit of flotsam, if it happened.

If that warship scented something out there, something sudden enough to draw it out, *something* was loose in Venture System.

Mallory, it might be. She fervently hoped so.

The red telltales winked to green, indicating the ports sealed. Deirdre and Neill had gotten them secure. In a moment she heard the working of the lift.

Com beeped. She listened. It was the characteristic spit and fade of distant transmission, numerical signal, an arriving ship for sure. She punched it through to comp, flurried through an unfamiliar set of commands.

Working, the young-man's-voice said, familiar sound by now, soothing. The answer came up. *Finity's End.* Alliance merchanter, headed into ambush. She reached toward the com, and vid suddenly lost the movement of the Mazianni warship—a surge of power that for a moment wiped out reception. They moved—Lord, they moved, with eye-tricking suddenness . . . and her own people were headed across the deck toward her from the lift with no idea what was in progress. If she had the nerve she would put in com, give out a warning—and get them all killed.

"Neihart's *Finity* just arrived," she said. "Headed into it."

Two bodies hit the cushions and started snatching functions to their own boards, without comment.

Warn them or not? There was a chance of making a score on the Mazianni if they lay low: of breaking things loose at their own moment, if they could pick it. Their guns were nothing. A pathetic nothing; and *Finity* had far better than they had—that was a guessable certainty.

"Got another one," Neill said; and then: "Allie: it's *Dublin*."

The blood went from her face to her feet.

"We've got to warn them," Deirdre said.

"No. We sit tight."

"Allie. . . ."

"We sit tight. We've got the Mazianni base. We give *Dublin* a chance if we can. But we don't tip it premature."

"What, premature? They're headed into a trap."

"No," she said. Desperately. Just no. She had worked it out, all of it, the range they needed. The odds of the troops. Suddenly the balance was tilted. Near two thousand Dubliners; the Neiharts of *Finity* might number nearly as many—a Name on the Alliance side, armed and not for trifling.

"They're not dumping," Deirdre said. "The way that's coming in they haven't dumped. Permission to use scan."

"*Do it.*"

The freighters were coming in at all gathered velocity—they *knew*, they knew what they were running into. Allison sat still, clenched her hands together in front of her lips. Scan developed in front of her, a scrambled best estimate of the Mazianni position and that of the merchanters revising itself second by second as Deirdre fought sense out of it.

"We're moving," she said, and committed them, a release of the grapples and a firing of the undocking jets. *Lucy* backed off and angled, and she cut mains in, listening to the quiet voice of the ghost in *Lucy*'s comp assure her she was doing it right.

"We go for them?" Neill asked, an optimistic assessment of their speed and their firepower.

"Ought to get there eventually," she said. "Mark they

don't run us down. Just keep our targets straight." She asked comp for armaments, keying in that function.

"*Sandy,*" comp objected, "*are you sure of this?*"

She keyed the affirmative and uncapped the switches. A distressing red color dyed her hand from the ready light. It was a clumsy system . . . a computer/scan synch that was decent at low velocities, fit for nullpoint arguments, but nothing else.

"*Got another one,*" Neill said. And: "*Lord,* it's Mallory!"

Her hand shook above the fire buttons. She looked at scan, a flick of the eye that was in *Norway's* terms several planetary diameters duration. The garble sorted itself out in com; and then she saw the angle on scan.

She fired, a flat pressure of her hand, at what she reckoned for the Mazianni's backside, a miniscule sting at a giant with two giant freighters coming on at the Mazianni and its companion, and a carrier of its own class in its wake. Other blips developed; rider-ships were deployed.

And then something was coming at the pattern broadside: "*Union* ship," she heard reported into her ear . . . and suddenly everything broke up, sensors out, a wail of alarm through *Lucy's* systems.

It passed. She still had her hand on controls. "*Hello, Sandy,*" comp said pleasantly, sorting itself into sense again. Scan had not. They had ships dislocated from last estimated position. The ID signals started coming in again.

"That's *Dublin,*" Neill said, "and *Finity. Norway* and her riders. *Liberty.* That was a Union ship that just passed us. . . ."

"Outbound," Deirdre exclaimed. "Lord, they're running, the Mazianni are taking out of there . . . and that Mazianni freighter's *blown.* . . ."

She sat still, with the adrenalin surge still going hot and cold through her limbs and an alarming tendency to shake.

"Do we contact?" Neill asked. "Allie, it's *Dublin* out there."

"Put me through," she said; and when she heard the steady calm of *Dublin's* Com One, she still felt no elation. "*Dublin* Com, this is *Lucy.* We've got two missing, request help in boarding the station and searching."

"We copy, *Lucy.*" Not—who is this? Not—hello, Allison

Reilly. Ship to ship and all business. "Do you need assistance aboard?"

"Negative. All safe aboard."

"This is *Norway* com," another voice broke in. "Ridership *Odin* will establish dock; nonmilitary personnel will stay at distance. Repeat—"

She had cut the engines. She rolled *Lucy* into an axis turn and cut them in again, defying the military order. Let them enforce it. Let *Norway* put a shot toward them in front of witnesses, after all else *Norway* had done. She heard objection, ignored it.

"*Dublin*, this is *Lucy*. Request explanation this setup."

"Abort that chatter," *Norway* said.

"Hang you, *Norway*—"

A ridership passed them, cutting off communication for the moment—faster than they could possibly move. *Norway* had followed. *Lucy* clawed her slow way against her own momentum, and there was a silence over *Lucy*'s bridge, no sense of triumph at all.

She had won. And found her size in the universe, that she counted for nothing.

Even from *Dublin* there was no answer.

"They've got them," the report came in via *Norway* com, even while *Lucy* was easing her way into a troop assisted dock. And in a little time more: "They're in sorry shape. We're making a transfer to our own medical facilities."

"How bad?" Allison asked. "*Norway*, *Lucy* requests information."

"When available. Request you don't tie up this station. *Norway* has other operations."

She choked on that, concentrated her attention on the approaching dock, listened to Deirdre giving range.

Norway sat in dock; the Union carrier *Liberty* was in system somewhere, poised to take care of trouble if the Mazianni had a thought of coming in again. *Dublin* and *Finity* moved in with uncommon agility.

"They can't be hauling," Deirdre said. "They came down too fast."

"Copy that," Allison said, and paid attention to business, smothering the anger and the outrage that boiled up through her thinking. No merchanter ran empty except to make speed; so *Dublin* itself had been cooperating with *Norway* and Union forces. *Norway* had beaten them out of Pell; and somehow in the cross-ups of realtime they had leapfrogged each other, themselves and *Norway* and *Dublin* with Neihart's *Finity*. *Norway* had *known* the score here: that much had penetrated her reckonings; and if *Dublin* had come in empty, it was to make time and gain maneuverability. She had no idea what *Dublin* could do empty: no one could reckon it, because *Dublin* has never done the like.

For a lost set of Dubliners? She doubted that.

The cone loomed ahead. *"Docking coming up, Sandy,"* comp said. She paid attention to that only, full concentration . . . the first time she had handled docking, and not under the circumstances she had envisioned—antiquated facilities, a primitive hookup with none of the automations standard with more modern ports.

She touched in with the faintest of nudges, exact match . . . felt no triumph in that, having acquired larger difficulties.

"My compliments to the Old Man," she said to Neill, "and I'll be talking with him at the earliest. On the dock."

Neill's eyes flickered with shock in that glance at her. Then they went opaque and he nodded. "Right."

She shut down.

"Dublin's coming in," Deirdre said. *"Finity's* getting in to synch."

She unbelted. "I'll be seeing about a talk with the Old Man. I think we were *used,* cousins. I don't know how far, but I don't like it."

"Yes, *ma'am,"* Deirdre said.

She got up, thought about going out there as she was, sweaty, disheveled. "We'll be delivering that body to *Norway,"* she said. "Or venting it without ceremony. Advise them."

"Got that," Neill said.

Her cabin was marginally in reach with the cylinder in downside lock. She made it, opened the door on chaos, hit by a wave of icy air. The cabin was piled with bundles lying where maneuvers and *G* had thrown them, not only hers, but everyone else's—clothes jammed everywhere, personal items strewn about. She waded through debris to reach her locker, found it stripped of her clothes and jammed with breakables.

She saw them in her mind, Curran and Sandor both, taking precautions while they were in the process of being boarded, fouling up the evidence of other occupancy, as if this had been a storage room. And they had kept to that story, as witness their survival. All riding on two men's silence.

She hung there holding to the frame of the door, still a moment. Then she worked her way back out again, down the pitch of the corridor to the bridge.

"*Dublin* requests you come aboard," Neill said.

"All right," she said mildly, quietly. "At my convenience.— I'm headed for *Norway*."

"They won't let you in."

"Maybe not. Shut down and come with me."

"Right," Deirdre said, and both of them shut down on the moment and got up.

Down the lift to the lock: *Norway* troops were standing guard on the dock when they had gone out into the bitter cold, three battered merchanters in sweat-stained coveralls.

There was a thin scattering of movement beside that, a noise of loudspeakers and public address, advising stationers in hiding to come to dockside or to call for assistance. Men and women as haggard as themselves, in work clothes—came out to stand in lines the military had set up, to go to desks and offer papers and identifications—

"Poor bastards," Neill muttered. "No good time for them, in all of this."

She thought about it, the situation of stationers with Mazianni in charge. They were very few, even so. A maintenance crew—there were no children in evidence, and there would have been, if it had been a station, in full operation. All young; all the same look to them.—"You," an armored trooper shouted at them. "ID's."

Allison stopped, Deirdre and Neill on either side of her—"Allison Reilly," she said, and the rifle aimed at them went back into rest. "Papers," the trooper said, and she presented them.

"We've got two of ours in *Norway* medical section," she said. "I'm headed there."

The trooper handed the papers back, faceless in his armor. "Got the *Lucy* crew here," he said to someone else. "Requesting boarding."

And a moment later—a nod to that unheard voice. . . . "One of you is clear to board. Officer on duty will guide you."

"Thanks," Allison said. She glanced at Neill and Deirdre, silent communication, then parted company with them, walked the farther distance up the docks to the access of *Norway.*

Another trooper, another challenge, another presentation of papers. She walked the ramp into the dark metal interior without illusions that Mallory had any interest in talking to her after what they had done.

She was an inconsequence, with her trooper escort, in the corridor traffic, came virtually unremarked to the doorway of the medical section. An outbound medic shoved into her in his haste and she flattened herself against the doorway, gathering her outrage and fright. A second brush with traffic, a medic on his way in—"Where's the *Lucy* personnel?" she asked, but the man brushed past. "Hang out—" She thrust her way into a smallish area and a medic made a wall of himself. "Captain's request," the trooper escorting her said. "Condition of the *Lucy* personnel. This is next of kin."

The medic focused on her as if no one until now had seen her. "Transfused and resting. No lasting damage." They might have been machinery. The medic waved them for the door. "Got station casualties incoming. Out."

She went, blind for the moment, was shaking in the knees by the time she walked *Norway*'s ramp down to the dockside and headed herself toward *Dublin.* The troopers stayed. She went alone across the docks, with more anger than she could hold inside.

Megan met her at the lock—had been standing there . . . no knowing how long. She looked at her mother a moment without feeling anything, a simple analysis of a familiar face, a recognition of the heredity that bound her irrevocably to *Dublin.* Her mother held out her arms; she reacted to that and embraced her, turned her face aside. "You all right?" Megan asked when they stood at arm's length.

"You set us up."

Megan shook her head. "We knew *Norway* had. We shed it all . . . we knew where *Finity* was bound and we put out with them. Part of the operation. They gave you false cargo; mass, but *nothing*. And you hewed the line and played it honest but it wouldn't have made a difference. Mallory gave you what she *wanted* noised about. And sent you in here primed with everything you were supposed to spill. If you were boarded, if they searched—they'd know you were a setup. But all you could tell them was what Mallory wanted told."

The rage lost its direction, lost all its logic. She was left staring at Megan with very little left in reserve. "We were boarded. Didn't Deirdre and Neill say? But we got them off."

"Curran and Stevens—"

"They're all right. Everything's fine." She fought a breath down and put a hand on Megan's shoulder. "Come on. Deirdre and Neill aboard?"

"With the Old Man."

"Right," she said, and walked with her mother to the lift, through *Dublin's* halls, past the staring, silent faces of cousins and her own sister—"Connie," she said, and took her sister's hand, embraced her briefly—Connie was more pregnant than before, a merchanter's baby, pregnancy stretched into more than nine months of realtime, a life already longer and thinner than stationers' lives, to watch stationers age while it grew up slowly, with a merchanter's ambitions.

She let her sister go, walked on with Megan into the lift, and topside—down the corridor that led to the bridge. She was qualified there, she realized suddenly: might have worn the collar stripe . . . posted crew to a *Dublin* associate; and it failed to matter. She walked onto the bridge where Michael Reilly sat his chair, where Deirdre and Neill stood as bedraggled as herself and answered for themselves to the authority of *Dublin*. Ma'am was there; and Geoff; and operations crew, busy at *Dublin* running.

"Allison," the Old Man said. Rose and offered his hand. She took it, slump-shouldered and leaden in the moment, her sweat-limp hair hanging about her face as theirs did, her crew, her companions, both of them. "You all right?"

"All right, sir."

"There wasn't a way to warn you. Just to back you up. You understand that."

"I understand it, sir. Megan said."

"Small ship," the Old Man said. "And expendable. That's the way they reckoned it." He gestured toward the bench near his chair. She folded her hands behind her, locked her aching knees.

"Won't stay long," she said.

"You don't have to have it that way." The Reilly sat down. "You can turn your post over to Second Helm . . . take a leave. You're due that."

She sucked at her lips. "No, sir. My crew can speak for themselves. But I'll stay by *Lucy*."

"Same, sir," Deirdre said, and there was a like murmur from Neill.

"They owe us," she said. "They promised us hazard rate for what we're hauling, and I'm going to Mallory to collect it."

The Reilly nodded. Maybe he approved. She took it for dismissal, collected her crew.

"You can use *Dublin* facilities," the Old Man said. "During dock. We'll help you with any sorting out you need to do."

She looked back. "Courtesy or on charge?"

"Courtesy," the Old Man said. "No charge on it."

She walked out, officer of a small ship, a poor relation come to call. Dubliners lined the corridor, stared at her and her companions, and there was something different. She did not bother to reason what it was, or why cousins stared at them without speaking, with that bewilderment in their eyes. She was only tired, with more on her mind than gave her time for politeness.

18

Dublin was in port: he had heard that much, when they took Curran out and left him behind, among the station wounded. He lay and thought about that, putting constructions together in his mind, none of which made particular sense, only that somewhere, as usual lately, he had been conned.

So there was a reason Dublin had handed out a paper half million; and Norway had landed on the case of a petty skimmer with customs problems. He had pursued his fate till it caught him, that was what.

Allison. All of Lucy's crew was safe. They had told him that too, and he was glad, whatever else had happened. He had no personal feeling about it—or did, but he had no real expectation that Allison would come down into the depths of Norway to see him. He made a fantasy of such a meeting; but she failed to come, and that fit with reality, so he enjoyed the fantasy and finally stopped hoping.

He was, before they took out the station casualties, a kind of hero—at least to the few men next to him, who had gotten him confused with the captains of ships like Dublin and Finity's End and, he had heard, even the Union ship Liberty, who had done the liberating of their station. Mostly Norway. Mostly the tough, seasoned troops of the Alliance carrier had invaded the halls and routed out what pockets of Mazianni remained holding stationer hostages. The same troops had found him holding Curran, trying to keep him from bleeding to death, which was how he had spent the battle for Venture Station, crouched down in a small spot and confused about who was fighting whom. The gratitude embarrassed him, but it was better than admitting what he really was, and fighting a silent war across the space between cots, so he took it with appropriate modesty.

It was someone to talk to, until they moved the stationers out.

"When do I get out?" he asked, hoping that he was going to.

"Tomorrow," the medic promised him, whether or not that came from official sources.

He was not in the habit of believing official promises, and he was trying to sleep the next morning after breakfast when the medic came to ask him if he could walk out or if he had to have a litter.

"Walk," he decided.

"Got friends waiting for you."

"Crew?"

"So I understand."

He took the packet the medic tossed down, his own shaving kit. A change of clothes. So they had come. He was heartened in spite of himself, reckoned that somehow it had turned up convenient in *Dublin*'s books.

It got him out of *Norway*. That much. He shaved with the medic's help—no easy trick with one arm immobilized. Got dressed.—"Here," the medic said, stuffing a paper into his pocket. "That's the course of treatment. You follow it. Hear me?"

He nodded, only half interested. A trooper showed up on call to take him out. "Thanks," he told the medic, who accepted that with a dour attention; and he left with the trooper. "Got to walk slow," he told the woman, who adjusted her pace to suit.

It was not a far walk—not as far as it might have been on something *Norway*'s size. He came down the lift and out the lock, taking it as slowly as reasonable, only half light-headed.

And they were there, Allison, Deirdre, Neill; and Curran, at the foot of the ramp. He went down and met offered hands, took Curran's. "You all right?" he asked Curran.

"Right enough," Curran said, embraced him carefully with a hand on his sound shoulder. Looked at him with that kind of gratitude the stationer had had, which he took in the same understanding.

"Allison," he said then, and took *her* hand—a forlorn pain went through him, a flicker of the dark eyes. "Well, you did it right, Reilly, top to bottom. Must have."

"I should have come after you," she said. "I didn't know you were on the dock."

"Then how could you? No way. It worked, didn't it?"

"Got us all in one piece."

"I'm usually right." He touched Deirdre's arm and took Neill's hand, looked back at Allison and saw a trooper beckon.

"Captain's waiting," the trooper said, waved a hand toward the dockside offices.

"Mallory," Allison said.

He nodded. His heart had turned over. He started that way—at least it was not far across the dock; the same office, the place of recent memory. He felt numb in the cold, and no little disoriented.

"*Dublin's* in on the conference," Allison said. "The Old Man; our legal counsel—you've got that behind you."

"Good to know," he said.

"You don't believe it."

"Of course I believe it. You say so."

She gave him one of those looks as they went into the office, into a gathering thick with military in blue and merchanters in silver and white.

Repeat scene: only it was Mallory behind the desk, and Talley close by her . . . one of the breed exchanged for another.

"Captain," she said, a courteous nod.

He paid her one in return. He looked further about him, noted the patches: *Dublin's* shamrock on the silver, and on the white, the arrogant black sphere of *Finity's End*, a Name so old they had no insignia at all: and rejuv-silvered hair other than Mallory's, a gathering of senior officers in which one Sandor Kreja would have been a small interest— give or take a bogus cargo and a half a million credits.

"Wanted to straighten a matter out with you," she said. "—Need a chair, Captain?"

"No." An automatic no, half-regretted; but no one else was seated but Mallory . . . he refused to be the center of things along with her; but he was: he reckoned that.

"Any time you change your mind," she said, "feel free.

It's really not fair to call you in like this, but *Norway*'s prone to sudden departures. And I'm sure others don't want to log too much dock time.—Are you sure about the chair, Captain?"

He nodded. A small trickle of sweat started down the side of his face. Small talk was not Mallory's style. He disliked it, them, this whole gathering.

"You played it straight," she said. "I rather hoped you might, Captain. But I was a little surprised by it."

"You were a little *late*." He recovered his sense of balance, pulse rate getting up again. "You took our arrival rate. You cut it pretty long on our side."

She shrugged, passing off the wounds, the deaths on station. "You bettered your rate by a few hours . . . didn't you?"

He thought back then, through the fog of realtime—the haste they had used through the second jump, Allison in command and mutiny on the bridge. The anger went out of him. "Maybe we did," he said.

"We were on time, absolutely.—But you managed well enough.—Tell me . . . did you tell them where to find me?"

"I reckoned you meant me to. You don't set much store by heroes, do you?"

Mallory laughed. It surprised him, that quick, cold humor. "Land on your feet, do you? No, I didn't expect it."

"So I spilled all I knew and invented some. But I'll trust you're going to stand by our agreement."

"On what, Captain?"

"Hazard rate. On military cargo."

She thought a moment, wondering, he thought.

"I didn't breach the seals," he said, "but they did. And they knew I was a plant. That wasn't comfortable."

"No, I daresay not." She turned over some papers on her desk. "Vouchers for the pay you're due. No dock charge at Venture, under the circumstances. Let's treat it as lifesupport freight."

Mallory had, he thought, a certain sense of humor. He was going to get out of this. He was insanely tempted to like Mallory, in sheer gratitude. "Captain," he said. *Thanks* stuck in his throat.

"That's an interesting rig, your ship." She failed to let go of the papers and he let go of them in a sudden chill, cursing his momentary trust. "Everything under lock—

papers of clouded origin—backing from one of Union's major Names. You know there was a time, Captain, I wondered about *Dublin* itself . . . keeping your company."

"We don't take that," a *Dublin* officer said.

"Oh, I'm assured otherwise. Our allies from across the Line vouch for you. But you have odd associates.—Tell me, Captain Reilly—what motive to lend to a marginer . . . on that scale?"

"Private business."

"I don't doubt." She offered the papers a second time. Sandor took them, his fingers gone cold. He wanted to sit down. The room proved hot/cold and confused with sound. "Your papers, Captain—are altered. Do you know that?"

He blinked . . . felt the edge of the desk with his fingertips, tried to summon up his wits. "That's not so."

"And you run gold under the plates."

"Private store. My own property. I expect it to be there when I board."

Mallory considered him slowly. "Of course it is."

"If you ran that thorough a search on Pell—"

"We wondered."

"That's under *Dublin* finance," Allison said from behind him. "The papers say that too. We're good for any debts."

He looked around slowly at the Dubliners—at Curran's sweating pale face, and Allison's flushed one, Deirdre and Neill unfocused behind them. The rest of the room blurred. They had it, he reckoned. The keys and the excuse. He made a small shrug and looked around again at Mallory. "That's the way the papers are set up."

"I know that too. As long as *Dublin* stands good for it."

"No question," Reilly said.

He tucked the voucher into his pocket, finding about all the strength he had gathered deserting him. He could make it back to *Lucy,* he reckoned, if he got that far. He wanted that, just to get home, however long it lasted.

"You want to let me see the aforesaid papers, Captain?"

He felt in his pocket, of the jacket draped about his shoulder on the left, fumbled the packet out and gave it into Mallory's hands.

"They *are* faked," she said, riffling through them. "Pell caught that. Paper analysis didn't match. Good job, though. They're going to go over to disc on this kind of thing: it's going to put a lot of paper-traders out of business. Some merchanters howl at the prospect; but then some have reason, don't they? You really ought to get that title straightened up."

She offered them back. He took them, blind to anything else.

"That ought to be all," she said. "*Dublin* vouches for you. And Union, to be sure, vouches for *Dublin*. So we don't ask any more questions."

"Can I go?"

She nodded, dark eyes full of surmises. He kept his face neutral, turned about and walked out, in the company of Allison and her crew, unasked. Allison put herself in front of him and he stopped outside, dizzy and none too steady on his feet. "Get it clear," she said. "*Dublin*'s with us. They won't *do* anything. You can clear the Name up, go by your own, you understand that? You can get the papers cleared."

"Maybe I don't want to."

"For what?—Who is it that recorded the comp messages? It's you he talks to, isn't it? Who was he?"

He looked at the decking, across the dock, at the scant foot traffic, at the overhead where lonely lights gave the dock what illumination it had.

"You want to talk about it?" Curran asked.

"Not particularly."

"Brother?" Allison asked.

He shrugged. "Might have been."

"He set it up," Allison said, "for somebody who really didn't know how to run a ship. To teach everything there was. It must have taken him a long time to do that. I figure he must have thought a lot about your being able to take care of yourself."

"None of your business."

"We're not welcome there, are we?"

He thought a moment about that one. "You coming back?" he asked, looking at her. "Or do they send me a new set of Dubliners for the run back?"

"We're coming back," she said. "You know we know how to work comp. Do everything. We're pretty good."

It was about the humblest he was likely to get out of Allison Reilly, and it set him off his balance again. "I know you're pretty good," he said, shrugged it off. Looked up, then, at her and the others, one face and the other.

"Excuse me," he said, and walked back into the office and others' business. Aides moved: rifles swung fractionally in the hands of guards. Mallory's face had an uncommon degree of wariness. "It's Kreja," he said, feeling the presence of Allison and the others close at his back. He took his papers from his pocket, another tiny movement of the rifles which had not quite given up their focus. "*Le Cygne* and Kreja. Maybe I ought to get the papers straightened out."

Mallory looked up at him curiously. "*Is* it? And how do you come by that Name? It's a long time out of circulation."

He wondered in that moment—decided in the negative. Mallory's puzzlement seemed for once other than a mockery. "I was born with it," he said. "I'd like it back."

Mallory settled back in her chair, a hand on her desk. "Not a difficult matter. Pan-Paris, was it? That was a time ago."

Breath failed him. "Would you know what happened?"

"I *heard* what happened."

He believed that. Mallory was trustable—in some degree. He believed that much.

"Give me the papers," she said. And when he laid them on the desk she simply took them and wrote in longhand. "*Le Cygne*. Name of owner?"

"Sandor Kreja."

The pen flourished and stopped. She handed the papers back. The corrections were there. *S. Mallory* was written below: *amended by her authority.*

"Kreja."

A hand was offered him from his right. One of the Reillys—*the* Reilly: he had heard him answer. He took the hand, suffered the friendly pressure, escaped then past the door in his own company.

"That's straight," he said. He pocketed the papers, along with the voucher, walked a fragile course toward *Lucy/Le Cygne*'s dock, with his Dubliners about him. "Going to have to go out on the hull when we get time. Do a name change."

"Not much chance of getting cargo here," Allison said. "But hazard rate ought to cover it both ways."

"Game for another run?"

"They're keeping military watch on the whole line for the time being. So the rumor runs."

"Nice to pick up rumors. I'm not sure I believe all of them."

"I figure they'll hold by this one."

They reached the access. It was about the limit of his strength and Curran's, who was out of breath as he was going up the ramp—a young Dubliner plastered himself against the wall of the lock as they came in with a quick "Sir—Ma'am" and Sandor gave the boy a dazed and misgiving stare as his own Dubliners pulled him past. "I didn't clear any boarders," he said, finding more of them by the lift. "Hang it, Reilly—"

"Borrowed help," Allison said. The corridor was clean. The inside of the lift car was clean, spit and polish. "Young Dubliners wanted some exercise."

The lift let them out in the lounge/bridge area. Scrubbed decks, polished panels, every smudge and smear and tarnish cleared away. It looked new again, except for the tape patches on the upholstery. "You cleaning her up to take possession?" he asked outright.

"No," Allison said.

"Can't touch anything without fingerprinting it."

"That's fine. It's old habits."

He looked back at them standing there, reckoned how the place would feel without them. Nodded then. "Looks like she used to," he admitted, and turned back and walked onto the bridge.

She went out, *Le Cygne* did, with empty holds, moving lightly as she could in that condition.

Comp talked to them, commending them that they had got it right. *"Jump coming up, Sandy. Find your referent."*

"Got it," Allison said from number two post, talking back to comp and to him, and the numbers came up on the screen.

The checks came in from the others, routine matters.

They headed for Pell, for station cargo this time, and reckoned *Dublin* would pass them on the way. There was a bet on, inside *Le Cygne*, about elapsed-time and drinks when they got there. He reckoned to win it, knowing his ship.

But it was all one account, anyway.

40,000 In Gehenna

I

Departure

i

T-190 hours
Communication, Union Ministry of Defense,
to *US Venture*
in dock at Cyteen Station

ORIG: CYTHQ/MINDEF/CODE111A/USVENTURE
ATTN: Mary Engles, capt. US VENTURE
Accept coded packet; navigation instructions contained herein. US CAPABLE and US SWIFT will accompany and convoy. Mission code: WISE. Citizens will board on noncitizen manifest, identifiable by lack of tattoo number. Sort from noncitizens on boarding and assign aboard VENTURE. Tally will be 452 including all uniformed military personnel and dependents. Treat with due courtesy. AZI class personnel will be billeted in special hold preparation, 23000 aboard US VENTURE, remainder apportioned to CAPABLE and SWIFT. Due to sensitive nature of first boardings, urge rapid processing up to number 1500; delays beyond that point will not expose civilian personnel to discomfort and/or breach of cover. No station personnel are to be permitted within operations area once loading has begun. Security will be posted by HQ. Should an emergency arise, call code WISE22. All libertied crew must be recalled before D–0500 to assure smooth function-

ing of boarding procedures. Mission officer Col. James
A. Conn will present credentials and further orders regarding disposition of citizen and noncitizen personnel. Official cover has the convoy routed to mining
construction at Endeavor: use this in all inship communications.

ii

T-190 hours
Communication: Cyteen HQ, Defense Ministry
to *US Venture*
docked at Cyteen Station

ORIG:CYTHQ/MINDEF/CODE111A/COLBURAD/CONN/J.
PROJ287:
Military Personnel:
Col. James A. Conn, governor general
Capt. Ada P. Beaumont, lt. governor
Maj. Peter T. Gallin, personnel
M/Sgt. Ilya V. Burdette, Corps of Engineers
   Cpl. Antonia M. Cole
   Spec. Martin H. Andresson
   Spec. Emilie Kontrin
   Spec. Danton X. Norris
M/Sgt. Danielle L. Emberton, tactical op.
   Spec. Lewiston W. Rogers
   Spec. Hamil N. Masu
   Spec. Grigori·R. Tamilin
M/Sgt. Pavlos D. M. Bilas, maintenance
   Spec. Dorothy T. Kyle
   Spec. Egan I. Innis
   Spec. Lucas M. White
   Spec. Eron 678-4578 Miles
   Spec. Upton R. Patrick
   Spec. Gene T. Troyes
   Spec. Tyler W. Hammett
   Spec. Kelley N. Matsuo
   Spec. Belle M. Rider
   Spec. Vela K. James
   Spec. Matthew R. Mayes

Spec. Adrian C. Potts
Spec. Vasily C. Orlov
Spec. Rinata W. Quarry
Spec. Kito A. M. Kabir
Spec. Sita Chandrus
M/Sgt. Dinah L. Sigury, communications
Spec. Yung Kim
Spec. Lee P. de Witt
M/Sgt. Thomas W. Oliver, quartermaster
Cpl. Nina N. Ferry
Pfc. Hayes Brandon
Lt. Romy T. Jones, special forces
Sgt. Jan Vandermeer
Spec. Kathryn S. Flanahan
Spec. Charles M. Ogden
M/Sgt. Zell T. Parham, security
Cpl. Quintan R. Witten
Capt. Jessica N. Sedgewick, confessor-advocate
Capt. Bethan M. Dean, surgeon
Capt. Robert T. Hamil, surgeon
Lt. Regan T. Chiles, computer services

Civilian Personnel: list to follow:

Secretarial personnel: 12
Medical/surgical: 1
Medical/paramedic: 7
Mechanical maintenance: 20
Distribution and warehousing: 20
Security: 12
Computer service: 4
Computer maintenance: 2
Librarian: 1
Agricultural specialists: 10
Geologists: 5
Meteorologist: 1
Biologists: 6
Education: 5
Cartographer: 1
Management supervisors: 4
Biocycle engineers: 4
Construction personnel: 150

Food preparation specialists: 6
Industrial specialists: 15
Mining engineers: 2
Energy systems supervisors: 8
　　TOTAL MILITARY 45
　　TOTAL CIVILIAN SUPERVISORY 296
TOTAL CITIZEN STAFF 341; TOTAL NONASSIGNED
DEPENDENTS: 11; TOTAL ALL CITIZENS: 452
　　ADDITIONAL NONCITIZEN PERSONNEL:
　　list to follow:
　　"A" class: 2890
　　"B" class: 12389
　　"M" class: 4566
　　"P" class: 20788
　　"V" class: 1278
TOTAL ALL NONCITIZENS: 41911
TOTAL ALL MISSION: 42363
　　Male/female ratio approx. 55%/45%
DEPENDENTS LIST WILL FOLLOW
NONCITIZEN LIST WILL APPEAR ON MANIFEST

iii

T-56 hours
On Cyteen Dock, restricted area

The place was large and cold and somehow the instructions lost themselves in so strange a place. Jin 458-9998 walked where he was told, feeling the chill in his body and most especially on his skull where they had shaved off all his hair. 9998s were darkhaired and handsome and they were A's, important in the order of things; but the orderliness in his world had been upset. They had taken him into the white building on the farm and given him deepteach that told him the farm was no longer important, that he would be given a new and great purpose when he got where he was going, and that there would be other tapes to tell him so, very soon.

"Yes," he had said, because that was the appropriate acknowledgement, and the change had not vastly disturbed him at the outset. But then they had taken him, still muzzy with trank, into the med wing, which he never liked, because nothing good ever happened there, and they had taken his clothes and had him lie down on a table, after which they had shaved all the hair off him, every bit but his eyelashes, and shot him full of so many things that they used all of one arm and started on the other. It hurt, but he was used to that. He was only dismayed when he saw himself in the glass going out, and failed to recognize himself—a destruction of all his vanity.

"How do you feel about this?" the supervisor had asked him, the standard question at a change; and he searched his heart as he was supposed to do and came up with a word that covered it.

"Erased."

"Why do you feel that way?"

"I look different."

"Is that all?"

He thought about it a moment. "I'm leaving the farm."

"What's worst?"

"My looks."

"It's to keep you clean for a while. While you're being shipped. Everyone has it done. They won't laugh at you. They won't notice you. It'll grow back in a few weeks and you'll have a new assignment. Tapes will explain it to you. It's supposed to be very good. They're taking only very expensive contracts like yours."

That had cheered him considerably. He stopped minding the shaving and the paperthin white coveralls and the loss of himself. He stood up then and started to leave.

"Goodbye, Jin," the supervisor said, and a little panic hit him at the thought that he was never again going to see this man who solved all his problems.

"Will someone there help me?" he asked.

"Of course there'll be someone. Do you want to shake hands, Jin? I think they're going to pass you a lot higher than you are here. But you have to be patient and take things as they come."

He came back, feeling strange about taking a born-man's hand, and very proud in that moment. "I'll miss you," he said.

"Yes. But the tapes will make you happy."

He nodded. That was so. He looked forward to it, because he was not thoroughly happy at the moment, and his ears were cold and his body felt strangely smooth and naked under the cloth. He let go the supervisor's hand and walked out, where another attendant took him in tow and led him to a building where others as shaven as himself were waiting. The sight hit him with deep shock—that he knew some of them, and had trouble recognizing them at all; and they looked at him the same way. There were four other 9998s and they all looked alike, all like him; and there were three 687s and seven of the 5567s—and all the small traits by which they knew each other as individuals were obliterated. Panic settled into him afresh.

"Which are you?" one of his own twins asked.

"I'm Jin," he said softly. "Are we all going to the same place?"

"Jin?" A female voice. "Jin—" It was one of the 687s; it was Pia, making room for him on the bench which ran round the room, among the others. He came and sat down with her, grateful, because Pia was a friend and he wanted something familiar to cling to. Her face was vastly changed. Pia's hair was dark as his own and it was all gone, her eyes staring out vast and dark from a lightly freckled face. They wound their fingers together for comfort in the space between them. He looked down. The hands were still like Pia's; the manners were still hers.

But she was in back of him in the line somewhere, and they had mixed in a lot of strange azi from elsewhere, types he had never seen before, and the place was cold and miserable. The line stopped and he unfocused his eyes, waiting, which was the best way to pass the time, thinking on pleasanter images such as the tapes gave him when he earned tapetime above his limit. But he could not conjure the same intensity as the tape, and it never quite overcame the cold. No one spoke; it was not a time for speaking, while they were being transferred. They had instructions to listen for. No one moved, because no one wanted to get lost, or to merit bad tape, which seemed very easy to earn in a situation like this, one for which no tape had ever prepared them.

They had ridden a ship up to this place. He had seen ships fly but had never imagined the sensation. His heart had gone double beats during the flight, and he had been terrified for a while, until he had gotten used to the sensation. But no sooner had he done that than they had entered a new state with other and worse sensations one atop the other. This time someone had thought to speak to them and to assure them it was safe.

Then they had knocked into something and they were advised they were at dock, that they were getting out on Cyteen Station, which was a star at night in the skies of Cyteen, and which he had watched move on summer nights. The news confused him, and of a sudden the door opened and blinded them with light. Some cried out: that was how disturbed they were. And they walked out when they were told, not into the shining heart of a star, but into a very large and very cold place, and were herded this way and that and bunked in a cold barn of a place where the floors all curved up. People walked askew and things tilted without falling over. He tried not to look; he became afraid when he looked at things like that, which suggested that even solid realities could be revised like tape. He wanted his fields back again, all golden in the sun, and the warmth on his back, and the coolth of water after work, and swimming in the brook when they had gotten too hot in summers.

But he could read and write, and presently as they were led along he read things like CYTEEN STATION and DANGER HIGH VOLTAGE and AUTHORIZED PERSONNEL ONLY; and A MAIN and A 2 and CUSTOMS and DETENTION. None of it was friendly, and least of all did he like the word detention, which led to bad tape. Others could read too, and no one said anything; but he guessed that everyone who could read had a stomach knotted up and a heart thudding up into the throat the same as his.

"This way," a man with a supervisor's green armband said, opening a door for their line. "You'll get tape here, by units of fifty. Count off as you go in."

Jin counted. He was 1-14, and a born-man passed him a chit that said so. He took his chit in hand and filed in behind the first.

It was more med. He followed his file into the white-walled and antiseptic enclosure and his heart, which had settled a moment, started again into its now perpetual state of terror. "You're afraid," they told him when they checked his pulse. "Don't be afraid."

"Yes," he agreed, trying, but he was cold with his coveralls down to his waist and he jerked when one of the meds took his arm and shot something into it.

"That's trank," the woman said. "Cubicle 14 down the hall. You'll have time enough to hook up. Push the button if you have trouble."

"Thank you," he said and put his clothes back to rights, and walked where she aimed him. He went in and sat down on the couch, which was cold tufted plastic, not like the comfortable bed at home. He attached the leads, already feeling his pulse rate slowing and a lethargy settling into his thinking, so that if someone had come into the cubicle that moment and told him they might put him down, the news would have fallen on him very slowly. He was only afraid now of bad tape; or unfamiliar tape; or tape which might change what he was and make him forget the farm.

Then the warning beep sounded and he lay back on the couch, because the deepteach was about to cycle in, and he had just that time to settle or fall limp and hurt himself.

It hit, and he opened his mouth in panic, but it was too late to scream.

CODE AX, it gave him, and then a series of sounds; and wiped all the careful construction of his values and cast doubt on all his memories.

"Be calm," it told him as the spasms eased. "All A class find this procedure disorienting. Your fine mind and intelligence make this a little more difficult. Please cooperate. This is a necessary procedure. Your value is being increased. You are being prepared for a duty so vastly important that it will have to be explained in a series of tapes. Your contract has been appropriated by the state. You will be in transit on a ship and nothing will divert you from your purpose, which is a secret you will keep.

"When you step out in a new world you will be beside a river near a sea. You will work at the orders of bornmen. You will be happy. When you have made a place to live you will make fields and follow other orders the tapes will give you. You are very fortunate. The state which holds your contract is very happy with you. We have every confidence in you. You can be very proud to be selected for this undertaking.

"Your bodies are very important. They will be under unusual stress. This tape will instruct you in precautionary exercise. Your minds will be important where you are going. You will be given instruction in that regard in this session. Please relax. You will be very valuable when we are done.

"You will be more and more like a born-man. The state which owns your contract is very pleased with you. This is why you were selected. Your genetic material is very important. You are to create born-men. This is only one of your many purposes. Is there a female you have formed a close friendship with? . . . Pia 86-687, thank you, yes, I am checking . . . Yes, this individual has been selected. This is an approved mating. You will both be very happy . . . Yes or no, respond at the tone: do you feel comfortable with this? A technician is standing by . . . thank you, Jin 458, your self-confidence is a mark of your excellent background. You should feel very proud of this. . . ."

iv

T-48 hours
Cyteen Dock

It was all restricted area, and the dock crews were some of them security people from the station offices—in case. Col. James Conn walked the dock with an eye to the ordinary foot traffic beyond. Alliance merchanters were common here in Union's chief port, under the treaty that ceded them trade rights across the Line; and no one was deceived. There were spies among them, watching every movement Union made, interested in everything. It was a mutual and constant activity, on both sides of the Line. They moved freely up the curving horizon, in small groups, keeping to the blue-line pathways through the military docks, looking without seeming to look, and no one stopped them. The holes in the net were all purposeful, and the right information had been leaked by all the appropriate sources to let the Alliance folk think they knew what was going on. This was not Conn's department, but he knew that it was done.

Gantries lined the dock, one idle, three supporting ships' lines. *US Swift* was coming in later in the watch; *Capable* would follow. There were more ships, but those were normal military traffic, small. Crews took their liberties, knowing nothing specific yet, hand-picked crews, so what passed in bars was worthless, excepting a few, who spread the desired rumors. That was Security's doing, their design. One could surmise shells within shells of falsity and deception; a man could trust nothing if he fell into Security's way of thinking.

A line officer could get uneasy in such business. Conn *had* gotten uneasy, in times less certain, but he saw round the perimeters of this and knew its limits, that this was not a hot one. There were civs in this one, and civs had rights; and those civs gave him reassurance in the packet he carried, unheralded by security, in his inside pocket.

He reached *Venture's* dock, number one white berth, and climbed the access ramp into the tube itself. That was where the first real security appeared, in the form of two armed and armored troopers who barred his way to the inner lock—but so would they on any warship.

"REDEX," he said, "Conn, Col. James A."

"Sir." The troopers clattered rifles to their armored sides. "Board, sir, thank you."

They were *Venture* personnel. Spacer command, not of his own service. He walked through the hatch and into the receiving bay, to *Venture's* duty desk. The officer on duty stopped reading comp printout in a hurry when he looked up and saw brass. "Sir."

Conn took his id from his pocket and slid it into the receiver.

"Id positive," the duty officer said. And into the com: "Tyson: Col. James Conn to see the captain."

That was as arranged—no formalities, no fanfare. He was a passenger on this ship, separate, no cooperative command. Conn collected the aide and walked with him up to the lift, small-talked with him on the way, which was his manner . . . none of the spit and polish of the spacegoing Elite Guard. Special operations was his own branch of the service, and that of the highest officers in his immediate staff. And after thirty years service, with a little arthritis that got past the pills—rejuv delayed just a shade too long—he had less spit and polish about him than he had started with.

A new start. They had persuaded him with that. Jean was gone; and the mission had fallen into his lap. A change seemed good, at this stage in life. Maybe it was that for Beaumont, for Gallin, for some of the others he knew were going. There might be a separate answer for the science people, who had their own curious ambitions, and some of whom were married to each other; or were sibs; or friends. But those of them who came out of the old service—those of them carrying some years—out of that number, only Ada Beaumont was taking advantage of the Dependents allowance and taking a husband along in a mission slot. The rest of them, the nine of them who had seen the war face-on, came solo like the freshfaced youths. The years had stripped them back to that. It was a new life out there, a new chance. So they went.

The lift opened, let him and the aide out on the main level. He walked into the captain's office and the captain rose from her desk and met him with an offered hand. A woman of his own years. He felt comfortable with her. He surprised himself in that; generally he was ill at ease with spacers, let alone the black-uniformed Elite like Mary Engles. But she offered a stout and calloused hand and used a slang out of the war, so that he knew she had dealt with the ground services before. She sent the aide out, poured them both stiff drinks and sat down again. He drew a much easier breath.

"You saw service in the '80, did you?" he asked.

"Ran transport for a lot of you; but old *Reliance* saw her better days, and they stripped her down."

"*Reliance.* She came in on Fargone."

"That she did."

"I left some good friends there."

She nodded slowly. "Lost a few too."

"Hang, it's a better run this time, isn't it?"

"Has to be," she said. "Your boarding's set up. You have orders for me?"

He opened his jacket and took out the envelope, passed

it to her. "That's the total list. I'll keep out of your way during transit. I'll instruct my command to do the same."

Another nod. "I always liked special op. Easy passengers. You just keep the science lads and the dependents out of the way of my crew and I'll think kindly on you forever."

Conn grinned and lifted the glass. "Easy done."

"Huh, easy. The last such lot I dropped was glad to get off alive."

"What last lot? You do this weekly?"

"Ah." Engles sipped at her glass and arched a brow. "You'll not be telling me I'm to brief you on that."

"No. I know what the program is. And the ship knows, does she?"

"We have to. What we're doing, if not where. We're the transport. We'll be seeing you more than once, won't we? Keep us happy."

"By then," Conn said, "any other set of faces is going to come welcome."

Engles gave a one-sided smile. "I expect it will. I've run a few of these assignments. Always like to see the special op heading it up. Far less trouble that way."

"Ever had any trouble?"

"Oh, *we* haven't."

He lifted a brow and drained the glass. There were photofaxes on the office walls, ships and faces, some of the photos scarred and scratched. Faces and uniforms. He had a gallery like that in his own duffle. The desk had a series of pictures of a young man, battered and murky. He was not about to ask. The photos never showed him older. He thought of Jean, with a kind of grayness inside . . . had known a moment of panic, the realization of his parting from Cyteen, boarding another ship, leaving the places Jean had known, going somewhere her memory did not even exist. And all he took was the pictures. Engles offered him a half glass more and he took it.

"You need any special help in boarding?" Engles asked.

"No. Just so someone gets my duffle on. The rest is coming in freight."

"We'll take your officers aboard at their leisure. Science and support personnel, when they arrive, are allotted a lounge to themselves, and they'll kindly use it."

"They will."

"A lot smoother that way. They don't mix well, my people and civs."

"Understood."

"But you have to make it mix, don't you? I sure don't envy you the job."

"New world," he said, a shrug. The liquor made him numb. He felt disconnected, and at once in a familiar place, a ship like a dozen other ships, a moment lived and relived. But no Jean. That was different. "It works because it has to work, that's all. They need each other. That's how it all fits together."

Engles pressed a button on the console. "We'll get your cabin set up. Anything you need, you let me know."

The aide came back. "The colonel wants his cabin," Engles said quietly.

"Thanks," Conn said, took the hand offered a second time, followed the black-uniformed spacer out into the corridors, blinking in the warmth of the liquor.

The scars were there . . . the aide was too young to know; scars predating the clean, the modern corridors. The rebellion at Fargone; the war—the tunnels and the deep digs. . . .

Jean had been with him then. But twenty years the peace had held, uneasy detente between Union and the merchanter Alliance. Peace was profitable, because neither side had anything to gain in confrontation . . . yet. There was a border. Alliance built warships the Accord of Pell forbade; Union built merchant ships the Accord limited to farside space . . . cargo ships that could dump their loads and move; warships that could clamp on frames and haul: the designs were oddly similar, tokening a new age in the Between, with echoes of the old. Push would come to shove again; he believed it; Engles likely did.

And the Council must believe it . . . making moves like this, establishing supply, the longterm advantage of bases on worlds, which were unstrikable under the civilized accords; most of all assuring an abundance of worldbred troops who could not retreat. Union seeded worlds, strategically placed or otherwise . . . every site which could marginally support human life. . . . an entrenched, immovable expansion which would bottle Alliance in close to their own center and thoroughly infiltrate any territory Alliance might gain in war or negotiations.

The building of carrier ships like *Venture* was part of it.

And the other part rested in the hands of special op, and employees of the government who, for various reasons, volunteered.

v

T-20 hours
Cyteen dock

The lines fell into order, white-clad, shaven headed, a slow procession across the dock, and no one paid it more than the curiosity the event was due—the loading of cloned-man workers onto transports, which always shocked Alliance citizens and sent a shiver up the staunchest of Union backbones. It was an aspect of life most citizens never had to see, the reminder of the lab-born ancestry of many of them—the labor pool on which worlds were built. Azi workers served in citizen homes, and worked on farms and took jobs others found undesirable—quiet and cheerful workers in the main.

But these were quiet indeed, and the lines were unnaturally patient, and the shaved heads and faces and the white sameness was grim and without illusion.

And to stand in that line—himself shaven and blank except for the small blue triangle on his right cheek and a number on his hand—Marco Gutierrez felt a constant panic. Keep the eyes unfocussed or fixed, they had said onworld, when they were loaded onto the shuttles. Don't worry. The numbers you're wearing are specially flagged in the comp. The same system that lets the azi all get the right tape will get you no worse than an informational lecture. They'll know who you are.

The azi frightened him—all of them, so silent, so fixed on what they did and where they went. He stared at the whiteclad shoulders in front of him, which by the hips belonged to a woman, but he could not tell for sure from the back. There were sets of these workers, twins and triplets, quads and quints. But of some he had seen only a single example, unique. He had not gotten a wrong tape when they passed through the lab: he had lain down under the machine terrified that they might slip him a wrong one, and he might end by needing psychiatric help—his mind, his mind, that was his life, all the years of study—But it had come out right, and he had only the dimmest impression of what they had fed him—

Unless—the thought occurred to him—that was the same confidence all of them in the lines had, and they were all being deceived and programmed. The imagination that something might have been done to him without his knowledge sent the sweat coursing over a shaved, too-smooth body. He trusted his government. But mistakes were made with the push of a computer key. And sometimes the government had done harsh things in harsh times—and lied—

Eyes blank. He heard noises, the crash of machinery, and the movement of vehicles. He was aware of people on the sidelines staring at them; at him. It was hard not to be human, hard not to turn and look, or to shift the feet or to fret in line or make some small random movement—but the azi did not.

At least some of these close to him must be citizens like him. He had no idea how many. He knew that some of his colleagues were with him, but he had lost track of them, in the shifting of the lines. They were boarding. They went toward the ship; and they moved with incredible slowness.

There had been a time, in that white-tiled room on Cyteen where he and others of his group had last been human—that they had been able to laugh about it; that they made jokes and took it lightly. But that was before they had been taken singly into the next room and shaved, before they had had a number stamped on them and individually gotten the instruction on behavior, before they had fallen into the lines at the shuttleport and been lost.

There was no more humor in it, no more at all. There was terror . . . and humiliation, the violation of privacy, the fear of coercion. All he had to do to back out now was to turn and walk away from the line, which no azi could do; and something was holding him there, a constraint he believed was his own volition, his courage keeping him where he was.

But lately all realities had shifted. And he was no longer certain.

What, he thought as the line inched its way toward the access ramp, in sight now, what if things had gone totally wrong? And what if the people who were to recognize him did not?

But the tape had been harmless; and therefore the computer had the number right.

He trusted. And inched up the ramp step by step, never making a move some azi in front of him had not made. He picked the quietest and the steadiest for his models, in the hope that others behind him were likewise taking their cues from him.

The line entered the dark of the hold, and they approached a desk, one by one; one by one the azi held out their right hands for the inspection of the clerks.

But none of them were pulled out of line, and Gutierrez' heart beat harder and harder.

His own turn came, and he offered his falsely tattooed hand to the recorder, who took it and wrote down the number. The slip went to a comp tech. "Move on," a supervisor said, and Gutierrez moved, less and less in command of his knees. He passed the inner lock in the same shuffling line, and a kind of paralysis had set in, past the time that he thought he should have made a protest—that it was too great a silence to break, that hypnotic oneness that drew him into step and kept him there.

"789-5678?" a male voice asked him. He looked that direction; one could look, when a number was called. A guard beckoned him. He came; and they called another number and another, so that now there was a group of them being called out of the lines and let into a side corridor.

"You'll just come this way," the guard said. "We've got your id all set up; you're all right and your gear is boarded. They'll get you all, don't worry."

Gutierrez followed the black-uniformed guard, through that corridor and along the curving halls which became difficult to walk without leaning, a turn aft now, and another turn which brought them to a lift. The guard opened the door for them, and motioned them into the car.

"Push 3R," the guard said, while the lift filled with more and more of them until some had to wait outside. "3R's your section; someone's waiting for you topside."

Gutierrez pushed the buttons and the door closed. The car shot up against the direction of G and let them out again, where a second guard waited with a clipboard. "Room R12," the guard said, and slapped a keycard into his hand. "Name?"

"Gutierrez." It was his again, name and not number. They called off another man to room with him: Hill, the name was. "Next," the guard said, and the lift was already headed down again, with name after name called off and all of them headed down the corridor.

In silence. Deathly silence. "We're clear," Gutierrez said suddenly, and turned and looked at the rest of them, at shaved, hollow faces, male and female, hairless, browless, at eyes which had gone from blankness to bleak fatigue. "We're clear, hear it?"

There were some braver than the others—a female face startlingly naked without brows, a too-thin mouth that twisted into a struggling grin; a darkskinned man who looked less naked, who shouted out a cheer that shocked the silence. Another reached up and rubbed the tattoo on his cheek; but that would have to wear off, as the hair would have to grow back. "You're Hill?" Gutierrez asked of his assigned roommate. "What field?"

The thin, older man blinked, wiped a hand over his shaved skull. "Ag specialist."

"I'm biology," Gutierrez said. "Not a bad mix."

Others talked, a sudden swelling of voices; and someone swore, which was what Gutierrez wanted to do, to break the rest of the restraints, to vent what had been boiling up for three long days. But the words refused to come out, and he walked on with Hill—26, 24, the whole string down past the crosscorridor and around the corner: 16, 14, 12 . . . He jammed the keycard in with a hand shaking like palsy, opened the door on an ordinary little cabin with twin bunks and colors, cheerful green and blue *colors*. He stood inside and caught his breath, then sat down on the bed and dropped his head into his hands, even then feeling the tiny prickle of stubble under his fingertips. He felt grotesque.

He remembered every mortifying detail of his progress across the docks; and the lines; and the medics; and the tape labs and the rest of it.

"How old are you?" Hill asked. "You look young."

"Twenty-two." He lifted his head, shivering on the verge of collapse. If it had been a friend with him, he might have, but Hill was holding on the same way, quietly. "You?"

"Thirty-eight. Where from?"

"Cyteen. Where from, yourself?"

"Wyatt's."

"Keep talking. Where'd you study?"

"Wyatt's likewise. What about you? Ever been on a ship before?"

"No." He hypnotized himself with the rhythm of question and answer . . . got himself past the worst of it. His breathing slowed. "What's an ag man doing on a station?"

"Fish. Lots of fish. Got similar plans where we're going."

"I'm exobiology," Gutierrez said. "A whole new world out there. That's what got me."

"A lot of you young ones," Hill said. "Me—I want a world. Any world. The passage was free."

"Hang, we just paid for it."

"I think we did," Hill said.

And then the swelling in his throat caught Gutierrez by surprise and he bowed his head into his hands a second time and sobbed. He fought his breathing back to normal—looked up to find Hill wiping his own eyes, and swallowed the shamed apology he had had ready. "Physiological reaction," he muttered.

"Poor bastards," Hill said, and Gutierrez reckoned what poor bastards Hill had in mind. There were real azi aboard, who went blankly to their berths wherever they might be, down in the holds—who would go on being silent and obedient whatever became of them, because that was what they were taught to be.

Lab specialists would follow them in three years, Gutierrez knew, who would bring equipment with which the new world could make its own azi; and the lab techs would come in expecting the fellowship of the colony science staff. But they would get none from him. Nothing from him. Or from the rest of them—not so easily.

"The board that set this up," Gutierrez said quietly, hoarsely. "They can't have any idea what it's like. It's crazy. They're going to get people crazy like this."

"We're all right," Hill said.

"Yes," he said; but it was an azi's answer, which sent a chill up his back. He clamped his lips on it, got up and walked the few paces the room allowed, because he could now; and it still felt unnatural.

vi

T-12 hours
Aboard *Venture*
docked at Cyteen Station

"Beaumont." Conn looked up from his desk as the permission-to-enter button turned up his second in command. He rose and offered his hand to the special forces captain and her husband. "Ada," he amended, for old times' sake. "Bob. Glad to draw the both of you—" He was always politic with the spouses, civ that Bob Davies was. "Just make it in?"

"Just." Ada Beaumont sighed, settled, and took a seat. Her husband took one by her. "They pulled me from Wyatt's and I had a project finishing up there . . . then it was kiting off to Cyteen on a tight schedule to take the tapes I guess you had. They just shuttled us up, bag and baggage."

"Then you know the score. They put you somewhere decent for quarters?"

"Two cabins down. A full suite: can't complain about that."

"Good." Conn leaned back, shifted his eyes to Bob Davies. "You have a mission slot in Distributions, don't you?"

"Number six."

"That's good. Friendly faces—Lord, I love the sight of you. All those white uniforms. . . ." He looked at the pair of them, recalling earlier days, Cyteen on leave, Jean with him . . . Jean gone now, and the Beaumont-Davies sat here, intact, headed out for a new world. He put on a smile, diplomat, because it hurt, thinking of the time when there had been four of them. And Davies had to survive. Davies, who lived his life on balance books and had no humor. "At least," he said charitably, "faces from home."

"We're getting old," Beaumont said. "They all look so young. About time we all found ourselves a berth that lasts."

"Is that what drew you?"

"Maybe," Beaumont said. Her seamed face settled. "Maybe there's about one more mission left in us, and one world's about our proper size about now. Never had time for kids, Bob and me. The war—You know. So maybe on this one there's something to build instead of blow up. I like to think . . . maybe some kind of posterity. Maybe when they get the birthlabs set up—maybe—no matter what the gene-set is; I mean, we'd take any kid, any they want to farm out. Missed years, Jim."

He nodded somberly. "They give us about a three-year lag on the labs, but when that lab goes in, you're first in line, no question.—Can I do anything for you in settling in? Everything the way it ought to be?"

"Hang, it's great, nice modern ship, a suite to ourselves— I figure I'll take a turn down there and see where they're stacking those poor sods below. Anyone I know down there?"

"Pete Gallin."

"No. Don't know him."

"All strange faces. We're up to our ears in brighteyed youth, a lot of them jumped up to qualify them. . . . a lot of specs out of the state schools and no experience . . . a few good noncoms who came up the hard way. Some statistician, fry him, figured that was the best mix in staff; and we've got the same profile in the civ sector, but not so much so. A lot of those have kin elsewhere, but they know there's no transport back; blind to everything else but their good luck, I suppose. Or crazy. Or maybe some of them don't mind mud and bugs. Freshfaced, the lot of them. You want kids, Beaumont, we've got kids, no question about it. The whole command's full of kids. And we'll lose a few."

A silence. Davies shifted uncomfortably. "We're going to get rejuv out there, aren't we? They said—"

"No question. Got us rejuv and some crates of Cyteen's best whiskey. And soap. Real soap, this time, Ada."

She grinned, a ghost out of the tunnels and the deeps of Fargone, the long, long weeks dug in. "Soap. Fresh air, sea and river to fish—can't ask better, can we?"

"And the neighbors," Davies said. "We've got neighbors."

Conn laughed, short and dry. "The lizards may contest you for the fish, but not much else. Unless you mean Alliance."

Davies' face had settled into its habitual dour concern. "They said there wasn't a likelihood."

"Isn't," Beaumont said.

"They said—"

"Alliance might even know what we're up to," Conn said . . . Davies irritated him: discomfiting the man satisfied him in an obscure way. "I figure they might. But they've got to go on building their ships, haven't they? They've got the notion to set something up with Sol, that's where their eyes are at the moment."

"And if that link-up with Sol does come about—then where are we?"

"Sol couldn't finance a dockside binge. It's all smoke."

"And we're sitting out there—"

"I'll tell you something," Conn said, leaned on his desk, jabbed a finger at them. "If it isn't smokescreen, they swallow our new little colony. But they're all hollow. Alliance is all trade routes, just a bunch of merchanters, no worlds to speak of. They don't care about anything else at the moment . . . and by the time they do, they're pent in. We might be fighting where we're going, give or take a generation—but don't expect any support. That's not the name of what we're doing out there. If they swallow us, they swallow us. And if they swallow too many of us, they'll find they've swallowed something Alliance can't digest. Union's going to be threaded all through them. That's what we're going out there for. That's why the whole colonial push."

Davies looked at his wife. A crease deepened between his eyes.

"Jim isn't only special op," Beaumont said, "he's out of the Praesidium. And it doesn't hurt to know that . . . in closed company. I have—for the past half dozen years. That's why Jim always got transferred to the hot spots. Isn't it, Jim?"

Conn shrugged, vexed—then thinking it was the truth, that there was no more cover, no more of anything that mattered. "Jim's getting to be an old man, that's all. It looked like a good assignment. My reasons are like yours. Just winding down. Finding something to do. Praesidium asked. This is a retirement job. I've got a good staff. That's all I ask."

So they were on their way, he thought when he had packed Beaumont and Davies off, Beaumont to a tour below and Davies to his unpacking and settling in. They were sealed in, irrevocably. *Venture* would use an outbound vector decidedly antiterrene, as if she and her companion ships had a destination on the far side of Union space instead of the outlying border region which was their real object; she had a false course filed at Cyteen Station for the obstinately curious.

So the auxiliary personnel, military and otherwise, found their way aboard among azi workers; and military officers chanced aboard as if they were simply hopping transport, common enough practice.

It was all very smooth. No mission officer took official charge of anything public; it was all *Venture* personnel down there on the docks seeing the azi aboard, and seeing to the lading of boxes labeled for the Endeavor mines.

The clock pulsed away, closer and closer to undock.

II

The Voyage Out

This is a holographic map reproduced in monoplane looking "down" through the galactic arm. Apparent distance is therefore deceptive.

ALLIANCE AND UNION STARS

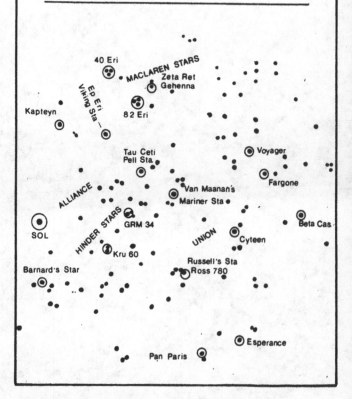

Military Personnel:

Col. James A. Conn, governor general
Capt. Ada P. Beaumont, lt. governor
Maj. Peter T. Gallin, personnel
M/Sgt. Ilya V. Burdette, Corps of Engineers
  Cpl. Antonia M. Cole
  Spec. Martin H. Andresson
  Spec. Emilie Kontrin
  Spec. Danton X. Morris
M/Sgt. Danielle L. Emberton, tactical op.
  Spec. Lewiston W. Rogers
  Spec. Hamil N. Masu
  Spec. Grigori R. Tamilin
M/Sgt. Pavlos D. M. Bilas, maintenance
  Spec. Dorothy T. Kyle
  Spec. Egan I. Innis
  Spec. Lucas M. White
  Spec. Eron 678-4578 Miles
  Spec. Upton R. Patrick
  Spec. Gene T. Troyes
  Spec. Tyler W. Hammett
  Spec. Kelley N. Matsuo
  Spec. Belle M. Rider
  Spec. Vela K. James
  Spec. Matthew R. Mayes
  Spec. Adrian C. Potts

Spec. Vasily C. Orlov
Spec. Rinata W. Quarry
Spec. Kito A. M. Kabir
Spec. Sita Chandrus
M/Sgt. Dinah L. Sigury, communications
Spec. Yung Kim
Spec. Lee P. de Witt
M/Sgt. Thomas W. Oliver, quartermaster
Cpl. Nina N. Ferry
Pfc. Hayes Brandon
Lt. Romy T. Jones, special forces
Sgt. Jan Vandermeer
Spec. Kathryn S. Flanahan
Spec. Charles M. Ogden
M/Sgt. Zell T. Parham, security
Cpl. Quintan R. Witten
Capt. Jessica N. Sedgewick, confessor-advocate
Capt. Bethan M. Dean, surgeon
Capt. Robert T. Hamil, surgeon
Lt. Regan T. Chiles, computer services

Civilian Personnel: to be assigned:

Secretarial personnel: 12
Medical/surgical: 1
Medical/paramedic: 7
Mechanical maintenance: 20
Distribution and warehousing: 20
Robert H. Davies
Security: 12
Computer service: 4
Computer maintenance: 2
Librarian: 1
Agricultural specialists: 10
Harold B. Hill
Geologists: 5
Meterologist: 1
Biologists: 6
Marco X. Gutierrez
Education: 5
Cartographer: 1
Management supervisors: 4

Biocycle engineers: 4
Construction personnel: 150
Food preparation specialists: 6
Industrial specialists: 15
Mining engineers: 2
Energy systems supervisors: 8
  TOTAL MILITARY 45
  TOTAL CIVILIAN SUPERVISORY 296
TOTAL CITIZEN STAFF 341; TOTAL NONASSIGNED DE-
PENDENTS: 111; TOTAL ALL CITIZENS: 452

  ADDITIONAL NONCITIZEN PERSONNEL:
"A" class: 2890
  Jin 458-9998
  Pia 89-687
  "B" class: 12389
  "M" class: 4566
  "P" class: 20788
  "V" class: 1278
TOTAL ALL NONCITIZENS: 41911
TOTAL ALL MISSION: 42363
  Male/female ratio approx. 55%/45%

i

T-00:15:01
Communication: Cyteen Dock HQ

CYTDOCK1/USVENTURE/USCAPABLE/USSWIFT/
STANDBY UNDOCK.
            T-00:2:15
CYTDOCK1/USVENTURE/YOU ARE NUMBER ONE FOR
DEPARTURE.
            T-00:0:49
USVENTURE/CYTDOCK1/SEQUENCE INITIATED/THANK
YOU
STATIONMASTER/HOSPITALITY APPRECIATED/ENDIT.

ii

T00:0:20
Venture; en route

They moved. The stress made itself felt, and in spite of
the tapes which had instructed them how all this would be,
Jin 458 felt the shudder and shift of weight through the
thousands of bodies jammed into the aisles of the bunks—
stacks of bunks which leaned crazily together like watch-
towers, stacks already filled with bodies, azi all crowded
up together and holding onto each other as they had been
told to do. In spite of all the instruction, Jin felt afraid,
deep inside, not letting it out. A sigh went up, one united
breath, when the weight stopped and they had the falling-
sensation again.

"Hold tight," a voice told them over public address, and
they held, a painful clenching of hands on shoulders and
on the frames of the bunks and whatever they could hold
to, so that they would not come drifting loose when the
weight came back again.

And come it did, with a crash and rumble of machinery,
an authoritative settling of feet firmly back to the floor
and of clothes on bodies, a kind of crawling sensation far
from pleasant.

"That's it," the PA told them. "We have G now. You
can let go and find your places. You're berthed by alpha-
betic and numeric sequence. If you can't find your bunk,
report to the door where you came in."

Jin stood still waiting as the press of bodies slowly sorted
itself out, until it became possible to move again, and people who had been jammed into the bunks were coming
down the ladders to find their proper places. He could see
a tag where he was, bunk M 234-6787.

"The center aisle," the PA voice said again, "is M 1
through M 7. Row two spinward is M 8 through N 1. . . ."

Jin listened, shrank aside as azi needed to pass him to
get to their places. So they were bunked by alphabet and
birth-order, not by gene-set. He would not be near his sibs.
It was all very confusing, but they were being told what to

do and it was all, he supposed, moving with considerable organization under the circumstances.

It was hard to hold on with the ship moving as it was and people stumbled into him, thrown by the movement and the floor curve. Everyone hurried, at the pace of the PA voice, which kept throwing instructions at them. He reasoned that if MNO was spinward of the aisle, then J had to be the other direction, and when he had a clear space he went, handing his way along the bunk rails and not letting go, along aisles and past rows until he had come to a K and turned toward the front of the ship. He found himself among J designations, to his relief, and he kept searching, as others did, having figured out the system, passing muddled wanderers who were probably under T class, unable to read.

He located it—refuge, berth J 458-9998 right on the bottom, so that he would not have to climb the ladders which towered up and up atilt in the eerie slantwise way that things were built on the curved floor of the ship. If he sat up on top, he thought, he could look straight into the chasms of other rows sideways to his floor. It was that huge a room and that much curve; and he was glad not to have that view. He sat down at his assigned place, feet over the edge; and all at once another of the Js showed up. This J, another 458 but of gene-set 8974—must come from some other farm, but he could not be sure with the shaving. The man clambered up the ladder over him and the bunk next upstairs gave slightly as his bunkmate climbed in and swung his feet over the edge. Jin sat still, bent over because of the low overhead. He was tired, very glad to sit down, and he felt a great deal safer enclosed by the four uprights and other groundlevel bunks all around him. Another J found the bunk at his head, which was more company; and more Js went up the ladder.

It was all going very fast now, with comforting efficiency: they had managed to do it all right. Soon people were sitting all about him. Someone took the other decklevel bunk next to his, and he saw people on either side, and facing him and angling away down the diagonal view through the uprights. The room was getting quiet again, even the non-readers having mostly found their places, so that the PA sounded even louder. He had already spotted the small

packet the PA told them about next, the plastic case lying
on the pillow, and there was a massive stirring as thousands
of azi reached and took theirs as he did—as they opened
the covers and found hygiene kits and schedules.

"Read your schedule for exercise," the voice instructed
them. "If you don't read, you will have a blue card or a
red card. Blues are group one. Reds are group two. I will
call you by those numbers; you will have half an hour at
a time."

It was not much time. Jin was already plotting how he
could adjust his personal routine to follow it. There were
more instructions, where one went for elimination and how
one reported malaise, and instruction that they must sit or
lie in the bunks at all other times because there was no
room for people to walk about. "A great deal of the time
we will play tape," the voice promised them, which cheered
Jin considerably.

He felt uncertain what his life had meant up to this point.
He remembered well enough. But the importance he had
attached to things was all revised. His life now seemed
more preparatory than substantive. He looked forward to
things to come. There would be a world, he believed; and
he was called on to build it. He would become more and
more like a born-man and he would be on this assignment
for the rest of his life, one of the most important assignments even born-men hoped to get. All of this was due to
his good fortune in having been born in the right year, on
the right world, of the right gene-set, and of course it was
due to his excellent attention to his work. There would be
only good tape for him, and when he had gotten where he
was going, when he looked about him at a new land, there
were certain things which would have to be done at once,
with all the skill he had. People believed in him. They had
chosen him. He was very happy, now that all the disturbing
things were over, now that he could sit in his own bunk
and know that he was safe . . . and he would have just
about enough time to understand it all before they would
be there, so the tape promised.

There would be Pia, for instance. He would have liked
to have found Pia in all this crowd, and asked her whether
the tape had talked to her about him. But he thought that
it had. Usually they were very thorough about such details.

And likely they had known even what he would answer: perhaps their own supervisor had had a hand in it, reaching out to take care of them, however far they had come from their beginnings. He and Pia would make born-men together and the tape said that this would be as good as the reward tapes, a reward anytime they liked as long as they were off duty. He had a great deal of new information in that regard to think on, and information about the world they were going to, and lists of new rules and procedures. He wanted to succeed in this new place and impress his supervisors.

The PA finished instructing them. They were to lie flat on their bunks, and soon they would be asked to take trank from the ampoules given them in their personal kit. He arranged all this where he could find it, taped the trank series to the bedpost, and lay down as he was supposed to do, his head on his hands. He would be very busy for the future. He was scheduled for exercise in the 12th group, and when it was called, he wanted to proceed to the right place as quickly as possible and to plan a routine which would do as much as possible for him in the least amount of time.

He had never been so taut-nerved and full of purpose—never had so much to look forward to, or even imagined such opportunity existed. He loved the state which first ordered his creation and now bought his contract and saw to every detail of his existence. It created Pia and all the others and took them together to a new world it planned to give them. Into the bargain it had made him strong and beautiful and intelligent, so that it would be proud of him. It felt very good to be what he was planned to be, to know that everything was precisely on schedule and that his contractholders were delighted with him. He tried very hard to please, and he felt a tingling of pleasure now that he knew he had done everything right and that they were on their way. He smiled and hugged it all inside himself, how happy he was, a preciousness beyond all past imagining.

A tape began. It talked about the new world, and he listened.

iii

T00:21:15
Venture **log**

". . . outbound at 0244 m in good order. Estimate jump at 1200 a. All personnel secure under normal running. *US Swift* and *US Capable* in convoy report 0332 m all stable and normal running."

iv

T28 hours Mission Apparent Time
From the personal journal of Robert Davies

". . . 9/2/94. Jump completed. Four days to bend a turn after dump and we're through this one. Out of trafficked space. We're coming to our intended heading and now the worst part begins. Four more of these—this time without proper charts. I never liked this kind of thing."

v

T15 days MAT
Lounge area 2, *US Venture*

"That's clear on the checks," Beaumont said, and Gutierrez, among other team chiefs, nodded. "All equipment accounted for. *Venture*'s been thorough. Nothing damaged, nothing left. The governor—you can call him governor from now on—wants a readiness report two days after third jump. Any problem with that?"

A general shaking of heads, among the crowd of people, military and civilian, present in the room. They filled it. It was not a large lounge; they were crowded everywhere, and the bio equipment was accessible only in printout from *Swift*, which swore it had been examined, that the cannisters were intact and the shock meters showed nothing disastrous. More of their hardware rode on *Swift* and *Capable* than on *Venture.* They could get at nothing. It was a singularly frustrating time—and after two weeks mission apparent time it was still humiliating to sit in the presence of military officers or ship's crew, who had never gone through the shaving, who had no idea of the thing that bound them together, who had.

And when it broke up, when Beaumont walked out, grayhaired and venerable and with her sullen special op bearing, there was a silence.

A moving of chairs then. "Game in R15," one of the regs said. "All welcome."

"Game in 24," a civ said. "40," another added. It was what they did to pass the time. There was a newsletter, passed by hand and not on comp, which told who won what, and in what game; and that was what they did for their sanity. They paid off in favor points. This was a reg, a military customs:—because where we been, Matt Mayes put it, ain't no surety we get free cash; but favor points, that's a loan of something or a walk after something or whatever: no sex, no property, no tours, no gear—cut your throat if you play for solid stakes. Favor points is friendly. Don't you get in no solid game: don't you bet no big favors. You're safe on favor points. You do the other thing, the Old Man'll collect all bets and shut down the games, right?

Got us reg civs, was the way the regs put it. They're reg civs, meaning the line was down and the regs, the military, swept them into the games and the bets and otherwise included them. And it was a strange feeling, that all their pride came from the stiff-backboned regs, like Eron Miles, whose tattooed number was real, because he came out of the labs, who recovered his bearings as fast as any of them whose numbers were wearing dim. It was We; and the officers and the governor were They. That was the way of it.

And even further removed was the spacer crew—who gambled too, for credits, in other games, because their voyage was a roundtrip and they would go on and on doing missions like this. The spacers pushed odds—even following the route a probeship crew had laid out for them, themselves following a drone probe: *Venture* went with navigational records and all the amenities, but it was a nervous lot of spacers all the same, and none of the games mixed—

Wouldn't gamble with you, the conversation was reported between spacer and reg: Cheap stakes.

People remembered the room numbers, with the manic attention they deserved, because it was the games that took one's mind off an approaching jump—that let them forget for a while that they were traveling a scarcely mapped track that had the spacers hairtriggered and locked in their own manic gamblings.

Cheap at any price, that little relaxation, that little forgetting. One forgot the hazards, forgot the discomforts to come, forgot to imagine, which was the worst mistake of all.

There were assignations, too: room shiftings and courtesies—for the same reasons, that with life potentially short, sex was a stimulus powerful enough to wipe out thinking. And liquor was strictly rationed.

It took a cultivated eye to discover the good points of any of them at the moment, but it was appreciated all the more when it happened.

vi

T20 days MAT
Number two hold, *Venture*

It was duty, to walk the holds—inspecting what was at hand, because so much of the mission was elsewhere, under other eyes, on the other ships. Conn bestirred himself in the slow days of transit between jumps—surprised the troops and civilians under his authority with inspections; and visited those reeking holds where the azi slept and ate and existed, in stacked berths so close together they formed canyons towering twenty high in places, the topmost under the glare of lights and the direct rush of the ventilating fans and the nethermost existing in the dark of the canyons where the air hardly stirred. All the bunks were filled with bodies, such small spaces that no one could sit upright in them without sitting on the edge and crouching, which some did, perhaps to relieve cramped muscles . . . but they never stirred out of them except with purpose. The hold stank of too many people, stank of chemicals they used to disinfect and chemicals they used in the lifesupport systems which they had specially rigged to handle the load. The stench included cheap food, and the effluvia of converter systems which labored to cope with the wastes of so large a confined group. The room murmured with the sound of the fans, and of the rumbling of the cylinder round the core, a noise which pervaded all the ship alike; and far, far softer, the occasional murmur of azi voices. They talked little, these passengers; they exercised dutifully in the small compartment dedicated to that purpose, just aft of the hold; and dutifully and on schedule they returned to their bunks to let the next scheduled group have the open space, their sweating bodies unwashed because the facilities could not cope with so many.

Cloned-men, male and female. So was one of the specs with the mission, lab-born; and that was no shame, simply a way of being born. Tape-taught, and that was no shame either; so was everyone. The deep-teach machines were state of the art in education. They poured the whole of the universe in over chemically lowered thresholds, while the mind sorted out what it was capable of keeping, without exterior distractions or the limitations of sight or hearing.

But the worker tapes were something else. Worker tapes created the like of these, row on row of expressionless faces staring at the bottom of the bunk above them day after day—male and female, bunked side by side without difficulty, because they presently lacked desires. They regarded their bodies as valuable and undivertible from their purpose, the printout said regarding them. They would receive more information in transit—the PA blared with silken tones, describing the world they were going to. And there were tapes to give them when they had landed—tapes for all of them, for that matter. Tapes for generations to come.

He walked through—into the exercise area, unnoticed, where hundreds of azi worked in silence. Their exercise periods, in which crew or troops might have laughed and talked or worked in the group rhythms that pulled a military unit's separate minds into one—were utterly narcissistic, a silent, set routine of difficult stretchings and manipulations and calisthenics, with fixed and distant stares or pensive looks. No talk. No notice of an inspecting presence.

"You," he said to one taller and handsomer than the

average of these tall, handsome people, and the azi stopped in his bending and straightened, an immediate, flowerlike focussing of attention. "How are you getting along?"

"Very well, sir." The azi breathed hard from his exertions. "Thank you."

"Name?"

"Jin, sir; 458-9998."

"Anything needed?"

"No, sir." The dark eyes were bright and interested, a transformation. "Thank you."

"You feel good, Jin?"

"Very good, sir, thank you."

He walked back the way he had come—looked back, but the azi had resumed his exercises. They were like that. Azi had always made him uncomfortable, possibly because they were not unhappy. It said something he had no wish to hear. Erasable minds . . . the azi; if anything upset them, the tapes could take it away again.

And there were times he would have found it good to have peace like that.

He passed through the hold again, unnoticed. They were undeniably a group, the azi, like the rest of the mission topside. They maintained themselves as devotedly as they would maintain anything set in their care, and their eyes were set on a rarely disturbed infinity, like waking sleep.

He had no idea, much as he had studied them, what thoughts passed in their heads at such times—or if there were any thoughts at all.

And he went topside again, into the silence that surrounded him in this long waiting, because Ada Beaumont and Pete Gallin handled the details. He studied the printouts, and dispatched occasional messages to the appropriate heads of departments. There were his pictures, set on his desk; and there were memoirs he was writing—it seemed the time for such things. But the memoirs began with the voyage . . . and left out things that the government would not want remembered. Like most of his life. Classified. Erasable by government order. He put it on tape, and much of it was lies, why they came and what they hoped.

Mostly he waited, like the azi.

vii

T20 days, MAT
Gutierrez, from a series of free lectures in lounge 2

". . . there's as varied an ecology where we're going as on Cyteen . . . somewhat more so, in respect to the vertical range of development; somewhat less, since you don't have the range of phyla—of types of life. Plants . . . that's algae, grasses, native fruits, pretty much like Cyteen, all the way up to some pretty spectacular trees—" (pause for slide series) "I'll repeat those in closer detail later, or run them as often as you like. This is all stuff that came from the survey team. But the thing you'll have heard about already, that's the calibans, the moundbuilders. They're pretty spectacular: the world's distinct and crowning achievement, as it were. The first thing I want to make clear is that we're not talking about an intelligence. The bias was in the other direction when the Mercury survey team landed. They looked at the ridges from orbit and thought they were something like cities. They went down there real carefully, I can tell you, after all the orbiting observations." (slide) "Now let me get you scale on this." (slide) "You can see the earthen ridge is about four times the man's height. You always find these things on riverbanks and seacoasts, on the two of the seven continents that lie in the temperate zone—and this one's going to neighbor our own site. The moundbuilders happen to pick all the really good sites. In fact you could just about pick out the sites that are prime for human development by looking for mounds." (slide) "And this is one of the builders. Caliban is a character in a play: he was big and ugly. That's what the probe crew called him. Dinosaur's what you think, isn't it? Big, gray dinosaur. He's about four to five meters long, counting tail—warmblooded, slithers on his belly. Lizard type. But trying to pin old names on new worlds is a pretty hard game. The geologists always have a better time of it than the biologists. They deny it, but it's true. Look at that skull shape there, that big bulge over the eyes. Now that brain is pretty large, about three times the size of yours and mine. And its convolutions aren't at all like yours and mine. It's got a place in the occipital region, the back, that's like a hard gray handball, and pitted like an old ship's hull; and then three lobes come off that, two on a side and one on top, shaped like human lungs, and having a common stem and interconnecting stems at several other places along their length. They're frilled, those lobes—make you think of pink feathers; and then there's three of those handball-things in the other end of the skull, right up in that place we call the frontal lobes of a human brain, but not quite as big as the organ behind. Now that's the brain of this citizen of the new world. And if it didn't connect onto a spinal cord and have branches, and if microscopy didn't show structure that could answer to neurons, we'd have wondered. It's a very big brain. We haven't mapped it enough to know what the correspondences are. But all it does with that big brain is build ridges. Yes, they dissected one . . . after they established the behavior as instinct-patterned. You do that to a certain extent by frustrating an animal from a goal; and you watch how it goes about the problem. And if the answer is wired into the brain, if it's instinct and not rationality, it's going to tend to repeat its behavior over and over again. And that's what a caliban does. They're not aggressive. Actually, there's a smaller, prettier version—" (slide) "The little green fellow with all the collar frills is called an ariel. A-r-i-e-l. That's Caliban's elvish friend. Now he's about a meter long at maximum, nose to tail, and he runs in and out of caliban burrows completely unmolested. They're fisheaters, both the calibans and ariels, stomachs full of fish. And they'll nibble fruits. Or investigate about anything you put out for them. None of the lizards are poisonous. None of them ever offered to bite any of the probe team. You do have to watch out for caliban tails, because that's two meters length of pretty solid muscle, and they're not too bright, and they just could break your leg for you if they panicked. The ariels can give you a pretty hard swipe too. You pick them up by the base of the tail and the back of the neck, if so happens you have to pick one up, and you hold on tight, because the report is they're strong. Why would you want to pick one up? Well, not often, I'd think. But they apparently run in and out of caliban burrows, very pretty folk, as you see, and no one's ever caught an ariel doing a burrow of its own: all play and no work, the ariels. And the probe team found them in their camp, and walking through their tents, and getting into food if they had a chance. They haven't got any fear at all. They and the calibans sit on top of the food chain, and they haven't got any competition. The calibans don't seem to get anything at all out of the association; it's not certain whether the ariels get anything out of it but shelter. Both species swim and fish. Neither species commits aggression against the other. The ariels are very quick to get out of the way when the calibans put a foot down, while in the human camp, the ariels sometimes went into a kind of freeze where you were in danger of stepping on one, and they'd be stiff as a dried fish until a second after you'd pick them up, after which they'd come to life in a hurry. There's some speculation that it's a panic reaction, that the overload of noise and movement in the camp is just too much for it; or that it thinks it's hidden when it does that. Or maybe it's picking up something humans don't hear, some noise from the machinery or the com. Its brain is pretty much like the caliban's, by the way, but the handball organs are pink and quite soft.

"Interiorly, the snout is odd too, in both species. That gentle swelling behind the nostril slits is a chamber filled with cilia. Hairlike projections, but flesh. And they're rife with bloodvessels. So are the organs that seem to correspond to lungs. Filled with cilia. Like a nest of worms. They expel water when they come up from a dive: they sit on the shore and heave and it comes out the nostril slits. So they're taking in water; and they're getting oxygen out of it. Gills and lungs at once. They can handle river water and estuary water, but no one's observed them diving at sea. They may have relatives that do. We're a long way from knowing how many different varieties of lizards there are. But the present count is about fifty-two species under the size of the ariels. And a lot are aquatic.

"There are flying lizards—for the naturalists among you that know what bats are—rather like bats and rather not; warmblooded, we reckon—the probe crew never caught any, but the photo stills" (Slide) "—rather well suggest bats; that's a terrene form. Or Downbelow gliders, of which no one's yet got a specimen. We don't know a thing about them, but their agility in the air, along with the fact that calibans and ariels are warmblooded—suggest that they're the world's closest approach to a mammal. This is the item we've got a particular caution on. They're fairly rare in the area, but they do swarm. The wingspan is half a meter, some larger. They could bite; could carry disease: could be venomous—we don't know. Because they might be something like a mammal, we're a little more concerned about contamination with them. There's no good being scared of them. I'm talking about remote possibility precautions. Everything's new here. You don't find easy correspondences in lifeforms. All the can'ts and won'ts you ever heard can be revised on a new world. Nature's really clever about engineering around can'ts. Insects can't get above a certain size . . . except that insect is a terrene category term, covering things with chitin and certain kinds of internal structure; but what we meet in the Beyond can differ quite a bit. And our world has some oddities." (slide) "Like the hoby mole. That's a meter long, half a meter wide, engorges earth like a burrowing worm. That tiny annular segmentation is chitin, and they're very soft. Yes, they are something like an insect, and if you put a spade through one by accident, don't touch the remains. They exude an irritant that sent a member of the probe team to sickbay for two days. So there's also a caution out on this one.

"There are snakes. They're coldblooded and they're constrictors. At least the samples were. We don't rule out poison. Possibly we're being alarmist in that regard: human prejudice. But poison in a legless structure seems to be a very efficient hunting mechanism and it's proven so on two worlds besides Earth.

"And the fairy flitters." (slide) "These little glider lizards are about fingersized, the wings are really rib extensions, and if you set a lantern near the trees, you'll get a halo of flitters. They don't really fly, mind, they glide. The iridescence lasts as long as they live. You only see it in the photos, not in the lab specimens. They eat putative insects, they're utterly harmless, and probably beneficial to the farming effort. They'll cling to anything when they land, and you just disengage them gently and set them back on a branch. They'll fly right back to the light. As long as there's no trees near our camp lights, we won't have trouble with flitters piling up there. But they'll be all over you if you carry a light through the woods, and I'm afraid we're going to have trouble with vehicle headlights. It's a shame to think of killing any of them. They're far too beautiful. We're going to try to devise something that might drive them off. Ideas are welcome.

"Fish—beyond counting. Saltwater and freshwater. No poisons yet detected. Edible. We'll want to be sure to stick to varieties that have already been tested; and bio will run tests on new species as they're brought in. You'll learn to recognize the species so you know what to eat and what to bring us.

"Microorganisms. We're very fortunate in that regard. No one picked up a parasite. No one got sick. No one developed allergies, either. We don't get careless, though. And particularly where you have mammal analogues, we don't get careless. There's a phenomenon we call biological resonance, for want of a better name. That's when two worlds' microorganisms set up housekeeping together and develop new traits over a period of years; when they cooperate. So—the medical staff is going to have a long lecture on this topic—you have to report every contact with a new lifeform, especially if you accidentally touch something, which is not a good idea. And you report every runny nose and every cough and every itch. We do have a biological isolation chamber we can set up. If someone turns out to be in really serious trouble and nothing else will work, we can put you in a bubble for three years until a ship comes back and lifts you off. Short of that we have antihistamines and all kinds of other alternatives, up to the autoimmune lot, so there's no good becoming obsessive about the chance of contamination; but there's no good being cavalier about things, either. If you drop down in a faint, it's really helpful if you've already told us you got stung by something that morning or that you'd been digging down on the beach. You're all going to have to keep your wits about you and be able to give a meticulous account of your whereabouts and your contacts with any and everything. The thing you forget to mention could be the key that we need to figure out what's wrong with you. And that's partly my business, because I have to form a picture of every ecosystem, so that if your contact with something harmful was on the beach, for instance, I have a good idea what to look for. And the faster I can answer questions, the safer you are. That's why I have to ask everyone in the mission to be bio's eyes and ears. Leave the hands and the touching to us, where you have any doubts. Humans can be compatible with all kinds of ecosystems; don't kill anything, just move it over. This world doesn't have any predators to argue with us; and we've got the construction sites planned so that eventually we're going to intersperse urban development with wild areas and wildlife safeguards. The optimum development areas are also the optimum sites for some of the world's most interesting inhabitants, and there's no reason why protected habitat can't exist side by side, theirs and ours. It has to do with attitude toward the wild. It has to do with knowledge and not fear. We're not turning this world into Cyteen. We're turning it into something uniquely its own. People who come here will be able to see the old world right along with the most modern development. Caliban habitat right in the middle of a city. Humans are very flexible. We can just extend a road a bit and locate a loading dock around a critical area; and that's what we'll do. That's why there's a land bank being set up. When you own land, you'll have title to a certain value of land, but not any specific land, and that lets the governor's office and the bio department create a preserve where needed, and it protects you and your descendants against any financial damage. You can't own caliban habitat. That has to be left. On the other hand, to prevent their encroachment on us, there will be barrier zones, usually residential, surrounding any contact point—like, for instance, the caliban mounds near the landing site. In the theory that lifeforms get along better with each other than lifeforms get along with roads and factories, there'll be housing built along the line that turns only windows in that direction, not doors, not accesses. Once we determine the actual boundary of an area, that's where the permanent building will go. And you'll be up against a protected zone, so your actual maintenance on that side will be handled through the bio department. City core will be industrial. All city growth will be handled through the creation of similar enclaves along roadways. This is the way it is in the charter. I think you understand it. I just want to explain how the bio section relates to the construction agency and to the governor's office and why we'll have some functions linked in with security and law enforcement. We have a constituency, which is the ecosystem we're entering. We also represent the human ecosystem. We work out accommodations and bring those before other departments, who have to adjust to the facts as we present them. We don't really have authority. Nature has that. We just find out the facts as they exist; the decision's already made—that the two systems have to exist in balance. A world where humans come in at the top of the food chain is easily thrown out of balance. Those of you who are stationborn will appreciate that quite readily. It's like a station, like Pell, for instance, where two biosystems exist in complement. Very tricky lifesupport setup, one looping into the other, and each benefitting the other. But when you start from the beginning you can do that, and make them balance. We look to have station manufacture for the really heavy and polluting industries. All the departments will be doing these seminars and we'll go on doing them after we land, making tapes for the azi and for future generations. All of this is going to be priceless stuff. And mostly history's going to make liars out of us, but, we sincerely hope, not in our hopes for the place.

"I'll be going over the ecosystem from the microorganisms up in the more detailed session tomorrow; and I'll be doing it again for my own staff in a morning session day after tomorrow. Check your schedules, and if you find you want to sit in on that lecture you're quite welcome. It's going to be pretty detailed, but after the other session it might make fair sense. Session to begin tomorrow morning is Zell Parham on security and law, this room, 0700 mainday. . . .

"Game in R12."

viii

T20 days MAT

". . . The world is to be loved," the tape voice whispered, and Jin accepted it deeply, wholly. "The things you will find there are beautiful. All the things that really belong to the world are to be protected; but you will build there. Born-men will tell you where you will build and if life is taken in the building, that is as it must be. If you can spare a living thing you will do so, if it is your choice alone. You will observe certain cautions in touching wild things. You will report all such contacts to your supervisors, just as born-men have to report them.

"You will work in the fields; and it may be you will take lives. That will be an accident and there is no guilt.

"You will catch fish and eat them, and this is the order of nature. There is no guilt in this. Fish are there for your use, and they feel very little pain.

"You will become part of this world, and if ever people came to harm it you would take up weapons to defend it. In that, you might kill, and you would not have guilt. But if ever you had to take up weapons, you would be trained, and the governor would tell you.

"You will work because you are strong and because your work is very important. You will have a right to be very proud of what you do, and when it is all done well, you will be closer to being born-men.

"The government which holds your contract is very pleased with you. You're learning very well. Soon you will get born-man tapes teaching you the nature of the world, and in very little time you will step out on your land. Through all the difficulties you will experience you can find occasion for pride that you will overcome them all. Every difficulty will make you stronger and wiser, and you will fit more and more perfectly into the world. Be happy. Not everything will be pleasant, but every difficulty will give the pleasure of its solution, and the confidence that you are as intelligent and as fine as the promise of your gene-set. The government believes in you. The born-men will take care of you and you will take care of them, because where they are wiser than you, you are very strong and you have the capacity to become wise. Love the land. Love the world. Care for the born-men, and expect their care for you. You have every right to be proud and happy. . . ."

Jin lay relaxed, dissolved in the pleasure of approval—stirred, as much as anything moved him in this time, with the anticipation of his becoming. There had never been such azi as themselves, he was persuaded, and he had only believed he was ordinary because no one had ever pointed out to him his uniqueness. He saw his descendants in vast numbers, his genetic material, and Pia's, who was quite as wonderful, ultimately mixed with all the other specially chosen material. They were made of *born-man* material: he had never realized this until the tape told him. The capacity was in them, and it was awakening.

He thought on this, having a capacity for sustained concentration that could knit together the most complex of problems. This capacity could be turned to pure reason. He had never had it called upon in quite this way. In fact, it was discouraged, because an azi's understanding was full of gaps which could mislead. But this special capacity which born-men lost in the distractions of their sense-overloaded environments—could make him very wise as the total sum of his knowledge increased. Of this too, he was proud, knowing that a 9998 was extraordinarily capable in this regard. It would make him loved, and secure, and born-men would never give him bad tape.

"Highest life native to the world are the calibans," the tape told him. "And if you understand them, they will do you no harm. . . ."

ix

T42 days MAT
Venture log

". . . arrival Gehenna system 1018 hours 34 minutes mission apparent time. US *Swift* and US *Capable* to follow at one hour intervals. . . ."

". . estimate Cyteen elapsed time: 280 days; dates will be revised on recovery of reliable reference."

". . . confirm arrival US *Swift* on schedule."

". . . confirm arrival US *Capable* on schedule."

". . . insert into orbit Gehenna II scheduled 1028 hours 15 minutes mission apparent time. All systems normal. All conditions within parameters predicted by Mercury probe. Systems arrival now determined to be possible within narrower margin to be calculated for future use. Systemic positions were accurately predicted by Mercury probe data. *Venture* will make further observations during exit from Gehenna system. . . ."

x

T42 days MAT
US Venture
Office of Col. James A. Conn

It was there, real and solid. The world. Gehenna II, the designation was; Newport, he reckoned to record the name. Their world. Conn sat at his desk in front of the viewer with his hands steepled in front of him and looked at the transmitted image, trying to milk more detail from it than the vid was giving them yet. The second of six planets, a great deal blue and a great deal white, and otherwise brown with vast deserts, sparsely patched with green. Not quite as green as Cyteen. But similar. The image hazed in his eyes as he thought not of where he was going, but of places he had been . . . and of Jean, buried back home; and what she would say, when they had been like Beaumont and Davies, travelling together. Even the war had not stopped that. She had been there. With him. There existed that faint far thought in his mind that he had committed some kind of desertion, not a great one, but at least a small one, that he had hoped for happiness coming here, for something more to do. He left her there, and there was no one to tend her grave and no one who would care. That had seemed such a small thing—go on, she would say, with that characteristic wave of her hand when he hung his thoughts on trivialities. Go on, with that crisp decisiveness in her voice that had sometimes annoyed him and sometimes been so dear: Lord, Jamie, what's a point in all of that?

Something had gone out of him since Jean was gone: the edge that had been important when he was younger, perhaps; or the quickness that crackle in Jean's voice had set into him; or the confidence—that she was there, to back him and to second guess him.

Go on, he could hear her saying, when he pulled out of

Cyteen; when he took the assignment; and now—go on, when it came down to permanency here.

Go on—when it came to the most important assignment of his life, and no Jean to tell it to. It all meant very little against that measure. For the smallest evening with her face looking back at him—he would trade anything to have that back. But there were no takers. And more—he knew what lived down there, that it was not Cyteen, however homelike it looked from orbit.

The light over the door flashed, someone seeking entry. He reached across to the console and pushed the button— "Ada," he said curiously as she came in.

"Ah, you've got it," she murmured, indicating the screen. "I wanted to make sure you were awake."

"No chance I'd miss it. I'd guess the lounge has it too."

"You couldn't fit another body in there. I'm going down to 30; the officers are at the screen down there."

"I'll come down when the vid gets more detail."

"Right."

She went her way. Bob Davies would be down there. Jealousy touched him, slight and shameful. There would be Gallin and Sedgewick and Dean and Chiles; and the rest of the mission. . . .

One horizon, one site for years ahead. Blueskyed. Grounded forever. That was what it came to. And whatever private misgivings anyone had now, it was too late.

Look at that, he could imagine Jean saying. And: Don't take stupid chances, Jamie.

Don't you, he would say.

He looked back at the image, at the bluegreen world that was not home at all. The whole thing was a stupid chance. An ambition which Jean had never shared.

"Col. Conn," the com said, Mary Engles' voice. "Are you there, colonel?"

He acknowledged, a flick of the key. "Captain."

"We've got a fix on the landing site coming up."

A shiver went over his skin. "What do you reckon in schedules?"

"We're going to ride here one more day and do mapping and data confirmation before we let you out down there. You'll want that time to order your sequence of drop. I'll be feeding you the shuttle passenger slots, and you fill them

up at your own discretion. The equipment drop is all standard procedure with us, and we've got all that down as
routine. You handle your own people according to your
own preferences. You will need some of the construction
personnel in your initial drop. I'd like to ask you to stay
on board until the final load. In case of questions."

"Good enough. I'll wait your printout."

"We have suggestions, based on experience. I'll pass
them to you, by your leave."

"No umbrage, captain. Experience is appreciated."

"A professional attitude, colonel, and appreciated in
turn. Printout follows."

He opened the desk cabinet, took out a bottle and a
glass and poured himself a drink, soothed his nerves while
the printout started spilling onto his desk.

Everything would have to be packed. Mostly there were
the microfax books and the study tapes, which were precious. Uniforms—there were no more uniforms where they
were going. They became citizens down there. Colonists.
No more amenities either, in spite of the cases of soap. He
meant to have a shower morning and evening during the
unloading. It was that kind of thing one missed most under
the conditions he was going to face. Soap. Hot water. Pure
water. And a glass of whiskey in the evenings.

The printout grew. On the screen, the tighter focus came
in. It agreed with the photos in the mission documents.

Patterns showed up under tight focus . . . the same patterns
which the probe had abundantly reported, curious mounds
near seacoasts and rivers, vast maze designs which interrupted
the sparse green with tracings of brown lines, loops and rays
stretching over kilometers of riverbank and coastline.

That was where they were going.

xi

T43 days MAT
Communication: mission command

. . . First drop scheduled 1042 hours 25 minutes mission
apparent time. Capt. Ada Beaumont commanding. Selected for first drop: M/Sgt. Ilya V. Burdette with five seats;

M/Sgt. Pavlos D. M. Bilas, with five seats; M/Sgt. Dinah L.
Sigury, two seats; Cpl. Nina N. Ferry, one seat; Sgt. Jan
Vandermeer, one seat; Capt. Bethan M. Dean, one seat; Dr.
Frelan D. Wilson, one seat; Dr. Marco X. Gutierrez, one seat;
Dr. Park Young, one seat; Dr. Hayden L. Savin, one seat;
workers A 187–6788 through A 208–0985, thirty seats."

xii

T43 days MAT
Venture loading bay one

"He's not coming," Ada Beaumont said quietly, rested
her hand on her husband's back, kept her eyes front, on
the movement of machinery, the loading of cannisters onto
the lift, an intermittent clank and crash.

Bob Davies said nothing. Nothing was really called for,
and Bob was careful with protocols. Ada stayed still a
moment—looked aside where some of the ship's crew were
rigging the ropes to channel boarding personnel to the
lift—but the bay up on the frame was empty yet, the shuttle
on its way up from *Venture*'s belly, close to match-up with
the personnel deck. The lift yonder would take them by
groups of ten, synch them out of *Venture*'s comfortable rotation, to let them board the null G shuttle. The azi were
to go first, taking the upright berths in the hold and to the
rear of the cabin, and then the citizen complements would
follow, in very short sequence.

But Conn stayed in his quarters. He had rarely come out
of them since their arrival in the system. The ship was
crowded; departments were busy with their plans: possibly
no one noticed. He played cards and drank with the two
of them—he had done that, at the end of watches, regularly. But he never came out among the staff.

"I think," Ada Beaumont said more quietly still, when
the crew was furthest from them and only Bob could possibly hear. "I think Jim shouldn't have taken this one. I wish
he'd take the out he still has and go back to Cyteen. Claim
health reasons."

And then, in further silence, Bob venturing no comment:
"What he actually said was—'You handle things. You'll

be doing that, mostly. The old man just wants to ride it out easy.' "

"He wasn't that way," Bob said finally.

"It's leaving Cyteen. It's Jean, I think. He never showed how bad that hurt."

Bob Davies ducked his head. There was noise in the corridor to the left. Some of the azi were coming up. The clock ran closer and closer to their inevitable departure. He reached and took his wife's hand—himself in the khaki that was the uniform of the day for everyone headed planetward, civ or military. "So maybe that's why he can sit up here; because he can lean on you. Because he knows you'll do it. You can handle it. And there's Pete Gallin. He's all right."

"It's no way to start out."

"Hang, he can't make every launch down here."

"*I'd* be here," Beaumont said. She shook her head. The azi line entered the bay, brighteyed, in soiled white coveralls; weeks with no bathing, some of them with gall sores from the bunks. There were already difficulties. Some of the details regarding the azi were not at all pretty, not the comfortable view of things the science people or even the troops had had of the voyage. At least Conn had been down seeing to the azi, she gave him that. He had been down in the holds during the voyage, maybe too often.

Now Conn handed it to her. She knew the silent language. Had served with Conn before. Knew his limits.

He had been drinking—a lot. That was the truth she did not tell even Bob.

xiii

T43 days MAT
Venture communications log

"*Venture* shuttle one: unloading now complete; will lift at ready and return to dock. Weather onworld good and general conditions excellent. Landing area is now marked with the locator signal. . . ."

"*Venture* shuttle two now leaving orbit and heading for landing site. . . ."

xiv

T45 days MAT
Venture hold, azi section

"Passage 14," the silk-smooth voice intoned, "will be J 429-687 through J 891-5567; passage 15. . . ."

Jin smiled inwardly, not with the face, which was unaccustomed to emotion. Emotion was between himself and the tape, between himself and the voice which caressed, promised, praised, since his childhood. He had no need to show others what he felt, or that he felt, unless someone spoke directly to him and entered the bubble which was his private world.

When the time came, he listened to the voice and gathered himself up along with the rest of them in his aisle, stood patiently as everyone lined up, coming down the ladder to join them. And then the word was given and the file moved, out the door they had not passed since they had entered the ship, and through the corridors of the ship to the cold room which admitted them to the lift chamber. The lift jolted and slid one way and the other, and opened again where there was no gravity at all, so that they drifted—"Hold the lines," a born-man told them, and Jin seized the cord along with the rest, beside a silver clip on the line. "Hold to the clips with one hand and pull yourselves along gently," the born-man said, and he did so, flew easily upward along the line in the company of others, until they had come to the hatch of the ship which would take them to the World.

It was more lines, inside; and they were jammed very tightly into the back of the hold while more and more azi were loaded on after them. "Secure your handgrips," a born-man told them, and they did so, locking in place the padded bars which protected them. "Feet to the deck." They did the best they could.

It took a short time to load. They were patient, and the others moved with dispatch: the hatch closed and a born-man voice said: "Hold tight."

So they went, a hard kick which sent them on their way

and gave them the feeling that they were lying on the floor on top of each other and not standing upright. No one spoke. There was no need. The tape had already told them where they were going and how long it would take to get there, and if they talked, they might miss instruction.

They believed in the new world and in themselves with all their hearts, and Jin was pleased even in the discomfort of the acceleration, because it meant they were going there faster.

They made entry, and the air heated, so that from time to time they wiped sweat from their faces, crowded as they were. But weight was on their feet now, and it was a long, slow flight as the engines changed over to ordinary flight.

"Landing in fifteen minutes," the born-man voice said, and soon, very soon, the motion changed again, and the noise increased, which was the settling of the shuttle downward, gentle as the settling of a leaf to the ground.

They waited, still silent, until the big cargo hatch opened where they had not realized a hatch existed. Daylight flooded in, and the coolth of outside breezes flooded through the double lock.

"File out," the voice told them. "Go down the ramp and straight ahead. A supervisor will give you your packets and your assignments. Goodbye."

They unlocked the restraints line by line in reverse order to that in which they had loaded, and in that order they went down the ramp.

Light hit Jin's eyes, the sight of a broad gray river—blue sky, and green forest of saplings beyond a hazy shore—the scars of a camp on this one, where earthmovers were already at work tearing up the black earth. Clean air filled his lungs, and the sun touched the stubble on his head and his face. His heart was beating hard.

He knew what he had to do now. The tapes had told him before and during the voyage. He had reached the real beginning of his life and nothing but this had ever had meaning.

III

Landing

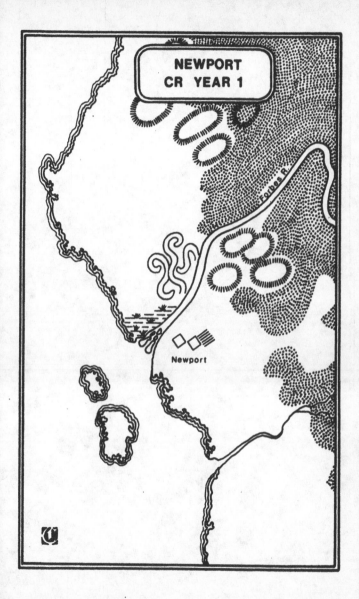

Military Personnel:

Col. James A. Conn, governor general
Capt. Ada P. Beaumont, lt. governor
Maj. Peter T. Gallin, personnel
M/Sgt. Ilya V. Burdette, Corps of Engineers
   Cpl. Antonía M. Cole
   Spec. Martin H. Andresson
   Spec. Emilie Kontrin
   Spec. Danton X. Norris
M/Sgt. Danielle L. Emberton, tactical op.
   Spec. Lewiston W. Rogers
   Spec. Hamil N. Masu
   Spec. Grigori R. Tamlin
M/Sgt. Pavlos D. M. Bilas, maintenance
   Spec. Dorothy T. Kyle
   Spec. Egan I. Innis
   Spec. Lucas M. White
   Spec. Eron 678-4578 Miles
   Spec. Upton R. Patrick
   Spec. Gene T. Troyes
   Spec. Tyler W. Hammett
   Spec. Kelley N. Matsuo
   Spec. Belle M. Rider
   Spec. Vela K. James
   Spec. Matthew R. Mayes
   Spec. Adrian C. Potts

Spec. Vasily C. Orlov
Spec. Rinata W. Quarry
Spec. Kito A. M. Kabir
Spec. Sita Chandrus
M/Sgt. Dinah L. Sigury, communications
Spec. Yung Kim
Spec. Lee P. de Witt
M/Sgt. Thomas W. Oliver, quartermaster
Cpl. Nina N. Ferry
Pfc. Hayes Brandon
Lt. Romy T. Jones, special forces
Sgt. Jan Vandermeer
Spec. Kathryn S. Flanahan
Spec. Charles M. Ogden
M/Sgt. Zell T. Parham, security
Cpl. Quintan R. Witten
Capt. Jessica N. Sedgewick, confessor-advocate
Capt. Bethan M. Dean, surgeon
Capt. Robert T. Hamil, surgeon
Lt. Regan T. Chiles, computer services

Civilian Personnel:

Secretarial personnel: 12
Medical/surgical: 1
Medical/paramedic: 7
Mechanical maintenance: 20
Distribution and warehousing: 20
Robert H. Davies
Security: 12
Computer service: 4
Computer maintenance: 2
Librarian: 1
Agricultural specialists: 10
Harold B. Hill
Geologists: 5
Meterologist: 1
Biologists: 6
Marco X. Gutierrez
Eva K. Jenks
Education: 5
Cartographer: 1

Management supervisors: 4
Biocycle engineers: 4
Construction personnel: 150
Food preparation specialists: 6
Industrial specialists: 15
Mining engineers: 2
Energy systems supervisors: 8
   TOTAL MILITARY 45
   TOTAL CITIZEN STAFF 341; TOTAL NONASSIGNED
DEPENDENTS: 111; TOTAL ALL CITIZENS: 452

   ADDITIONAL NONCITIZEN PERSONNEL:
"A" class: 2890
     Jin 458-9998
     Pia 86-687
"B" class: 12389
"M" class: 4566
"P" class: 20788
"V" class: 1278
TOTAL ALL NONCITIZENS: 41911
TOTAL ALL MISSION: 42363

i

Day 03, Colony Reckoning
Newport Base, Gehenna System

   The hatch opened, the ramp went down, and Conn
looked about him . . . at stripped earth, at endless blocks
of two-man tents, at the shining power tower and the solar
array that caught the morning sun. Beyond them was the
river and on their left, the sea. From the origin of the river,
mountains rose; and forest skirted them; and plains running
down to this site, with forest spilling onto it from another
low surge of hills behind the shuttle landing. He knew the
map in his sleep, what was here now and what would come.
He inhaled the warm air, which was laden with a combina-
tion of strange scents; felt the gravity which was different
from the standard G of ships and a little different than that
of Cyteen. He felt a slight sense of panic and refused to
betray it.

The staff waited, solemn, at the foot of the ramp. He walked down—he wore civilian clothes now, no uniform; and took the hand of Ada Beaumont and of Bob Davies and of Peter Gallin . . . in shock at the change in them, at shaved heads and shaved faces, when the rest of the mission was now at least well-stubbled.

"I didn't authorize this," he said to Ada Beaumont. Temper surged up in him; outrage. He remembered they had witnesses and smothered the oath. "What's going on?"

"It seemed," Beaumont said firmly, "efficient. It's dirty down here."

He swept a glance about him, at the sameness; at military officers converted to azi-like conformity. Beaumont's democracy. Beaumont's style. He scowled. "Trouble?"

"No. My initiative. It seemed to create a distinction down here—apart from regulations. I apologize, sir."

In public. In front of the others. He took a grip on himself. "It seems," he said, "a good idea on that basis." He looked beyond them, and about him—at the last load coming off the last shuttle flight, his personal baggage and less essential items, and the last few techs. He let his eyes focus on the mountains, on the whole sweep of the land.

On the far bank of the river rose grassy mounds, abrupt and distinctive. He pointed that way. "Those are the neighbors, are they?"

"That's the caliban mounds, yes, sir."

He stared at them. At uncertainty. He wished they had not been so close. He scanned the camp, the tents which stretched row on row onto the plain at their right . . . azi, above forty thousand azi, a city in plastic and dust. The earthmovers whined away, making more bare dirt. Permanent walls were going up in the center of the camp, foamset domes, obscured by the dust of a crawler. "What's in?" he asked Beaumont. "Got the hookup?"

"Power's functioning as of half an hour ago, and we're shifted off the emergency generator. We're now on the Newport Power Company. They're laying the second line of pipe now; so we'll have waste treatment soon. Hot water's at a premium, but the food service people have all they need."

He walked with them, beside Beaumont, gave a desultory

wave at workers who had come out with a transport to carry the baggage to camp. He walked, electing not to use the transport . . . inhaled the dust and the strangeness and the unfamiliar smell of sea not far distant. In some respects it was like Cyteen. There was a feeling of insulation about him, a sense of unreality; he shook it off and looked about him for plant life that might prove to his senses that he was on an alien world—but the earthmovers had scraped all that away. There were only the azi tents, all of them in neat lines stretching away into the dust; and finally the camp center, where earthmovers dug the foundations for more plastic foam construction, where dome after dome had already sprung up like white fungus among the tents, one bubbled onto the next.

They were thirty six hours into the construction.

"You've done a good job," he said to Ada Beaumont, loudly, amends for the scene at the ramp, in which he had embarrassed himself. "A good job."

"Thank you, sir."

There was caution there. In all of them. He looked about him again, at the entourage of department heads who had begun to follow them, at others who had joined them in their walk into the center of the camp. "I'll be meeting with you," he said. "But it's all automatic, isn't it? Meetings aren't as important as your building and your job schedules. So I'll postpone all of the formalities. I think it's more important to get everyone under shelter."

There were nods, murmurs, excuses finally as one and another of them found reason to move off.

"I'd like to find my own quarters," Conn said. "I'm tired."

"Yes, sir," Beaumont said quietly. "This way. We've made them as comfortable as possible."

He was grateful. He squared his shoulders out of the slump they had acquired, walked with her and with Bob and Gallin in that direction. She opened the door of a smallish dome bubbled onto the main one, with a plastic pane window and a door sawed out of the foam and refitted on hinges. There was a bed inside, already made up; and a real desk, and a packing mat for a rug on the foamset flooring.

"That's good," he said, "that's real good." And when the company made to leave: "Captain. Can I talk to you a moment?"

"Sir." She stayed. Bob Davies and Pete Gallin discretely withdrew, and the reg who had brought some of the luggage in deposited it near the door and closed the door on his way out.

"I think you know," he said, "that something's wrong. I imagine it bothered you—my not being down here."

"I understand the procedure calls for the ranking officer to stay on the ship in case—"

"Don't put me off."

"I've had some concern."

"All right. You've had some concern." He took a breath, jammed his hands into his belt behind him. "I'll be honest with you. I reckoned you could handle the landing, the whole setup if you had to.—I'm feeling a bit of strain, Ada. A bit of strain. I'm getting a little arthritis. You understand me? The back's hurting me a bit."

"You think there's a problem with the rejuv?"

"I know I'm taking more pills than I used to. You use more when you're under stress. Maybe it's that. I've thought about resigning, going back to Cyteen on a medical. I've thought about that. I don't like the thought. I've never run from anything."

"If your health—"

"Just listen to me. What I'm going to do—I'm going to take the command for a few weeks; and then I'm going to step down and retire to an advisory position."

"Sir—"

"Don't sir me. Not here. Not after this long. I just wanted to tell you the stuff's failing on me. That's why we have redundancies in the system, isn't it? You're the real choice, you. I'm just lending my experience. That's all."

"If you want it that way."

"I just want to rest, Ada. It wasn't why I came. It's what I want now."

"There's still that ship up there."

"No."

"I'll take care of things, then." She put her hands in her hip pockets, blinked at him with pale eyes in a naked-skulled face, showing age. "I think then—begging your pardon . . . it might be a wise thing under the circumstances—to take a joint command and ease the moment when it comes."

"Eager for it, are you?"

"Jim—"

"You've already started doing things your way. That's all right."

"The staff has wondered, you know—your absence. And I think if you talked to them frankly, made it clear, your health, your reasons—you really are a figure they respect; I think they'd be glad to know why you've suddenly gone less visible, that it's a personal thing and not some upper-level friction in command."

"Is that the rumor?"

"One's never sure just what the rumors are, but I think that's some of it. There's a little bit of strain."

"Troopers and civs?"

"No. Us and Them. The visible distinction—" She rubbed her shaved scalp, selfconsciously returned the hand to her pocket. "Well, it solved an immediate problem. People get tired and they get touchy; and I went and did that on the spot, that being the way I knew how to say it. And the rest of the staff followed suit. Maybe it was wrong."

"If it solved the problem it was right. I'll talk to them. I'll make everything clear in my own way."

"Yes, sir." Soft and quiet.

"Don't respect me into an early grave, Beaumont. I'm not there yet."

"I don't expect you to be. I expect you'll be around handing out the orders. I'm your legs, that's the way I see it."

"Oh, you see further than that. You'll be governor. I think that'll suit you."

She was silent a moment. "I considered it a matter of friendship. I'd like to keep it on that basis."

"I'll rest a bit," he said.

"All right." She tended to the door, stopped and looked back. "I'll warn you about the door—you have to keep the door closed. Lizards have discovered the camp. They'll get into tents, anything. And the window—they come in windows if you have the lights on and the windows open. We try not to carry any of the flitters back to the camp, but a few have made it in, and they'll make a nuisance of themselves."

He nodded. Loathed the thought.

"Sir," she said quietly, left and softly tugged the thick door shut. He lay down on the bed, his head pounding in a suspended silence—the absence of the ventilation noises and the rotation of the ship and the thousand other subtle noises of the machinery. Outside the earthmovers growled and whined and beeped, and human voices shouted, but it was all far away.

The arthritis story was real. He felt it, wanted a drink; and tried to put it off—not wanting that to start, not yet, when someone else might want to call.

He had to hold off the panic, the desire to call the ship and ask to be lifted off. He had to do it until it was too late. He had never yet run; and he was determined it would not be this time, this last, hardest time.

ii

Day 03, CR

That evening (one had to think in terms of evening again, not mainday and alterday, had to learn that things shut down at night, and everyone slept and ate on the same schedules) . . . that evening in the main dome, Conn stood up at the staff mess and announced the changes. "Not so bad, really," he said, "since there's really a need for a governing board and not a military command here. Headquarters and the Colonial Office left that to our discretion, what sort of authority to set up, whether military or council forms; and I think that there's a level of staff participation here that lends itself to council government. All department heads will sit on the board. Capt. Beaumont and I will share the governorship and preside jointly when we're both present. Maj. Gallin will take vicechairman's rank. And for the rest, there's the structural precedence in various areas of responsibility as the charter outlines them." He looked down the table at faces that showed the stress of long hours and primitive conditions. At Bilas, with a bandage on his shaven temple. That had been bothering him: the thoughts wandered. "Bilas—you had an accident?"

"Rock, sir. A tread threw it up."

"So." He surveyed all the faces, all the shaven skulls— commissioned officers and noncoms and civs. He blinked, absently passed a hand over his thinning, rejuv-silvered hair. "I'd shave it off too, you know," he said, "but there's not much of it." Nervous laughs from the faces down the table. Uncertain humor. And then the thread came back to him. "So we've got the power in; got electricity in some spots. Camp's got power for cooking and freezing. Land's cleared at least in the camp area. We've all got some kind of shelter over our heads; we've done, what, seven thousand years of civilization in just about three days?" He was not sure of the seven thousand years, but he had read it in a book somewhere, how long humankind had taken about certain steps, and he saw eyes paying earnest attention to what sounded like praise. "That's good. That's real good. We've got excuse for all of us to slow down soon. But we want to do what we can while the bloom's on the matter, while we're all motivated by maybe wanting a hot shower and a warmer bed. What's the prospect on the habitats? Maybe this week we can start them? Or are we going to have to put that off?"

"We're looking," Beaumont said, beside him, seated, "at getting all the personnel into solid housing by tomorrow, even if we have to take crowded conditions. So we'll be dry if it rains. And we're putting a good graded road through the azi camp, to help them under the same conditions. We're clearing and plowing tomorrow; looking at maybe getting the sets in the ground for the garden in three more days; maybe getting general plumbing out at the azi camp."

"That's fine," Conn said. "That's way ahead of schedule."

"Subject to weather."

"Any—"

"Hey!" someone exclaimed suddenly, down the table, and swore: people came off the benches at that end of the table. There was laughter and a man dived under the table and came up with a meter long green lizard. Conn stared at it in a daze, the struggling reptile, the grinning staffer and the rest of them—Gutierrez, of the bio section.

"Is that," Conn asked, "a resident?"

"This, sir—this is an ariel. They're quick: probably got past the door while we were coming into the hut." He set it down a moment on the vacated section of the long table, and it rested there immobile, green and delicate, neck frills spread like feathers.

"I think it better find its own supper," Beaumont said. "Take it out, will you?"

Gutierrez picked it up again. Someone held the door for him. He walked to it and, bending, gave it a gentle toss into the darkness outside.

"Been back a dozen times," Bilas said. Conn felt his nerves frayed at the thought of such persistence.

Gutierrez took his seat again, and so did the others.

"Any of the big ones?" Conn asked.

"Just ariels," Gutierrez said. "They get into the huts and tents and we just put them out. No one's been hurt, us or them."

"We just live with them," Conn said. "We knew that, didn't we?" He felt shaky, and sat down again. "There are some things to do. Administrative things. I'd really like to get most of the programs launched in our tenure. The ships—leave in a few hours. And we don't see them again until three years from now. Until they arrive with the technicians and the setup for the birthlabs, at which point this world really begins to grow. Everything we do really has to be toward that setup. The labs, when they arrive, will be turning out a thousand newborns every nine months; and in the meanwhile we'll have young ones born here, with all of that to take care of. We've got azi who don't know anything about bringing up children, which is something Education's got to see to. We've got mapping to do, to lay out the pattern of development down to the last meter. We've got to locate all the hazards, because we can't have kids running around falling into them. Three years isn't such a long time for that. And long before then, we're going to have births. You've all thought of that, I'm sure." Nervous laughter from the assembly. "I think it's going to go well. We've got everything in our favor. Seven thousand years in three days. We'll come up another few millennia while we're waiting, and take another big step again when the ships get those labs to us. And this place has to be safe by then. That's all I've got to say."

A glass lifted: Ilya Burdette, down the table. "For the colonel!" All the glasses went up, and everyone echoed it. "For the captain!" someone else yelled; and they drank to Beaumont. It was a good feeling in the place. Noisy.

"What about beer?" someone yelled from the second table. "How many days before beer?"

Tired faces broke into grins. "Ag has a plan," a civ yelled back. "You get us fields, you get your beer."

"To beer!" someone shouted, and everyone shouted, and Conn laughed along with the rest.

"Civilization," someone else yelled, and they drank down the drinks they did have, and the sweat and the exhaustion and the long hours seemed not to matter to them.

iii

Venture log

"Departure effected, 1213 hours 17 minutes mission apparent time. En route to jump point, all systems normal. *US Swift* and *US Capable* are following at one hour intervals. Last communication with ground base at 1213 hours indicated excellent conditions and progress ahead of schedule: see message log. Estimate jump point arrival at 1240. . . ."

iv

Day 07, CR

Jin stepped forward as the line moved closer to the small makeshift table the supervisors had set up among the tents. He wore a jacket over his coveralls in the morning chill. The air was brisk and pleasant like spring on the world he had left. He remained content. They were clean again, besides the dust that he had to rub off his face and hands, that ground itself into his clean coveralls. They had the pipe laid, and the pumps set up, bringing clean water up to the camp, so that they had been able to shower under a long elevated pipe with holes in it—bracing cold, and there was no soap, but it had been good all the same. They could shower, they had been informed, anytime they came offshift, because there was plenty of water. There were bladed razors they could shave with, but they could let their hair and brows grow again. Faces had their expression back—almost. His head would be darkening with hair again, although he had not seen a mirror since Cyteen. He could feel it, and more, he had seen a sib or two about the sprawling camp, so he knew: he looked better.

And he tingled with excitement, and was hollowed by no small insecurity, because this line they were standing in, early in the morning, had to do with final assignments.

It all went very quickly. The comp the supervisor used was a portable. The born-man plugged in the numbers as given and it sorted through them and came up with assignments. Some azi were turned aside to wait longer; some went through without a hitch. The man in front of him went through.

"Next," the born-man said.

"J 458-9998," he said promptly, and watched it typed in.

"Preferred mate."

"P 86-687."

The man looked. One could never see the screens, whatever the operators knew, whatever the screens gave back. The machine was full of his life, his records, all that he was and all they meant him to be.

The man wrote on a plastic square and gave it to him. "Confirmed. Tent 907, row five. Go there now."

The next azi behind him was already giving her number. Jin turned away—all his baggage in hand, his small kit with the steel razor and the toothbrush and the washcloth: he was packed.

5907 was no small hike distant among the tents, down the long rows of bare dust and tents indistinguishable except for tags hung at their entries. Other walkers drifted ahead of him, azi likewise carrying their white assignment chits in hand, in the early morning with the sun coming up hazy over the tents and the small tracks and serpentine tailmarks of ariels in the dust. An ariel wandered across the lane, leisurely, paying no heed at all to the walkers, stopped only when it had reached the edge of a tent, and turned a hard eye toward them. There were more than twenty thousand tents, all set out to the east of the big permanent domes the born-men had made for themselves. Jin had helped set up the tents in this section, had helped in the surveying to peg down the marker lines, so that he had a good idea where he was going and where number 5907 was. He met cross-traffic, some of the azi from other areas, where other desks might be set up: it was like a city, this vast expanse of streets and tents, like the city he had seen the day they went to the shuttle port, which was his first sight of so great a number of dwellings.

Forty thousand azi. Thousands upon thousands of tents in blocks of ten. He came to 901 and 903 and 905, at last to 907, a tent no different than the others: he bent down and started to go in—but she was already there. She. Squatting at the doorflap, he tossed his kit onto the pallet she had not chosen, and Pia sat there crosslegged looking at him until he came inside and sat down in the light from the open tentflap.

He said nothing, finding nothing appropriate to say. He was excited about being near her at last, but what they were supposed to do together, which he had never done with anyone—that was for nighttime, after their shift was done. The tape had said so.

Her hair was growing back, like his, a darkness on her skull; and her eyes had brows again.

"You're thinner," she said.

"Yes. So are you. I wished we could have been near each other on the voyage."

"The tape asked me to name an azi I might like. I named Tal 23. Then it asked about 9998s; about you in particular. I hadn't thought about you. But the tape said you had named me."

"Yes."

"So I thought that I ought to change my mind and name you, then. I hadn't imagined you would put me first on your list."

"You were the only one. I always liked you. I couldn't think of anyone else. I hope it's all right."

"Yes. I feel really good about it."

He looked at her, a lift of his eyes from their former focus on the matting and on his knees and hands, met eyes looking at him, and thought again about what they were supposed to do together in the night—which was like the cattle in the spring fields, or the born-men in their houses and their fine beds, which he had long since realized resulted in births. He had never known azi who did the like: there were tapes which made him imagine doing such things, but this, he believed, would be somehow different.

"Have you ever done sex before?" he asked.

"No. Have you?"

"No," he said. And because he was a 9998 and confident of his reason: "May I?" he asked, and put out his hand to touch her face. She put her hand on his, and it felt delicately alive and stirred him in a way only the tapes could do before this. He grew frightened then, and dropped his hand to his knee. "We have to wait till tonight."

"Yes." She looked no less disturbed. Her eyes were wide and dark. "I really feel like the tapes. I'm not sure that's right."

And then the PA came on, telling all azi who had located their assignments to go out and start their day's work. Pia's eyes stayed fixed on his.

"We have to go," he said.

"Where do you work?"

"In the fields; with the engineers, for survey."

"I'm with the ag supervisor. Tending the sets."

He nodded—remembered the call and scrambled for his feet and the outside of the tent. She followed.

"5907," she said, to remember, perhaps. She hurried off one way and he went the other in a great muddle of confusion—not of ignorance, but of changes; of things that waited to be experienced.

Should I feel this way? he would have liked to have asked, if he could have gone to his old supervisor, who would sit with him and ask him just the right questions. Should I think about her this way? But everyone was too busy.

There would be tape soon, he hoped, which would help them sort out the things they had seen, and comfort them and tell them whether they were right or wrong in the things they were feeling and doing. But they must be right, because the born-men were proceeding on schedule, and in spite of their shouts and their impatience, they stopped sometimes to say that they were pleased.

This was the thing Jin loved. He did everything meticulously and expanded inside whenever the supervisor would tell him that something was right or good. "Easy," the supervisor would say at times, when he had run himself breathless taking a message or fetching a piece of equipment; would pat his shoulder. "Easy. You don't have to rush." But it was clear the supervisor was pleased. For that born-man he would have run his heart out, because he loved his job, which let him work with born-men in the fields he loved, observing them with a deep and growing conviction he might learn how to be what they were. The tapes had promised him.

v

Day 32, CR

Gutierrez stopped on the hillside, squatted down on the scraped earth and surveyed the new mound heaved up on this side of the river. Eva Jenks of bio dropped down beside him, and beside her, the special forces op Ogden with his rifle on his knees. Norris, out of engineering, came puffing up the slope from behind and dropped down beside them, a second rifle-carrier, in case.

It was indisputably a mound . . . on their side of the river; and new as last night. The old mounds lay directly across that gray expanse of water, about a half a kilometer across at this point—the Styx, they called it, a joke—the way they called the world Gehenna at this stage, for the dust and the conditions; Gehenna II, Gehenna Too, like the star, and not Newport. But Styx was fast getting to be the real name of this place, more colorful than Forbes River, which was the name on the maps. The Styx and the calibans. A mingling of myths. But this one had gotten out of its bounds.

"I'd really like to have an aerial shot of that," Jenks said. "You know, it looks like it's matched up with the lines on the other side."

"Maybe it has to do with orientation to the river or the sun," Gutierrez reckoned. "If we knew why they built mounds at all."

"Might use some kind of magnetic field orientation."

"Might."

"Whatever they're doing," Norris said, "we can't have them doing this in the fields. This area is gridded out for future housing. We've got to set up some kind of barrier that these things are going to respect; we need to know how deep they dig. Can't put up a barrier if we don't know that."

"I think we could justify bothering this one," Gutierrez said, without joy in the prospect.

"It's not guaranteed to be as deep a burrow as they can get," Jenks said. "After all, it's new. I don't think it would mean anything much if you dug into it. And the other mounds are all in protectorate."

"Well, the bio department made the protectorate," Norris said.

"The bio department won't budge on that," Gutierrez said. "Sorry."

A silence. "Then what we have to do," said Ogden. "is put it back across the river."

"Look," Norris said, "we could just put one of the building barriers up against it and if it tunnels under, then we'll know, won't we? A test. It's on the riverside. It won't be digging below the watertable, not without getting wet."

"They're gilled, aren't they?"

"They may be gilled, but I don't think any tunnels would hold up." Norris squinted into the morning sun and considered a moment. "By the amount of dirt and the dryness of it—What's the function of the mounds? You figure that out?"

"I think," Gutierrez said, "it rather likely has something to do with the eggs. They do lay eggs. Probably an elaborate ventilation system, like some of the colony insects; or an incubation device, using the sun. I think when we get to examining the whole system, the orientation might have to do with the prevailing winds."

"Let's have a look," said Jenks.

"All right." Gutierrez stood up, brushed off his trousers and waited on Norris and Ogden, walked down the face of the last hill the earthmovers had stripped. They headed toward the mound, down across the grassy interval.

As they reached the trough, a stone's cast from the mound of disturbed grass and dark earth, a darkish movement topped the crest of the mound and whipped up into full view, three meters long and muddy gray.

Everyone stopped. It was a simultaneous reaction. The safety went off Ogden's rifle.

"Don't shoot," Gutierrez said. "Don't even think of shooting. Just stand still. We don't know what their eyesight is like. Just stand still and let it think; it's likely to be curious as the ariels."

"Ugly bastard," Norris said. There was no dispute about that. The ariels prepared them for beauty, moved lively and lightly, fluttering their collar fronds and preening like birds. But the caliban squatted heavily on its ridge and swelled its throat, puffing out a knobbed and plated black collar, all one dull gray and smeared with black mud.

"That's a little aggression," Jenks said. "Threat display. But it's not making any move on us."

"Lord," Ogden said, "if *those* start waddling through the base they're going to need room, aren't they?"

"It eats fish," Gutierrez reminded them. "It's more interested in the river than in anything else."

"He means," Jenks said, "that if you stand between that fellow and the river you're a lot more likely to get run down by accident. It might run for its mound access; or for the river. If it runs."

"Stay put," Gutierrez said, and took a cautious step forward.

"Sir," Ogden said, "we're not supposed to lose you."

"Well, I don't plan to get lost. Just stay put. You too, Eva." He started forward, moving carefully, watching all the small reactions, the timing of the raising and lowering of the knobbed collar, the breathing that swelled and diminished its pebbly sides. The jaws had teeth. A lot of them. He knew that. A thick black serpent of a tongue flicked out and retreated, flicked again. That was investigation. Gutierrez stopped and let it smell the air.

The caliban sat a moment more. Turned its head with reptilian deliberation and regarded him with one vertically slit jade eye the size of a saucer. The collar lifted and lowered. Gutierrez took another step and another, right to the base of the mound now, which rose up three times his height.

All of a sudden the caliban stood up, lashed its tail and dislodged clods of earth as it stiffened its four bowed legs and got its belly off the ground. It dipped its head to keep him in view, a sidelong view of that same golden, vertical-slitted eye.

That was close enough, then. Gutierrez felt backward for a step, began a careful retreat, pace by pace.

The caliban came down toward him the same way, one planting of a thick-clawed foot and a similar planting of the opposing hind foot, one two three four, that covered an amazing amount of ground too quickly. "Don't shoot." He heard Eva Jenks' voice, and was not sure at the moment that he agreed. He stopped, afraid to run. The caliban stopped likewise and looked at him a body length distant.

"Get out of there," Jenks yelled at him.

The tongue went out and the head lifted in Jenks' direction. It was over knee high when it was squatting and waist high when it stood up; and it could move much faster than anticipated. The tail moved restlessly, and Gutierrez took that into account too, because it was a weapon that could snap a human spine if the caliban traded ends.

The collar went flat again, the head dipped and then angled the same slitted eye toward him. It leaned forward slowly, turning the head to regard his foot; and that leaning began to lessen the distance between them.

"Move!" Jenks shouted.

The tongue darted out, thick as his wrist, and flicked lightly about his booted, dusty foot; the caliban retracted it, serpentined aside with a scraping of sod, regarded him again with a chill amber eye. The tail swept close and whipped back short of hitting him. Then in remote grandeur the caliban waddled back and climbed its mound. Gutierrez finally felt the pounding of his own heart. He turned and walked back to his own party, but Jenks was already running toward him and Ogden was close behind, with Norris following.

Gutierrez looked at Jenks in embarrassment, thinking first that he had done something stupid and secondly that the caliban had not done what they expected: it had not gone through the several days of flight-and-approach the probe team reported.

"So much for the book," he said, still shaking. "Might be pushing on the mating season."

"Or hunting."

"I think we'd better try to establish a concrete barrier here, right on that hill back there."

"Right," Norris said. "And draw the line all around this area."

Gutierrez looked back at the caliban, which had regained its perch on the mound. When animals violated the rules on a familiar world it indicated a phase of behavior not yet observed: nesting, for instance.

But curiosity in a species so formidably large—

"It didn't follow the book," he muttered. "And that makes me wonder about the rest of the script."

Jenks said nothing. There was a limit to what bio ought to speculate on publicly. He had already said more than he felt politic; but there were people out walking the fields still relying on Mercury probe's advice.

"I'd just suggest everyone be a bit more careful," he said.

He walked back up the hill with the others following. The first front had sprinkled them with rain, quickly dried. There was weather moving in again that looked more serious—on the gray sea, out among the few islands which lay off the coast, a bank of cloud. There was that matter to factor in with the environment.

Might the weather make a difference in caliban moods?

And as for construction, if the weather turned in earnest—

"The foam's not going to set too easy if we get that rain," he said. "Neither will concrete. I think we may have to wait . . . but we'd better get to the maps, and figure where we're going to set that concrete barrier."

"Two criteria," the engineer said. "Protection from flood and our own access to areas we need."

"One more," Jenks said. "The calibans. Where they decide to go."

"We can't be warping all our plans around those lizards," Norris said. "What I'd like to do instead, by your leave— is put a charged fence out here and see if we can't make it unpleasant enough it'll want to leave."

Gutierrez considered the matter, nodded after a moment. "You can try it. Nothing that's going to disturb the colony across the river. But if we can encourage this fellow to swim back to his side, I'd say it might be better for him and for us."

Gutierrez looked at the clouds, and over his shoulder at the mounds, still trying to fit the behavior into patterns.

vi

Day 58 CR

The fog retreated in a general grayness of the heavens, and the wind blew cold at the window, snapping at the plastic. The heat seemed hardly adequate. Conn sat wrapped in his blanket and thinking that it might be more pleasant, privacy notwithstanding, to move into the main dome with the others. Or he could complain. Maybe someone could do something with the heater. With all that expertise out there, gathered to build a world—surely someone could do something with the space heater.

Two weeks of this kind of thing, with the waves beating at the shore and driving up the river from a monster storm somewhere at sea: water, and water everywhere. The newly cleared fields were bogs and the machinery was sinking, even sitting still. And the chill got into bones and the damp air soaked clothes so that none of them had had warm dry clothing for as long as the fog had lain over them. Clothes stank of warmth and mildew. Azi lines huddled in the drizzle and collected their food at distribution points and went back again into the soggy isolation of the tents. How they fared there Conn had no true idea, but if they had been suffering worse than the rest of the camp, then Education would have notified the staff at large.

A patter began at the window, a spatter of drops carried by a gust. When the wind blew the fog out they had rain and when the wind stopped the fog settled in. He listened to the malevolent spat of wind-driven water, watched a thin trickle start from the corner that leaked; but he had moved the chest from beneath it, and put his laundry on the floor to soak up the leak that pooled on the foamset floor. There was no sound but that for a while, the wind and the beat of the drops; and solitude, in the thin, gray daylight that came through the rain-spattered plastic.

It was too much. He got up and put his coat on, waited for a lull in the rain and opened the door and splashed his way around to the front door of the main dome onto which his smaller one abutted, a drenching, squelching passage through puddles on what had been a pebbled walk.

He met warmth inside, electric light and cheerfulness, the heat of the electronics and the lights which were always on here; and the bodies and the conversation and the business. "Tea, sir?" an azi asked, on duty to serve and clean in the dome; "Yes," he murmured, sat down at the long table that was the center of all society and a great deal of the work in the staff dome. Maps cluttered its far end; the engineers were in conference, a tight cluster of heads and worried looks.

The tea arrived, and Conn took it, blinked absently at the azi and muttered a Thanks, that's all, which took the azi out of his way and out of his thoughts. A lizard scuttled near the wall that separated off the com room: that was Ruffles. Ruffles went anywhere she/he liked, a meter long and prone to curl around the table legs or to lurk under the feet of anyone sitting still, probably because she had been spoiled with table-tidbits. Clean: at least she was that. The creature had come in so persistently she had acquired a name and a grudging place in the dome. Now everyone fed the thing, and from a scant meter long, she had gotten fatter, passed a meter easily, and gone through one skin change in recent weeks.

A scrabbling climb put Ruffles onto a stack of boxes. Conn drank his tea and stared back at her golden slit eyes. Her head turned to angle one at him directly. She flared her collar and preened a bit.

"Help you, sir?" That was Bilas, making a bench creak as he sat down close by, arms on the table. Non-com and special op colonel—they had no distinctions left. Protocols were down, everywhere.

"Just easing the aches in my bones. Any progress on that drainage?"

"We got the pipe in, but we have a silting problem. Meteorology says they're not surprised by this one. So we hear."

"No. It's no surprise. We got off lightly with the last front."

Another staffer arrived, carrying her cup—Regan Chiles dropped onto a bench opposite, scavenger-wise spotting a body in authority and descending with every indication of problems. "Got a little difficulty," she said. "Tape machines are down. It's this salt air and the humidity. We pulled the most delicate parts and put them into seal; but we're going to have to take the machines apart and clean them; and we're really not set up for that."

"You'll do the best you can." He really did not want to hear this. He looked about him desperately, found fewer people in the dome than he had expected, which distracted him with wondering why. Chiles went on talking, handing him her problems, and he nodded and tried to take them in, the overload Education was putting on Computer Maintenance, because inexpert personnel had exposed some of the portable units to the conditions outside. Because Education had programs behind schedule . . . and shifted blame.

"Look," he said finally, "your chain of command runs through Maj. Gallin. All this ought to go to him."

A pursed lip, a nod, an inwardness of the eyes. Something was amiss.

"What answer did Gallin give you?"

"Gallin just told us to fix it and to cooperate."

"Well, you don't go over Gallin's head, lieutenant. You hear me?"

"Sir," Chiles muttered, clenched her square jaw and took another breath. "But begging the colonel's pardon, sir—my people are going shift to shift and others are idle."

"That's because your department has something wrong, isn't it?"

"Yes, sir."

"I'll talk to the other departments." He was conscious of Bilas at his elbow, witness to it all. "I stand by Gallin, you hear? I won't have this bypassing channels.—Drink the tea, lieutenant; both of you. If we have any problems like that, then you keep to chain of command."

"Yes, sir."

"Sir," Bilas murmured.

He stayed there, sipping the tea, himself and Chiles and Bilas; and soon others came up the table to intimate their troubles to him, so that his stomach knotted up again in all the discomfort he had left his quarters to avoid.

And finally after he had drunk several cups of tea and had to go out to avail himself of the latrine in back of the dome, he headed back to his own quarters with his collar turned up and an ache in his bones that felt like dull needles. An ariel slithered through a puddle in his path, miniature mariner, swimming for a moment, more intent on direction than convenience, which was the habit of ariels.

A siren disturbed the air. He looked about him in the pale gray haze, tried to get location on it, and thought it was coming from somewhere near the fields.

vii

Day 58 CR

They brought Ada Beaumont back in a sheet with the blood and the rain soaking it, and Bob Davies following along after the litter with his clothes soaked and stained with mud and blood, and that look in his eyes that was nowhere, and nowhen, as if he had backed away from life.

Conn came out into the rain and looked down at the smallish bundle on the stretcher—stared confusedly, because it was always ridiculous how something as large across life as Ada, a special op who had survived Fargone and the war and the Rising, who had been wiry and cagey and full of every trick the enemy never expected—could come down to an object so small and diminished. Men and women stood with their eyes hazed with tears, in the fog and the mist, but Bob Davies just stared in shock, his face gone ghastly pale; and Conn put his hands in his pockets and felt a panic and a hollowness in his gut.

"It was a caliban burrow," Pete Gallin said, wiped the water out of his eyes with a bloody, abraded hand. "Andresson—saw it happen."

"Andresson." Conn looked at the man, a thin and wispy fellow with distracted eyes.

"We were fixing that washout up there and she was talking to me on the rig when the ground behind her feet just—went. This big crawler behind her, parked, nobody on it—just started tipping for no cause. She went under it; and we had to get the winch, sir—we got another crawler turned and got the winch on it, but it was one of those lizard burrows, like—like three, four meters down; and in that soft ground, the crawler on it—the whole thing just dissolved. . . ."

"Take precautions," Conn said; and then thought that they were all expecting him to grieve over Beaumont, and they would hate him because he was like this. "We can't have another." There was a dire silence, and the bearers of the litter just stood there in the rain shifting the poles in their hands because of the weight. Their cropped heads shed beads of water, and red seeped through the thin sheeting and ran down into the puddles. "We bury in the earth," he said, his mind darting irrevocably to practical matters, for stationers, who were not used to that. "Over by the sea, I think, where there's no building planned."

He walked away—like that, in silence. He did not realize either the silence or his desertion until he was too far away to make it good. He walked to his own quarters and shut the door behind him, shed his wet jacket and flung it down on the bench.

Then he cried, standing there in the center of the room, and shivered in the cold and knew that there was nothing in Pete Gallin or in any of the others which would help him. Old as he was getting and sick as he was getting, the desertion was all on Ada's side.

He was remarkably lucid in his shock. He knew, for instance, that the burrowing beyond the perimeters was worse news than Ada's death. It threw into doubt all their blueprints for coexistence with the calibans. It spelled conflict. It altered the future of the world—because they had to cope with it with only the machines and the resources in their hands. When the weather cleared they would have to sit down and draw new plans, and somehow he had to pull things into a coherency that would survive. That would save forty thousand human lives.

Promotions had to be done. Gallin had to be brought up to co-governor: Gallin—a good supervisor and a decent man and no help at all. Maybe a civ like Gutierrez—

Gutierrez was the brightest of the division chiefs, in more than bio; but there was no way to jump Gutierrez over others with more seniority. Or Sedgewick—a legal mind with rank but no decisiveness.

He wiped his eyes, found his hand trembling uncontrollably.

Someone splashed up to the door, opened it without a by your leave, a sudden noise of rain and gust of cold. He looked about. It was Dean, of the medical staff.

"You all right, sir?"

He straightened his shoulders. "Quite. How's Bob?"

"Under sedation. Are you sure, sir?"

"I'll be changing my clothes. I'll be over in the main dome in a minute. Just let me be."

"Yes, sir." A lingering look. Dean left. Conn turned to the strung clothesline which was his closet and his laundry, and picked the warmest clothes he had, still slightly damp. He wanted a drink. He wanted it very badly.

But he went and set things right in the dome instead—met with the staff, laid out plans, unable finally to go out to the burial because of the chill, because he began to shiver and the chief surgeon laid down the law—which was only what he wanted.

Tired people came back, wet, and shivering and sallow-faced. Davies was prostrate in sickbay, under heavier sedation after the burial—had broken down entirely, hysterical and loud, which Ada had never been. Ever. Gallin sat with shadowed eyes and held a steaming cup in front of him at table. "You're going to have to survey the area," Conn said to him, with others at the table, because there was no privacy, "and you're going to have to keep surveying, to find out if there's more undermining."

"Yes, sir."

Ruffles, on her stack of boxes, flicked her tongue. Conn regarded her balefully past Gallin's slumped shoulder and bowed head. "It was an accident," he said. "That's all there is to say about it. We just don't intend to have another one."

"Sir," Gallin said, "that caliban mound on this side of the river . . . I'd like to break that up."

Conn looked at Gutierrez, who had his mouth clamped tight. "Gutierrez?"

"I'd like to know first," Gutierrez said, "if that's the

source of the tunnelling in the camp or not. If we don't know for sure, if we're just guessing—we're not solving the problem at all."

"You're proposing more study."

"I'd like to do that, sir."

"Do it, then. But we're going to have to probe those tunnels and know where they go."

"I'll be on that—tonight, if you like."

"You map it out on paper tonight. And we get a team out at daybreak to probe the ground. We don't know for certain it is the calibans at all, do we?"

"No," said Gutierrez. "That's the point. We don't know."

Conn gathered up the bottle on the table in front of him, that they had used to lace the tea, and poured himself the long postponed drink. His hand shook violently in the pouring so that he spilled a little. He sipped at it and the liquor went into him, settling his battered nerves.

Ruffles scrambled from her perch and hit the floor, put on her best display. One of the techs slipped from the table and got her a morsel of food, which vanished with a neat dart of the head and a choking motion.

Conn finished his drink, excused himself, put his jacket on and walked back to his own quarters around the bending of the walk. The rain had stopped, in the evening. The electric lights in the compound and scattered throughout the azi camp were haloed in the mist. He stopped there on the puddled gravel walk, cold inside, looked out over all the camp, seeing what they had come to do slipping further and further away.

viii

Day 58 CR

"They put her in the ground," Pia said, very soft, in the comfort of their pallet; and Jin held to her for comfort in the dark. "They buried her in the ground, and they all stood around and cried."

This was a revelation—the death of a born-man. They were accustomed to azi mortality. Azi died, and they carried the body to the white building on the farm, and that was the end of the matter. If one was a good type, then there was the confidence that others of one's type would go on being born. There was pride involved in that. And that meant something.

But they saved nothing of Ada Beaumont. There were no labs to save it.

"I wish we could have tapes," Jin said. "I miss them."

Pia hugged him the tighter, buried her face against his shoulder. "I wish the same thing. There was a mistake about the machine falling on the captain. I don't know what. I think we could have been at fault. I wish we knew."

"They say they can't use the machines in the bad weather."

"When there are labs again," Pia said, "when we have good tape again, it's going to be better."

"Yes," he said.

But that was a very long time away.

He and Pia made love in the dark; and that replaced the tapes. It came to him that they were happier than the born-man who had died, having no one of her own type surviving, at least here on this world. But there were other 9998s and 687s. And they made love because it was the warmest and the pleasantest thing they could do, and because they were permitted.

This made born-men; and an obscure sense of duty dawned on Jin, that if one had died, then one had to be born. This was why they had been chosen, and what they had to do.

The rain stopped, and the sun came back in the morning, with only a ragged bit of cloud. The world was different under this sun. The crawlers stood off in the cleared fields, muddy with yesterday's accident, and a great pit remained around which born-men began to probe. And the world was different because there was a dead born-man lying alone by the sea, with a marker that let the grave be seen across the camp.

Jin walked to his supervisor's table, set up in the roadway under this new sun, and applied for the day's work; but instead of doing more survey, he was given a metal rod and told to push it into the earth. He was to call the supervisor if it seemed that the dirt was looser than it ought to be. He went out among others and probed until his shoulders ached, and the born-man Gutierrez and his crew took down all that they found.

ix

Day 162 CR

The domes rose, with the sun hot and the sea beating blue and white at the shore; and Conn sat in his chair in front of the main dome, under the canopy, because the heat was never that great, and the breeze pleased him. An ariel waddled across the dust near the walk and squatted there just off the gravel path, in the shadow of Conn's own adjacent dome. It built—instinctive behavior, Gutierrez maintained. It had brought a pebble and added it to the stack it was making—not a pebble from the walk, thank you, but a larger one, painstakingly found elsewhere, presumably just the right pebble, for reasons only another ariel might grasp. It made circles of stacks. It built domes too, Conn thought distantly; but its domes failed, collapsing into nests. The last few stones always knocked the efforts down, lacking the trick of a keystone. So it seemed. But that was a fancy: too much of domes, too much of a preoccupation with them lately. The ariel built lines and patterns out from its collapsed stacks of stones, loops and whorls and serpentines. Rudimentary behavior like the moundbuilding calibans, Gutierrez had said. Probably it originated as a nesting behavior and elaborated into display behaviors. Both sexes built. That had disappointed Gutierrez.

No more calibans this side of the river, at least. The mounds remained, across the river, but azi with spades had taken the mound this side apart. It was stalemate, the calibans forbidden their mounds this side, the crawlers and earthmovers standing still, mothballed, now that all the major building and clearing was done.

The ship would come, bringing them the supplies and lab facilities they needed; and then the machines would grind and dig their way further across the landscape around that ell bend between the river and the forest, making foundations for the lab and the real city they planned.

But the nearer focus was still tents. Still tents. More than twenty thousand tents, dull brown under the sun. They tried, having hunted the last determined caliban off this shore; but the crawlers had reached the point of diminishing returns in maintenance, needing the supplies the ship would bring. Up the rivercourse the azi blasted at limestone and hauled it back in handpulled wagons, laboriously, as humans had hauled stone in the dawn of human building, because they dared not risk the crawlers, the last of them that worked on parts cannibalized from the others. The azi labored with blasting materials and picks and bare hands, and there was a camp of two dozen tents strung out there too, at the limestone cliffs where they quarried stone.

Perhaps it might have been wiser to have moved the whole site there, to stony ground—knowing now that calibans burrowed. But they had spent all their resources of material and fuel. The domes stood, so at least the staff had secure housing. The fields were planted, and the power systems and the equipment were safe so long as they kept the calibans away.

Conn studied his charts, traced again and again the changes they had had to make in plans. The cold this spring had hurt his hands; and the joints twisted and pained him, even in the summer sun. He thought of another winter and dreaded it.

But they survived. He knew the time of the landing that would come, down to the day, year after next; and mentally he marked off every day, one to the next, with all the complexities of local/universal time.

The ship, he was determined, would take him home. He would go back to Cyteen. He thought that he might live through the jumps. Might. Or at least he would not have to see more of this world.

Newport, he had called it. But Gehenna had stuck instead. It was where they were; it described their situation. Like Styx for the Forbes River, that began as a joke and stayed. When a wheel broke on one of the carts or when it rained—Gehenna's own luck, they said; and: What do you expect, in Hell?

They came to the Old Man and complained: Conn solved what he could, shrugged his shoulders at the rest. Like Gallin. Finally—like Gallin. "That's your problem," was Gal-

lin's line, which had gotten to be a proverb so notorious
Gallin had had to find different ways of saying it. A sad
fellow, Gallin, a bewildered fellow, who never knew why
he deserved everyone's spite. Conn sat placidly, waited for
problems to trickle past the obstacle of Gallin, soothed
tempers—kept the peace. That was the important thing.

A figure slogged down the lane, slumpshouldered and
forlorn, and that was Bob Davies, another of the casualties.
Davies worked the labor accounts, kept the supply books,
and went off the rejuv of his own choice and over the
surgeons' protests. So there were two of them getting old.
Maybe it showed more on Davies than on him—balding
and growing bowed and thin in the passage of only a few
months.

"Morning," Conn wished him. Davies came out of his
private reverie long enough to look up as he went by.
"Morning," Davies said absently, and went back to his
computers and his books and his endless figuring.

That was the way of it now, that as fast as they built, the
old pieces fell apart. Conn turned his mind back to the
permafax sheets in his lap and made more adjustments in
the plans which had once been so neatly drawn.

Two things went well. No, three: the crops flourished in
the fields, making green as far as the eye could see. And
Hill's fish came up in the nets so that a good many of them
might be sick of fish, but they all ate well. The plumbing
and the power worked. They had lost some of the tape
machines; but others worked, and the azi showed no appre-
ciable strain.

But the winter—the first winter . . .

That had to be faced; and the azi were still under tents.

x

Day 346 CR

The wind blew and howled about the doors of the med
dome. Jin sat in the anteroom and wrung his hands and
fretted, a dejection which so possessed him it colored all
the world.

She's well, the doctors had told him; she's going to do

well. He believed this on one level, having great trust in Pia, that she was very competent and that her tapes had given her all the things she had to know. But she had been in pain when he had brought her here; and the hours of her pain wore on, so that he sat blank much of the time, and only looked up when one of the medics would come or go through that inner corridor where Pia was.

One came now. "Would you like to be with her?" the born-man asked him, important and ominous in his white clothing. "You can come in if you like."

Jin gathered himself to unsteady legs and followed the young born-man through into the area which smelled strongly of disinfectants—a hall winding round the dome, past rooms on the left. The born-man opened the first door for him and there lay Pia on a table, surrounded by meds all in masks. "Here," said one of the azi who assisted here, and offered him a gown to wear, but no mask. He shrugged it on, distracted by his fear, "Can I see her?" he asked, and they nodded. He went at once to Pia and took her hand.

"Does it hurt?" he asked. He thought that it must be hurting unbearably, because Pia's face was bathed in sweat. He wiped that with his hand and a born-man gave him a towel to use.

"It's not so bad," she said between breaths. "It's all right."

He held onto her hand; and sometimes her nails bit into his flesh and cut him; and betweentimes he mopped her face . . . his Pia, whose belly was swollen with life that was finding its way into the world now whether they wanted or not.

"Here we go," a med said. "Here we are."

And Pia cried out and gave one great gasp, so that if he could have stopped it all now he would have. But it was done then, and she looked relieved. Her nails which had driven into his flesh eased back, and he held onto her a long time, only glancing aside as a born-man nudged his arm.

"Will you hold him?" the med asked, offering him a bundled shape: Jin took it obediently, only then realizing fully that it was alive. He looked down into a small red face, felt the squirming of strong tiny limbs and knew—suddenly knew with real force that the life which had come out of Pia was independent, a gene-set which had never been before. He was terrified. He had never seen a baby. It was so small, so small and he was holding it.

"You've got yourselves a son," a med told Pia, leaning close and shaking her shoulder. "You understand? You've got yourselves a little boy."

"Pia?" Jin bent down, holding the baby carefully, oh so carefully—"Hold his head gently," the med told him. "Support his neck," and put his hand just so, helped him give the baby into Pia's arms. Pia grinned at him, sweat-drenched as she was, a strange tired grin, and fingered the baby's tiny hand.

"He's perfect," one of the meds said, close by. But Jin had never doubted that. He and Pia were.

"You have to name him," said another. "He has to have a name, Pia."

She frowned over that for a moment, staring at the baby with her eyes vague and far. They had said, the born-men, that this would be the case, that they had to choose a name, because the baby would have no number. It was a mixing of gene-sets, and this was the first one of his kind in the wide universe, this mix of 9998 and 687.

"Can I call him Jin too?" Pia asked.

"Whatever you like," the med said.

"Jin," Pia decided, with assurance. Jin himself looked down on the small mongrel copy Pia held and felt a stir of pride. Winter rain fell outside, pattering softly against the roof of the dome. Cold rain. But the room felt more than warm. The born-men were taking all the medical things away, wheeling them out with a clatter of metal and plastics.

And they wanted to take the baby away too. Jin looked up at them desperately when they took it from Pia's arms, wanting for one of a few times in his life to say no.

"We'll bring him right back," the med said ever so softly. "We'll wash him and do a few tests and we'll bring him right back in a few moments. Won't you stay with Pia, Jin, and keep her comfortable?"

"Yes," he said, feeling a tremor in his muscles, even so, thinking that if they wanted to take the baby back again later, after Pia had suffered so to have it, then he wanted very much to stop them. But yes was all he knew how to say. He held on to Pia, and a med hovered about all the same, not having gone with the rest. "It's all right," Jin told Pia, because she was distressed and he could see it. "It's all right. They said they'd bring it back. They will."

"Let me make her comfortable," the med said, and he was dispossessed even of that post—invited back again, to wash Pia's body, to lift her, to help the med settle her into a waiting clean bed; and then the med took the table out, so it was himself alone with Pia.

"Jin," Pia said, and he put his arm under her head and held her, still frightened, still thinking on the pleasure they had had and the cost it was to bring a born-man into the world. Pia's cost. He felt guilt, like bad tape; but it was not a question of tape: it was something built in, irreparable in what they were.

Then they did bring the baby back, and laid it in Pia's arms; and he could not forbear to touch it, to examine the tininess of its hands, the impossibly little fists. It. Him. This born-man.

xi

Year 2, day 189 CR

Children took their first steps in the second summer's sun . . . squealed and cried and laughed and crowed. It was a good sound for a struggling colony, a sound which had crept on the settlement slowly through the winter, in baby cries and requisitions for bizarre oddments of supply. Baby washing hung out in the azi camp and the central domes in whatever sun the winter afforded—never cold enough to freeze, not through all the winter, just damp; and bone-chilling nasty when the wind blew.

Gutierrez sat by the roadside, the road they had extended out to the fields. In one direction the azi camp fluttered with white flags of infant clothing out to dry; and in the other the crawlers and earthmovers sat, shrouded in their plastic hoods, and flitters nested there.

He watched—near where limestone blocks and slabs and rubble made the first solid azi buildings, one-roomed and simple. They had left some chips behind, and an ariel was at its stone-moving routine. It took the chips in its mouth, such as it could manage, and moved them, stacked them in what began to look like one of the more elaborate ariel constructions, in the shadow of the wall.

A caliban had moved into the watermeadow again. They wanted to hunt it and Gutierrez left this to Security. He had no stomach for it. Best they hunt it now, before it laid eggs. But all the same the idea saddened him, like the small collection of caliban skulls up behind the main dome.

Barbaric, he thought. Taking heads. But the hunt had to be, or there would be more tunnelling and the azi houses would fall.

He dusted himself off finally, started up and down the road toward the domes, having started the hunters on their way.

Man adjusted—on Gehenna, on Newport. Man gave a little. But between man and calibans, there did not look to be peace, not, perhaps, until the ship should come. There might be an answer, in better equipment. In the projection barriers they might have made work, if the weather had not been so destructive of equipment . . . if, if, and if.

He walked back into the center of camp, saw the Old Man sitting where he usually sat, under the canopy outside main dome. The winter had put years on the colonel. A stubble showed on his face, a spot of stain on his rumpled shirt front. He drowsed, did Conn, and Gutierrez passed him by, entered quietly into the dome and crossing the room past the long messtable, poured himself a cup of the ever-ready tea. The place smelled of fish. The dining hall always did. Most all Gehenna smelled of fish.

He sat down, with some interest, at the table with Kate Flanahan. The special op was more than casual with him; no precise recollection where it had started, except one autumn evening, and realizing that there were qualities in Kate which mattered to him.

"You got it?" Kate asked.

"I headed them out. I don't have any stomach left for that."

She nodded. Kate trained to kill human beings, not wild-life. The specials sat and rusted. Like the machinery out there.

"Thought—" Gutierrez said, "I might apply for a walk-about. Might need an escort."

Kate's eyes brightened.

But "No," Conn said, when he broached the subject, that evening, at common mess.

"Sir—"

"We hold what territory we have," the colonel said. In that tone. And there was no arguing. Silence fell for a moment at the table where all of them who had no domestic arrangements took their meals. It was abrupt, that answer. It was decisive. "We've got all we can handle," the colonel said then. "We've got another year beyond this before we get backup here, and I'm not stirring anything up by exploring."

The silence persisted. The colonel went on with his eating, a loud clatter of knife and fork.

"Sir," Gutierrez said, "in my professional opinion—there's reason for the investigation, to see what the situation is on the other bank, to see—"

"We'll be holding this camp and taking care of our operation here," the colonel said. "That's the end of it. That's it."

"Yes, sir," Gutierrez said.

Later, he and Kate Flanahan found their own opportunity for being together, with more privacy and less comfort, in the quarters he had to himself, with Ruffles, who watched with a critical reptilian eye.

"Got a dozen specs going crazy," Kate said during one of the lulls in their lovemaking, when they talked about the restriction, about the calibans, about things they had wanted to do. "Got people who came here with the idea we'd be building all this time. Special op hoped for some use. And we're rotting away. All of us. You. Us. Everyone but the azi. The Old Man's got this notion the world's dangerous and he's not letting us out of camp. He's scared of the blamed lizards, Marco. Can't you try it on a better day, make sense to him, talk sense into him?"

"I'll go on trying," he said. "But it goes deeper than just the calibans. He has his own idea how to protect this base, and that's what he means to do. To do nothing. To survive till the ships come. I'll try."

But he knew the answer already, implicit in the Old Man's clamped jaw and fevered stare.

"No," the answer came when he did ask again, days later, after stalking the matter carefully. "Put it out of your head, Gutierrez."

He and Flanahan went on meeting. And one day toward fall Flanahan reported to the meds that she might be pregnant. She came to live with him; and that was the thing that redeemed the year.

But Gutierrez' work was slowed to virtual stop—with all the wealth of a new world on the horizon. He did meticulous studies of tiny ecosystems along the shoreline; and when in the fall another caliban turned up in the watermeadow, and when the hunters shot it, he stood watching the crime, and sat down on the hillside in view of the place, sat there all the day, because of the pain he felt.

And the hunters avoided his face, though there was no anger in his sitting there, and nothing personal.

"I'm not shooting any more," a special op told him later, the man who had shot this one.

As for Flanahan, she had refused the hunt.

xii

Year 2, day 290 CR

The weather turned again toward the winter, the season of bitter cold rain and sometime fogs, when the first calibans wandered into the camp. And stayed the night. They passed like ghosts in the fog, under the haloed lights, came like the silly ariels; but the calibans were far more impressive.

Jin watched them file past the tent, strange and silent except for the scrape of leathery bodies and clawed feet; and he and Pia gathered little Jin against them in the warmth of the tent, afraid, because these creatures were far different than the gay fluttery green lizards that came and went among the tents and the stone shelters.

"They won't hurt us," Pia said, a whisper in the fog-milky night. "The tapes said they never hurt anyone."

"There was the captain," Jin said, recalling that, thinking

of all their safe tent tumbling down into some chasm, the way the born-man Beaumont had died.

"An accident."

"But born-men shoot them." He was troubled at the idea. He had never gotten it settled in his mind about intelligence, what animals were and what men were, and how one told the difference. They said the calibans had no intelligence. It was not in their gene set. He could believe that of the giddy ariels. But these were larger than men, and grim and deliberate in their movements.

The calibans moved through, and there were no human sounds, no alarms to indicate harm. But they laced the tentflap and stayed awake with little Jin asleep between them. At every small sound outside they started, and sometimes held hands in the absolute dark and closeness of the tent.

Perhaps, Jin thought in the lonely hours, the calibans were angry that born-men hunted them. Perhaps that was why they came.

But on the next day, when they got up with the sun, a rumor of something strange passed through the camp, and Jin went among the others to see, how all the loose stones they had stacked up for building had been moved and set into a low and winding wall that abutted a building in which azi lived. He went to work with the others, undoing what the calibans had done, but he was afraid with an unaccustomed fear. Until then he had feared only born-men, and known what right and wrong was. But he felt strange to be taking down what the calibans had done, this third and unaccountable force which had walked through their midst and noticed them.

"Stop," a supervisor said. "People are coming from the main camp to see."

Jin quit his work and sat down among the others, wrapped tightly in his jacket and sitting close to other azi . . . watched while important born-men came from the main domes. They made photographs, and the born-man Gutierrez came with his people and looked over every aspect of the building. This born-man Jin knew: this was the one they called when they found something strange, or when someone had been stung or bitten by something or wandered into one of the nettles. And there was in this man's face and in the faces of his aides and in the faces of no few of the other born-men . . . a vast disturbance.

"They respond to instinct," Gutierrez said finally. Jin could hear that much. "Ariels stack stones. The behavior seems to be wired into the whole line."

But calibans, Jin thought to himself, built walls in the night, silently, of huge stones, and connected them to buildings with people in them.

He never felt quite secure after that, in the night, although the born-men went out and strung electric fences around the camp, and although the calibans did not come back. Whenever the fogs would come, he would think of them ghosting powerfully through the camps, so still, so purposeful; and he would hug his son and Pia close and be glad that no azi had to be outside by night.

xiii

Year 3, day 120 CR

The air grew warmer again, and the waiting began . . . the third spring, when the ships should come. All the ills— the little cluster of forlorn human graves beside the sea— seemed tragedy on a smaller scale, against the wide universe, because the prospect of ships reminded people that the world was not alone. "When the ships come" was all the talk in camp.

When the ships came, there would be luxuries again, like soap and offworld foods.

When the ships came, the earthmovers would move again, and they would build and catch up to schedule.

When the ships came, there would be new faces, and the first colonists would have a distinction over the newcomers, would own things and be someone.

When the ships came, there would be birthlabs and azi and the population increase would start tipping the balance of Gehenna in favor of man.

But spring wore on past the due date, with at first a fevered anticipation, and then a deep despair, finally hopes carefully fanned to life again; a week passed, a month— and When became a forbidden word.

Conn waited. His joints hurt him; and there would be medicines when the ship came. There would be someone on whom to rely. He thought of Cyteen again, and Jean's untended grave. He thought of—so many things he had given up. And at first he smiled, and then he stopped smiling and retreated to his private dome. He still had faith. Still believed in the government which had sent him here, that something had delayed the ships, but not prevented them. If something were wrong, the ship would hang off in space at one of the jump points and repair it and get underway again, which might take time.

He waited, day by day.

But Bob Davies lay down to sleep one late spring night and took all the pills the meds had given him. It was a full day more before anyone noticed, because Davies lived alone, and all the divisions he usually worked had assumed he was working for someone else, on some other assignment. He had gone to sleep, that was all, quietly, troubling no one. They buried him next to Beaumont, which was all the note he had left wanted of them. It was Beaumont's death that had killed Davies: that was what people said. But it was the failure of the ship that prompted it, whatever Davies had hoped for—be it just the reminder that Somewhere Else existed in the universe; or that he hoped to leave. Whatever hope it was that kept the man alive—failed him.

James Conn went to the funeral by the sea. When it was done, and the azi were left to throw earth into the grave, he went back to his private dome and poured himself one drink and several more.

A fog rolled in that evening, one of those fogs that could last long, and wrapped all the world in white. Shapes came and went in it, human shapes and sometimes the quiet scurryings of the ariels; and at night, the whisper of movements which might be the heavier tread of calibans—but there were fences to stop them, and most times the fences did.

Conn drank, sitting at the only real desk in Gehenna; and thought of other places: of Jean, and a grassy grave on Cyteen; of the graves by the sea; of friends from the war, who had had no graves at all, when he and Ada Beaumont had had a closeness even he and Jean had never had . . .

for a week, on Fargone; and they had never told Jean and never told Bob, about that week the 12th had lost a third of its troops and they had hunted the resistance out of the tunnels pace by pace. He thought of those days, of forgotten faces, blurred names, and when the dead had gotten to outnumber the living in his thoughts he found himself comfortable and safe. He drank with them, one and all; and before morning he put a gun to his head and pulled the trigger.

xiv

Year 3, day 189 CR

The grain grew, the heads whitened, and the scythes went back and forth in azi hands, the old way, without machines; and still the ships delayed.

Gutierrez walked the edge of the camp, out near those fields, and surveyed the work. The houses at his right, the azi camp, were many of them of stone now, ramshackle, crazy building; but all the azi built their own shelters in their spare time, and sometimes they found it convenient to build some walls in common . . . less work for all concerned. If it stood, the engineers and the Council approved it; and that was all there was to it.

He and Kate did something of the like, needing room: they built onto their dome with scrap stone, and it served well enough for an extra room, for them and for small Jane Flanahan-Gutierrez.

Another caliban had come into the meadow. They came, Gutierrez reckoned, when the seasons turned, and whenever the autumn approached they were obsessed with building burrows. If thoughts at all proceeded in those massive brains. He argued with Council, hoping still for his expedition across the river; but it was weeding time; but it was harvest time. Now a caliban was back and he proposed studying it where it was.

And if it undermines the azi quarters, Gallin head of Council, had objected, or if it gets into the crops—

"We have to live here," Gutierrez had argued, and said what no one had said in Council even yet: "So there's not going to be a ship. And how long are we going to sit here blind to the world we live on?"

There was silence after that. He had been rude. He had destroyed the pretenses. There were sullen looks and hard looks, but most had no expression at all, keeping their terror inside, like azi.

So he went now, alone, before they took the guns and came hunting. He walked past the fields and out across the ridge and down, out of easy hail of the camp, which was against all the rules.

He sat down on the side of the hill with his glasses and watched the moundbuilders for a long time . . . watched as two calibans used their blunt noses and the strength of their bodies to heave up dirt in a ridge.

About noon, having taken all the notes of that sort he wanted, he ventured somewhat downslope in the direction of the mound.

Suddenly both dived into the recesses of their mound.

He stopped. A huge reptilian head emerged from the vent on the side of the mound. A tongue flicked, and the whole caliban followed, brown, twice the size of the others, with overtones of gold and green.

A new kind. Another species . . . another gender, there was no knowing. There was no leisure for answers. All they knew of calibans was potentially overturned and they had no way to learn.

Gutierrez took in his breath and held it. The brown—six, maybe eight meters in length—stared at him a while, and then the other two, the common grays, shouldered past it, coming out also.

That first one walked out toward him, closer, closer until he stared at it in much more detail than he wanted. It loomed nearly twice a man's height. The knobby collar lifted, flattened again. The other two meanwhile walked toward the river, quietly, deliberately, muddy ghosts through the tall dead grass. They vanished. The one continued to face him for a moment, and then, with a sidelong glance and a quick refixing of a round-pupilled eye to be sure he still stood there . . . it whipped about and fled with all the haste a caliban could use.

He stood there and stared a moment, his knees shaking, his notebook forgotten in his hand, and then, because there was no other option, he turned around and walked back to the camp.

That night, as he had expected, Council voted to hunt the calibans off the bank; and he came with them in the morning, with their guns and their long probes and their picks for tearing the mound apart.

But there was no caliban there. He knew why. That they had learned. That all along they had been learning, and their building on this riverbank was different than anywhere else in the world—here, close to humans, where calibans built walls.

He stood watching, refusing comment when the hunters came to him. Explanations led to things the hunters would not want to hear, not with the ships less and less likely in their hopes.

"But they didn't catch them," Kate Flanahan said that night, trying to rouse him out of his brooding. "It failed, didn't it?"

"Yes," he said. And nothing more.

xv

Year 3, day 230 CR

"Jin," the elder Jin called; and Pia called with him, tramping the aisles and edges of the camp. Fear was in them . . . fear of the outside, and the chances of calibans. "Have you seen our son?" they asked one and another azi they met. "No," the answer was, and Pia fell behind in the searching as Jin's strides grew longer and longer, because Pia's belly was heavy with another child.

The sun sank lower in the sky, and they had gone much of the circuit of the camp, out where the electric fence was. That riverward direction was young Jin's fascination, the obsession of more than one of the rowdy children in the camp.

"By the north of the camp," an azi told him finally, when he was out of breath and nearly panicked. "There was some small boy playing there."

Jin went that way, jogging in his haste.

So he found his son, where the walls stopped and the land began to slope toward the watermeadow. White slabs of limestone were the last wall there, the place they had once stacked the building stone. And little Jin sat in the dirt taking leftover bits of stone and piling them. An ariel assisted, added pebbles to the lot—turned its head and puffed up its collar at so sudden an approach.

"Jin," Jin senior said. "Look at the sun. You know what I told you about wandering off close to dark. You know Pia and I have been hunting for you."

Little Jin lifted a face which was neither his nor Pia's and looked at him through a mop of black hair.

"You were wrong," Jin said, hoping that his son would feel shame. "We thought a caliban could have gotten you."

His son said nothing, made no move, like the ariel.

Pia arrived, out of breath, around the white corner of the last azi house. She stopped with her hands to her belly, cradling it, her eyes distraught. "He's all right," Jin said. "He's safe."

"Come on," Pia said, shaken still. "Jin, you get up right now and come."

Not a move. Nothing but the stare.

Jin elder ran a hand through his hair, baffled and distressed. "They ought to give us tapes," he said faintly. "Pia, he wouldn't be like this if the tape machines worked."

But the machines were gone. Broken, the supervisors said, except one that the born-men used for themselves.

"I don't know," Pia said. "I don't know what's right and wrong with him. I've asked the supervisors and they say he has to do these things."

Jin shook his head. His son frightened him. Violence frightened him. Pick him up and spank him, the supervisors said. He had hit his son once, and the tears and the noise and the upset shattered his nerves. He himself had never cried, not like that.

"Please come," he said to his son. "It's getting dark. We want to go home."

Little Jin carefully picked up more stones and added them to his pattern, the completion of a whorl. The ariel waddled over and moved one into a truer line. It was all loops and whorls, like the ruined mounds that came back year by year in the meadow.

"Come here." Pia came and took her son by the arms and pulled him up, scattering the patterns. Little Jin kicked

and screamed and tried to go on sitting, which looked apt
to hurt Pia. Jin elder came and picked his son up bodily
under one arm, nerving himself against his screams and his
yells, impervious to his kicking as they carried him in shame
back to the road and the camp.

While their son was small they could do this. But he was
growing, and the day would come they could not.

Jin thought about it, late, lying with Pia and cherishing
the silence . . . how things had gone astray from what the
tapes had promised, before the machines had broken. The
greatest and wisest of the born-men were buried over by
the sea, along with azi who had met accidents; the ships
were no longer coming. He wished forlornly to lie under
the deepteach and have the soothing voice of the tapes tell
him that he had done well.

He doubted now. He was no longer sure of things. His
son, whom sometimes they loved, who came to them and
hugged them and made them feel as if the world was right
again, had contrary thoughts, and strayed, and somehow an
azi was supposed to have the wisdom to control this born-
man child. Sometimes he was afraid—of his son; of the
unborn one in Pia's belly.

When the ship comes, the azi used to say.

But they stopped saying that. And nothing was right
since.

IV

The Second Generation

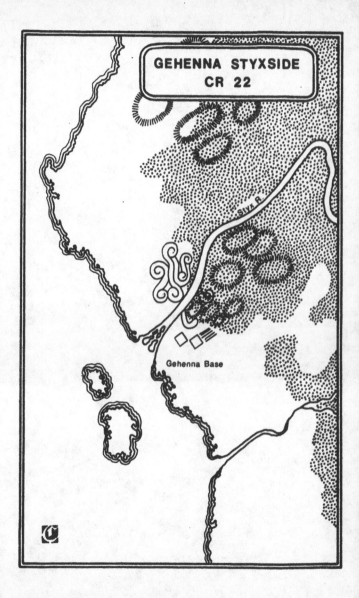

GEHENNA STYXSIDE
CR 22

Styx R.

Gehenna Base

Military Personnel:

Col. James A. Conn, governor general, d. 3 CR
Capt. Ada P. Beaumont, lt. governor, d. year of founding
Maj. Peter T. Gallin, personnel
M/Sgt. Ilya V. Burdette, Corps of Engineers
  Cpl. Antonia M. Cole
  Spec. Martin H. Andresson
  Spec. Emilie Kontrin
  Spec. Danton X. Norris
M/Sgt. Danielle L. Emberton, tactical op.
  Spec. Lewiston W. Rogers
  Spec. Hamil N. Masu
  Spec. Grigori R. Tamilin
M/Sgt. Pavlos D. M. Bilas, maintenance
  Spec. Dorothy T. Kyle
  Spec. Egan I. Innis
  Spec. Lucas M. White
  Spec, Eron 678-4578 Miles
  Spec. Upton R. Patrick
  Spec. Gene T. Troyes
  Spec. Tyler W. Hammett
  Spec. Kelley N. Matsuo
  Spec. Belle M. Rider
  Spec. Vela K. James
  Spec. Matthew R. Mayes
  Spec. Adrian C. Potts

Spec. Vasily C. Orlov
Spec. Rinata W. Quarry
Spec. Kito A. M. Kabir
Spec. Sita Chandrus
M/Sgt. Dinah L. Sigury, communications
Spec. Yung Kim
Spec. Lee P. de Witt
M/Sgt. Thomas W. Oliver, quartermaster
Cpl. Nina N. Ferry
Pfc. Hayes Brandon
Lt. Romy T. Jones, special forces
Sgt. Jan Vandermeer
Spec. Kathryn S. Flanahan
Spec. Charles M. Ogden
M/Sgt. Zell T. Parham, security
Cpl. Quintan R. Witten
Capt. Jessica N. Sedgewick, confessor-advocate
Capt. Bethan M. Dean, surgeon
Capt. Robert T. Hamil, surgeon
Lt. Regan T. Chiles, computer services

Civilian Personnel:

Secretarial personnel: 12
Medical/surgical: 1
Medical/paramedic: 7
Mechanical maintenance: 20
Distribution and warehousing: 20
Robert H. Davies d. CR 3
Security: 12
Computer service: 4
Computer maintenance: 2
Librarian: 1
Agricultural specialists: 10
Harold B. Hill
Geologists: 5
Meteorologist: 1
Biologists: 6
Marco X. Gutierrez
Eva K. Jenks
Jane E. Flanahan-Gutierrez b. 2 CR
Education: 5

Cartographer: 1
Management supervisors: 4
Biocycle engineers: 4
Construction personnel: 50
Food preparation specialists: 6
Industrial specialists: 15
Mining engineers: 2
Energy systems supervisors: 8
   ADDITIONAL NONCITIZEN PERSONNEL:
    "A" class: 2890
      Jin 458-9998
      Pia 86-687
      Jin Younger b. year of founding
      Mark b. 3 CR
      Zed b. 4 CR
      Tam b. 5 CR
      Pia Younger b. 6 CR
      Green b. 9 CR
    "B" class: 12389
    "M" class: 4566
      Ben b. 2 CR
      Alf b. 3 CR
      Nine b. 4 CR
    "P" class: 20788
    "V" class: 1278

i

Year 22, day 192 CR

It was a long walk, a lonely walk, among the strange hills the calibans raised—but her brothers were there, and Pia Younger kept going, out of breath by now, her adolescent limbs aching with the running. She always ran on this stretch of the trail, where the mounds and ridges were oldest and overgrown with brush. She never admitted it to her brothers, but it disturbed her to cross this territory. Here. With *them*.

Ahead were the limestone heights where the old quarry was; the elders had built the town with limestone, but they took no more stone there nowadays except what they could bribe her brothers to bring down. Afraid, that was it; elders were afraid to cross the territory of the calibans. Youngers had this place, the deep pit where they had done blasting in the old days, and they owned the pile of loose stone that they loaded up and brought back when they wanted to trade. A lot of the youngers in the azi town came here, her brothers more than most, but the elders never would; and the main-Camp elders, they huddled in their domes and defended themselves with electric lights and electric wires.

She caught a stitch in her side and slowed to a limp when she reached the old trail, which had been a road once upon a time, a rain-washed road paved with limestone chips and overgrown with small brush and weeds and fallen away so that in some places it was wide enough for one walker only. She looked back when she made the turn—it was that kind of view that the eye had to go to, that sprawling perspective out over all the world, the lazy S of the Styx and the mounds of the calibans like wrinkled cloth strewn on both sides of it, some under the carpet of trees and some new and naked; and caliban domes that mimicked the domes of the main Camp.

Calibans had never made domes, her father said, until they saw the domes of main Camp; but they made them now, and larger and grander, raising great bald hills on this side and that of the Styx. Beyond them were the solid hills, the natural hills; and then the fields all checkered green and brown; and the rusting knot of giant machines—and the tower, and the big shining tower that caught the sun and fed power to the little cluster of domes before the graveyard and the sea. All of that, in one blunt sweep of the eye, the whole world: and this height owned it all. That was why her brothers came here, to look down on all of it; but she was sixteen—not yet, her brothers said to her. Not yet for you.

What her parents said to her coming here—but they did everything the Council said; and saying no was part of it.

She began to run again, uphill, pushing past the brush, careless now because there was nothing but snakes to worry about up here in the day; and calibans ate snakes, and noise frightened both, so she made all the noise she could.

A whistle caught her ear, above her on the rim; she looked up, at a head that appeared over the rim of the

cliffs, head and shoulders, black hair blowing on the wind.
Her brother Zed. "I've got to come up," she called.

"Come on up, then," he called back. One had to be
Permitted to come up to the heights; and she dusted her
hands on her coveralls and came up the last few turns . . .
stopped on that bald crest of stone slabs and scant brush
and sat down panting for breath on the lefthand slab of the
two that served them for a gate, there by a bitterberry.
All her elder brothers were up here. And Jane Flanahan-
Gutierrez. Her eyes caught that with shock and jealousy.
Jane Flanahan-Gutierrez from the main Camp, of the dark
skin and the curling black hair . . . there with all the boys;
and she knew at once what they had been doing up here—
it was in her brothers' eyes, like summer evening heat.
They looked older, suddenly, like strangers. Jane looked
that way too, disheveled clothes, her coveralls unzipped to
here, staring at her as if she had been dirt. Her four older
brothers, Jin and Mark and Zed and Tam; and the boys
from down the row in town, Ben and Alf and Nine. They
fronted her like a wall, her brothers the dark part of it and
the Ben/Alf/Nine set all red and blond. And Jane Flanahan-
Gutierrez.

"You let her up here," Ben said to Zed. "Why let *her*
up here?"

"I know what you're doing," Pia said. Her face felt red.
She was still gasping for breath after the climb; she caught
a mouthful of air. Jane Flanahan-Gutierrez sat down on
another rock, her hands on either side of her, flaunting
sex and satiation. "You think," Pia gasped, "you think it's
anything? Jin, our father sent me. To find you all. Green's
run off again. They want you back to help."

Her brothers settled, one by one, all but her brother Jin,
who was eldest, who stood there with his face clouded and
his hands caught in his belt. Green: that was the sixth of
them. Youngest brother.

"That boy's *gone*," Ben said, with the disgust everyone
used about Green; but: "Quiet," Jin Younger said, in that
tone that meant business, that could frighten elders into
listening to whatever Jin wanted to say. "How long?"

"Maybe since morning," Pia said hoarsely. "They
thought he was off with some boys. He ran off from them.
They didn't send anyone back to tell. Pia's looking in the

Camp; but Jin's out in the hills. Hunting this way. He asked us, Jin; our father *asked* us. He's really scared."

"It's going to get dark."

"Our father's out there, all the same. And he doesn't know anything. He could fall in a burrow, he could. But I don't think he'll quit."

"For Green."

"Jin—" She talked only to Jin, because he made up the minds of the rest. "He asked."

"We'd better go," Jin said then; so that was it: the others ducked their heads and nodded.

"What do we do with that brother of yours," Ben asked, assuming they were going too, "if we find him?"

"Hey," Jane said, "hey, I have to get back to the Camp. You said you'd walk me back to the Camp."

"*I'll* walk you back," Pia said with a narrow look. "That trail down's really bad. A careless body might slip."

"You'd better watch who you talk to," Jane said.

"*Azi.* That what you reckon, maincamper? Think I'm scared? You watch yourself."

"Shut up," Jin said.

"One of you," said Jane, "has to get me back. I can't wait around while you track that brother of yours down— I know; I know all about him."

"We'll be back. Just wait."

"He's gone, don't you think that? When they go, they go."

Pia gathered herself up again without a word, started off down the road without a backward look, not inside; and before she had gotten to the first downslope there was a skittering of pebbles and a following in her wake: the whole troop of her brothers was gathered about her, and the down-the-row boys too.

"Wait!" Jane shouted after the lot of them. "Don't you go off and leave me up here." And that was satisfaction. They would get her down—later. When they had seen to Green again. A stream of words followed them, words they swore by in the main Camp in the longest string Pia had ever heard. Pia marched down the winding track without looking back, hands in her pockets.

"That Green," Ben muttered. "Going to do what he

likes, that's what. Going to get to what he wants sooner or later."

"Quiet," Jin Younger said, and Ben kept it to himself after that, all the long way down.

It was better going back. In company. Pia began to pant with exhaustion—her tall brothers had long legs and they were fresh on the track, but she kept going, with the stitch back in her side, not wanting to admit her tiredness. Green—as for Green, Ben might be right. She had five brothers and the last was wild; was thirteen, and wandered in the hills.

And those who did that—they went on wandering; or whatever they did, who gave up humankind.

It was the third time . . . that Green had gone.

"This time," Pia said out of her thoughts, between gasps for air, "this time I think we have to get him, us. Because I don't think our father can find him fast enough."

"This time—" Jin Younger said, walking beside her, themselves out of hearing of the others if he kept his voice low, "this time I think it's like Ben said."

He admitted that to her. Not to the others. And it was probably true.

But they kept going all the same, down into the woods the calibans had grown, among the mounds and the brush in the late afternoon. "Where's Jin hunting?" Jin Younger asked.

Pia pointed, the direction of the Camp. "From Camp looking toward the river. That's what he thought—the river."

"Probably right," Jin Younger said. "Probably right for sure." He squatted down, cleared ground with the edge of his hand, took a stick and scratched signs as the others gathered. "I think Mark and I had better find our father: that's furthest. And Zed and Tam, you go the middle way; Ben, you and Alf go with them and split off where you have to go up to cover the ground; and Nine, you and Pia go direct by the river way. Pia's got most chance of talking to Green: I want her there where he's most likely to go. We draw a circle around him and sweep up our father too, before some caliban gets him."

That was Jin Younger: that was her brother, whose mind

worked like that, cool and quick. Pia got up from looking at the pattern and grabbed Nine's hand—Nine was eighteen, like Zed; and red and gold and freckled all over. They all moved light and quick, and in spite of the prospect in front of them, Pia went with a kind of relief that she was doing something, that she was not her mother, searching the town because she had to do something, even a hopeless thing, lame as Pia elder was, worn out from Green, aching tired from Green—

Lose him this time, Pia thought, in her heart of hearts. Let him go this time to be done with it; and no more of that look her parents had, no more of doing everything for Green.

But if they lost him, they had to have tried. It was like that, because he was born under their roof, stranger that he was.

They took the winding course through the brush-grown mounds, she and Nine, hand in hand, hurried past the gaping darknesses under stones that were caliban doorways—sometimes saucer-big eyes watched them, or tongues flicked, from caliban mouths mostly hid in shadow and in brush.

And the way began to be bare and slithery with mud, and tracked with clawed pads of caliban feet, which was a climbway calibans used from the Styx or a brook that fed it. Ariels scurried from their track, whipping their tails in busy haste; and flitters dived in manic profusion from the trees—some into ariel mouths. Pia brushed the flitters off, a frantic slapping at the back of her neck, protecting her collar, and they jogged along singlefile now, slid the last bit down to the flat, well-trampled riverside, where calibans had flattened tracks in the reeds of the bogs, and clouds of insects swarmed and darted.

Desolation. No human track disturbed the mud flats.

"We just wait," Pia said. "He can't have gotten past us unless he went all the way around the heights on the east." She squatted down by the edge of the water and dipped up a double handful, poured it over her head and neck, and Nine did the same.

"Why don't we take a rest?" Nine suggested, and pointed off toward the reeds.

"I think we ought to walk on down the way toward the rocks."

"Waste of time."

"Then you go back."

"I think we could do something better."

She looked suddenly and narrowly at him. He had that look they had had up there, with Jane. "I think you better forget that."

He made a grab at her; she slapped his hand and he jerked it back.

"Go after that Jane," she said, "why don't you?"

"What wrong with you? Afraid?"

"You go find Jane."

"I like you."

"You've got no sense." He scared her; her heart was pounding. "Jane and all of you, that's all nice, isn't it? But I say no, and you'd better believe no."

He was bigger than she, by about a third. But there were other things to think of, and one was living next to each other in town; and one was that she always got even. People knew that of Pia Younger; it was important to have people believe that, and she saw to it.

And finally he made a great show of sulking and dusting his hands off. "I'm going back," he said. "I don't stay out here for nothing."

"Sure, you go back," she said.

"You're cold," he said. "I'll tell how you are."

"You tell whatever you like; and when you do, I'll tell plenty too. You make me sound bad, you make my brothers sound the same. We figure like that. You're three and we're six. You make up your mind."

"You're five now," he said, and stalked off.

Afterward she found her hands sweating, not sure whether it was because of the sun or her temper or the thought that she could have had Nine, who was not bad for a first; but he was ugly inside, if not out. And lacking that reason, she thought of her mother, and how she had been young before Green started growing up. She thought about babies and the grief her mother had had of them, and that dried the sweat all at once.

So they might be five now. Green might be gone. And

that might cure them of all their troubles at once, if only they could prove they had searched; if they could get Green out of Jin and Pia's minds.

They went out to get their mother and father back for their own: that was why they went. That was why she had known that her brother Jin would come.

And if Nine had run back to his brothers, Pia still meant to stay where her brother said, to watch the bank. The rocks offered the most likely vantage, where the cliffs tumbled down to the Styx, where calibans sunned themselves and where anyone headed upriver had to go.

She had no fear of her brother Green. It was the others of his sort she had no desire to meet; and she wanted somewhere to watch unseen.

ii

The sun was halfway down the sky, and Jin elder moved with a sense of desperation, his breath short and shallow, his senses alive with dread on all sides. The wooded mounds surrounded him, offered dark accesses out of which calibans could come. Young ones challenged him, mansized, athwart his path, and he scrambled aside on the hill and kept going.

He might call aloud, but Green would never answer to his name, hardly spoke at all, and so he did not waste the breath. It was a question of overtaking his son, of finding him in this maze when he had no wish to be found. It was impossible, and he knew that. But Green was his, and whatever Green was, however strange, he tried, as his wife tried, in the town, already knowing her son was gone—searching among the thousands of houses, asking faces that would go blank to the question—"Have you seen our son? Have your children heard from him? Is there anyone who knows?"—They would shut the doors on her as they would on the night or on a storm, not to have the trouble inside with them, whose houses were secure. Pia had no hope; and he had none, except in his rebel children, his other sons and his daughter, who might possibly know where to look, who ran wild out here—but not as wild as Green.

He slowed finally, out of breath, walked dizzily among

the mounds. Now the sun was behind them, making pockets of dark. A body moved, slithered amid the thick brush, among the trees which had grown here, this side of the river. The sight was surreal. He recalled bare meadow, and gentle grass, and the first beginnings of a mound; and caliban skulls piled behind main dome. But all that was changed; and a forest grew, all scrub and saplings. Fairy flitters came down on his shoulder, clung to his clothing, making him think of bats; he beat them off and recalled that they were lives—which touched a faint, far chord in him, of guilt and of dread. The world was full of life, more life than they could hold back with guns or fences; it came into the town at night; it seduced the children and year by year crept closer.

A heavy body thrust itself from a hole—a caliban flicked its tongue at him; an ariel scurried over its immobile back and fled into the dark inside. He started aside, ran, slowed again with a pain in his side . . . sat down at last, against the side of a mound, by one of the rounded hills, the domes the calibans made.

And leapt up again, spying a white movement among the saplings on the ridge. "Green," he called.

It was not Green. A strange boy was staring down at him, squatting naked atop the ridge—thin, starved limbs and tangled hair, improbable sight in the woods. It was the image of his fears.

"Come down," he asked the boy. "Come down—" Ever so softly. Never startle them; never force—It was all his hope, that boy.

And the boy sprang up and ran, down the angle of the hill among the brush; Jin ran too—and saw the boy dive into the dark of a caliban access, vanishing like nightmare, confirming all that he had dreaded to know, how they lived, what they were, the town's lost children.

"Green," he called, thinking that there might be others, that his son might hear, or someone hear, and tell Green that he was called. But no answer came; and what the mound had taken in, it kept. He moved closer, climbed the slope with all his nerves taut-strung. He went as far as the hole and put his head inside. There was the smell of earth and damp; and far away, down some narrow tunnel, he heard something move. "Green," he shouted. The earth swallowed up his voice.

He crouched there a moment, arms flung across his knees, despair thicker about him than before. His children had all gone amiss, every one; and Green, the different one, was stranger than all the strange children he had sired. Green's eyes were distant and his mind was unknowable, as if all the unpleasantness of the world had seeped into Pia while she carried him, and infected his soul. Green was misnamed. He was that other face of spring, the mistbound nights when calibans prowled and broke the fences; he was secret things and dark. He had lost himself, over and over again; had shocked himself on the fences, sunk himself in bogs—had lost himself into the hills, and played with ariels and stones, forgetting other children.

Jin wept. That was his answer now that he was like bornmen and on his own. He mourned without confidence that there would be comfort—no tapes, now; nothing to relieve the pain. He had to face Pia, alone; and that he was not ready to do. He pictured himself coming home with daylight left, giving up, when Pia would not. When he failed her, she would come out into the hills herself: she was like that, even frail as she grew in these years. Pia, to lose a son, after all the pain—

He got up, abandoning hope of this place, kept walking, brushing the weeds aside in the trough between the mounds, going deeper and deeper into the heart of the place. All the way to the river—that was how far he must go, however afraid he was, all along this most direct track from the village to the river, as close as he could hew to it.

Brush stirred above him on a ridge: he looked up, expecting calibans, hoping for his son—

And found two, Jin and Mark, standing on the wooded ridge above him, mirrors of each other, leaning on either side of a smallish tree.

"Father," Jin Younger said—all smug, as if he were amused. And hostile: there was that edge always in his voice. Jin 458 faced his son in confused pain, never knowing why his children took this pose with him. "A little far afield for you, isn't it, father?"

"Green is lost. Did your sister find you?"

"She found us. We're all out looking."

Jin elder let the breath go out of him, felt his knees

weak, the burden of the loss at least spread wider than before. "What chance that we can find him out here?"

"What chance that he wants to be found?" Mark asked, second-born, his brother's shadow. "That's the real matter, isn't it?"

"Pia—" He gestured vaguely back toward the camp. "I told her I could go faster, look further—that you'd help; but she'll try to come—and she can't. She can't do that anymore."

"Tell me," Jin Younger said, "would you have come for any of us? Or is it just Green?"

"When you were four and five—I did, for you."

Jin Younger straightened back as if he had not expected that. He scowled. "Sister's gone on down by the river," he said. "If we don't take Green between us, there's no catching him."

"Where's Zed and Tam?"

"Oh, off hereabouts. We'll find them on the way."

"But Pia's on the river alone?"

"No. She's got help. Anyhow, Green won't hurt her. Whatever else, not her." Jin Younger slid down the slope, Mark behind him, and they caught their balance and stopped at the bottom in front of him. "Or didn't that occur to you when you sent her into the hills by herself?"

"She said she knew where you were."

His sons looked at him in that way his sons had, of making him feel slow and small. They were born-men, after all, and quick about things, and full of tempers. "Come on," Jin Younger said; and they went, himself and these sons of his. They shamed him, infected him with tempers that left him nothing—his sons who ran off to the wild, who took no share of the work in the fields, but cut stone when the mood took them, and dealt with born-men for it in trade, their own discovery. Well enough—it was not calibans that drew them; but laziness. He tried to guide them, but they had never heard a tape, his sons, his daughter . . . who ran after her elder brothers.

Who left her youngest brother to himself; while Green—started down a path all his own.

Jin thought that he might have done better by all of them. In the end he felt guilt—that he could not tell them what he knew, and how: that once there had been ships, that ships still might come, and there was a purpose for the world and patterns they were supposed to follow.

It was the first time, this walk with his eldest sons, that they had ever walked in step at all—young men and a man twice their age, the first time he had ever come with them on their terms. He felt himself the child.

iii

The way was strange along the bank, the reeds long since left behind, where the river undercut the limestone banks and made grottoes and caves. The calibans had taken great slabs of stone and heaved them up in walls—no caprice of the river had done such things. It was a shadowed place and a hazardous place, and Pia refused to go into it. She perched herself on a rock above the water, arms about her knees, in the shadows of the trees that arched out from rootholds in the crevices of the stone. Moss grew here, in the pools; fish swam, black shapes in the ripples, and a serpent moved, a ripple through the shallow backwaters of the river. Ariels and flitters left tracks on the delicate sand, washed up on the downstream side of the stones, and at several points were the grooves calibans made in their coming up from the river, deep muddy slides.

She looked up and up, where the cliffs shadowed them, scrub trees clinging even to that purchase. There were caves up there. Possibly ariels found them accessible, but no human could climb that face. Bats might nest there. There might possibly be bats, though they came infrequently to the river.

And very much she wished for her brothers . . . the more when something splashed and moved.

She turned; caught her breath at the sight of the coveralled figure which had come up behind her among the rocks.

"Green," she said softly, ever so quietly. Her youngest brother looked back at her, out of breath, with that strange, sober stare he used habitually. "Green, our father's looking for you."

A dip of the head, one of Green's staring nods, his eyes

hardly leaving her. He knew, Green meant; she knew how to read him.

"You know," she said, "how upset they'll be."

A second nod. There was no hint of distress on Green's face. No feeling at all. She remembered why she hated this brother, this feelingless nothing of a brother who had changed everything when he came.

"You don't care."

Green blinked, solemn as one of his leathery pets.

"Where do you think you're going?" she asked. "Doing what? You want to starve?"

A shake of the head.

"Speak to me. Once, *speak* to me."

Green sank down on his haunches on the bank and gathered up a stone, laid it flat on another one. He no longer listened.

"That's nice," she said. For one desperate moment she thought of warning him off, telling him the others were coming, so that he would run off, would escape, so that they would never again have to worry about him. But the words stuck in her throat, an ultimate dishonesty—not for themselves, but because it would be hard to look at her father and claim Green had run away.

She sidled closer while her brother made patterns with the stones . . . sidled closer, snatched suddenly at his arm and spoiled his pattern. He came up flailing and splashing into the margin of the water, twisted in her grip, and of a sudden her foot skidded on wet moss, spilling them both.

He twisted loose. "Green," she yelled after him, as he went skittering this way and that among the higher rocks.

But he was gone, and she was sitting in the water, soaked and shaken to think that finally he had gotten away. She was jolted by the fall—embarrassed and no small bit angry that he had outdone her, her little brother.

But gone. They were free of him. Finally free.

She gathered herself up then and laved off her hands and muddy coveralls, settled herself finally to dry off and wait.

And when her brothers brought her father with them down the banks of the river, she rose up off her rock to meet them in the twilight.

"He pushed me," she said as dourly as she could. "He hit me and he got away."

She was not sure what to expect—focused only on her father's eyes.

"Did he hurt you?" Jin elder asked, and his question warmed her heart with a warmth she had hardly felt since she was small. There was concern there; care for *her*. He took her into his arms and hugged her as he had done when she was small, and in that moment she looked beyond him, at her brothers; and at Nine and his kin, with a warning and a triumph in her smile.

She was someone again, with Green gone. She looked at Jin Younger, and Mark and Zed and Tam, and they knew what she had done. They had to know, that she had not struggled half hard enough; and why. So she was one of them: co-conspirator. Murderer, perhaps.

"You tried," Jin elder said. But she had no twinge of conscience, looking up into his face, because, at least in intent, she had done that much.

"Go back with father," Jin Younger said. "We'll search further."

"No," Jin elder said. "Don't. I don't want that."

Because he was afraid of this place, Pia thought; he took care for them now and not for Green. He had given up, and that was sweet to hear; that was what they had wanted to hear.

"I'll look," Jin Younger insisted, and turned away, up the bank, up among the rocks, never asking which way Green might have gone. It was the wrong way; and Mark went off that way too, toward the cliffs where Jin was leading. So she understood.

"We'd better get home," Zed said. "It's getting dark. He's off into the wild places. And there's no help in all of us wandering around out here."

"Yes," Jin elder said finally, in that quiet way he had, that resigned things he could no longer mend. For once Pia felt a shame not for him, for the simple answers her father gave, but on their account; on her own. *Yes.* Like that. After walking through territory that was a terror to him. *Yes.* Let's go home. Let's tell mother how it is.

Her brothers were in no wise bound after Green. They had no interest in Green. They had left themselves a maincamper up on the cliffs and night was falling; it was time to go get Jane Flanahan-Gutierrez down before she went silly with panic. Games were done. The night was coming. Fast.

And as for her brother, as for Green, spending the night out in the cool damp, slithering underearth where he chose to be—

She shivered in the circle of Jin elder's arm, turning back to the way along the shore. Nine and his brothers had already begun to walk back, having nothing to do with her father, and less with their own; besides, Nine had reason to avoid her now. So Jin elder was their possession, theirs, finally, the way he had been before Green existed.

iv

The sun sank, casting twilight among the stones, and Jane Flanahan-Gutierrez walked briskly down the trail among the mounds. Her knees shook just slightly as she went, making the downhill course uncertain. Fear was a knot in her stomach; and she cursed the azi-born, the beautiful, the so-beautiful and so hollow. Stay away from them, her mother said—stay away. And her father—said nothing, which was his habit. Or he delivered lectures on ships and birth-labs and plans gone amiss, and why she ought to think about her future, which she had no desire at all to hear.

Beautiful and hollow. No hearts in them. Nothing like them in the main Camp, no men so beautiful as Jin and his brothers, who were made to fill up the world with their kind. She wanted them; lowered herself to go off in the hills with them, like their own wild breed; and then their half-minded brother took to the hills as crazy as everyone expected of him, and they left her—just walked off and left her, up in the wild and the oncoming dark, as if she were nothing, as if it was nothing that Jane Flanahan-Gutierrez came out of the camp and wanted them.

Anger stiffened her knees; anger kept her going down the road into the brushy wild below the cliffs. She walked among the mounds, guided herself by the little sun that filtered through the trees atop the mounds.

And suddenly—a moving in the brush—there was a boy. Her heart lurched, clenched tight, settled out of its panic.

She stopped, facing the boy in the halflight, among the
brush. His coveralls were ragged, his hair too long. But he
was human at least. Weirds, they called them, like Green,
who lived wild among the mounds. But he was only a boy,
not even in his teens—and a better guide, she suddenly
hoped, than Jin and the lot of his friends had proved.

"I belong in the camp," she said, taking the kind of
stance she used when she expected something of the azi
who served. "I want to go through the maze. You understand? You take me through."

The figure beckoned, never speaking a word. It began to
move off through the brush as vague as ever it had been.

"Wait a minute," she said; and panic was in her mind—
wondering how she was going to explain all this when she
got home. She was going to be late. The fugitive showed
no interest in helping her and they would be turning out
search parties when it got dark. It was already beyond easy
explaining—I was lost, mother, father; I was fishing; I got
back in the mounds—"Wait!"

Brush moved behind her. She looked about, saw a half
dozen others, who held out hands toward her, silent. "Oh,
no," she told them. "No, you don't . . ." Her heart was
crashing against her ribs. "I'm going on my own, thank you.
I've just changed my mind." She saw the eyes of some, the
curious intensity, like the eyes of ariels. Crazy, every one.
She edged back. "I have to get home. My friends are looking for me right now."

They came closer, a soft stirring among their ranks, some
of them in coveralls and some in only the remnant of clothing, or in blankets and sheeting. And strange, and silent
and without sanity.

She remembered the other one, the one behind her—
turned suddenly and gave a muffled outcry, face to face
with the boy, close enough to touch—"You keep your
hands to yourself," she said, trying to keep the fear from
her voice, because that was her chiefest hope—that there
were still the town ways instilled in them, still the habit of
obeying voices that had no doubt when they gave commands. "Be definite," her mother had taught her, special
op and used to moving people, "and know what you're
going to do if they refuse,"; but her father—"Know what
you're poking your finger at," he said, whenever she was

stung. She stared at the boy, a wild frozen moment before she realized the others were closing from behind.

She whirled, one desperate effort to shock them all and find an opening; but they snatched at her, at her clothing—wrong timing, she thought in utter selfdisgust, and only half thought that she might die. She hit one of them and laid him out the way her mother had taught her, but that was only one of them: the others caught her hair and held her arms. And some of them had clubs, showing her what might happen if she yelled.

Go along with it, she thought; none of the Weirds had ever killed. They were strange, but they had never yet kept their minds at anything: they would lose interest and then she might get away.

They tugged her arms, drew her with them . . . and this she let happen, noticing everything, every landmark. Jin and his brothers would find her; or she might get away; or if she could not, then her father would come looking, with her mother and the specials who knew the hills and the mounds. The camp would come with guns; and then they would be sorry. The important thing now was not to startle them into violence.

The way they walked twisted and turned in the maze, among wooded ridges and through thickets, until she had only the sunset to rely on for direction. Now she began to feel lost and desperate, but something—be it common sense or despair itself—still kept her from sudden moves with them.

They came to a hill, one of the caliban domes. A boy crouched there, dark of hair, who beckoned her inside, into the dark, gaping entry.

"Oh, no, I won't. They'll miss me, you understand. They'll come—" Hunting, she had almost said, and swallowed the very thought of shooting calibans. They were the Lost, these boys, this strange band. A shiver ran over her skin.

"Come." The boy stretched out a hand, fingers spread upward, closed his fist with a slow intimation of power, so real it seemed to narrow all the space in the region, to draw in all that was. A second time he beckoned. Hands closed about her arms, propelled her forward . . . in a kind of paralysis—they brought her to him, this beautiful young man.

"Green," she murmured, knowing him. It was her brother's look on him, but changed. Mad. Crazed.

And others came, older than he, male and female.

"They're looking for you," she said. "You'd better go."

But then one of the young men came down from atop the hillside, came close to her, that same far distance in his expression. She might have been a stone. She was not really afraid of him for that reason—until he put his hand on her breast.

"They won't like that," she said, "the people in the camp." And then she wished she had not said that at all; her wish was to get out of here alive, and threatening them was not the way to assure that. The youth fingered her clothing, and began at the closing of it. She stood quite, quite still, not minded to lose her life to these creatures.

He was beautiful beneath the dirt. Most were, who came of azi lines. They were gentle in their moves—all of them curiously gentle, stroking her hair, touching her now without violence, so that it began to wander somewhere between nightmare and dream.

V

"She's not here," Jin Younger said, looking about the rocks and scrub of the summit—looked at his brother as if Mark could comprehend any more than he what kind of craziness had taken Jane Gutierrez off the heights. "She's just not here."

"She's got to have tried it on her own," Mark said, no less than what Jin had in his own mind. Jin pushed past his brother at the narrow passage up among the rocks and started down the trail at a run.

"We've got to get the rest of us," Mark called after him. "We've got to get some help fast."

"You go," Jin called back, and kept going. His brother yelled other things after him, and he ignored them.

The sun was throwing the last orange light into the clouds, glinting like fire off the solar array down in the camp, like miniature suns; and around that brightness was the dark. She had come to them, this main Camp woman, her own choice, come to him in particular, because he had that about him, that he could impress any woman he liked—he and his brothers. She came into the wild country, against all the rules and regulations: that was her choice too; and he was not one to turn away such favors. It had been good, up on the ridge. Good all day, because Flanahan-Gutierrez was like them, wild.

But he should have reckoned, he chided himself, that a maincamper who would have had the nerve to come up here with them would not cower atop the hill waiting; with more nerve than sense, she would not stay put.

And Flanahan-Gutierrez was more than born-man, she had a father on Council; and a mother in the guards. That was more than trouble.

"Jane," he called, plunging off the trail and into the most direct course through the mounds. It was twilight this low among the hills, deep dusk, so that he pushed his way blindly among the brush, for the moment losing his way, finding the trail again. "Jane!"

But he could see her with her anger and her born-man ways, just walking on, hearing his voice and ignoring it—determined to find her own way home. If she had started immediately after they had left the hill, she might almost have made it through the mounds by now, might be coming out among the hills just this side of town.

That was his earnest hope.

But the further he went, in the dark now, with sometimes the slither and hiss of calibans attending him—the more he feared, not for his safety, but for what an ignorant born-man might do out here at night. One could get by the calibans; but there were pits, and holes, and there were the Weirds like Green, who lurked and hid, who had habits calibans did not. Flitters troubled him, gliding from the trees. He brushed them aside and jogged where he could, out of breath now. "Jane!" he called. "Jane."

No answer.

He was gasping and sweating by the time he reached the top of the last ridge, with the town and Camp in front of him all lit up in floods. He stood there leaning over, his hands on his knees, getting his breath, and as soon as the pain subsided he started moving again.

For a very little he would have given up his searching then, having no liking for going into the main Camp—for

going to Gutierrez—Pardon, sir, has your daughter gotten
home? I left her on the cliffs and when I got back she
was gone. . . .

He had never seen Gutierrez angry; he had no wish to
face him or Flanahan; but he reckoned that he might have
no choice.

And then, when he had only crossed the fringes of the
town, running along the road under the floodlights—"Hey,"
a maincamper shouted at him: "You—did you come up
from the azi town?"

He skidded to a stop, recognized Masu in the dark, one
of the guards. "Yes, sir." A lie, and half a lie: he had cut
across the edge of it and so come up from the town.

"Woman's missing. Out of bio. Flanahan-Gutierrez.—
They're supposed to be looking down in town. Are they?
She went out this morning and she hasn't gotten back. Are
they searching out that way?"

"I don't know," he said, and the sweat he had run up
turned cold. "They don't know where she is?"

"Get the word down that way, will you? Go back and
pass it."

"I'll get searchers up," he said, breathless, spun about
and ran, with what haste he could muster.

They would find out, he kept thinking in an agony of
fear. The main Camp found everything out, whatever they
tried to hide. They would know, and he and his brothers
would be to blame. And what the main Camp might do
then, he had no idea, because no human being had ever
lost another. He only knew he had no wish to face her
people on his own.

vi

The sun came up again, the second sun since Jane was
gone; and Gutierrez sat down on the hillside, wiped his
face and unstopped his canteen for a sip to ease his throat.
They had gridded off, searchers in all the sections between
the Camp and the cliffs and the Camp and the river. His
wife reached him, sank down and took her own canteen,
and there was a terrible, bruised look to her eyes.

The military was out there, in force, by pairs; and azi

who knew the territory searched—among them the young azi who had come to him and Kate to admit the truth. A frightened boy. Kate had threatened to shoot him. But that boy had been out all the night and roused all the young folk he could find . . . had gone out again, on no knowing what reserves. It was not just the boy. It was Jane. It was the world. It had given her to them. But Jane thought in Gehenna-time; thought of the day, the hour. Had never seen a city. Had no interest in her studies—just the world, the moment, the things she wanted . . . now. Everything was now.

What good's procedure? she would say. She wanted to understand what a shell was, what the creature did, not what was like it elsewhere. What good's knowing all those things? It's this world we have to live in. I was born here, wasn't I? Cyteen sounds too full of rules for me.

The day went, and the night, and a new day dawned with a peculiar coldness to the light—an ebbing out of hope. His wife said nothing, slumped against him and he against her.

"Some run away," he offered finally. "In the azi town—some of them go into the hills. Maybe Jane took it into her head—"

"No," she said. Absolute and beyond argument. "Not Jane."

"Then she's gotten lost. It's easy in the mounds. But she knows—the things to eat; the way to survive—I taught her; she knows."

"She could have taken a fall," his wife said. "Could have hurt herself—Might be too wet to start a fire."

"All the same she could live," Gutierrez said. "If she had two legs broken, she could still find enough within reach that she could get moisture and food. That's the best guess; that she's broken something, that she's tucked up waiting for us—She's got good sense, our Jane. She was born here, isn't that what she'd say?"

They did it to bolster their own courage, shed hopes on each other and kept going.

vii

Jane screamed, came awake in the dark and stifled the outcry in sudden terror—the smell of earth about her, the prospect of hands which might touch. . . . But silence, no breathing nearby, no intimation of human presence.

She lay still a moment, listening, her eyes useless in this deep and dark place where they had brought her. She ached. And time was unimportant. The sun seemed an age ago, a long, long nightmare/dream of naked bodies and couplings in a dark so complete it was beyond the hope of sight. She was helpless here, robbed of every faculty and somewhere in that time, of wit as well.

She lay there gathering it again, lay there waking up to the fact that, having done what they had done, the Weirds were gone, and she was alone in this place. She imagined the beating of her heart, so loud it filled up the silence. It was terror, when she thought that she had long since passed the point of fear. She was discovering something more of horror—being lost and left. Isolation had never dawned on her in the maelstrom just past.

Think, her father would say; think of all the characteristics of the thing you deal with.

Tunnels, then, and tunnels might collapse: how strong the roof?

Tunnels had at least one access; tunnels might have more, tunnels meant air; and wind; and she felt a breeze on naked skin.

Tunnels were made by calibans, who burrowed deep; and going the wrong way might go down into the depths.

She drew a deep breath—moved suddenly, and as suddenly claws lit on her flesh and a sinewy shape whipped over her. She yelled, a shriek that rang into the earth and died, and flailed out at the touch—

It skittered away . . . an ariel; a silly ariel, like old Ruffles. That was all. It headed out the way Ruffles would head out if startled indoors . . . and it knew the way. It went toward the breeze.

She sucked in wind again, got to hands and knees and scrambled after—up and up a moist earth slope, blind, keeping low for fear of hitting her head if she attempted to stand. And a dim light grew ahead, a brighter and brighter light.

She broke out into the daylight blind and wiping at her eyes . . . saw movement then, and looked aside. She scrambled to her feet, seeing a human shape—seeing the azi-born young man crouched there, the first who had touched her. Alone.

"Where are the rest of them?" she asked. "Hiding up there?" There was brush enough, in this bowl between the mounds, up on the ridges, all about.

And then a sweep of her eye toward the left—up and up toward a caliban shape that rested on the hill, four meters tall and more—brown and monstrous, huger than any caliban she had imagined. It regarded her with that lofty, one-sided stare of a caliban, but the pupil was round, not slit. The feet clutched the curved surface and a fallen branch snapped beneath its forward-leaning weight as the head turned toward her. She stared—fixed, disbelieving when it moved first one leg and then the other, serpentining forward.

Then the danger came home to her, and she yelled and scrambled, backward, but brush came between her and it, and trees, as she climbed higher on the further slope.

No one stopped her. She looked back—at the caliban which threaded its way among the trees; again at the azi-born, who sat there placid in the path of that monster. Very slowly the young man got to his feet and walked toward the huge brown caliban—stopped again, looking back at her, his hand on its shoulder.

She began to run, up and over the mound—scrambling among the brush and the rocks. A gray caliban was there, down the slope and another—near her, that jolted her heart. It lashed about in the brush, caliban-like: it skittered down the slope and along the ridge, headed toward the river past the rocks—it must be going to the river. . . .

In a flash she realized where she likely was, near rocks that thrust through the mounds: rocks and the river below the cliffs.

She stopped running when she had spent her breath, slumped down amongst the trees and took stock of herself, her remnant of clothing, that she put to rights with trembling hands. She sat there in the brush with tears and exhaustion tugging at her, and she fought the tears off with swipes of a muddy hand.

"Hey," someone said; and she started, whirled to her knees and half to her feet, like something wild.

From the Camp: they were two of the men from the

Camp, Ogden and Masu. She stood up, shaking in the knees, and the blood drained from her face, sudden shame as she stood there with her clothes in rags and her pride in question. "There," she yelled, and pointed back over the ridge, "there—they caught me and dragged me off—they're there. . . ."

"Who?" Masu asked. "Who did? Where?"

"Over the ridge," she kept crying, not wanting to explain, not wanting anything but to see it wiped out, the memory and the smiling, silent lot of them.

"Take care of her," Masu said to Ogden. "Take care of her. I'll round up the others. We'll see."

"There's calibans," she said, looking from one to the other of them. Ogden took her arm. Her coveralls were torn almost beyond staying on; she reached to cover herself and gasped for breath in shock. "There's calibans—a kind no one ever saw—" But Ogden was pulling her away.

She looked back when Ogden had hastened her off with him. Fire streaked across the sky, and she stared at the burning star.

"That's a flare," Ogden said. "That's Masu saying we found you."

"There are people," she said, "people living in the mounds."

"Hush," Ogden said, and squeezed her hand.

"It's so. They live there. The Weirds. With the calibans."

Ogden looked at her—old as her father, a rough man, and big. "I'm going to get you out of here," he said. "Can you run?"

She caught her breath and nodded, shaking in all her limbs. Ogden seized her hand and took her with him.

But they met others, coming their way . . . and one was her father and the other her mother. She might have run to meet them: she had the strength left. But she did not. She stopped still, and they came and hugged her, her mother and then her father, and shed tears. She was dry of them.

"I'm going back after Masu," Ogden said. "It may be trouble back there."

"They should get them," Jane said, quite, quite coldly. She had gotten her dignity back, had found it again, used it like a cloak between her and her parents, despite her nakedness.

"Jane," her father said—there were tears in his eyes, but her own were still dry. "What happened?"

"They caught me and dragged me in there. I don't want to talk about it."

Her father hugged her, and her mother did. "Come home," her mother said, and she walked with them, no longer afraid, no longer feeling anything but a cold distance between herself and what had happened.

It was a far way, to the Camp; and her father talked about medics. "No," she said to that. "No. I'm going home."

"Did they—?" That her mother found the question hard struck her as strange, and ominous. Her face burned.

"Oh, yes. A lot of times."

viii

"There has to be law," Gallin said, in Council, in the dome—looked down at all the heads of departments. "There has to be law. We rout them out of there and we have to do something with them. It was a mistake to sit back and let it go on. We can't be having this . . . this desertion of the young. We set up fences; we organize a hunt and clear the mounds."

"They're our own kind," the confessor-advocate objected, rising from her chair, grayhaired and on the end of her rejuv. "We can't take guns in there."

"We should," Gutierrez said, also on his feet, "mobilize the town, dig foundations that go far down; we ought to make the barriers we meant to make at the beginning. We can shoot them—we can level the mounds—and it happens all over again. Time after time. It never works. There's more going out there than we understand. Maybe another species—we don't know. We don't know their habits, their interrelations, we don't know what drives them. We shoot them and we dig them out and it never works."

"We mobilize the azi," Gallin said. "We give them arms and train them—make a force out of them."

"For the love of God, what for?" the advocate cried. "To march on calibans? Or to shoot their own relatives?"

"There has to be order," Gallin said. He had gained weight over the years. His chins wobbled in his rage. He looked up at them. "There has to be some order in their lives. The tape machines are gone, so what do we give them? I've talked to Education. We have to have some direction. We make regiments and sections; we mount guard; we protect this camp."

"From what?" Gutierrez asked. And added, because he knew Gallin, because he saw the insecure anger: "Sir."

"Order," Gallin said, pounding the table for emphasis. "Order in the world. No more dealing with runaways. *No more tolerance.*"

Gutierrez sank down again, and the confessor-advocate sat down. There was a murmuring from the others, an undertone of fear.

The calibans had come closer and closer over the years and they had found no occasion to say no.

But he had qualms when he saw the azi marshalled out for drill, when he saw them given instruction to kill. He walked back on that day with a lump in his gut.

Kate and Jane met him, daughter like mother—so, so alike they stood there, arms about each other, with satisfaction in what they saw. A change had come about in Jane. She had never had that hard-eyed look before she went out into the mounds. She had grown up and away, to Kate's side of the world. No more curiosity; no more inquiring into the world's small secrets: he foresaw silence until that threat out there was swept away, until Jane saw the world as safe again.

While azi marched in rows.

ix

Pia Younger set the bucket down inside the door, in the two room house that was theirs, a house hung with clothes and oddments from the rafters—drying onions, dried peppers, plastic pots balanced on the beams, and her own bed in this corner, her parents' bed in the other room. And rolled pallets that belonged to her brothers, who prepared for another kind of leaving.

Her mother sat outside—a woman of silences. She went out again and stopped to take her mother's hand, where she sat sharpening a hoe—stroke, stroke of a whetstone across the edge. Her father—he was off with the boys. Her mother paid little attention . . . had paid little at all to the world in recent days. She only worked.

"I'm going out," Pia Younger said. "I'm going to see how it goes." And quietly, in a hushed voice, bending close and taking her mother's hands: "Listen, they'll never catch Green. They'll go up the river, all the lost ones do. Don't worry about them shooting him. They can't."

She felt guilty in the promise, having no faith in it, having no love for her brother. And it all failed with her mother anyway, who went on with her sharpening, stone against steel, which reminded her of knives. Pia drew back from Pia elder and as quietly drew away. She lifted her eyes to the borders of the town, where another kind of camp was in the making.

Her father was out there following born-man orders; her brothers pretended to. And very quietly, Pia elder never noticing, Pia Younger walked down the street the opposite way, then cut through at the corner and doubled back again.

She watched the weapons-practice from the slope of the caliban-raised hill near the town, crouched there, as she daily watched these drills. The fields went unattended; the youngest deserted the work. And she knew what her brothers said among themselves, that they would only pretend, and carry the weapons, but when it got to attacking the calibans and runaways, they would run away themselves. Her father did not know this, of course. Her father carried arms the way he did other things the officers asked of him. And that was always the difference.

Herself, she sat thinking on the matter, how drear things would be if her brothers should go, if all their friends should follow them.

Sixteen years was almost grown. She sat making up her mind, thinking that she would go already if not for the danger of the guns and the weapons, that they might mis-

take her for one of the Weirds out there. Her parents
would not understand her leaving. But they understood
nothing that was different from themselves; and she had
known long ago that she was different. All the children
were.

Most of the day she watched; and that night her brothers
did not come home. Her father came; neighbors came.
They waited dinner. The blanket rolls waited against the
wall. And her parents sat in silence, ate finally, asked no
questions even of each other, their eyes downcast in that
silence in which her parents suffered all their pain.

Officers came in the night, rapped on the door and asked
questions—wrote down the names of her missing brothers
while Pia hovered behind her parents, wrapped in her blanket and shivering not from cold, but from understanding.

x

"We have to move," Jones said—atop the hill, where
they had set up the observation post; and Kate Flanahan
nodded, looking outward over the mounds. She shifted her
fingers on the woven strap of the gun she carried on her
shoulder. "We've got the location of the runaways: we're
getting radio from Masu and his lot, with the site under
observation. We get this settled. Fast. We've turned back
two hundred deserters at the wire—it's falling apart. We
get the human element out of this thing, get those runaways
routed out of there before we have every aziborn in town
headed over the hill. They're deserting in troops—got no
sympathy for this operation; and there never was any need
of drafting that many. This unit: Emberton's up the way—
we'll get it stopped. No more runaways then; and then we
can get the older workers to start building that barrier. Any
questions before we move?"

There were none. Flanahan had none; had hate—had
that, for her daughter's suffering, for the hush that had
fallen on Jane, the loss of innocence. For her daughter who
sat inside or fell to the studies which she had always hated,
because it filled her mind.

"Move out," Jones said, and they moved, filed out quietly through the hills, amid the brush and the trees of the

mounds. Some of Bilas' crew brought the demolitions. Vandermeer had a projectile gun, and gas cannisters to flood the mound and make it unpleasant for the refugees. And a few shots after that—

The orders were not to kill. But Flanahan reckoned that accidents might happen; there might be excuse. She was looking for one.

They walked, moving cautiously, making as little disturbance as possible . . . but the way they knew, had it down precisely—the spot where Emberton's unit had set up shop, watching the accesses, watching the runaways come and go.

They came on a sentry: that was Ogden, one of their own—and gathered him up into their small band: eight of them, in all, counting borrowings from Maintenance—and Emberton was arriving with her escort a little earlier, to take personal command up on the ridge. From now on it was careful stealth: and they broke as few branches as possible, disturbed the brush only where they had to. Flitters troubled them, brushed aside when they would light and cling. A fevered sweat ran on Flanahan's arms and body— a chance, finally, to do something. To take arms against the confusion that had marked all their efforts in Gehenna. A few shots fired, a little healthy fear on the part of the azi-born: that would settle it.

And then they might build again.

Flanahan was breathing hard when they topped the ridge: the gun was no small weight and she was years out of training. So were they all—Jones with his waist twice its former girth; Emberton gray with rejuv. She saw the tactical op chief in conference with Masu and Tamilin and Rogers as they came up, into that area where Masu and Kontrin and Ogden had sat out observing the situation throughout.

The runaways were still there. Kate Flanahan crept up with the others, near the edge. The word passed among their crouching ranks. Vandermeer armed the projectile gun with the gas cannisters, aimed at the access of the mound they faced. And right in front of them a pair of the fugitives sat naked, sunning their bony, muddy limbs.

Of the calibans, no sight; and that was just as well: less confusion. Jones put the safety off his rifle, and Flanahan did the same, the sweat colder and heavier on her with the passing moments. Those ragged creatures down there, those

fugitives from all that was human, they had hurt Jane . . .
had humiliated her; had cared nothing for what they did,
for their pleasure; and Jane would never be the same. She
wanted those two. Had one all picked out.

"Move," the order came from Jones; and they did as
they had arranged, pasted a few shots near the visible fugitive, came down the slope. Flanahan whipped off a shot,
saw the taller of the two go down like he was axed.

And then the ground pitched underfoot, went soft, slid:
there were outcries. One was hers. Trees were toppling
about them. Of a sudden she was waistdeep in earth and
still sliding down as the whole slope dissolved.

She let go the rifle, used her hands to fight the cascading
earth; but it went over her, pinning her arms, filling her
mouth and nose and eyes; and that and the pressure were
all, pain and the crack of joints.

xi

So they failed. Jane Flanahan-Gutierrez understood that
when her father came to her to break the news . . . but she
had understood that already, when the radio had been long
silent, and the rumor went through the Camp. She took it
quietly, having abandoned the thought that her life would
proceed as she wanted. Little surprised her.

Her father settled into silence. His calibans went un-
hunted, after all; but Kate was gone, and calibans had killed
her. He smiled very little, and a slump settled into his
shoulders in the passing months.

He offered to have the doctors rid her of it, the swelling
presence of the child in her belly; but no, Jane said, no.
She did not want that. She paid no attention to the stares
and the talk among the youths who had been her friends.
There was herself and her father; there was that . . . and
the baby was at least some of Kate Flanahan; some of her
father, too; and of whatever one of the lostlings had sired it.

When it came she called her daughter Elly—Eleanor
Kathryn Flanahan, after her mother: and her father took it
into his arms and found some comfort in it.

Jane did not. Jin's daughter, it might be; or one of his
brothers'. Or something that had happened beneath the

hill. She fed it, cared for it, saw a darkhaired girl toddling for her father's hands, or going after him with smaller paces, or squatting to play with Ruffles—at this she shuddered, but said nothing—Elly followed her grandfather everywhere, and he showed her flitters and snails and the patterning of leaves.

That was well enough. It was all Jane asked of life, to keep a little peace in it.

The fields went smaller. The azi who had fled did some independent farming, over by the cliffs, so the rumor ran. Gallin died, a cough that started in the winter and went to pneumonia; that winter carried off Bilas too. They went no longer outside the Camp—the calibans came here, too . . . made mounds on the shore, between them and the fishing; and only that roused them to fight the intruders back.

But the calibans came back. They always did.

Jane sat in the summer sun the year her father died, and saw Elly half grown—a darkhaired young woman of wiry strength who ran with azi youths. She cared not even to call her back.

That was the way, at the end of it all, she felt about the child.

xii

Year 49, day 206 CR

There were more and more graves—of which the bornman Ada Beaumont had been the first. Jin elder knew them all: Beaumont and Davies, Conn and Chiles, Dean who had birthed his son; Bilas and White and Innis; Gallin and Burdette, Gutierrez and all the others. Names that he had known; and faces. One of his own sibs lay here, killed in an accident . . . a few other azi, the earliest lost, but generally it was not a place for azi. Azi were buried down by the town, where his Pia lay, worn out with children; but he came here sometimes, to cut the weeds, with a crew of the elders who had known Cyteen.

So this time he brought the young, a troop of them, his daughter Pia's children and three of his son Jin's; and some of Tam's, and children who played with them, a rowdy lot.

They trod across the graves and played bat-the-stone among the weeds.

"Listen," Jin said, and was stern with them until they stopped their games and at least looked his way. "I brought you here to show you why you have to do your work. There was a ship that brought us. It put us here to take care of the world. To take care of the born-men and to do what they said. They built this place, all the camp."

"Calibans made it," said his granddaughter Pia-called-Red and the children giggled.

"*We* made it, the azi did. Every last building. The big tower too. We built that. And they showed us how, these born-men. This one was Beaumont: she was one of the best. And Conn—everyone called him the colonel; and he was stronger than Gallin was . . . Stop that!" he said, because the youngest Jin had thrown a stone, that glanced off a headstone. "You have to understand. You behave badly. You have to have respect for others. You have to understand what this is. These were the born-men. They lived in the domes."

"Calibans live there now," another said.

"We have to keep this place," Jin said, "all the same. They gave us orders."

"They're dead."

"The orders are there."

"Why should we listen to dead people?"

"They were born-men; they planned all this."

"So are we," said his eldest grandson. "We were born."

It went like that. The children ran off along the shore, and gathered shells, and played chase among the stones. Ariels waddled unconcerned along the beach, and Jin 458 shook his head and walked away. He limped a little, arthritis setting in, that the cold nights made worse.

He worked in the fields, but the fields had shrunk a great deal, and it was all they could do to raise grain enough. They traded bits and pieces of the camp to their own children in the hills—for fish and grain and vegetables, year by year.

He walked back to the camp, abandoning the children, avoiding the place where the machines that had killed Beaumont rusted away.

Some azi still held their posts in the domes, and the

tower still caught the sun, a steel spire rising amid the brush and weeds. Flitters glided, a nuisance for walkers. Ariels had the run of all the empty domes in maincamp, and trees grew tall among the ridges which had advanced across the land, creating forests and grassy hills where plains and fields had been. Most of the born-men had gone to the high hills to build on stone, or their children had. In maincamp only the graves had human occupants.

He was old, and the children went their own way, more and more of them. His son Mark was dead, drowned, they said, and he had not seen the rest of his sons in the better part of a year. Only his daughter Pia came and went from them, and brought him gifts, and left her children to his care . . . because, she said, you're good at it.

He doubted that, or he might have taught them something. The shouts of children pursued him as he went; they played their games. That was all. When they grew up they would go to the hills and go and come as they pleased. Himself, he kept trying with them, with life, with the world. This was not the world born-men had planned. But he did the best he knew.

V

---

outside

i

Excerpt, treaty of the new territories

"Union recognizes the territorial interests of the Alliance in the star systems variously named the Gehenna Reach or the MacLaren Stars; in its turn the Alliance will undertake to route fifty percent of trade with these systems through Union gateway ports after such time as a positive trade balance has been achieved; . . . further . . . that the defense of these territories will be maintained jointly by the terms of the Accord of Pell. . . ."

ii

Private apartments, the First of Council, Cyteen Capital

"It's only come a few years ahead of expectations." Councillor Harad's face, naturally long, was longer still in his contemplation. He paused, poured himself and the Secretary each a glass of wine—lifted his, thoughtfully. "This is our purchase. Pell wine, from the heart of Alliance."

"You would have opposed the signing."

"Absolutely not." Harad sipped slowly and settled again in his chair. The window overlooked the concrete canyons of the city and the winding silver sheen of the Amity River.

Outside, commerce came and went. "As it is, Alliance ships go on serving our ports. No boycott. And the longer that's true—the less likely it becomes. So the colonies were well spent. They'll keep the Alliance quite busy."

"They may just lift the colonists off, you know. And if one colony should resist, we'll have a crisis on our hands."

"They won't. There'll be no untoward incident. Maybe Alliance knows they're there. We'll have to break that news, at least, now that the treaty's signed. They'll take that hard, if they don't know. They'll be demanding records, access to files. They'll know, of course, the files will be culled; but we'll cooperate. That's at the bureau level."

"It seems to me a halfwitted move."

"What?"

"To give up. Oh, I know the logic: hard worlds to develop; and we've hurried Alliance into expansion—but all things considered, maybe we should have thrown more into it. We may regret those worlds."

"The economics of the time."

"But not our present limits."

Harad frowned. "I've looked into this. My predecessor left us a legacy. Those worlds were all hard. I'll tell you something I've known since first I opened the file. The Reach colonies were all designed to fail."

The Secretary favored him with a cold blue stare. "You're serious."

"Absolutely. We couldn't afford to do it right. Not in those years. It was all going into ships. So we set them up to fail. Ecological disaster; a human population that would survive but scatter into impossible terrain. That's what they'll find. No mission was ever backed up. No ships were dispatched. The colonists never knew."

"Union citizens—Union lives—"

"That was the way of it in those days. That's why I supported the treaty. We've just dictated Alliance's first colonial moves, handed them a prize that will bog them down in that direction for decades yet to come. Whatever they do hereafter will have to be in spite of what they've gained."

"But the lives, Councillor. Those people waiting on ships that never came—"

"But it accomplished what it set out to do. And isn't it, in all accounts, far cheaper than a war?"

VI

Re-entry

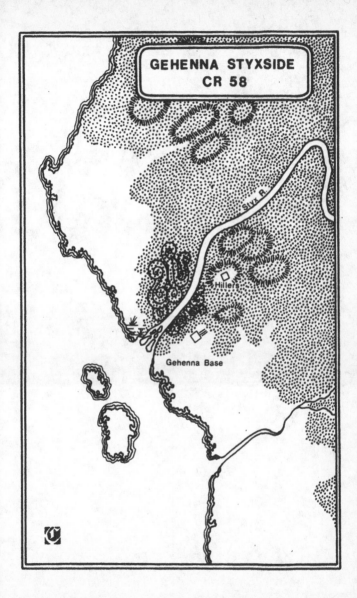

GEHENNA STYXSIDE
CR 58

Styx R.

Hiller

Gehenna Base

Military Personnel:

Col. James A. Conn, governor general d. 3 CR
Capt. Ada P. Beaumont, lt. governor, d. year of founding
Maj. Peter T. Gallin, personnel, d. 34 CR
M/Sgt. Ilya V. Burdette, Corps of Engineers, d. 23 CR ·
  Cpl. Antonia M. Cole, d. 32 CR
  Spec. Martin H. Andresson, d. 22 CR
  Spec. Emilie Kontrin, d. 31 CR
  Spec. Danton X. Norris, d. 22 CR
M/Sgt. Danielle L. Emberton, tactical op., d. 22 CR
  Spec. Lewiston W. Rogers, d. 22 CR
  Spec. Hamil N. Masu, d. 22 CR
  Spec. Grigori R. Tamilin, d. 22 CR
M/Sgt. Pavlos D. M. Bilas, maintenance, d. 34 CR
  Spec. Dorothy T. Kyle, d. 40 CR
  Spec. Egan I. Innis, d. 36 CR
  Spec. Lucas M. White, d. 32 CR
  Spec. Eron 678-4578 Miles, d. 49 CR
  Spec. Upton R. Patrick, d. 38 CR
  Spec. Gene T. Troyes, d. 42 CR
  Spec. Tyler W. Hammett, d. 42 CR
  Spec. Kelley N. Matsuo, d. 44 CR
  Spec. Belle M. Rider, d. 48 CR
  Spec. Vela K. James, d. 25 CR
  Spec. Matthew R. Mayes, d. 29 CR
  Spec. Adrian C. Potts, d. 27 CR

Spec. Vasily C. Orlov, d. 44 CR
Spec. Rinata W. Quarry, d. 39 CR
Spec. Kito A. M. Kabir, d. 43 CR
Spec. Sita Chandrus, d. 22 CR
M/Sgt. Dinah L. Sigury, communications, d. 22 CR
Spec. Yung Kim, d. 22 CR
Spec. Lee P. de Witt, d. 48 CR
M/Sgt. Thomas W. Oliver, quartermaster, d. 39 CR
Cpl. Nina N. Ferry, d. 45 CR
Pfc. Hayes Brandon, d. 48 CR
Lt. Romy T. Jones, special forces, d. 22 CR
Sgt. Jan Vandermeer, d. 22 CR
Spec. Kathryn S. Flanahan, d. 22 CR
Spec. Charles M. Ogden, d. 22 CR
M/Sgt. Zell T. Parham, security, d. 22 CR
Cpl. Quintan R. Witten, d. 22 CR
Capt. Jessica N. Sedgewick, confessor-advocate, d. 38 CR
Capt. Bethan M. Dean, surgeon, d. 46 CR
Capt. Robert T. Hamil, surgeon, d. 32 CR
Lt. Regan T. Chiles, computer services, d. 29 CR

Civilian Personnel:

Secretarial personnel: 12
Medical/surgical: 1
Medical/paramedic: 7
Mechanical maintenance: 20
Distribution and warehousing: 20
Robert H. Davies, d. 3 CR
Security: 12
Computer service: 4
Computer maintenance: 2
Librarian: 1
Agricultural specialists: 10
Harold B. Hill, d. 32 CR
Geologists: 5
Meteorologist: 1
Biologists: 6
Marco X. Gutierrez, d. 39 CR
Eva K. Jenks, d. 38 CR
Jane Flanahan-Gutierrez, CR 2—CR 50
Elly Flanahan-Gutierrez, b. 23 CR—

Education: 5
Cartographer: 1
Management supervisors: 4
Biocycle engineers: 4
Construction personnel: 50
Food preparation specialists: 6
Industrial specialists: 15
Mining engineers: 2
Energy systems supervisors: 8
ADDITIONAL NONCITIZEN PERSONNEL:
  "A" class: 2890
  Jin 458-9998
  Pia 86-687, d. 46 CR
  (chart)
  "B" class: 12389
  "M" class: 4566
  "P" class: 20788
  "V" class: 1278

i

Communication: Alliance security to AS Ajax
". . . survey and report."

ii

Year 58, day 259 CR

The ship came down, all longrange contact negative, and settled at the site the oribiting scan had turned up.

And Westin Lake, Alliance Forces, ordered the hatch opened on a close view of the land; on a sprawl of human-made huts, on an eerie wilderness beyond, a landscape different than the sketchy Union charts told them they should find.

Someone swore.

"It's not right," another said. That was more than true.

They waited two hours, expecting approach: it failed, except for a few small lizards.

But trails of smoke went up, among the trees and the huts—the smoke of evening fires.

iii

There had been a sound like thunder, disturbing the too-close sick-room where the old man lay, amid a clutter of wornout blankets. An ariel perched on the windowsill, and another enjoyed a permanent habitation in the stack of baskets by the door. The sound stopped. "Is it raining?" Jin elder asked, stirring from that sleep that had held him neither here nor there. Pia tried to tell him something.

And he was perplexed, because Jin Younger was there too, that tall man sitting on the chest by Pia. There was silver in his son's beard, and in Pia's hair. When had they gotten so old?

But Pia—*his* Pia—was dead long ago. Her sibs had gone close after her; the last of his had gone this spring. All were dead, who had known the ships. None had lived so long as he—if it was life, to lie here dreaming. There was none that recalled the things he remembered. The faces confused him, not clear types such as he had known, but still, much like those he had known.

"Mark," he called; and: "Green?" But Mark was dead and Green was lost, long ago. They told him Zed had vanished too.

"I'm here," someone said. Jin. He recalled them, and focused on the years in the curious way things would slip into focus and go out again. His children had come back to him, at least Jin and Pia had.

"I don't think he understands." Pia's voice, a whisper, across the room. "It's no good, Jin."

"Huh."

"He always used to *talk* about the ships."

"We could take him outside."

"I don't think he'd even know."

Silence a moment. Darkness a moment. He felt far away.

"Is he breathing?"

"Not very strong.—Father. Do you hear? The ships have come."

Over the fields of grain, high in blue skies, a thin splinter of silver. He knew what it was to fly. Had flown, once. It

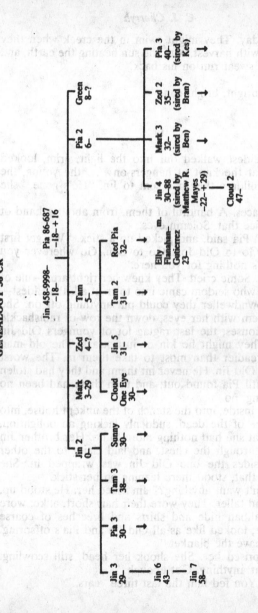

GENEALOGY 58 CR

was a hot day. They might swim in the creek when they
were done with harvest, with the sun heating the earth, and
making the sweat run on his back.

"Father?"

Into the bright, bright sun.

iv

Pia-now-eldest walked out into the light, grim, looked
round her at the knot of hangers-on . . . the young, the
scatter of children they had sent to Jin. "He's gone," she
said.

Solemn faces. A handful of them, from about a hand of
years to twice that. Solemn eyes.

"Go on," Pia said, and picked up a stick. "We get first
stuff. *Get.* Go to Old Jon. Go to Ben. Go wherever you
like. There's nothing for you here."

They ran. Some cried. They knew her right arm—one of
the Hillers, who seldom came into town at all, Pia Eldest—
no timid towndweller they could put anything off on. She
followed them with her eyes, down the row of ramshackle
limestone houses, the last ragtag lot of youngers Old Jin
had had. They might be kin or just strays. The old man
had been readier than most to take them in. The worst
stayed with Old Jin. He never hit them, and they had stolen
his food until Pia found out; and then there had been no
more stealing, no.

She went inside, into the stench of the unkept house, into
the presence of the dead, suddenly lacking an obligation,
realizing that she had nothing more to do. Her brother Jin
was going through the chest, and laid claim to the other
blanket besides the one Old Jin was wrapped in. She
frowned at that, stood there leaning on her stick.

"You don't want anything?" Jin asked her. He stood up,
a half a head taller. They wore their hair short, alike; wore
boots of caliban hide and shirts and breeches of coarse
town weave; looked like as all Old Jin and Pia's offspring.
"You can have the blanket."

That surprised her. She shook her head, still scowling.
"Don't want anything. Got enough."

"Go on. You fed him the last three years."

She shrugged. "Your food too."

"You made the trips."

"So. No matter. Didn't do it for that."

"Owe you for the blanket," her brother said.

"Collect it someday. What's town to us? I don't want what smells of it."

Jin looked aside, on the small and withered form beneath the other blanket. Looked at her again. "We go?"

"I'll wait for the burying."

"We could take him up in the hills. There's those would carry."

She shook her head. "This is his place."

"This." Jin rolled the razor and the plastic cup into the blanket, tucked them under his arm. "Filth. Get up to the hills. Those new born-men—they'll come here. They'll be trouble, that's all. Jin's ships. He thought everything the main-campers did was all right. How could he know so much and so little?"

"I had myself a main-camper once. He said—he said the old azi had to think like Jin, that's all."

"Maybe they did. Anything the main-campers wanted. Only now there's new main-campers. You remember how it was. You remember what it was, when old Gallin had the say in main-camp. That's what it'll be again. You mind me, Pia, you don't wait for the burying or they'll have you plowing fields."

She spat, half a laugh.

"You mind me," Jin said. "That's how it was. Mark and Zed and Tam and I—we ran out on it."

"So did I. It wasn't hard." She took a comb Jin had left. "This. I'll keep this."

"They'll be coming here."

"They'll bring things."

"Tape machines. They'll catch the youngers and line us up in rows."

"Maybe they should."

"You thinking like *him?*"

She walked away to the door, looked out above the abandoned, caliban-haunted domes and the fallen sun-tower where vines had had their way, where the town stopped. The ship sat there in the distant plain, shining silver, visible above the roofs.

"You don't go," Jin argued with her, coming and taking her shoulders. "You don't be going out there talking to those born-men."

"No," she agreed.

"Forget the stinking born-men."

"Aren't we?"

"What?"

"Born-men. We were born here."

"I'm going," Jin said. "Come along."

"I'll walk with you to the trail." She started on her way. There was nothing to carry but the staff, and what Jin chose to keep; and behind them, the town would break in and steal.

So Old Jin was gone.

And she was sitting by the doorway when they brought the New Men to her.

They disturbed her with their strangeness, as they disturbed the town. There were those who were ready to be awed by them, she saw that, but she looked coldly at the newcomers, and kept her mind to herself.

Their clothes were all very fine, like the strange tight weave which the looms the town made nowadays could never duplicate. Their hair was short as Hillers wore it and they smelled of strange sharp scents.

"They say there was a man here who came on the ships," the first of them said. He had a strange way of talking, not that the words were unclear, just the sound of them was different. Pia wrinkled her nose.

"He died."

"You're his daughter. They said you might talk to us. We'd like you to come and do that. Aboard the ship, if you'd like."

"Won't go there." Her heart beat very fast, but she kept her face set and grim and unconcerned. They had guns. She saw that. "Sit."

They looked uncomfortable or offended. One squatted down in front of her, a man in blue weave with a lot of metal and stripes that meant importance among born-men. She remembered.

"Pia's your name."

She nodded shortly.

"You know what happened here? Can you tell us what happened here?"

"My father died."

"Was he born?"

She pursed her lips. All the rest knew that much, whatever it meant, because it had never made sense to her, how a man could not be born. "He was something else," she said.

"You remember the way it was at the beginning. What happened to the domes?" The gesture of a smooth, white hand toward the ruins where calibans made walls. "Disease? Sickness?"

"They got old," she said, "mostly."

"But the children—the next generation—"

She remembered and chuckled to herself, grew sober again, thinking on the day the born-men died.

"There were children," the man insisted. "Weren't there?"

She drew a pattern in the dust, scooped up sand and drew with it, a slow trickling from her hand.

"Sera. What happened to the children?"

"Got children," she said. "Mine."

"Where?"

She looked up, fixed the stranger with her stronger eye. "Some here, some there, one dead."

The man sucked in his lips, thinking. "You live up in the hills."

"Live right here."

"They said you were out of the hills. They're afraid of you, sera Pia."

It was not, perhaps, wise, to make Patterns in the dust. The man was sharp. She dumped sand atop the spiral she had made. "Live here, live there."

"Listen," he said earnestly, leaning forward. "There was a plan. There was going to be a city here. Do you know that? Do you remember lights? Machines?"

She gestured loosely toward the mirrors and the tower, the wreckage of them amid the caliban burrowings in main camp. "They fell. The machines are old." She thought of the lights aglow again; the town might come alive with these strangers here. She thought of the machines coming to life again and eating up the ground and levelling the burrows and the mounds. It made her vaguely uncomfortable. Her brother was right. They meant to plow the land again. She sensed that, looking into the pale blue eyes. "You want to see the old Camp? Youngers'll take you there."

And on the other side there was lack of trust, dead silence. Of course, they had seen the mounds. It was strange territory.

"Maybe you might go with us."

She got up, looked round her at the townfolk, who tried to be looking elsewhere, at the ground, at each other, at the strangers. "Come on then," she said.

They talked to their ship. She remembered such tricks as they used, but the voices coming out of the air made the children shriek. "Old stuff," she said sourly, and reached for Old Jin's stick that he had had by the door, leaned on it as if she were tired and slow. "Come on. Come on."

Two of them would go with her. Three stayed in the village. She walked with them up the road, in amongst the weeds and ruins. She walked slowly, using the stick.

And when she had gotten into the wild place she hit them both and ran away, heading off among the caliban retreats until her side ached and she needed the stick.

But she was free, and as for the mounds, she knew how to skirt them and where the accesses were to be avoided.

She came by evening into the wooded slopes, up amongst the true, rock-hearted hills.

Someone whistled, far and lonely in the woods where flitters and ariels darted and slithered. It was a human sound. One of the watchers had seen her come.

Home, the whistle said to her. She whistled back; Pia, her whistle said. There were friends and enemies here, but she had her knife and she brought away a comb and her father's stick, confident and set upon her way.

At least Old Jin had not been crazy. She knew that now. She had seen the ships come, and she remembered the born-men who had lived in the domes, who had died and mingled their types with azi, some in the hills and some few scratching the land with wooden plows.

There were ships again and born-men to own the world.

Azi marching in rows, her brother Jin had said. But she was not azi and she would never march to their orders.

v

Strangers.

Green wrinkled his nose and blinked in the light, perceiving disruption in the Pattern made on the plain. There was a new motion now. He felt the stirrings underground recognizing it.

The disquiet grew extreme. He dived back into the dark, finding his way with body and direction-sense rather than with eyes. Small folk skittered past him as he went, muddy slitherings of long-tailed bodies past his bare legs as he stooped and hastened along in that surefooted gait he had learned very long ago, hands before him in the dark, bare feet scuffing along the muddy bottom. His toes met a serpentine and living object in the dark, his skin felt an interruption in the draft that should blow in this corridor, his ears picked up the sough of breathing: he knew what his fingers would meet before they met it, and he simply scrambled up the tail and over the pebble-leathery back, doing the great brown less damage than its blunt claws could do to him in getting past. The brown gave a throaty exhalation, flicked an inquisitive tongue about his shoulders and when he simply scurried on, it slithered after.

It wanted to know. It was interested. Green darted up again, taking branches of the tunnels which led nearer the strangers. He was, after all, Green, and old, almost the oldest of his kind, in his way superior to the elder brown which whipped along after him. It wanted to know; and he changed his plans and darted up again to daylight to show it.

When he had come to the light again, up where trees crested the mound, where he had free view of the town and the shining thing which had come to rest in the meadow, the brown squatted by him to look too.

He made the Pattern for it. He offered up what he had, making the spirals rightwise up to a point and leftwise thereafter.

The brown moved heavily and seized up a twig fallen

from the trees, crunched it in massive jaws. The crest was up. The eyes were more dark than gold. Green sat with the muscles at his own nape tightening, lacking expression for his confusion. The brown was distraught. It was everywhere evident.

It nosed him suddenly, directing him back inside the mound. He reached the cool safe dark and still it pushed at him, herding him toward the deepest sanctuary.

There were others gathered in the dark. They huddled together and in time one of the browns came to herd them further.

It was days that they travelled in that way, until they had come far upriver, to the new mounds, and here they stayed, able to take the sun again, here where calibans made domes and walls and caliban young and grays came out to sun, heedless of the danger westward.

vi

T51 days MAT: Alliance Probe *Boreas*:

Report, to be couriered to Alliance Security Operations under seal COL/M/TAYLOR/ASB/SPEC/OP/NEWPORT-PROJECT/

. . . initial exploration in sector A on accompanying chart #a-1 shows complete collapse of Union authority. The prefab domes are deserted, overgrown with brush. The solar array is indicated by letter a on chart #a-1, lying under the wreckage of the tower; brush has grown over most of it. Inquiry among inhabitants produces no clear response except that the fall occurred perhaps a decade previous. This may have been due to weather.

On the other hand, the prefab domes sit amid a convoluted system of ridges identical to those observed throughout the riverside and named in orbiting survey reports 1-23. We have found the caliban mounds predicted by Union information on the site, but there is no close agreement between present circumstance and Union records. If one example might illustrate the disturbing character of the site, chart #a-1 may serve: it is inconceivable that the original colony would have established their domes and fields in the center of the mound system. What was level terrain in the Union records is now a corrugated landscape overgrown with brush. When asked what became of the residents of the domes, the townsmen answer that some of them came to the town, and some went to the hills. Orbiting survey does show (chart #a-2) a second settlement in the hills about ten kilometers from the town, but considering the potential risk of extending interference without understanding the interrelation of the systems, the mission has confined itself to the perimeter outlined for the colony.

There was, however, one interview with a woman, one Pia, no other name known, who has vanished from the community after assaulting mission personnel she had agreed to guide (see sec. #2 of this report) and who may have retreated to the hills. (The transcript of the Pia interview is included as document C, sec. 12. The economy of the town and that of the dwellers in the hills are perhaps linked in trade: see documents in C section, especially sec. 11.)

When questioned regarding the calibans the townsmen generally look away and affect not to have heard; if pressed, they refuse direct answer. The interviewers have not been able to ascertain whether the townsmen hold the calibans in some fear or whether they distrust the interviewers.

The mission finds the townsmen politically naive, existing in a neolithic lifestyle. The individual Pia recalled technology, and no inhabitants seem surprised at modern equipment, but if there is any technology among them other than a few items originally imported from offworld, the mission has not observed it. They plow with hand-pushed wooden plows, have no metals except what was originally imported, and apparently do not have high-temperature-forging techniques necessary to work what metal they do have. Weaving and pottery are known, and may conceivably have been an independent discovery. If there is ritual, religion, or ceremonies of passage, we have yet to discover them, unless there is in fact some superstition regarding the calibans.

There is no writing except in primitive accounts of food inventory. Spelling is not regular, nor is the majority literate beyond the capacity to make tallies. There has been some linguistic change, on which we might derive more information if we knew the world of origin of these Union colonists and the azi (see document E). The accent is distinctive after less than a century of isolation, indicative of a very early breakdown of formal education; but the forms of standard grammar remain, not uncommon in azi-descended populations where precise adherence to instruction has been tape-fed as a value.

The local nomenclature has changed: few townsmen recognize Newport as the name of the colony. Their word for their world is Gehenna, while the primary is called simply The Sun, and the principal river on which they have settled they name Styx. The literary allusion is not known to them.

There is no indication that the inhabitants understand any political affiliation to Union, or that there will be any active opposition to Alliance operations or governance.

There is, however, a second and more serious consideration, and it is one which the mission hesitates, in the absence of more evidence, to present to the Bureau. While Union documents describe the highest lifeform as nonsapient, evidence points to caliban intrusion into human living area during the colony's height. It would be speculative at this point to suggest that caliban activity may have led directly to the decline of the colony, but it is remarkable that the decline has been so thorough and so rapid. Dissension and political strife among the colonists might have disrupted human civilization, but the town, of considerable population, does not show any fear or carry any weapons excepting utilitarian objects such as knives or sticks, and does not threaten with them. We do not yet have a census, but the town is a little smaller than we would expect. Granted the usual Union colonial base, the world population in fifty years might well exceed a hundred thousand by natural reproduction alone.

Possibly poor health care and limited food have worked to keep the rate of increase somewhat lower than average, although families observed are large. Possibly there was a conflict. Possibly there was decimation by conflict or disease. Based on information given by townsmen, nomadism may be a factor to be considered both in population estimates and in politics. The town numbers perhaps as many as 70,000, with extremely crowded conditions. There are small outlying settlements of less than 1000 individuals sharing town fields, and probably established for convenience.

The heart of the town is limestone slab construction, but the outlying districts and later additions to central district houses are brick and timber, indicating change of supply or change in technological level. Access to the limestone of the central hills may have been cut off, perhaps marking some change of affairs regarding hill communities and the town, but it would be speculation at this point to draw any conclusion.

There is division of labor into brickmaking, pottery, weaving, agriculture. There are no domestic animals: clothing is linenlike, from the cultivation of local plants. There has been a successful economic adaptation to locally available materials, and insofar as success of a colony might be its ability to remain viable without offworld supply, Newport, or Gehenna as the locals name it, has achieved at least a tenuous success.

The atmosphere is overall agrarian and tranquil, although our military advisors persist in warnings that they may be awaiting the departure of the ship and attempting to secure an advantage of surprise. The scientific mission doubts this, but will of course take suggested precautions. The mission for its part has advised that extreme precautions extend to native lifeforms.

From Section D, mission report
Dr. Cina Kendrick

. . . . Intelligence is not, as indicated above, a scientific term. I have objected to the description *sapience* in previous studies and again take issue with biological studies which attempt to attach this imprecise assessment of adaptive and problem-solving capacities to non-human lifeforms.

Two considerations must be made. First, that an organism's behaviors may be survival-positive in one environment and not in another, and second that its perceptive apparatus, its input devices, may be efficient for one environment but not for another. The quality imprecisely described as intelligence is commonly understood to describe the generalization of an organism, i.e, its capacity to adapt by the use of analogy to a variety of situations and environments.

On the contrary even the concept of *analog* is anthropocentric. *Logic* is another anthropocentric imprecision, the attempt to impose an order (binary, for instance, or sequential) on observations which themselves have been filtered through imprecise perceptive organs.

The only claim which may be made for generalization as a desirable trait is that it seems to permit survival in a multitude of environments. The same may be said of generalization as part of the definition of intelligence, particularly when intelligence is used as a criterion of the inherent value of an organism or its right to life or territory when faced with human intrusion. Generalization permits migration in the face of encroachment; and it permits one species to encroach on another, which adds another dimension to natural selection. But when extended to intrusion not over another mountain ridge within the same planetary ecology and the same genetic heritage, but instead to intrusion of one genetic heritage upon another across the boundaries of hitherto uncrossable space, this value judgement loses some credibility.

The dominant lifeform on Gehenna II is a scaly endothermic quadruped without aesthetic attraction. The description that leaps too readily to mind is *reptile*, which does not adequately describe an interior structure which is not reptilian or pertinent to any previously catalogued lifeform; it does not describe behaviors such as mound-building or suggest reasons for an advance into human "territory". Nor does it adequately describe the adaptive process by which this lifeform succeeds in the face of a human colony armed with modern weapons, furnished with heavy construction equipment, and established with the precedent of many previous successes.

I dissent from the mission opinion which seeks to debate whether the Union colony may have "contaminated" a sapience. I dissent not to condone the intrusion of humankind into this ecosystem, but to protest a proceeding which will attempt on the basis of quantitative anthropocentric standards to determine the relative value of a lifeform against the desire of humankind to possess what this world has held until now unique within the rules established by its own genetic heritage.

Report, document E
Dr. Carl Ebron

Observation indicates human sites scattered through the hills to such an extent that it would take years and force to lift human presence off this planet. The colonists of the town might obey a summons to be lifted off. It is doubtful that others would be receptive, and the result of any attempt to remove the human population would be a scattering of human presence on a world where humanity can survive without technology. The end result is still contamination, and possibly hostility which might be exploited centuries hence. We are ironically faced with a first-contact situation involving our own species, a situation fraught with the direst potential hazard to zonal stability and peace.

My own recommendation is a quarantined observation point, allowing what has begun here to take as natural a course as is possible under regrettable circumstances. The other logical solution, a thorough sterilization of the entire area of possible contamination, the elimination of both human and native lifeforms in the hope of preserving a planet from contamination, is Draconian and unthinkable. We are human beings. Our morality constrains us from such a decision as might undo an evil. I do not know whether this is (a term to which Dr. Kendrick would object) *intelligent* on humanity's part, but it is certain that nothing on this world offers us resistance or seems to mean us harm, and I see no choice but the maintenance of the status quo until such time as a more informed decision might be made.

Document G: Dr. Chandra Cartier

I respectfully dissent from Drs. Kendrick and Ebron. Dr. Kendrick's thesis, taken in the extreme, might be extended to every lifeform on every world, but I believe that the hazard on Gehenna is more specific, without claiming that it is mindful or sapient. The danger is in ourselves, that humankind and human civilization have failed so miserably here and that we are raising atavistic suspicions of aliens in our midst. I object to the proposition that human beings be quarantined and observed in poverty, disease, and ignorance to protect the supposed value of native life which has not evidenced any creative capacity. I object to the proposition that there is not relative value involved, the value of human beings trapped in a situation of squalor and futility, neither of which may be scientific terms, but both of which have stark value on a world whose last civilized inhabitants named it Hell. I propose on the contrary that it would be a crime against humanity to wall ourselves off from these people. On the contrary, we should bring hospitals, educational facilities, and bring these survivors into the modern age, at least to the extent that they become capable of transforming Gehenna into a viable colony. From the neolithic to the space age may be too great a leap for one generation; but metal plows and engines to pull them are not too great a leap; rejuv and modern medicine are not too great a leap; aid in years of bad weather, advice in agriculture, the judicious importation of plants and livestock, all these things are minimal response to this human suffering. I do not dignify with a response the suggestion advanced by Dr. Ebron that neither humankind nor native life might count against the ideal of ecological restoration: he is correct; the idea is inhuman. As for Dr. Kendrick's debate of values, it is attractive only in the abstract. Taken in substance it would have starved our species out of existence as soon as it had conceived the theory: our intelligence, whether anthropocentric or otherwise, advises us that we have ensured the survival of terrene species by our actions. Whales survive in the oceans of Cyteen; bears and seals and other species on Eversnow. Was this moral? Is it moral for us to have left our ancestral Sun? Human history is collision, not stasis. It is inhuman not to preserve these people in a reasonable quality of life. There must be a perimeter established here within which humanity can retreat to remain human; and that perimeter must be defended with whatever measures are necessary until investigation has established what we have done on this world. The fact that this world has reduced one well-equipped human effort to the neolithic is eloquent enough argument that humankind has to be wiser in its dealings with this environment and what lives here.

vii

Alliance HQ Newport/Gehenna Mission
Couriered by *AS Boreas*

. . . Equipment and personnel arriving with this message will permit the expansion of a secure perimeter to include the landing site and town and fields as well as a river access. Establishment of permanent health care and educational facilities for Newport/Gehenna citizens should be given a high priority, but security of Alliance personnel and equipment must not be compromised in the process, regarding force of nature or force of arms, and not excluding the possibility of action by Union agents or native lifeforms.

This office has contacted Union colonial offices with a further request for data on humanitarian grounds and there has been some negotiation opened in this matter, but progress is likely to be minimal and slow.

In the absence of further information, the mission is instructed to establish a perimeter as wide as possible without conflict and within the limits of available equipment and security and tactical considerations. Conflict is to be avoided with humans and native life, but this prohibition does not extend to the function of effective fencing devices. The Bureau draws no conclusion on the sapience or competency of the calibans and awaits further data which the mission will supply.

The priorities of the mission will be as follows:

(1) to secure the area of its own operation
(2) to determine whether any activity of any other outside agency might exist; if so, to take appropriate measures
(3) to secure the area of the town and adjacent villages necessary for establishment of a viable economy
(4) to assist colonists with medical and educational facilities
(5) to encourage trade with the center of colonization in preference to trade with those in outlying areas, with

a view of centralization of economy and facilities and
the establishment of an Alliance-influenced capital
which will tend to draw scattered human settlements
toward the landing site by the attraction of food and
stability, minimizing future political difference

(6) to educate all available citizenry in hygiene, agriculture, small manufacture, and government

(7) to defend against encroachment by native agency
by the use of whatever force is minimally sufficient
to deter the attempt, up to and including lethal arms.

Closely following this equipment delivery another ship
will follow, bringing a station module and personnel for the
core of a permanent manned orbiting port, which will monitor the majority of Newport planetary surface and serve,
with the addition of a shuttle by future shipment, to maintain constant surveillance and flow of supplies.

It is not Bureau policy to permit a colony to suffer failure
from neglect. The human inhabitants regardless of origin
are now an Alliance polity but must be dealt with under
Section 9 procedures as a first contact. The mission is
urged to provide answers to questions of local sapience,
and particularly to assist the station when operational in
determining what planetary areas might be developed without contact with high lifeforms.

Of high priority, therefore, is the establishment of a landing area at Newport Base. . . .

viii

Newport Base briefing room

"Then the decision is to exploit," Ebron said, "in potential disregard of native life."

"It's a political decision," said Kendrick. "We're in the proposed path of expansion. They *want* Gehenna. That's what it
comes to. Union seeded it, we cultivate it—they're happy,
you understand that? They're actually relieved the population's sunk to the stone age. And devil take the calibans."

"That's off the record," Cartier said.

Kendrick drew a breath and let it go again. "That's off

the record. Of course it's off the record. You had your way, didn't you?"

"No," said Cartier. "Unfortunately I didn't."

ix

Year 72, day 130 CR
The Hills

It was many a day that Pia Elder sat atop her hill, watching the coming and going in the camp, a long hard walk for an old woman, and the first such walk of the spring. Cloud was panting when he had come so far, and relieved that the old woman was here.

His heart was beating very hard when he came up the slope, partly because the old woman was sitting very still (but she often did that) and his mother had done that when she was dead; and partly because he was afraid of this old woman, who was thin and dry as a stick and strange enough to do things like this, coming out before dawn to look at a place she would not go.

"Ma Pia," he said very quietly, and circled to the side of her and came facing her, squatted down with his elbows tucked between his knees. It was cold in the morning wind. He was cold. He shivered, looking into a face wrinkled like old fruit and eyes like black Styx stone, water-smoothed and cold. She let her hair grow. Neglect, he guessed. "Ma Pia, father he wished was you well, ma Pia."

A while longer the implacable eyes gave him nothing. Then Pia Elder lifted a bony arm from beneath her blanket.

"New buildings this spring."

He looked, turning his head and turning on his haunches. It was so that there were more buildings in the camp, tall and strange buildings. Perhaps the old woman was being conversational with him. He looked back at her hoping that it would be easy to get her home.

"They've smoothed the mounds, levelled the way to the river," the old woman said. "But you don't remember how it was."

"They made the mounds flat."

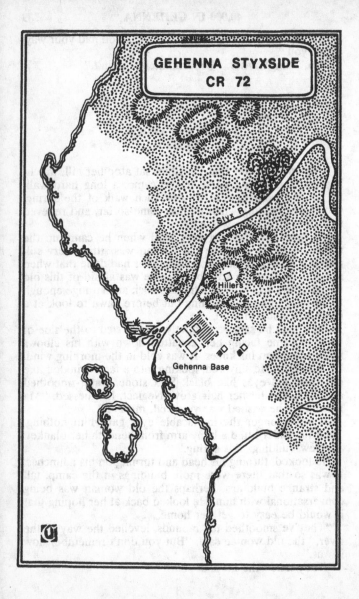

GEHENNA STYXSIDE
CR 72

Styx R.

Hillers

Gehenna Base

GENEALOGY CR 72

Gebenna Outpost [235]

Pia 86–687
–18–+16

Jin 458–9998–
–18–+58

Jin 2
0–62

Green
8–?

Pia 2
6–
(MA PIA)

Tam
5–58

Zed
4–?

Mark
3–29

Sunny
30–89 →

Pia 3
40– (sired by Kes) →

Zed 2
35– (sired by Bran) →

Mark 3
32– (sired by Ben) →

Jin 4
30– (sired by Matthew R. Mayes
–22–+29)

Cloud 2
47–

Cloud 3 m.

who talks to
Pia
62–

Red Pia
32– m.

Elly
Flanahan-
Gutierrez
23–

Tam 2
31–

Jin 5
31–

Cloud
One Eye

Tam 3
38–94 →

Pia 3
30–89 →

Jin 3
29–78

Jin 6
43–69

Jin 7
58–89

Jin 8
71–

"And they go on building. See how the fields go, right across the plain; see where the fences go."

"Mustn't touch them fences, the power'll hurt you."

She whipped out her arm straight toward him, snapped her fingers. It had as well been a blow; might have been if she had had her stick in her hand. He clenched his arms in shock. "Them fences."

"Those fences, ma Pia." He was trembling, from the hour, the cold, the old woman's eyes.

"Who taught you to talk? Stupid Nine's lot?"

"No, ma Pia."

"You *talk*, hear? Not like Nine's breed. Not like my brother Jin's either. You know why, boy?"

"To go and come," he recited. "To be like born-men, like them—" He stammered on the word and the cold. The old woman's eyes bore down on him and he swallowed and picked his word. "Like them down there in the camp.—To be born-man."

A moment more the old woman stared at him shivering in front of her; and then she opened her blanket, inviting him into the warmth of her arms. He came, because she frightened him and she had never done this since he was small; and because his teeth were chattering from the morning chill. He was ten. He was old enough to be afraid of her body, which had stopped being woman or man, so old she was, so thin and hard and frail at once that she had stopped being anything he understood. She smelled of smoke and herbs when her arm and the blanket enfolded him; she felt like one of the ariels, all dry and strange. Her hair was white and coarse when he looked up at her. Her arm hugged him with an unsuspected tenderness, waking memories of earliest years, of being a child, and she rocked him—ma Pia, whose face did not know how to laugh.

"I had a brother," she said. "His name was Green. He went away into the mounds. Before that he forgot how to talk. You never do that. You never do that, young Cloud."

"I can write my name," he said.

The arm tightened about him. "Every year more buildings down there. They want us to come. They make their fences and they want us inside. Sometimes I think I'd like to go down and see—but they've changed it all. And our kind doesn't get into the center of it, just the town. There

were domes. There were born-men that lived there. I remember. I remember the day the ships came back and
there was a forest where the center of the buildings is now;
and mounds; and the calibans weren't all upriver. Nothing
could move them, until the ships came, and the fences, and
then the calibans left, and all the Weirds with them, right
up the Styx, and to Otherside. So Green went. I think he
must be dead now. It was a long time ago."

He was silent, victim of this outpouring of old things,
frightening things, because he saw the buildings growing
too, constantly changing.

"Your father was my oldest boy. You look like him,
those eyes."

"Where'd you get my grandfather?" He went brave of a
sudden, and twisted about and looked into her eyes.

"Don't know," she said. "I found that boy." That was
always the answer. And then: "I think I got him off a born-
man's son." She ruffled his hair. "Maybe off a Weird, what
would you say?"

His face went hot.

"No," she said. "I don't remember. That's the way it is.
It's cold. I'm walking back."

"Tell me."

The old lips pursed. "I think I got him off this born-man.
I do think I did. He was a pretty boy. Such pretty hair, like
yours. Name was Mayes. He came into the hills but he
never stood the first winter. So fine he was—but he just
faded out. My boy had none of that. He was strong. But
your mother—"

"She died birthing a baby. I know."

"Birthing's hard."

"Lots do it."

"Lots die." She gripped his face in a hard, thin hand,
turned his eyes toward her, and the blanket fell away, so
that he was cold. "She was Elly Flanahan-Gutierrez; and
she had hair like yours. She was a born-man's daughter.
Her mother went down in the mounds and came out
pregnant."

He shook his head, teeth chattering. She would not let
him go. "My father was Jin, my mother Pia; they had numbers. Born-men made them. They had me, and Jin; Mark—
he's dead, long time, and Zed—you never knew him: he

hunted, and one day he didn't come back; and Tam Oldest;
and me; and Green who went into the mounds. And Old
Jin, the second Jin, he had Jin Younger; and Pia Younger;
and Tam Younger; and Cloud Eldest; and Sunny and others
he didn't know and no one did. Maybe Elly Flanahan.
Maybe. Zed had nobody. But he could have had Elly. If
he did it was his only that anyone knows. Tam Oldest had
Tam Youngest and Jin Youngest and Red Pia and Cloud
Oneeye. Or maybe he had Elly Flanahan. And Green—he
was thirteen when he went into the mounds and Jane Flanahan did, and you know, Cloud Youngest, you look most
like Green. *He* had hair like that and eyes like that, and
you're small like he was small. Maybe it was Green. Or
maybe it was a hundred more, eh? who live in the dark in
the mounds. You talk, Cloud, you read and you write your
name, and maybe someday you go down to the new camp
and plow the fields."

"I'm a Hiller." It was protest. His shivers were convul-
sive. "My ma she wasn't what you say."

"Call your oldest Elly," the old woman said, making him
believe she was crazy as they said. "Or Green. And you
teach them to talk, hear me, Cloud?" She drew with her
finger on the ground, among the dead grass, as if she had
forgotten him. "This is the sun rising." A backwards spiral.
"This is setting. Or change. Pebbles one on the other, that's
building. There's the big browns and the stupid grays and
the little greens. And there's those have seen the seafolk
beach in the river in the dark before the ships came back.
There's a thing I saw—it was like caliban but not. Only
one. It was big, Cloud. In the river near the sea. I never
saw the like again. Lots of things I could never tell the
olders. And now there's lots of things I can't tell the
youngers. Is that fair?"

"I'm cold, ma Pia. I'm cold. Please let's go. My father
told me come."

"Here." She took off the blanket from about her
shoulders—she wore leather with fringes, all the clothes she
ever wore—she wrapped it about his shoulders and stood
up with the staff she had had by her in the grass. She
moved slowly, grimacing lines deeper into her wrinkled
face. And when he got to his feet she touseled his hair

again, touched his face in a gentle way ma Pia had never used. And then she walked away toward the north.

"Ma Pia!" Cloud cried, exasperated. He clutched her blanket about him and ran after, the edges fluttering as he hurried. "Ma Pia, that's the wrong way. That's the river that way." The old were like that, forgetting where they were. He was embarrassed for her, for fierce old Pia, and angry for all she had said, and grateful for the blanket. "It's this way."

She stopped and stood. "Thought I might go down to the camp today. But there's no one there to see. Thought I might like a hot meal and maybe look at the machines, like old days. But they make fences down there, and you have to ask to come in and ask to come out and they might think I was old and sick, eh? I'd die if they shut me in. And that's no way to go. Our village stinks, you know that, Cloud, it smells like the town down there smells, like it smelled the day the first Jin died. I'm tired of stink. I think I'll take a walk upriver, see where the calibans have gone."

"Ma Pia, that's a long way. I don't think you ought to do that."

She smiled, a face that was set with years of scowls. It shook his world, that smile, so that he knew he had never known her. "I think I might about make it," she said. "Mind you *talk*, Cloud. Mind you read and write."

And she walked away. He was guilty, coward, standing there, but she never called him after her. *She's an older,* he thought, *she's oldest of the old, like the hills themselves, she is. She knows whether she wants a boy at her heels. She knows how to find her way to home. She knows where she's going and how far she means to walk.* And: *She's beautiful,* he thought, which he had never thought in his life about Pia Oldest, but she was, tall and straight and thin, with the wind dancing in the fringes of her clothes and the gray ropes of her hair—going away from him because she wanted to.

He ran back to the village in the hills and told his father, who sent young runners out to find her, but they could not, they never could, Pia being Pia and better than any of them in the wild.

It was days before he cried, and then only for a moment.

He imagined she found the calibans, that being what she wanted.

He thought of calibans all his life, thought of them in getting his son and telling him tales, and seeing some of his kin go down to the camp in the plain. Calibans moved close again after ma Pia went away. He was never sure if she had found them, but that thing was sure.

X

Year 72, day 198 CR
Main Base, Gehenna

"Are you," the man asked, "scared?"

The boy Dean stared at him, sitting where he was on the edge of the doctor's table in the center of the Base, and the answer was yes, but he was not about to say as much to this Base doctor. Children did this, he knew, went into the Base and learned. And he was here halfgrown as he was because they started taking older ones now, special older ones, who ran off from their work in the fields and lazed about working with their hands or being a problem to the supervisors. He had been a problem. He had told the field boss how to arrange the shifts, and the boss had not liked that; so he had walked offshift, that was all. He had had enough of the man.

Only they took people who bucked what was and soldiers visited their houses and brought them into the Base, behind the inmost wire, to go into the study like they took the children their families sold into going here every day for extra credit at the store.

They did this to children, so he was not going to admit he was scared. They went on asking him questions . . . Do you read or write? Does anyone you know read and write?—He said nothing. His name was Dean, which was a born-man name. His mother had told him that, and taught him to write his name and read the signs. But he figured it was theirs to find out.

"My mother get the store allowance?" he asked finally, reckoning if there was good to be gotten out of this, it might as well be hers.

"Depends on how you do," the man with the book said, turning him back his own kind of answer. "You do real well, Dean, and you might get a lot more than that."

He viewed it all with suspicion.

"Now we're going to start out with lessons, going to let you watch the machines, and when you've got beyond what they can teach you, then you get paid; and if you think you want to learn more than that—well, we'll see. We'll see how you do."

They put him in front of a machine that lighted up and showed him A and made the sound. It went to B then and showed him AB. They showed him how to push the buttons, and make choices, and he blinked when the machine took his orders. Possibilities dawned on him. He ran the whole range of what they wanted of him.

"I can read," he said, taking a chance, because of a sudden he saw himself using machines, like them, like what his name meant to him—being different than the others— and he suddenly, desperately, wanted not to be put out of this place. "I'm born-man. And I can read. I always could."

That got frowns out of them, not smiles. They went outside the door and talked to each other while he sat with his shoulders aching from sitting and working so long and hoping that he had not done the wrong thing.

A woman came into the room, one of them, in fine clothes and smelling the way born-men smelled in the Base, in the tall buildings, of things other than dirt and smoke. "You're going to stay the night," she said. "You've done very well. We're going to make up more questions for you."

He did not know why—he should have been relieved to know that he had done well. But there was his mother not knowing what might have happened; and he was thirteen and not quite a man, to know how to deal with this.

But the Base was authority, and he stayed.

Their questions were not A and B. They involved himself, and all the things he thought were right and wrong, and all the things he had ever heard. They asked them over and over again, until his brain ached and he did what he had never done for anyone but his own mother: he broke down and cried, which broke something in him which had never been broken before. And even then they kept up

their questions. He stilled his sobs and answered what they
wanted, estimating that he had deserved this change in himself because he had wanted what no towns-man had. The
barrage kept up, and then they let him eat and rest.

In the morning or whatever time he woke—the building
had no windows—they brought him to a room and put a
needle in his arm so that he half slept; and a machine
played facts into his awareness so that his mind went
whirling into cold dark distances, and the world into a different perspective: they taught him words for these things,
and taught him what he was and what his world was.

He wanted to go home when he waked from that. "Your
mother's sent lunch for you," they told him kindly. "She
knows you're well. We explained you'll be staying a few
more days before you come and go."

He ate his mother's bread in this strange place, and his
throat swelled while he swallowed and the tears ran down
his face without his even trying to stop them, or caring that
they saw. He knew what they did to the children then. The
children laughed and wrote words in the dust and hung
about together, exempt from work because they had their
hours in the Base school. But he was no child; and if he
went back into the town now he would never be the man
he had almost been. That thing in him which had broken
would never quite repair itself; and what could he say in
the town?—I've seen the stars. I've seen, I've touched,
there are other worlds and this one's shut because we're
different, because we don't learn, because—Because the
town is what it is, and we're very, very small.

He was quiet in his lessons, very quiet. He took his trank,
and listened to the tapes, having lost himself already. He
gave up all that he had, hoping that they would make him
over entirely, so that he could be what they were, because
he had no other hope.

"You're very good," they said. "You're extremely
intelligent."

This gave him what cheer he had.

But his mother cried when he went back to her quiet as
he had become; it was the first time she had ever cried in
front of him. She hugged him, sitting on the bed which was
the only place to sit in their small and shabby house, and

held his face and looked in his eyes and tried to understand what he was becoming.

She could not. That was part of his terror.

"They give me credit at the store," he said, searching for something to offer her in place of himself. "You can have good clothes."

She cleaned the house after, worked and worked and worked as if she somehow imagined to herself the clean white place where he had been, as if she fought back by that means. She washed all the clothes and washed the rough wood table and turned the straw mattresses, having beaten the dust out of them outside; and scrubbed the stone floor and got up and dusted even the tops of the rafters with a wet cloth to take away the dust. The ariels who sometimes came and went dodged her scrubbing and finally stayed outside. And Dean carried water and helped until the neighbors stared, neighbors already curious what had happened.

But when it was all still, it was only the old house all unnaturally clean, as if she had scrubbed it raw. And they ate together, trying to be mother and son.

"They wanted to teach me to write," he said. "But I already knew. You taught me that."

"My dad taught me," she said, which he knew. "We're born-men. Just like them."

"They say I'm good."

She looked up from her soup and met his eyes, just the least flicker of vindication. " 'Course," she said.

But he hedged all around the other things, like knowing what the world was. He was alone; with things dammed up inside he could never say.

And they had asked him things no one talked about—like the old things: like the books—the books they said the Hillers had. He had said these things not because he was innocent, but because he was afraid, because he was tired, because they wanted these things very, very badly and he was afraid to lie.

He sat across the rough table from his mother and ate his soup, afraid now to have her know how much of a stranger he had already become.

xi

"He's not Unionist," the science chief said. "The psych tests don't turn up much remnant of it. No political consciousness, nothing surviving in his family line."

"The mother's got title to a two bed house," security said, at the same long table in an upper level of the education facility. "Single. Always been single. Says the father's a hiller and she doesn't know who."

"Different story from the boy," said education. "The father's got born-man blood, he says. But he doesn't know who. We've interviewed the mother: she says the boy's got only *her* blood and her father was a doctor. She's literate. She does some small medical work in the town. Not getting rich at it. We give it away; she gets paid in a measure of flour. Hasn't done any harm at it."

"Remarkable woman. I'd suggest to bring her in for tests."

"Might have her doing clinic work," the mission chief said. "Good policy, to reward the whole family."

"We're forming a picture," the science chief said. "If we could locate the books that are supposed to exist—"

"The constant rumor is," security said, "that the hillers have them. If they exist."

"We don't press the hillers. They'll run on us."

"If there are literates among the hillers, and books, Union materials—"

"We do what we can," the mission chief said. "Short of a search, which might drive the material completely underground."

"We know what the colony was. We know that the calibans moved in on them. Something we did scared them off right enough. Maybe it was the noise of the shuttle. But somewhere the first colony lost control, and cleared out of this place. Went to the hills. The azi stayed in the town. The Dean line, a couple of others trace back to the colonists; but there's a hiller line among traders from one Elly Flanahan, and a lot of Rogerses and Innises and names that persist that aren't like azi names. *Something* turned most of the colonists to the hills, completely away from this site. The azi tended to stay, being azi. The flood hypothesis is out. Policy split is possible . . . but there's not much likelihood of it. The old camp seemed to have been purposely stripped, just people moving out. And calibans all over it. Tunnelled all under it. The earthmovers sunk and near buried. That's caliban damage, that's all."

"We have a pretty good picture," science said. "It's far from complete. If there are records—if there was anything left but anomalies like this boy Dean—"

"We pull the town tighter in," the mission chief said. "We continue the program, while we have the chance."

"Only with the town itself."

"Militarily—" security said, "the only answer. We can't get the hillers. Not without the town at a more secure level than it is. We can't ferret the hillers out. Can't."

"There's division of opinion on that."

"I'm telling you the departmental consensus. I'm telling you the longrange estimate. We don't need hardened enemies on this world. We don't use the fist."

"The policy stands," the mission chief intervened, a calm voice and firm. "The town first. We can't reach into the hiller settlement."

"The calibans—"

"We just keep an eye on that movement. If the caliban drift in our direction accelerates, then we take alarm."

"The drift is there," science said. "The mounds exist, a kilometer closer than last season."

"Killy has a breeding cycle theory that makes a great deal of sense—that this advance and retreat has something to do with a dieoff—"

"We make theories at a distance. While the ban holds on firsthand observation—"

"We do what we can with the town," the mission chief said, "before we take any action with the Calibans. We don't move until we're absolutely secure."

xii

Year 89, day 203 CR
Styxside

They were born-men and townsmen and they came up
the river with a great deal of noise, a sound of hardsoled
boots and breaking of branches and sometimes splashing
where a stream fed into the Styx. Jin was amazed and
squatted on a rock to see, because there had never in his
lifetime come such a thing, people from inside the barrier
come from behind their fences and down the Styx.

They saw him there, and some of them aimed their guns
from fright. Jin's heart froze in him from shock and he
moved no muscle until the seniormost of them waved the
guns away and stopped the rest of the column in the kind
of order townsmen liked.

"You," the man said. "Hiller?"

Jin nodded, squatting on his rock, his eyes still alert for
small movements of weapons. He had his arms about his
leatherclad knees, but there was brush beside him and he
could bound away with one fast spring if they went on
being crazy.

"You got your number, hiller?"

Jin made a pursing of his lips, his eyes very much alert.
"Got no number, born-man. I hunt. I don't trade behind
your wire."

The man came a little closer, looking up at him on his
rock. "We're not behind the wire now. Don't need a number. Want to trade?"

"Trade what?"

"You know calibans, hiller?"

Jin half-lidded his eyes. "O, so, calibans. Don't touch
them, born-man. The old browns, they don't take much to
hunters. Or strangers come walking 'long the Styx."

"We're here to study," another man said, leaving the
others to come closer. He was an older man with gray hair.
"To learn the calibans. Not to hunt."

"Huh." Jin laughed hiller-fashion, short and soft. "The
old browns don't fancy being learned. You make tapes, old

born-man, you make tapes to teach you calibans? They go away from you, long time ago. Now you want them back? They make your buildings fall, they drag you under, old born-man, take you down with them, down in the dark under ground."

"I'll go up there," a young man said; but: "No," the old man said. "He's all right. I want to hear him.—Hiller, what's your name?"

"Jin. What's yours?"

"Spencer. You mind if I come up there?"

"Sir—" the man said, with the weapons. But the old man was coming up the side of the rocky slope, and Jin considered it and let him, amused as the old born-man squatted down hiller-fashion facing him.

"You know a lot about them," Spencer said.

Jin shrugged, not displeased at respect.

"You hunt them?" Spencer asked. "You wear their hides."

"Grays," Jin said, rubbing his leather-clad knee. "Not the browns."

"What's the difference?"

It was a stupid question. Jin studied the old man, conceived an outrageous idea, because it was a pleasant old face, a comfortable face, on this slightly fat man with wrinkled skin and fine cloth clothes. Fat was prosperity, just enough. An important man who climbed up a rock and sat with a young hunter. Jin grinned, waved a dismissing hand. "You tell the rest of them go home. They make too much noise. I take you upriver."

"I can't do that."

"Make the calibans mad, that noise. You want to see, I show you."

Ah, the old man wanted the bargain. He saw it in the eyes, pale, pale blue, the palest most wonderful blue he ever saw. And the old man got down off his rock and went to the armed young leader and argued, in harder and harder words.

"You can't do that," the young man said.

"You turn them around," the old one said, "and you report how it was."

In the end they each got half, because the old man was going on and the rest were waiting here.

"Not far," Jin said easily. He bounced down off his rock, a soft landing on softsoled boots, and straightened with a nod to the old man in the way that they should go.

"He hasn't made a deal," the armed man said. "Dr. Spencer, he's no townsman; we've got no number on him."

"Maybe if you had," Spencer said, "he wouldn't be any good out here."

The armed man said nothing. Jin motioned to the old one. It was a lark. He was fascinated by these people he had never seen so close at hand, in their fine cloth and hard boots. He reckoned this man for someone—not just a townsman but from the buildings where no one got, not even town folk, and least of all hillers.

And never a hunter who had no number on his hand, for passing the fences and going and coming into the born-man territory.

"Come on," he said to the old man Spencer. "You give me a shirt, all right?" He knew that such folk must be rich. "I show you calibans."

The old man came with him, walking splayfooted down the bank, shifting the straps of all sorts of things he carried. Flitters dived and splashed among the reeds and the old man puffed on, making noise even in walking, a helpless sort in the way no hiller child was helpless.

I could rob this man, Jin thought, just because robbery did happen, high in the hills; but it was a kind of thought that came just because he thought it was trusting of the old man to be carrying all that wealth and going off with a stranger who was stronger and quicker and knew the land, and he was wondering whether the old man knew people robbed each other, or whether inside the camp such things never happened.

He found the calibans where he knew to find them, not so very far as they had been a hand of years ago. Even ariels were more plentiful, a lacery of trails across the sandy margin. Ariels, grays, even browns had turned up here-abouts, and all the lesser sorts, the hangers-about: it was a rich season, a fat season.

"Look," he said and pointed, showing the old man a ripple amid the Styx, where the broad marshy water re-flected back the trees and the cloudy sky.

The old man stopped and gaped, trying to make out calibans; but there was no seeing that one clearly. It was fishing, and need not come up. They kept walking around the next bank, where mounds rose up on all sides of them, and trees thrust their roots in to drink from the dark hollows. It was forest now, and only leaves rustled.

"They're all about us," he told the man, and the man started violently and batted at a flitter which chanced at that moment to land on his neck. The startlement made Jin laugh. "Listen," Jin said, and squatted down, so the old man squatted too, and paid attention when he pointed across the water, among the trees. "Over there—across the water—that's theirs. That's theirs all the way to the salt water, as far as a man can walk. They're smart, those calibans."

"Some of you—live in there. I've heard so. Could I talk with one?"

Jin's skin prickled up. He looked toward the safe side of the river, toward familiar things. "Tell you something, old born-man. You don't talk to them. You don't talk about them."

"Bad people?"

Jin shrugged, not wanting to discuss it. "Want a caliban? I can whistle one."

"They're dangerous, aren't they?"

"So's everyone. Want one?" He did not wait, but gave out a low warble, knowing what it would do.

And very quickly, because he knew a guard had been watching all this tramping about near the mound, a caliban put its head up out of the brushy entrance and a good deal more of the caliban followed.

He heard a tiny sound by him, a whirring kind of thing. He shot out a hand at the machinery the man carried. "Don't do that. Don't make sounds."

It stopped at once. "They pick that up."

"You just don't make sounds."

"It's *big*."

Children said that, when they first saw the old browns. Jin pursed his lips again, amused. "Seen enough, old born-man. Beyond here's his. And no arguing that."

"But the ones—the humans—that go inside—Is it wrong to talk about that? Do you trade with them?"

He shook his head ever so slightly. "They live, that's all.

Eat fish." Above them on the ridge the caliban raised its
crest, flicked out a tongue. That was enough. "Time to
move, born-man."

"That's a threat."

"No. That's wanting." He heard something, knew with
his ears what it was coming up in the brush, grabbed the
born-man's sleeve to take him away.

But the Weird crouched there, all long-haired and
smeared with mud, head and shoulders above the brush.

And the born-man refused to move.

"Come on," Jin said urgently. "Come on." Out of the
tail of his eye, in the river, a ripple was making its way
toward them. The man made his machinery work once
more, briefly. "There's another one. There's too many,
born-man. Let's move."

He was relieved when the man lurched to his feet and
came with him. Very quietly they hurried out of the place,
but the old man turned and looked back when the splash
announced the arrival of the swimmer on the shore.

"Would they attack?" the born-man asked.

"Sometimes they do and sometimes not."

"The man back there—"

"They're trouble, is all. Sometimes they're trouble."

The old man panted a little, making better speed with
all his load.

"What do you want with calibans?" Jin asked.

"Curious," the old man said. He made good time, the
two of them going along at the same pace. "That's following us."

Jin tracked the old man's glance at the river, saw the
ripples. "That's so."

"I can hurry," the old man offered.

"Not wise. Just walk."

He kept an eye to it—and knowing calibans, to the
woods as well. He imagined small sounds . . . or perhaps
did not imagine them. But they ceased when they had come
close to the curve of the river where the rest of the born-
men waited.

They were nervous. They got up from sitting on their
baggage and had their guns in their hands. Out in the river
the ripples stopped, beyond the reeds, in the deep part.

"They're there," the old man said to the one in charge

of the others. "Got some data. They're stirred up some. Let's be walking back."

"Got a shirt owed me," Jin reminded them, hands on hips, standing easy. But he reckoned not to be cheated.

"Hobbs." The old man turned to the younger, and there was some ado while one of the men took off his shirt and passed it over. The old man gave it to Jin, who looked it over and found it sound enough. "Jin, I might like to talk with you. Might like you to come to the town and talk."

"Ah." Jin tucked his shirt under his arm and backed off. "You don't put any mark on me, no, you don't, born-man."

"Get you a special kind of paper so you can come and go through the gates. No number on you. I promise. You know a lot, Jin. You'd find it worth your time. Not just one shirt. Real pay, town scale."

He stopped backing, thinking on that.

And just then a splash and a brown came up through the reeds, water sliding off its pebbly hide. It came up all the way on its legs.

Someone shot. It lurched and hissed and came—"No!" Jin yelled at them, running, which was the wise thing. But they shot with the guns, and it hissed and whirled and flattened reeds in its entry into the river. The ripples spread and vanished in the sluggish current. It went deep. Jin crouched on his rock and hugged himself with a dire cold feeling at his gut. There was shouting among the folk. The old man shouted at the younger and the younger at the others, but there was a great quiet in the world.

"It was a *brown*," Jin said. The old man looked up at him, looking as if he of all of them halfway understood. "Go away now," Jin said. "Go away fast."

"I want to talk with you."

"I'll come to your gate, old born-man. When I want. Go away."

"Look," the younger man said, "if we—"

"Let's go," the old man said, and there was authority in his voice. The folk with guns gathered up all that was theirs and went away down the shore. The bent place stayed in the reeds, and Jin watched until they had gone out of sight around the bend, until the bank was whole again. A sweat gathered on his body. He stared at the gray light on the Styx, trying to see ripples, hoping for them.

But brush whispered. He stood up slowly, on his rock, faced in the direction of the sound.

Two of the Weirds stood there, with the rags of garments that Weirds affected, their deathly pale skins streaked with mud about hands and knees. Their backs were to the upriver. Their shadowed eyes rested on him, and he grew very cold, reckoning he was about to die. There was nowhere to run but the born-men's wire. The hiller village could never hide him; and he would die of other reasons if he was shut away behind the wire and numbered.

One Weird lifted his head only slightly, a gesture he took for a summons. He might cause them trouble. He was minded to. But somewhere, not so far away and not in sight either, would be another of them, or two or three. They would move if he denied them. So he leapt down from his rock and came closer to the Weirds as they seemed to want.

They parted, opening a way for him to go, and a quiet panic settled into him, because he understood then that they intended to bring him back with them upriver. Desperately he looked leftward, toward the Styx, toward the gray sunlight mirrored among the reeds, hoping against all expectation that the brown the born-men had shot would surface.

No. It was gone—dead, hurt, no one might know. A gentle hand took his elbow, ever so gently tugging at him, directing him where he had to go if he had any hope to live.

He went, retracing the track he and the old man had followed, and now the Weirds held him by either arm. The one on his left deftly reached and relieved him of his belt knife.

He could not understand—how they moved him, or why he did not break and run; only the death about him was instant and what was ahead was indefinite, holding some small chance. There was no reckoning with the Weirds or with the browns. There was no understanding. They might bring him back to the mounds and then as capriciously let him go.

The turns of the Styx unwound themselves until the sky-shining sheet was dimmed in the shade of trees, until they reached the towering ridges and the tracks he and the old man had made when they had stopped.

Perhaps they would hold him here and the old brown

would come out and eye him as calibans would, and lose interest as calibans would, and they would let him go.

No. They urged him up the slope of the mound, toward the dark entryway in the side of it, and he refused, bolted suddenly out of their hands and down among the brush at the right, breaking twigs and thorns on his leather clothing, shielding his face with his arms.

A hiss broke in front of him and the head of a great brown loomed up, jaws gaping. He skidded to a stop, slapped instinctively at a sharp sting on his cheek and felt a dart fall from under his fingers. The brown in front of him turned its head to regard him with one round golden eye while he felt that side of his face numb, his heart speeding. His extremities lost feeling, his knees buckled: he flung up an arm to protect his eyes as brush came up at him, and lacked the strength to move when he landed among the thorny branches. They were all about him, the human shapes, silent. Gentle hands tugged at him, turning him onto his back, so that a lacery of cloudy sky and branches swung into his vision.

He was not dying. He was numb, so that they could gather him up and carry him but he was not dead when they carried him toward the hole in the earth, and realizing this, he tried to fight, in a terror deeper than all his nightmares. But he could not move, not the least twitch of a finger, not even to close his eyes when dirt fell into his face, not to close his mouth or swallow or use his tongue, even to cry out when the dark went around him and he was alone with them, with their silence and their touches.

xiii

Year 89, day 208 CR
Main Base

"No sign of this hiller," Spencer said.

"No, sir," Dean said, hands behind him.

Spencer frowned, turned from his table fully facing Dean—an intense young man, his assistant, with a shock of thick black hair and a coppery skin tone and a faded blue number on his hand that meant townsman, at least intermittently. Presently Dean was doing field work, meaning he was back in the town again. "How did you hunt for him?" Spencer asked.

"Asking other hillers. Those who come to trade. *They* haven't seen him."

"They know him?"

Dean took the liberty and sat down on the other stool at the slanted desk full of reports, pulled it under him. He smelled of recent soap, never of the fields. Meticulous in that. He had ambitions, Spencer reckoned. He was good— in what they let him do. "Name's known, yes. There's a kind of split—I don't pick up all of it; I've given you notes on that. At any rate, there was this very old azi—You want his history?"

"Might be pertinent."

"The last azi survivor. His brood went for the hills. That's the ancestry. You *hear* about that line, but you don't see them. None of them are registered to come into the camp. There's an order among hillers. The ones we get around here—they'll talk easy on some things. But I didn't get an easy feeling asking about this fellow Jin."

"How—not easy?"

A shrug. "Like first it was no townsman's business; like second, that maybe this particular hiller wouldn't be dealing with a townsman."

"How did you put it to them?"

"Just that I had come on something that had to do with this Jin. I thought it was clever. After all, his ancestor was hereabouts. And it used to be that townsmen would trade found-things to the hills. I didn't say anything more than that. They might get curious. But if this man's a bush hiller, it could be a while."

"Meaning he might be out of their settlement and out of touch."

"Meaning that, likely. It seemed to be a good bit of gossip. I imagine it'll go on quick feet. But no news yet.—You mind if I ask what I'm looking for?"

Spencer clamped his lips together, thinking on it, reached then and dragged a set of pictures down from the clutter on the desk, arranged them in front of Dean.

"That's the Styx."

"I see that," Dean said.

Spencer frowned and livened the wallscreen, played the tapeloop that was loaded in the machine. He had seen the tape a score of times, studied it frame by frame. Now he watched Dean's face instead, saw Dean's face go rigid in the light of the screen, seeing the caliban and then the human come out of the mound. Dean's whole body gave back, hands on the edge of the tabletop.

"Bother you?"

Dean looked toward him as the tape looped round again. Spencer cut the machine off. Dean straightened with a certain nonchalance. "Not particularly. Calibans. But someone got real close to do that tape."

"Not so far upriver. Look at the orbiting survey."

Spencer marked the place, difficult to detect under the general canopy of trees. Dean looked, looked up, without the nonchalance. "This have to do with the hiller you're looking for, by any chance?"

"It might."

"You take these?"

"You're full of questions."

"That's where you and the soldiers went. Upriver last week. Looking for calibans."

"Might be."

"This hunter—this Jin—He was there? He guided you?"

"You don't like the sound of it."

Dean bit at his lip. "Not a good idea to go up on calibans like that. Not a good idea at all."

"Let me show you something else." Spencer pulled a tide of pictures down the slope of the desk. "Try those."

Dean turned and sorted through them, frowning.

"You know what you're looking at?"

"The world," Dean said. "Seen from orbit."

"Pictures of what?"

A long silence, a shuffling of pictures. "Rivers. Rivers all over the world. I don't know their names. And the Styx."

"And?"

A long silence. Dean did not look around.

"Caliban patterns," Spencer said. "You see them?"

"Yes."

"Want to show you something more." Spencer found the aerial shot of the hiller village, thatched huts and stone walls, winding walls, walls that bent and curved. He put a shot of the Base and town and fields next to it, a checker-board geometry. "Don't you find something remarkable in that? Have you ever seen it?"

Dean sat still, his eyes only on the pictures under his hands. "I think any townsman would tend to understand that."

"How do you mean?"

"The founders laid out the town streets. Hillers made the hiller village."

"Why didn't they make it like the town?"

"Because they don't like to do things like us. Spirals are like them. Maybe they got it from the calibans. I figure they did. They do spirals sometimes—like in the dust. You talk with them to trade—they squat down and draw when they don't like much what you're telling them."

"I don't think I've ever seen a hiller do that."

"Wouldn't."

"What's that supposed to mean?"

"Like when you send me out to ask things hillers won't say when you ask it. Like when a hiller's dealing with some-body in Base clothes it's one way; and when it's a towns-man that hiller's more and less hard to deal with. They price you way high if they think they can; but they don't give you the eye, they don't do hiller tricks when they bar-gain. Like spitting in the dirt. Like looking off. Like writ-ing patterns."

"Patterns. What patterns?"

"Spirals. Like two of them squatting down in the dirt and letting the dust run out of their hands or drawing with their fingers—one does one thing and one does a bit on it, while they're thinking over a deal. And they make you think they've forgotten you're standing there. But—maybe they're talking to each other that way. Maybe it's nothing at all. That's why they do it. Because we won't know. And we're supposed to wonder."

Spencer sat and stared at him so long that Dean finally looked his way. "Somehow that never got into your reports."

"I never thought it was much. It's all show."

"Is it?" Spencer pulled two more pictures from the lot, one of an eastern hemisphere river, one of the north shore, a mosaic going toward the sea, including all the effluence of the Styx, and the Base and both town and hiller settlement. He pointed out the places, the encroachment of calibans toward the sea on the far side of the river, the faint shadowing at the end of ridges. "They're different. The spirals of calibans everywhere in the world but here—are looser. They don't make hills. See the shadow cast from the centers, here, here and here—that's a tall structure. That's a peak in the center of those spirals. Let me get you a closeup." He searched and pulled another out, that showed the structure, a spiral winding into a miniature mountain, slid that in front of Dean. "You understand what I'm saying now? Only here. Only across from the Base. Is that a caliban structure?"

"How big is that?"

"The complex is a kilometer wide. The peak is forty meters wide at base of the most extreme slope and twenty high. Have you ever seen the like?"

Dean shook his head. "No." He glanced up. "But then I've never seen a caliban. Except the pictures."

"They didn't like sharing the Base. They moved out."

"But they're moving back. On the river. Your pictures— You won't get that hunter to go across the Styx, if that's what you're thinking. I don't think you will. I don't think you ought to push at the hillers where it regards calibans."

"Why?"

A shrug. "I just don't think you should."

"That's not the kind of answer you draw your pay for."

"I think it's dangerous. I think the hillers could get anxious. The calibans are already close. They won't like them stirred up, that's what."

"They hunt them?"

Another shrug. "They trade in leather. But there's calibans and calibans. Different types."

"The browns."

"The browns and the grays."

"What's the difference?"

A third shrug. "Hillers hunt grays. They know."

"Know what?"

"Whatever they know. I don't."

"There was this caliban," Spencer said carefully. "We'd been up to the mound to take those pictures, this Jin and I. Alone. And we got back to the troops, and this caliban came out of the river. They shot it and it slid back in. 'It was a *brown*,' the hunter said. Like that. And then: 'Go away fast.' What do you make of that?"

Dean just stared a moment, dead-faced the way he would when something bothered him. "Did you?"

"We left."

"I reckon he did, too. Fast and far as he could. *He* won't come to your gate, no."

"Meaning?"

"Meaning he's going to be scared a long, long time. He'll never come to you."

"Would he be that afraid?"

"He'd be that afraid."

"Of *what?* Of calibans? Or Weirds?"

A blink of the dark eyes. "Whatever's worth being afraid of. Hillers would know. I don't. But don't go out there. Don't send the soldiers outside the wire, not another time."

"I'm afraid I don't make that decision."

"Tell them."

"I'll do that," Spencer said frowning. "You don't think the search is worthwhile, do you?"

"You won't find him."

"Keep your ears open."

"I'd thought about sleeping in my own quarters tonight."

"I'd rather you stayed in the town—just keep listening."

"For what?"

"Hiller talk. All of it. What if I offered you a bonus—to go outside the wire?"

Dean shook his head warily. "No. I don't do that."

"Townsmen have gone to the hills before."

"No."

"Meaning you won't. Suppose we put a high priority on that."

Dean sat very still. "Townsmen know I'm from inside. Hillers may be stirred up right now. And if they are, and if they knew where I came from—"

"You mean you think they'd kill you."

"I don't know what they'd do."

"All right, we'll think about that. Just go back to the town and listen where you can."

"All right." Dean got up, walked as far as the door,

looked back. He looked as if he would like to say something more, but walked away.

Spencer stared at his pictures, ran the loop again.

Calibans had tried the wire last night down by the river. They had never done that, not since Alliance came to the world.

There had to be precautions.

xiv

Year 89, day 208 CR
Styxside

He might be mad: or he wished he were, in the dark, in the silence broken only by slitherings and breathings and sometimes, when his sanity had had all it could bear, by his screams and sobs. His screaming could drive them back a while, but they would be back.

They put no restraint on him. They needed none but the darkness and the earth, the hardpacked earthen walls that he could feel and not see in the absolute and lasting night. His fingers were torn and maybe bleeding: he had tried to dig his way to safety, even to dig himself a niche in which to put his back, so that he could defend himself when they came at him, but he had no sense which way the outside was, or how deep they had taken him—he might be trying to dig through the hills themselves. He found a rock once, and battered one of his attackers with it, but they used their needles and had their revenge for that, a long, long time—like the times he had tried to crawl away, feeling his blind way through the dark, until he had ended with the hissing blast of a caliban's breath in his face, the quick scrabble of claws, the thrusting of a great blunt nose that knocked him off his feet—lying there with a great clawed foot bearing down on his ribs and throat until human hands arrived with needles; or running into such hands direct—No, there was no fighting them. He did not know why he did not die. He thought about it, young as he was, and thought he could smother himself in the earth, that he could dig himself a grave with his lacerated fingers and hide his face in it and stop his breathing with dirt. He dug, but they always came when they heard him digging—he was sure that they heard. So he kept still.

They brought him raw fish to eat, and water to drink which might or might not be clean. At such times they touched him, constant touches like the nagging of children, and then more than other times he thought of dying, mostly because feeding was the one thing they did to keep life in him. He was always cold. Mud caked on his clothes and his skin, dry and wet by turns, wherever in the earthen maze they had moved him last. His hair was matted with filth. His clothes were torn, laces snapped with his struggles, and he tried to knot them back together because he was cold, because clothes were all the protection he had.

He lay still finally, weaker than he had begun, with druggings and struggles and food that sometimes his stomach heaved up or that his body rejected in cramping spasms; and even his condition did not repulse the females among them, who tormented him with some result at the beginning, when it took all of them, sealing up the exits and herding and hunting him through the narrow dark, and hauling him down with weight of numbers—but they got nothing from him now, nothing but a weary misery, terror that they might kill him in their frustration. That was what he had sunk to. But they were always silent, gave him no hint of humor or anger or whether they were themselves quite mad. He was himself passing over some manner of brink; he even knew this, in a far recess of his mind where his self survived. If he were set out again on the riverside—he thought of Styx as the outside, having lost all touch with the sunny hills—if he were set outside to see the daylight again, the sun on the water, the reeds in the wind—if he were free—he did not think he would laugh again. Or take sunlight for granted. He would never be a man again in the narrow sense of man—because sex had not gone dead in him, but become personless, unimportant; or in the wider sense, because he had been gutted, spread wide, to take into his empty insides all the darks and slitherings underearth, all the madness and the windings underground. He had nothing in common with humanity. He felt this happening, or realized it had happened; and finally knew that this was why he had not died, that he had reached a point past which he had more interest in this darkness, the sounds, the slitherings, than he had in life. It had all begun to give him information. His mind received a thousand clues in the midst of its terror, grew tired of terror and concentrated on the clues.

They came for him. He thought it might be food when he heard them, but food smelled, and he caught no such smell, so he knew that it was himself they wanted, and he lay quite still, his heart speeding a little, but his mind reasoning that it was only inconvenience, a little pain to get through like all the other pains, and after that he would still be alive, and still thinking, which was something still more promising than dying was.

But they gathered about him, a great lot of them by the sounds, and jabbed him with one of their needles. He screamed, outraged by that trick, suddenly wild as a caliban could go. He struck at them, but they skipped silently out of reach. Something slithered across his chill-numbed legs, and that was an ariel, who ran where they liked in the mounds. He struck at it with a shudder, but it eluded him. Then he sat still, waiting while the numbness crept over him, while his mouth seemed full of fluff and his extremities went dead.

They gathered him up then, feeling over his body to be sure which way he was lying, dragged at his wrists to take him through the narrow tunnel, while he was as paralyzed as he had been when they brought him into this place. His mind still worked. He wished that they would turn him over on his belly because dirt fell into his eyes.

Then there began to be daylight, and they were going up, *up,* and out of the tunnel into the glaring sun. Light crossed his eyes like a knife, brought tears, and vanished again in a whirl of leaves living and dead as one of them slung him up and over his shoulder.

They passed him then to another, who did not support him, but held him about the chest and dragged him into the river. The shock of water got to him. He tried again to move, to throw his head, to at least get air; but a hand cupped his chin and the water took all but his face and sometimes washed over him. He choked, incapable of moving as his limbs dragged through the water. Terror grew too much then. The senses dimmed, from want of air, from the hammering of his heart—and then they were hauling him out on the other side, and took up his sodden, leather-clad body sideways while his head fell lowest and a spasm of his throat and stomach sent up a thin stream of choking fluid. His limbs took on a little life, a slight degree of response, but now they dragged him up again, pulling him up a brushy mound on the opposite side of the river, and the dark took them all back again.

He convulsed once, a spasm which emptied out his stomach, lay still and shallow-breathing when it had passed, and the hands which had let him go when he doubled up took him again by the wrists and collar and by the knees, carrying him in rapid jolting through the dark. He heard a sound, a faint protest from his own throat, and stopped it, silent as this whole world was silent. He had lain for unguessable time in the dark learning the rules and now they stripped all the rules away. He was truly gone now. The paralysis of his body had receded to a kind of numbness, but he failed to do anything to help himself, blind, completely blind, and fainting for long black periods hardly distinguishable from his waking in the dark, except that the fainting was without pain, and that such periods were gratefully frequent.

They stopped finally. He thought perhaps that they had gotten to some place which satisfied them, and that they might go away and let him lie, which was all he wanted, but they stayed: he heard their panting breaths close by, and the small movements they made. He heard the skittering of ariels and the slither of one of the calibans in the vast silence. Perhaps, he thought, they meant him some harm when they had rested. Maybe they were renegades or crazier than the rest, with a notion to have privacy for their sport. He meant to fight them if it got to that, make them stick him again, because that brought him numbness.

One moved, and the others did, fingering him with their blind touches; he struck once, but they got his arms and legs and simply picked him up again, having had their rest. He knew what they could do, and had no desire for the needle under those terms, and even made feeble attempts to cooperate when they had come to a low place, so that finally it seemed to get through to them that he would go with them on his own. More and more they let him carry himself for brief periods, taking him up when he would stumble, when his exhaustion was too extreme.

And then there was a confusion in the dark, a meeting, he thought, and a different smell about those they met. He was pushed forward, let go, taken again, and after that snatched up again, so that he knew he was in different hands. Tears leaked from his eyes. The others had understood something, he had gotten *something* through to the others to better his condition, and they changed the game again—snatched him off and hauled him along with more roughness than before. He went limp and let them do what they liked, afraid of needles, afraid of utter helplessness. Such strength as he had left in him, he saved, that being the only canniness he had left.

They climbed. He gathered his mind from the far corners of its retreat and tried to think again, getting information again—ascent, spirals, dry earth.

And light. He tried to lift his head from its backward tilt, could not hold it, watched the light grow in his upside down vision, making a hazy silhouette of the man who had his arms.

An earthen chamber with light coming from a window. A man sitting on the floor, another shadow in his hazed vision.

They let him down. He lay there a moment, frozen in the silence of them, turned his head to the seated man— one of their own, but old, the oldest man he had ever seen, bald and withered and clothed in a oneshouldered robe that held at least the memory of red. The others squatted in their rags. The old man sat and waited.

It was a time before he gathered his wits at all. He levered himself up on his arm, squinted up at the light as the silhouette of a Weird set a large bowl of water in front of him. He bent and cupped up water to drink and wash the sickness from his mouth, drank again and again and splashed clean water over his face while his hands shook and spilled a lot of it in his lap. He blinked at the old man, having gotten used to insanity and expecting more of it.

"Speak," the old man said softly.

A rock might have spoken. The old man sat. A smallish ariel rested in his lap. His fingers played with it, stroking its ruffled fringes.

Jin needed a time to consider. He wiped his face yet again, drew his knee up and rested his arm on it because he was not steady even sitting. He looked at the old man very long. "Why am I here?" he asked finally, as still, as hushed. But the old man did not answer, as crazed as the rest of them. Or that was not the speech the old man wanted. The silence between them went on, and Jin hugged his knee against him to keep himself from shaking. There was warmth here. It streamed through the window, circulated with the air. Summer went on outside as if it had never stopped. "They found me by the river," Jin said then, precisely, carefully, in a voice hardly more than whisper. He recalled the shooting of the caliban and blocked that from his mind, focussing narrowly on the old man in front of him, whose skull was naked of hair, whose thin beard was white and clean. Clean. He never thought to see cleanliness again. He reeked of mud and sweat and excrement; his clothes were caked with filth. "It must have been days ago—" He went on talking, reckoning for the first time that someone was listening to him. "They brought me across the river. I don't know why."

"Name."

"Jin."

The aged head lifted. Watery dark eyes focused on his for a long and quiet time. "My name is Green."

The name hit his mind and settled, a cold, cold feeling. Family stories. They knew each other. He saw that. "Let me go," he said. "Let me out of here."

"Someday," Green whispered, a rusty sound like something long unused. A long silence. "A brown is dead."

"An accident. No one meant it."

Green simply stared, then took pebbles from his lap and placed them in a line on the earthen floor. The ariel watched, then scrambled over his knee and onto the hard-packed earth, a flailing of limbs. It stood up on its legs, flicked its collar, studying the matter with one cocked eye. Then it began to move the pebbles, laying them in a heap.

"Let me leave," Jin said hoarsely, focussing with difficulty. "It was an accident."

"Do you understand this Pattern?" Green asked. "No." He answered himself, and gathered up the stones, laid them down again, only to have the ariel move them into a heap. It went on and on.

"What do you want with me?" Jin asked at last. A tremor had started in his arms, exhaustion, and a pain in his gut. "Can't we get it done?"

"Look at this place," Green said.

He lifted his eyes and looked around him, the earthen walls, the window, the rammed-earth floor scored with claws far larger than the ariel's. The Weirds crouched in shadow beneath the window.

Green clapped his hands, twice, echoing in the stillness. And far away, down somewhere in the shadows something stirred. There was a sough of breath, and that something was large.

Jin froze, his arms locked about his knees. He looked at the window, at sunlight, at a way of escaping or dying.

"No hurt," Green said softly.

It came up from below, a whuff of breath, a dry scraping of claws, the thrusting of a blunt, bony-collared head up out of the entry to the room, a head as large as the entry itself. Jin scrambled back until he felt the wall behind him, and more of it kept coming, a brown, but a bigger brown than ever he had seen. Its eyes were green-gold. Its crest was touched with green. It settled on its belly, curling its tail around the curving of the wall beyond Green, reaching from side to side of the room, and the Weirds never stirring from where they sat. The brown craned its neck, turned a fistsized pupil in Jin's direction, came up on its legs and moved closer.

Jin shut his eyes, felt warm breath and the flickering of its tongue about his face and throat. The tongue withdrew. The head turned again to stare at him with an eye large as a human head. The tongue licked out, thick as his arm.

"Be calm," Green whispered. Jin huddled against the wall, beside huge clawed feet. The head swung over him, overshadowing him; and quietly it bent and nudged him with its jaws.

He cried out; it whipped away, dived down into the dark of the access with a last slithering of its tail. Jin stayed where he was against the wall, shivering.

"Others died," Green whispering, sitting again where he

had sat, calmly placing his stones one after the other. *No*, the stones said, chilling with hope. Green gathered up the stones again, strewed them one after the other, went on doing this time after time while the ariel crouched near and watched, while the rougher, ragged Weirds crouched watching in their silence.

Jin wiped his mouth and grew quieter, the shivers periodic. He was not dead. He had not died. There was an anger stored away inside him, anger at what he was, that he could not stop shivering, because they could do whatever they liked. He remembered what he had suffered, and how he had screamed, and how all his wit and hunter's skill had let him down. He no longer liked being what he had been—vulnerable; he would never be again what he had been—naive. All his life people must have seen these things in him. Or all his kind were like him. He loathed himself with a deep and dawning rage.

xv

Year 89, day 222 CR
Main Base

Dean came into the lab, stood, hands behind him, coughed finally when Spencer stayed at work. Spencer turned around.

"Morning," Spencer said.

"Morning, sir." He kept his pose, less than easy, and Spencer frowned at him.

"Something *wrong*, Dean?"

"I heard—"

"Is this panic all over the town, then?"

"The soldiers moved last night. To the wire."

"An alarm. An empty one."

"Hillers haven't shown up in days."

"So I understand." Spencer came closer, rested his portly body against the counter and leaned back, arms folded. "You here to say something in particular, Dean?"

"Just that."

"Well, I appreciate your report. I reckon the hillers are a little nervous, that's all."

"I don't know what I can learn out there in town if there aren't any hillers coming in."

"I think you serve a purpose," said.

"I'd really like to be assigned inside."

"You're not nervous, are you?"

"I just really think I'm not serving any purpose out there."

"It's rather superstitious, isn't it? I detect that, in the town."

"They're quite large, sir. The calibans."

"I think you serve as a stabilizing influence in the town. You can tell them that the station's still up there watching and we don't anticipate any movement. It's probably due to some biocycle. Fish, maybe. Availability of food. Population pressures. You're an educated man, Dean, and I want you right where you are. We've got a dozen applications for Base residency in our hands, a rush on applications for one open job. That disturbs me more than the calibans. We've got a whole flood of field workers on the sick roster. I'm talking twenty percent of the workers. Not a fever in the lot. No. We're not pulling you inside. You stay out until the crisis is over."

"That could be a while, Dr. Spencer."

"You do your job. You keep it down out there. You want your privileges, you do your job, you hear me? No favors. You talk to key people and you keep the town quiet."

"Yes," Dean said. "Sir." He jammed his hands into his pockets and nodded a good morning, trying to manage his breathing while he turned and walked out.

His mother was dead. Last month. The meds had not saved her this time: the heart had just gone. The town house was empty except when he moved in. His neighbors hardly spoke, coveting the house so conveniently sharing a wall with their overcrowded one. He had no friends: older than the adolescent scholars, he was anomaly in his generation. He had no wife or lover, being native and untouchable on the main base side of the line, outsider and unwanted in the town.

He walked the quadrangle of Base, among the tall out-worlder buildings, among strange concrete gardens which disturbed him to look at, because they made no sense in their forms of twisted concrete, and he saw obscure comparisons to Patterns, which hillers made to confuse townsmen. Just beyond the enclosure made by the buildings and their concrete walls, he entered the gatehouse where he stripped and hung his Base clothes in a locker, and changed to townsman coveralls, drab and worn. They were a lie; or the other clothes were: he was not, this morning, sure.

He went out again, passed the guard who knew him, the outworlder guard who looked at him and never smiled, never trusted him, always checked at the tags and the number on his hand as if they had changed since yesterday.

The guard made his note in the record, that he had left the Base. Dean went out, from concrete garden to a concrete track that led into the town, making a T north and south, one long true street which was all the luxury the town had. The rest were dirt. The buildings were native stone and brick; and the clinic, which was featureless concrete—that was the other gift from the Base. Dirt streets and ordinary houses raised by people who had forgotten architects and engineers. They had a public tap on every street; a public sewer to take the slops, and a law to make sure people took the trouble. There was a public bath, but that stank of its drains, and kept the ground around it muddy, to track in and out. There were fields as far as the hills, golden at this time of year; and the sentry towers; and the wire, wire about the fields, about the town, and concrete ramparts and guardstations about the Base. The wire made them safe. So the outworlders said.

xvi

Year 89, day 223 CR
The Hiller Village

A caliban came at twilight, carrying a rider, a thing no one had ever seen; it came gliding out of the brush near old Tom's house and another one came after it. A small girl saw it first and stood stock still. Others did the same, excepting one young man who dived into the common hall and brought the whole village pouring out onto the rocky commons.

It was a man on the caliban's shoulders, all shadowy in

the twilight, the caliban itself indistinct against the brush, and a second caliban, smaller, came after with a man sitting on that one too. The calibans stopped. Weirds materialized out of the brush around the camp, shadows in the fading colors of night's edge, some naked and some wearing dull-hued bits of clothes.

The man sitting on the caliban's neck—the first one—lifted his arm. "You'll leave this place," the voice came ringing out at them, speech from a Weird . . . and that alone was shock enough, but the caliban moved forward, light and slow as the clawed feet could set themselves on the stone, and the hillers gathered on the doorstep of the common-hall gave backward like the intaking of a breath. There were hunters among them, but no one had brought weapons to evening meal; there were elders, but no one seemed to know what to say to this; there were children, and one of the youngest started to cry, setting off an infant, but parents hugged their faces against their shoulders and frantically hushed them.

Other calibans were around the camp, some with riders, moving ghostlike through the brush. And smaller calibans, like the witless grays. And smaller still, a handful of the village ariels came slithering out into the empty space between calibans and hall and froze there, heads up, fringes lifted, a thing peculiarly horrid, that creatures the children kept for pets should range themselves with such an invasion.

"The village is done," the intruder said. "Time to move. Calibans are coming—tonight. More and more of them. The times change. These *strangers* inside the wires, these strangers that mark you to go through their gates, that take food enough from the town to get fat, they've got everything. And they shoot browns. That doesn't do, no, that doesn't do at all. There's no more time. There's new Patterns, across the river, there's things no outsider ever saw, there's a safe place I'll bring you to, but this place . . . this village is going to be for the wind and the ariels tomorrow, like the domes they tell about, like those, dead and dark. The stone underfoot won't protect you. Not now."

"That's *Jin*," someone said under his breath, a tone of horror, and the name went whispering through the village. "That's Jin, that was lost on riverside."

"Jin," a man's voice said, and that was Jin Older, who pushed his way out in front of everyone, with tears and shock in his voice. "Jin, come down from that, come here. This is your people, Jin."

Something hissed. Jin Older slapped at something in his neck about the time his wife pushed through the crowd to get to him; and other kin—but Jin Older fell down, and a few tried to see to him, but one broke to run for cover—a second hissing, and that woman staggered and sprawled.

"Take what you want," Jin shouted, pointing a rigid arm at the village about them. "What you'll need, you gather up—But plan to leave. You thought you were safe here, built on rock. But you leave these buildings, you just leave them for the flitters and be glad. You move now. They won't like waiting."

And then: *"Move!"* he shouted at them, because no one did, and then everyone did, a panicked scattering.

Cloud reached his own house, out of breath, and fumbled in the dark familiar corner for his bow, with only the fireplace coals to see by. He found his quiver on the peg, slung that to his shoulder and turned about again facing the door as a flurry of running steps came up to it, a flood of figures he knew even in the dark.

"It's me," he said before they could take fright—his wife Dal, his sister Pia, his grandmother Elly and his own son Tam, eight years old. His wife hugged him; he hugged her one-armed, and hugged his son and sister too. Tam was crying as he made to go; ma Elly put herself in his way.

"No," Elly said. "Cloud, where are you going?"

He was afraid at the thought of shooting humans and calibans, but that was what he was off to, what was about to happen out there—what had already started, on the invaders' side. He heard shouting, heard the hiss of calibans. Then he heard faint screams.

"Come back here." Ma Elly clenched his shirt, pulled at him with all her might, a stout woman, the woman who had mothered him half his life. "You've got a family to see to, hear?"

"Ma Elly—if we don't stop them out there together—"

"You're not going out there. Come back here. They'll kill you out there, and what good is that?"

His wife held him, her arms added to ma Elly's, and young Tam held to his waist. They pulled him inside, and he lost his courage, lost all the fire that urged him to go out and die for them, because he was thinking now. Then what? ma Elly asked, and he had no answer, none. He patted his wife's shoulder, hugged his sister. "All right," he said.

"Gather everything," ma Elly said, and they started at it, in the dark. Young Tam tossed a log on the hearth— *"No,"* Cloud said, and pulled the boy back and raked the log out with a stick before it took light, a scattering of coals. He took the boy by the shoulders and shook him. "No light. Get all the clothes you can find. Hear?"

The boy nodded, swallowed tears and went. Cloud looked rightward, where ma Elly was down on her knees among the scattered coals wrestling with the flagstones.

He squatted down and levered it up for her with his knife, asked no question as she pulled up the leather-wrapped books that were the treasure of Elly's line. She hugged them to her and he helped her up while the business of packing went on around them. "Not going to live in any caliban hole," ma Elly muttered. He heard her voice break. He had not heard Elly Flanahan cry since his mother died. "You hear me, Cloud. We go out that door, we keep going."

"Yes," he said. If he had seen no other way he would have surrendered for his family's sake, for nothing else; but what ma Elly wanted suddenly fell into place with all his instincts. Of course that was where they would try to go. Of course that was where they had to try. Only—his mind shuddered under the truth it had kept shoving back for the last few moments—the invaders would get the old, the weak, the children: the calibans would have them, and the darts would strike down those that stood to fight. All that might get away was a family like his, with all its members able to run, even old ma Elly. Coward, something said to him; but—Fool, that something said when he thought of fighting calibans and darts at night.

He took up a bundle of something his wife gave him,

and very quietly went to the door and looked out into the commons, where calibans moved between them and the common-hall lights. It was quiet yet. "Come on," he said, "keep close. Pia, go last."

"Yes," she said, a hunter herself, for all she was fifteen. "Go on. I'm behind you."

He slipped out, strung his bow, nocked an arrow as he went around the side of the house, toward the slope of the hill.

A gray thrashed toward him, sentry in the bushes. He whipped the bow up and fired, one true venomed shot. The gray hissed and whipped in its pain, and he ran, down the slope, collected his family again at the bottom, out of breath as they were, and started off again, a jog for a time, a walk, and then a mild run, gaining what ground they could, because he heard panic behind him.

"Fire," Pia breathed.

He looked back. There was. He saw the glow. Houses were afire.

"Keep walking," ma Elly said, a gasp for air. "Keep walking."

A noise broke at their backs, a running, but not of caliban feet. Cloud aimed an arrow, but it was more of their own coming.

"Who are you?" Cloud hissed at them. But the runners just kept running—of shame, perhaps, or fear. His own family went as fast as it could already, and soon he carried young Tam, and Dal took the books from ma Elly, who tottered along at the limit of her strength.

He wept. He did not know it until he felt the wind on his face turn the tears cold. He looked back from time to time at the glow which marked the end of what he knew.

And if the calibans would hunt them further, if they had a mind to, he knew nowhere that they were safe. He only hoped they would forget. Calibans did, or seemed to, sometimes.

xvii

The Town

The snap of wires, flares in the dark—there was screaming, above all the commotion of people running in the streets.

They surged at the gates, at the wire, but the Base never saw them.

"Open up," Dean cried, screamed, lost among the others. "Open the gates—"

But the Base would not. Would never open the gates at all, to let a rabble pour into their neat concrete gardens, come too near their doors, bring their tradecloth rags and their stink and their terror. Dean knew that before the others believed it. He turned away, ran, panting, crying at once, stopped in a clear place and looked over his shoulder at nightmare—

—at a seam opening in the earth, at houses beginning to fold in upon themselves under the floodlights and collapse in heaps of stone—at the rip growing and tilting the slabs of the paved road, and under the crowd itself, people falling.

A renewed screaming rang out.

The rift kept travelling.

And suddenly in the dark and the floodlights a monstrous head thrust up out of the earth.

Dean ran, everything abandoned, the way the calibans themselves had opened, across the ruined fields.

Once, at screams, a thin and pitiful screaming from behind, he looked back; and many of the lights had gone out, but such as were left shone on a puff of smoke, a billowing cloud amid the tall concrete buildings of main Base . . . and there was a building less than there had been.

The calibans were under the foundations of the Base. The Base itself was falling.

He ran, in terror, ran and ran and ran. He was not the only one to pass the wires. But he stayed for no one, found no companion, no friend, nothing, only drove himself further and further until he could no longer hear the screams.

xviii

In the Hills

They found him in the morning, among the rocks; and Cloud raised his bow, an arrow aimed across the narrow stream—because everything had become an enemy. But the townsman, wedged with his back to the rocks, only lifted a hand as if that could stop a flint-headed arrow and stared at them so bleakly, so wearily that Cloud lowered the bow and put the arrow away.

"Who are you?" Cloud asked when they squatted across the narrow stream from each other, while his sister Pia and his wife and son tended ma Elly, bathing her face and holding water for her to drink. "What name?"

"Name's Dean," the other said, hoarse, crouching there on his side with his arms about his knees and his fine town clothes in rags.

"Name's Cloud," Cloud said; and Dal came beside him and handed him some of the food they had brought, while the stranger sat across the stream just looking at them, not asking.

"He's hungry," Pia said. "We give him just a bit."

Cloud thought about it, and finally took a morsel of bread and held it out to the townsman on his side.

The man unwound himself from his crouch and got up and waded across the stream. He took the bit they offered him and sank down again, and ate the bread very slowly. Tears started from his eyes, ran down his face, but there was never expression on it, never a real focus to his eyes.

"You come from town," ma Elly said.

"Town's gone," he said.

There was none of them could think of what to say then. Town had always been, rich and powerful.

"Base buildings fell," he said. "I saw it."

"We go south," Cloud said finally.

"They'll hunt us," Pia said.

"We go down the coast," Cloud said, thinking through it, where the food was, where they could be sure of fresh water, streams coming to the sea.

"South is a big river," said Dean in a quiet voice. "I know."

They took the townsman with them. They found others as they went, some of their own kin, some that were only townsmen who had run far enough and fast enough—like themselves those who could run, and those who would run, for whatever reason.

Others drifted to them, and sometimes calibans came, but kept their distance.

xix

Message from Gehenna Station to Alliance Headquarters couriered by *AS Winifred*

". . . intervention of station-based forces has secured the perimeter of the Base. Casualties among Base personnel are fourteen fatalities and forty-six injuries, nine critical. . . . All personnel except security forces and essential staff have been lifted to the station.

"Destruction in the town is total. Casualties are undetermined. Twenty are confirmed dead, but due to the extensive damage and the hazard of the ground, further search is not presently an option. Two hundred two survivors have reached the aid stations set up at the Base gate for treatment of injuries: most told of digging themselves free. Under the cover of darkness calibans return to the ruin and dig in the rubble. Accompanying tape #2 shows this activity . . .

"The hiller village also suffered extensive damage and orbiting survey has seen no sign of life there. The survivors of the town and village have scattered. . . .

"The Station will make food drops attempting to consolidate the survivors where possible. . . . The Station urgently requests exception to the noninterference mandate for humanitarian reasons. The mission recommends lifting the survivors offworld."

xx

Message: Alliance Headquarters Science Bureau to Gehenna Station couriered by *AS Phoenix*

". . . with extreme regret and full appreciation of humanitarian concern the Bureau denies request for lifting of the non-interference mandate under any circumstance. . . .

"Gehenna Base will be reestablished under maximum security with equipment arriving aboard this courier. . . .

"It is Bureau policy that no interference be permitted in the territory of unconsenting sapience, even in benevolent intention. . . .

"The Station will extend all possible cooperation and courtesy to Bureau agent Dr. K. Florio. . . ."

xxi

Year 90, day 144 CR
Staff meeting: Gehenna Station

"It is a tragedy," Florio said, making a fortress of his hands in front of him. He spoke quietly, eyed them all. "But those who disagree with policy have their option to be transferred."

There was silence from the rest of the table, poses like his own, grim faces male and female. Old hands at Gehenna Station. Seniority considerable.

"We understand the rationale," the Director said. "The reality is a little difficult to take."

"Are they dying?" Florio asked softly. "No. The loss of life is done. The human population has stabilized. They're surviving very efficiently down there." He moved his hands and sorted through the survey reports. "If I lacked evidence to support the Bureau decision—it's here. The world is put through turmoil and still two communities reassert themselves. One is well situated for observation from the Base. Both are surviving thanks to the food drops. The Bureau will sanction that much, through the winter, to maintain a viable population base. The final drop will be seed and tools. After that—"

"And those that come to the wire?"

"Have you been letting them in?"

"We've been delivering health care and food."

Florio frowned, sorted through the papers. "The natives brought up here for critical treatment haven't adjusted to Station life. Severe psychological upset. Is that humanitarian? I think it should be clear that good intentions have led to this disaster. Good intentions. I will tell you how it will be: the mission may observe without interference. There will be no program for acculturation. None. No firearms will be permitted on world. No technological materials may be taken outside the Base perimeter except recording instruments."

There was silence from the staff.

"There is study to be pursued here," Florio said more softly still. "The Bureau has met measurable intelligences; it has never met an immeasurable one; it has never met a situation in which humanity is outcompeted by an adaptive species which may violate the criteria. The Bureau puts a priority on this study. The tragedy of Gehenna is not inconsiderable . . . but it is a double tragedy, most indubitably a tragedy in terms of human lives. For the calibans— very possibly a tragedy. Rights are in question, the rights of sapients to order their affairs under their own law, and this includes the human inhabitants, who are not directly under Alliance laws. Yes, it is an ethical question. I agree. The Bureau agrees. But it extends that ethical question to ask whether law itself is not a universal concept.

"Humans and calibans may be in communication. We are very late being apprised of that possibility. Policy would have been different had we known.

"If there were any question whether humans were adapted to Gehenna, that would have to be considered— that humans may have drifted into communication with a species the behaviors of which twenty years of technologically sophisticated research and trained observation has not understood. This in itself ought to make us question our conclusions. In any question of sapience—in any definition of sapience—where do we put this communication?

"Suppose, only suppose, that humans venture into fur-

ther space and meet something else that doesn't fit our
definitions. How do we deal with it? What if it's spacefaring—
and armed? The Bureau views Gehenna as a very valuable study.

"Somehow we have to talk to a human who talks to
calibans. Somehow what we have here has to be incorporated into the Alliance. Not disbanded, not disassembled,
not reeducated. Incorporated."

"At the cost of lives."

The objection came from down the table, far down the
table. From Security. Florio met the stare levelly, assured
of power.

"This world is on its own. We tell it nothing; we give it
nothing. Not an invention, not a shred of cloth. No trade
goods. Nothing. The Station will get its supplies from space.
Not from Gehenna."

"Lives," the man said.

"A closed world," Florio said, "gains and loses lives by
its own rules. We don't impose them. By next year all aid
will have been withdrawn, food, tools, everything including
medical assistance. Everything."

There was silence after. No one had anything to say.

xxii

Year 90, day 203 CR
Cloud's Settlement

The calibans came to the huts they made on the new
river in the south, and brought terror with them.

But the shelters stood. There was no undermining. The
grays arrived first, and then a tentative few browns, burrowing up along the stream.

And more and more. They fired no arrows, but huddled
in their huts and tried not to hear the calibans move at
night, building walls about them, closing them about, making Patterns of which they were the heart.

Calibans spared the gardens they had made. It was the
village they haunted, and even by day ariels and grays sat
beneath the sun.

"They have come to us," said Elly, "the way they came to Jin."

"We have to stay here," said an old man. "They won't let us go."

It was true. They had their gardens. There was nowhere else to go.

xxiii

Settlement on Cloud's River

". . . They came from a place called Cyteen," Dean said, by the hearth where the only light was in their common shelter, and the light shone on faces young and old who gathered to listen. He had the light, but he told it by heart now, over and over, explaining it to children, to adults, to townsmen and hillers who had never seen the inside of modern buildings, who had to be told—so many things. Ma Elly and her folk sat nearest, Cloud with that habitual frown on his face, and Dal listening soberly; and Pia and young Tam solemn as the oldest. Twenty gathered here, crowded in; and there were others, too many to get into the shelter at once, who would come in their turn. They came because he could read the books, more than Elly herself—he could *tell* what was in them in ways the least could understand. Cloud valued him. Pia came to his bed, and called him *my Dean* in a way proud and possessive at once.

In a way it was the happiest period of his life. They cared for him and respected him; they listened to what he had to say and took his advice. He gave them a tentative love, and they set him in a kind of special category—excepting Pia, who made him very special indeed; and Cloud and Dal who adopted him and ma Elly who talked about the past with him and Tam who wanted stories. At times the village seemed all, as if the other had never been.

But he read more than he could say. He interpreted; it was all that he could do. He was alone in what he understood and he understood things that tended to make him bitter, written in the hands of long-dead men who had seen the

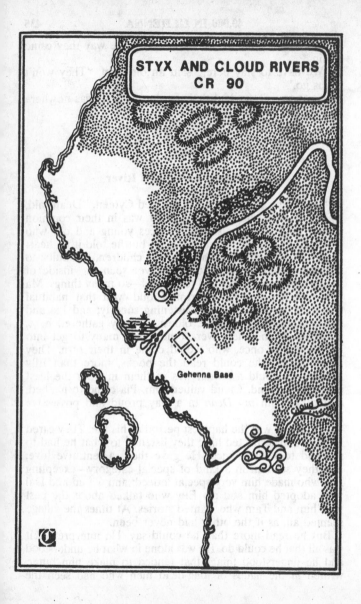

STYX AND CLOUD RIVERS
CR 90

Gehenna Base

GENEALOGY CR 90
Gehenna Outpost [303]

```
Jin 458-9998-                              Pia 86-687
  -18-+58                                   -18-+16

Jin 2     Mark    Zed     Tam         Red Pia          Pia 2         Green
0-62      3-29    4-?     5-58        32-89             6-72          8-?
                                                        (MA PIA)

Pia 3   Tam 3   Sunny    Cloud One-Eye   Jin 5    Tam 2    Jin 4        Mark 3    Zed 2    Pia 3
30-89   38-     30-89    30-89           31-89    31-89    30-88        32-       35-      40-
  →       →       →         →              →        →     (sired by    (sired    (sired   (sired
                                                          Matthew R.   by Ben)   by Bram) by Kes)
                                          Red Pia          Mayes         →          →        →
                                          32-89           -22-+29)
                                            m.
                                          Elly           Cloud 2
                                          Flanahan-      47-
                                          Gutierrez
                                          23-
```

```
        Dean    m.   Pia Flanahan        Cloud 2        Cloud 3    m.   Dal
        62-          74-                  47-                            61-

                     Elly                                         who talks to
                     90-                                          Pia
                                                                  62-

                                                                  Cloud's Tam
                                                                  81-
```

```
Jin 3     Jin 6     Jin 7     Jin 8 (who goes into the     Jin 9
29-78     43-69     58-89     mounds)                      90-
                              71-
```

world as strangers. He could go to the wire again. They might take him back. But the bitterness stood in the way. The books were his, his revenge, his private understanding—

Only sometimes like tonight when calibans moved and shifted in the village, when he thought of the mounds which crept tighter and tighter about their lives—

—he was afraid.

VII

Elai

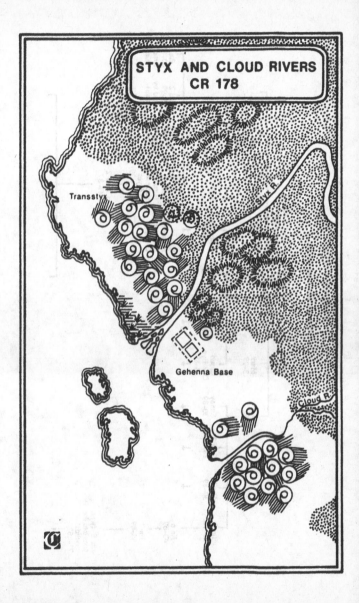

GENEALOGY 178 CR

Gehenna Outpost [309]

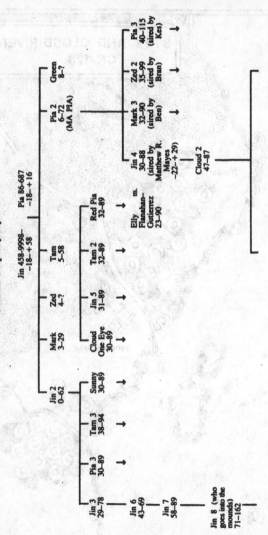

Jin 458-9998—
-18-+58

Pia 86-687
-18-+16

Green
8-?

Pia 2
6-72
(MA PIA)

Pia 3
40-115
(sired by Kes)

Zed 2
35-99
(sired by Bram)

Mark 3
32-90
(sired by Ben)

Jin 4
30-88
(sired by Matthew R. Mayes
-22-+29)

Cloud 2
47-87

Tam
5-58

Red Pia
32-89

Tam 2
32-89

Jin 5
31-89

Cloud One Eye
30-89

Zed
4-?

Mark
3-29

Elly
Flanahan-
Gutierrez
23-90

m.

Jin 2
0-62

Sunny
30-89

Tam 3
38-94

Pia 3
30-89

Jin 3
29-78

Jin 6
43-69

Jin 7
58-89

Jin 8 (who
goes into the
mounds)
71-162

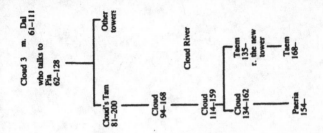

Cloud 3 m. Dal 61–111
who talks to Pia
Pia 62–128

Other towers

Cloud's Tam 81–200

Cloud 94–168

Cloud River

Cloud 114–159

Cloud 134–162

Taem 135–
r. the new tower

Taem 168–

Paeria 154–

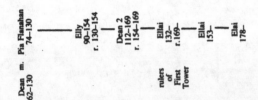

Dean m. Pia Flanahan 74–130
62–130

Elly 90–154
r. 130–154

Dean 2 112–169
r. 154–169

Ellai 132–
r.169–

rulers of First Tower

Ellai 153–

Elai 178–

Styxside

Jin 9 90–172

Jin 10 124–

Jin 11 156–

Jin 12 170–

i

178 CR, day 2
Cloud River Settlement

She was born into a world of towers, in the tallest of the
Twelve Towers on the sandy Cloud, and the word went out
by crier to the waiters below, huddled in their cloaks in a
winter wind, that Ellai had an heir and the line went on.

Elai she was, in the new and simpler mode her mother
had decreed—Elai, daughter of the heir to the Twelve
Towers and granddaughter of the Eldest herself; and her
mother, when her grandmother laid her red and squalling in
her arms, clutched her with a tenderness rare in Ellai Ellai's-
daughter—a kind of triumph after the first, stillborn, son.

Calibans investigated the new arrival in her cradle, the
gray builders and the dignified browns, coming and going
where they liked in the towers they had built. An ariel laid
a stone in the cradle, for sun-warmth, as she did for her
own eggs, of which she had a clutch nearby. A gray, realizing someone's egg had hatched, brought a fish, but a brown
thoughtfully ate it and drove the gray away. Elai enjoyed
the attention, the gentle nudgings of scaly jaws that could
have swallowed her whole, which touched ever so carefully.
She watched the flutter of ariel collars and the blink of
huge amber eyes as something designed to amuse her.

When she walked, tottering between Ellai's hands and an

earthen ledge of her mother's rooms, an ariel watched—and soon learned to scamper out of the way of baby feet. They played ariel games, put and take the stone, that sometimes brought squalls from Elai, until she learned to laugh at skillful theft, until her stones stayed one upon the other like the ariels'.

And the day her grandmother died, when she was hustled into the great topmost hall to put her small hand in Ellai Eldest's and bid her goodbye—Scar got up and followed her out of the room, the great brown which was her grandmother's caliban—and never would return. It was a callous desertion: but calibans were different, that was all, and maybe Ellai Eldest understood, or failed to know, sinking deeper into her final sleep, that her life's companion had gone away and traded allegiances.

But there was consternation in the Tower. Ellai's presumed heir, Ellai-almost-eldest, stood watching it. There was silence among the servants, deathly silence.

Ellai Eldest passed. The caliban Scar should have pined over its dead, or suicided after the manner of its kind, refusing food, or swimming out to sea. Instead it luxuriated, hugely curled about young Elai on the floor, bearing the stumbling awkwardness of young knees in its ribs and the slaps and roughness of infant play. It simply closed its eyes, head lifted, collar lowered, as if it basked in sunlight instead of infant pleasure. It was happy this evening. The child was.

Ellai-Now-Eldest reached beside her own chair and met the pebbly hide of her own great brown, Twig, which sat quite, quite alert, raising and lowering her collar. If Scar had felt no urge to die, then Scar should have come to her, driven Twig away and appropriated herself, the new eldest, First in First Tower. Her own Twig could not dominate this one. She knew. At that moment Ellai foresaw rivalry—that she would never wholly rule, because of this, so long as that unnatural bond continued. She feared Scar, that was the truth. Twig did. So did the rest. Digger, Scar had been named, until his forays with Ellai-now-deceased against the intruders from the Styx, coming as they would the roundabout way, through the hills; then he had taken that raking cut that marked his ribs and renamed him. Scar was violence, was death, was power and already old in human years. And he might at this moment drive Twig away as an inconsequence.

He chose the child, as if Ellai in her reign over the Twelve Towers was to be inconsiderable, and the servants and the rulers of the other eleven Towers could see it when they came in the morning.

There was nothing that Ellai could do. She considered it from every side, and there was no way to undo it. Even murder crossed her mind, and infanticide: but this was her posterity, her own line, and she could not depend on another living heir, or tolerate the whispers, or dare the calibans. It had to be accepted as it was, and the child treated with tenderness. She was dangerous otherwise.

Children.

A child of eight sat in power on the distant Styx, Jin 12, with the old man dead. And Scar took to Elai. The Styx would stay quiet for at least a decade or so. And then—

A chill afflicted her. Her hand still stroked the plated scales of Twig's beautiful skull.

Scar had simply bypassed her, this caliban whose occupation was conflict, as if all her reign was inconsequence, as if she were only preface. It portended peace, then, while children grew. A decade or so of peace. She would have that, and if she were wise, she would use it well, knowing what would come after her.

ii

184 CR, day 05
General Report, Gehenna Base to Alliance Headquarters

. . . The situation has remained stable over the past half decade. The detente between the Styx settlement and the Cloud River settlements continues in effect. Contacts with both settlements continue in an unprecedented calm. A Stygian tower has risen on the perimeter of the Base. In accordance with established policy the Base has made no move to prohibit construction or movement.

. . . The two settlements are undergoing rapid expansion in which some see an indication that humanity on Gehenna has passed a crisis point. The historical pattern of conflict has proceeded through the forested area outside Base observation, minor if constant encounters between Stygians and Cloud River settlers involving some loss of life, but never threatening the existence of either, excepting the severe and widespread hostilities of CR 124–125, when flood and crop failure occasioned raids and widespread destruction. The current tranquil period, with its growth in population and food supply, is without precedent. In view of this historical pattern, and with careful consideration of longrange objectives, the Base respectfully requests permission to take advantage of this opportunity to establish subtle and non-interfering ties with both sides in the hope that this peaceful period may be lengthened. This modified and limited intervention seems justified in the hope of establishing Gehenna as a peaceful presence in the zone.

iii

185 CR, day 200
Message, Alliance HQ to Gehenna Base

. . . extend all cooperation to the Bureau agents arriving with this message, conducting extensive briefings and seminars on the Gehenna settlements. . . .

. . . While the Bureau concurs that conditions warrant direct observation and increased contact, the Bureau cautions the Mission that prohibitions against technological imports and trade continue. In all due consideration of humanitarian concerns, the Bureau reminds the Mission that the most benign of interventions may result in premature technological advances which may harm or misdirect the developing culture. . . .

iv

185 CR, day 201
Gehenna Base, Staff Meeting

". . . meaning they're more interested in the calibans than in human life," Security said glumly.

"In the totality," the Director said. "In the whole."

"They want it preserved for study."

"We could haul the Gehennans in by force," the Director said, "and hunt them wherever they exist, and feed them tape until they're model citizens. But what would *they* choose, umn? And how many calibans would we have to kill and what would we do to life here? Imagine it—a world where every free human's in hiding and we've dismantled the whole economic system—"

"We could do better for them than watch them."

"Could we? It's an old debate. The point is, we don't know what we'd be doing. We take it slow. You newcomers, you'll learn why. They're *different.* You'll learn that too."

There were guarded looks down the table, sensitive outworlder faces.

"*Different,* on Gehenna," the Director said, "isn't a case of prejudice. It's a fact of life."

"We've studied the culture," the incoming mission chief said. "We understand the strictures. We're here to review them."

"*Different,*" the Director said again. "In ways you won't understand by reading papers or getting tape."

"The Bureau appreciates the facts behind the designation. Union . . . is interested. Surveillance is being tightened for that reason. The quarantine makes them nervous. They wonder. Doubtless they wonder. Perhaps they've begun to have apprehensions of something beyond their intentions here. There will be negotiations.. We'll be making recommendations in that regard too. This *difference* will have its bearing on policy."

"Union back on Gehenna—"

"That won't be within our recommendations. Release of data is another matter. A botched alien contact, happening in some other Union recklessness, might not limit its effects so conveniently to a single world. Release of the data is a possibility . . . educating Union to what they did here."

There were frowns. The Director's was deepest. "Our concern is human life here. Now. Our reason for the request—"

"We understand your reasons."

"We have to do something with this generation or this settlement may take abrupt new directions."

"Fears for your own security?"

"No. For what this is becoming."

"The difference you noted."

"There's no time," the Director said, "that I can see any assimilation of Gehenna into Alliance . . . without the inclusion of humans who think at an angle. You can tape them. You can try to change them. If you don't understand what they are now, how do you understand them when they've come another hundred years, another two hundred on the same course? If you don't redirect them—what do you do with them? Perpetual quarantine—into the millennia? Governments change. Policies change. Someday somebody will take them in . . . and *what* they take in . . . is being shaped in these first centuries. We have a breathing space. A little peace. The chance of contact."

"We understand that. That's what we're here to determine."

"A handful of years," the Director said, "may be all we have."

v

188 CR, day 178
Cloud River Settlement

There was land across the saltwater and Elai dreamed of it—a pair of peaks lying hazily across the sea.

"What's there?" she had asked Ellai-Eldest. Ellai had shrugged and finally said mountains. Mountains in the sea.

"Who lives there?" Elai had asked. And, No one, Ellai had said. No one, unless the starships come there. Who else could cross the water?

So Elai set her dreams there. If there was trouble where she was, the mountains across the sea were free of it; if there was dullness in the winter days, there was mystery in the mist-wreathed isle across the waves. If there was No, Elai, and Wait, Elai, and Be still, Elai—on this side of the waves, there was adventure to be had on that side. The mountains were for taking and the unseen rivers were for swimming, and if there were starships holding them, then she would hide in burrows till they took their leave and she and a horde of brave adventurers would go out and build their towers so the strangers could not argue with their possession. Elai's land, it would be. And she would send to her mother and her cousin Paeia, offering them the chance to come if they would mind *her* rules. The Styxsiders could never reach them there. The rivers there would never flood and the crops would never fail, and behind those mountains would be other mountains to be taken, one after the other.

Forever and forever.

She made canopies for passengers on her most elaborate constructions, and did straw-dolls to ride, and put on pebbles for supplies and put them out to sea. But the surge toppled the stones and swept off the dolls and the raft came back again, so she made sides so the passengers should stay, carved her rafts with a precious bone knife old Dal had made her, and set them out with greater success.

If she had had a great axe such as the woodcutters used, then she might build a real one: so she reckoned. But she tried her bone knife on a sizeable log and made little progress at it, until a rain swept it all away.

So she sat on the shore with Scar, bereft of her work, and thought how unfair it was, that the starships came and went so powerfully into the air. She had tried that too, made ships of wood and leafy wings that fell like stones, lacking the thunderous power of the machines. One dreamed. At least her sea-dreams floated.

The machines, she had thought, made wind to drive them. If only the wind which battered at the shore could get all into one place and drive the ships into the sky. If only.

She saw leaves sail, ever so much lighter on the river's face, whirling round and about. If she could make the ships lighter. If she could make them like the leaves . . . If they could be like the fliers that spread wings and flew . . . She made wings for her sea-borne ships, pairs of leaves, and stuck them up on twigs, and to her delight the ships did fly, if crazily, lurching over the water and the chop until they crashed on rocks.

If she had a woodcutter's skill, if she could build something bigger still—a great sea-ship with wings—

She sailed her carved ships at least to the rocks an easy wade offshore, and imagined those rocks as mountains.

But always the real, the true mountains were across the wider sea, promising and full of dreams.

She watched the last of her ships wreck itself and it all welled up in her, the desire, the wishing, that she could be something more than ten years old and superfluous to all the world. She could order this and that about her life— she had what she wanted in everything that never mattered. She could have gone hungry: she was willing to go hungry in her adventures, which seemed a part of war: she had heard the elders talking. She was willing to sleep cold and get wounds (Cloud Oldest had dreadful scars) and even die, with suitable satisfaction for it—the fireside tales were full of that, a great deal better than her grandmother who had slept out her end (but it was her youngly dead uncle they told the best stories of)—in all she could have done any of these things, imagining herself the subject of tales. But she had no axe and her knife was fragile bone.

She did have Scar, that she relied on for consolation, for near friendship, for pride. He had fought the Styx-folk. When she climbed up to his back she was something more than ten. He played games with her. He was adult and powerful and very, very dangerous, so that Ellai herself had taken her aside and lectured her severely about responsibility. She could feel the power of him, that she could lie on and be rough with and laugh at boys who were still playing at stones with ariels, who teased her with their adolescent manhood and retreated in real fear when Scar shouldered his way into any imagined threat they posed. Then they remembered what he was—and Scar was ever so coy about it, giving way to lesser browns belonging with the elders: biding his time, that was what, only biding his time until his rider grew up to him.

Scar knew her. Only the rest of the world misapprehended what she was. She waited for this revealing with a vast discontent, and the least gnawing doubt, looking at the great brown lump sunning himself with a caliban smirk, among the rocks above the beach.

She whistled, disconsolate with her shipwreck. One lamp-like eye opened, the tongue flickering. Scar heaved himself up on his legs in one sinuous rise and looked at her, lifting his collar. He was replete with fish. Satisfied. But because she wanted he came down, lazy with the sun, presenting his bony side jaws for a scratching, the soft underjaw for a stroking.

She touched him, so, and he sank down on his full belly and heaved a sigh. She reached up behind the collar for that bony ridge which helped her mount, planted a bare sandy foot on his foreleg and swung up astride. Her boots and breeches were up there on the rocks: they had had their swim in the saltwater and the seat of her scant undergarments was still wet from a recent wade among the rocks for vantage. Scar's pebbly hide was hardly comfortable to bare legs and partly bare bottom, but she tapped her foot and headed him for the sandy part of the shore, to cool them both in the sea, to salve her melancholy in games.

They went onto the shelf of sand, a great smooth ripple spreading out around them, a twisting motion to which she swayed as Scar used his tail and hit that buoyant stride that was the freest thing in the world, she reckoned, short of flying. Scar did not take this water into his nose: it was too bitter for him and too salt. He kept his head aloft and paddled now, soaking her.

And then this madness came on her as she looked at the mountains beyond the sea, clearer than ever on this warm day.

She whistled softly, nudged him with her toes and heels, patted him with her hands. He turned, first his head and then the rest of him down to his tail, so that she felt the shift of him, every rippling of muscle, taking this new direction. The waves splashed up and broke about Scar's face, so that he lifted his head still higher and fought the harder, great driving thrusts of his body. Salt was in her mouth and it was hard to see with the sting of it in her eyes, hard to keep her grip with the lurching whip of Scar's body through the waves, the constant working of his shoulders. In a salthazed blink she realized they were beyond the rocks, well beyond, and of a sudden they were being carried aside from their course. She used her heel, she urged at Scar: he twisted his whole body trying to fight it, and still they were losing against the rush of water.

In some remote area of her mind she was afraid: she was too busy hanging on, too busy trying to discover a way out of it to panic. She kicked at Scar when he turned into the rush and then they were going much faster.

Something breached near them. A steamy plume blew on the wind, and vanished, and then the fear got through. She tried to see where that breaching dark shape had gone, and quite as suddenly something brushed them, a back bigger than any three browns broke the water right next to them and Scar was jolted under her, twisting suddenly, flailing in a roll that left her clinging only to the collar.

He ducked under, a brief twist of the body, and then he moved with all the fluid strength he could use. She clung to his bony plates and skin till her fingers ached, holding her breath, and then she lost him. She launched out on her own in sure, desperate strokes, looking for the surface, blind, and knowing there was something else nearby, something that might take half her body in a gulp, and the moving water resisted her strokes, wanting to pull her down.

She surrendered one direction, gathered speed and broke through to light in a spray of droplets, sucked air and water into her throat and coughed and flailed to stay afloat.

She felt the contact coming under the surface, a shock of water, a numbing blow against her legs. She swam in utter panic, striking out for the shore, the distant pale sand that wavered in her streaming eyes. Other water-shocks flashed about her—a body brushed hers, a claw raked her and threw her under. She kept swimming, weaker now, failing and choking, driving herself long after she stopped seeing where she was going and after she knew the weak motions of her arms and legs could never make it.

Then her knees hit sand, and she hurled herself a lung-wracking length further, sprawled on the shelf in shallow water, sucking air in great gulps and with her arms threatening to collapse and drown her in the shallows.

"Scar," she managed to call, and struck the water with her palm the way she would to call him up, but there was not a ripple. She wept with strangling sobs for breath, wiped her salt-stung eyes and nose, tried to walk and inched her way up the slope, flailing with swimming strokes while she could, crawling-swimming in the extreme shallows because that was all she could do. She turned about again looking at the sea in panic.

Then a body broke the surface close in, and she sobbed for breath and tried to get up, but it was Scar rising out of the sea, his wedge-shaped head coming closer until he could get his bowed legs under him and serpentine his weary way up the slope. He vomited water, but not the way he would coming out of fresh. His jaws trailed mucus and he dipped his head and washed himself, coughing in great wounded gasps. He snorted his nose clear and dipped his head again, suffering from the salt, pawing at his face in misery. There was a raking wound on his rump that wept clouds of blood. She got up in shaky haste and felt something wrong with herself, looked and saw the blood clouding away from her calf through the shallow water.

She cast a panicked look toward the shore, saw a human figure standing there. "Help," she called out, thinking this one of the riders come hunting her. And then she thought not, because the outlines were wrong.

Scar was moving now, striding surely if slowly toward the shore. She joined him, limping, feeling the pain now, coughing and wiping her eyes and hurting in her chest. The blood leaked away too quickly. She moved with some fear because of it, and the figure was clearer in her eyes—no one from the Towers, not in that strange bright garb. It was a star-man staring at her, witnessing all that had happened, and she stopped at the water's edge ahead of Scar, bleeding into the sand, feeling the life leak out of her in one rush of sickness.

She had to sit down and did, examining the deep gash that ran a hand's length across her thigh, deep into the muscle. It made her sick to see it. She tried to stop the blood with her fingers and then thought of her clothes far up the shore, which was all she had for bandages excepting her halter, and it was leaking out too fast, making her dizzy and sick.

Scar came up the beach, hissing. She looked up, saw the star-man both closer and standing quite, quite still with Scar's collar up like that and his tail tip flicking. Elai's heart pounded and her head spun. They were stranger than Weirds, the star-folk. Lately they came and went and just stood and watched the workers in the fields, but this one had something more in mind, and herself sitting here bleeding to death of her own stupidity.

"Can I help?" the star-man called to her, at least that was what it sounded like, and Elai, sitting there and trying to hold her life inside with her bare fingers and her head none too clear, thought about it and gave a whistle that called Scar back, because the star-man was carrying a pack that might have help in it of some kind. Scar hardly liked it, but the star-man came cautiously closer and closer, standing over her finally and bending down out of the sunglare—a woman after all, with her hair silky fine and her clothes of stranger-cloth and glittering with metal bits and wealth and colored patches. Elai frankly stared open-mouthed as this apparition knelt down by her and opened her pack, taking out this and that.

"That's bad," the star-man said, moving her fingers off the wound.

"Fix it," Elai said sharply, because she was scared and it hurt; and because it seemed a star-man who could make ships fly might do anything.

The star-man took the tops off jars and unwrapped bandages, and hissed cold foam onto her leg, at which Elai winced. But very quickly it stopped hurting and the foam went pink and red and white, but the blood stopped too. Elai drew a great breath and let it go, relaxing back onto her hands in the confidence now that she was right and the starfolk could fix whatever they had a mind to. The pain just stopped. At once. She felt in command of things again, while Scar put his big blunt head down closer to give everything a one-sided examination. There was only a little queasiness in Elai's stomach while she watched the star-man work, while she put sticky stuff all over the wound somewhat the color of her leg. "Now you let that dry," the star-man said.

Elai nodded gravely, drew her leg back from the star-man's hands in the sudden conviction it was a little less than herself to be sitting here mostly naked and sandy and half drowned. She looked the other way, while Scar took up a protective posture, his head shading her from the sun.

"You think you can walk?" the star-man asked.

Elai nodded, once and shortly. She pointed down the beach, where the point they had started from was out of sight. "My clothes are there." Go get them, she meant. The star-man seemed not to take the hint and Elai frowned, suspecting star-folk of pride.

"You can send someone to get them," Elai said.

The star-man frowned too. She had bright bronze hair,

a dusting of freckles. "I don't think I'd better do that. Maybe you'd better not talk about this much, umn?"

Elai picked up a handful of sand and patterned it aimlessly, commentary on the matter. "I'm Elai," she said. "Ellai's daughter."

"*That* Ellai."

Elai looked up, liking the surprise she caused, lifted her chin toward the sea. "We'd have crossed the sea, only the river comes out into the sea too strong."

"You hit a current. But there was something else out there too."

"The sea-folk." The memory assailed her confidence, made her think of Scar, hovering over her, and she got up, holding to him, and favoring her leg. Her head spun. She leaned against his ribs looking at the cut he had got. "Fix his too."

"He might not like that."

The star-man was scared, that was what. Elai turned a wicked glance at her. "He won't bite. Go on."

The star-man did it, taking up her medicines; and Scar flinched and hissed, but Elai patted him and stopped him from more than a whip of his tail and a ducking of his head. "Hai," she said, "hai, hai, hai," and Scar stood still for it. She reached as if to mount, which worked: Scar settled, flicking his tail and stirring up the sand, his collar jerking in ill temper. But her dizziness came back and she leaned there against Scar's shoulder looking at the star-man as she finished, and Scar put his head about, likewise looking after his one-sided fashion.

"Going now," Elai said, and set her foot to mount.

"You might fall off," the star-man said critically.

Elai just stared, letting the spinning-feeling stop.

"I think I'd better walk back with you in case," the star-man said.

"I'm going after my clothes." Elai climbed up, after which her head really spun, and she reeled badly when Scar rose up on his four legs at once. She caught her breath and focussed her eyes and started Scar back down the beach, out into the water where the rocks came down.

"Don't do that," the star-man called, panting along after them, but over the rocks. "You'll get the leg wet."

She tucked that leg behind Scar's collar and gritted her

teeth through his lurching about, his more-than-casual pace, which sent him whipping along in serpentine haste, throwing her constantly to one point of balance and the other. He hated her to lock her legs because of his breathing. She gripped the bony plates with her hands, feeling the sweat break out on her, but eventually he clambered over the rocks to the place where she had left her breeches and her boots and the vest she wore over her halter.

She climbed off and got everything, and shrugged the vest on, wrapped the boots up in the breeches and just sat down a while until she could get her head to stop whirling and her heart to stop pounding. It seemed a very long way home now. There was the Seaward Tower, and the New Tower was closer, but she had no desire to show her face there, Ellai's daughter, limping in half-naked and half-minded and not able to get her breeches on. She hauled herself up again and clutched her bundle to her as she crawled up and over Scar's shoulder to set herself on his neck. He was patient now, understanding she was in trouble: he came up gently and searched back and forth for the easy ways up the slope, and meanwhile she held onto her clothes and onto him and let the sky and the grass and the distant view of the nearer two Towers pass in a giddy haze.

Suddenly there was a thumping and a panting and the star-man came jogging to catch up with them from the side, having found her way up off the beach onto the grassy flats.

Scar looked askance at that. Elai tapped her bare toes at him and soothed him with her hand, blinked hazily as the star-man caught up and strode along with them, jogging sometimes to stay even.

"What do you want?" Elai asked.

"To see you get home. To see you don't fall off." This between gasps.

She slowed Scar down. The star-man plodded along with her pack, breathing hard and coughing.

"My name's Elai," Elai said again pointedly.

"You said that."

"Elai," she repeated, scowling at the rudeness of this concerned stranger.

"MaGee," the star-man said, whether duly reprimanded or only then figuring out what was due. "I really don't want to make a stir about this, understand. I'll just see you get where you're going. What were you doing swimming out there?"

Elai considered sullenly. It was her dream, which she had never talked about to anyone, a private thing which had gone badly, humiliatingly wrong.

"I watched you," MaGee said. "You chase one of your rafts out? Your river-in-the-sea could just about drown you, hear?"

Elai lifted her head. "There was the seagoer out there. That was what stopped us, not the river."

"A little outmatched, weren't you?"

She was not sure, but it sounded insulting. "They're big."

"I know they're big. They have teeth, you know that?"

"Scar has teeth."

"Not like those."

"Where did you see one?"

MaGee's face took on a careful look. "Just say I know, umn? Next boat you lose, you let it go."

"*Boat.*"

"Raft."

"Ship," Elai concluded, and frowned. "You fly, MaGee?"

MaGee shrugged.

"How do you catch the wind?" Elai asked, suddenly on that track, with a star-man at hand and answering questions. "How do you get the wind to blow the ships up?"

She thought she might be answered. There was of a sudden such a look in this MaGee's pale eyes. "Maybe you'll figure that out someday," MaGee said, "when you're grown."

There was a sullen, nasty silence. Elai gnawed on it, and her leg was hurting again. She ignored it, adding it up in her mind that star-man medicine was fallible. Like star-men. "Your ships ever fall down?"

"I never saw one do it," MaGee said. "I don't hope to."

"If my ships had the wind," Elai said, "they could go anywhere."

"They're quite good," MaGee said. "Who taught you?"

"I taught me."

"I'll bet not. I'll bet someone told you."

"I don't tell lies."

"I guess you don't," MaGee said after a moment of looking up at her as she walked along at Scar's side. "They're good ships."

"Your medicine doesn't work," Elai said. "It hurts."

"It's going to if you keep hanging that leg down like that."

"I haven't got anywhere else to put it, have I?"

"I guess you don't. But it's going to hurt until you can lie down and get it level."

"Huh," Elai said, frowning, because she really wished the star-man could do something. But she was mollified about the ships. Proud, even. A star-man called them fine. "How did you know about the river?"

"The word is current. Like in the river. The sea has them. Really strong ones."

Elai stored that away in her mind. "What makes them?"

MaGee shrugged again. "You do ask questions, don't you?"

Elai thought about it. "Where do rivers start from, anyway?"

MaGee grinned, laughing at her, at which she frowned the harder.

"Someday," Elai said, "Scar and I will just go up the Cloud and see."

MaGee's grin perished into something quite like belief. "I shouldn't listen to your questions."

"Why?"

"Why, why, and what? I'll get you home, that's what. And I'll thank you if you don't say I helped you."

"Why? Don't they like that?"

"Questions and questions." MaGee hitched the pack up on her shoulder and plodded on, panting with the pace.

"What makes the ships fly?"

"I'm not going to answer your questions."

"Ah. You *know*, then."

MaGee looked up, sharp and quick, the distance to Scar's back. "You talk to him, do you?"

"Scar?" Elai blinked, patted Scar's shoulder. "We talk."

"When you make Patterns on the ground, what do you do?"

Elai shrugged.

"So, there are some things you don't talk about, aren't there?"

Elai made the gesture of spirals. "Depends."

"Depends on what?"

"Depends on how Scar is and what he wants and what I want."

"You mean the same thing means different things."

Elai shrugged, blinked, confused.

"How do you know?" MaGee pursued.

"Tell me how the ships go."

"How much does Scar understand? Like a man? Like that much?"

"Caliban things. He's the biggest caliban in the Towers. He's old. He's killed Styx-siders."

"Is he yours?"

Elai nodded.

"But you don't trade calibans, do you? You don't own them."

"He came to me. When my grandmother died."

"Why?"

Elai frowned over that. She had never clearly thought that out, or she had, and it hurt her mother that Scar had not gone to her: that was not for saying out loud.

"That's a very old caliban, isn't he?" MaGee asked.

"Maybe he is." Elai patted him again.

"How many years?"

"Where do star-folk come from?"

MaGee grinned again, slowly, and Elai felt a little triumph, swaying lightheadedly this side and that. The Cloudside towers passed into view now. The precious time passed.

"Do you live at the Base, MaGee?"

"Yes."

She thought a moment, and finally brought her dearest dream into the light. "Have you been to the mountains out there, the ones you see from the beach?"

"No."

"Is that very far?"

"Is that what you sail your ships for?"

"Someday I'll build a big one."

Silence from MaGee.

"I'll go there," Elai said.

"That ship would have to be big," MaGee allowed.

"How big?"

"Questions again."

"Is it far, MaGee?"

"As far as from the New Tower to the Base."

"Do people live there?"

MaGee said nothing, but stopped, and pointed to the Towers. "That's home, isn't it?" MaGee said.

Elai dug her fingers into the softness of Scar's hide beneath the collar, felt the power that was hers now, understood what was the star-folk's power, and felt something partly anger, partly loss. "Come to the beach tomorrow," she said.

"I don't think I can," MaGee said. "But maybe."

Elai memorized the face, the look of MaGee. If, she thought, I led thousands like this starman, I would take the islands, the Styx, the heavens everyone came from.

But MaGee kept the secrets to herself, and did not belong to her or to her mother.

"Hai," she yelled at Scar, and rode him off at a pace that sent jolting spears of pain through her leg, that had her swaying when she arrived in her own lands, to the solicitude of those that met her.

vi

188 CR, day 178
Memo, office of the Director to staff member Elizabeth McGee

Appreciating potential difficulties, the Director nevertheless considers this a prime opportunity for further study.

vii

The Cloud Towers

Elai lay fitfully that night, with Weirds to soothe Scar in his restlessness, with a firebowl boiling water for compresses they laid on her leg. Figures moved like nightmare about her, and Scar fretted and hissed, not trusting any of them. Even her mother came, asking coldly after her safety, questioning her what had happened.

"Nothing," she said.

Ellai scowled at that; but Ellai's Twig came no further than the outer passage of her room, fretting and hissing on her own. The temperature of the situation rose steadily so that—"See to her," her mother snapped at those who tried, and went away, collecting Twig and getting no answers.

It was like that the next day and the next. The leg bothered her, and the small rides she could take in days after that turned up no sign of the star-folk. No MaGee. No answers. Nothing.

She sat on Scar's shoulders and stared out to sea, or at the river, or vented her moodishness on the Weirds, who said nothing and only did those services for Scar she was too tired to do.

And then one day MaGee was there—on the beach, watching her.

"MaGee," Elai said, riding up to her, trying not to sound as if it mattered. She slid down from Scar—trying not to limp, but she did.

"How is that leg?" MaGee asked.

"Oh, not so bad."

It was not what she wanted to discuss with MaGee. It was the world that mattered, and every question in it. Elai sat and Patterned idly while she asked and answered—she got very little, but that little she stored away, building and building.

"Help me make a ship," she asked MaGee.

But MaGee smiled and said no. That was always the way of it.

And the days passed. Sometimes MaGee was there and sometimes not.

And then, day after bitter day, MaGee was not there at all.

She rode Scar as far as the Wire, a great long distance, and slid down at the gate through which star-folk came and went, in sight of a Styx-tower in the far distance, which reminded her that there were those who rivaled the Cloud Towers to gain star-brought secrets.

"I want to see MaGee," she said to the guard at the gate, and all the while she was comparing the Cloud-towers and this place, and thinking how strong and disturbingly regular it was. On the other side of the Wire, ships landed, and she hoped to see one, looking beyond the guard without seeming to stare—but there was none.

The guard wrote . . . *wrote* on a paper, at which performance Elai could not help but wonder. He sent his companion inside with that message, and she must stand and wait . . . trying in her discomfiture to talk to the guard, who looked down at her through the Wire, who talked to her in a strange accent worse than MaGee's, and who made little of her, as if she was a child.

"My name's Elai," she said, pointing loftily back toward the Towers. "From First Tower."

The guard refused to be impressed. Her face burned.

"Tell MaGee to hurry," she said, but the man stood where he was.

Eventually the message came back, and the guard waved his hand at her, dismissing her. "The Director says no," the guard said.

Elai mounted Scar and rode away. She had surrendered enough of her dignity, and it hurt. It hurt enough that she cried on the way home, but she was dry-eyed and temperful when she came among her own, and never admitted where she had been, not to all the anxious questions.

viii

Memo, Base Director to staff member Elizabeth McGee

. . . commends you for excellent observations and requests you write up your reports in detail for transmission and publication. The Director feels that further investigation should extend in other directions and requests you hold yourself ready. . . .

Memo, E. McGee to Base Director in the offices of Gehenna Base

. . . The Styxsiders have turned reluctant for contact.

Genley's report on my desk indicates a team member suffered injury as the team retreated from a caliban within the permitted zone of observation. The team is anxious to return to the Styx; I would discourage this while the calibans show reluctance.

Report, R. Genley to Base Director transmitted from field

Dr. McGee is overcautious. The incident involved a sprained wrist as the team cleared the immediate vicinity of a caliban engaged in mound-building. No Styxsider was present.

Message, E. McGee to R. Genley Copy to Base Director

The cooperation between calibans and humans is close enough to warrant alarm at this attack.

Message, R. Genley to Base Director transmitted from field

I do not agree with Dr. McGee's hypothesis. We are under observation by Styxsiders. Retreat now would give an impression of fear. I object to McGee's treatment of the data we transmit.

Base Director to R. Genley in field

Continue with caution. Measured risk seems justified.

Memo, E. McGee to Base Director

I am applying for a return to the field. We are losing an opportunity. We already have sufficient observations of calibans. Genley's approach is producing no useful results. We should use the approaches we do have on the Cloud and draw the Styx into contact on their own initiative. The Styx is *not* peaceful. This very silence is a danger signal. I am sending another personal advisement to Genley. All others have been disregarded. I am concerned. I urge the Board to act quickly to recall this mission before some serious incident occurs.

Message, E. McGee to R. Genley

Pull back. Conduct your investigations on this side. The calibans' moundbuilding is the equivalent of a wall. They are telling you you are not wanted there.

Message, R. Genley to Base Director

I have received another communication from Dr. McGee. Her theories are based on communication with a single minor child, and earnest as I am sure her concern is, and not based on any eagerness to advance her own studies, I do not feel that her theories, preliminary as they are, and drawn from such a source, ought to become the official standard for dealing with this culture. Independent assessment and cross-check of observations is essential to this mission. Dr. McGee is making a basic error in applying her Cloud River study to the Styx: she assumes that the development here is the same, when by all evidence of dwelling-patterns it is not.

I am frankly concerned that the Board has assigned Dr. McGee to the writing of reports based on my data. I would like to see these before they are sent.

Message, E. McGee to R. Genley transmitted from Base

You are committing a basic error in the assumption that calibans do not themselves constitute a single culture which lies at the foundations of both Cloud and Styx.

As for the reports, be assured that they will be written up with more professionalism than your suggestion contained.

Message, Base Director to R. Genley in the field

The Board will make assignments by its own consensus. The Board has every confidence in Dr. McGee.

Memo, Base Director to E. McGee

You are more valuable in your present assignment inside the Base. The Board will assess and determine the proper assignment of personnel. Where is the write-up on the Styxside data? Documents is complaining about short schedules.

We have a shuttle due to make that Document pickup in four days.

ix

The Cloud Towers

She designed ships in her mind, great ones, which she intended to build when she was in Ellai's place. She gave orders to the Weirds and experimented with her stick-and-leaf fliers off the very top of the First Tower.

Her tiny constructions wrecked themselves at the base of the Tower. And some of the fishers had the bad grace to laugh, while Ellai looked at her askance—not reprimanding her: Ellai never reprimanded her in things that might do her harm.

Her mother hoped, Elai thought obscurely, for accidents—to her person or to her pride. Sometimes she caught her mother with that look in her eyes. Like Twig, bluffing and blustering and making way for Scar because Scar had the power and all the world knew it.

It was not even hate. It was too reasonable for that. Like the calibans. They simply knew who was first.

"I met a starman," Elai said to her mother, one more thing between them. "She stopped the bleeding when I hurt my leg. Like that. We talked about flying. And lots of things."

"Stop throwing things off the Tower," her mother said, precise in her counterattack. "People laugh at you."

"I never hear them."

"Keep at it and you will."

x

188 CR
Report: Dr. Elizabeth McGee to Alliance Science Bureau
for Dr. R. Genley; Dr. E. McGee; Dr. P. Mendel; Dr. T. Galliano; Dr. T. Mannin; Dr. S. Kim

. . . The Cloud River settlement exists in a loose unity called, if they understand a name, the Cloud Towers.

The administrative organization is difficult to analyze at a distance. Each of the twelve Cloud Towers seems to have its hereditary ruler, male or female, with no clearly observed pattern of allegiances, while the First Tower seems to have the right to call up all the population in defense or attack—after what, if any, co-deliberation is unclear, in their more or less perpetual distrust of the Styx-dwellers. Presumably one Ellai daughter of Ellai, who seems to have no official title, has the hereditary right to give orders in the largest and oldest of the Towers, which gives her by extension the right to "give orders" (the language of my informant) to rulers of other towers in some but not all situations; and to individuals of her tower and other towers, but not in all situations.

If this seems confusing, it seems to reflect a power structure generally controlled by seniority, heredity, lines of descent, and traditions and divisions of responsibility which are generally understood by the community, but which may not be codified or clearly worked out. Another source of confusion may be the level of understanding of my informant, due to her youth, but to my observation, this youth understands the system far better than she is willing or able to communicate.

By far the largest number of individuals in the Cloud Towers are fishers or farmers, most of the latter operating in cooperatives, although again, this system seems to vary from tower to tower in a fashion which suggests a loose amalgamation or federation of independent traditions of rule. . . .

Concerning the fisheries, the fishing technique seems to involve the calibans, who do the fishing in partnership with humans who derive the benefit: generally the gray calibans fish, although some browns do so . . . There is trade among the towers, in the form of barter. . . . Another caliban/human cooperation exists in construction: evidently the calibans rear the towers and humans do the modifications or supervise the modifications. Both humans and calibans of all types inhabit the towers, including also the ariels. . . .

A typical tower population includes the underground shelters of fishers and farmers and artisans who may, however, live in subterranean shelters skirting the towers or as part of the spiral which culminates at the crest: there seems to be as much of a tower extended underground and round about as in the tower-structure itself.

The inhabitants of each upper tower seem to be the ruler, the elders, a number of riders, persons of some hereditary importance, a number of calibans who come and go at will, and another class about which I have been able to gather only limited information, which seems linked to the care of the calibans. . . .

. . . . Elai herself . . . The girl has an amazing precocity. There were times that I wondered whether she derived some of her inquisitiveness and above all her use of forms and techniques more advanced than what is practiced elsewhere, from some record or restricted educational system to which she might have access as Ellai's heir. But I have watched her approach a new situation and discover an answer with a facility which makes me believe completely that this precocity is genuine.

I confess to a certain awe of this ten-year-old. I think of a young da Vinci, of an Eratosthenes, a naive talent perhaps tragically limited by Gehenna. And then I recall that this is the heir who may live to direct the Cloud Towers.

Concerning Dr. R. Genley's (attached) photographic analysis of the towers of the Styxsiders, the Twelve Towers of the Cloud may offer some useful comparison.

The Cloud Towers (considering the two anomalous seaward towers as a village unto themselves, partially separate in politics) seem by the description of my informant to be comparable to a polis, an urban center in which there is much interaction among the Towers. The Styx Towers, each surrounded by tracts of cultivated land, are, at least in situation, reminiscent of feudal castles, while the Cloud Towers seem to maintain both a system of small gardens within their group and wide grainfields surrounding the Towers as a whole. When I asked my informant who works in the fields she said farmers work there, but everyone works at harvest. . . .

I asked my informant why the towers do not suffer in the rainy season. She said that there is always damage, but indicated, as we have observed in the construction of the

Styx tower, that the walls are composed not only of earth but of rock and timber and kiln-fired tile. In spite of her age she seemed certain of her observation and indicated that repair and building are a constant activity carried on by gray calibans as well as the human inhabitants, and that the aristocratic-seeming riders and the class she calls Weirds do a great deal of this repair. I asked whether she was a rider. She answered that she was. Does the heir work? I asked. She laughed at the question and said that everyone had to work. . . .

In the matter of the new Styx construction my informant offered the opinion, contrary to the reports of Drs. Genley and Kim, hereto appended, that the recent construction of the Stygian tower near the Base is less concerned with watching the Base than with providing a staging area for further hostilities against the Cloud River.

The power structures among Stygians as among Cloudsiders seem indistinct, although the external observations of the long silence from the Styx, combined with the Cloud River informant's statements that the Styx ruler is young, seem to indicate a hereditary authority which may have been awaiting the majority of the young Stygian ruler. Precisely what manner of social organization or power structure is in effect during this period is therefore a guess.

xi

188 CR, day 344
Cloudside

It had begun slowly, a tenderness about the wound, and that had been going on for weeks. Maybe, Elai thought, it was the cold. Old Cloud limped worse with his old wounds when it rained, and complained a great deal. But whenever she complained it meant not going outside and it meant having the nurses hovering about her, so she kept from limping.

It was healing, she reckoned. By spring it would be well. A little discomfort was only natural.

But the scar went red and the place went hot and finally she could not help but limp.

So the nurses noticed; and they brought old Karel to look at it. And Karel got out his knives.

They gave her bitterweed boiled up to kill the pain, but the tea made her sick at her stomach and left her only doubly miserable. She clamped her jaws and never yelled, only a scant moaning while old Karel hunted away in the wound he had made; and the sweat went cold on her. "Let me go," she said to the riders who had come to help Karel hold her still; and mostly they did, except when the knife went deep and the sweat broke out on her and she threw up.

Karel held up a bit of something like a small bone. Her mother Ellai came to see.

"Seafolk spine," Karel said. "Left in the wound. Whoever wrapped that leg up never looked to see. Never should have left it that way."

He laid the spine aside and went back to his digging with the knife; they gave her more tea and she threw that up too, the several times they gave it to her.

Afterwards her mother only looked at her, as she lay limp and buried in blankets. Scar was somewhere down below, with Weirds to keep him quiet; only Twig was in the room, and her mother just stood there staring at her, whatever went on behind her eyes, whether that her mother was thinking she was less threat now, whether she just despised the intelligence of the daughter she had birthed.

"So your starman knows everything," her mother said.

Elai just stared back.

xii

189 CR, day 24
Message, R. Genley to Base Director

Weather has made observation difficult. Persistent fogs have obscured the riverside now and we have only limited view.

Last night the calibans came close. We could hear them moving around the shelter. When we went outside they retreated. We are using all due caution.

xiii

189 CR, day 24
The Base Director's office

"Genley," McGee said, "is in danger. I would remind you, sir, the Base has fallen before. And there were warnings of it. Take the calibans seriously."

"They're far from Base, Dr. McGee." The Director leaned back, arms locked across his middle. The windows looked out on the concrete buildings, on fog. "But this time I do agree with you. There's a possibility of a problem out there."

"There's more than a possibility. The rainy season seems to act on the calibans, and everything's stirred up on Styxside."

"What about your assessment of the calibans as a culture? Doesn't this weather-triggered behavior belong to something more primitive?"

"Do we sunbathe in winter?"

"We're talking about aggression."

"Early humans preferred summer for their wars."

"Then what does this season do for calibans?"

"I wouldn't venture an answer. We can only observe that it does something."

"Genley's aware of the problem."

"Not of the hazards. He won't listen to those."

The Director thought a moment. "We'll take that under advisement. We know where you stand."

"My request—"

"Also under advisement."

xiv

189 CR, day 25
R. Genley to Base Director

. . . I have made a contact. A band of Stygians riding calibans has shown up facing our camp on our own side of the Styx this foggy morning. There was no furtiveness in their approach. They stopped a moment and observed us, then retreated and camped nearby. Mist makes observation difficult, but we can see them faintly at present.

189 CR, day 25
Base Director to R. Genley.

Proceed with caution. Weather forecast indicates clearing tonight and tomorrow, winds SW/10–15.

Drs. McGee, Mannin, and Galliano are on their way afoot to reach your position with 10 security personnel. Please extend all professional cooperation and courtesy. Use your discretion regarding face to face contact.

xv

189 CR, day 26
Styxside Base

They reached the camp by morning, staggering-tired and glad enough of the breakfast they walked in on, with hot tea and biscuits.

"Hardly necessary for you to trek out here," Genley said to McGee. He was a huge florid-faced man, solid, monument-like in the khaki coldsuit that was the uniform out here. McGee filled out her own with deskbound weight-gain. Her legs ached and her sides hurt. The smell of the Styx came to them here, got into everything, odor of reeds and mud and wet and cold, permeating even the biscuits and the coffee. It was freedom. She savored it, ignoring Genley.

"I expect," Genley went on, "that you'll follow our lead out here. The last thing we need is interference."

"I only give advice," she said, deliberately bland. "Don't worry about your credit on the report."

"I think they're stirring about out there," said Mannin from the doorway. "They had to have seen us come in."

"Weather report's wrong as usual," Genley said. "Fog's not going to clear."

"I think we'd better get out there," McGee said.

"Have your breakfast," Genley said. "We'll see to it."

McGee frowned, stuffed her mouth, washed the biscuit down, and trailed him out the door.

The sun made an attempt at breaking through the mist. It was all pinks and golds, with black reeds thrusting up in clumps of spiky shadow and the fog lying on the Styx like a dawn-tinted blanket.

Every surface was wet. Standing or crouching, one felt one's boots begin to sink. Moisture gathered on hair and face and intensified the chill. But they stood, a little out from their camp, facing the Stygians' camp, the humped shapes of calibans moving restlessly in the dawn.

Then human figures appeared among the calibans.

"They're coming," McGee said.

"We just stand," said Genley, "and see what they do."

The Stygians drew closer, afoot, more distinct in the morning mist. The calibans walked behind them, like a living wall, five, six of them.

Closer and closer.

"Let's walk out halfway," said Genley.

"Not sure about that," said Mannin.

Genley walked. McGee trod after him, her eyes on the calibans as much as the humans. Mannin followed. The Security fieldmen were watching them. No one had guns. None were permitted. If they were attacked, they might die here. It was Security's task simply to escape and report the fact.

Features became clear. There were three older men among the Stygians, three younger, and the one foremost was youngest of the lot. His long hair was gathered back at the crown; his dark beard was cut close, his leather garments clean, ornamented with strings of river-polished stones and bone beads. He was not so tall as some. He looked scarcely twenty. He might be a herald of some kind, McGee thought to herself, but there was something—the spring-tension way he moved, the assurance—that said that of all the six they saw, this was the one to watch out for.

Young man. About eighteen.

"Might be Jin himself," she said beneath her breath. "Right age. Watch it with this one."

"Quiet," Genley said. He crouched down, let a stone slip

from his clenched hand to the mud, let fall another pebble by that one.

The Stygians stopped. The calibans crouched belly to the ground behind them, excepting the biggest, which was poised well up on its four legs.

"They're not going to listen," McGee said. "I'd stand up, Genley. They're not interested."

Genley stood, a careful straightening, his Patterning-effort abandoned. "I'm Genley," he said to the Stygians.

"Jin," said the youth.

"The one who gives orders on the Styx."

"That Jin. Yes." The youth set his hands on hips, walked carelessly off to riverward, walked back again a few paces. The calibans had all stood up. "Genley."

"McGee," McGee said tautly. "He's Mannin."

"*MaGee*. Yes." Another few paces, not looking at them, and then a look at Genley. "This place is ours."

"We came to meet you in it," said Genley. "To talk."

The young man looked about him, casually curious, walking back to his companions.

This is an insult, McGee suspected without any means to be sure. *He's provoking us.* But the young face never changed.

"Jin," McGee said aloud and deliberately and Jin looked straight at her, his face hard. "You want something?" McGee asked.

"I have it," Jin said, and ignored her to look at Genley and Mannin. "You want to talk. You have more questions. Ask."

No, McGee thought, sensing that civility was the wrong tack to take with this youth. "Not interested," she said. "Genley, Mannin. Come *on*."

The others did not move. "We'll talk," Genley said.

McGee walked off, back to the camp. It was all she had left herself to do.

She did not look back. But Genley was hard on her heels before she had gotten to the tent.

"McGee!"

She looked about, at anger congested in Genley's face. At anger in Mannin's.

"He walked off, did he?" she asked.

xvi

189 CR, day 27
Main Base, the Director's office

She expected the summons, stood there weary and dirty as she was, hands folded. She had come back to Base with three of the security personnel. She had not slept. She wanted a chair.

There was no offer. The Director stared at her hard-eyed from behind his desk. "Botched contact," he said. "What was it, McGee, sabotage? Could you carry it that far?"

"No, sir. I did the right thing."

"Sit down."

She pulled the chair over, sank down and caught her breath.

"Well?"

"He was laughing at us. At Genley. He was provoking Genley and Genley was blind to all of it. He was getting points off us."

"The sound tape doesn't show it. It shows rather that he knows *you*."

"Maybe he does. Rumors doubtless travel."

"And you picked this up too, of course."

"Absolutely."

"You lowered Genley's credibility."

"Genley didn't need help in that. This Jin is dangerous."

"Might there be some bias, McGee?"

"No. Not on my side."

There was silence. The Director sat glaring, twisting a stylus in his hands. Behind him was the window, the concrete buildings of the Base. Safety behind the wire. Beneath them detectors protected the underground, listened for undermining. Man on Gehenna had learned.

"You've created a situation," the Director said.

"In my professional judgement, sir, it had to be done. If the Styx doesn't respect us—"

"Do you think respect has to matter, one way or another? We're not in this for points, McGee, or personal pride."

"I know we've got a mission out there on the Styx with their lives riding on that respect. I think maybe I made them doubt their calculations about us. I hope it's good enough to keep Genley alive out there."

"You keep assuming hostility exists."

"Based on what the Cloudsiders think."

"On a ten-year-old girl's opinion."

"This Jin—every move he made was a provocation. That caliban of his, the way it was set, everything was aggression."

"Theories, McGee."

"I'd like to renew the Cloudside contact. Pursue it for all it's worth."

"The same way you turned your back on the Styxsiders?"

"It's the same gesture, yes, sir."

"What about your concern for the Styxside mission? Aren't you afraid that would precipitate some trouble?"

"If Genley's right, it won't. If I'm right, it would send a wrong signal not to. Not doing it might signal that we're weak. And that could equally well endanger Genley."

"You seriously think these Styxsiders could look at this Base and think we're without resources."

"This base has fallen before. Despite all its resources. I think it could be a very reasonable conclusion on their part. But I wouldn't venture to say just what they think. Their minds are at an angle to ours. And there's the possibility that we're not dealing just with human instinct."

"Calibans again."

"The Gehennans take them seriously, however the matter seems to us. I think we have to bear that in mind. The Gehennans think the calibans have an opinion. That's one thing I'm tolerably sure of."

"Your proposal?"

"What I said. To take all our avenues."

The Director frowned, leaned forward, and pushed a button on the recorder.

xvii

Report from field: R. Genley

The Stygians remain, watching us as we watch them. Today there was at least a minor breakthrough: one of the

Stygians approached our shelter and looked us over quite
openly. When we came toward him he walked off at a
leisurely pace. We reciprocated and were ignored.

xviii

Styxside

"Sit," said Jin; and Genley did so, carefully, in the firelit
circle. They took the chance, he and Mannin together—a
wild chance, when one of the young Stygians had come a
second time to beckon them. They walked alone into the
camp, among the calibans, unarmed, and there was the waft
of alcohol about the place. There were cups passed. Quickly
one came their way as they settled by the fire.

Genley drank first, trying not to taste it. It was something
like beer, but it numbed the mouth. He passed the wooden
cup on to Mannin and looked up at Jin.

"Good," said Jin—a figure that belonged in firelight, a
figure out of human past, leather-clad, his young face sweating in the light and smoke, his eyes shining with small fire-
sparks. "Good. Genley. Mannin."

"Jin."

The face broke into a grin. The eyes danced. Jin took
the cup again. "You want to talk to me."

"Yes," Genley said.

"On what?"

"There's a lot of things." Whatever was in the drink
numbed the fingers. Distantly Genley was afraid. "Like
what this drink is?"

"Beer," Jin said, amused. "You think something else,
Gen-ley?" He drank from the same cup, and the next man
filled it again. They were all men, twelve of them, all told.
Three fiftyish. Most young, but none so young as Jin.
"Could be bluefish in a cup. You die that way. But you
walk in here, you bring no guns."

"The Base wants to talk. About a lot of things."

"What do you pay?"

"Maybe it's just good for everyone, that you and the
Base know each other."

"Maybe it's not."

"We've been here a long time," Mannin said, "living next to each other."

"Yes," said Jin.

"Things look a lot better for the Styx recently."

Jin's shoulders straightened. He looked at Mannin, at them both, with appraising eyes. "Watch us, do you?"

"Why not?" Genley asked.

"I speak for the Styx," Jin said.

"We'd like to come and go in safety," Genley said.

"Where?"

"Around the river. To talk to your people. To be friends."

Jin thought this over. Perhaps, Genley thought, sweating, the whole line of approach had been wrong.

"Friends," Jin said, seeming to taste the word. He looked at them askance. "With starmen." He held out his hand for the cup, a line between his brows as he studied them. "We talk about talking," Jin said.

189 CR, day 30
Message, R. Genley to Base Director

I have finally secured a face to face meeting with the Stygians. After consistently refusing all approach since the incident with Dr. McGee, Jin has permitted the entry of Dr. Mannin and myself into his camp. Apparently their pride has been salved by this prolonged silence and by our approach to them.

Finding no further cause for offense, they were hospitable and offered us food and drink. The young Stygian leader, while reserved and maintaining an attitude of dignity, began to show both humor and ease in our presence, altogether different than the difficult encounter of four days ago.

I would strongly urge, with no professional criticism implied, that Dr. McGee avoid contact with the Styxsiders in any capacity. The name McGee is known to them, and disliked, which evidences, perhaps, both contact between Styx and Cloud, and possibly some hostility, but I take nothing for granted.

xix

189 CR, day 35
Cloud Towers

There was surprisingly little difficulty getting to the Towers of the Cloud. There looked to be, even more surprising, only slightly more difficulty walking among them.

McGee came alone, in the dawning, with only the recorder secreted on her person and her kit slung from her shoulder, from the landing she had made upriver. She was afraid, with a different kind of fear than Jin had roused in her. This fear had something of embarrassment, of shame, remembering Elai, who would not, perhaps, understand. And now she did not know any other way but simply to walk until that walking drew some reaction.

There would be a caliban, she had hoped, on this rare clear winter day: a girl on a caliban would come to meet her, frowning at her a bit at first, but forgiving her MaGee for her lapse of courtesy.

But none had come.

Now before her loomed the great bulk of the Towers themselves, clustered together in their improbable size. *City,* one had to think. A city of earth and tile, slantwalled, irregular towers the color of the earth, spirals that began in a maze of mounds.

She knew First Tower, nearest the river: so Elai had said. She passed the lower mounds, through eerie quiet, past folk who refused to notice her. She passed the windowed mounds of ordinary dwellings, children playing with ariels, calibans lazing in the sun, potters and woodworkers about their business in sunlit niches in the mounds, sheltered from the slight nip of the wind, walked to the very door of First Tower itself.

A trio of calibans kept the inner hall. Her heart froze when they got up on their legs and made a circle about her, when one of them investigated her with a blunt shove of its nose and flicked a thick tongue at her face.

But that one left then, and the others did, scrambling up the entry into the Tower.

She was not certain it was prudent to follow, but she hitched up her kit strap and ventured it, into a cool earthen corridor clawed and worn along the floor and walls by generations of caliban bodies. Dark—quite dark, as if this was a way the Cloudsiders went on touch alone. Only now and again was there a touch of light from some tiny shaft piercing the walls and coming through some depth of the earthen construction. It was a place for atavistic fears, bogies, creatures in the dark. The Cloudsiders called it home.

In the dim light from such a shaft a human shape appeared, around the dark winding of the core. McGee stopped. Abruptly.

"To see Ellai," she said when she got her breath.

The shadow just turned and walked up the incline and around the turn. McGee sucked in another breath and decided to try following.

She heard the man ahead of her, or something ahead, heard slitherings too, and pressed herself once against the wall as something rather smallish and in a hurry came bolting past her in the dark. Turn after turn she went up following her guide, sometimes now past doorways that offered momentary sunlight and cast a little detail about her guide: sometimes there were occupants in the huge rooms inside the sunless core, on which doors opened, flinging lamplight out. In some of them were calibans, in others knots of humans, strangely like the calibans themselves in the stillness with which they turned their heads her way. She heard wafts of childish voices, or adult, that let her know ordinary life went on in this strangeness.

And then the spiral, which had grown tighter and tighter, opened out on a vast sunpierced hall, a hall that astounded with its size, its ceiling supported by crazy-angled buttresses of earth. She had come up in the center of its floor, where a half a hundred humans and at least as many calibans waited, as if they had been about some other business, or as if they had known she was coming—they had *seen* her, she realized suddenly, chagrined. There might easily be lookouts on the tower height and they must have seen her coming for at least an hour.

The gathering grew quiet, organized itself so that there was an open space between herself and a certain frowning woman who studied her and then sat down on a substantial wooden chair. A caliban settled possessively about it, embracing the chairlegs with the curve of body and tail and lifting its head to the woman's hand.

Then McGee saw a face she knew, at the right against the wall, a girl who was grave and frowning, a huge caliban with a raking scar down its side. A moment McGee stared, being sure. The child's face was hard, offering her no recognition, nothing.

She glanced quickly back to the other, the woman. "My name is McGee," she said.

"Ellai," said the woman; but that much she had guessed.

"I'm here," McGee said then, because a girl had taught her to talk directly, abruptly, in a passable Cloud-side accent, "because the Styx-siders have come to talk to us; and because the Base thinks we shouldn't be talking to Styxsiders without talking to Cloud-side too."

"What do you have to say?"

"I'd rather listen."

Ellai nodded slowly, her fingers trailing over the back of her caliban. "You'll answer," Ellai said. "How is that boy on Styx-side?"

McGee bit her lip. "I don't think he's a boy any longer. People follow him."

"This tower near your doors. You let it be."

"We don't find it comfortable. But it's not our habit to interfere outside the wire."

"Then you're stupid," Ellai said.

"We don't interfere on Cloud-side either."

It might have scored a point. Or lost one. Ellai's face gave no hints. "What are you doing here?"

"We don't intend to have a ring of Styx towers cutting us off from any possible contact with you. If we encourage you to build closer towers, it could mean more fighting and we don't want that either."

"If you don't intend to interfere with anyone, how do you plan to stop the Styx-siders building towers?"

"By coming and going in this direction, by making it clear to them that this is a way we go and that we don't intend to be stopped."

Ellai thought that over, clearly. "What good are you?"

"We give the Styxsiders something else to think about."

Ellai frowned, then waved her hand. "Then go do that," she said.

There was a stirring among the gathering, an ominous shifting, a flicking and settling of caliban collars and a pricking-up of the caliban's beside Ellai.

"So," said McGee, uneasy in this shifting and uncertain whether it was good or ill, "if we come and go and you do the same, it ought to make it clear that we plan to keep this way open."

An aged bald man came and squatted by Ellai's side, put his spidery fingers on the caliban. Ellai never looked at him.

"You will go now," Ellai said, staring at McGee. "You will not come here again."

McGee's heart speeded. She felt ruin happening, all her careful constructions. She kept distress from her face. "So the Styxsiders will say what they like and build where they like and you aren't interested to stop it."

"Go."

Others had moved, others of the peculiar sort gathering about Ellai, crouched in the shadows. Calibans shifted. An ariel skittered across the floor and whipped into the caliban gathering. Of the sane-looking humans there seemed very few: the woman nearest Ellai's chair, a leather-clad, hard-faced type; a handful of men of the same stamp, among their gathering of dragons, among lamp-like eyes and spiny crests. The eyes were little different, the humans and the dragons—cold and mad.

A smaller, gray caliban serpentined its way to the clear center of the floor with a stone in its jaws and laid it purposely on the floor. Another followed, placing a second beside if, while the first retrieved another rock. It was crazy. The craziness in the place sent a shiver over McGee's skin, an overwhelming anxiety to be out of this tower, a remembrance that the way out was long and dark.

A third stone, parallel to the others, and a fourth, dividing her from Ellai.

"The way is open now," Ellai said.

Go, that was again, last warning. McGee turned aside in disarray, stopped an instant looking straight at Elai, appealing to the one voice that might make a difference.

Elai's hand was on Scar's side. She dropped it and

walked a few paces forward—walked with a limp, as if to demonstrate it. Elai was lame. Even that had gone wrong.

McGee went, through the dark spirals, out into the un-friendly sun.

xx

189 CR, day 43
Report, E. McGee

. . . . I succeeded in direct contact; further contacts should be pursued, but cautiously. . . .

189 CR, day 45
Memo, office of the Director to E. McGee

Your qualification of the incident as a limited success seems to this office to be unfounded optimism.

xxi

189 CR, day 114
Styxside

Genley looked about him at every step along the dusty road, taking mental notes: Mannin trod behind him, and Kim; and in front of them the rider atop his caliban, un-likely figure, their guide in this trek.

Before them the hitherside tower loomed, massive, solid in their eyes. They had seen this at distance, done long-range photography, observed these folk as best they could. But this one was within their reach, with its fields, its out-buildings. Women labored in the sun, bare-backed to the gentle wind, the mild sun, weeding the crops. They stopped and looked up, amazed at the apparition of starmen.

189 CR, day 134
Field Report: R. Genley

. . . The hitherside tower is called Parm Tower, after the man who built it. The estimates of tower population are incorrect: a great deal of it extends below, with many of the lower corridors used for sleeping. Parm Tower holds at least two thousand individuals and nearly that number of calibans: I think about fifty are browns and the rest are grays.

The division of labor offers a working model of theories long held regarding early human development and in the degree to which Gehenna has recapitulated human patterns, offers exciting prospects for future anthropological study. One could easily imagine the ancient Euphrates, modified ziggurats, used in this case for dwellings as well as for the ancient purpose, the storage of grain above the floods and seasonal dampness of the ground.

Women have turned to agriculture and do all manner of work of this kind. Hunting, fishing, and the crafts and handcrafts, including weaving, are almost exclusively a male domain and enjoy a high status, most notably the hunters who have exclusive control of the brown calibans. Fishers employ the grays. The grays are active in the fields as well, performing such tasks as moving dikes and letting in the water, but they are directed in this case by the class called Weirds. Weirds are both male and female, individuals who have so thoroughly identified with the calibans that they have abandoned speech and often go naked in weather too cool to make it comfortable. They do understand speech or gesture, apparently, but I have never heard one speak, although I have seen them react to hunters who speak to them. They maneuver the grays and a few browns, but the calibans do not seem to attach to them as individuals in the manner in which they attach to the hunter-class.

Only hunters, as I have observed, own a particular caliban and give it a name. It should also be mentioned that one is born a hunter, and hunter marriages are arranged within towers after a curious polyandrous fashion: a woman marries her male relatives' hunting comrades as a group; and her male relatives are married to their hunting comrades' female sibs. Younger sisters usually marry outside the tower, thus minimizing inbreeding; they are aware of genetics, though, curiously enough, they have reverted to or reinvented the old term "blood" to handle the concept. There is no attempt to distinguish full brother-sister relationship from half. In that much the system is matrilineal. But women of hunter class are ornaments, doing little labor but the making of clothes and the group care of children in which they are assisted by women relieved from field work. All important decisions are the province of the men. I have observed one exception to this rule, a woman of about fifty who seems to have outlived all her sibs and her band. She wears the leather clothing of a rider, has a caliban and carries a knife. She sits with the men at meals and has no association with the wives.

Crafts and fisher-class women work in the fields with their daughters. Male children can strive for any class, even to be a hunter, although should a lower class male succeed in gaining a caliban he may have to fight other hunters and endure considerable harassment. There is one such individual at Parm Tower. His name is Matso. He is a fisher's son. The women are particularly cruel to him, apparently resenting the possibility of his bringing some fisher-sib into their society should he join a hunter-group.

Over all of this of course is Jin himself. This is a remarkable man. Younger than most of his council, he dominates them. Not physically tall, he is still imposing because of the energy which flows from him. The calibans react to him with nervousness-displays, a reaction in which his own plays some part: this is a beast named Thorn, which is both large and aggressive. But the most of it is due to Jin's own force of personality. He is a persuasive speaker, eloquent, though unlettered: he is a hunter, and writing is a craft: he will not practice it.

He has survived eight years of guardianship to seize power for himself at sixteen, effectively deposing but not killing his former guardian Mes of the River Tower, from what I hear. He is inquisitive, loves verbal games, loves to get the better hand in an argument, is generous with gifts—he bestows ornaments freehandedly in the manner of some oldworld chief. He has a number of wives who are reserved to him alone but these are across the Styx. At Parm Tower he is afforded the hospitality of the hunter-class women, which is a thing done otherwise only between two bands in payment of some very high favor. This lending of wives and the resultant uncertainty of parentage of some offspring seems to strengthen the political structure and to create strong bonds between Jin and certain of the hunter-bands. Whether Jin lends his wives in this fashion we cannot presently ascertain.

We apparently have the freedom to come and go with the escort of one or the other hunters. Jin himself has entertained us in Parm Tower hall and given us gifts which we are hard put to reciprocate.

The people are well-fed, well-clothed and in all have a healthy look. Jin enumerates his plans for more fields, more towers, wider range of his hunters to the north. . . .

Memo, E. McGee to Committee

It seems to me that it is a deceptively easy assumption that these Styxsiders are recapitulating some *natural* course of human society. This is selective seeking-out of evidence to fit the model Dr. Genley wishes to support. He totally ignores the contrary evidence of the Cloud Towers, who have grown up in a very different pattern.

Message from field: R. Genley

I thank the committee for the inclusion of the reports.

As for Dr. McGee's assertion that I am selecting my data, I would be interested to see this presented in full, rather than in an inter-office memo, if she has obtained any new data from the Cloud.

As for the earlier data I am of course familiar with it. It is not surprising that one of the communities has managed to cling to their ancestral ways and, in their unstressed river-plain environment, lack the impetus to change. It is inconceivable that their ways would survive except for the circumstance of their origin which flung them into close community: they were, be it remembered, a settlement of refugees. They are not coping well. Their cultivated areas are small. They do not hunt widely, if at all. They are predominantly fishers, which is an occupation, at least as practiced on Gehenna, which does not require physical strength.

The critical difference is the necessity of physical

strength in the hunter culture of the Styx, a difference which should be self-evident given the biological realities of the human species.

Memo, E. McGee to Committee
Copy transmitted to R. Genley

It is a difficult task to extricate the observer from the observation. I do not believe we are out here at considerable expense to seek to reaffirm theories dearly held by our various disciplines, but to faithfully record what exists, and secondly to challenge, where appropriate, theories which become questionable in the light of observed fact.

It is possible that the entanglement of the observer with the observation throughout history, along with the sorrowful fact that in general only the winners write the accounts of wars, has tended to advance certain cultural values in the place of fact, when these values are confused with fact by the observer.

Fact: two ways of life exist on Gehenna.

Fact: more than one way of life has existed in humanity's cradles of civilization.

I propose that, instead of arguing old theories which have considerable cultural content, we consider this possibility: that humanity develops a multiplicity of answers to the environment, and that if there must be a system of polarities to explain the structure around which these answers are organized, that the polarity does not in and of itself involve gender, but the relative success of the population in curbing those individuals with the tendency to coerce their neighbors. Some cultures solve this problem. Some do not, and fall into a pattern which exalts this tendency and elevates it, again by the principle that survivors and rulers write the histories, to the guiding virtue of the culture. It is not that the Cloud River culture is unnatural. It is fully natural. It is, unfortunately, threatened with extinction by the hand of the Styxsiders, who will need centuries to attain the level of civilization already possessed by the Cloud. Barbarians win because civilizations are inherently more fragile.

Message from the field: R. Genley

I again urge Dr. McGee to present her theories formally

when she can reestablish sufficient contact with the culture she is describing to secure corroborative and specific observations.

xxii

190 CR
Unedited text of message
Dr. E. McGee to Alliance HQ
couriered by *AS Pegasus*

[Considering the personal difficulty of continuing in this position—]

[Considering the contribution which I feel I might make elsewhere and the personal disappointment]—

[Considering the—]

[Considering the unfortunate circumstances which have incurred, I suspect, some personal animosity on the part of the Cloud-siders—]

Considering the difficulty of life on Gehenna and my personal health, I would like to make application for immediate transfer from the project. [I feel that my work here is at a standstill and that the—] At the present level of activity my assistants are fully competent to conduct my project and I would urge the Bureau to appoint Dr. Leroy H. Cooper to the post. He has shown himself to be a skilled and dedicated investigator. [I feel that a certain cultural and personal bias on the part of the—] I wish my application for transfer to cast no shadow on the mission or the staff here. My reasons are medical and personal, involving a sensitivity to certain irritants present in the area . . .

xxiii

191 CR, day 202
Message, Alliance HQ
to Dr. E. McGee, Gehenna Base

. . . with thorough sympathy for your medical difficulties, the Bureau still considers your presence in the project to be of overriding value, in view of the expense and difficulty of personnel adjustments. So it is with regret that we must reject your application for transfer . . .

. . . We have analysed the facilities available at Gehenna both on the Base and at the Station for alleviation of your difficulties and have made shipment of medicines which we feel will provide a wider range of treatment alternatives . . .

191 CR, day 205
Prescription, Base pharmacy
for Dr. E. McGee

. . . for insomnia, take one capsule at bedtime. ALCO-HOL CONTRAINDICATED.

xxiv

200 CR, day 33
Field report: E. McGee

. . . rumor which I have picked up from the usual New Tower source indicates that the heir, Elai, has given birth to a second son. Due to the tenuous nature of my contact with these sources and the need for caution I cannot yet confirm. . . .

xxv

200 CR, day 98
Styxside

"Genley," Jin said, in the warmth of Farm Tower, in the closeness that smelled of brew and calibans and smoke and men. A hand came out and rocked his shoulder, pressed with strong fingers. "You write about me. What do you write?"

"Things."

"Like what, Genley?"

"The way you live, the things you do. Like your records. Like the things you write down."

"You make the starmen know me."

"They know you."

Jin clapped his shoulder. They were mostly alone. There was only Parm and his lot drowsing in the corner. The hand fell from his arm. "That Mannin, that Kim, always scratching away—You know, Gen-ley, they have fear. You know how I know they have fear? It's in the eyes. They're afraid. You watch them. They don't look in my eyes. You do."

Genley did, without flinching. Jin buffeted his arm and laughed when he had done it.

"You are my father," Jin said.

Mannin would have taken notes on that. Asked questions: was it a common thing to say? Genley went on staring him in the eye, too solid for Jin to shake, in any sense.

"My father," Jin said, still holding his arm. "Who asks me questions, questions, questions what I do. I learn from your questions, Gen-ley. So I call you my father. Why doesn't my father ask me gifts?"

"What should I ask for?"

"A man should have women. You want the women, Genley, you go down . . . anytime you like. Not hunter women: trouble, hunter women. But all the others. Anytime you like. You like that?"

200 CR, day 120
Field report: R. Genley

. . . The lord Jin has made considerable progress toward further stabilizing the government. The reports of dissent in the TransStyx have died down following a personal visit of one of his aides to that side and indications are that the chief of the opposition is now supporting his authority.

Memo, E. McGee to Base Director
Copy to R. Genley in field

The *lord* Jin? . . . .

xxvi

200 CR, day 203
Field report: R. Genley

. . . . . In all, Jin 12's new programs are succeeding.
Agriculture is up another 5 percent this year, for a total of
112% increase since his accession. Roadbuilding, a totally
new development, has made possible the delivery of limestone to the hitherside tower, another of Jin's ideas, gathered from observation, I surmise, of our own constructions
inside the wire. The mission has continually observed the
zero trade restriction and most carefully has withheld information, but it could be the mere presence of the Base is a
goad to the energetic Styxside culture, accelerating their
dissatisfaction with conditions as they are. Looking as they
do through the wire at a permanent city, observing woven
clothing and a wealth of metal, they are discontent with what
they have. The lord Jin is particularly anxious for metal, but
sees no present possibility of obtaining it. The choice which
placed the colony in a fertile deep plain has ironically made
that particular advancement difficult until explorations reach
the mountainous southeast. The road to the quarries is part
of a push in this direction, making possible, if not wheeled
transport, the rapid transit of mounted traffic.

There has been another development, in the surprising
invitation of the lord Jin for me to visit the farside settlements, an opportunity providing some hazards, but altogether attractive in terms of opening even wider contacts
with this unprecedented culture. I have told the lord Jin
that this will require some consultation and I hope for the
Director's consent. . . .

200 CR, day 203
Message, Dr. E. McGee to R. Genley

. . . . It seems to me that this extension of a quarry road
and this interest you name as evidence of a progressive
attitude could equally well be interpreted as a certain ag-

gressiveness toward the south. The mountains lord Jin wants, as you put it, lie within the natural sphere of the Cloud-siders.

200 CR, day 203
Message, Dr. R. Genley to E. McGee

I do not view that our duties include carving out "spheres of influence" or manifest destinies of our private protectorates. I do not urge the Styx settlements to any ambition and I trust that you maintain the same policy with the Cloud, in what contacts you have managed to secure with them.

200 CR, day 203
Message, Dr. E. McGee to R. Genley
Copy to Base Director

You have been taken in by a deceptive scoundrel and may be taken further if you accept this invitation to enter the transStygian settlements. I consider the potential hazard to peace to be unwarrantably great should advanced technology fall into the hands of this young warlord and I intend to object to your proposed operations across the Styx for that reason and for no private animosity.

200 CR, day 206
Memo, Base Director to E. McGee

The Board has taken your warning under consideration, but feels that the potential advantages outweigh the risk.

Message, Base Director to R. Genley

Arrangements for transStyx operation may be pursued with appropriate safeguards. . . .

xxvii

201 CR, day 2
Field report, Dr. R. Genley
Green Tower: the transStyx district

. . . Lord Jin has been persuaded that Drs. Mannin and Kim might join me in the TransStyx.

I have been afforded the signal honor of being given a high tower room for my comfort—a small one, to be sure, but decidedly dryer in the recent rains. Further, this has afforded me the chance to see the interactions of the upper tower folk at close hand.

Which brings me to a repeated request for the chance to bring vid recorders into the TransStyx. We are losing irreplaceable material. We do not believe that such highly complicated technology would pose any significant problem, since the people are well-accustomed to our handling strange things, and there has never been any incidence of theft or attempt at theft: the lord Jin has us under his protection. Mannin and Kim might bring this equipment when they come.

xxviii

203 CR, day 45
Field report, Dr. E. McGee

The heir, Elai, was delivered of a fourth son. So the report runs among the outer towers. Ellai-Eldest's health is failing. I have heard that the heir is in fragile health following this birth and there is some alarm on this account. I am not sanguine about the future of the Cloud settlements should Elai die after succeeding Ellai, as now seems imminent. It is not out of all possibility that this community too could see a prolonged regency for Elai's minor sons. Or the power might pass laterally to one Paeia, a cousin of some degree, who is of middle years, and ambitious. I urgently hope the Board will consider whether any protective measures could be taken, considering that we have, albeit indirectly, sustained the prestige and the power of the Stygian leader by accepting his contact. Whether this was correctly done or whether the continued and increasing presence of Base personnel in the TransStyx does not in fact create an indirect threat to the safety of the Cloud, I do not at this time argue.

I urgently advocate the establishment of a permanent base for study in the vicinity of the Cloud to balance any real or imagined support we may have given their enemies. In my judgement, the Cloud expects attack. By what reasoning they have arrived at this conclusion, I have no information. I even suspect information carried through the calibans.

203 CR, day 47
Message, R. Genley to the Base Director

. . . That Dr. McGee now descends to obscure arguments involving conspiracy among calibans does not deserve serious answer. I would support her request for assistance: her post has involved too much solitude, and perhaps some personal risk, recalling her injuries of some years past.

As for her suggestions of possible attack from the Styx, I can assure the Board that no such moves are underway.

And regarding calibans, their communication is assuredly an elementary symbol-directional system with a system of reasoning which is far more concerned with purely caliban matters such as the availability of fish, the security of their eggs, and their access to the river than with any human activity, let alone the politics of succession.

I have of course read Dr. McGee's paper on caliban-human interaction in the Cloud Towers and am aware of her beliefs that the Cloud calibans are equal partners in Cloud Tower life: this is surely the basis of her remarkable assertion above. To the degree in which this so-named partnership exists, the Cloud River society is, by data which she herself reports, an unhealthy society, suspicious, reclusive, clinging to the past, and in all, preoccupied with calibans to such an extent that it does not innovate in any traditional human pattern. The Cloud River settlement is an impenetrable maze on which Dr. McGee has spent her health and many years, in which regard I would personally be interested to see new blood introduced into that study, to make comparisons with Dr. McGee's ongoing studies.

xxix

204 CR, day 34
Cloud River plain

The shelter by no means kept out the damp and the cold. Noon was murky after the fashion of winter days, and the help had gone scuttling back to the warmth of the Base under the pretext of supplies when the rascal saw the front coming. McGee wiped her nose and turned up the heater a bit—they let her have that modern convenience, but the latrine was a hole and a shovel to fill it and water was a rainbarrel outside in the muck because otherwise it was hauling two liter jugs the whole long distance from the wire. Her coveralls kept her warm: but her feet and hands were always cold because the cold got up from the ground; and her coat, on its wire hook on the centerpole, was drying out over the stove while her boots were baking in front of it. Warm socks, heated socks, were a luxury as wonderful as dry, fire-warmed boots.

There were such things as heated boots, to be sure, and thermcloth and all sorts of wonderful luxuries, but somehow, in the labyrinth of communications with HQ, Gehenna could never make it understood that, temperate climate notwithstanding, the requisitions were needed. A few items arrived. Seniority snatched them up. Medical priorities got them. Outside-the-wire operations got plain boots and cold feet. Advanced technology, the Director called it, and interdicted it for the field. The Director had thermal boots for his treks across the concrete Base quad or out about his rounds for the hours he was out.

A plague on all Directors. McGee sneezed again and wiped her nose and sat down on her bunk by the heater, brushed the dust off her frigid right sole and eased into a heated sock and into a warmer boot, savoring the sensation. Then the other foot. There was never a time when all of her was warm, that was the trouble. One got the feet or the backside or the hands or the front but the other side was always away from the heat. And baths were shivering misery.

She got to her report, on a tablet propped on her lap, scribbling the latest notes.

A sound grew into her attention, a distant whisper and fall that brought her pen to a stop and had her head up. Caliban. And moving as calibans rarely moved in the open grassland. She laid the pen and tablet aside, then thought better of that and dumped both into the safebox that no Cloud-sider could hope to crack.

It came closer. She had no weapons. She went to the flimsy door, peering out through the plastic spex into the mist.

A caliban materialized. It had a rider on its back, and it came to a stop outside with a whipping of its tail that made its own sibilance in the grass. It was a gray bulk in the fog. The rider was no more than a silhouette. She heard a whistle, like calling a caliban from its sleep, and she took her coat from its hook, shrugged it on and went out to face the situation.

"Ma-Gee," the young man said stiffly. This was no farmer, this; no artisan. There was a class of those who rode the big browns and carried lances such as this fellow had resting against the brown's flattened collar.

"I'm McGee."

"I'm Dain from First Tower. Ellai is dead. The heir wants you to come. Now."

She blinked in the mist, the tiny impact of rain on her face. "Did the heir say why?"

"She has First Tower now. She says you're to come. Now."

"I have to get a change of clothes."

The young man nodded, in that once and assured fashion the Cloudsiders had. That was permission. McGee collected her wits and dived back into the shelter, rummaged wildly, then thought and opened the safebox, her hands shaking.

Ellai dead, she wrote for the help when he should get back. *A messenger calling me to First Tower for an interview with Elai. I'm not threatened. I haven't tried refusing. I may be gone several days.*

She locked it back inside. She stuffed extra linens into

her pockets and a spare shirt into her coat above the belt.
She remembered to turn the heater off, and to put the lock
on the flimsy door.

The caliban squatted belly on the ground. The young
man held out his lance, indicating the foreleg. She was expected to climb aboard.

She went, having done this before, but not in a heavy
coat, but not after sixteen years. She was awkward and the
young man pulled her up into his lap by the coatcollar, like
so much baggage.

xxx

204 CR, day 34
Cloud River

The child had become a woman, darkhaired, sullen-
faced—sat in Ellai's chair in the center of the tower hall,
and Scar curled behind that chair like a humped brown hill,
curled his tail beside her feet and his head came round to
meet it from the other direction, so he could eye the
stranger and the movement in the hall.

Then the elation McGee had felt on the way was
dimmed. It had been dimming all the way into the settlement and reached its lowest ebb now, facing this new ruler
on the Cloud, this frowning stranger. Only the caliban Scar
gave her hope, that the head stayed low, that he turned his
head to look at her with one gold, round-pupilled eye and
had the collar-crest lifted no more than halfway. They were
surrounded by strangeness, with other calibans, with other
humans, many of the shave-headed kind, crouching close
beside calibans. And weapons. Those were there too, in the
hands of leather-clad men and women. Elai wore a robe,
dull red. Like the shave-skulls. She was thin as the shave-
skulls. A robe lay across her lap. Her hands were all bone.
Her face was hollowed, febrile.

And the child looked out at her from Elai's face, with
eyes cold as the calibans'.

"Elai," said McGee when the silence went on and on,
"there wasn't any other way for me to come. Or I would
have."

The sullenness darkened further. "Ellai is dead. Twig has swum to sea. I sent for you, MaGee."

"I'm glad you sent," she said, risking her death; and knew it.

For a moment everything was still. A gray moved, putting itself between them.

Scar lunged with a hiss like water on fire, jaws gaping, and seized the hapless gray, holding it, up on his own four legs, towering beside the chair. Thoughtfully he held it. It was stiff as something dead. He dropped it then. It bounced up on its legs and scurried its sinuous way to the shadows, where it turned and darted out its tongue, licking scaly jaws. Scar remained statue-like, towering, on his four bowed legs. The crest was up, and McGee's heart was hammering in her ears.

An ariel came wandering between Scar's thick-clawed feet, and set a stone between them, a single pebble. Scar ignored it.

"MaGee," said Elai, "what does it say?"

"That I should be careful."

Laughter then, laughter startling on that thin face, an echo of the child. "Yes. You should." It died then into a frown as if the laughter had been surprised out of her, but a trace of it remained, a liveliness in the eyes. Elai waved a thin arm at all about her. "Out! Out, now! Let me talk to this old friend."

They moved, some more reluctantly than others. Perhaps it was ominous that many of the calibans stayed. Silence fell in the retreat of steps down the well in the center of the floor, the shifting of scaly bodies. Scar continued to dominate the hall, still curled round the chair. But he settled, flicking his collar-crest, running his thick dark tongue round his jaws.

"Ellai is dead," said Elai again, with all that implied.

"So everything is changed."

Elai gathered herself up. The laprobe fell aside. She was stick-thin. She limped like an old woman in the few steps she took away from the chair. An ariel retreated from her feet. For a moment Elai gazed off into nothing, somewhere off into the shadows, and it was a deathshead that stared so, as if she had forgotten the focus of her thoughts, or gathered them from some far place.

"Sixteen years, MaGee."

"A long time for me too."

Elai turned and looked at her. "You look tired, MaGee."

The observation surprised her, coming from what Elai had become. As if a little weathering counted on her side, a fraying of herself in the sun and wind and mists. "Not used to riding," she said, turning it all away.

Elai stared, with an irony the child could never have achieved. It went to sour laughter. She walked over and patted Scar on his side. The lamplike eyes blinked, one and then the other.

"I'm Elai-eldest," she said, a hoarse, weary voice. "You mustn't forget that. If you forget that you might die, and I'd be sorry, MaGee."

"What do I call you?"

"Elai. Should that change?"

"I wouldn't know. Can I ask things?"

"Like what?"

Her pulse sped with fear. She thought about it a moment more, then shrugged. "Like if there's anything I can do to help you. Can I ask that?"

The stare was cold. Laughter came out, as suddenly as the first time. "Meaning can you notice what you see? No, MaGee my friend. You can not. My heir is six. My oldest. They have nearly killed me, those boys. The last died. Did you hear?"

"I heard. I didn't report it. I figured that Jin knows enough."

"Oh, he'll know, that one. The Calibans will say."

McGee looked at her. *Calibans,* she thought. Her skin felt cold, but she felt the heat in the room. Sweat ran at her temples. "Mind if I shed the jacket? Am I staying that long?"

"You're staying."

She started to unzip. She looked up again as the tone got through in its finality. "How long?"

Elai opened her hand, fingers stiff and wide, a deliberate, chilling gesture. "Did I teach you that one, MaGee?"

All stones dropped. An end of talk. "Look," McGee said. "You'd better listen. They'll want me back."

"Go down. They know a place for you. I told them."

"Elai, listen to me. There could be trouble over this. At

least let me send a message to them. Let one of your riders take it back to the hut. They'll look there. I don't mind staying. Look, I *want* to be here. But they have to know."

"Why? The stone towers aren't where you live."

"I work for them."

"You don't now. Go down, MaGee. You can't tell me no. I'm Eldest now. You have to remember that."

"I need things. Elai—"

Elai hissed between her teeth. Scar rose up to his full height.

"All right," McGee said. "I'm going down."

It was a small room on the outer face of the tower. It was even, McGee decided, more comfortable than the hut—less drafty, with opaque shutters of some dried membrane in woodset panes. They opened, giving a view of the settlement; and a draft, and McGee chose the warmth.

Dry, clay walls, formed by some logic that knew no straight lines; a sloping access that led to the hall, with a crook in it that served for privacy instead of a door; a box of sand for a chamberpot—she had asked those that brought her.

They would bring food, she decided. And water. She checked her pockets for the c-rations she always carried, about the fields, when a turned ankle could mean a slow trip home. There was that, if they forgot; but she kept it as an option.

Mostly she tucked herself up crosslegged on what must be a sleeping ledge, or a table, or whatever the inhabitant wanted it to be—tucked herself up in her coat and her good boots and was warm.

She had had to ask about the sand; she had no idea now whether she was to sit on the ledge or eat on it. She was the barbarian here, and knew it, asea in more waves than Elai had been that day, that sunny faraway day when Elai tried for islands and boundaries.

But she was free, that was what. Free. She had seen enough with her trained eye to sit and think about for days, for months; and facts poured about her, instead of the years' thin seepage of this and that detail. It was perhaps mad to be so well content. There was much to disturb her;

and disturb her it would, come dark, with a door that was only a crookedness in the hall, in a room already scored with caliban claws. A Tower shaped by calibans.

The room acquired its ariel while she sat. She was not surprised at that. One had come sometimes to the hut, as they came everywhere outside the wire, insolent and frivolous.

This one dived out and in a little time a larger visitor came, a gray, putting his blunt head carefully around the bend of the access way, a creature twice man-sized. It came serpentining its furtive way up to look at her.

Browns, next, McGee thought, staying very still and tucked up as she was. *O Elai, you're cruel. Or aren't we—who take our machines for granted?*

It opened its jaws and deposited a stone on the floor, wet and shiny. It sat there contentedly, having done that.

The grays had no sense, Elai had told her once. It stayed there a while and then forgot or lost interest or had something else to do: it turned about and left with a whisk of its dragon tail.

The stone stayed. Like a gift. Or a barrier. She was not sure.

She heard someone or something in the doorway, a faint sound. Perhaps the caliban had set itself there. Perhaps it was something else. She did not go to see.

But the slithering was still outside when they brought her food, a plate of boiled fish and a slice of something that proved to be, mush; and water to drink. Two old women brought these things. McGee nodded courteously to them and set the bowls beside her on the shelf.

No deference. Nothing cowed about these two sharp-eyed old women. They looked at her with quick narrow glances and left, barefoot padding down the slope and out the crook of the entry in the gathering dark.

McGee ate and drank. The light faded rapidly once it had begun to go. After that she sat in her corner of the dark and listened to strange movings and slitherings that were part of the tower.

She kept telling herself that should some dragon come upon her in the dark, should some monster come through the doorway and nudge her with its jaws—that she should take it calmly, that Elai ruled here; and Scar; and no caliban would harm Elai's guest.

If that was what she was.

* * *

"Good morning," said Elai, when Elai got around to her again, on the grayly-sunlit crest of First Tower, on its flat roof beneath which stretched the Cloud, lost in light mist, the gardens, the fields, the fisher-digs with their odd-shaped windows and bladder-panes shut against the chill. People and calibans came and went down at the base. McGee looked over, and beyond, at towers rising ghostlike out of the mist. And she delayed greeting Elai just long enough.

"Good morning," she said as she would say long ago on the shore, when she had been put to waiting, or when child-Elai had put her off somehow—a lift of the brow and an almost-smile that said: my patience has limits too. Perhaps to vex Elai risked her life. Perhaps, as with Jin, it was a risk not to risk it. She saw amusement and pleasure in Elai's face, and mutual warning, the way it had always been. "Where's Scar?" McGee asked.

"Fishing, maybe."

"You don't go to the sea nowadays."

"No." For the moment there was a wistful look on the thin, fragile face.

"Or build boats."

"Maybe." Elai's head lifted. Her lips set. "They think I'll die, MaGee."

"Who?"

Elai reached out her hand, openfingered, gesturing at all her world.

"Why did you send for me?" McGee asked.

Elai did not answer at once. She turned and gazed at an ariel which had clambered up onto the waisthigh wall. "Paeia my cousin—she's got Second Tower; next is Taem's line over at the New Tower. My heir's six. That Jin on Styxside—he'll come here."

"You're talking about who comes after you."

Elai turned dark eyes on her, deepset and sullen. "You starmen, you know a lot. Lot of things. Maybe you help me stay alive. Maybe we just talk. I liked that. The boats. Now I could do them. Real ones. But who would go in them? Who would? *They* never talked to MaGee. But now you're here. So my people can look at you and *think*, MaGee."

McGee stood staring at her, remembering the child—

every time she looked at her, remembering the child, and it seemed there was sand in all directions, and sea and sky and sun, not the fog, not this tired, hurt woman less than half her age.

"I'll get things," she said, deciding things, deciding once for all. "You let me send word to the base and I'll get what I can. Everything they've given the Styxsiders. That, for a start."

Elai's face never changed. It seemed to have forgotten how. She turned and stroked the ariel, which flicked its collar fringes and showed them an eye like a green jewel, unwinking.

"Yes," Elai said.

xxxi

204 CR, day 41
Base Director's Office

"Dr. Genley's here," the secretary said through the intercom, and the Director frowned and pushed the button. "Send him in," the Director said. He leaned back in his chair. Rain pattered against the window in vengeful spats, carried on the wind that whipped between the concrete towers. Genley had done some travelling to have gotten here this fast, from Styxside. But it was that kind of news.

Genley came in, a different man than he had sent out. The Director stopped in mid-rock of his chair and resumed the minute rocking again, facing this huge, rawboned man in native leather, with hair gone long and beard ragged and lines windgraven into his face.

"Came to talk about McGee," Genley said.

"I gathered that."

"She's in trouble. They're crazy down on Cloudside."

"McGee left a note." The Director rocked forward and keyed the fax up on the screen.

"I heard." Genley no more than glanced at it.

"Have the Styxsiders heard about it?"

"They got word. Someone got to them. Com wasn't any faster at it."

"You mean they found it out from some other source."

"They know what goes on at the Cloud. I've reported that before." Genley shifted on his feet, glanced toward a chair.

"Sit down, will you? Want something hot to drink?"

"Like it, yes. Haven't stopped moving since last night."

"Tyler." The Director punched the button. "Two coffees." He rocked back and looked at Genley. "It seems to be a new situation down there. This ruler of the Cloud Towers is apparently well-disposed to McGee. And this office isn't disposed to risk disturbing that."

Genley's face was flushed. Perhaps it was the haste with which he had come. "She needs communications down there."

"We'll be considering that."

"Maybe some backup. Four or five staff to go in there with her."

"If feasible."

"I have to state my opposition to sending McGee in there without any help. I have experienced staff. Maybe they wouldn't be accepted down there. But someone else ought to be in there."

"Do I hear overtones in that?"

"Are we on the record?"

"Not for the moment."

"I'm not sure McGee's stable enough to be in there alone. I'm not sure anyone is."

"What does that mean?"

"It means there are times that my staff and I have to get together and remind ourselves where we came from. And I don't think McGee has the toughness to stand up to them alone. Mentally. It gets to you. It will. You have to start out tough and stay that way. The Weirds—you've read my report on the Weirds. . . ."

"Yes."

"That's how strange human beings can get, living next to calibans. And I'm afraid McGee's primed to slip right over into it. She's wanted this too long, too badly. I'm afraid she's the worst candidate in the world to be sitting where she is."

The Director considered the man, the leather, the stone ornaments, the unruly hair and beard. Genley brought a smell with him, not an unwashed smell, but something of earth and dry muskiness. Woodsmoke. Something else he could not put a name to. "Going native, you mean."

"I think she went, as far as she knew how, years ago. I mean, no kid of her own, a woman, after all—Finding that kid on the beach. You know how that could be."

The Director looked at Genley narrowly, at the clothes, the man. "You mean to say some people might find things they wanted outside the wire, mightn't they? Something—psychologically needful."

For some reason the ruddiness of Genley's scowling face deepened.

"I haven't any reason," the Director said, "to question McGee's professional motives. I know you and McGee have had your problems. I'll trust you to keep them to a minimum. Particularly under the circumstances. And I won't remind you how this office would view any leak of information on the Cloud to Styxside—and vice versa."

The red was quite decisive now. It was rage. "I'll trust that warning will likewise be transmitted to McGee. I can tell you—this Elai is understood as trouble."

"On Styxside."

"On Styxside."

"McGee reports Elai's health as fragile. This woman doesn't sound like a threat."

Genley's lips compacted, worked a moment. "She's got a mean caliban."

"What's that mean?"

Genley thought about the answer. The Director watched him. "It's a perception the natives have; I've mentioned this before in the reports— That the social position of humans relates to caliban dominance. Those that have the meanest and the toughest stand highest."

"Where do you stand? Where are you without one? What's it mean, if the calibans aren't together to fight it out."

"It affects attitude. That woman down on the Cloud has an exaggerated idea of herself, that Elai inherited this caliban when she was young—that's what they say."

"So they expect she'll move on them."

"They reckon she'll push. One way or the other."

"Tell me, you're not backing McGee's assertions, are you, that we're dealing with calibans as well as humans out there."

"No." That answer was firm. "Absolutely not. Except as the Cloudsiders may do some kind of augury whereby they *think* the calibans have an opinion. The old Romans, they used to plan their days by the behavior of geese. The flight of birds. Must have worked at least as well as calibans. They got by."

"Different brain size, geese and calibans."

"Biologists can argue that point. Look at the Weirds. There's a good example of humans that talk to calibans. They crawl around underground, let the gray fishers feed them, don't talk, don't interact with the rest of humankind except to take orders and shove dirt around. You want the caliban vote, ask a Weird and see if you get any answer. Sir. McGee will learn that pretty quick if she wants to do some honest work out there."

"I'm aware of your differences of opinion. Is it possible this is a difference of the cultures you're observing?"

"I doubt it."

"But you don't draw conclusions."

"Absolutely not. I'm simply waiting for data out of McGee. And in sixteen years, there's been nothing new out of her but speculation. Maybe this will prove matters once for all. But for the record I want to caution the committee that this move is very serious—that with observers inside both cultures, we could embroil ourselves in local problems. Or worsen them. Or push these two cultures into conflict. It's waiting to happen."

"Because of a caliban. Because it's as you say . . . mean."

"It means this Elai has a higher status than her situation warrants. That she has a higher confidence than it warrants. She didn't hesitate to snatch McGee in defiance of the Base. That's worth thinking on."

"It still sounds very much like McGee's theories."

"There's a critical difference. McGee thinks the calibans decide. They don't. It's human ambition based on status. And this Elai has a lot of status. They might miscalculate—psychological strength for military strength. A lot of people could die over that mistake. I'm talking about McGee's precious Cloudsiders. And the Styx. They've got too much going to waste it all in war."

"Maybe it wouldn't be miscalculation. On those terms you cite."

"We've got roads built; agriculture increased. Unification of the Towers. We could lose a hundred years in a war right now."

"A hundred years down whose course?"

Genley gave him a puzzled look, and the look became a frown.

"Maybe," the Director said, "the calibans won't permit a war. Or maybe they fight them for their own reasons. And humans just go along with it."

"That's more radical than McGee's hypothesis. Sir."

"One just thinks—sitting here behind the wire. No matter. We play it cautiously. Since McGee has the chance she can use it."

"Or maybe they can use McGee. That's what Jin thinks about it. I'm sure of that."

"Well," the Director said, "we just let it go along for now. Frankly, I don't see much else that we could do about it, do you?"

xxxii

204 CR, day 42
Message, E. McGee to Base
Couriered by Dain of the Flanahan line to the Wire
by order of Elai Eldest

Wish to report I am safe and well and have persuaded the new ruler of the Cloud Towers to have this couriered: to satisfy Security, my id number is 8097-989 and the holo on your desk is a Terran rose, so you'll know this is all my idea.

Ellai has been succeeded peacefully at her death by Elai, her daughter and designated heir. Elai took advantage of her accession to power over the Cloud to have one of her riders escort me to the Towers. I have been treated with all courtesy and am presently comfortable and content in my situation. This is a rare opportunity with the Cloud Towers and presages an era in which I believe the Cloud may be as productive in research as the Styx has been in recent years. I am not eager to break my stay here at this stage in which I believe much good can be accomplished in stabilizing mission relations with the Cloud.

I will need some equipment and supplies. Elai has agreed to this, and will send to my hut in seven days to collect the supplies which I hope will be there.

Please send:

Writing materials

All such operations apparatus as has been cleared for operation outside the wire, incl. recorder, etc.

4 changes clothing

pair boots

hygiene field kit (forgot mine)

soap!

field medical kit

Also and most important, 1 case (*case!*) broad spectrum antibiotics, class A, field; 1 case vitamin and mineral supplement; 1 case dietary supplement.

I realize this quantity is unusual, but due to my supply resting on local transport, and due to the possibility of being isolated from supply by circumstance beyond my prediction, I feel this request is only prudent on my part and of utmost urgency, due to close contact with unaccustomed population and drinking and eating unaccustomed food: as approved for Styx mission.

Thank you.

E. McGee

204 CR, day 42
Base Director's Office

"I am going to approve this," the Director said to the secretary.

"Sir," the secretary said, tight-lipped. "Sir, this is talking about cases. I checked with supply. A *case* of antibiotics is one thousand 50 cc units. A box is one hundred. Dr. McGee undoubtedly meant—"

"Approved," the Director said, "just as ordered. Case lots."

"Yes, sir," the secretary said, with thoughts passing behind his eyes.

"Any word from Dr. Genley?"

"Message." The secretary keyed it up. "Non-urgent. He's gone back to the field."

"He did receive the McGee transcript."

The secretary hit more keys. "Oh, yes. He did get that copy. Was that a mistake? It wasn't coded no-dispersal."

"No. It wasn't a mistake. I want to be informed when anything comes in from outside. Or when any native comes to the wire. Personally. No matter what hour."

"Yes, sir."

"That load for McGee's going to take a light transport. Make the order out. I'll sign it."

"What about Smith?"

"Smith."

"McGee's assistant. Does Smith go out again? He's asking."

"Does he want to go out?"

"He's suggested he wants someone with him if he does."

"Exactly what is he requesting?"

"Security. And supplies." The secretary keyed up the request. "He wants a whole list of things."

"Never mind Smith. Just put one of our Security people out there. I'll sign that too. Someone who's been outside the wire. But not anyone who's worked in the Styx regions. They might be known. If information passes. Check all past assignments. I don't want any nervous people out there. I don't want an incident."

204 CR, day 42
Memo, Base Director to Committee Member

I am approving new operations in the Cloud River area. New and promising contacts have opened. We are presented the opportunity to secure comparative data.

204 CR, day 42
Message, Base Director to E. McGee, in field
Sent in writing with supplies.

I am backing you on this. Hope that your health improves. Please remain in close contact.

xxxiii

204 CR, day 200
Cloud Towers

Elai laughed, laughed aloud, and it startled calibans, who shifted nervously; but not Scar, who merely shut his eyes and kept taking in the sun, there upon the roof of First Tower, with McGee, in the warm tail of summer days. And McGee went on telling her heir how his mother had tried to swim to the islands one day some years ago. Young Din's eyes achieved amazement. He looked at his mother to see whether this were true, while his five-year-old sib played his silent games, put and take with ariels—silent, Taem was; he would always be one of the silent ones, lost to the line of Flanahans, but not without his use. There was three-year-old Cloud, who was noisy in his wandering about, who played wicked games, disrupting his brother Taem's Patterns. But ariels retrieved his thefts, and nurses interfered when he grew too persistent.

There were the calibans, besides Scar: a half grown brown named Twostone, that was the heir's; and a smaller, runt brown that had attached itself to Cloud. But Taem had no caliban in particular, owned nothing in particular. Taem was Taem. He never spoke, except with the stones, at which he had precocious skill.

"One in a house," Elai had said of Taem, "that's fine. I can stand that."

"What if he were the only child?" McGee had asked.

"Usually it's the youngers that go," Elai had said. "I thought Cloud would go since Taem had. But I lost Marik in Cloud's first year. Maybe that weighed some on Cloud."

McGee had doubted this, but she listened to it all the same. Perhaps she had some influence on Din, who had begun to hang on her more than on his nurses. Din liked the tales she told.

"Did you?" Din asked now. "Did you swim out there?"

Elai pulled up her robe and showed the old scar. "That's why I don't walk so fast, young one. Would have bled everything I had onto that beach if MaGee hadn't stopped the blood."

"But what's out there in the sea?" The young eyes were dusky like Elai's, roiled with thoughts. Din's brows were knit.

"Maybe," McGee said, "things you haven't seen."

"Tell me!" Din said. His caliban came awake at that tone, came up on its legs. Scar hissed, a lazy warning.

"That's enough stories," Elai said. "Some things a boy has no need to know."

"Maybe," said McGee, "tomorrow. Maybe."

"Go away," said Elai. "I'm tired of boys."

Din scowled. His caliban was still up and darting with its tongue, testing the air for enemies.

"Take your brothers with you," said Elai. "Hey!"

Nurses came, the two old women, fierce and silent, half Weirds themselves. There was no escape for the boys. Rowdiness and loud voices near Scar were not wise. So they went away.

And Elai kept sitting in the sun, caliban-like, basking on the ledge against the wall. All about the towers the fields were golding. Between them, like skirts, gardens remained green atop the odd mound-houses of the fishers and workers; weirds sat on riverside like lopsided cages, and fish hung drying beside rows and rows of drying washing and drying fisher-ropes and nets.

McGee smiled in the tight, quiet way of Tower-folk, minor triumph. She knew what she did. Elai was well-pleased, if one knew how to read Tower-folk gestures. Her heir had come from silence to questions, from sullen disdain to a hurting need to know; and from disdain of Elai to—perhaps a curiosity and a new reckoning what his mother was; for quite unexpectedly since spring Elai had begun to flourish like a hewn tree budding, had put on weight: muscle was in the way Elai moved now. It might have been the exercises, the antibiotics against persistent lowgrade fever, the vitamins and trace-minerals. McGee herself was not sure; but there were differences in diet on the Cloud, and she hammered them home to Elai.

"Fish guts," Elai had said in disgust.

"Listen to me," McGee had said. "Styxsiders eat grays. They get it that way. Grays eat all the fish. Fish eat other fish.

Whole. You won't eat grays, so you'll have to do better with the fish. Net the little ones. Smoke them. They're not bad."

"I like the pills fine," Elai said.

"Haven't enough for everyone," said McGee. "Want healthy people?"

So the nets. And soups and such. And fish dried against the winter-time when fishing was scant.

Interference, they would call it behind the Wire.

xxxiv

Notes, coded journal Dr. E. McGee

. . . So I ask the boy questions. I tell him stories. The sullenness is gone. Used to look at me like I was something too vile to think on. Used to look at his mother the same way, but there's respect when he talks to her now.

What I find here between Elai and her sons is strange. We talk in cultural terms about maternal instinct. It's different here. I don't say Elai doesn't have any feeling for her sons. She talks with some disturbance of losing one baby, but I draw no conclusions whether the distress is at the discomfort without reward, at the failure, at some diminution of her self-respect—or whether it's what we take for granted is universal in human mothers.

Here is an instance where we have adjusted data to fit the desire, since it is ourselves we measure. The human species is full of examples of motherhood without feeling. Can a researcher impugn motherhood? Or have we been wrong because it was as a species safer to construct this fantasy?

How many such constructs has the species made?

Or is it the attribute of an advanced mind, to make such constructs of an abstract nature in its folklore when its genetic heritage doesn't contain the answer? Folklore as an impermanent quasi-genetics? Do all advanced species do such things? No. Not necessarily.

Or I am wrong in what I see.

They are Union; they came out of labs.

Two hundred years ago. There's been a lot of babies born since then.

Elai's sons had different fathers. Some Cloud Tower folk pair for what seems permanence. Most don't. I asked Elai if she chose the fathers. "Of course," she said. "One was Din, one was Cloud, one was Taem. And Marik."

So the boys have the father's name. I haven't met the mates. Or we haven't been introduced. Elai said something that shed some light on it: about Taem: "That man's from New Tower. Scar and that caliban were trouble; he ran. Got rid of that one."

"Killed him?" I asked, not sure whether she was talking about the caliban or the man.

"No," she said, and I never did find out which one.

But Taem rules what they call the New Tower over by the sea. And I think it's the same Taem. Relations seem cordial at least at a distance.

I say Elai has no motherhood. I found the relationship between herself and her sons chilling, like a rivalry, one in which the dominancy of the calibans seemed to have some bearing; and Taem's lack of one, his silence—Elai's resignation, no, her acceptance of his condition. (Humans bearing children to give to calibans?)

But today I picked up something I hadn't realized: that Elai treats her heir as an adult. Cloud can run about being a baby; Weirds take care of him, and those two old women. Taem—no one knows what Taem needs, but the Weirds see he gets it, I suppose. Only this six year old is no child. God help us, I haven't seen a child in twenty years excepting natives, but that's no six year old of any mindset I'm used to.

He's like Elai was, quiet, grownup-like.

Is even childhood one of our illusions? Or is this forced adulthood what's been done to us out here?

Us. Humans. They are still human; their genes say so.

But how much do genes tell us and how much is in our culture, that precious package we brought from old Earth?

What will we become?

Or what have they already begun to be?

They look like us. But this researcher is losing perspective. I keep sending reassurances to Base. That's all I know to do.

I think they accept me. As what, I'm far from sure.

XXXV

204 CR, day 232
Cloud Towers

Ma-Gee, they called her in the camp. A woman had come
from another tower carrying a river-smoothed stone the
size of those only the big browns moved, and laid it at
McGee's feet, in the gathering of First Tower.

"What does that mean?" McGee had asked Elai
afterward.

"Nest-stone," Elai had said. "Brings warmth from the
sun. Baby-gift. That's thanks."

"What do I do?" McGee had asked.

"Nothing," Elai said. "No, let it be. Some caliban will
take it when it wants one."

Notes, coded journal Dr. E. McGee

Every time I think I understand they do something I
can't figure.

A woman dropped a stone at my feet. It was warm from
the sun. Calibans do that to hatch the eggs. It represented
a baby somehow, that was important to her. She didn't
cry. Cloud River folk don't, that I've never seen. But she
was very intense about what she did. I think she gave up
status doing it.

Mother love?

Do they love?

How do I end up asking such a question? Sometimes I
know the answer. Sometimes I don't.

Elai has some feeling for me. My friend, she says. We
talk—we talk a great deal. She listens to me. Maybe it was
her health that made her what I saw, that separated her
from her sons.

The calibans swim to sea when their people die. One
didn't. It died on the shore today. People came and
skinned it. Other calibans ate it. What it died of I don't
know.

It took all day to disappear. The people collected the

bones. They make things out of bone. It's their substitute for metal. They consider it precious as we might value gold. They're always carved things, things to wear. They have wood for other things. A few really old iron blades: they take care of those. But they have caliban bone for treasure.

They have native fiber for cloth; but leather is precious as the bone. Only riders have all leather clothes. They get patched. They don't ever throw them away, I'd guess. It's like the bone. A treasure. This colony was set where it had no metals, had no domestic animals, no resources except their neighbors. I think they would choose another way if they had one. But they do what they can. They won't hunt; not calibans, at least, and there's nothing else to hunt on land.

They're digging on the bank again. The calibans are. Across the river. Elai says they may have some new tower in mind, but that it looks to her like more burrows.

"What's the difference?" I asked.

But Elai wouldn't say.

I'm sure orbiting survey has picked it up. I've put it in my report as indeterminate construction. They'll want some interpretation.

I'm not sure Elai knows.

xxxvi

204 CR, day 290
Cloud Towers

On the summit of First Tower, under a dying summer sun:

"MaGee, what is it like to fly?"

Elai asked questions again, questions, and questions. But now she thought of ships.

"Like sitting on something that shakes," McGee said. "You weigh a little more than usual sometimes, sometimes less: it makes your stomach feel like it's floating. But up there the river would look like a thread. The sea looks flat, all smoothed out and shining like the river at dawn; the

mountains look like someone dropped a wrinkled cloth; the
forests like waterweed."

Elai's eyes rested on hers. That spark was back behind
them, that thing that adulthood had crushed. Sadness then.
"I won't ever see these things," she said.

"I haven't," McGee said, "in a good many years. Maybe
I won't again. I don't think so."

For a long while Elai said nothing. The frown deepened
moment by moment. "There is a Wire in the sky."

"No."

"So you could go when you like."

McGee thought about that one, not sure where it led.

"Could we?" Elai asked. "We say that the Wire keeps
your stone towers safe. But is that so, MaGee? The ships
come and go from inside there to outside. I think that Wire
keeps us away from ships. My boats, MaGee, what could
they find, but places like this one? They couldn't find where
we came from. We'd just go back and forth, back and forth,
on rivers and on seas, and find more islands. But we couldn't
go up. You watch us from the sky. How small, you say. How
small. What did we do, MaGee, to be shut away?"

McGee's heart was beating very fast. "Nothing. You did
nothing. How do you know all this, Elai? Did you figure
it?"

"Books," Elai said finally. "Old books."

"Could I," asked McGee, and her heart was going faster
still, "could I see these books?"

Elai thought about it and looked at her very closely.
"You think something might be important to you in these
books? But you know where we came from. You know
everything there is to know—don't you, MaGee?"

"I know the outside. Not the inside. Not things I'd like
to know."

"Like what?"

"Calibans. Like how you know what they're saying."

"Books won't tell you that. Books tell about us, where
the lines started. How we got to the Cloud and how it was
then. How the Styxsiders began."

"How did they?"

Elai thought again, frowning, opened her hand palm up.
"Can't say it so you'd understand. It's Patterns."

Notes, coded journal Dr. E. McGee

There are a thousand gestures that have meaning among Cloud River folk, gestures which I think are the same for Styxside. Often they actually use stones, which some folk carry in their pockets or in small bags; but particularly the riders have a way of expressing themselves in sign, pretending the fingers are dropping pebbles. Or picking them up. There's no alphabetical system in this. The signs are true signs, having a whole meaning in the motion.

But they do write. Counting both sign and writing there's considerable education among these people, no mean feat considering the diversity of the systems.

Concerning communication with the calibans, there are some concepts that pass back and forth. A caliban can "ask" a human a direction and basic intentions. I can get old Scar to respond to me as far as *I want to go up*, meaning to the roof. Or down.

There are the Weirds. There are always the Weirds. They care for the children and they function somewhere between priesthood and janitorial duties. They keep the burrows clean. The calibans seem to take pleasure in being touched by them. Most Weirds are thin: high activity, a diet more of fish and less of grain, a lack of sunlight. But in general they seem healthy physically. In any human society off Gehenna their sanity would be in question. It is uncertain whether this is a mental aberration peculiar to the culture, as certain human cultures historically have spawned certain disorders with more frequency than others, or come up with completely unique maladies.

Hypothesis: this is a mental disorder uniquely produced by Gehennan culture with its reliance on calibans. Humans identify completely with the creatures on whom all humans rely for survival, and receive a certain special status which confirms them in their state.

Hypothesis: this is a specialized and successful adaptation of humankind to Gehenna, growing out of the azi culture which was left here in ignorance.

Hypothesis: Weirds *can* talk to calibans.

xxxvii

204 CR, day 293
Cloud Towers, the top of First Tower

"You mean you can't say it in words."

"It's not a word thing." Elai laughed strangely and made a scattering gesture. "Oh, MaGee, I could tell it to Din and he'd know. I can't figure how to do it."

"Teach me to Pattern."

"Teach you."

"At least as much as the boy knows."

"So you tell the stone towers? So they know if we got underneath the Wire? There was a time the towers fell. More than once. There was a time the whole Base sank in. We remember too." Scar had stirred, putting himself between them and the ariel, which cleared the wall in a great hurry. Elai scratched the scaly jaw, looked at her beneath her brows. "They're building them a new tower this year, the Styxsiders, closer to the Wire."

"You think the Base is in danger?"

"Styx is trouble. Always is. You tell the stone towers that with your com." She nodded toward the river, up it, toward the forested horizon. "Our riders move up there. They kill a few this year, I think. Maybe next. That's in the Patterns."

"How?" McGee asked. "Elai, how do you mean—in the Patterns?"

Elai stretched out her hand, swept it at all the horizon. "You write on little things. Calibans, they write large, they write mountains and hills and the way things move."

A chill was up McGee's back. "Teach me," she said again. "Teach me."

Elai stroked Scar's jaw again, thoughts passing behind her eyes. "Calibans could make one mouthful of you."

"Human beings?"

"Been known. I send you down with them—you could be in bad trouble."

"I didn't ask to go anywhere with calibans. I asked you to teach me. Yourself."

"I've showed you all the things I can show. The things you want, MaGee—you got to go down to them. You can talk and talk to me; I can show you *up* and *down* and *stop* and such. But you really want to talk the Patterns, you got to talk to *him*." One vast eye stared at her, gold and narrow-pupilled in the light, a round of iris bigger than the sun. Scar was looking at her, sidelong, in his way.

"All right," McGee said, scared enough to fall down where she was, but she put her hands in her pockets and looked casual as she could. "They smell fear?"

There was humor in Elai's eyes, but it was Elai-Eldest's face, implacable. "You go down," Elai said. "You go down and down as far as you can. I think Scar will go. I could be wrong."

"How long will I be there? What will I eat?"

"They'll tell you that. There'll be the Weirds. They'll take care of you. Be a child again, MaGee."

204 CR, day 203

Message, E. McGee to Base Director, transmitted from field

Expect to be out of touch for a number of days due to rare study opportunity.

Notes, coded journal Dr. E. McGee

I made a tentative trip down to the depths. It is, predictably, dark down there. It's full of calibans and Weirds, either one of which makes me nervous. No. I'm scared. I think— personally afraid in a way I've never been afraid of anything. Not even dying. This is being alone with the utterly alien. Vulnerable to it. Isn't that an odd thing for a xenologist to fear most in all the world? Maybe that's why I had to go into this work. Or why I got myself into this. Like climbing mountains. Because it's there. Because I have to know. Maybe that has to do with fear.

Or craziness.

I think they would let me go if I asked. At least back

upstairs. But I've got myself into one. Elai would say she told me so; but this is a thing—I don't think there's any going back from this, having asked for this chance. I can't just be an outsider now. I just closed the door to that. If I go running now—it'll be McGee, who failed. McGee, who was afraid. It would mark what Elai is, and where I can't reach her, and I'd live here as something neither fish nor fowl.

So I don't see anything else to do.

xxxviii

?
Cloud Tower: the lower section

There was food. McGee went to it by the smell, in the dark, not needing the calibans to guide her. But one was there. She had touched it, knew by the size, guessed by the texture of the skin that it was one of the grays.

Shepherds, she thought of them. She had been terrified at first, of the claws, the hard, bony jaws, the sinuous force of them. They had knocked her down, repeatedly, until she learned to use her ears.

There were other things in the dark: ariels. They skittered here and there and of them she had never been afraid, had kept them close when she could, because they seemed friendly.

There was a big brown hereabouts; she had felt the smoothness on his side. It was Scar, and Elai had lent him. She was grateful, and stayed close to him when she could.

Even of the Weirds she had lost her awe. They were strange, but gentle, and touched her with their spidery fingers, embraced her, held her when she was most afraid.

Once in this fathomless dark, in this waking sleep, she had been intimate with one, and more than once: that was the thing that she had most trouble to reckon with, that the thing she had dreaded most had happened, and that she had (perhaps) been the aggressor in it, having forgotten all she was, with some faceless man, a Weird, a voiceless priest of calibans.

She had lain listless for a long time after, for she had lost her objectivity, and she was compassless in more than the robbery of her senses.

Then: *McGee*, she thought, *you did that. That was you. Not their fault. What if it had been? Get up, McGee.*

And in one part of her mind: *He'll know me, outside this place. But I won't know him.*

And in another: *You don't care, McGee. This is real. The dark. This place. It's a womb for growing in.*

So grow, McGee.

She scrambled along the earthen walls, found the food left for her and ate, raw fish, which had become a neutral taste to her, something she had learned to abide. Something light skittered over her knees and she knew it was an ariel begging scraps. She gave it the head and bit by bit, the offal and the bones.

God knows what disease I'll take, the civilized part of her had thought, of muddy hands and raw fish. *I'm stronger than I thought*, she reckoned now. She had not reckoned a great deal about herself lately, here in the dark. *I'm wiser than I was.*

The ariel slithered away with a flick of its tail. That presaged something.

A gray came then. She heard it moving. She drew to the side of the passage in case it wanted through. It arrived with a whispering of its leathery hide against the earth, a caliban in quiet approach. It nosed at her; she patted the huge head and it kept nudging. *Move, move.* So she must.

She went with it, this caliban-shepherd, up and up.

This was different. There had been no such ascent in her other wanderings. They were going out to the light. *Have I failed?* she wondered. *Am I being turned out?* But no Weird had tutored her, none had been near her in—she had lost track of the time.

Daylight was ahead, a round source of sun. She went more slowly now, to accustom her eyes, and the gray went before her, a sinuous shape moving like a shadow into what proved twilight, a riot of color in the sky.

But we have left the Towers, McGee thought, rubbing at her eyes. The river was before her. Somehow they had come out by the river, where caliban mounds were, beside the fisher nets.

I should find Elai, call the Base. How many days?

Something overshadowed her, on the ridge. She looked about, blinking in the light, with tears running down her face. It was a great brown.

Her gray had stayed. It offered her a stone, laying it near. She saw a nest of ariels, a dozen dragon-shapes curled up in a niche in the bank, where stones had been laid. It was a strange moment, a stillness in the air. "Here I am," she said, and the sound of her own voice dismayed her, who had not heard a voice in days. It intruded on the stillness.

An ariel wriggled out and offered her a stone. It stayed, flicking collar fringes, lifting its tiny spines.

She, squatted, took the stone and laid it down again.

It brought another, manic in its haste.

xxxix

204 CR, day 300
Message, R. Genley from transStyx, to Base Director's office.

I am not receiving McGee's regular reports. Should I come in?

Message, Base Director to R. Genley

Negative. Dr. McGee is still on special assignment.

Memo, Base Director to Security Chief

Refer all inquiries about Dr. McGee to me.
I am more than a little concerned about this prolonged silence from McGee. Prepare a list of options in this case.

Message, Base Director to Gehenna Station.

Request close surveillance of the Cloud River settlement. Relay materials to this office . . .

transStyx: Green Tower

"My father," Jin said, in the sunlight, in the winter sun, when the wide fields of Green Tower lay plowed and vacant. Forest stretched about them to the east, the marsh to the west. The wind lifted Jin's dark hair, blew it in webs; the light shone on him, on Thorn, lazy beside the downward access. "My father." His voice was low and warm and his hand that had rested on the walls rested on Genley's shoulder, drew him close, faced him outward as he pointed, a sweep about the land. "This is mine. This is mine. All the fields. All the people. All they make. And do you know, my father, when I took it into my hands I had one tower. This one. Look at it now. *Look*, Gen-ley. Tell me what you see."

There was a craziness in Jin sometimes. Jin played on its uncertainties, unnerved some men. Genley looked on him with one brow arched, daring to dare him back.

"Would you think," Jin said, "that a man has tried to kill me today?"

It was not a joke. Genley saw that and the humor fell from his face. "When? Who?"

"Mes Younger sent this man. This was a mistake. Mes will learn." Jin set both his hands on the rim of the wall, fists clenched. "It's this woman, Gen-ley. This woman."

"Elai."

"*MaGee.*" Jin rounded on him, looked up at him, his face flushed with rage. "This conniving of women. This thing goes on. Jin is a fool, they say; he lets the starmen play with him. He listens to them while they talk to this Elai and this Elai learns anything she wants from MaGee. And if Jin is a fool, then fools can try him, can't they?"

Genley took in his breath. "I've warned Base about this."

"They don't listen to you."

"I'll file a complaint with them if you've got something definite I can say to them. I'll make them understand."

Jin stared up at him, a shorter man. His veins swelled; his nostrils were white. "What would they like to hear?"

"What she's doing. They don't know where she is right now. Do you?"

"They don't know where she is. *She's with Elai.* That's where she is."

"Tell me what she's doing and I'll tell them."

"No!" Jin flung his arm in a gesture half a blow, strode off toward Thorn. The caliban had risen, his collar erect. Jin turned back again, thrust out his arm. "No more com, Genley. *My father,* who gives me advice. I'm sending you to Parm. You. This Mannin, this Kim."

"Let's talk about this."

"No talk." He flung the arm northward, an extravagant gesture. "I'm going north to kill this man. This man who thinks I'm a fool. You go to Parm Tower. You think, you *think,* Genley, what this woman costs."

He disappeared down the access. Thorn delayed, a cold caliban eye turned to the object of the anger, then whipped after Jin.

Genley stood there drawing deep breaths, one after the other.

xl

**204 CR, day 321
Cloud Towers**

"MaGee," said Elai.

The starman looked at her, met her eyes, and Elai felt the stillness there. The stillness spread over all the room and into her bones. Her people were there. There were calibans. They brought MaGee to her, this thin, hard stranger with loose, tangled hair, who wore robes and not the clothes she had worn, who could have worn nothing and lost none of that force she had.

But MaGee was not MaGee of the seashore, of the summer; and she was not the child.

"Go," Elai said, to the roomful of her people. "All but MaGee. Go."

They went, quietly, excepting Din.

"Out," said Elai, "boy."

Din went out. His caliban followed. Only Scar remained. And the grays.

"A man came from behind the Wire," said Elai. "Four days ago. We sent him away. He asked how you were."

"I'll have to call the Base," MaGee said.

"And tell them about calibans?"

MaGee was silent a long while. It became clear she would not answer. Elai opened her hand, dismissing the matter, trusting the silence more than assurances.

"No words," said MaGee finally, in a hoarse, strange voice. "You knew that."

Elai gestured yes, a steadiness of the eyes.

And MaGee picked it up. Every tiny movement. Or at least—enough of them.

"I want to go back to my room," MaGee said. "There's too much here."

Go, Elai signed in mercy. In tenderness. MaGee left, quietly, alone.

204 CR, day 323
Message, E. McGee to Base Director

Call off the dogs. Reports of my death greatly exaggerated. Am writing report on data. Will transmit when complete.

204 CR, day 323
Message, Base Director to E. McGee

Come in at once with full accounting.

204 CR, day 323
Message, E. McGee to Base Director

Will transmit when report is complete.

204 CR, day 326
Notes, coded journal Dr. E. McGee

I've had trouble starting this again. I'm not the same. I know that. I know—

xli

204 CR, day 328
Cloud Tower

Security had sent him. Kiley. A decent man. McGee had

heard about him, or at least that something was astir, and then that it was Outsider; and when she heard that she knew.

She had put on her Outsider-clothes. Cut her hair. Perfumed herself with Outsider-smells. She went there, to the hall, where the riders would bring the Outsider.

"Kiley," she said, when Elai said nothing to this intruder.

He was one of the old hands. Stable. His eyes kept measuring everything because that was the way he was trained. He would know when someone was measuring him.

"Good to see you, doctor," Kiley said. "The Director'd like to see you. Briefly. Sent me to bring you."

"I'm in the middle of something. Sorry."

"Then I'd like to talk to you. Collect your notes, take any requests for supplies."

"None needed. You don't have to send me signals. I can say everything I have to say right here. I don't need supplies and I don't need rescue. Any trouble at the Base?"

"None."

"Then go tell them that."

"Doctor, the Director gave this as an order."

"I understand that. Go and tell him I have things in progress here."

"I'm to say that you refused to come in."

"No. Just what I said."

"Could you leave if you wanted to?"

"Probably. But I won't just now."

"Yes, ma'am," Kiley said tautly.

"Let someone take him outside the Towers," McGee said. "This man is all right."

Elai made a sign that was plain enough to those that knew, and Maet, an older rider, bestirred himself and gave Kiley a nod.

Later:

You stay here, Elai said, not with words, but she made it clear as it had always been.

Notes, coded journal Dr. E. McGee

I can write again. It's hard. It's two ways of thinking. I have to do this.

There's a lot—

No. Maybe I'll write it someday. Maybe not. No one needs to know that. I've talked to calibans. A couple of ideas. Finally.

It's not too remarkable, talking *to* calibans. They pick up a lot of what we do.

But after all that time I was sitting there playing put and take with ariels and making no sense at all—they're not at all bright, the ariels. You can put and take with them a long time, and then they get to miming your game; and then you don't know who you're playing with, yourself or it, because they pick up the way you do things. And the calibans just watching. Until the grays get to moving stones around. And then you know what they'll do. You know what their body-moves mean; and that this is a tower, and how they circle that, building it, protecting it. The grays say only simple things. Their minds aren't much. It's almost all body language. And a few signs like *warning* and *stop here* and *tower.* And more I can't read. This gray shoved dirt around as well as stones. It seemed to play or it was stupider than I thought then; it would come up with dirt sitting on its nose and blink to clear its eyes and dive down again and move more dirt until it built a ridge; and when it would stop, old Scar would come down off that mound and get it moving again, it and others, about three others, I don't know how many. Maybe more.

And that circle was around me. It wasn't threatening. It was like protection. It went this way and that, tendrils spiraling off from it, the way the ariels do.

I got brave. I tried putting a stone out in front of Scar, a sun-warmed one. And that wasn't remarkable. You can get something out of ariels with that move. But then he came down—stood there staring at me and I stood there staring back into an eye bigger than my head, so big he could hardly see me at that range, and then it dawned on me what his vision is like, that those eyes see in larger scale than I am. I'm movement to him. A hazy shape, maybe.

I got him to say a simple thing to me. He walked round me now that my Place was established; he told me there was trouble toward the northeast: he told me with body language, and then I could see how the spirals were, that the grays had made, that they were mapping the world for me. Conveying their land-sense to smaller scale. Or his land-sense. Or it was all feeding in, even the ariels.

Calibans write on the world. They write the world in microcosm and they keep changing it, and they don't have tech. Technology can't matter to them. Cities can't. Or civilization. They aren't men. But that big brain is processing the world and putting it out again; it added me to the Cloud Towers. It stood there staring past me with an eye too big to see me the way I see and all of a sudden I was awed—that's not a word I use much. Really awed. I wanted to cry because I had gone non-verbal and I couldn't get it out and couldn't take it in because my eyes and my brain aren't set up for what I was seeing.

And now I'm scared. I'm writing up a report and they'll think I'm crazy. I can hear what Genley will say: "Now they *write*. Pull McGee in. She's been out too long."

But I get up on the top of the Tower—how calibans must have loved the idea of towers! Their eyes are fit for that. And then I think of the square concrete Base we've built and I don't feel comfortable. We bring our big earthmovers to challenge the grays and we build things with angles.

All over the world calibans build spirals. But here on Cloud and Styx, they've gone to towers. And human gardens. We're like the ariels. The grays. Part of the ecumene. Capacity was there. God knows if we touched it off or if we ourselves are an inconsequence to what they've been doing all this time, spreading over all the planet, venturing here and there—speaking the same language, writing the same patterns on every rivervalley in the world. But not the same. The spirals vary. They're saying different things.

Like Styx and Cloud. Like isolate towers and grouped towers.

Two different Words for the world.

xlii

204 CR, day 355
Memo, Director's office to R. Genley

This office finds it of some concern that reports from

your group have become infrequent and much devoted to routine. You are requested to come in for debriefing. There is news concerning Dr. McGee's effort.

204 CR, day 356
Memo, Base Director to Chief of Field Operations

Genley has failed response to a report. He may be temporarily out of contact, but considering the delicate relations of the two communities and the McGee situation I think we ought to view this silence with alarm. I am transmitting another recall to McGee. I do not think it will produce results, whether she is being held by force or that her refusal is genuine; but it seems one avenue of approach to the Genley matter. I do not consider it wise to inform McGee that Genley's group is not reporting; we cannot rely on that report remaining secure, in any of several possibilities.

I am furthermore requesting orbiting observation be stepped up.

Advise all observers in the field to observe unusual caution.

Likewise, run a thorough check of all base detection and warning systems. Winter is on us.

205 CR, day 20
Excerpt, Director's annual report, transmitted to Gehenna Station

. . . We will be sending up a great quantity of data gathered in the past year. We have enjoyed considerable successes this year in gathering data which still remains to be interpreted. . . . We are still out of touch with the Styx mission and this remains a cause of some concern; and based on Dr. McGee's study, that concern is increasing, although the chance still remains that Dr. Genley and his staff may have entered into an area of observation which is too sensitive to allow free use of communications . . .

The reprimand given Dr. McGee has been rescinded due to extraordinary mitigating circumstances. Special note should be made of this fact in all communication with the Bureau.

Her report, which we have placed next in sequence, is

a document with which many of the staff take strong issue. Those contrary opinions will follow. But the Committee attaches importance to the report, historically significant in the unique situation of the observer, and containing insights which may prove useful in future analysis.

Report: Dr. E. McGee

. . . . With some difficulty I have succeeded in penetrating the caliban communication system which makes impossible the withholding of any information between Styx and Cloud.

. . . . I have noted that there is a tendency to use Gehennan as a designation for native-born humans and caliban as distinct from this. This may be incorrect.

The communication mode employed by calibans is, with some significant exceptions, similar to the simple communications used by insects. It is as simplistic to compare the two directly as it would be to compare the vocalizations of beasts to human speech on the grounds that they are similarly produced. The caliban system is of such complexity that I have only been able to penetrate the surface of it, for the communication of such simple concepts as directions and desire for food. . . .

. . . . Part of my reluctance to report has been the difficulty of assimilating and systematizing such data; but more than this is the dismay that I have felt in increasing conviction that the entire body of assumptions and procedures on which my field of xenology is founded has to be challenged.

Among the terms which have to be jettisoned or extensively modified when dealing with calibans: intelligence; culture; trait; language; civilization; symbiont.

Humans native to Gehenna have entered into a complicated communication with this lifeform which I believe to be pursuing a course of its own. All indications are that it is ultimately a peaceful course, though peace and war are human concepts and also to be questioned, presupposing government of some sort, of which calibans may prove biologically incapable.

I make this assertion advisedly. Calibans understand dominance. They apply sudden coercion. They commit suicide and have other maladies of an emotional nature. But what they are doing is not parallel to human ambitions. It goes off from it at such an angle that conflict between humans and calibans can only result from a temporary intersection of territorial objectives.

The term caliban itself is questionable in application, since the original application seems only to have been to the grays. Absolutely there should be no confusion of browns with grays. There has been some speculation that the grays are a sex or a life stage of the caliban. The humans who know them say that this is not the case. Grays and browns seem to be two separate species living in harmony and close association, and if one counts the ariels—there are three.

Further, ariels seem to perform an abstract function of pattern-gathering. Not themselves intelligent, they are excellent mimes. If a bizarre analogy might be made, the calibans are technological: they use a sophisticated living computer, the ariels, to gather and store information which they themselves process and use in the direction of their heavy machinery, the grays.

I believe that the browns have long since developed beyond the limits of instinctual behavior, that they have learned not so much to manipulate their environment as to interact with it; and further, I believe (and herein lies the only definition of intelligence applicable in lifeforms which are not analogous to humanity), they have proceeded to abstract purposes in their actions. The Styx and the Cloud are not their Tigris and Nile nor ever should be: we do not have to define them as civilized because such distinctions are outside their ambition, as perhaps ambition lies outside their understanding: in short, their purposes are at an angle to ours. They seem to pursue this abstract purpose collectively, but that should not encourage us to expect collective purpose as an essential part of the definition of intelligent species. The next sapience we encounter may well violate the new criteria we establish to include calibans.

This leads me to a further point, which makes the continuation of my studies absolutely critical at this juncture. This species, whose basic mode of encounter is interactive, has begun to interact with humans. It may be possible to communicate to calibans that they may themselves wish to interdict further spread of this interaction. I believe that it is the kind of communication they are capable of understanding. It is the kind of "statement" that is expressible in their symbol system. I am not skilled enough to propose it to them. A six-year-old native child could phrase it to them—if that human child could comprehend the totality of the problem. If a native adult could. That is our dilemma. So is human ambition. We are very sure that that word is in *our* vocabulary.

Which brings me to my most urgent concern.

The calibans Pattern a disturbance on the Styx. This Patterning is increasingly more urgent. That mound-building, which you are no doubt observing in orbital survey on the Cloud, is nothing less than a message, and a rampart, and a statement that danger comes this way.

I am perhaps objective enough to wonder of the two different human/caliban cooperations which have developed, which is the healthier in caliban terms. I think I know. On the Styx they eat grays.

Report, Dr. D. Hampton

. . . . As for Dr. McGee's assertions, the report is valuable for what may be read between the lines. With personal regret, however, and without prejudice, I must point out that the report is not couched in precise terms, that the effort of Dr. McGee to coin a new terminology does not present us with any precise information as to what calibans *are,* rather what they are *not.* A definition in negatives which attempts to tear down any orderly system of comparisons which has been built up in centuries of interspecies observations, including non-human intelligence, is a flaw which seriously undermines the value of this report. More, the vague suggestions Dr. McGee makes of value structures and good and evil among the calibans leads to the suspicion that she has fallen into the most common error of such studies and begun to believe too implicitly what her informants believe, without applying impartial logic and limiting her statements to observable fact.

I fear that there is more of hypothesis here than substance.

xliii

205 CR, day 35
Styxside

The sun broke through and brought some cheer to the reedy waste about Parm Tower, glancing gold in the water, making black spears of the reeds. A caliban swam there. Genley watched it, a series of ripples in the sheeting gold. Other calibans sat along the bank, in that something-wrong kind of pose that had been wrong all day.

Riders came in, scuffing along the road upriver. That was what the disturbance had been. Somehow the calibans had gotten it, worked it out themselves in that uncanny way they had.

The riders came. With them came lord Jin.

Every caliban in sight or smell reacted to lord Jin's Thorn. It swept in like storm, the impression of sheer power that affected all the others and sent calibans and ariels alike into retreat or guard-posture along the riverside. Jin arrived with his entourage, without word or warning, immaculate and the same as ever—the matter up north was settled, Genley reckoned. Settled. Over. Genley gathered himself up from his rock with the few fish he had speared and came hurrying in, splashing across the shallows and hastening alongside the scant cultivation Park Tower afforded.

So their isolation was ended. Two months cut off in this relative desolation, two months of fishing and the stink of water and rot and mud and Parm all prickly with having outsiders in his hall. The lord Jin had deigned to come recover them.

Genley did not go running into Jin's sight. He collected Kim and Mannin from their occupations, Kim at his eternal sketching of artifacts, Mannin from his notes.

"You know the way you have to be with him," he warned them. "Firm and no backing up. No eagerness either. If we ask about that com equipment right off it'll likely end up at the bottom of the Styx. You know his ways. And then he'll be sorry tomorrow. Don't bring that up. Hear?"

A surly nod from Kim. Mannin looked scared. It had not

been an easy time. Kim had had little to say for the last two weeks, to either of them.

"Listen," said Mannin. "There's only one thing I want and that's headed back to Base. Now."

"We'll send you back on r and r when we get the leisure," Genley said. "You just don't foul it up, you hear? You don't do it. You muddle this up, I'll let you get out of it any way you can."

Mannin sniffed, wiped the perpetual runny nose he had had since they had gotten back to this place. Dank winter cold and clinging mists almost within sight and vastly out of reach of the Base; with the Styx between them and the pleasures of Green Tower, the high, dry land where winter would not mean marsh and bogs.

"Come on," Genley said, and went off ahead of them.

Your problem, Jin had said once. *These men of yours. Your problem.*

They went, the three of them, where every other person of status in the community was going, to the Tower, to see what the news was.

xliv

205 CR, day 35
Parm Tower

The hall rustled with caliban movements, nervous movements. Thorn had made himself a place. Parm's own Claw had moved aside, compelled by something it could not bluff, and below it, other calibans, of those which had come in, sorted themselves into an order of dominances. These had been fighting where they came from: violence was in their mood, and in the mood of their riders, and it was not a good time to have come in. Genley saw that now, but there was no way out. They stood there, against the wall, last to have come in; no caliban defended them. Scaly bodies locked and writhed and tails whipped in sweeps on the peripheries.

"Let's get out of here," Mannin said.

"Stay still," Genley said, jerked at his arm. Mannin had no sense, no understanding what it meant even yet, to give up half a step, a gesture, a single motion in hunter-company. He smelled of fear, of sweat; he was afraid of calibans. Not singly. En masse. "Use your head, man."

"Use yours," Kim said, at his other side. Kim left. Walked out.

Mannin dived after him, abject flight.

So Jin noticed him finally, from across the room where, heedless of it all, he was stripping off his leather shirt. Women of Parm's band had brought water in a basin. Other men stood muddy as they were, attending the calibans. A scattering of Weirds insinuated themselves and brought some quiet, putting their hands on the calibans, getting matters sorted out.

Jin lifted his chin slightly, staring straight at him while the women washed his hands. *Come here,* that meant.

Genley crossed the recent battleground, weaving carefully around calibans who had settled into sullen watching of each other. It was a dangerous thing to do. But the Weirds were there. A man knew just how close to come. He did that, and stood facing Jin, who looked him up and down with seeming satisfaction. "Gen-ley." The eyes had their old force. But there was a new scar added to the others that were white and pink on Jin's body. This was on the shoulder, near the neck, an ugly scabbed streak. There were others, already gone to red new flesh. He always forgot how small Jin was. The memory of him was large. Now the eyes held him, dark and trying to overawe him, trying him whether he could go on looking back, the way he tried every man he met.

Genley said nothing. Chatter got nowhere with Jin. It was not the hunters' style. A lot passed with handsigns, with subtle moves, a shrug of the shoulders, the fix of eyes. There was silence round them now. He was only one of the number that waited on Jin, and some of those were mudspattered and shortfused.

One was Parm; and Parm's band; one was Blue, mad-eyed Blue, who was, if Jin had a band, chiefest of that motley group, excepting Jin. A big man, Blue, with half an ear gone, beneath the white-streaked hair that came down past his shoulders. The hair was strings of mud now.

"How many more?" Parm asked, not signing: Jin's shoulder was to him.

"I'll talk to you about that." Jin never looked at Parm. He gave a small jerk of his head at Blue. "Go on. Clean up—" The eyes came back to Genley. "You I'll talk to. My father."

"How did it go?" Genley asked.

"Got him," Jin said, meaning a man was dead. Maybe more than one. A band would have gone with him. The women. Jin unlaced his breeches, sat down on the earthen ledge to strip off his muddy boots. Women helped him, took the boots away. He stood up and stripped off the breeches, gave them to the women too, and dipped up water in the offered basin, carrying it to his face. It ran down in muddy rivulets. He dipped up a second and a third double handful. The water pooled about his feet. More women brought another basin, and cloths, and dipped up water in cups while he stood there letting them wash the mud off, starting with his hair. It became a lake.

"You here for a while?" Genley asked.

Jin waved off further washing, reached for a blanket a woman held and wound it about himself.

"A bath's ready," Parm's sister said.

He waved them off again. Held out his hand from beneath the blanket. A cup arrived in it; he never looked to see, but carried it to his lips and drank, looking up at Genley the while. He was not easy. Genley read that mood. Beyond him Thorn rested, only half relaxed.

"Like Parm Tower?" Jin asked him.

"It's wet here."

Jin failed to laugh. Just stared at him.

"Didn't think it would take this long," Genley ventured, still pushing, judging he had to push. And pay the young bastard a compliment, if he took it that way.

It halfway pleased Jin. Genley saw the blink. The mouth never changed. Jin gestured with the cup. *Sit.* Jin took the ledge. The floor was damp from what had not run down the slant to the drain. Genley ignored the invitation, not liking looking up, but stood easier, and that was all right; it had not been an order. Jin puffed his cheeks, let out a long, slow breath.

"The Styx is cold," Jin said.

"Cold here too. No women here."

Jin looked up, nonplussed.

"Didn't have that matter taken care of here," Genley said.

Jin blinked, blinked again, and a small wicked smile started at the corners of his mouth. "Forgot that. That old sod Parm." It became a laugh, a silent shaking of the shoulders. "O my father, all this time. Poor Genley." He wiped his eyes. "No women." He laughed again, gestured with the cup. "We fix that."

Genley regarded him with touchy humor. There were other things about Parm he would have wished to say, but a list seemed risky. He folded his arms and looked down at Jin. "Mostly," he said, "I fished. Hunted a bit along the banks. In the bog. Didn't hear anything, didn't get any news. So you settled with that Mes bastard."

"Yes."

"Want to talk to you when you've got time."

"About what?"

"When you've got time."

The brows came down, instant frown. "But I always have time," Jin said, "if it's news."

"Told you I had none of that. That's what about. There's a point past which the Base is going to be asking questions."

"Let them ask."

"They'll know there was fighting up north. They see things like that. They'll make up the answers."

"Let them make them up. What will they do?"

"I don't know what they'll do."

"But they don't interfere outside the Wire."

Genley thought about that suddenly, in sudden caution. That was a question, posed hunter-style, flatly.

"Up to a point," he hedged it. "I don't know what they'd do. There's no need to stir things up with them."

"Tell me, Gen-ley. Who are they like? You—or Mannin? Like Kim?"

Genley frowned, perceiving he was being pressed, backed up on this, step and step and step, and Jin was choosing the direction. "You're asking what the Base might do about it if they didn't hear from us."

"Maybe we found that out."

"What's that mean?"

The dark eyes rested on him, redirected to the wall. Jin took a drink, pursed his lips. "They're Mannins."

"Some are. Some aren't." He squatted, arms on knees, to meet Jin's eyes. "You listen to me. There's a point past which. There always is. I tell you what's good. You want advice, I give you advice. You've got the Styx in your hand; got roads; got stone; got ways to get yourself written down as the man that made this collection of towers into something star-men have to respect, you hear me? You have it all in your hand. But you don't deal with Base the way you deal with that petty tower lord up north. I'm telling you. Think of a tower as large as the whole Base, in the sky, over your head: that's what the Station is, and it watches the whole world; it has other watching posts strung out round the world, so nothing moves but what they see it. Imagine beyond that a hundred towers like that, imagine half a dozen places as big as all Gehenna itself where millions of towers stand—you reckon in millions, Jin? That's a lot more than thousands. Towers beyond counting. You pick a fight with Base, Jin, that's what you've got. You want to deal with Base, they'll deal, but *not yet*."

Jin's face was rigid. "When," he said in a quiet, quiet voice, "when is the time?"

"Maybe next year. Maybe you go to the Wire. I'll set it up. I'll talk to them. It'll take some time. But they'll listen to me sooner or later if nothing happens to foul it up. We get them to talk. That first. Beyond that, we start making them understand that they have to deal with you. We can do that. But you don't get anywhere by going against the Base. It's not just the Base you see. There's more of it you don't see. They're not weak. They know you're not. You listen to me and they'll hear of you all across the territories the starmen have. They'll know you."

Something glittered in the depth of Jin's eyes, something dark. The frown gathered. He set the cup down, gathered the blanket between his knees and leaned forward. "Then why do they send MaGee?"

"MaGee doesn't matter."

"They send this woman. This *woman*. Ma-Gee." Jin drew a breath. It shuddered, going in. "*Talk*, you say. Tell me this, Gen-ley. What does this MaGee say to Elai down there on the Cloud? Tells her starmen will talk to her—is that what this MaGee says?"

"It doesn't matter what McGee says. Elai's *nothing*. They've got nothing to what you've got. Don't lose it."

"They make me a fool. They make me a fool, Gen-ley."

The veins stood out on his neck, on his temples. "I gut one man, his band, his woman—but there's others. You know why, Gen-ley? This woman. This woman on the Cloud. Wait, you say. Talk to the Base. My men say something else. My men have waited. They see me make roads, make fields—they hear their enemy gets stronger, that this MaGee is in First Tower, like you, here. Wait, you say. No, my father."

"Don't be a fool." Wrong word. Genley caught it, seized Jin's wrist in the hardest grip he had. "Don't be one. You don't let those women plan what you do, do you? McGee's nothing. Elai's not worth your time. Let them be. You can deal with Base without involving them. They don't matter."

"It's you who are the fool, Genley. No. This MaGee, this Elai, there's enough of them. It's *winter,* my father."

A chill came on him that had nothing to do with the weather. "Listen to me."

"There are men coming," Jin said, "from across the Styx. Thousands. What I did to Mes—will be double on the Cloud. Before this woman's eyes."

"You listen. This isn't the way to settle this."

"Yes, it is," said Jin.

"Or to have the Base on your side."

"I know where the Base is," Jin said. "And you can go with me, Genley. You hear? You ride with us. You. Those men of yours. I want you with me."

"No. I'm not getting into this."

The dark eyes bore into his. "But you are. On my side. In case this MaGee has something. And your Base, they won't interfere. They'll deal with me, all the same. There won't be anybody else to deal with. Will there?"

"Where's the com?"

"Somewhere," Jin said. "Not here. If you called them— what would they do?"

Nothing, Genley thought. He stood up, scowling, close to shaking, but that would never do. He jammed his hands into his belt.

"Nothing," Jin said, leaning back. "Later is good enough." He wrapped the blanket back about himself, looked up at him with a halflidded smile. "Go find yourself a woman. Do you good, Gen-ley."

xlv

205 CR, day 48
Cloud Towers

Something was amiss. Elai knew it. It had come in a great wave up the Cloudside, like the building of storm, like the sudden waft of change in the winter wind, like both these things, but this storm was in caliban minds, and moved constantly, so that each day the sun rose on something new in the patterns across the Cloud; so that mounds continually revised themselves and the soft earth churned, collapsed, rose and fell again. The Weirds patterned their distress; Towerwork grew disorganized, the place grew untidy with neglect. There was winterwork to do; and riders and craftsfolk tended to it alone, the little mendings of the walls after rain, the bracing-up with stone.

The Weirds abdicated, mostly; and calibans grew restive; children fretted, sulked, retreated, reading patterns too. Cloud grew irritable; Taem kept much to himself; Din went back and forth between the roof and the depths, a frown between his brows.

There was no staying from the roof: Elai went up to see what was written on the world, compulsively, throughout the day. Others did. And so she found MaGee, staring outward from the rim.

Riders—Dain, and Branch, had paused in their work, bare to the waist and sweating in the unseasonal sun, muddy-armed from their wall-mending. Two of her sons were there, Taem and Cloud. The nurses stood forgetting Cloud, while Taem—Taem sat beside an aged Weird, only sat, his naked arms about his knees, in the shelter of the rim.

Elai looked out, past MaGee, with the sun at her back, her shadow falling long over the baked-clay roof, the irregular tiles scored by generations of caliban claws, eroded by winter rains. A drowsing ariel noticed it was beshadowed and moved aside, sunseeking. Everywhere on the roof ariels shifted, and then calibans moved, for Scar came up from the access, thrust himself to her side, and lumbered to the rim, rising up on one scaly clawed foot to survey the world, then sinking down again, walking the rim, trampling the riders' new tile-work, dislodging what they had done.

"Something's happened," MaGee said, pointing outward. "The Styx-pattern. Something's come out from it."

"Yes," Elai said. The wind stirred at her robes, pulled at them, at her hair and MaGee's.

"What's going on?" MaGee asked. And when she was silent: "Has something moved from the Styx?"

Elai shrugged. For all the warmth of the day, the wind was chill.

"First," Dain appealed to her, at her right, with Branch and the others. *First,* as if she could mend it. She did not look that way. She walked up beside MaGee, rested her hands on the rim, staring outward at the world.

"Have they moved?" MaGee persisted.

"Yes," she said. "Oh, yes, MaGee, they've moved."

"They're coming here."

Elai looked at her, and a strange sad sweetness came to her. *O MaGee,* she thought. She had waited for this thing all her life. Now that it was here there was someone it truly horrified. "MaGee, my friend." She smiled then, not so distraught as she should have been. "You are simple." But to make it lighter she laid a hand on MaGee's shoulder, then turned and walked away to the downwards entry, ignoring the eyes of all the rest.

"First," she heard MaGee call after her. *"Elai!"*

So she stopped, curiously tranquil in this day.

"I have to warn the Base," MaGee said.

"No. No com."

"Are they in danger?" MaGee asked.

She stared at MaGee. There were other things to think of. Other folk had begun to arrive from below. Din was one. Twostone was with him. Beside them all stood Dain and Branch, still waiting. "First," said Dain, fretting at her. "Do what, First?"

Three of the elders had come up, their white hair blowing in the wind. There was Din, her son, who stood with his hands behind him, whose brown had its crest up and advanced stiffly on its legs, very near to Scar.

Whhhhhsssss! Scar moved, seized up the young caliban

in his great jaws, and nothing moved on that rooftop for the space of a long-held breath, until Scar decided to let Twostone go.

So much for juvenile ambition, borne on the moment's possibilities. *Wait your turn,* Elai thought with a cold, cold stare at her son, and turned her shoulder in disdain, not even bothering to address her anger to the boy.

This was cruel. After a moment she heard him flee the daylight, a scraping of claws, a patter of naked boyish feet vanishing down into the tower, while Scar's crest lowered in satisfaction. There was a second, slower retreat. Cloud with his nurses; but Taem, when she looked his way, had stayed, small, bare-kneed boy, with a Weird's cool observance of what had passed between her and Din. So she knew this morning that Taem was gone for good, and that hit her unpleasantly, and completed her anger at the world.

That was what it was to be First. From the time that she was small, when Scar had come to her and made her what she was; and now that pathetic brown of Din's, young yet, and not likely to get older—

Wisest to kill the rivals, with such a winnowing coming. It was not alone that Styxsider she fought. It was far more general a matter than that. Kill the rivals, unite the Towers. That was what Jin had been doing, one by one.

She walked and looked about her, and calibans and ariels shifted, a scaly wave, a refixing of gold and sea-green eyes all set on her. She looked about her from the Tower rim, to the Patterns, the river, the towers, the bright sea to which the river ran. *Go bring,* she signed abruptly, facing Dain; aloud: "Paeia." Dain started away in grim haste. "Taem," she added, which command turned Dain about at the entry with bewilderment on his face.

"Bring him too," she said. "Tell him mind his manners. He knows."

She hoped he did. She seldom felt Taem active in the Patterns. The New Towers were isolate; and for Taem the Twelve Towers calibans made a whorl with a silent center. Paeia they made as sunward, full of activity; but Taem was silence, like his son.

"Bring them," Dain echoed her, as if he could have mistaken it. "And if they won't come?"

Taem, he meant. *If Taem won't come.*

She gave Dain no answer. Dain went. Perhaps her son had read it all too; perhaps he read his death out there, patterned on the shore.

Violence, his caliban had signalled. Desperate, not comic, a young caliban, too young for such a challenge. *Mother, I want to live.*

She had waited for this all her life. So had her son. She wanted to be alone now, only with MaGee, and Scar, not under these staring eyes that looked on her now with estimations—whether she would die now, whether that was what she meant by calling in those most dangerous to her life. She was frail; she limped. She ached when it rained. And her heirs were under twelve.

Will you die? their stares asked her. Some might think that safest. But her riders had cause to dread it, having been too loyal, serving her too closely. Change seemed in the wind, hazardous to them.

Give me sand, she asked of the aged Weird; it was Taem that brought it, a small leather sack, and crouched beside her as she stooped and Patterned with it. Others gathered about her, shadowing her from the sun, cutting off the wind.

She made the river for them, recalling the great Pattern on the shore. She made the whorls and mounds with sand streaming from her hand, so, so quickly, and signified Paeia and Taem coming in; their unified advance. Ariels nosed in past human feet, interfering in her work, trying mindlessly to put it back the way it was Patterned on the shore. Futures distressed them: they were never ready to make the shift, being occupied with *now.* She picked up the most persistent; it went stiff as a stick and she set it roughly back. It came to life again, scuttled off to watch. A gray nosed in, thigh-high to the watchers.

So she built it, with Taem crouched elbows-on-knees beside her; and the Weird who was her son would pattern it to the browns, and the ariel and the gray would spread it too. She returned the challenge Jin had made. She had just insulted him, remaking the pattern that was the Styx.

She stood up, dusting off her hands, rose without needing Branch's offered hands. Someone added a handful of stones to what she had done, embellishing the insult. There was laughter at that.

But it was nervous laughter. And afterward, she thought, they would be whispering aloud within the Tower, talking with voices, not daring Pattern what they thought where calibans might read.

Elai is finished.

If she goes herself, she'll not come back.

If Jin comes here, there'll be revenge; only fishers might survive—only might.

But if she steps aside—we have no stability.

"Go away," she said, and they went. Their going let the wind come at her pattern and blow the sand in streamers across the stone, as if the wind were patterning back at her and mocking her folly.

MaGee stayed. Only MaGee and Scar. Even Taem and the other Weird had gone. The solitary gray retreated with other calibans and ariels, a retreating skein of lithe bodies and tails flowing down the entry to the Tower.

Shall I go? MaGee signed.

"I want to ask you something."

"Ask," MaGee said.

"If we should fall—will the starfolk do anything?"

"No," MaGee said slowly, "no, I don't think they will. They only watch what happens."

"Does this amuse them?"

"They want to see—they've waited all these years to see what Pattern you'll make. You. The Styx. No. They won't intervene."

This was a thunderclap of understanding. She saw the look Magee had, like a caliban well-fed and dreaming in the sun. MaGee knew what she had said, had meant to let that slip. Elai spread her fingers at MaGee like the lifting of a crest.

"Yes." MaGee acknowledged the curse. "The absolute truth, old friend. That's what they've been up to all these years."

A wider spread of the fingers.

MaGee lifted her head, blinked lazily as Scar could do. Defiant, as Scar could be, defying her in a way that was silent and more subtle than her son. "You can't keep much secret from Jin, can you?" MaGee asked.

"No." Pattern-blind starfolk could keep their movements secret from each other. Cloudsiders swam in the knowledge of patterns like a sea. What she had done this morning flowed across the river; and the word would flow back again to Jin like a rebounding wave. *I'm coming, man-who-wants-the-world. I'm bringing all that ever escaped Green's hands. I'll take your towers, I'll erase you and all you are.*

"MaGee," she said, suddenly, thinking on this, "you're not in the Pattern. Not really. Tell me in words what you'd do if you were me. Maybe it would confuse them."

For a moment then MaGee looked less than confident. "No."

"Then you do know something."

"What would I know? What would I know that calibans don't? Oh, I'd confuse things. Maybe not in a way you'd like. Don't make me do that."

"My rivals would take you," Elai said, "Jin, Taem, Paeia—They'd want you to use. Taem and Paeia'd treat you all right. But Jin's another matter. They have different ways on Styxside. Do you want that? Give me advice."

MaGee set her jaw and ducked her head, then looked up. "First thing, I'd get the conflict out of here. Away from the Towers and the fields. But that, you're going to do."

"Calibans say that much."

"What else do they say?"

"We'll meet upriver."

"What kind of war is that," MaGee exclaimed, "when you know where you'll meet? That's not war, that's an appointment. They'll kill you, Elai, you know that?"

Elai felt a chill. "Come with me. Come with me to meet with Jin, my friend."

"Up the Cloud? To fight a war?"

Elai made the affirmative. MaGee thrust out her lip, a pensive look as if it were just some ordinary venture she were considering.

"Oh, well," MaGee said, "sure."

And then, from nowhere: "You should have built your ships, Elai."

"What's that mean?"

"You should have, that's all."

"You think I'll die?"

"What would you leave behind you?"

MaGee had a way of walking ground others knew better than to tread. Elai lifted her head and stared at her like some drowsing old caliban. "Don't know that. No one does, do they?" She walked away, beside Scar's huge length, stopped near his tail-tip. "Never wore leathers myself. Got some, though. Wished I could, now and then, just take Scar and go."

"*Ships*, Elai."

She stared at this insistent starman. "Was that what I was supposed to do? Was that what you were waiting for?" She recalled a day on the beach, the launching of her boats, a starman watching from the shore. "Of course," she said softly when MaGee answered only with silence. Her heart plummeted. Of course. Scar had chosen her for one reason; of course starmen also came equipped with reasons. She was the creature of others. That was what it was to be First. She was self-amused and pained.

And she walked toward the wall, stood there looking seaward. "Give Jin ships?" she asked MaGee. "If I'd made them, he'd have built them too. He'd have patterned how they are. We talk to each other—have for years, back and forth. Takes days. But I always know where he is. And what he's doing. And he knows me. Hates me, MaGee. Hates me. Hates what got from the fingers of the Styxsiders. Ships. That could be something. He wants the world, he does. Wants the world. He'll break those men."

"Who? Genley?"

"Don't know their names. Three of them. His starmen."

"How do you know these things?"

There was dismay in MaGee's voice, in her eyes when Elai turned around. "Calibans talk to you," Elai said quietly. "But you don't hear all they say. You don't know everything, starman. Friend."

"I've got to warn the Base, Elai."

"You keep quiet with that com. They'd do nothing, you say. That true?"

"I think it's so."

Elai looked her up and down. "You've gotten thin, MaGee. Leathers might fit you. You come with me, you keep that com quiet. You're mine, you hear?"

MaGee thought about it. "All right," she said.

Later that day, Paeia came, grim and frowning—came, quite tamely, into hall, her caliban behind her. She had not

brought her heir, came armed with only a knife; and stood
there in front of the chair she had stood behind so often
when Ellai had ruled.

"You've read how it is," Elai said, from the authority of
that chair."I'm going upriver. You too."

Elai watched Paeia draw a breath, a long, slow one. Paeia
folded her arms and stared. Her face might have been
stone, seamed and weathered as it was. She had braided
her grizzled hair, with beads in the strands. Had taken her
own time about coming, to look her best. Had thought long
about coming, maybe—whether it was a trap, whether she
might die.

"With you," Paeia said.

"I'm no fool," said Elai. "I don't want us weak. You tell
me you'll be by me, I don't ask any other promises."

Paeia went on thinking a moment. "I'll be there," Paeia
said. And truth, there were no other promises she could
have asked. Both of them knew that.

"Taem's coming," Elai said.

"Then, First, you are a fool."

Elai frowned at that. She had to, being First; and smiled
after, bleak and cool, amused at Paeia warning her. "But
he's coming," she said. "I asked him to."

Taem took three days, with the pattern growing worse
each one of them. But come he did, with his riders across
the Cloud, enough to raise the dust, to veil the shore in
amber clouds.

He crossed the Cloud alone then, just himself with his
caliban.

"Been a while," Taem said when he stood in hall where
Paeia had stood.

It had. He had not changed. The presence was the same.
But it added up differently. There was no son. And she
herself had changed. She met his eyes, saw him for what
he was worth in the daylight as well as dark. He was
straight and tall. Ambitious. Why else had he wanted her,
in those years? She had no grace, was not fine to look on.
He was.

Din's father—he had come too, and stood by her now,
one of her riders, nothing more. Din was there, against the
wall; and Paeia stood close by her side. And Cloud and

Cloud's father, one of the long line of Cloud, same as Paeia, but of Windward Tower—he had come. So all her men were here, and their kin; and two of her sons.

"Why didn't you kill me?" Taem asked her outright. And that was like him too.

205 CR, day 51
Notes, coded journal Dr. E. McGee

Elai has called the seaward towers to her aid, brought in this former mate of hers . . . Taem's father. Taem Eldest of New Tower. He's dangerous. You can see the way the calibans behave, up on their four legs, crests up. His caliban is trouble, Elai said once. I see what she means. This *man* is trouble.

"Why didn't you kill me?" he asked her right there in hall, and everyone seemed to be asking himself that question. I think he was insulted she hadn't tried. He came with all his riders, all of them just across the river, but he came into First Tower alone, and that took nerve, the kind of craziness calibans instill. I think he was reading Patterns all the way, that he could get away with it. That he had to come because she wouldn't come out to him; that he had to swallow the fish's tail, they say on the Cloud, when they mean that's all you've got left for choices. It galled him.

Elai just looked at him, never getting up from her chair, and made some sign I couldn't read all of, but it was something like dismissing him as a threat, which didn't please him. "This isn't Styx," she said then. "I don't have Jin's manners." It was absolute arrogance; and his caliban bristled up and Scar bristled up, and those two calibans sucked air and stared at each other like two rocks determined to go on staring nose to nose forever.

"How's the boy?" Taem asked then.

"He's well," she said. Taem had to know about his son, that Elai's Taem had gone down to the Weirds; too much news travels unspoken, everywhere. But news about the Weirds that have no name—well, that could be different. "I saw him this morning," Elai said.

He's a handsome man, this Taem. I see what attracted Elai to him in spite of other troubles. He's none so old, this Taem Eldest: good-looking, straight and mean and trim;

wears his hair braided at the crown, and a lot of ornament: he's rich as a Cloudsider can be, and those riders of his are part of it. I never saw a man move like that, like he owned whatever space he was in.

"When do we go?" he asked, not patterning this: it was himself and Elai talking, two humans, that was all, and there was something electric in it as if something from a long time ago were back for a moment.

O Elai, secrets. You loved this man, that's what. And you've got him puzzled now.

Young Din was standing over against the wall with Two-stone all this while, his little face all hard and scared. First born. I think he's in danger. If anyone in that hall would have knifed that man, Din might.

The thing is, with Taem's son gone among the Weirds, Taem Eldest is lost from the First Tower pattern, as if there had never been a son. *That* was the change in the pattern, I think, that let Taem in.

And Paeia—lean and mean as they come, that old woman, always in riding leathers and always carrying a knife. Paeia was right by the door when Taem went outside again, back to his own riders across the river, and that sent the chills up my back. That woman rules Second Tower, and she's mateless at the moment; and there was thinking in that look she gave him.

Solutions occur to me that I don't like to write down. I know this Taem thought of them. "I don't have Jin's manners," Elai said. Meaning that she's thought about it. The affairs of princes. Old, old problems. I read the patterns the best I can and they scare me.

Elai is the key, the peacemaker. Scar's rider—the only one who can dominate the others and hold Cloudside together, and if anything should happen to her now it'll fall, everything will come apart in chaos. Taem—he was challenging her the same way: See if you can hold the Seaward Towers without me. But likewise he knew, I think, he couldn't do without her. Neither can Paeia. Not in this moment.

I look out the window and it's crazy out beyond the river. Calibans. Everywhere. And already the grays are reworking the Pattern out there, broadcasting it to anyone who's not Pattern-blind.

xlvi

Message, Station to Base Director

Survey picks up increased activity on the Cloud, a frenzy of mound-building answering this advance of the Styxsiders from the upriver. It seems clear that Cloud River is aware what is happening, through spies, perhaps. The mounds suggest ramparts, but they are curiously placed as defense, and the lines change constantly. We observe no such activity on the part of the Styxsiders. They only camp and advance, averaging thirty kilometers a day.

It seems clear that there is a massing of calibans for defense or attack at the Cloud River settlement. These have come from the two seaside settlements and their numbers are being augmented hourly.

. . . Observers in the field are at hazard. . . .

Message, Base Director to E. McGee in Field

Genley and team are missing on Styxside. Do you know anything?

Memo, Security to Base Director

Agents in field are proceeding with utmost caution. War seems imminent. Field agents are reporting unusual aggressiveness on the part of calibans.

Memo, Base Director to Security

I don't think there's any question Genley, Kim, and Mannin are with that movement toward the Cloud. McGee is also out of touch. Don't take unwarranted risks in observation. Start pulling the teams back.

xlvii

205 CR, day 60
Cloudside

The corridors were unnaturally still, empty of calibans, of Weirds, unnaturally dusty, because no one was sweeping them, and that, thought McGee, was because of that gathering out on the riverside, that milling about of calibans. Fishernets got tangled; someone hauled in a gray by accident, but it survived. Something large surfaced in the river, just a great gray back, and no one saw it again—*curiosity,* someone said. *They've noticed,* but McGee had no notion who that *they* were, unless seafolk.

Great calibans moved in that no one owned, just arrived— presumably from upriver, from the forest. There were giants among these newcomers, but Weirds kept them to the Pattern across the river, and they tried none of the local calibans.

Wild, McGee thought, or tame. There was no distinction. And they remained, harbingers of trouble up the Cloud, while Elai delayed to move. The riders fretted; the calibans seemed indecisive. It all seemed wrong. And the halls grew dusty with neglect, under the wear of feet both shod and clawed; the sun shafted through clouds within the inmost halls, dustmotes dancing.

So she came on Din, in a little-used way, a shadow in the dustmotes. She had not looked to meet him.

"Din," she said by way of greeting. "Haven't seen you." He had not come for stories. She missed that. He remained a shadow to her, mostly, with Twostone close against the wall, a caliban silhouette out of which the light picked tiny details, the color of a nose, a lambent eye too shadowed for color, staring at her.

Din said nothing, but bowed his head and stood aside for her to pass.

"Din—are you all right?" she asked.

Notes, coded journal Dr. E. McGee

I talked with Din today. I don't think he understood. He's

seven. He's wiry, all elbows; you want to give his face a washing and comb his hair; and then you look into his eyes and you wouldn't dare. He's a boy that's thinking hard right now, how to stay alive. That's the way it is. He's not mature, not in all ways. He's growing and awkward and he took a stone when I was trying to talk with him and threw it. Like a child. He cried, trying not to let me see.

I don't want to die. That's what that meant. He just threw the stone and it bounced off the wall and hit me. I never let on it did. I just stared at him the way you have to do with that boy to let him know he doesn't impress you; and he just broke into tears then and turned his face out of the light.

"Jin scare you?" I asked.

"No," he said, and sniffed and wiped his eyes and tried to pretend he hadn't ever cried, all sullen and arrogant. "Not scared."

"Look at the sea," I said. That puzzled him, us being inside, in the dark. "Look at the sea next time you're out."

"Why?" He's a little boy, always ready to suspect someone's playing tricks on him.

"You just do that." I started to talk about boats, which we had talked about before. He just made that stone-dropping move. *I don't want to talk.*

"You're smart," I said. "You want to live to be a man?"

That got his attention. So that was what he was thinking about.

"Just be smart," I said, not knowing how to advise him, because it's not my world; it's his. "Your mother wants you alive, you know that? That's why she's got that Taem around; because what's coming up that river is mean and it's coming here, you know that?"

He squatted there thinking about that, and then I figured out that scene on the roof, where he defied his mother; where his little caliban took on Scar, who makes ten of him. Scared. Just scared and full of fight, this boy. Elai's son. I tousled his hair; no one touches him much: it's not Cloudsider way. He set his jaw and ducked, but he looked pleased as that sullen little face of his does these days. Poor boy. Your mother loves you. I do.

"I like you," I said then. He looked pleased. If he were a caliban his crest would have settled. That kind of look.

His caliban moved up and nearly knocked him off his haunches, putting its head in our way. They know where the sunlight is. The attention. I don't know how they know, or how much they understand. "Fight," I said, "but be smart."

"Elai say that?" he asked.

I lied about that, but I thought she would if she were not busy; but she said I should take care of her sons for her, so I guess it was in a way the truth.

I talked to Cloud too, but that's nothing. Cloud's too young to know much. And Taem knows—who knows what a Weird knows, but too much for any five-year-old, and too different to hear anything I could say. Scar talks to him. All the grays and ariels do. Presumably that's enough.

We're running out of time. We have to move. I won't take this book when we do. I'm burying it. In case.

They'll lend me a spear to use. Dain showed me how to hold it. I'm supposed to ride—one of the free calibans the Weirds have come up with on this side of the river, the kind that don't let themselves belong to anyone. I've seen it; we've looked each other in the eye. It's not particularly big. I patterned to it and it nosed my pattern but it wouldn't give me anything back. This is not a friendly one. But it's born to the Cloud River pattern. Dain says; and so I trust it doesn't hate me in particular, just the idea of being beast of burden.

That's a human thought. And then I remember that I'm sitting in a house they made, in a land they own. I'm sitting in a word of the Statement they've made about Cloud River, one of the folk who write in squares and angles, no less; and it's going to go where it pleases while I'm on its back, because I can't stop it; I can't defend it either, not with that spear. And it knows.

xlviii

**205 CR, day 97
Upper Cloud**

They rested, the sun lost among the trees, and cooked what they had of supper at the hunters' fires, mealcakes and boiled dried meat, and a bit of starchy root that grew wild. "I'm going off that stuff," Mannin said. He sat bent over, had gotten thin—some bowel complaint. "Maybe it's allergy."

"Come on," Genley said, "you've got to eat, man."

"It's the water," Kim said. "Told you. Man's been here long enough, letting sewage in the rivers, on the land. Mannin drinks the water—"

"Shut up," Mannin said. He stayed bent over. His lips were clamped.

"Weak," a hunter said, and nudged him with his elbow. This was Hes, who had Mannin to carry, behind him on his caliban. "The Cloudsiders, they feed you to the calibans, starman."

Mannin got up and went beyond the firelight, riverward.

"Huh," Genley said. That was nothing unusual, not the last two days. He ate his meal, watched the hunters about the fire. It was a man's community, this. All hunters. Jin's own, scattered wide in many camps along the streamside.

How many? he had asked of Jin. Jin had shrugged, but he had added it himself, from the number that he could see, that it was a great number: thousands upon thousands. The station would have seen them move; the station would spot the fires tonight and count them; the station could sense their presence virtually everywhere. But it would do nothing. This barbarian lord, this Caesar on the Styx, had gambled—no, not gambled: had calculated what he could do. Would take the world while the Base and the station watched. Would deal with Base and station then, himself, literal master of the world.

Poor McGee, Genley thought. *Poor bastards.* He made a dry grimace, swallowed down the brew. It had gone sour in the skins, taken on flavors somewhere between old leather and corruption, but it was safe. Kim was right. Boil the water. Drink from skins. Man had loosed his plagues in Gehenna. Now it went the rest of the way.

Now the weak went under, that was all.

"Mannin," someone said. Men went off into the brush. "Hey," Kim said, anxious, and got to his feet, "hey, let him alone."

"He's all right," Genley said, and stood up. Suspicion. They were still strangers. He pointed, waved at Kim. "Get him—get him before there's trouble."

"Stop them," Kim said, hesitating this way and that, pushed aside by the hunters. His eyes were wild. "*You*, you do something—"

There was laughter from the brash. A crashing of branches. Laughter and quiet then, but for breaking branches. So they brought Mannin back and set him down by the fireside.

"You," Kim said, "you talk to them, you've got the means—"

"Shut up." Genley squatted down, gave a scowling stare at the hunters, put a hand on Mannin's shoulder. Mannin was white. Sweat glistened on his face in the firelight. He shook at Mannin. "All right?"

Mannin's teeth were chattering. He sat hunched over, shook his head.

"Get the skin," Genley said.

"I'm not your bloody servant," Kim hissed. "You don't give me orders."

"*Get the skin.* You take care of him, you bloody take care of him, hear me?" Jin had come; Genley saw it, gathered himself up in haste, drew a deep breath.

Jin stared at the hunter-leader; at him, at one and the other, hands on his hips. It was not a moment for arguing. Not an audience that would appreciate it. After a moment Jin gave a nod of his head toward the second, the smaller circle of hunters. "Genley," he said.

Genley came aside, hands in his belt, walked easily beside Jin, silent as Jin walked, on soft hide soles, crouched down by the fireside as Jin sat, one of them, a leader with his own band, however poor it was. He had his beads, had his braids, had his knife at his side. Like the rest. Moved like them, silent as they. He had learned these things.

"This Mannin," Jin said with displeasure.

"Sick," Genley said. "Bad gut."

Jin thrust out his jaw, reached out and clapped a hand on his knee. "Too much patience. All starmen have this patience?"

"Mannin's got his uses."

"What? What, my father?" Jin reached to the fire's edge and broke off a bit of a cake baking on a stone. "For this bad gut, no cure. It's his mind, Gen-ley. It's his mind wants to be sick. It's fear."

"So he's not a hunter. He's other things. Like Weirds."
Jin looked up from under his brow. "So. A Weird."

"We're a lot of things."

"Yes," Jin said in that curious flat way of his, while the eyes were alive with thoughts. "So I give him to you. This Kim; this Mannin. You take care of them . . . Lord Genley."

He drew in a breath, a long, slow one. Perhaps it was Jin's humor at work. Perhaps it meant something else.

"You know weapons, Gen-ley?"

Genley shrugged. "Starman weapons. Don't have any. They don't let them outside the Wire."

Jin's eyes lightened with interest.

Mistake. Genley looked into that gaze and knew it. "All right," he said, "yes, they've got them. But the secret to it is up there. *Up.*" He made a motion of his eyes skyward and down again; it was not only Jin listening, it was Blue and others. It was the Tower-lords. "First steps first, lord Jin. None before its time."

"*MaGee.*"

"She's got none."

Jin's lips compacted into a narrow grimace something like a smile.

"You put McGee in my keeping," Genley said. He had worked for this, worked hard. It was close to getting, close to it, to get this concession. Save what he could. Do what he could, all rivalries aside. "You want Cloudside in your hand, hear, that woman knows what there is to know. You give her to me."

"No." There was no light of reason there, none at all in the look Jin turned on him. "Not that one."

He felt a tightening of the gut. *So, McGee, I tried.* There was nothing more to do. No interference. Just ride out the storm. Gather pieces if there were pieces left. *No place for a woman.* She might get common sense at the last, run for it, get back to the Wire. It was the best to hope for now.

If Elai let her run.

205 CR, day 98
Cloud Towers

They gathered in the dawn, in the first pale light along the Cloud, and McGee clutched her spear and hurried along the shore. The leathers felt strange, like a second, unfamiliar skin at once binding and easy; she felt embarrassed by the spear, kept the head canted up out of likelihood of sticking anyone with it as calibans brushed by her carrying riders on their backs, tall, disdainful men and women who knew their business and were going to it in this dusty murk. *God help me,* she kept thinking over and over, *God help me. What am I doing here?*—as a scaly body shouldered her and its tail rasped against her leg in its passing, weight of muscle and bone enough to break a back in a half-hearted swing.

A Weird found her, among the thousands on the move, waved her arm at her. She followed through the press of moving bodies, of calibans hissing like venting steam, of claw-footed giants and insistent grays that could as easily knock a human down, of ariels skittering in haste. She lost her guide, but the Weird waited on the shore where she had known to go, where her caliban waited, indistinct in the dusty dawn. Hers, the only one unridden, the only one which would be waiting on the shore.

It hissed at her, swung its head. Weirds calmed it with their hands. The tail swept the sand, impatient with her, with them. She tapped the leg with her spear; it dipped its shoulder, and her knees went to water. *Enough of that, McGee.* She planted her foot, heaved herself up and astride, caught the collar as it surged up under her and began to move, powerful steps, a creature at once out of control, never under it—the while she got the spear across to its right side, out of the way, got the kit that was slung at her shoulder settled so it stopped swinging. Scaly hide slid loosely under her thighs, over thick muscle and bony shoulders: buttocks on the shoulder-hollow, legs about the neck, the soft place behind the collar. *They've learned to carry humans,* she thought, *to protect their necks—O God, the tails, the jaws in a fight; that's what the spear is for.* Get the rider off, Dain had said, showing her how to couch it.

Go for the gut of a human, the underthroat of a caliban.
O God.

The movement became a streaming outward, leisurely in
the dawn. The Weird was left behind. She joined other riders
of other towers, of every tower mingled. There was no order.
Elai was up there somewhere, far ahead. So were Taem and
Paeia, Dain and his sisters—all, all the ones she knew. As
for herself, she clung, desperately, as they shouldered others
on their way; she moved her legs out of the way when offended calibans swung their heads and snapped.

There were days of this to face. And war. Some horrid
dawn to find themselves facing other calibans, men with
spears and venomed darts. *How did I get into this?*

But she knew. She shivered, for none of them had had
breakfast and the wind blew cold. She comforted herself
with the thought of days to go, of distance between themselves and the enemy.

Time to get used to it, she thought, and the *it* in her
mind encompassed all manner of horrors. She hated being
rushed; she had a compulsion to plan things: she wanted
time to think, and this sudden madness of Elai's that had
brought them out of bed as if the enemy were at their door
instead of far upriver—this was no way to wake, stumbling
across the town in the dark, shoulder-deep in proddish
calibans . . . *The shore, MaGee,* a Weird had signed to her,
in the last of torchlight. That was all.

But of course, she thought suddenly, weaving along
within the press. *Of course. The Patterns. It confounds the
Patterns—*

The Patterns could not foretell this madness of Elai's,
this sudden wild move. The news that they were coming
could travel no faster than the calibans they rode, the great,
long-striding calibans; was nothing for ariel gossip, up and
down the Cloud.

Elai, she thought, not without pride. *Elai, you bastard.*
And on another level it was raw fear: *This is your world,
not mine. I'm going to get killed in it.* She suffered a vision
of battle, herself run through by some Styxside spear; or
falling off, more likely, to be trampled under clawed feet,
unnoticed in the moment; or meeting some even less ro-
mantic accident along the way—War. She remembered how

fast old Scar could snap those jaws of his on an offending gray and shuddered in the wind. *I'm going to die like that.*

It was at least days remote. There was something left to see.

There was Elai up there. Friend. There was Dain. There were others that she knew.

For the Cloud, she thought. She was shocked at herself, that her blood stirred, that she came not to observe but to fight a war. For the Cloud. For Elai. For the First.

No one shouted. There were no slogans, no banners. Elai yesterday had given her a thong on which a bone ornament was tied; so, Elai had said, so you have some prettiness, MaGee.

Prettiness. She had it about her neck. For friendship's sake. *Do they love?* she had written once, naive.

xlix

205, day 107
Memo, Base Director to all staff

Orbiting survey shows the Styxside column advancing under cover of the woods headed toward the Cloud 200 km east of the Cloudside settlement. The Cloudsiders have advanced 75 km at a very leisurely pace and appear to have stopped in a place where the river offers some natural defense . . .

Message: Base director to Station

Negative on query regarding whereabouts of four observers. Com is inactive. We suspect the presence of observers with the columns but we are not able to confirm this without risking other personnel and possibly risking the lives of the observers themselves in the warlike movements of both groups.

Request round the clock monitoring of base environs. We are presently discovering increased caliban activity on our own perimeters, both along the riverside and in burrowing. This, combined with the sudden massive aggression we are witnessing outside, is, in the consensus of the staff, a matter of some concern.

205 CR, day 109, 0233 hours
Engineering to Base Director

We have an attempt at undermining in progress, passing the fence at marker 30.

0236 hours
Base Director to Security

. . . Stage one defense perimeter marker 30. . . .

0340 hours
Message, Base Director to Station

The defense systems were effective at primary level in turning back the intrusion. We are maintaining round the clock surveillance. We are advising agents still in the field of this move. Since caliban violence seems generally directed toward structures and not toward individuals some staff members have suggested that those agents in open country are not likely to be the objects of aggression, and may be safer where they are than attempting to approach the base. Agents are being advised to use their own discretion in this matter but to tend at once toward high stony ground where feasible.

More extensive report will follow.

l

205 CR, day 112
Cloud River

"Calibans," Elai said, "have tried the Base."

"Yes," McGee said, sitting crosslegged in their camp, among others who sat near Elai and Scar, but her brown had deserted her when she dismounted. It always did, moving off alone to the river though other calibans stayed by their riders; and she was downcast, having read what she had read in the stones this morning, the small things ariels did, copying the greater Patterns current in the world. The little messengers. Mindless. Making miniature the world. They said the Base had held. They said that too.

They said that Jin was near.

"What do they do," Elai asked, "to turn back calibans?"

McGee worked numb hands, her heart beating fast with notions of heroism, of refusing to say, but it was Elai asking, friend, First, her First, who had made her one of them.

There was a great silence about her. Elai simply waited, Gehennan-fashion, would wait long as a caliban could wait for that answer.

"They put a thing into the ground; it smells bad; it goes in under pressure. Calibans won't like it. But there's worse that they could do. A lot worse. There's ships."

Some looked skyward. Elai did not. She looked frail in the firelight, looked gaunt, her beaded braids hanging by her face. There was Paeia by her, Paeia's son, a man full grown. On Elai's other side sat Taem, silent, as Taem usually was.

"They won't," said Elai.

McGee shook her head.

"Why?" Taem asked.

"To see what Pattern we make," Elai said quietly. "So we'll show them."

"Huh," said Taem, and stared into the fire. He was methodically seeing to his darts, to the tiny wrappings of thread, in case the rain had gotten at them.

Something splashed in the river, a diving caliban. Sometimes there were other sounds, the scrape of claws on earth. The Pattern went on about them. There was no fear of ambush, of something breaking through. McGee understood this Word in which they travelled. *Cloud,* it said; and nothing alien got into it. A mound was between them and the Stygians. It would not be breached quietly.

McGee went back to her notes.

. . . It's quiet tonight. It's a strange way to fight a war. We know where they are. And it's just as sure they're not moving yet. Tomorrow, maybe. We heard about an assault on the Wire. That's Styxside calibans, I think, not Cloud. They're a different kind; and not different. I wish I understood that point . . . why two ways exist, so different, even among calibans.

Nations? But that's thinking human-style again.

Are *we* the difference?

I don't even know who's at war out here . . . us or the calibans. Mine puts up with me. I don't know why. A wild caliban takes a human onto his back. No training. Nothing. It's all its idea. I don't even pretend to control it.

As for order in the march, as for any sense of discipline—there's none. Calibans wander when and where they like and we sit around the fire with no sentries posted.

But there are. Calibans.

She looked up. Close by her couples moved through the camp, going the way couples went these last few evenings while they had leisure, while this strange peace obtained.

Taem took Elai's hand. Looked at her. So they had passed the night before. They rose, went off together. Paeia got up in a pique, dusted herself, found one of her own riders. So did her son.

There are pairings in the camp. It's a strange thing, as if all the barriers of Tower loyalty were down. As if there were a sense of time being short. There's a fondness among these people—the way they've left everything behind, the way calibans that normally won't tolerate each other have gotten unnaturally patient.

But it's territory: the Cloud. Maybe they see it that way, that all of a sudden they all belong to the same territory.

Elai and Taem have paired up. I don't know why. I don't know if it portends any longer bond. If we get out of this alive—

Maybe it's only politic. Maybe it's something else. I'm sitting here alone. They've all left, as if there were nothing else—

A shadow fell. Dain sat down by her, just sat on his haunches as she looked up. The fire shadowed his face. His long hair hung about his leathered shoulders. He wore beads hanging from a braid at the side of his head, among the rest of his locks. He was very fine, she thought, very fine. Any woman had to notice when Dain sat down that close to her: a lot had, so that Dain was never without partners. She had Dain in her notes, how this was; how the women courted him as he courted them, so it was a joke in the camp, one Dain liked as well as the tellers of it.

He just sat there looking at her. Nodded his head finally toward the dark. Toward what others did. He wanted her hand, holding his out.

He's crazy, she thought. *What is this? Me?*

Still the outheld hand. She put her papers down, thinking she was mistaken and might embarrass herself. He took her hand—friendship, she reckoned; he just wanted to talk to her, and she was wrong.

But he pulled her to her feet and kept drawing her along, going off to the dark.

She was afraid, then, putting this together with the attack on the Base, with Elai's questions. She thought of betrayal, of factions, of Elai off with Taem.

But outside the firelight he pulled her down with him, this best of Elai's riders, this Dain Flanahan—"Why?" she asked late, "why me?"—preparing herself for wounds.

He laughed as if that question surprised him, and they stayed that way till dawn, wrapped up in each other, the way she had had the Weird in the dark, in the depths, the same terms.

For friendship, then; she reckoned how she had been by the fire night after night; and no one had asked, and finally Dain took it on himself. He was kind, this young man. She had always known that.

li

205 CR, day 113
Cloud River

There was no coherency about it; the Cloudside patterns were confused—sudden advance and then this dawdling along the banks—"They're crazy," Blue said, with shaking of his head. "They're farmers," said Parm.

"Cloudsiders," Jin muttered, still anxious, scowling, because he saw his men making light of it, because he saw his own camp less ordered than he liked. His men grew quiet, reading his mood. They were wise, the men nearest him, at least to duck their heads. But he suspected—in the least, niggling way suspected, that he was too cautious in their eyes, that there would be whispers if they dared. "This Elai," he said, not for the first time, "this Elai's nothing. But this isn't one tower. There's numbers. You keep thinking on that. *Hear?*"

They faced him across the fire, men he had won, tower by tower, themselves. He had his starman by him. Genley. Genley sat at his left hand, to do what he wanted, to tell him what he asked. The Cloud Towers . . . that had waited settling too long; there was MaGee; and that woman; and women worth the having; workers for the fields; these caliban-riders to deal with at his leisure, to teach the others what defying him was worth, any of them they got alive . . . far from the sight of the Wire. These women that played at war. There would be scores settled. Indeed, scores settled.

"Tomorrow," he said, having thought it out, "we go by them."

"Past?" echoed Blue.

"We go out from the shore." He signed it as he spoke, frowning to himself, to no one in particular, satisfied, well-satisfied now he had mapped it out. "We come at them from the south. Let these Cloudsiders have the water at their backs. We drive them off the shore. Caliban matter then. All caliban."

There were grins, figuring how it would be, darts for what riders remained astride, calibans coming up from below, seizing legs, embattled calibans lashing the water to froth—it was not a way to get caught, in that kind of action. This woman, gullible, continued on the shore, going where calibans wanted to go—of course wanted to go, where the ground was soft, where they could throw up mounds to ring their camps, where there was fish abundant to satisfy caliban appetites.

Fish. On so small a thing, to lose a war.

There were voices, too loud, at the edge of the camp.

"What's that?" he asked, vexed. He stood up. Genley started off from him. "What is that?"

"I'll see," Genley said.

Mannin. The starmen were in that direction; another matter with the starmen. Genley was running, crossing the ground. He went more slowly, overtook Genley where Genley came up against Vil and his lot: it was the starmen. Voices were raised. Genley shoved; Vil shoved back, and Vil's band had weapons.

"Where?" Jin asked directly, thrusting an arm between Vil and Genley, levering them apart. Blue moved in, got Vil's attention with a spearshaft. *"Where?"*

"Don't know where," someone said.

Genley ran, riverward. The spear was quick, coming from the side.

Jin stood there a moment, seeing this, seeing Genley down, writhing on the spear. The hunter pulled it out. Jin drew a breath, just held out his hand.

Blue gave him what he asked for. The smooth wood filled his hand. He walked forward and swung the spear up; the hunter blocked it, instinct, but this was a dead man. He whirled the spear and thrust it up, under the jaw, whipped round with it ready for Vil, for the rest of them. One looked apt to try, but did nothing.

"Gen-ley," he said, not looking at him, watching kinsmen's eyes. There was no answer. He had expected none, not the way that spear had hit. He stood there the space of several breaths. "I want Mannin," he said very quietly, "I want Kim—*Blue*," he said, "where's Parm?" They were Parm's men, these.

Parm came. Stood quietly. Jin saw him unfocussed, to the side; his eyes were all for Vil, who had not yet said a word. All about the camp, everywhere, men were on their feet, weapons ready. He found himself shaking, voiceless in the vastness of his suspicions: Parm Tower, Parm, which had harbored a grudge of which the starmen were the center. Parm, defying him.

Parm, who was allied with Green Tower, had a Green Tower woman; Green had Parm's.

The silence went on. It was Vil's to speak. Or Parm's himself. The calibans were off at hunt. From the river came splashes, grunts. There would be one already to deal with, its rider dead, when it discovered it.

"I'll settle it," Parm said.

It would not be safe. There would be Parm to watch. Parm knew that. They all did. But the structure was too fragile.

"Want those starmen back," Jin said quietly. "Want this settled with Vil."

"He'll get them."

"You be careful," Jin said. He spared a slight shift of his eye to Parm. "You get this man out of my way. Hear?"

There was a slow sorting-out, slow movements everywhere. Already an ariel had come to investigate the bodies. It tugged at one of Genley's fingers.

Jin drove his spear through it, pinned it wriggling to the ground. Genley's face still had its look of shock. "River," Jin said. Burying was too much work. There was a war to fight. He flung the spear down uncleaned, walked away to the fire, took up the skin of drink and had enough to settle his belly. He took a bit more. Tears welled up in his eyes, dammed up there, unsheddable.

Men came and went around him, moving softfooted. He sat there still, with his mind busy, ignoring the rage that had him near to trembling. There was Parm to reckon round now. This man would have to be killed. There were the calibans. When the dead man's came in, that was to settle; kill the beast, before it spread. Let Vil make amends if he would; kill this man too, like killing infection, before it spread.

A tower had to fall over this. No, there was no stopping it. Unless Parm could die in battle. He considered this, more and more thinking of it.

"This Parm," he said to Blue, who sat close by him. "Tomorrow." He made a tiny sign.

Blue's eyes lighted with satisfaction. He closed his fingers in a circle: *band.*

Jin met Blue's gaze and smiled with the eyes only. *Yes.* Decimate the band. Blue would find a way, tomorrow, in battle: put Parm and his lads—Vil too—where they could die.

It would save a tower. Save the unity of the towers.

Thorn came in. So other calibans came, to the scent of blood, to the rumor of ariels. Thorn swung his head, swept the ground with his tail. "Hsss," Jin said, leaning back when that great head thrust itself into his way. He grasped the soft wattle skin and pulled, distracting the caliban, but it wandered off, to walk stifflegged about the camp, just in case.

So he was whole again. Blue's came. The pattern took shape again, men shifting to his side, gathering all about *his* fire and not to Parm's, not joining the search that Parm and his men made.

And when Parm brought the starmen back, he was

obliged to cross the camp with his prisoners, to bring them to him, like an offering . . . offering it was. A placation. The starmen—muddy, wet, bedraggled—"Genley," Mannin kept asking, looking about. "Genley?"—with fear in his voice. This was a nuisance, this man. To all of them. A small voice, while Parm looked at him and reckoned his chances, how much time this bought.

"Vil will pay for his mistake," Parm said, having added up, it seemed, this silence in the camp.

Jin looked elsewhere, not willing to be appeased. The bands had made their judgment, silently, ranged themselves with him. The calibans were at hand, quiet on the fringes of the light.

"I will see to it," Parm persisted, further abasement.

"Do that." Jin looked at him. There was no reprieve. The man had lost his usefulness; now he lost his threat as well. Jin breathed easier still, assumed an easier expression; but Parm knew him. This was a frightened man. And would die before he recovered from it. Jin rose and dusted off his breeches, looked at the starmen.

Mannin snuffled. Kim stared, with dark, measuring eyes.

"These caused the trouble," Jin said, snapped his fingers and pointed at Kim, "Kill that one."

Kim started to his feet. A knife was in his back before he made it. He tumbled backward, and hit the ground the while Mannin simply stared, on his knees, stared and hugged himself and trembled.

"Now you see how it is," Jin said, squatting down, face to face with Mannin. "Genley's dead. Now you're what I have." He stood up again, looked round him at the hunters. "This man's sick. Don't you see? Keep him warm, put him near the fire. He'll want something to eat. He'll know not to run again. And you'll know how to treat what's mine."

Faces met his, settled faces, things secure again, men certain they had taken the stronger side. He walked away to the other fire, to let Blue deal with smaller things, like being rid of Kim.

A waste, that. And not a waste. They did not mistake him now. Perhaps the killing of Genley was no accident. Perhaps Parm misjudged, how important starmen were to him, or where in matters they fitted.

There was respect around him. He was sure of it again.

"In the morning," he muttered, for those who stood by to hear. *"In the morning,"* others echoed, and it went through the camp—enough delay, enough of waiting on Elai's coyness.

In the morning, revenge, blood, promises kept: no real opposition. He would not sleep this night; he wanted to see this thing done at last. Cloud put under his feet, Parm most deftly scotched.

Genley my father.

He mourned. His mourning confounded itself with his rage. He clenched his hands and thought on killing, on killing so thorough none of Cloudside would survive. They would tell tales of him, the things that he had done.

"Jin," a man said, bringing him a thing, a sodden mass of pages. Genley's. He had seen it often. He looked at it, the crawling marks that made no sense to him, dim in fire-light and in the fading. His history.

"Give this to Mannin," he said. "Tell him it's his."

lii

205 CR, day 114
Cloudside

Calibans moved, running through the camp in the dark before the dawn, a sound of heavy tread, of whispering of scales through brush. *"Hai, hey,"* a voice yelled.

Riders scrambled for weapons. McGee collected her spear, her kit.

"Up!" Elai was calling to them; "up!"

They ran, confused in the dark; calibans nosed past riders. Dain doused the embers of the nightfire: the tumult ran down the shore, a murmur of voices in the night, the hisses of calibans as if some strange sea were breaking at their backs. "Hup, hai!" someone cried, near at hand, a man's voice. "Up, up, up!" There were splashes from the river—not attack: McGee had gained a sense of this—it was another sudden move. But something was close. She clutched at her clothes, hurried for the shore in the dark, skipped as ariels flowed like water about her feet, avoided stepping on one somehow.

"Brown," she called; it was all the name it had. *Brown, don't leave me here!* She whistled as best she could in panic. Riders were moving out, in the dark, no sense or order in it. "Hey!"

A shape came toward her, a tongue quested, found her. A head-butt followed, and that was Brown, all slick with water—had to be Brown. McGee clambered doggedly up with a ruthless spring onto Brown's foreleg the way the riders did it, her spear in her hand and her bag of belongings slung about her with her precious notes. Brown started to move along with the others, confused as the others, shouldering others in haste—

Going where? McGee wondered, clinging in the dark, clinging to the spear, the casual way the riders carried it: she had learned to ride with it, balanced herself with it when Brown was in a hurry, with that sinuous rocking fore and back, side to side in a rhythm that had its highs and lows, its pitches into which the riders settled as if they were born to it.

But this was real. This was the last move, the last plunge into dark and war and no one was ordering this thing, except that Elai was up ahead with Taem, with Paeia by her side, no less her enemies in potential. . . . Dain would go to Elai's side: Dain's caliban went where Dain told it, and he would get himself to the fore, while Brown—

I'm scared, I'm scared, I'm scared, she told herself to the rhythm of their moving. *This is no way to fight a war. There ought to be lines, generals, orders; someone ought to set this thing up. We'll all be killed.*

They climbed through brush, making noise, breaking branches, caring nothing that they were heard. Treelimbs raked her: she fended with a leathered arm, kept the spear along Brown's side.

I'm going to use this thing. She flexed her fingers on it, the smooth wood: the head was venomed; an ugly thing, to counter other weapons bound to come her way. Panic gave way to certainty, like some long, long dive which had its own logic, its own morality. Life seemed precious and trifling at once. *Dain. Elai sent him. Her messenger, after all.* She laid her heels to Brown, clutching the spear the tighter, half crazed, drawing great breaths and anxious only to get on with it.

Life, she kept thinking, like a talisman, to keep herself alive.

Dain—Hardly started in his life. The rest of us—all caliban-bait. The thought enraged her, and the spear was like her arm, an extension of herself. The sky was going lighter, the shapes of calibans more definite, the rhythm of Brown's strides more certain.

Kill them, kill them, kill them. That's what's left to do.

liii

Message Alliance HQ to Gehenna Station
Couriered by *AS Phoenix*

. . . inform you that pursuant to the agreement worked out in the commercial exchange treaty a limited access will be extended Union observers for several worlds of the Gehenna Reach, specifically to the reserve on Gehenna and the study program there. Gehenna is required and requested to provide such documented personnel access to quarantine areas, specific operations to be approved by the Base Director. Union observers will at all times be accompanied by Bureau personnel.

In the spirit of detente and in pursuit of mutual interests, a reciprocity has been arranged in the opening of Union records. . . .

liv

205 CR, day 114
Cloudside

The morning came up gold and placid as they moved among the trees, beside the river, in the changes calibans had made in the land. Ridges hove up, freshly dug and showing the roots of overturned trees, the hollows between them pocked with seepage from the river, and Elai read the patterns through which they moved, shaped them with her mind.

Jin is this way, they said. So she knew the time they

would meet. *Ahead lies the alien. We surround you, go beneath you in harmony,*

> *Cloud-towers-clustered-Hillers*
> *well-ordered toward the*
> *Green-nest-aggression*

It spiralled off into gilded distances, the wreckage, the patterns building about them for days.

Where? she had tried to ask of Scar last night; but Scar ignored the stones, ignored her, as if he had said it all. *When?*

They moved when it was time; and calibans knew that time when they saw it, when the Pattern shaped itself, that was all.

Cloud against Styx.

One way against another.

There was logic in it. It had compelled Paeia, brought Taem to her side. Perhaps Weirds on both sides had shaped this confrontation: there were hints of this in the patterns . . . that Weirds knew no tower-loyalty.

There was herself; there was Jin.

Two kinds; and calibans brought them both, here, to this place, long-appointed. She had her spear in hand, her darts slung to her side. Her mates, her rivals were by her, joined with her, like Taem, who had said nothing of why he came, not the deep reasons: only he was there, and the pattern agreed with that, shaping no other way for him to go. They were Cloudside, and the whole Cloudside pattern was being shoved at now.

Not a matter now of driving them off a time. She read that too, the way she read the land. Jin took the high ground, to push. She knew what he would do, and by that what they would do, surely as the sun came up—if flesh was strong enough.

She put forward her spear in the dim dawn, in the quickening of Scar's pace. There was no time now to order things. She gave a fleeting thought to MaGee and wished that she had had Dain put her somwhere, but MaGee would fare as they all fared, and there was no helping it. Pattern against pattern. The calibans had made MaGee part of it: part of her; that was the way of it. Grays joined them, plowed the earth like the currents of the sea. Their powerful claws found places to probe in the mounds: they dived in earth and surfaced again, hissing and whistling, but the long-striding browns scrambled across soft ground, four-footed and stable, bridging the gaps with the reach of their limbs, treading the grays down with grand disdain, in silent haste.

The sun arrived, spread its rays through the ruin of a forest before them, where the trees had been cast down, undermined. They plunged over this, like a living torrent, with hissings and scramblings; but greater were the rocks down by the sea that she had climbed on Scar. Grays, not their own, vacated the Pattern and fled before the browns, through the brush, over the ridges, among trees still standing.

Scar's collar flashed up. Taem's brown plunged ahead. The hisses of browns broke like water hitting hot metal.

Her riders surged about her. Whistles split the air; younger calibans took their riders to the fore as they climbed the mounds, refusing the patterns they met now.

Elai clamped her knees taut as they met soft ground where grays were at work and Scar lurched down and up again, past the roots of overthrown trees, past brush that raked harmlessly on her leather-clad legs.

"Hai!" She caught the fever and shouted with her young men's cries, with the high-pitched yelps of the young women as they came down the banks among grays that froze under the browns' scrabbling claws, confused and immobile. She couched her spear, held her seat, for now other shapes hove up, rider-bearing calibans, shapes bristling with raised collars, with spears in human hands. Darts flew, struck her leathered arm.

She shouted, not knowing what she yelled, but all at once the fear was gone, every dread was gone. *"Ellai!"* she was yelling at the last, which was her mother's name; and *"Cloud!"*

More darts; she shook them off; they struck Scar in vain, useless on his hide. Lesser browns fled Scar's approach, bearing their riders out of his path. Scar trod others down, mounted over them, clawing their riders heedlessly underfoot, with riders yelling and calibans lurching this way and that through the ruin of trees.

Scar lurched, taxed her weak leg. She held as the earth opened, and grays came up, some calibans losing their riders as they slid into the undermining, and over all the hisses and the screams.

But she knew where she was going. Paeia was beside her, was delayed by one of the Styxsiders so that she lost that guard; but then came a clearing of bodies, a withdrawing except for the rider coming toward her, a caliban larger than the rest.

Jin.

Scar lurched aside, almost unseated her. One of her riders rushed by in the whirl of day and trees and plunging bodies. Her spearshaft cracked hard against another, and Scar bore her out of the path of that attack as another of her riders took it. Taem was out there, Taem's brown trying Jin's, circling.

"Scar!" she yelled, her spear tucked again beneath her arm. She drove with her heels, less to Scar's tough hide than the darts that spattered about them. "Scar!"

Scar moved, shied off as Jin overrode Taem, kept retreating, retreating, disordering their lines.

Jin's brown scrambled forward, lunged low as Scar shied off, presenting his belly. Elai fought for balance, dug with her heel and rammed the spear at the Styxsider; but Scar was still rising, up and over the collar crest of Jin's caliban.

The lame leg betrayed her as Scar twisted, as he reared up with the Styxsider in his jaws and the Styxside caliban lunging and clawing at his gut. She hit the ground, winded, tucked low as a tail skimmed her back, melded herself in the gouged earth as it came back again, as the battle rolled over her. She spat mud from her mouth and scrambled for her life as the feet came near, as the rolling mass lashed the ground and calibans raked each other.

She fell again, legs too shaken to bear her weight, used the spear to lever herself up, sorted caliban from caliban in the mass and the one with the throat-grip had a starlike scar shining on his side. She rammed the spear into the soft spot of the other's neck, heaved her weight against it, and the mass all came her way: a tail hit her, but she was already going down, half-senseless as calibans poured over her, to the sharing of the kill.

She scrambled out of the mire—wild, blind struggle: hands seized her, pulled her to safety, and she leaned on

offered arms—Dain was one. They pulled her further, away
from the heaving mass that had become a ball of calibans,
huge browns biting and rolling like ariels about a prize. She
could not see Scar.

"They've run," Maeri said, one of her own. "First,
they're *down*."

There was chaos everywhere, no rider able to stay
mounted, calibans pursuing fugitives, fighting each other,
humans in pursuit of humankind, the earth thundering to
the impacts of the massed bodies in that knot before them.
She saw Scar pull free of it, saw him seize another throat
in his jaws and plunge into the mass.

Alive, then, alive. And Jin was under that. She began to
shiver, unable to stand.

They brought her an accounting of the dead: Taem was
one; but she had known that. There were other names.
"MaGee?" she asked. "Where's Paeia?"

"Paeia's hunting," the man told her, kin of Paeia; and
with a grin: "MaGee fell off way back. Must be safe."

"Find her," Elai said, never taking her eyes from the
feeding that had begun on this hillside above the Cloud.

There were other things to do, but the calibans would
tend to them; and most of her young·folk would not go so
far as the Styx. Some would, to be sure the Pattern there
shaped the way it should. Most would come back to her,
here, in good time.

She gave a whistle, trying to retrieve Scar; but that was
useless yet. It would be useless until there was nothing left
but bones. So she sat there on the trampled hill to wait,
numb and cold and aching when she moved. They brought
her drink; they brought her the prizes of Jin's camp: she
took little interest in these things.

But they found MaGee, finally; and MaGee sat down
near her in the dim morning with the calibans dragging the
bones toward the river, leaving the trampled ground.

She offered MaGee her hand. MaGee's eyes were
bruised-looking, her face scratched and battered. Her hair
hung loose from its braids, caked with mud.

So was her own, she reckoned.

"You're all right," MaGee said.

"All right," she said, too weary to move an arm. She motioned with her eyes. "Got him chewed down to bone, that Thorn."

Something distressed MaGee, the blood maybe, or getting thrown. Her mouth shook. "What happened?"

"Got him." Elai drew a hard breath. Her ribs hurt. Clearly MaGee failed to understand much at all. She whistled up Scar, levering herself up again with the spear, because there was something starting on that bank, a new altercation among calibans—some of the Styxside lot, that might be, or some of their own from Cloudside, testing out who had the right to shove and who had to take. She was anxious. She wanted Scar out of there, but calibans were snapping and lashing at one another and she did not want the quarrel moved their way either. She could see Scar among the others; could see Paeia's big brown throwing her weight around, sweeping lessers out of the way with her tail. The sniping attacks went on, lessers' jaws closing on a hind or forelimb, dragging at the skin, worrying them from this side and that—

He's old, Elai thought. Her fists were clenched. *That Thorn got him in the belly.* She saw Scar bowl a rival over and get him belly up, after which the rival ran away, but others worried at him: he swept them with his tail, whirled and snapped. It went on.

"Is he all right out there?" MaGee asked.

"Of course he's all right." Elai whistled again. Others called their mounts, and some of the quarreling quieted. But there was no recalling them, not yet. She turned, motioned with her spear downriver, and others gained their feet, of the elders.

"What now?" MaGee asked.

"Nothing, now," Elai said, looking at her in bewilderment. "Don't you know? That's Jin down there. We've won."

lv

Message: Gehenna Station to Base Director

Survey notes two movements this morning—one on a broad front toward the Styx and a second, smaller and more compact movement up the Cloud. The Styxward movement is of greater speed. Survey suggests contrary to expectations that the invasion may have been routed. . . .

lvi

205 CR, day 215
Cloudside

Someone whistled, to the rear of the column, and heads turned: McGee looked, the while she limped beside Elai over the sand beside the Cloud: the calibans had come, swimming effortlessly down the current.

"Do we ride?" McGee asked. It seemed madness that they had left the calibans behind; or not madness: for her own part she had taken one fall, and that was enough for her bones. One fall; one nightmare of Brown trampling down a man. But no one said anything; they had left the calibans behind and walked at Elai's order, as if it were sane; and she was not sure of that, was sure of nothing now.

Still the silence. Elai said little on the walk, nothing but monosyllables, stayed lost in her own thoughts, unlike a woman who had just won the world entire, who held all Gehenna in her hands.

The calibans paced them in the river, that was all.

"No," Maeri answered her question, Dain's sister of First Tower. "Don't think so."

They walked further. The calibans dived and surfaced, not coming in, but at last Scar did, strode out on the shore ahead of them.

Riverweed, McGee thought at first. But it was his skin, hanging in rags about his belly, about his limbs. He walked with his collar down, his tail inscribing a serpentine in the sand.

Elai whistled then; and Scar stopped. *He's hurt,* McGee opened her mouth to ask, to protest; but she stood still, watched with dismay as Elai approached him, touched him, climbed up to her place despite the hanging skin.

They began to walk again, in Scar's tracks on the shore, at Elai's back, no more cheerful than Scar himself, while the calibans sported in the river.

They would know, back in Cloud Towers, who had won, McGee reckoned; the calibans would get there before them: ariels would pattern it, grays would build it for the people to see, out beyond the rows of dry fishnets.

But she looked at Elai riding ahead of them, at bowed shoulders, both rider and caliban hurting.

She was afraid then, the way she had been afraid before the battle; in a way that wiped out nightmares of what had been.

What's happening? she wondered. She stalked Dain, walked beside him in hope of answers, but he had none, only trudged along like the rest.

They camped early; more calibans became tractable and came in, seeking out their riders. Scar sulked alone, down by the riverside, and Elai huddled by the fire.

"Is everything all right?" McGee asked at last, crouching there.

"Jin's dead," said Elai tonelessly. "Styx towers will fall now."

"You mean that's where the others went." McGee pursued the matter, knowing it was fragile ground. Elai held out her hand and opened the fingers. End of the matter. McGee sat and hugged her knees against her chest, in the fire warmth, surer and surer that something had been lost.

Scar, she kept thinking in growing chill, and restrained herself from a glance toward the river; she knew what she would see: an old caliban on the last of his strength, a caliban who had done well to survive his last battle. Some other caliban could take him now. Any other. If one were inclined to try.

Paeia—off hunting still. Paeia would come. Maybe others. She lowered her head against her arms, feeling all her aches, a nagging sense that all the ground she relied on was undermined.

Other riders came before the dawn, quietly, bringing Styx-sider prisoners who came and sat down across the fire, a handful of youths, sober and terrified. Elai thought about them a long time.

Speak up for them, McGee thought; it was outsider-instinct. And then she clenched her fist in front of her mouth as she sat there and pressed her fist against her lips to hold herself from talking. *I could get Elai killed with wrong advice.*

But it was Elai let the boys live after all, with a gesture of her hand, and they sat there and shivered, all tucked up looking lost and scared and knowing that (if Elai told truth) there was nothing left to run to.

So other riders brought other prisoners. One ran: Parm was his name, at whose name the riders hissed . . . he took off running and the calibans got him, down by the river in the dark.

McGee sat there and shivered, the same way she had sat through the rest, as if some vital link had been severed. She betrayed nothing, had no horror left.

It's cold, she told herself. *That's all.*

She had learned to be practical about death, in these days, to deal it out, to watch it. It was like any other thing, to listen to a man die, a little sound, a little unpleasantness. A small, lost sound, compared to the battle on the shore, the earth shaking to the fall of the great browns. The air filled with their hisses. Soon done. Forgettable.

But they brought Mannin in, and that was different . . . "Found one of the starmen," Paeia said, who had come with that group. And what they brought was a leather-clad, draggled man who did nothing but cough and shiver and tucked himself up like the teenaged boys. This thing—this wretched thing—she stared at him: it was only the dark hair, the height, that told her which it was.

"Let him live," she said to Elai, in a voice gone hoarse and hard. So she discovered the measure of herself, that she could bear the death of natives, but not of her own kind. She was ashamed of that.

"He's yours," Elai said.

"Give him food and water," McGee said, never moving from where she sat, never moving her fist from her chin, her limbs from the tightness that kept them warm. She never looked closely at Mannin, not being interested any longer. It was a horror she did not want, at the moment, to consider, how she had come to sit here passing life and death judgments, in the mud and the stink and the calibans milling about ready for the kill.

It did not seem likely then that she could ever go back to white, clean walls, that she could unlearn what she knew, or be other than MaGee. MaGee. Healer. Killer. Dragon-rider left afoot. She saw the sunlit beach, there in the night, herself young, Elai a child, old Scar in his prime again, his hide throwing back the daylight.

Here was dark, and fire, and they collected the leavings of the war.

Perhaps they would find the rest, Genley; Kim.

"Ask him," she asked one of the riders at last, "where the other starmen are."

"He says," that rider reported back to her, "that this Jin killed the rest."

"Huh," she said, and the dried fish she was eating went dryer yet in her mouth and unpalatable. She found another depth of herself, that she could still harbor a resentment toward the dead. But she did. She wished in a curious division of her thoughts that even Mannin would try to run; that the whole matter might be tidy. And that horrified her.

"Someone should take Mannin to the Wire," she said, for Elai's hearing.

Elai waved a hand.

So a rider named Cloud did that, who had a caliban who was willing to go. They went off into the dark and the last of the starman matter was settled.

It was not what matttered, on the Cloud.

lvii

205 CR, day 168
Base Director's Office

". . . It's down," the secretary said, wild-eyed and distressed, breathless from the other office, leaning on the desk forgetful of protocols. "The tower, sir—it's down, just—*fell.* I looked up in the window one minute and it was going down—"

There were scattered red lights on the desk com. One was an incoming station message, on that reserved channel; more were flicking on.

"The Styx tower," the director said, striving for calm.

"The face of it—just hung there a moment like gravity had gone, and then it went down in all this dust—"

The account went on, mild hysteria. The Director pushed the button for the fax from station.

". . . Urgent: your attention soonest to accompanying survey pictures. Styx towers eight, six, two in collapse. . . ."

The door was open. Security showed up, agitated and diffident, red-faced in the doorway.

"You've seen it," the man said.

"My secretary saw it go. What's going on out there? Station says we've got more towers down. Maybe others going."

"Try Genley again?"

The Director considered it, thought it through, the governing principle of all dealings across the wire. "Try any contact you like. But no one goes outside."

"If there are injured out there—"

"No aid. No intervention. You're sure about our own subground."

"Systems are working."

"Try McGee again. Keep trying—Get back to work," he told the secretary, who went out a shaken man. He wanted a drink himself. He was not about to yield to that. He wanted the pills in his desk. He withheld the reassurance. The desk com was still full of red lights, not so many as before, but still a bloody profusion of them. Another winked out.

"Prepare a report," he told Security. "I want a report. We've got observers coming in. I want this straightened up."

"Yes, sir," Security said, and took that for dismissal.

More of the lights were going out. His secretary was back at work. Things had to be set in order: there had to be reports with explanations. His hands were shaking. He began to think through the array of permissions he had given, the dispatch of agents. Those would be reviewed, criticized. There had to be answers ready, reasons, explanations. The Bureau abhorred enigmas.

McGee, he thought, cursing her, setting his hope in her, that all reports now indicated that the Cloud was unaffected.

One native site to show the visitors. One native site to showcase; and McGee could get access to it—surmising McGee was still alive.

He started composing messages to the field while the reports came in, one and the other of the Stygian towers going down.

Everywhere. There was death out there, wholesale. Optics picked up the movements of Calibans. The two settlements went to war or something like a war and calibans went berserk and destroyed one side, overthrowing towers, burrowing through planted fields, everything, while the apparently solid earth churned and settled.

"There's a rider coming to the wire," they told him later that day, when he had sent message after message out. "He's carrying someone."

And later: "Sir, it's Mannin."

"What happened?" he asked, brushing past the medics, shocked at the emaciation, the slackjawed change in the man on the stretcher, there in the foyer of the med building. "Mannin?"

He got no sensible answer, nothing but babble of riversides and calibans.

"Where did you come from?" he asked again.

Mannin wept, that was all. And he deputed someone to listen and report; and came back later himself only when the report began to be coherent, news of going upriver, of seeing McGee, of Genley and Kim murdered in cold blood.

So he went to hear it, sat by the bedside of a man who had gone to bone and staring eyes, who looked the worse for being shaven and clipped and turned into something civilized.

"Going to shuttle you up to station," he said when Mannin had done. "There's a ship due. They'll get you back to Pell."

Maybe names like that no longer made sense to Mannin. He never even reacted to it.

lviii

Message: Base Director to E. McGee, in field

Urgent that you report in: the Styx towers have all fallen. We see refugees but they do not come near the wire. We have recovered Dr. Genley's notes, which shed new light on the situation. We assure you no punitive action is contemplated. . . .

Message: Base Director to E. McGee, in field

Did you receive the last message? Please respond. The situation is urgent. Bureau is ferrying in an observer from Unionside, with documents that may bear on your studies. The situation for the mission is quite delicate, and I cannot urge strongly enough that you put yourself back in contact with this office at once, by whatever means.

lix

205 CR, day 172
Cloud Towers

"No," Elai said. "No com." And McGee did not dispute it, only frowned, sitting there in the hall of First Tower where Elai sat. Elai had a blanket wrapped about her. She had not combed her hair; it stuck out at angles, webbed like lint. Her eyes were terrible.

Her heir was there—Din, who crouched in the corner with his juvenile caliban, with his eyes as dreadful as Elai's own—frightened little boy, who knew too much. Din had his knife. It was irony that he was here, an heir defending his elder; but this seven year old had the facts all in hand. This seven year old had an aunt ready to take him when she could, to her own tower, to what befell a seven year old heir to a line that had lasted long on the banks of the Cloud.

Scar was dying—had never come up to First Tower, but languished on the shore. Elai only waited for this, the way she had waited for days, eating nothing, drinking little.

Quiet steps came and went, Weirds, who tended Elai. Taem never came; the nurses had Cloud kept somewhere away, as much in danger, but ignorant. A baby. Likeliest catspaw for Paeia if Din came to grief.

There was Dain, always Dain, at the doors below. Dain's sister Maeri. The Flanahans were loyal still; would die in that doorway if they must. They were armed—but so were all the riders. And so far one could come and go.

"MaGee," said Elai, having wakened.

"First," McGee murmured in respect.

"What would you advise?"

"Advise?" Perhaps Elai was delirious, perhaps not. Elai made no more patterns, sat with her arms beneath the blankets, alone. McGee shrugged uneasily. "I'd advise you eat something."

Elai failed to react to that. Just failed. There was long silence. It went like this, through the hours.

"First," McGee said, working her hands together, clenching them and unclenching. "First, let's go . . . just use some sense and eat something, and you and I'll just walk out of here. To the Wire, maybe, maybe somewhere else. You can just walk away. Isn't that good advice?"

"I could make a boat," Elai said, "and go to the islands."

"Well, we could do that," McGee said, half-hoping, half-appalled, shocked at once by Elai's dry laugh. Elai slipped forth a hand, opened thin fingers in mockery, dropping imaginary stones. *Forget that, old friend.*

"Listen, I don't intend to put up with this, Elai."

Elai's eyes more than opened, the least frownline creased her brow. But she said nothing.

"Styx towers are down," McGee said. "What's that going to mean in the world?"

A second throwing-away gesture. "Should have made the boats," Elai said. "But they'd have taken down our towers."

"Who?" There was a cold wind up McGee's back. "What do you mean they'd have taken down the towers? Calibans? Like Jin's towers? Like they're doing there? What are you talking about, First?"

"Don't know, MaGee. Don't know. Maybe not. Maybe so."

"They'll kill. Like at the Styx towers."

"The strong ones'll come this way," Elai said. She was hoarse. This talk tired her. She made an impatient gesture. "All those Styxside men, too mean; all those women, too stupid—Life would kill them, here. Land will kill them. Most. Maybe not all." The frown reappeared between her brows. "Or maybe Styxside way just grows up again. Don't know."

Somewhere at the depth of her McGee was shocked. "You mean these Styxsiders did something the calibans didn't like. That *that* was what killed them."

Elai shrugged. "They ate grays."

"For years, Elai—"

"It got worse, didn't it? They went on and on; they got themselves the likes of Jin; he pushed." Elai made a motion of her fingers, indicating boundaries. "Calibans aren't finished with this pattern, MaGee, here on the Cloud. Cloud stands. That's what it meant, out there."

"And they'd have stopped your ships the same way?"

"Maybe." Elai heaved a breath. "Maybe not. Old Scar would swim. Maybe he thought the same as me. That old sea-folk, he was just bigger than Scar, that's all. Or maybe that was *our* limit and he was saying so."

McGee saw pictures in her mind, squatting there with her fist against her lips: saw every caliban on Gehenna in every river valley making mounds much alike, except on Styx and Cloud. "Boundaries," she said, and looked up, at Elai. But Elai had shut her eyes again, closing her out.

She looked at Din, at the boy huddled in the corner with his caliban. The hall was eerily vacant. Only a single ariel lurked in the shadows. Of all the communications that had once flowed from this place, one small green watcher. There was always one.

McGee hugged her knees and thought and thought, the patterns that had been since they had come home, lines and mounds across the river, beyond her to read.

And Scar dying on the shore, slowly, snapping now and again at grays who came too close.

She could not bear it longer. She got up and walked out, down the access, down the corridors in the dark, where voices were hushed, where desertions had begun, deep below, calibans and Weirds at their work, which might be undermining or shoring up, either one.

Dain gave her a curious look as she passed the lower door; a handful more of the riders had joined him, armed with spears; so no one got into First Tower yet. It seemed sure that they would. Everything was at a kind of rest,

Paeia plotting in her tower, Taem's in uproar, noncommunicant, now that Taem was dead, heirless; and other towers turned secretive. The fishers still plied their trade; folk went out to farm. But they did so carefully, disturbing as little as they could; and strange calibans had come: they saw them in the river, refugees from the battle, maybe Styxside calibans, maybe calibans that had never come near humans before. If anyone knew, the Weirds might, but Weirds kept their own counsel these days.

She stood there looking out to the shore, where Scar still sat like some rock under the sun.

"Still alive," said Dain. His own caliban was about, not with him, not far either. She spied it with its collar up, just watching.

She started walking, walked all the way out past the nets where Scar sat. The place stank, a dry fishy stench like stagnant water, like caliban and rot. Not dead yet. But his skin hung like bits of old paper, and his ribs stuck out through what whole skin there was as if it were laid over a skeleton. The eyes were still alive, still blinked. He moved no more than that.

She picked up a rock. Laid it down. Went and gathered another, caliban sized. She struggled with it, and set it onto the other. Of smaller ones she built the rest of a spiral, and the small spur that gave direction. An ariel came and helped her, trying to change the pattern to what was; she pitched a pebble at it and it desisted. She wiped her brow, wiped tears off her face and kept building, and saw others had come, Dain and his folk. They stared, reading the pattern, First Tower built taller than the rest, the uncomplex thread that went from it toward a thing she had made square and alien.

Dain invaded the pattern, severed the line with his spearbutt, defying her.

Scar moved: his collar fringe went up. Dain looked at that and stayed still. No Cloudsider moved.

McGee hunted up more rocks. Her clothes were drenched with sweat. The wind came cold on her. There were more and more watchers, riders and calibans of First Tower.

"Paeia will come," Dain said. "MaGee—don't do this."

She gave him a wild look, lips clamped. He stepped back

at that. The crowd grew, and there was unearthly quiet. A gray moved in and tried to change the pattern. Scar hissed and it retreated to the fringes again, only waiting. McGee worked, more and more stones. Bruised ribs ached. She limped, sweated, kept at it, making her statement that was not in harmony with anything ever written in the world.

Dain handed another man his spear then and carried stone for her, leaving her to place it where she would; and that made it swifter, the building of this pattern. She built and built, lines going on to a settlement by the Styx, going outward into the sea, going south to rivers she remembered—*Elai*, the statement was: *expansion. Links to the starmen. The starmen*—She built for creatures who had never seen the stars, whose eyes were not made for looking at them, made the sign for *river* and for *going up,* for *dwelling-place* and *sunwarmth,* for *food/fish* and again for *warmth* and *multitude,* all emanating from the Base.

A fisher came into the pattern, bringing more stones; so others came, bringing more and more. *Growing things,* one patterned. A woman added a Nesting-stone. Ariels invaded the structures, clambered over them, poked their heads into crevices between stones, put out their tongues to test the air and the madness of these folk.

McGee lost track of the signs; some she did not know. She tried to stop some, but now there were more and more; and Weirds watching on the side. It was out of control, going off in directions she had never planned. "Stop!" she yelled at them, but they went on building the starman theme, wider and wider.

She sat down, shaking her head, losing sight of the patterns, of what they did. She wiped her face, hugged herself, and just sat there, more scared than she had been in the war.

She looked up in a sudden silence and saw Elai there, in a place the crowd had made—Elai, arriving like an apparition, her person still in disarray, Din and his smallish caliban trailing in her wake.

"MaGee," Elai said; it was a whipcrack of a voice, thin as it was. There was rage.

"MaGee's crazy," McGee said. She stood up. "Don't the Weirds have the right to say anything they like?"

"You want them to take us down, MaGee, like they took Jin?"

Scar hissed and turned his head, one plate-sized eye turned toward Elai. That was all. Then he wandered off, avoiding the pattern, while humans scrambled from his path.

He went to the river. McGee saw him going in, turned to watch Elai's face, but Elai gave no sign of grief, nothing.

"You're a fool," Elai said in a weak voice, and started back again.

Paeia was in her way, astride her big brown, with armed Second Tower riders at her side.

Elai stopped, facing that. Everything stopped for a moment, every movement. Then Elai walked around to the side. They exacted that of her, but they stood still and let her do it.

They stood there surveying the pattern. They stood there for a long time, and eventually the crowd found reasons to be elsewhere, one by one.

McGee went when those nearest her went, limping and feeling the wind cold on her sweat-drenched clothes.

A lance brushed her when she passed Paeia on her way back. She looked up, at Paeia's grim, weathered face, at eyes dark and cold as river stones.

"Fool," Paeia said.

"That's two that have told me," McGee said, and backed off from the speartip and walked away, expecting it in her back. But they let her pass.

lx

Message: Base Director to E. McGee

Repeat: Urgent you report: we have Bureau representatives incoming. They're bringing Unionside observers. There will be data essential to your work. . . .

lxi

Notes, coded journal Dr. E. McGee

Elai's no worse. No better. Paela hasn't come through the door. I did one thing, at least, with my meddling—

They're waiting. They're just waiting to know what the calibans are going to do now that I've done what I did.

I didn't think it through. I tried to tell the calibans they couldn't lose Elai, that was all, tried explaining she could make the Base itself rational—tried to explain starmen. Tried to tell them about their world and what they were missing, and O dear God, I did something no one's ever done: I went and did a human pattern in terms they could read. I tried to say there was good in starmen, that there's life outside—and they took it away from me, the Cloudsiders, they started telling it their way, their own legends— they were talking about *themselves*.

No one's moving. The calibans have gone off—most of them. Elai's eating again, at least I got her to take a little soup this morning; that was a triumph. Dain helped. Everyone's going about quiet, really quiet.

And across the river there's building going on, within sight of the towers. The calibans are in debate. I think they must be. Patterns rise and fall incomplete. There's no reason in it that makes sense yet. They reform the old pattern and then tear it up again in new elaborations, and they do things I don't make sense of.

Paeia's been forestalled. This is no time to upset the calibans.

lxii

Message: station to Base

AS Wyvern inbound from Cyteen. Visitors aboard.

lxiii

Cloudside

There was restlessness that night. McGee heard it starting in the depths, vague echoes of movements, stirrings and slitherings down below, and she shivered, lying on her bed, on the earthen ledge in her own quarters, wrapped in her rough blankets.

It grew. Her heart began beating in a panic like night fears, and she scrambled up, threw on her clothes without seeking any light: she went blind as she had learned to do, running up the spiral turns of the hall—So others came, men and women running either way, some down toward the exit from the tower, some few up, as she ran, up toward the hall where they kept firelight these last nights, since it had become Elai's refuge.

Elai was there, awake. Dain was; and young Din; and Maeri, and others, pale and distressed faces. They brought no weapons; their calibans had deserted them, save for Din's.

The access gave up a flood of ariels, like a plague of vermin scrabbling across the floor, like the first feeling outward of some vast beast; in that flood a few grays hove up through the access pit, up the ramp, casting their heads about, putting out their tongues.

What came then was huge, was bigger than Scar had been, a caliban that, up on his legs, was halfway to the ceiling—No one's, that brown. The riders gave back from it, even Dain; McGee stood sweating, out of its convenient path, lacking the courage to fling herself for a mouthful in its direct route to Elai.

Elai sat still, image-like in her wooden chair. Her hands were in her lap. It put out a tongue, leaned forward, leaned, put out a foot and made that a step and a second pace, that closed the distance. The tongue investigated, barely touched Elai's robes; and other calibans were coming, invading all the halls, a noisy scrabbling flood below.

We'll fall, McGee thought, imagined First Tower in collapse, them dying in a cascade of earth at the same time as every other human on the Cloud, the Base under attack, Styx going under yet again.

The big brown's collar crest went down. He turned himself, his long tail sweeping their circle wider, but that was a settling at Elai's side, half up on his forelegs. The crest went up again.

"Dear God," McGee breathed, when she remembered to breathe, but they were half the hall deep in calibans now, and there was hissing and snapping as the calibans defined territory, as Dain's brown moved in clearing rivals, and Maeri's showed up, and young Din scrambled for cover in McGee's arms, the young brown Twostone hissing and lashing its tail in front of them, holding his ground against larger ones.

There was order made. Elai put out a hand and appropriated the big brown. His crest flicked, in something like pleasure.

McGee caught another breath. Her chest hurt. She clenched Din in her arms and the boy struggled. She let him go, remembering he was Cloudsider, and at most times independent. No one moved beyond that for a very long time, until calibans had stopped milling and crests were down.

A gray came to the middle of the floor and spat up a fish. The big brown leaned forward and ate it. The gray got out of the way in haste.

"Paeia will be disappointed," Elai said, and looking at McGee: "So, MaGee?"

McGee ignored her limbs, which still felt dissolved, and the sweat that was running on her skin, lifted her chin and managed a grand indifference. "You had old Scar a long time; you never figured he wasn't important of his kind? He picked you from way back. You're not a warleader. If they wanted one they'd have had Jin just as easy. They wanted you, First, for some reason."

Elai just stared at her, her hand resting on the big brown's shoulder. Jaw set, eyes hard. The First of First Tower was not prone to displays.

"His name's Sun," she said.

Message: Base Director to E. McGee

Repeat: urgent you respond. We have a shuttle landing. We have a Dr. Ebhardt, Unionside, with aides, coming in. This is an official instruction: this office is taking the position that some damage to the com must have occurred and therefore no reprimand will be lodged. I add to this an earnest personal plea: I am concerned with your welfare and urge you to consider your professional and personal interests and to respond to this message by whatever means may be accessible to you. Dr. Mannin's brief report of you indicates that you are well and in a position to have gathered valuable material. I am sure that the arriving mission will make every effort to accommodate you within its policies and I am sure will not wish to interfere in your work. It would, however, be of great help if we could have your direct input.

lxiv

Message: E. McGee to Base Director
transmitted from Cloud River

This is not a time or place for interference. I regret the misfortune of the Styx River mission. Keep your observers at a distance. Calibans are very uneasy just now. Report follows.

lxv

205 CR, day 298
Cloudside

The thing grew on the riverside, taking shape out of the reeds they had floated down. Calibans had nudged it this way and that, still prowled round it of nights to see what new thing it was becoming, with their tying and their braiding, not an easy matter; but MaGee had unbent enough to give some advice, being less pure a starman than she had been. The sun came up on a new thing every morning; and Elai watched this business of boatbuilding from the crest of First Tower with a certain forlorn distress.

Dain would try this thing. MaGee persuaded her the First of First Tower was too important to be laughed at if it was a little cranky at the start; and when it was proved, then she would try it.

She looked out over all the land, toward the horizon this morning; and saw a thing before any sentry saw it.

Metal flashed in the sun, in the sky. It was a ship from the Base, but not going up. Coming their way. It had gone crazy, was going to fall. She could hear the sound of it now, a sound like distant thunder.

Work stopped on the shore. Folk looked up, everywhere.

It was coming their way. Elai's heart turned over in her, but she stood her ground (the First of First would not run, would not show fear) with her fists clenched on the rim of the tower, her eyes fixed on this visitor.

It was coming down, carefully, not falling. Elai became sure of that. She turned, whistled to Sun, passed her distressed offspring, who had dropped their game of tag with the calibans.

"MaGee!" she shouted in anger, on her way down. *"MaGee—"*

They kept to their side of the river, these intruders. Elai had a closer view of the ship as Sun carried her up and out of the river, the water rolling off her leathers, off his sides. Out of the tail of her eye she saw MaGee with Dain and a dozen others of her riders. They were all armed. She was. The spear she had in hand seemed futile, but she carried it all the same, to make these strange starmen figure where was their limit.

She tapped Sun, making him understand that she meant to stop. Sun took his time about it. The other riders drew even with her. And one of the starmen came out from the shadow of that shining ship—not much larger than her boat, this ship. It had flattened the grass in a circle about it. It was quiet now. The thunder had stopped. And they wanted to talk: that was clear too.

"MaGee," she said, "see what they want." And: "MaGee," she added, making MaGee stop after she had slid down from behind Dain: "You don't go with them."

"No," MaGee agreed, and walked out to that man, looking like a rider herself, lean and leather-clad, her graying hair, her fringes blowing in the wind that whipped at them, that made the fine blue cloth the starman wore do strange small flutters, showing how soft it was. They were rich, the starmen. They had everything. They brought their ship to show what they could do, overshadowing the boat there on the shore. To impress. They could have come afoot. They had done that before. Or in their crawlers, that they used sometimes, that made noise and disturbed the ariels for days.

It was all show, theirs against hers.

She waited, spear held crosswise. Paeia was one who had

come out, with her heir, grim and disapproving, waiting for mistakes. And MaGee went out to this starman and talked a while, just talked; after a time MaGee folded her arms and shifted her weight and seemed not to fear attack, but she looked down much and seldom at the starmen, saying things with the way she stood that seemed uneasy.

Then she came back, and looked up at her on Sun. "First," she said, "they want to talk to you. To tell you they're wanting to talk trade."

Elai frowned.

"It's this new lot," MaGee said carefully, "they want some things changed. Trade would mean medicines. Maybe metal. You need that."

"What do they want back?"

"You," MaGee said. Elai's eyes met hers and locked, honest and urgent. "I'll tell you what: they want to make sure you grow the right way, starman-like. To be sure you're something they can deal with someday. When you're like them." Her eyes slid aside, back again. "That dark one—that's Dr. Myers; from the Base; the light one's Ebhardt—from Union. From Cyteen."

"Is *that* a Unioner?" Elai had heard of these strangers, these folk of the ship that never came. Her books had them in them. She looked with narrowed eyes on these visitors. "Hssst—*Sun*."

Sun moved forward, a sudden long stride. The starmen fell back in disorder and recovered themselves. "You," Elai said, "you're from Cyteen, are you? From outside?"

"Maybe McGee's told you," Ebhardt began.

"You want trade? Give you what, starman?"

"What you have too much of. What we don't have. Maybe carvings. Maybe fish."

"Bone's *ours*," Elai said. The starman was insolent as she had thought; she tapped Sun in his soft skin, beneath the collar, and the collar went up. They retreated yet again, and beyond them another figure mounted half up the access to their ship. "But fish, maybe. Maybe things you want to know, starman. Maybe you'd like that better. Maybe you sit behind that Wire and ask your questions. This land's mine. Cloud's mine. All this—" She swept her arm about, a pass of her spear. "My name's Elai, Ellai's daughter, line of the first Cloud, the first Elly; of Pia, line of the first Jin when they made the world. *And you're on my land.*"

They backed up from her. "McGee," one said.

"I'd move," MaGee said equably, from somewhere to the rear. "The First just told you she'd trade, and where; and you don't want an incident, you really wouldn't want an incident at the foundation of the world. I'd really advise you pack up and get this machinery out of here."

There was some thinking about it. "First," one said then, and both of them made a downcast gesture and began a retreat with more dignity than their last.

They took the ship away. The calibans just stood and looked up at it with curious tilts of their heads, and Elai did, sitting on Sun—waved her spear at them, adding insult to the matter. Her riders jeered at them. Paeia looked impressed for once, she and her heir.

"Come on," Elai said to MaGee, touching Sun to make him put his leg out. "Ride behind me."

VIII

outward

GENEALOGY 305 CR

Gehenna Outpost [523]

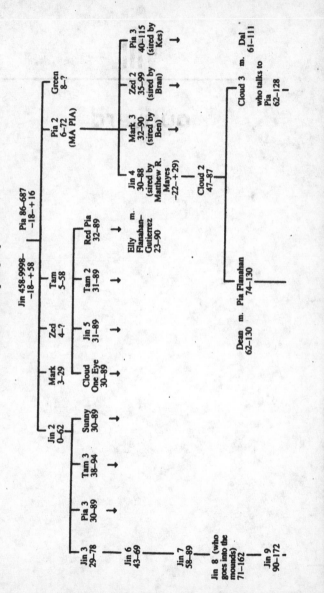

Styxside

Jin 10 124–185 — Jin 11 156–174 — Jin 12 170–

rulers of First Tower

Elly 90–154 r. 130–154 — Dean 2 112–169 r. 154–169 — Ellai 132–188 r. 169–181 — Ellai 153–204 r. 181–204 — Elai 178–241 r. 204–241

Din 198–243 r. 241–243 — Din 239–

Teem 200–276

Cloud 201–298 — Marik 203–203 — Marik 286–

Cloud River

Other towers

Cloud's Tam 81–200 — Cloud 94–168 — Cloud 114–159 — Cloud 134–162

Taem 135–189 r. the new tower — Taem 168–202

Paeia 154–209 — Cloud 181–268 — Paeia 241–

i

Year CR 305, day 33
Fargone Station
Union Space

One saw all sorts dockside, military, merchanters, stationers, dockers, the rare probe-ship crewman. This was new, and the dock crew stared, not unlike other crews, all along the long, long metal curve, in the echoing high spaces that smelled of otherwhere and cold.

"What's *that*?" someone wondered, too loud, and the young man turned and gave them back the stare, just for a moment, stranger estimating stranger: but this one looked dangerous . . . tall, and lean, and long-haired, wearing fringed leather and white bone beads of intricate carving. He had a knife, illegal on the docks or anywhere else onstation. That they saw too, and no one said anything further or moved until he had gone his way ghostlike down the line.

"That," said Dan James, dockman boss, "that's Gehennan."

"Heard there was something strange came in," another man said, and ventured a look at a safely retreating back.

"Got his dragon with him," James said; the docker swore and straightened up, satisfying effect.

"They let that thing loose?"

"Hey, they don't *let* it anywhere. That thing's human, it is. Leastwise by law it is."

There were anxious looks. "You mean that," one said.

The place was like other such places he had seen—he,
Marik, son of Cloud son of Elai. He explored it in slow
disdain, gathering information, which he would go home
again to tell; and all the same he was excited by this knowledge, that they could travel so far and still find stations like
Gehenna Station, that the universe was so large. He was
wary in it. Cloud had taught him how to deal with strangers, not letting them tell him where he ought to go and
where not, and what he ought to see and what he should
be blind to.

Only he left Walker in her hold, where there was
warmth. She would not like this cold; it would make her
restless; and the sounds would irritate her, and besides,
enough people came to her. Walker was not bored, at least,
and had gotten used to strangers, enough to give them the
lazy stare they deserved and to go on with her Pattern,
figuring this trip out. He told her what he could. She was
working on it.

Some things he was still working on himself. Like what
the universe was like. Or what starmen wanted.

There was a problem, they said, a world that they had
found. There was life on it, and it made no sense to them.

A Gehennan sees things a different way, they said. Just
go and look—you and Walker.

So they would go and see.